Praise for Eric Van Lust[...]

With each new volume. The Pearl Saga has bloomed and ramified like a gorgeous flowering vine. *The Mistress of the Pearl* is the best yet—those who have read the previous books will find new sources of excitement and enlightenment, as the evil Sauromicians seek to use banestones to bind a dragon, but this is also a great place to begin catching up with the series. Come to Kundala, and you too will be changed.

Kundala is Miina's world, created by that Goddess with the help of the dragons. But Miina is missing, and her people have been enslaved by the alien V'orn. Now a savior has come, the Dar Sala-at, a messiah promised by prophecy yet unlike anyone's expectations: within the body of a beautiful young woman is the mind and spirit of a unique Kundalan female who is joined in mystical partnership with the mind and spirit of Annon Ashera, a V'orn male, the last survivor of a noble family. Together the two adolescents have matured and merged into a new joint identity. Now their common destiny, and Kundala's, is in their own hands.

The Veil of a Thousand Tears

"Lustbader erects a strong armature of myth, magic, technology, and religion . . . World-building that should attract a new universe of fans."   —*Kirkus Reviews*

"Lustbader creates a unique tale with the compelling style that has distinguished his writing since his renowned Sunset Warrior fantasy cycle."   —*Publishers Weekly*

The Ring of Five Dragons

"Complex characterization, with a meticulously crafted background detailing history, culture and people will entice readers into this new saga."   —*Romantic Times*

"*The Ring of Five Dragons,* however, is not purely a fantasy novel. It . . . is a fusion, blending and breaking the barriers between technology and sorcery, pragmatism and mysticism. . . . Lustbader, as always, is full of surprises."

—*Chicago Sun-Times*

Tor Books by Eric Van Lustbader

The Ring of Five Dragons
The Veil of a Thousand Tears
Mistress of the Pearl

MISTRESS
OF THE
PEARL

Volume Three of The Pearl

ERIC VAN LUSTBADER

A TOM DOHERTY ASSOCIATES BOOK
NEW YORK

This is a work of fiction. All the characters and events portrayed in this book are either products of the author's imagination or are used fictitiously.

MISTRESS OF THE PEARL

Copyright © 2004 by Eric Van Lustbader

Edited by David G. Hartwell

A Tor Book
Published by Tom Doherty Associates, LLC
175 Fifth Avenue
New York, NY 10010

www.tor.com

Tor® is a registered trademark of Tom Doherty Associates, LLC.

ISBN 0-812-57235-1
EAN 978-0-812-57235-3

First edition: March 2004
First mass market edition: November 2005

Printed in the United States of America

0 9 8 7 6 5 4 3 2 1

In loving memory of my father,
Melvin Harry Lustbader
1912–2002

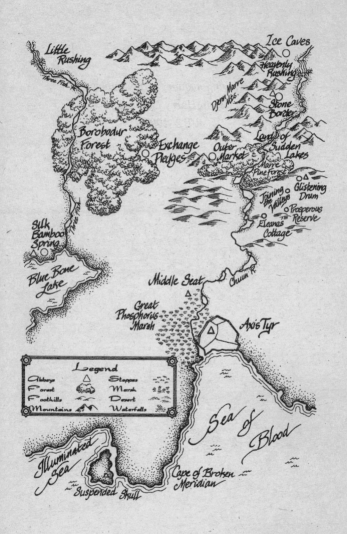

Unknown Territories

Djenn Marre Mts.

Great Rift

NORTH

Im-Thera   Site of Za Hara-at

Bandichire

Agachire

Shelachire   Okkamchire

The Korrush

The Great Voorg

Kundala
The Northern Continent

2002 AlexMitchell

MISTRESS
OF THE
PEARL

Prologue

So the black Chimaera says to the mermaiden, 'You have displeased me, and for this I will carve your heart out and feed it to you.' And the mermaiden says, 'I would not mind so much, but I am a vegetarian.'"

The small off-duty complement of Sarakkon laughed at the first mate's joke, and why not? The *Oomaloo* was nearing the end of its long journey north from the bustling port of Celiocco on the southern continent. The air belowdecks was turgid and sweet with laaga smoke. But they sprang to as they heard the lookout's long-awaited call of "Land-all!" and thundered up the companionway. Halfway there, however, their high spirits evaporated, as the ship abruptly heeled over. Thrown against the polished wooden bulkhead, they shook their heads as the ship righted itself. But now they could feel the thrumming of the heavy seas, and they heard the storm call even as they rushed on deck.

The captain stood amidships, his eyes tearing in the high wind. Like all Sarakkon, he was tall and slender, his skin, sun-washed, wind-scoured, the color of ripe pomegranates. One eye squinty from a fishhook through it in intemperate youth. He had a full beard, sign of his rank, and through its thick curling black hair were threaded carved blue-jade spheres, silver cubes, tiny conical striped shells. He wore a lightweight kilted skirt and the kaldea—a wide belt of cured sea grape that circled his waist and hung down in front in a complex series of knots, identifying his status as well as his lineage. The moment his crew appeared, he gestured them to their stations. Moments before, the wind moaning its intentions in his ear bones, he had signaled the lookout down from his nest. One glance to the northeast had confirmed what he knew: within minutes the storm would overtake them. Already they were being buffeted by fistfuls of sleet. Sensing the storm's powerful heart, he was reminded anew of how arrogant and small they all were.

Like virtually all Sarakkonian ships that made this long journey, the *Oomaloo* was a marvelously sleek three-masted merchanter, but loaded down as it was with valuable cargo, the ship was less maneuverable and thus more vulnerable to inclement weather. On top of that, the sleet, catching rigging and brass fittings, looked to bring down the sails. Although the captain was both clever and experienced, he was under an inordinate amount of pressure because of the nature of one piece of cargo. It was not something he had wished to transport, but he had been given no choice by the Orieniad, the Sarakkon ruling council.

The *Oomaloo*, borne by the last great storm of winter, heeled over, and the high slate seas overran its scuppers, flooding the deck. The next wave, more towering than the last, took three of the crew, his lookout among them, as it crashed obliquely across the deck. The howling wind drowned out their screams as they tumbled across the canted deck, carried overboard into the wild and punishing sea.

The second mate, a parsimonious devil, and therefore in charge of the larder, made an unwise lunge for them. The captain grabbed him from behind, kept him close to, thus ensuring that he would not lose a fourth member of his crew to the cruel Sea of Blood. Then he freed him aft to tie down rigging the gale had ripped loose.

Tearing his mind away from the tragedy, the captain yelled to the navigator to turn west. He and his first mate scrambled across a deck shin deep in sluicing water, the whorled tattoos that covered their shaved heads and bodies seeming to come alive with the actions of their muscles.

As he seized the mizzenmast, the other asked him what he meant to do.

"You will help us put the ship under full sail," the captain replied over the roar of the storm.

"Full sail?" The first mate, a knot of muscle, a face all gnawed bone, was aghast. "That will capsize us for certain." He turned his eyes fearfully to the mainsails already straining their sleet-grizzled grommets to the limit. "We should be furling all sail."

"We will founder and be taken under."

"Then we should be making all haste for Axis Tyr."

"We are now heading west, the same direction as the storm."

"But that is away from Axis Tyr. The port is our only—"

The captain was already unwinding the rigging from the brass stays. "We are going to use our sails to race ahead of it."

Still the first mate balked. "That is certain suicide," he shouted, wiping spume off his sharply triangular goatee.

The captain grabbed his first mate by the wet flaps of his tooled sharkskin vest, slammed his back against the mast. "Listen to us. Our only chance is to round the Cape of Broken Meridian, where the Sea of Blood meets the Illuminated Sea. There the ship will be protected. The ship will be safe!"

"Safe?" The mate shot him a horrified look. "No Sarakkon ship has sailed this part of the Illuminated Sea, and you know why. The legends—"

A wall of water smashed into the *Oomaloo*, and the ship dipped dangerously to port, taking on more water. The captain, seeing his navigator wrestling the recalcitrant tiller, bellowed at the second mate. With that worthy's help, the navigator put his shoulder into it and slowly, with a painful creaking, the ship turned her high, carved prow more quickly to the west.

"We have no time for superstition," the captain said to his first mate. His thick beard was rimed with salt water and spittle. The silver runes woven into it glistened in the dim light. "We have our lives to think of."

"Not *our* lives," the first mate shouted back. "The life of our passenger. It is evil luck to sail with a female on board."

"More superstition." The captain struck his first mate a massive blow to the side of his head. "You have not shipped with us before. Aboard the *Oomaloo* our word is law." A dirk with a wrapped shagreen handle bloomed in his fist. "Now unfurl all sail and make it quick!" The dirk's point grazed the side of the mate's neck. "Else we swear by Yahé's sweet lips we will slit your throat."

The first mate leapt to, but not without a look dark with ferment. He and the captain worked smoothly and efficiently, their muscles bulging, their booted feet planted wide on the pitching deck. Methodically, doggedly in the raging face of the storm, they repeated the same procedure with the sails on each of the *Oomaloo*'s masts. And as the ship came to full sail, it leapt forward as if propelled by the engine of a V'ornn hoverpod. Its hull fairly lifted from the boiling sea as it skimmed along on the leading gusts of the gale.

Waves had ceased to overrun the deck, and to starboard could be seen the rocky tip of the thick finger of land known as the Cape of Broken Meridian, beyond which lay the uncharted waters of the Illuminated Sea. The captain noted the fear in his first mate's eyes, but behind the *Oomaloo* was a growing wall of water, black and ugly and lethal. No matter what—if the legends were true or no—there was no turning back. A sure death rode their stern and would doubtless overtake them should their speed falter.

He strode aft, climbing the short, slippery companionway to where the navigator held the juddering tiller steady.

"When we come abeam of the cape make ready to turn her hard to starboard," he growled. "We want to get land between us and the storm as quickly as possible."

The navigator nodded. He had shipped with the captain since their youth. His teeth were gritted, and the cords of his neck stood out in stark relief with the effort of holding the *Oomaloo* on course. For an instant, he caught the captain's eye, and the look that passed between them served as silent tribute to the crew that had perished. Then they directed their attention to what lay ahead.

The area of ocean off the tip of the Cape of Broken Meridian was known as the Cauldron because it was aboil even in the calmest of weather. Its extreme turbulence could be seen, and ofttimes felt, by Sarakkon crews as they headed to and from the port of Axis Tyr. These deep and dangerous crosscurrents at the confluence of the two seas were fearful enough even without the alarming Sarakkonian legends attached to the Illuminated Sea.

The captain squeezed the navigator's shoulder. No need to voice his trepidation. The gale was hurling them directly into the heart of the maelstrom. Grey spume flew over the high prow, which was carved into a Protector—a composite image unique to each Sarakkonian ship. The *Oomaloo*'s was of the lithe body of Yahé crowned with the noble head of the paiha. In this way, the very bones of the ship were infused with the goddess's wisdom and the mythic bird of prey's great healing powers. As the *Oomaloo* began to pitch and roll in the fierce crosscurrents the captain knew that they would need all of their Protector's powers if they were to survive.

The ship dipped precipitously as they came abeam of the cape's tip. He could see the frothy spume geysering high into the turbid sky as the sea beat itself against the jagged black rocks. He saw the navigator pushing the tiller, trying to take them hard to starboard. Since the winds were still too high and unpredictable to risk sending a lookout up the mizzenmast, he dispatched the first mate to the prow to keep a sharp eye out for any sign of rock outcroppings or reefs.

A great shuddering began to work its way through the *Oomaloo* as the ship entered the perilous crosscurrents. The captain got his first look at the Illuminated Sea, and it was not reassuring. Despite its name, the water was dark as night, the same color as the rocks that jutted from the tip of the Cape of Broken Meridian. Even the most expert eye would have difficulty differentiating the two.

The speed of the ship, which had been their savior against the storm, now worked against them in these uncharted waters. The captain called for all sails to be reefed, and his crew sprang to. He was battening down the canvas when the first mate rushed up to him. His face was pale and pinched and his eyes rolled in his head.

"We gave you an order," the captain growled, now sorely vexed. "Why have you abandoned your post?"

"We have—" The first mate swallowed hard. "We have seen it, Captain."

"Seen what?" The captain had his hands full, prepared to order the navigator to alter course. "A reef?"

The mate shook his spume-wet head. "Not a reef. We—"

"Well, out with it then!" The navigator was winning the war with the crosscurrents. The ship was slowly but surely turned to starboard, putting the finger of the cape between it and the storm. "What did you see?"

"A Chimaera." The first mate was shaking. "A black Chimaera."

"First, we are in uncharted waters. We are relying on your eyes to keep us from breaking apart. The daemons out of your imagination—"

"But we did see it, Captain. By Yahé's full lips, we swear it. We saw a black Chimaera. The legends are true!"

At that moment, they were all pitched violently forward as, with a great grinding scream, the *Oomaloo*'s forward momentum came to an abrupt halt.

"Reef hoy!"

The navigator's cry was nearly drowned out by the grinding and rending of lacquered timbers. The captain, picking himself up off the deck, saw a crack like a finger of doom zigzagging up the side of the Protector, and he knew all was lost. They were impaled upon the thrice-damned obsidian reef. He knew his duty, the one he had been made to swear before he had set sail. Immediately, he made for the aft companionway, leaving the first mate's screams behind him.

Down the wet companionway he slid. The lower deck

was already awash with seawater, with more imminent. There were multiple rents in the forward hull, as if the sea were eating the *Oomaloo* alive, and the crosscurrents ground the ship against the jagged reef, as if to leave only wormy powder behind.

He reached his cabin, tore open the door. Krystren was standing as if anticipating his appearance. Sea-green eyes, a face of extremes, like iron and velvet. She was wrapped in her wine-dark sea greatcoat. Her hair, dark and glossy as sea wrack, was wound in a thick braid, like a coil of stout rope that wouldn't fray in the worst of winter weather.

Without a word, the captain grabbed her hand and hurried toward the aft companionway. Already the seawater was up to their shins. The ship gave a great lurch, tossing them to their knees. Up ahead, torrents began to pour through the widening rent. They regained their feet and ran.

Krystren was silent. What was there to say? She had seen he was a good captain, not that it made any difference; the sea would have the last word today. Up the companionway they clattered, while boiling seawater flooded belowdecks. As the captain appeared on deck, Krystren in his lee, the first mate fixed them with a murderous eye.

"We knew it!" the first mate crowed, advancing on them. "The accursed female!" He had drawn his dirk, an oddly small weapon, whose short, diamond-shaped blade seemed most unsuitable for hand-to-hand combat. "It is because of her that this voyage was doomed from the start!"

"See to your position!" the captain cried, interposing himself between Krystren and the first mate. "That is an order!"

The first mate laughed a cruel laugh. "Your ship is dying, captain. Your command is mercifully at an end. We have gathered what is left of the crew to our side."

"Impossible." The captain automatically looked to the helm. "You could not—" But the position was vacant, and now he saw the body of the navigator, facedown on the deck. Around him, blood mingled with seawater and the remnants of sleet.

The first mate grinned as the captain's gaze swung back to him. "Those who disagreed have gone to kiss Yahé's sweet lips." He waggled the point of his dirk. "We give the orders now. The small boats are in the water, but neither you nor she will board them. The sea gods have spoken. They have produced the black Chimaera. They demand her as sacrifice."

"Your fear has made you mad," the captain said. "We will see you hanged for this."

The *Oomaloo* gave another sickening groan, and the deck canted over as it began to list. The first mate waggled his filthy fingers. "No more talk, Captain. Hand her over, or you will feel our blade between your ribs."

"You know we cannot," the captain said, drawing his own dirk. "You know we will not."

With an almost casual gesture, the first mate flicked his wrist. The captain's eyes opened wide as the weapon pierced him to its hilt. Expertly cast, the narrow blade passed between his first and second ribs, puncturing his heart.

"You—" the captain said, blood already bubbling on his lips. "We should have guessed." Then he pitched onto the deck, his corpse sliding to the rail that was by then just above the waterline.

Already, the first mate had another dirk in his fist, the mate to the one that had killed the captain.

"*Sintire*," Krystren said.

The first mate spat. "You must be very valuable indeed. We will receive a fortune when we see to it that you never set foot on the northern continent."

"Who is paying you?" Krystren asked.

The first mate laughed. "Even if we knew, do you think we would tell you? We serve the Oath."

"How well we know," she said as she threw the small dirk she had been holding beneath her greatcoat.

The first mate's weapon struck the deck as his hands

clutched at his throat. Desperately, he clawed at the sea-cor hilt. He staggered back, falling to his knees as he drew out the narrow, diamond-shaped blade. He knelt, staring at it as his ragged breath sawed in and out of the wound.

"We serve it, as well."

"You are *Onnda*, bitch. You serve the Oath in perversity."

Krystren took her weapon from his nerveless fingers, kicked him over onto his back. He tried to speak, but blood bubbled out of his throat. She picked up his weapon, then knelt beside him.

"You will die. All of you." She turned the bloody blade of her dirk so that it glinted dully in the starlight. "This is my Oath, my religion."

The *Oomaloo* was fast breaking apart. Krystren rose and hurried to the rail. There, she saw two small boats, manned by what was left of the crew. They had not waited for the first mate and were more than three hundred meters away. They appeared to be making for an island to the north, whose dark and ominous cliffs loomed out of the storm haze. None of them looked back at the doomed ship that had been their home for months and, in some cases, years.

Krystren was obliged to grab on to the rail as the *Oomaloo* gave another lurch downward. Groaning mightily, it began its death throes. She looked over the side, saw in the wreckage spars and timbers large enough to support her. She was about to clamber over the rail when she heard frantic shouts floating over the turbulent water. To her right, she could see that something was happening around the lead boat. The sailors were pointing and gesticulating madly, at what she could not say. Then, all at once, there was a great fountaining of water in the midst of which she could just make out a huge shape, black as night. Then it opened enormous jaws and snapped the small boat in two. The Sarakkon screamed as they tumbled into the water, and the monstrous shape rose again. Its gaping jaws crashed closed, crunching through muscle, sinew, and bone. Blood and gore fountained in a rosy halo.

The Sarakkon in the following small boat had now changed course and were frenziedly rowing away from the island cliffs. No matter. The thing pursued them with relentless precision, so swiftly it took Krystren's breath away. Within moments, they shared the same doom as their compatriots.

Now she alone had survived the wreck of the *Oomaloo*, but she knew that would not long be the case unless she jumped from what was left of the ship. Without another thought, she threw off her greatcoat and leapt into the churning sea. The shock of the cold water ran up her spine with a jolt. She kicked upward, broke the surface, and swam to a section of the prow that had been sheared off. Wrapping her hands around the carved image of Yahé's body, she climbed on, straddling it. Retrieving a long piece of flotsam to use as a paddle, she tucked her legs under her and struck out toward the island. Behind her, she could hear an awful groaning as the last and largest of the *Oomaloo*'s beams shattered against the knife-toothed reef.

She bent her back, putting all her strength into steering through the crosscurrents. Happily, she was nearly out of the Cauldron. Up ahead, she could see the last vestiges of pinkish foam, all that remained of the two small boats and their crews. In order to make landfall, she would have to intersect the path the small boats had taken. She knew what had destroyed them; she knew the legends of the Illuminated Sea as well as any Sarakkon.

With each stroke of her improvised oar she was making greater headway as she left the swirling Cauldron behind. She concentrated on the island's cliff face, which looked high and sheer. Its top was obscured by a dense, roiling mist, doubtless a residue of the storm that was still raging on the other side of the Cape of Broken Meridian. Angry dark grey clouds scudded overhead, but the sleet had turned to a chill rain, and the brunt of the wind was being sheared away by the intervening landmass.

Now Krystren was oaring through the small boat debris field, a grisly insight into the origin of legends. She oared even faster, trying to redouble her pace. It was all she could do not to look around for the thing that had feasted terrifyingly on the others. She could only hope that its fearsome appetite had been at least temporarily sated. To occupy herself and also as an exercise in survival she turned her mind to estimating how far she was from the island. She judged it to be a half kilometer distant, perhaps a bit less. But if the blackness of the water was any guide, she was still in very deep water. Had the captain been with her, he would have been puzzled by how a reef could exist so close to the surface in such deeps, but she was no sailor and so remained ignorant of this conundrum.

Each stroke brought her closer to her goal. The island was, of course, nowhere near Axis Tyr, and when she reached it she would still have to find the means to make her way to the mainland. However, that question was for later, after she had rested, foraged for food, and availed herself of a good night's sleep. For the moment, she needed to concentrate on this last half kilometer of water. She could begin to see more clearly the creaming line of surf as it crashed and boomed at the base of the rocky cliff. Ignoring the growing stiffness in her shoulders and back, she continued to bend into each stroke. Now the sounds of the shoreline came to her across the bosom of the sea. She was breathing a sigh of relief, when the section of the Protector that carried her dipped so violently she was almost cast off it. Obliged to drop her oar, she gripped the splintered wood with both arms. In the process, the lower half of her legs slid into the water and she could feel the ripple of a very powerful current, and it took her a moment to realize that the current was localized beneath her, making her blood run cold. She felt the ripple again, stronger this time, and crouched atop her makeshift craft. Small tremors passed through the powerful muscles of her thighs. She knew what must be swimming below her. She looked around for her oar, but it was floating twenty meters behind her. Now she was at the mercy of the off shore tide, which in the interregnum was already exerting its force, pushing her farther west, rather than north toward the island. She tried to paddle with her hands, but it soon became apparent that doing so was an exercise in futility.

But then the direction of the tide became a moot point, for directly ahead of her rose an apparition out of a nightmare. The black Chimaera was huge—perhaps half as long as the *Oomaloo*. Its body looked to be all muscle, with a tapering forked tail and a trio of wicked-looking dorsal fins. Its cold red eyes took her in with what appeared to be daemonic intelligence.

Krystren's heart was in her throat. She had worked long and arduously to become *Onnda*, and her training had prepared her for death. But nothing could have prepared her for this.

As she watched, mesmerized with a mixture of fear and awe, the Chimaera waggled its wicked-looking tail and started moving toward her. It was so large that the fore wave had already reached her. If there had been something to do, she would have done it. There wasn't. Instead, she recited the Oath, repeating it as a kind of death prayer.

The Chimaera was up to speed, and she prepared herself to be crushed by its massive jaws. But the bite never came. Instead, at the last moment, it dived beneath her. Before she had a chance to turn her head, a powerful wave seized the Protector, pushing her due north, out of the tidal flow, toward the island. As she gripped the Protector more tightly, she could feel the vibration of the wave growing and extending until she fairly flew over the water on its crest. Risking a quick glance behind her, she saw to her astonishment the triple fins riding in her wake. The Chimaera was, in effect, propelling her toward the shore.

How could this be? she wondered. How could a monstrous beast that had just slain and devoured twelve Sarakkon help save her life? It made no sense at all, and yet it was undeniable. The cliff line was coming up fast, in fact too fast for her comfort. Those rocks, monstrous in themselves, were jagged and saw-toothed. Surely, at this speed they would instantly rend the Protector to smithereens.

Just then, she felt the wave behind her dissipating, and almost instantly she slowed. As the water at last grew shallow, she took one last look back and an intense shiver passed through her. There was the great black Chimaera, with a flick of its powerful forked tail gliding broadside, fixing her with its cold red eye.

Krystren rolled off the Protector and swam gingerly through the flying spume, trying her best to avoid the worst of the rock outcroppings. The air was sharp in her nostrils, thick with phosphorus and brine. Nearly out of breath, she stumbled through the suck and roar of the surf, her feet and shins scraped and bleeding. Flinging herself into a tidal pool that was more or less protected, she dragged herself onto the base of the cliff. There, she lay panting, her back against a barnacle-encrusted slab of rock that rose like a grave marker. Her eyes scanned the Illuminated Sea, but of the Chimaera or the *Oomaloo* there was no sign.

Almost at once, she fell into an exhausted slumber, from which she awoke hours later to find the twilit sky scrubbed clean. Long-winged pelagic birds called and swooped among crags iced with their droppings. Several first-magnitude stars twinkled in the pellucid heavens. A gentle onshore breeze nevertheless made her shiver in her wet clothes, urging her to get up and find food and suitable shelter. That was when she noticed that the tops of the cliff were still shrouded in dense mist.

Food proved to be no problem. The tidal pool was swarming with small-clawed crabs encased in shining greenish black shells, their flesh tender and sweet even when eaten raw. That left shelter. A brief reconnoiter of the cliff base located no sea cave that could protect her from the increasing chill of encroaching night. She lifted her head to where the mist lay and, choosing a likely series of foot- and handholds, commenced her climb.

The going was easier than she had expected. The scouring wind and rains had etched the cliff face with myriad chips and cracks ideal for ascent. Her chief concern was inadvertently disturbing a bird's nest, for the occupants were possessed of long, curving beaks that could puncture her flesh as efficiently as the blade of a dirk.

She was perhaps a quarter of the way up when she came upon a cave mouth invisible from below. Clambering onto its projecting lip, she quickly realized that it was unlike any cave she had ever seen before. For one thing, the interior was absolutely smooth, shiny as glass. For another, it appeared lit from within, for a sickening crimson luminescence revealed the interior to her. Hard as she searched, however, she could find no source for the light, which imparted an even glow to every section of the arched cave.

It did not take her long to discover that the cave, as wide as the hall of a grand palace, was quite shallow. That too, spoke to its unnaturalness. In the center of the rear wall, which was made out of the same smooth, vitreous substance as the rest of the interior, she came upon what could only be a door. *This clinches* it, she thought. The cave had been constructed by the hand of the Kundalan. Why? What was it for?

What was behind the door?

She ran her fingers over the almost seamless outline. There were no hinges or handle, no indentations or visible lock of any kind. She pushed on the door; unsurprisingly, it did not open.

Sighing, she sat down with her back against it. She had meant only to close her eyes and rest, but almost at once she dozed off.

A slight vibration transmitted to her spine broke her dream. She had been back in the Great Southern Arryx, a child racing after her older brother across an arid ochre landscape dominated by the chain of enormous volcanoes.

Then her eyes snapped open, and, turning, she pressed the flat of her hand to the door. It was moving!

She scrambled to her feet as, soundlessly, the door began to swing open. Darting behind it, she stood absolutely still, holding her breath as she heard a slight rustling of fabric. She craned her neck in her hiding place so that she could peer out. Into her field of vision emerged a male in flowing black robes. He was Kundalan, but unlike any she had encountered. His black hair was long on top, shaved at the sides of his skull. He had elongated earlobes, pierced by polished knucklebones, and, when he turned, she could see that there was barely any flesh on his face. The tallow-colored skin was pulled taut over razor-edged bone. In the center of his forehead a ruddy rune rose like a livid scar. His eyes were twin beacons, the pupils tiny and pulsing, as if with a mysterious energy.

He went up a flight of stairs carved out of the curving wall that she hadn't previously noticed and a moment later descended. He looked up, held out his hand.

"Come."

The one seemingly innocent word burst into the cave like shrapnel, penetrating into every nook and corner. Instinctively, Krystren wrapped her arms around her waist as if to ward off some kind of attack.

Another male came hesitantly down the stairs. A handsome youth, athletic-looking, dark of skin, hair and eyes. The black-robed spectre took him by the elbow and led him to the cave opening. The night was clear, the stars brilliant. The water was lit by the pale green light of three moons, their reflections trailing in the deep and inky water like brilliant ribbons on a birthday present. The two stood for a long while, gazing out over the Illuminated Sea and the tip of the Cape of Broken Meridian, to the east of which lay the capital of the northern continent, Axis Tyr.

"This is Kundala," the black-robed spectre intoned in

his eerie, sepulchral voice. "This is the vastness of the world." He put a spidery arm low around the youth's waist in a gesture that was at once intimate and lascivious. "*Your* world, Dar Sala-at."

The youth smiled, but Krystren could see that his eyes were glazed, his mouth half-open. Was he drugged or under a some kind of spell? She was still pondering this when the black-robed spectre said, "Come, Dar Sala-at. There is something I wish to show you."

Quickly, she darted into the open doorway, hid in shadows, using her unique skill to blend into the surroundings.

With his spidery fingertips at the small of the youth's back, the black-robed spectre propelled the youth back through the doorway. The poor boy looked terrified.

They were in a thick-walled keep, small and uncharacteristically windowless. If one did not know better, it might have been mistaken for a prison, so grim was its appearance, so solid was its fastness. In the center of the floor was what appeared to be an open hatchway. The spectre led the terrified boy down into the hole in the floor. A moment later, Krystren was startled by a whining sound.

She went to the open hatchway and peered down. A square pole ran down the full length of the vertical shaft. It was down this the two had somehow descended, perhaps using the grooves she saw in its sides. She spat on her palms; then, leaping onto the pole, she wriggled down it as fast as she dared. It was a very long slide. Nearing the bottom it grew hot, the air full of fumes that seared the back of her throat.

When she saw the two figures below her, she held her position, her hand, elbows, and knees gripping the pole hard. What she saw made her heart pound. At the bottom of the shaft was a huge chamber almost entirely filled by a cage that appeared to be made out of pulsing energy beams. That was astonishing enough. But what she saw inside the cage made her break out into a cold sweat.

It was a creature: gargantuan, blue-green, long of snout, large of teeth, winged and crowned with horns.

Great Mother Yahé, she thought. *It is a Dragon!*

Book One:

CROOKED SPRING GATE

To the novice, it doubtless seems a co-nundrum that lies can have their basis in fact. Consider, however, the individ-ual's need to have his or her desires met. This is fact. If lies are clever enough to fulfill this desire, they become a truth and, therefore, that much harder to dis-pel. Their power has its origin in Crooked Spring Gate.

—Utmost Source,
The Five Sacred Books of Miina

1

Mirror

An exceptionally frigid winter was at last drawing to a close. The low, dense cloud cover that had spread itself like a bird of prey over virtually all of Kundala's northern continent was being slowly rent by the sun, in which had begun to burn of late the glowing ember of spring. The basaara, the ceaseless north wind that had its origins in the lethal permafrost of the Unknown Territories beyond the Djenn Marre mountain range, had raged for a full six weeks, disgorging a suffocating stratum of snow on the bustling towns, the barren fields, the forested hillsides, and ceaseless strip mines, inconveniencing Kundalan and V'ornn alike. Though the technically superior V'ornn had occupied the planet for over a century, they had never adjusted to snow and ice from which, like seas and deserts, they could derive no profit. But of late the wind had shifted, meandering indolently from the southwest, bringing with it the sharp tang of the Illuminated Sea along with tantalizing hints of the southern continent's tropical climes.

The lower-lying areas were already shrugging off winter's punishing grip, the snow grudgingly receding like an aging glacier, but here, high in the rugged massif of the Djenn Marre, it was still as thick as ever it had been in midwinter.

The windowless chamber in which Riane stood was not large, but its ceiling, invisible in its extreme height, lay shrouded in the shadowed cavern, bearded with stalactites like upended candles, their wax cold, calcified with rheumy age. Amber light poured from reed torches bound in copper wire, and the polar stink of minerals seeping made the room reek like the hold of a ship. A mirror, tall as it was narrow, beveled like cut gemstone, gilt-framed, here and there cloudy as the sky, hung from a bare black bolt driven into naked limestone. Riane moved until her reflection appeared like a wraith from predawn mist. She stared at herself, wondering.

She was known to her friends and compatriots as the Dar Sala-at, the fabled savior, destined to lead the Kundalan uprising against their alien V'ornn oppressors. Her image—an oval face framed by long blond hair braided in the *mistefan*, the Druuge symbol of battle, startling blue eyes, a strong nose pierced with a gold stud, and a wide, generous mouth—looked back at her. Even three months ago she had felt a stranger. But lately she was coming to realize that the male V'ornn persona of Annon Ashera and the female Kundalan known as Riane had in many ways fused, becoming a single entity, capable of drawing on both Annon's V'ornnish knowledge and Riane's formidable physical prowess and limited memories. The result was becoming each day more comfortable for both of them. Now, most of the time, they thought as one.

Riane shifted the two leather-bound books, gold-stamped, thick, ancient, precious beyond imagining. *Utmost Source* and *The Book of Recantation*, the two most sacred texts of the Great Goddess Miina, rescued by her, their right and true keeper, from oblivion, as it had been written in prophecy. "I am ready," she said to Giyan.

The tall Kundalan—sorceress, priestess, seer—came and stood at her side, nodded and gripped her hand. She had a face to make the heart melt, powerful and lovely, thick copper-colored hair cascading past her shoulders, and large whistleflower-blue eyes.

From a small distance, Thigpen's whiskers twitched in her copper, black-and-white-furred muzzle. Though they were not far from her home—the home of all Rappa—a gigantic cavern deep within the bowels of the Djenn Marre, Thigpen had never been in this chamber before, never even knew of its existence. But the Ramahan did. Typical.

"I like this not, little dumpling," Thigpen said anxiously. "We Rappa have a healthy fear of mirrors. Their sorcerous power is legendary."

"Yes," Giyan responded, not unkindly. "Mariners fear whirlpools, Rappa fear mirrors."

Thigpen shuddered. "Shall I tell you tales of Rappa sucked into the Other Side by ensorceled mirrors?"

"No need," Giyan said. "There is nothing here to fear."

Still, the Rappa backed away on her six furry legs, wickedly curved nails skittering on rock. Her whiskers twitched ferociously.

"I don't understand," Riane said. "What is the Other Side? Not, surely, Otherwhere?"

"Oh, no," Thigpen called. "The Other Side is a squirming pit, a shallow grave, nasty, nasty."

"Think of a pinhole in our Realm," Giyan said in a far calmer voice. "Necromancers—when they once walked Kundala—would use their foul sorcery to shove those who displeased them through the mirror, through the pinhole, into the null-space that exists between Realms."

"No one ever returns from the Other Side," the Rappa said.

"Is this true?" Riane asked.

Giyan shrugged. "I have heard of none."

"That is because there are none!" Thigpen howled, causing Giyan to turn to her with a finger across her lips. "You may leave, if you wish, dear Thigpen. No one is holding you here."

"No one is holding any of us to life," the Rappa said shortly. "That does not mean we all won't be swept aside by Anamordor, the End of All Things."

"Anamordor is a Dragon's tale," Giyan said.

"It is not inevitable?"

Giyan smiled. "None of us may use that word, dear Thigpen. What is inevitable and what is not is for the Great Goddess Miina to determine."

Thigpen grumped and fussed with her fur, as if she had suddenly discovered a colony of nits.

Giyan smiled and turned back to Riane. "All right, then. Let us begin."

Solemnly, she held the sacred texts, back straight, eyes shining while Riane intoned the Venca spell. Then Riane saw her reflection in the mirror come toward her, and it seemed now to have all the appearance of a shell, a cara-pace much like the Gyrgon wore to hide themselves. An-non, too, was hiding inside Riane's body. Only Giyan knew the secret, and she would never tell another soul.

Riane raised her hands, pressed them against the mirror, *into* it. She felt a coolness, as if she had dipped her hands in a lake.

"All is in readiness," she said.

Giyan placed the heavy texts on her arms.

"Are you sure this is the wisest place to store them?" Thigpen piped up.

"It is by far the safest place," Giyan said. "There are at present too many enemies who would stop at nothing to destroy these texts." She was, of course, speaking of the sauromicians.

"And if by chance the banestones should—"

"That is enough!"

It was not wise to anger Giyan, but the Rappa were an obstinate species, as it was often enough said, none more so than Thigpen. Once she got going, she was difficult to derail.

"She does not know about the banestones, does she?"

"Why would she need to?" Giyan snapped. "The bane-stones are ancient history, lost for eons."

"Ever since the fall of Za Hara-at, yes. But the bane-stones can penetrate the Other Side. I have heard that this is where they derive their enormous power."

"Why are you talking about me as if I am not here?" Ri-ane addressing them both at once.

Giyan sighed. "I apologize. But you have more than enough on your plate without concerning yourself with banestones. There are all manner of ancient artifacts I could make you aware of, but what would be the point?"

"Forewarned is forearmed," the Rappa said portentously.

"It is true that the banestones use another kind of energy, one that even Ramahan have failed to understand. They are very dangerous, should not be touched, for to do so connects you to them, alters you subtly on the atomic level."

"Strange things happen when you acquire a banestone," Thigpen could not help adding. "Not what you wish for, and with the banestone—believe me—you wish for plenty. Because they were originally mined, dug out of the bowels of Kundala, by the daemons. Nine banestones, they found, and nine are needed, linked, to unleash all their power."

"Are you satisfied now?" Giyan asked her.

Thigpen sat up on her four hind legs, her forepaws crossed in stubborn anger. "Satisfied? No, it would take a great deal to satisfy me, or any Rappa," she said somewhat sullenly.

"You forgot to mention that the banestones were used in the foundations of the nine major temples at Za Hara-at. They were its power."

Riane looked from one to the other. "Can we get on with it now?" Her voice clipped with impatience. "There is much to be done." And that, for the moment at least, seemed to settle the matter.

"Pay attention." Giyan spoke softly but sternly. "We do not want any mishaps now, else the sacred texts will be lost in null-space, drifting like a ship with a broken rudder, impossible to track or retrieve."

Riane focused all her attention.

"Concentrate on the reflections only," Giyan told her, not for the first time. "They will show you the exact spot in null-space where the books will be stored."

Riane moved in a continuous motion until her arms vanished up to her shoulders. Then she backed away slowly and smoothly until the tips of her fingers reappeared. The books, however, were gone, with another

Venca spell, safe in their repository in the place Thigpen called the Other Side.

A nd the sea comes, comes and goes, rocking like a cradle. The sea is leagues wide and fathoms deep, rocking like a cradle. The sea is a stern mistress and a gentle lover, rocking like a cradle. Into the deep we consign the mortal remains of our beloved captain: Courion, first son of Coirn, of the House of Oronel—"

The sonorous voice broke off and Kelyx, ship's surgeon of the *Omaline,* looked at Kurgan Stogggul, whose face glimmered like a newly honed hatchet, beautiful and deadly, eyes like obsidian cabochons, blood in them; and if he was any judge of V'ornn, no remorse in them, none at all. Kelyx said, "You see what we mean? How can we give Courion a proper burial—how can we pay him the respect we all feel for him when we do not even know where his mortal remains are?"

The *Omaline,* Courion's sleek Sarakkon vessel, lay at its slip at Harborside. The high prow, carved into a figure either fantastical or grotesque depending on your esthetics, arched elegantly into the night sky. Its beaten-bronze running lamps were lit. Its full complement of crew stood at attention in a shallow semicircle. Kurgan knew them all by sight. Some, like Kelyx, Chron, the first mate, Kobon, the quartermaster, he knew through his friendship with Courion. This friendship—hard-won and prickly at the best of times—meant everything, for Kurgan was quite certain that he was the first V'ornn to be invited to attend a Sarakkon funeral service.

Kurgan had fought Chron in the Kalllistotos, had played warrnixx with Kobon. With Kelyx, he had surprisingly debated the pros and cons of religion versus a state of godlessness. It was the Sarakkon's contention that a belief in a supreme being of whatever nature provided a needed sense of hope. It was Kurgan's contention that science— or technomagic, as the Gyrgon preferred to call it— provided a needed sense of order. It seemed to astonish both of them that they agreed on the essential chaos of the Cosmos.

"I am sorry," Kurgan said. "I promised to find Courion, but his body has vanished." This was not true, and Kurgan knew it very well, for he had seen Courion dead, knew how he had died, knew where even now he lay.

"No blame accrues to you." Chron in his gruff manner.

"We owe you a debt for trying," Kelyx said, he of the delicate face and watchful eyes and quick smile.

This was typical Sarakkon thinking. They valued the attempt—and therefore the intent—more than the outcome.

"It was my duty to try," Kurgan said. "It was the least I could do."

"Still, it is passing strange, Captain disappearing like that," Chron said darkly. He was overmuscled, with glowering eyes and a hatchet jaw overrun with a wicked slash of waxed mustache, a triangular black beard from which were strung lacquered sharks' teeth and mica cubes.

"Captain had dealings with the Gyrgon," Kobon said, even more ominously. Big, though not overly tall, he, like all Sarakkon, was covered in tattoos, over skull, shoulders, arms, tattoos that told a story if one knew how to interpret them. "He was warned not to trust them."

"He dealt only with Nith Batoxxx," Kurgan said, "who now, too, is dead. Of the Gyrgon's death the Comradeship refuses to speak."

Kelyx shifted his feet. "And of Captain's?" His reddish curling beard was shot through with turquoise cubes and tigershell spheres. The tattoos across his shaved skull and glistening shoulders were tiny and intricate curls like the crooked fingers of babies.

"They profess to know nothing," Kurgan said.

Chron grunted. "Even though you are regent, you kowtow to Gyrgon."

Kurgan knew he meant no offense. In fact, it was a simple statement of truth. And yet, Kurgan found himself offended, as if he had been belittled in the crew's eyes.

"This is our caste system, the way it has always been," he

said. "Your council, the Orieniad, do they not also sometimes give you orders which you are bound to follow?"

"Enough," the first mate said, stepping forward. "We are
here to perform the Last Honors for our captain and our
friend." He held out his hand. "The winding-shell."

Kelyx shook his head. "We believe Captain would want
Kurgan Stogggul to have that responsibility."

A leaden silence reigned aboard the *Omaline*. Water
slapped against the curved hull, sluiced through its scuppers. The onshore wind rocked the ship. Grey clouds
studded the noonday sky like alloy bolts. The crew shuffled while Chron's face went pale. His fists clenched and
unclenched.

Kurgan knew he must quickly break the impasse. "Courion has bade me help say good-bye, Kelyx, from across
the Great Sea of Death. I am honored to comply."

There was a palpable sigh from the assembly as Kurgan
responded the way a Sarakkon would. No one would oppose him now or even think ill of him, even Chron, whose
face had returned to its normal rich pomegranate color.

Kelyx nodded. "Spoken well and true, as is a friend's
duty." He opened his hand to reveal a heavily banded
sienna-and-cream-colored shell, long and spiraled. The
whorl inside a delicate pink. "Hold out your hand."

Kurgan did as he was asked. From inside the winding-
shell emerged a pink tongue. But when touched it felt cool
and smooth and hard, just as a shell would.

"The winding-shell is used to shroud the body before it is
consigned to the deep," Kelyx explained for Kurgan's benefit. "In the absence of Captain's body, we will use this." He
produced a beautifully made dirk with a curved forged
blade and a handle of pebbled shagreen. A cabochon star
sapphire capped the butt end. "Captain's favorite sea dirk."

He placed the weapon on the band of pink shell, and it
immediately turned sienna and cream. In an instant, it began to spiral around the dirk, winding it in its peculiar
shroud.

"From the sea we came, from the sea we return," Kelyx

intoned. "In the bosom of the ocean, where all life begins, there is no ending, there is no regret, there are only new beginnings."

He nodded to Kurgan, who threw the shrouded dirk into the waves. It sank out of sight without even the vestige of a splash, vanishing as its master had vanished, without a trace.

Kurgan, watching the rolling sea, tried to think of Courion, as he had done for the entire time he was on the ship, but his thoughts were tangled up in the lies he was bound to tell the Sarakkon. If he had known himself better, he would have understood that he was caught up in the lies he had been telling himself ever since he returned from Za Hara-at. But he was a Stogggul; he could not know himself better. And so, instead of thinking about Za Hara-at and what had transpired there, instead of thinking of *her*, he had come down to Harborside, to Courion's funeral, to get away from feelings that were, in the end, impossible to deny. That did not stop him from trying. But, of course, even among the Sarakkon, he could not elude them. They darted, silver and gold, like fish beneath the waves, and made it difficult for him to feel anything for the Sarakkon captain he had called friend.

"It is over," Kelyx said. "Now our captain is part of history."

The crew dispersed, taking up, in twos and threes, their appointed chores.

"We sail within the half hour," Chron said.

Kurgan nodded. "I understand." And turned toward the gangplank.

"You are welcome to sail with us, Kurgan Stogggul," Kelyx said.

Kurgan paused. "My regrets, Ship's Surgeon." He gave a fastidious smile. "Another time it will be my pleasure." There was nothing he wanted less.

W hat are they doing in there?" Eleana stalking back and forth in the enormous cavern that led to Rappa territory. They looked out on semidarkness, overflowing with the murmurous conversations of the Rappa, so curious about everything, not the least of which this gathering of folk of neither their kind nor kin.

The Nawatir, thick blond hair and close-cropped beard, high cheekbones and wide mouth set in a globular Kundalan skull, glanced at her. "We will find out soon enough."

Her grey-green eyes clouded over. "If they tell us anything."

"Did you have such impatience when you were in the Resistance?"

"In truth, it is the Resistance I cannot get out of my mind," she said simply. "Each day that goes by the Khaggun kill more of them. What are we doing here?"

"I do not know."

"Neither do I, and that is my point." A swirl of luxuriant nut-brown hair, this is what defined her, and a full, generous mouth, leading to a face, overall, of defiance, of crafty stratagems, of moving forward in the advent of adversity. It was so bold you could not help but ask yourself what lay beneath. "Doesn't it ever concern you that the two of them—Riane and Giyan—keep so many secrets?"

"Yes. When it comes to Giyan it bothers me deeply." He was clad in dark red crosshatched tunic and trousers of a supple and lustrous fabric unknown on Kundala. From a thick belt hung two swords, their scabbards incised with Miina's runes. The long, gleaming blades, etched down their lengths, thrummed like beaten bass drums when he drew them.

"What is it, then? Do they not trust us enough?"

The Nawatir, his tongue seized up, said nothing. But Eleana, who knew his silence for brooding, would not let him be, and at length he gave in, not because he was weak, but because he did not want to keep secret the thorn in his heart.

"Perhaps it is a matter of love. I love Giyan so, and she says she loves me." He started out slow and halting, feeling his way, and Eleana stepped closer to him, and his strange, semisentient cloak curled around her protectively. He had told her that it was like a companion or a familiar. "But I ask myself how it can be so. I was a Khagggun Pack-Commander when she met me. I had pursued her charge, Annon Ashera, into these very hills, to her home at Stone Border. And when Annon died, she brought him out to me so that I would stop the killing of innocent Kundalan. I wonder now how I could have done those things. But having done them, I wonder how she could love me. Were our situation reversed—were I the Kundalan and she the V'ornn—I could not."

He stopped, a little dazed by how much he had revealed.

"And now you wonder whether her love for you is real?"

"How can it be?" he asked, anguished. "How can she forget who I was, what I did to her? No sooner had I delivered her dead charge to me than I took her as concubine. How she fought me. How she. . . ."

But he could not go on. He turned away from Eleana, and she put her hand out to reassure him, but thought better of it, and dug a hole in the pocket of her jerkin instead.

Eleana sighed to herself and shook her head. It pained her to see her friend in such an agony of despair. She understood all too well his longings and desperate fears. In Za Hara-at, she had said to Riane, *We must not be afraid to say what is in our hearts. When I see you I cannot cool my body down. I have never felt this way about anyone.* For she had come to know with the ineluctable surety of those in love that her beloved Annon was still alive, that somehow, by whatever sorcery, he abided inside Riane.

"I wonder at what you say because of late the question of love has been much in my mind." She spoke softly to the Nawatir's broad back. "Love is an insolvable mystery, where it comes from, why it strikes us, how it grabs hold and never lets go. We will never understand its nature. And here is all that can be fathomed of it. It is love that transforms us, not V'ornn technomancy or Kundalan sorcery, because it does so completely from the heart. But I also

know the longing that springs from wanting to go back to
the way you once were. As much as I love being a member
of the band of outsiders, that very name triggers desires in
me, for I miss desperately my life in the Resistance, where
every day I could see the difference I was making in the
cause of Kundalan freedom against the V'ornn."

He said nothing, his back and shoulders a heavily defended wall.

"We never know what we will become, Rekkk. Look at
you, born a V'ornn of Khagggun caste, trained from birth
to be a warrior, to kill and maim, to do the bidding of the
Gyrgon. And yet you stopped. You questioned everything.
Your love for Giyan transformed you. From that moment
on, you were in a sense no longer truly V'ornn. Why do
you question the similar transformation in her?"

She knew the answer, of course. His guilt at what he had
done plagued him. If she had learned anything during her
time with the Resistance is was this: the spectre of the past
made the present unendurable.

"It is true that I have been transformed again. When I
look into a mirror I do not even recognize myself. I am the
Nawatir, but I am only slowly beginning to explore the
powers I have been given. This cloak is sorcerous, yet I do
not yet know the extent of its magic." He shook his head in
bewilderment. "It is all so new, all so mysterious, and I am
not comfortable with secrets and mysteries." He was huge,
and yet now he seemed to have been swallowed by his
cloak. His face was a clenched fist, cheekbones like bared
white knuckles, ready to put someone, anyone, on their
back. "What if she doesn't love me, after all. What if she
is just using me, if this is some sort of revenge she has
schemed."

"Surely you cannot believe that."

"It is what, above all else, I fear."

He frightened her when he was like this. She worried he
was digging a grave for himself but felt helpless, unable to
grab the shovel from his grip.

She turned with relief at the sound of nails clacking on

stone. Thigpen was trotting toward them across the cavern floor—Thigpen, made voluble by her own anger, her own sense of abiding injustice that ran through the entire species like a rip current. Thigpen, who started telling them about banestones and couldn't stop.

2

A Host of Questions

When through a lattice of cruel sunlight and knife-edged shadow Kurgan Stogggul had seen Riane and Eleana standing close together in the ruins of Za Hara-at, he had felt his stone hearts shatter. Lying now in a sinister fen of jewel-toned cushions, the aromatic smoke from a laaga stick drifting from between his lips, he closed his eyes and returned in memory to his crouching place behind a gritty wall, incised with unknowable runes, deep in the heart of the excavation of the ancient city. Even the bleary drug-induced fog could not stop his teeth from grinding in fury. In Za Hara-at he, the V'ornn regent of all Kundala, had been reduced to a craven fugitive. In Za Hara-at he, the scion of the illustrious trading family of Stogggul, had been reduced to a panting pup, his avid gaze caressing the contours of the Kundalan female whom he had taken by force. On that sun-spangled day two years ago, he had pounded into her all of his rage and contempt for the race that continued to confound his own. But ever since then he had been haunted by her.

After a hundred blind alleys he had still been in the ruins. The center of nowhere, among great groaning slabs of incised stone, a forest that had grown up around him while he slept. Unraveling his sleeve, leaving a thread behind

him to guard against double-tracking, his greatest fear, he
had finally emerged. With haste, he had descended at the
head of a detachment of Khagggun, intending to take
Eleana, Riane, and Giyan prisoner. But, try as he might, he
could not find his way back to the place where he had seen
them. Every time he had been certain he had made the
right turn, his mind grew hazy, and he became unsure of
himself. Ordering the Khagggun to fan out and search in
ever-widening circles had proved fruitless as well, and, at
last, he had ordered the search abandoned.

A toxic blue light leaked in through the window of the
high tower, playing upon the spiderweb scrim of his closed
lids. Outside seethed Axis Tyr, once the capital of all the
northern continent, now the nerve center of the V'ornn occupation of Kundala.

Kurgan sprawled, half-insensate, dreaming his drug-
induced dreams in the kashiggen he had commandeered
for his own use. This was a pleasure palace he had all to
himself, a haven from the frustrating tangle of rules and
regulations that bound the regent in boredom. Being the regent was not all he had dreamed it would be. Protocol
stymied him; and he was, like all V'ornn, still a slave to
Gyrgon whim.

He had already smoked half his first laaga stick by the
time the dzuoko had brought him the salamuuun, the potent psychotropic drug whose distribution was controlled
by his mortal enemies, the Ashera family. Following a
sour flight that made forgetting even more imperative, he
had lighted another laaga stick, using the smoke to conjure
up Eleana.

He had overheard her name when, upon seeing her with
Riane, he had sidled closer. His first sight of her in Za
Hara-at—sun-browned hand resting with the assurance of
an enchantress or a goddess upon a ruined temple's
cornice—had so unnerved him that he had fled into the
maze of half-destroyed buildings. He should have left
then, but he could not budge, could not even turn his head
away from the sight of her. The pale down of her strong

brown arms had so affected him he had actually become dizzy. Like all V'ornn he was utterly hairless. Up until his encounter with Eleana he had thought himself immune to the common male fascination with Kundalan hair. While Eleana and Riane stood close talking softly, he drank in her dark thicket of hair, her wide-set, grey-green eyes, her strangely flushed cheeks, her long and shapely legs licentiously bared through a slit in her robes. Yearning for a scent of her, he had stifled a moan. His tender parts had swelled painfully, forcing him to kneel. His back bowed, his blood throbbing in his veins, he was helpless before his lust.

A delicious eternity, floating in exquisite limbo, given over to a shower of shivers, symptom of a longing previously unknown to him. His hands curled into tight fists. What unthinkable alchemy had she worked on him?

"You must have her for your own."

The unfamiliar voice made his eyes snap open. He sat up, and when he saw the tall, hooded figure, wrapped in a fluid, floor-length greatcoat, he clasped his left forearm.

"My okummmon has been quiescent." He tried desperately to clear his head. "I have not been Summoned to the Temple of Mnemonics in more than a fortnight."

"I suppose," the figure said in a deep booming voice, "you thought after Nith Batoxxx died, the Comradeship would be in such disarray you could do as you pleased." Veradium tassels at the greatcoat's hem winked and flickered like flames as the figure approached him. "Now you know the folly of that assumption. All Gyrgon are linked through the Comradeship's central neural net. I know everything Nith Batoxxx knew about you, regent."

Not everything, surely, Kurgan thought smugly.

The figure drew away the hood. Implanted in the pale amber skull from just above the crimson-irised eyes was a neural net of germanium and tertium wafers floating in a semiorganic material. No one knew whether the Gyrgon were born this way or were operated upon just after birth. Kurgan would give his left arm to know, for he longed to usurp the power the Gyrgon held over all the other V'ornn castes, both Great and Lesser.

"I am Nith Nassam," the Gyrgon said.

"Have you taken Nith Batoxxx's place?"

Nith Nassam glanced around the sybaritic kashiggen chamber with a look of mingled rectitude and disgust. A glowing network of biocircuits were constructed as a pair of stubby horns that sprouted from the top of his forehead.

The Gyrgon studied him with his eerie, glittery eyes. "I see that I was right about you, Stogggul Kurgan."

Kurgan tense and on guard. "In what way?"

"Periodically, through the okummmon, the regent is Summoned by us. We test him, digest his news, and give him orders, which he carries out unquestioningly. It has always been thus. We Gyrgon find it useful to rule through—"

"Fear."

"—proxy." Nith Nassam's poise appeared undisturbed. "But you are different. You do not fear us as others do. This doubtless was Nith Batoxxx's doing, since it was he who trained you. No, for you something of a more— improvisational nature—is in order." He grinned unexpectedly. "A traditional Summoning affords you altogether too much warning."

"So you found me here."

Nith Nassam circled him, as if inspecting a craggy bannntor. The inside of his greatcoat was a pustule yellow, the same metallic hue as his ion exomatrix. "My dear regent, as long as the okummmon is implanted in your arm I can find you anywhere." He spread his hands, over which, like all Gyrgon, he wore neural-net gloves. "Besides, why would you want to hide from me? Have you secrets you have not disclosed? Have you plans to which I am not privy?"

Kurgan held his ground, said nothing. Gyrgon delighted in lying, obfuscating, deliberately deceiving the other castes if only to see the resultant reactions. They were scientists, behavioral and otherwise. To them, the entire Cosmos was an experiment in progress. And their holy grail, the reason they kept the homeless V'ornn traveling among the stars, absorbing the knowledge of new cultures before ravaging them, destroying them? Nothing less than the secret of eternal life.

Nith Nassam had come close enough now that Kurgan could feel the ion pulses given off by the Gyrgon's gloves like the bites of tiny insects. At Nith Nassam's merest thought, these ion pulses could deliver either pain or death. How he would love to don a pair, to wield that power over others.

"Of course you do, Stogggul Kurgan. You eat and drink secrets; they make up the very air you breathe. You cannot live without them. Like this lust you exhibit for a Kundalan female." He grunted. "Spend yourself in tender flesh, lose yourself in laaga and salamuuun. Indulge yourself as you may, if that is your wish. What do I care about such low matters?" He shook his head. "Do you think the secrets you harbor matter to me? The mistake my brethren have made with you is in trying to discover them. I have no such designs on you." He stuck his face in Kurgan's. "But you *will* obey me, in all matters. Unquestioningly. Unhesitatingly."

Kurgan noted that he said "obey me," not "obey the Comradeship." He was only seventeen, but ever since he could remember he had been under the thumb of adults. In one way or another, he had managed to outwit them all. Now, just when he thought he was free, Nith Nassam wanted to extend his servitude.

"Nith Batoxxx was possessed," he said in response, "by a Kundalan archdaemon named Pyphoros. I know a great deal about this archdaemon."

Nith Nassam's eyes glittered evilly. "It would be wise of you not to persist in perpetuating such myths."

There was nothing to be gained by engaging in an argument with a Gyrgon. "My obedience is not without value. What I want in return—"

Nith Nassam flexed his fingers. "Think not of dictating terms to a Gyrgon."

"What I want is the salamuuun trade."

The Gyrgon's laugh was ghastly, as were the alarming teeth he bared. "Like the majority of your caste. The salamuuun trade is the dominion of the Ashera."

"But why?"

"It is Edict. It is Law."

"You are Gyrgon. You can bend the Law, change it—"

"You do not understand."

"This is my point."

"You are wasting my time. You would have to be Gyrgon to understand." Nith Nassam snapped his fingers. "Now, come. There is work to be done." And he spread his greatcoat, encompassing them both.

Riane was staring into the mirror when everything disappeared, her reflection included. She saw herself walking through a windswept landscape, knees held high as she crunched through deep snow. The sky was purple, the sun glaring. She squinted, shading her eyes against the glare. Now and again granulated ice swept off the mountain crest in chittering swarms. She continued trekking up the steep slope. Every detail was familiar to her, as if she were following a path unseen except in her mind.

She came at length to high walls and, fitting an enormous key into an iron lock, she opened the front gates of basalt slabs bound in incised bronze. The courtyard that confronted her was laid with pink gravel, carefully raked into a wave pattern. It was bisected by a black-basalt path. There was no snow, no ice. Not even a puff of wind to disturb the perfect pattern of the pink gravel and the thickly leafed sheared trees. A pair of pale carved-stone fountains were set in the gravel on their side of the path. The soft *plink-plink* of water was soothing. Overhead arced a perfectly cloudless sky of a piercing purple-blue.

As a dreamer would, she walked along the central path without seeming to move her legs. She stopped when she came abreast of the fountains. There were Venca runes carved into their massive basins. The ones on the right spelled out the word MEMORY. The ones on the left spelled out the word OBLIVION.

No one came here but her. No one knew of this place but her.

She was absolutely alone. . . .

She opened her eyes and gasped. Her heart was pounding hard in her chest.

"What is it?" The concern on Giyan's face deepened. "Ah, I know. It must be so hard seeing yourself like that."

Riane said with a lump in her throat, "Yes, it's difficult and disquieting. At times I feel as if I am broken in two, cut off, being driven insane. But why should I think of those things? Look what I have become. What I want, Giyan. I long for arduous quests, dark days, facing down evil."

"That is the V'ornn in you talking, Teyjattt. The Annon I remember, that I raised from an infant. Your Kundalan warrior hearts still beat strong. Had I the power to turn back time—"

"Please don't." Giyan's anguish was like a stone in her heart.

"In order to save your life I put your essence into the body of this dying Kundalan girl." Giyan's voice dropped to a whisper. "What else could I have done?"

"You did what you had to do. I would not be alive if you hadn't. I say that for Annon *and* Riane. You saved us both." Riane reached out. "Giyan, I feel closer to you than I did to my own mother. This is what had to be."

What had to be, Giyan thought. *Of course. I fell in love with Eleusis Ashera. It had to be. I secretly bore him a son named Annon. It had to be. I passed on my Gift to him. It had to be. And now I cannot bear to tell my beloved child the truth for fear he will hate me forever for lying to him.*

They needed, both of them, to return to the present. "What did you see, Teyjattt?" Using the affectionate name she had called Annon when he was a small child restored her inner equilibrium. The life of her child was so precious to her that Giyan would have gladly died that instant if it assured her safety. "Another fragment of Riane's life?" The original Riane had lost her memory in a fall. "Tell me what happened."

Riane stared again into the mirror. Her reflection wavered, dissipating like breath on a frosty day. An instant of sheer whiteness and then . . . She spoke to Giyan, describing everything as she traveled the pink-gravel courtyard in the shadow of the Great Rift high in the Djenn Marre. The twin fountains of MEMORY and OBLIVION were at her back, and she was moving farther down the black-basalt path.

On the far side of the courtyard lay a long, low, symmetrical building with a roof that curved up on either end, covered in celadon-colored tiles. It was the most beautiful structure she had ever seen. She crossed the sea of gravel on the basalt path and entered the building. It was cool and calm inside. She could hear the echo of her boot soles against the green-marble floor.

She was in a central vestibule. It was cubic; light was diffuse, neither too bright nor too dim. On either side stretched interminable corridors down which sound-dampening runners had been laid, but the floor of the vestibule itself was bare. In the center of the stone flagging was set a mosaic medallion depicting the face of a male with a flaming red beard. The corners of his blue eyes were crinkled, and he seemed to be smiling at her. He was so familiar she was on the verge of saying his name, but she could not remember it.

OBLIVION.

She moved along the corridors, past door after door. Each one had a brass plate affixed to it where she knew a rune would be engraved. All the plates were blank, all the rooms were locked.

At the end of the long corridor on her left were two doors, opposite each other. One held the rune for Moon. She opened the door, and there, chapter by chapter, page by page was *Utmost Source,* the sacred book of Miina she had memorized, carefully arranged in vertical files along the shelves that lined the room.

The door opposite held the rune for Night. She opened the door and there chapter by chapter, page by page was *The Book of Recantation,* the other sacred book she had memorized.

"So this is Riane's construct," Giyan said, when her child had returned from her vision. "The Riane before you entered her, Teyjattt. It is her memory that is eidetic."

"Ironic, since she can remember her past only in small disassociated shards."

"The construct allows her to store all the things she wanted to remember in the rooms."

"But so many are marked OBLIVION and are unavailable."

"You will simply have to work on that. There is no easy answer, no quick cure for memory loss. Even sorcery avails us little." Giyan shook her head. "Listen to me, Teyjattt, this female whose body you have inherited is a very special creature. Even though we are ignorant of her origins, we know three very important things about her: she possesses an eidetic memory, she is fluent in Venca, and she is an accomplished mountain climber. My advice is to keep these things in mind as you seek to solve the puzzle of her past."

"Could she have been a Ramahan?"

"Doubtful." Giyan shook her head. "I know of no abbey that taught Venca. Even the highest konara of Floating White have no expertise in it."

"She must be Druuge, then."

"That is a possibility, yes. But what would Druuge be doing so high in the Djenn Marre? They have settled in the desert, the Great Voorg."

"But they do travel. All over, if rumors are to be believed."

"I shall have to ask Perrnodt." She held out a hand. "Now show it to me please."

Riane handed over a small milk-white wand.

"So this is the infinity-blade."

"You activate it by pressing the tiny gold disc just there. But it won't work now. When Minnum gave it to me he said there were only two charges left in it. I used them up in the Korrush."

"And it is a goron-particle beam?"

"That is what Minnum told me." Riane took it back. "And he was right. With it I was able to kill Nith Settt."

Giyan frowned. "Where did it come from? It is not V'ornnish technology."

"No. And Minnum had no idea."

"If we had more of these, we could reclaim Kundala."

"It does no good wishing for lightning." She was staring at the wand, rolling it in her hand. "We have no other wands, and this one is now useless. I know of no way to repower it."

Giyan, attuned to her child's emotions, said, "What is it about the infinity-blade, Teyjattt?"

"I don't know." Rolling it back and forth from fingertips to base of thumb. "I could almost believe . . ." She put a hand to her temple, as if she could conjure the memory to life. "The feel of the wand in my hand is so familiar."

"Are you implying that Riane once had use of such a weapon?"

Riane shook her head. "I don't know why it feels right, or how."

"Leave the memory thread alone, and sooner or later it will be sure to surface." Giyan's hand was on her child's shoulder, squeezing reassuringly. "Put it away now, Teyjattt. We have more pressing matters to occupy us. With the archdaemons banished back to the Abyss, the Storehouse Door will now open for you. It is time you returned to your quest for The Pearl."

"I am more than ready."

Giyan nodded. "Let us gather the others and make our plans."

"Quickly, now." Riane leading the way as they strode into the larger cavern. "I have grown weary of this sunless underworld."

At once, darkness became visible. There was a sensation of falling, and Kurgan grew dizzy. In an instant, the greatcoat was pulled aside, like a theater curtain. They were on a narrow glassy catwalk. All around them loomed vast space and the throaty thrumming of massed engines. It was a sound with which he had become familiar. They were inside the Gyrgon Temple of Mnemonics.

As he followed Nith Nassam down the catwalk, Kurgan could dimly make out other such pathways, so many it seemed as if he was looking at a metropolis of spiderwebs. Presently, the thrumming became a roar, and he saw looming on his left a sphere, gleaming deep bronze. It was so enormous he could make out neither top nor bottom. From an opening a vivid rubicund glow infused the surrounding area, and through the thrumming he could hear the rhythmic beats as of a hammer striking an anvil.

"What is that?" Kurgan craned his neck; but they had passed it so quickly he was left with only a fleeting glimpse, compressed like dream memory, of ruddy clouds passing with unnatural swiftness over a kind of metallic landscape through which misshapen shadows flickered and darted like wraiths or flames.

Of course, Nith Nassam did not provide an answer, and Kurgan had an uncharacteristically vague feeling of anxiety, as if someone unseen had been probing his innermost organs.

Ever pragmatic, he shook off the freakish sensation and returned to the mind-bending task of trying to outwit yet another Gyrgon.

Within moments, they climbed aboard a moving catwalk, which even as it conveyed them forward, swung them horizontally through grey space. At length, they reached their destination, another enormous sphere. It, as Kurgan guessed, was accessed via a circular hatch, through which Nith Nassam bent, and disappeared. Kurgan hesitated one long breathless instant, then he, too, stepped through.

Thirteen tear-shaped globes spinning in an oval orbit spilled cold purple-blue light onto a lozenge-shaped chamber around which the Gyrgon sphere had been constructed. The original Kundalan murals, as fanciful as they were ornate, covered the walls, which were overgrown with a webwork of fragrant orangesweet vines. This was Nith Batoxxx's laboratory. Kurgan again passed his fingertips over the scar in the hollow of his neck. The last time he had been there it was as the prisoner of Pyphoros. That was where the slow drip of the archdaemon of daemons' saliva had burned the foul inverted crescent into his flesh.

"You have been here before," Nith Nassam was saying. "Do not bother denying it." He was activating vast holopanels that depended from the ceiling like cool, clear stalactites. He turned from the softly glowing panels, studying the sharp-edged planes of Kurgan's face before alighting on the predatory night-black eyes. "I would take that as a lesson, if I were you, regent."

There was nothing Kurgan despised more than being spoken to as if he were a child.

"The Comradeship was once of one mind," Kurgan said, seizing the offensive. "It must have come as quite a shock to discover that you had been betrayed by one of your own."

"Nith Batoxxx was not the true betrayer; Nith Sahor was," Nith Nassam said. "What excuse did Nith Sahor have for embracing Kundalan culture?" His thin bluish lips held a sneer. "But then, Stogggul Kurgan, you have had ample experience with betrayal. Your handpicked Star-Admiral, in league with a rogue Line-General, tried to assassinate you." The sneer had turned into a smirk. "Have you yet named a successor? The Khagggun cannot for long operate at full efficiency without a supreme commander. What army can?"

Kurgan was beginning to enjoy this. There was nothing like verbal jousting to keep the mind sharp. "It seems I was reckless with my first choice. I am being more circumspect with this one."

"That is wise. But I wonder whether it will be sufficient. Your father was imprudent in promising the Khagggun Great Caste status. Only resentment and ferment has come of it. The high command grows distracted by the pursuit of amassing fortunes like you Bashkir while the rank-and-file warriors are resentful of their superiors' growing wealth. In short, your father has put a razor-raptor in among the qwawd."

"And what do you propose for a solution?" Kurgan asked.

"I?" Nith Nassam waved a gloved hand, sending tiny ion arcs spinning. "I am not concerned with such mundane matters. This is a question for the regent to answer."

Kurgan did not for a moment believe him. There was a saying among the Bashkir: *What Gyrgon cannot control, they destroy.*

"Once the waste chute is open you cannot put the excrement back in," Kurgan said.

"I have heard that said amongst the Khaggun," Nith Nassam replied, without a trace of amusement.

"Because it has not been debated in Gyrgon convocation does not make it any less true." Kurgan glanced at the shiny surface of the sinister egg-shaped chamber that stood to one side of the laboratory, then studiously ignored it. "My task is to find and train a Khaggun who shares my views, not those of his caste."

His comment seemed to arouse Nith Nassam's interest. "You mean to name as Star-Admiral a Khaggun not currently of the high command?"

"That is precisely what I mean to do."

"Fleet-Admiral Pnin Arduss will not be pleased. Are you prepared for the consequences?"

"I have lived among the Khaggun, Nith Nassam. I know how they think. I know what they will fight for. I know for whom they will die. So, yes, all in all, I would say that I am prepared."

Nith Nassam turned back to the holoscreens, having apparently lost interest. Kurgan, for his part, was satisfied that at least in the early going of this unorthodox Summoning he had held his own. How well he knew that Gyrgon tended to look upon the Bashkir as slightly wayward children, requiring guidance and, at times, strict discipline to keep them functioning at peak capacity. In order to eke out a modicum of their respect one had to display decisiveness and commitment.

As Nith Nassam's fingers worked the holoscreen a circular door corkscrewed open in the egg-shaped chamber. "Do you know what this is?"

Kurgan shook his head, though he knew very well that it was a goron-wave chamber.

The Gyrgon turned to him. "You know what I found in there, don't you, regent?" He led Kurgan across the laboratory to the sloped edge of the chamber and gestured. "There was a Sarakkonian captain named Courion inside. He was quite dead. His teeth had disintegrated, and his eyeballs were entirely white. His heart was shriveled to the size of a clemett pip. What killed him was the same thing that killed so many of us at Hellespennn. Goron particles. This means that Nith Batoxxx was experimenting with the source of Centophennni weapons. It seems reasonable, then, to assume that he knew things he chose not to share with the rest of the Comradeship."

"I thought that was impossible," Kurgan said, though he knew perfectly well that Nith Batoxxx had found a way to go off-line without being detected. "The Comradeship is a kind of hive mind linked through the core databanks, is it not?"

Nith Nassam turned away as if he either had not heard or did not care. He stood staring into Nith Batoxxx's goron-wave chamber.

As far as the Comradeship was concerned, their sole interest in the Sarakkon was their handling of radioactive substances, techniques they readily shared with the Gyrgon in exchange for being left alone. The trouble was, the Sarakkon were immune to the radioactive effects of these substances and V'ornn were not. Judging by how Courion had died, however, the Sarakkon were as susceptible to goron particles as V'ornn were.

Nith Batoxxx had once told Kurgan that in the early

days of the occupation the Gyrgon had made selective experiments on Sarakkon, using very few so as not to engender suspicion. But all attempts to discover what it was about the Sarakkon that gave them immunity against radiation proved fruitless, and the experiments were halted. Then Courion had been bombarded with a goron wave. Curious. What *was* Nith Batoxxx up to?

Here was an opportunity, Kurgan knew, to be both bold and brave. And there was every chance that Nith Nassam's anger could be aroused. But Kurgan would never gain the power he sought over the Gyrgon unless he grabbed the opportunity by the throat.

"I have no idea what Nith Batoxxx wanted with Courion," he lied. "But I am willing to wager that if you allow me time in here, I can come up with the answer."

"Allow you access to a Gyrgon laboratory? You are delusional."

"My knowledge of the Sarakkon exceeds that of any other V'ornn." Kurgan peered into the interior, saw what was left of Courion. He had taken the chance that if Nith Nassam knew all the answers, the Gyrgon would not have bothered bringing him there in the first place. Which meant that something in the lab frightened even Gyrgon. "Besides, Courion was a friend. It is only fitting that you give me a chance to discover the manner of his death."

"You have no friends," Nith Nassam said. "That is known."

"What can I do to convince you of my sincerity?"

"Save the talk of sincerity for those foolish enough to listen."

"You are making a mistake."

"Enough!" The laboratory shuddered to the expression of Nith Nassam's wrath. "You think you can play your scheming games with me? In the performance of your duties, regent, you will say what I tell you to say. You will give the orders I direct you to give. Nothing more, nothing less." The Gyrgon pointed a finger. "I know what you want, Stogggul Kurgan, but let me assure you that the status of the salamuuun trade is fixed in stone. You cannot have it, and you will not be allowed to steal it."

Full of sudden fury, Kurgan bowed his head. It was at that moment he decided he must find a way to make Nith Nassam eat those words.

Reaching the caverns below the regent's palace will be the difficult part; once you are inside the Storehouse you are safe." Giyan rose, handing back the Nawatir's sword. They stood in a circle, the better to bind them to a common purpose. "The guardian of The Pearl is a Hagoshrin, and the Hagoshrin will be waiting for you, Dar Sala-at."

"How will it know me?" Riane asked.

"You will come to the Storehouse Door, you will put your finger through the Ring of Five Dragons and the Door will open. Only the Dar Sala-at can do that."

"And then what?"

"That is unknown," Giyan said. "But trust me when I tell you that the Hagoshrin are unlike any creatures you have ever encountered before. They are loyal, utterly fearless, and unbelievably ferocious. This is why one was chosen to guard The Pearl. He will tell you only the truth. He cannot lie. And so, in turn, you must speak truthfully to him."

"Now that it's settled," the Nawatir said, "what are we waiting for?"

"You and I must return to the Abbey of Floating White, both to ensure its safety and to help Konara Inggres return its functioning to Miina's original purpose," Giyan said. "I have a feeling that in the coming weeks it will become increasingly important to shore up its defenses." None of the band of outsiders questioned Giyan's intuition. "Besides," she went on, "too many of us skulking around Axis Tyr poses an unacceptable risk. The regent has ten thousand spies. We are bound to be spotted no matter how careful we are."

She turned to Riane. "You will take Thigpen. She will protect you."

"I think I should be the one to go with the Dar Sala-at," Eleana said at once. "I know the secret byways and hidden passages of Axis Tyr better than anyone here." She held up a hand at the sound of Giyan's protest. "Better than you, First Mother." Eleana's gaze swung to Riane. "Better even than Annon Ashera ever did."

Giyan and Riane exchanged a quick look.

This is a mistake, Teyjattt, Giyan whispered in Riane's mind.

I do not think so.

She had a difficult childbirth just a month ago.

No matter. She is a warrior. We are still very much fugitives from the regent and his Khaggun. As she said, I need her.

You are allowing your personal feelings to get in the way of—

This has nothing to do with how I feel about her.

It isn't that I don't understand, mind you. You have spent many months apart, Teyjattt. And those months have been, up until now, the most perilous of your lives. It is natural for you to resist parting again so soon.

It is that you still do not trust her, isn't it?

One of your band will betray you, Dar Sala-at. This is certain. It is written in Prophecy.

I would trust my life to Eleana. She would never harm me.

Still, I fear for her, as I fear for you.

At least she is Kundalan. Rekkk is, at hearts, a V'ornn.

As are you, Teyjattt. But of all of the band of outsiders, it is Eleana who suspects your true identity. It is useless to deny it. I see how she looks at you, as if you were still Annon Ashera. In that, her love makes her powerful. But if it should become known to even one of your many enemies that Annon Ashera is not, indeed, dead as they now believe, the danger to you, well, we are not yet ready to deal with such dire consequences.

And yet, if she does not go, who will get us safely through Axis Tyr?

Annon's memory should be sufficient

Annon was the regent's son. He never knew the secret passages made by the Resistance. Neither do you. Remember, without her knowledge we never would have gotten the Ring of Five Dragons to the Storehouse Door in time to save Kundala from being blown apart.

Giyan, still staring into her child's eyes, gave a curt nod, and addressed those assembled in clipped tones. "This is how it will be. Thigpen will accompany the Dar Sala-at to protect her in Axis Tyr and in the caverns. Eleana, it will be your responsibility to get them safely through Axis Tyr."

A look of relief washed over Eleana's face. "Thank you, First Mother."

Giyan drew Eleana away from the others. "Beware, my child. Guide them to the caverns, but go no farther. I fear there are dangers awaiting you in Middle Palace."

3

The Black Finger

The bandy-legged sauromician named Minnum, face as round and hairy as a thistle, kind eyes and a kinder heart, was looking for his razor to cut a noxious wart off a hoary knuckle when he discovered that the banestone was missing. He and Sornnn SaTrryn, working happily together at the vast archeological dig of Za Hara-at, had unearthed the banestone. It was twice as large as Sornnn's fist and astonishingly dense, causing Minnum to groan in unexpected strain when he had first picked it up. Not that he had used his bare hands. Cautioning Sornnn not to do so either, he fashioned a sling from an old hat he never wore and brought it up out of its deep hole as if it were a baby in its rocker.

It was shaped like the egg of some titanic reptile. Though its striated surface was smooth as obsidian, it absorbed light instead of reflecting it. The moment he lifted it he felt the agonizing echo of its power, and his blood ran cold. It was an evil omen; very evil, indeed.

He knew all too well the banestones' purpose for, like the legendary Pearl, they had been much coveted by the league of sauromicians.

Now it was gone. Frantic, he searched his quarters from top to bottom, then from bottom to top, and all the area around, using every method at his disposal, including spells. Alas, he could find no trace of it. It had vanished as completely as if it had never existed. Truth to tell, part of him was relieved, for a single banestone, like a lone spotted wolf, could only cause evil, and often the consequence of an attempt to use one was nothing like what the user had intended. Only by linking all of them, as had long ago been done in Za Hara-at, could they be relied upon absolutely. Quite naturally, another part of him was terrified; for he knew that during the events of the past several weeks, long-buried Za Hara-at had begun to come alive again, and Miina only knew what was left behind when the daemon constructors were banished. Ancient beasts and wyr-goblins stirred in its darkling bowels.

And so he sat, brooding in his wind-blasted tent, while the ruddy Kundalan sun, gravid with its dark purple spot, plunged behind the bloody-toothed lower jaw of the Djenn Marre. The mouth of night stole in like a longed-for lover, exhaling constellations of stars across the great steppe sprawling 250 kilometers northeast of Axis Tyr. It was at this time, especially, when he heard the voice of Za Hara-at, still half-drowned in the red sandy soil of the Korrush. It was a voice of secrets, of ancient battles, the murmurous agitation of scarred legions led to their deaths, creaking through the warren of streets and boulevards, temples, storehouses, structures whose purpose was yet to be discovered or might never be. So powerful had been the sorcery enacted there that its incandescent residue had leached into the very rockwork of the city. Even the rubble was precious, for it preserved in its dust a truth that transcended that which could be seen, touched, tasted, smelled, or heard.

All this Minnum was aware of, dancing tantalizingly beyond his ken. Even the eventual appearance of his newfound friend, Sornnn SaTrryn, could not rouse his spirits from blackness.

"I would have been here sooner, but I ran into a Khagggun patrol." With a gust of gritty wind, Sornnn strode in with a round of traditional flatbread in one hand and a flask of wine in the other. He was quiet for a V'ornn, instilled with the solemnity and serenity of the Korrush, well schooled by his father as well as the Rasan Sul spice merchants with whom he did business. He had thoughtful eyes and a mind like a chronosteel trap. "The Khagggun are supposed to be protecting the Mesagggun architects here to help rebuild Za Hara-at, not harass poor Bashkir like me." Minnum and Sornnn were both secretly members of the band of outsiders, consisting of both Kundalan and V'ornn, who had pledged themselves to the Dar Sala-at.

"And you the Prime Factor," Minnum grunted.

"It is because I am the arbitrator for all Bashkir disputes that they cannot understand why I would prefer to sleep in this tent rather than be tucked warm and cozy behind protective ion fields in the V'ornn compound half a kilometer away." Sornnn SaTrryn sat down beside the diminutive sauromician. He was handsome, tall, lean, well muscled. His hairless bronze skin was deeply burnished. "And it is because I am Prime Factor that I cannot remain here, though it would be my wish."

"You're not going to leave me here on my own?"

"My duties call me back to Axis Tyr. I have numerous disputes awaiting adjudication."

"Typical of my life!" Minnum tore off a hunk of flatbread. The dense jungle of wiry hair made a halo round his outsize, bearded head. "I don't care what anyone says. Those packs of Khagggun makes me uneasy."

Sornnn nodded. "I am all too familiar with the horrors they perpetrate." Though he was the head of the wealthy and powerful SaTrryn trading house, he had learned from his father to love the Kundalan. Hadinnn SaTrryn had spent almost all his time on Kundala here in the Korrush, trading for spices. From a very early age, Sornnn had gone with him. He was fluent in the languages of all the Five Tribes of the Korrush, knew their customs better than any V'ornn. "I have seen the aftermath of firefights, when the only ones moving are the Deirus, there to administer to the dead and the dying."

"Deirus make me uneasy, too." Nervously, Minnum cast an eye toward Sornnn, who was searching through the trove of artifacts they had unearthed and cataloged.

Sornnn, confirming the sauromician's worst fears, said, "Minnum, what have you done with the banestone?"

"Best to forget the banestone, my friend."

Sornnn turned and, with hands on hips, faced him. Minnum could barely meet his gaze.

"Minnum, where is it?"

Wincing, he told Sornnn that the banestone had vanished. "The banestone was buried here for millennia," he added hurriedly. "Perhaps it is all for the best that it has been lost again."

"Is that what you believe?"

Minnum spread his arms. "What other possibility is there?"

"There were other sauromicians here just weeks ago."

"Speak not to me of them. I severed my ties with the Dark League years ago."

Sornnn threw him a look, dark and penetrating. "I think it is high time you told me about the sauromicians." He had about him the utter stillness Minnum knew well from the Korrush, that patient, watchful demeanor so atypical of his quick-tempered race. Sornnn also possessed a seemingly infinite capacity to absorb Kundalan lore.

While Sornnn settled himself on a carpet, Minnum sighed and took another swig of wine, extradeep this time, to prepare him for the tale. Wiping his red lips with the back of a hairy paw, he began.

"Once the sauromicians were Ramahan in the service of the Great Goddess Miina. We were the male sorcerers, wholly integrated with the female priestesses. As you doubtless know, in those days well before the invasion, ours was a society where males and females were partners in everything. Then, one hundred and two years ago, a cabal of male Ramahan grew restive. I was one of them. We coveted The Pearl, from which all Kundala was born, from whose limitless power the future of our race would be fashioned. With force unknown before in the abbeys, we overthrew Mother, ripped from the Keeper's hands this Pearl. For our sins, Miina cast us down into darkness. In trying to escape her wrath we ran to the farthest ends of Kundala. But she found us all, and those who survived she marked with a sixth finger, black as night, even as she burned away parts of our memories."

"But you have no sixth finger, black or otherwise."

"The Druuge interceded for me when I agreed to become curator of the Museum of False Memory. I was on probation, you see, when I was enlisted to help the Dar Sala-at in her search for the Veil of a Thousand Tears."

"You were being tested."

Minnum nodded. "And then to protect the Dar Sala-at I killed a sauromician, right here in Za Hara-at. And not just any sauromician. Talaasa, one of the Dark League's archons."

"There are others?"

"Indeed, yes." Minnum took another quick, nervous swig and gulped, nearly choking. "There are three. Always three." A dribble of wine crawled into the thicket of his beard. "Doubtless they will be looking for the perpetrator of Talaasa's death."

"What if the sauromicians did steal the banestone? What would they do with it?"

"I don't want to know." Minnum shivered and stared out at the ruins of Za Hara-at, lit by torches within and without by the eerie bluish light thrown off by the nearby V'ornn encampment of Mesagggun architects and their Khagggun bodyguards. The wind dug its claws into corners, screeching. His expression was bleak. "And believe me when I tell you that you don't want to know, either."

Receiving Spirit had once been a Kundalan hospice that the V'ornn had turned into a medical facility. As such, it was run by the Genomatekk caste but, as in all things V'ornnish, it was directed in secret by the Gyrgon.

Kurgan felt a ripple of unexpected emotion run through him as he walked into the vast, high-ceilinged lobby. Though his younger brother Terrettt had been incarcerated there for many years, Kurgan had not once come to see him. That unsavory task he left to his sister Marethyn, who had taken on the role of Terrettt's nursemaid.

On the other hand, he owed his sister a debt of gratitude (not that he would ever tell her), for it was through her persistent probing of the Deirus who took care of the mentally unstable Terrettt that she had discovered that Nith Batoxxx had somehow managed to manipulate Terrettt's genes, doubtless causing his madness. Chillingly, he had discovered in Nith Batoxxx's laboratory not only Terrettt's birth caul, but his own. Could this mean that the Gyrgon had manipulated his genes as well? And if so, why?

And so he had finally come to the massive bone-white structure at the northern edge of Harborside, not so much to see Terrettt as to talk to the Deirus in charge of him to find out everything he knew. Leaving his Haaar-kyut guards to terrorize those unlucky enough to be in the lobby, he went up the wide filigreed stairs, which in typically ornate Kundalan style were built in the shape of a spiral mollusk's shell. He hoped he would not run into Marethyn. Ever since she had declared her independence, she had become an embarrassment to the family. She was Tuskugggun, of a caste inferior to males, and yet she refused to acknowledge the order of things. Worse, she rebelled against it, declaring to all who would listen that

Tuskugggun were the equal of males. He was still smart-
ing at the way she had barged into their father's Rescendance ceremony, approaching him as if she were a Great
Caste male, berating him for not allowing Terrettt to attend. As if he would ever have any intention of allowing
Terrettt to make a public spectacle of himself. He had
heard reports of his brother's violent outbursts, his spew-
ing of insane ideas. Perhaps his madness made him the
popular painter he had become among the Bashkir and
even several of the higher-echelon Khagggun, though
Kurgan could see no talent there.

On the third floor, he asked to see the Deirus in charge
of his brother's case. Not long after, a small, wiry individual appeared. He had the corpselike pallor of his clients.
He introduced himself as Kirlll Qandda.

"I imagine you are here to see your brother," the
Deirus said.

"My sister isn't here, is she?"

"Oh, dear, no," Kirlll Qandda said with a nervous laugh
Kurgan found instantly annoying. "I haven't seen her for a
number of days. Um, or is it weeks?"

"Well, which is it?" Kurgan said irritably. He had not
liked this place the moment he stepped in, and each moment he was there was making him more uncomfortable.

"Well, to be honest, I am so wrapped up in my work—
your brother's case, not to put too fine a point on it—I
hardly know the time, let alone what week it is."

"You mean you are here day and night?"

"Often, yes." The Deirus gestured. "Please, regent,
come this way. I will take you to see Terrettt."

He led Kurgan through a warren of corridors. As they
went, Kurgan was careful to keep his distance from Kirlll
Qandda. It was not that the Deirus cared for the dead.
Someone had to do it and better them than him. No, it was
the fact that the Deirus consorted with their own gender that
sickened him.

They entered another corridor and were thrust into a
bustle of Deirus, going about their grisly chores. Kurgan

saw few Genomatekks now. From time to time, he heard small anxious murmurings and soft pitiable cries. The air held a fist of bitter medicinal scents.

They paused at the doorway to a small cubicle rife with holoscreens and data-decagons.

"My home," Kirlll Qandda said, rather pathetically. "Your brother's room is just over here."

"Perhaps it would be better to have this discussion in your office," Kurgan said, not moving a millimeter.

Kirlll Qandda frowned, then ducked his head. "As you wish, regent." He was more nervous now, and a loud crash ensued from his overeager attempt to clear a space for the regent to sit. Kurgan was not interested in sitting anyway.

"I have heard," Kurgan said without preamble, "that my brother has been the subject of a Gyrgon experiment."

"I believe that is so"—Kirlll Qandda ducked his head again—"though I can tell you that I have spent months in a vain attempt to locate any records of it."

"You might as well stop trying," Kurgan said. "The experiments were performed by a particular Gyrgon, now deceased, who did not enter his work into the records of the Comradeship." However, that did not mean that he had kept no records. Kurgan was willing to wager heavy coin that those records existed somewhere in Nith Batoxxx's laboratory. That was why he had tried to convince Nith Nassam to allow him access.

Finding a niche of cleared space, he leaned back against the wall. "What exactly was done to my brother?"

Kirlll Qandda turned to a holoscreen and tapped the photonic interface. A profile of a V'ornn head appeared. The Deirus tapped the interface again, and the flesh and bone vanished, revealing a cross section. "Here we have a typical V'ornn brain." His finger stabbed out. "You see? The nine main lobes, dual forebrains, four transverse lobes, two in each side, here and here, and beneath these six, the sylviat, where the senses are decoded, the sinerea, the central lobe where cortasyne and other chemicals are manufactured in larger amounts in the Khagggun, you know, fascinating, a subject for future study." His finger moved again. "For our purposes, however, it is the ativar, the primitive brain that is of interest. You see how small and compact it is, almost like an afterthought, a vestigial area without known function."

Kirlll Qandda brought up another image on a second holoscreen. "Terrettt's brain. In all ways, it appears normal." Finger jabbing out. "Save here. His ativar is three times the normal size. Notice how it has developed extensions that have twined themselves around the sinerea."

Kurgan peering at the holoimage with great concentration. "What does this mean?"

"Considering the curious admixture of chemicals he manufactures I would say that the retroset ativar is stimulating the sinerea in ways we cannot yet fathom."

"You said retroset."

Kirlll Qandda nodded. "As you know the central core databank was severely damaged and partially destroyed in the cataclysm that obliterated our homeworld countless millennia ago. And you also know that much of the data that survived is unreliable and often false."

Kurgan waved a hand for the other to continue.

"Instinct drew me back to the surviving medical database. My research there has uncovered a fascinating fact."

The image on the first holoscreen vanished, and another appeared. Kurgan looked from one to another. "Is this another view of Terrettt's brain? The ativar on this one looks identical to his."

"You are looking at a cross section of the brain of a member of our species who lived hundreds of thousands of sidereal years ago."

Kurgan, enraged, shot erect. "What are you telling me?"

"If the ancient data can be believed, your brother's brain is like that of the V'ornn who first set out on our galactic quest."

Kurgan's mind was working overtime. What could Nith Batoxxx have wanted? "What was the point?"

The Deirus offered a wan smile. "Now you know why I have been working day and night. I do not know the point." He turned off the holoscreens. "But it may be that our own present-day ativar have atrophied. Who knows, it may be that Terrettt's brain is in some ways, at least, more normal than ours."

Kurgan frowning, disbelieving. "Then why the seizures, the violent episodes?"

Kirlll Qandda hesitated only an instant. "If I had to guess, I would say that whatever was done to him failed. It produced these unfortunate side effects."

"*Unfortunate* is an interesting description of insanity."

"Terrettt is not insane." Kirlll Qandda stood up. "Shall we pay him a visit?"

Across the corridor was a locked door with a crystal viewing panel set into it at eye level. Through it, Kurgan saw a chamber with a large south-facing window overlooking Harborside, the Promenade teeming, the Sea of Blood aboil with Sarakkon ships and fishing boats. On one wall hung a large color topographical map of the northern continent. There seemed to be a number of circles, smears, and scribbles on it, the sure sign, Kurgan thought, of a mad V'ornn.

Kirlll Qandda was saying, "He has scars, as you will see, but they are old. I can control the seizures better now."

Kurgan staring at the photon lock. "But you have been unable to stop them."

"The abnormal outflow from the stimulated sinerea, you see."

Again he heard the Deirus say, *Terrettt is not insane.* It was then that he caught a glimpse of his brother, and was startled at how alike they looked. Terrettt's eyes were wide and feverish as he came into view. Three paintbrushes were clutched in his fist. With a manic energy that could be felt even through the closed door, a wide-legged stance, and a tensely hunched back he began to apply pigment to canvas.

Kirlll Qandda had only opened the door a crack, when Kurgan said, "No, wait. I . . . He is at work."

"Oh, I am sure he will be most pleased to see you, regent."

The muscles in Terrettt's cheeks bunched and bulged like those in his back. "I do not wish to disturb him," Kurgan said.

"If you change your mind, I will be in my office." He was about to turn away when he said, "If I may ask, regent, when did you see your brother last?"

Kurgan could not recall. He was sorry he had seen him now.

The Abbey of Floating White was a spectral stone edifice, with nine slender minarets topped by silver-leaf domes, rising from the bedrock of the Djenn Marre like the very hand of the Great Goddess Miina. It was there that Giyan had been trained as a Ramahan before she and those other few Ramahan born with the Gift had been exiled.

Nowadays, the abbey was overseen by Konara Inggres, a solid piece of carpentry, strong of limb and will, red-cheeked, intuitive, resourceful, gifted. She had resisted the daemons infesting Floating White, and, with help, had ousted them. But evil had many guises, as she was beginning to learn.

At this moment, she was at supper in the large, skylit refectory that she had restored. She sat at the head of a table empty save for her visitors, Giyan, the Nawatir, and a Druuge named Perrnodt. She herself had answered the visitor's bell, welcoming them with open arms as they dismounted the magnificent night-black narbuck, the Nawatir's great single-horned steed.

She looked around the refectory with mixed emotions. There was the relief of being free from evil's clutches but also a deep and abiding sadness that less than half the tables were filled with Ramahan.

Konara Inggres sighed. "It is a great relief to have you returned to us, First Mother."

Giyan smiled. "You have been making excellent progress here since we exorcized the archdaemon and his sauromician minions. We are all very proud of you, Konara Inggres, which is why you have been named head of the Dea Cretan."

"Though our ruling body is but a shadow of itself," the konara said.

"And yet for the first time in centuries it is pure again." Perrnodt was tall and thin, skin pale and translucent, and she gave the false appearance of fragility. The traditional Druuge *mistefan* had to a great extent tamed her night-black hair, though unruly wisps escaped here and there, framing a face severe as a dagger blade. "This is a new beginning. We must rejoice in that."

Konara Inggres shook her head. "In truth, I can feel little joy. I would not believe it, so many of our sisters gone, bewitched by the sauromicians."

"It is easier to believe a fantasy," Perrnodt said, "than to face the struggle of reality."

Konara Inggres nodded. "Miina has been gone so long. Ever since the V'ornn came, ever since The Pearl was lost, many of my sisters have also lost hope. Their faith had been hollowed out, they had begun to worship their growing fears."

"This is what the sauromicians excel at." Perrnodt knew the tastes of the Druuge. "It was how they usurped power over a century ago, how they came into possession of The Pearl."

"And yet now they have enlisted many of my sisters. Their power waxes again. Surely they must have recruited allies."

"Coerced them, more likely," Giyan said, "for that is the Dark League's way."

A soft susurrus, wind through a field of glennan, swept through the refectory, a flurry of furtive glances in their direction and hushed whisperings.

"You must forgive my Ramahan, Perrnodt," Konara Inggres said. "They have never seen a Druuge. Some may have stopped believing in their existence."

Perrnodt smiled. "It is only to be expected."

"But, after all, the Druuge were the original Ramahan. You were the first to sense the growing evil."

"And for that reason I think there remains a degree of resentment." Perrnodt had finished with her food. "For we Druuge left the abbeys, withdrawing into the Great Voorg."

"Which reminds me." Giyan pushed away her plate. "Are you aware of Druuge in the high Djenn Marre?"

"Well, of course we move everywhere, when the need arises. But I am aware of no particular activity there."

"Still," Giyan said, "it is possible for Druuge to be moving through the slopes and passes."

Perrnodt nodded. "I suppose so, yes."

Konara Inggres, refilling the flagons with ice-cold water, was still concerned with the impression her Ramahan were making on her distinguished guest. "Perhaps resentment is too strong a word for what my charges feel. Do not judge them too harshly. I am quite certain they are only curious as to why you did not stay to fight the evil."

"Is that a question?" Perrnodt said with some asperity.

Konara Inggres flushed deeply. "If it would not offend you, I would ask it."

"We each do battle in our own way, Konara Inggres. The Druuge withdrew to the desert so that we might continue our work unimpeded. We did not flee, as some of you might believe. We fought the battle in other ways, by paving the way for the Dar Sala-at, for instance. Among other things, we gave her an ally in the sauromician Minnum."

"One sauromician?"

"Oh, he is special," Perrnodt said. "Yes, Minnum is very special, indeed." She looked down at Konara Inggres' feet, where lay one of the two Ja-Gaar, ferocious sacred felines of Miina, who now helped guard the abbey. "And we had a hand in bringing these to life." She drained her flagon. "There are many ways to join the battle. Raising your fist is only one of them."

"How then will you help us battle the return of the sauromicians?"

"Giyan and I have discussed that in depth," Perrnodt said. "It is clear that for years the sauromicians were being aided by the archdaemon Pyphoros. Now that he has once again been incarcerated in the Abyss with the rest of his kind, it would be logical to assume that we may easily return our sisters to the fold. But as I put no store in assumptions, the question must be researched further. But fret not. I will come to you just after midnight with the answer."

After leaving the pathetic husk of his brother, Kurgan uncharacteristically lost his way. He went down one unfamiliar corridor after another without encountering a soul. He was about to turn around when he spied a set of double doors. Through the barred panes of crystal he saw a number of Khagggun standing guard over a straggly line of half-naked children who stood shivering, silent, and fearful. He looked upon them with a certain distaste. Why the Gyrgon were bothering with such refuse was beyond him. The children were the repellent mixed-race progeny of the thousands of Kundalan females who had been raped by Khagggun packs. He had heard rumors of recombinant gene resequencing experiments being performed on them by the Genomatekks at Gyrgon behest. Why not kill them outright and be done with the mess? That would be his solution. The shadowy rumors doubtless made their way to the Resistance, fueling their rage, redoubling their determination.

"Like what you see, regent?"

Kurgan turned to see a Gyrgon in an exomatrix biosuit, his taloned and winged helm completely covering his face and skull.

"I am Nith Immmon."

"Are you in charge of the experiments?"

"The children are in my care," Nith Immmon said obliquely. "Would you care to interview one or two?"

"No."

A slow smile spread across alloyed lips. How they managed to manipulate metal alloy as if it were V'ornn flesh was a mystery. "I did not think so." He pointed a gloved finger. "The recombinant experiments were of particular interest to Nith Batoxxx. But I suppose being so close to him you knew that."

Kurgan did not, and he was smart enough to keep his mouth shut about it.

"That being the case," Nith Immmon said equably, "it has become the special interest of Nith Nassam."

Kurgan found this exchange fascinating. Gyrgon did not reveal information without a reason. If Nith Immmon wanted him to know that Nith Batoxxx and Nith Nassam had been allied, it was because he was their enemy. Sornnn SaTrryn had once told him of a Korrush saying: The enemy of my enemy is my friend. That went so against the V'ornn grain, which was to kill an enemy as soon as he was identified as such, it had made him laugh. In the present situation, however, there was nothing funny about it. It occurred to him, not without irony, that a Gyrgon ally could prove useful, at least in the short run.

"It seems," he said with perfect candor, "that Nith Nassam has a special interest in me as well."

"Doubtless, you would enjoy a stroll through the ward beyond this door," Nith Immmon said as if he had not heard Kurgan.

He pushed open the doors, and they went through. A forest of small cubicles within which Genomatekks were examining very young children. He saw the patients' pale faces fill with fear as he and the Gyrgon passed.

"What will happen to the half-breeds?" he said.

"That is Nith Nassam's decision."

"I find it interesting," Nith Immmon said. "No Summoning was scheduled."

"Nith Nassam's idea of a Summoning is that he appears anytime he wants, anywhere he chooses."

Nith Immmon clasped his hands behind his back and pursed his lips. "What was the purpose of this most recent Summoning?"

"You mean he did not report it to the Comradeship?"

When Nith Immmon did not reply, Kurgan went on. "He asked me what I knew about Nith Batoxxx's experiments."

"This Summoning occurred where?"

"Nith Batoxxx's laboratory."

Nith Immmon stopped and turned to Kurgan. "You mean he took you into the Temple of Mnemonics?"

"Everything was as it had been left. Not even the corpse of the Sarakkon Courion had been removed." Kurgan searched the Gyrgon's eyes beneath the helm for clues. "He is extremely curious about Nith Batoxxx's experiments."

"He has no authorization to stick his snout into the investigation."

"That fact has not stopped him," Kurgan said.

"It is time to speak of you, Stogggul Kurgan." The Gyrgon's hands were once again clasped behind his back. "Make no mistake. There is a darkness about you. How shall I characterize it in a term you may understand? A penumbra, perhaps. In any event, it sets you apart." Nith Immmon lowered his voice, though every Deirus they passed shied away from them. "Though it goes against protocol, I will be candid. There are those in the Comradeship—chief among them the late Nith Batoxxx—who believe you to be a destroyer, the culmination, so to speak, of the storied Stogggul line. This faction expects a great deal from you. They see you as the great fist of the V'ornn." Greenish ion sparks arced off his upraised forefinger. "But there are others who interpret this darkness in another way. Their faction believes you to be irredeemably tainted by the hand of the Kundalan archdaemon. That faction wishes you dead."

Nith Immmon waited for a moment, then turned to Kurgan. "How does it feel to be threatened by Gyrgon?"

"There isn't a day in my life when I haven't felt threatened by Gyrgon," Kurgan said. "And yet, here I am."

Nith Immmon gave a little chuckle in which rows of very sharp yellow teeth glistered in the fusion lamplight. "You have been taught well, Stogggul Kurgan. I will give Nith Batoxxx that much."

* * *

T hree weeks!" Sornnn shook his head. "Three weeks and I have heard no word of Marethyn."

"Ah, yes." Minnum nodded as he brushed grit off Item 358b from their dig. "The regent's wayward sister."

"I should never have allowed her to join the Resistance."

Item 358b was carved into the shape of a figure seated cross-legged. Minnum picked up Item 358a, a head they had unearthed several days earlier, placed it onto the broken neck of the idol. The fit was just about perfect.

"Well, I suppose you could have bound and gagged her."

Sornnn paused, staring at the little sauromician. Then his lips curled in a wry smile. "You are right, of course. There was no way to stop her."

"Precisely. So put it out of your mind."

"I cannot. I worry about her safety."

An idol, no doubt about it, and a most curious one at that. Minnum turned the small, beautifully crafted figure around and around. Half-female, half-male. The breasts and nipples seemed swollen as if full of milk, the male member long and rigid, curving upward against the idol's belly, like a scimitar. He frowned. It was not a statue of Miina or any of her sacred creatures. Who was it, then? And what race had left it there in numinous Za Hara-at?

"Then it is well that you are leaving for Axis Tyr tomorrow," Minnum said.

Sornnn stared out into the utter stillness of the night. "Tomorrow is a long way off."

"Ah, love!" Minnum affixed the idol's head to its broken body. "I simply don't understand it. A sauromician's life is a lonely one, and none more than mine. During my long years of exile here in the Korrush and then, later, as curator of the Museum of False Memory in Axis Tyr I grew used to my solitude."

"Then I pity you, my friend."

Minnum shrugged. "There are benefits to being alone."

"Name one," Sornnn said shortly.

"You are beholden to no one."

"That is a benefit?"

"You know your problem? You are an inveterate romantic." Minnum started packing up their excavation gear. "And don't worry about me. I can manage quite well on my own. I always have."

Sornnn laughed.

Perrnodt was down in the triangular-shaped Kell, one of three such chambers where, in ancient days, the Great Goddess would periodically appear to monitor the holy work of her disciples. Perrnodt had come to this particular Kell because the triangle was Miina's most sacred symbol, representing as it did the three medial points: the Seat of Dreams, at the heart, the Seat of Truth, at the crown of the head, and the Seat of Deepest Knowledge, at the center of the forehead.

These were the body's power spots and she touched them with the forefinger and index finger of her left hand as she knelt in the center of the chamber. Her gaze lingered upon the image of Miina's sacred butterfly graven into the stone wall. Slowly, she allowed her eyes to close. Her breathing slowed until it became imperceptible. In her lap lay her closed left hand, and in it an opal nestled. For millennia, the most powerful Ramahan konara had used opals to communicate and to divine the nature of far-off things. Gradually, after the Druuge retreated to the Great Voorg, that skill was lost. So far as she knew, among Ramahan, only Giyan possessed the skill to cast the opals' power.

A slight tremor had begun to loosen Perrnodt's lower lip. As if it were a creature with a life of its own, this tremor proceeded down her arm, coursing over her breast, through her abdomen, into her pelvis and thighs. When it reached the soles of her feet, it rose, rippling through her body into her shoulders, down her arms, until it reached her left hand.

Her fingers were flung open as if plucked by unseen strings. The opal, vibrating, rose off the palm of her hand

and began to rotate. Throwing off sparks—green, blue, red—that bathed her in their milky light. Flashes of color, winking faster and faster until they blended together.

Perrnodt's eyes opened, but it was with a fixed stare that she peered deeply through the linkage of light into the opal's depths. She was seeking the Ramahan of the abbey who had been lost to the sauromicians' pernicious blandishments. To her they were like cor, momentarily led astray by poachers offering the promise of richer food, warmer quarters, and the power to defend themselves against snow-lynxes. She fully expected to find them abandoned and confused, trying to fend for themselves, unsure of the greeting they would find when they returned to the abbey they had so foolishly betrayed.

Through the lens of the opal's light the northern continent throbbed in her head. A pain began just behind her eyes, spreading rapidly to enclose her brain in a vise that exerted an intolerable pressure.

Perrnodt whimpered a little, but pressed on, the trail moving west, ever west, past the town of Exchange Pledges, bustling with the business brought to it by the V'ornn strip mines to the north. In the dense smoky depths of the Borobodur forest, the pain brought her low. Her chest constricted, she labored to take a breath. Through lips that could barely move, she invoked Crossed-Wrists, a Venca defensive spell. The cessation of the pain made her weep with relief, but within moments it was back, more agonizing than ever. She was obliged to cast ever more powerful spells, but even with that the periods of relief became shorter and shorter.

That confused and frightened her, for she felt certain that it was the Dark League that had turned their collective face in her direction in order to keep her from finding the abbey's Ramahan. The lens of the opal had turned opaque. No matter what she tried, it would not clear. From what infernal source were the sauromicians drawing their energy? She had heard stories—whispered, clandestine even among the Druuge—of the alleged power of necromancy, but, of course, that was impossible. Even the sauromicians would not dare to keep the dead from their cosmic fate.

She invoked Dragonfly in an attempt to use the opal to reveal to her the source of the sauromicians' newfound power. The opal began to shudder and shake as if it were trying to shatter itself against the sorcerous barrier it had come up against. And, then, all at once, the lens revealed to her a flash so horrific her mind could barely contain it. She saw the corpses of young Ramahan priestesses. Saw the look of fury frozen on their faces. In a frenzy, they had turned on each other.

Pain exploded, a searing fireball in her head, bursting nerves and blood vessels alike. She fell onto her back, her mouth working silently. Her heart thudded heavily in her chest. Her eyes were full of blood, and a blackness engulfed her that, gradually, she realized would not dissipate.

4

Return to Axis Tyr

Kurgan had been shadowing Nith Immmon for ten minutes along stone-clad corridors, through waiting areas flagged with agate tiles, down green-onyx and cor-blood-red-porphyry staircases, across abandoned skylit plazas, studded with obsidian plinths that had once held the trembling bodies of animals sacrificed to the Kundalan goddess Miina.

Kurgan, making a decision purely from intuition, had not walked out of Receiving Spirit after concluding his interview. Instead, as Nith Immmon had glided down the corridor away from him, moving deeper into the labyrinth the V'ornn had made of Receiving Spirit, he had hurried on silent feet after the Gyrgon.

Nith Immmon's gait now shortened, and Kurgan saw that he was approaching a heartwood door bound in bands of thick bronze incised with Kundalan runes. It was fitted with a complicated lock of Gyrgon manufacture. Nith Immmon put his palm against the lock, which opened with a sigh to reveal a space of utter blackness. Nith Immmon vanished through the open door, and a moment later it began to swing shut. Kurgan sprinted to it just in time to throw himself sideways through the opening. The door clicked shut behind him.

Pressing himself against the closed door, he scarcely dared breathe. Where was Nith Immmon? The question was soon answered as a pool of lambent blue light illuminated a corridor composed of rough stone blocks, white as the facade of the building. Up ahead, he saw the origin of the light, a glowing ball that hung suspended in midair just above Nith Immmon's cupped hand. The Gyrgon was moving away from him.

Kurgan, following Nith Immmon, made his cautious way down the corridor, which, unlike those on the other side of the door, was cramped and low-ceilinged, the sides sloping inward as they went up. The utter silence pressed in on him, as if even the sound of his breathing was being muffled.

Presently, the corridor made a ninety-degree turn to the left, and Kurgan came to a halt. Thrown upon the far wall was a ruddy glow, dim and flickering. It reminded him of something, but he could not immediately think of what. Nevertheless, he felt a crawling in his belly, as of insects stirring to life. It was then that a shadow flitted across the ruddy glow, and he knew where he had encountered this before: the sphere Nith Nassam had led him past on his way to Nith Batoxxx's laboratory.

He craned his neck, peering around the corner. The corridor ended a short way farther on, debouching onto a spherical chamber, lit by a series of fusion lamps exuding the reddish light. It had a metallic floor that was smaller than the chamber itself by perhaps three meters. It was connected to the corridor by a narrow walkway that spanned the waterless moat. The floor contained a number of horizontal chambers shaped like laaga sticks connected by photon lines to what he thought must be Gyrgon fusion engines, though they did not conform to any design he had ever seen.

Nith Immmon, his helm held in the crook of one arm, was standing before one of them. He had a long, mournful face and small ears that rather comically stuck out from his skull. The lobes glowed with implanted biocircuits, and there was a small germanium stud above each eye winking to the rhythm of his pumping blood. He was looking upward and, when Kurgan followed the tilt of his skull, he saw a great shadow descending from near the top of the sphere where another set of chambers hung in an ion stasis field.

As the shadow dropped into the ruddy light, Kurgan saw to his astonishment that it had wings, which folded as it alighted in front of Nith Immmon. Kurgan could see that the figure was carrying something in its arms, but he was for the moment too fascinated by the creature itself to take heed.

His astonishment doubled, for it was as tall as Nith Immmon, the hairless conical head clearly V'ornnish, the amber hue paler but, again, distinctly V'ornnish. But the eyes, large and expressive, had in the center of their black irises pure white pupils. Then, his breath was taken away by another detail. A string of Gyrgon biocircuits spiraled up the skull. *What is this thing?* he asked himself.

He shifted slightly in order to better his field of view. From there he could see that the creature was naked. Its breasts marked it as a female, but then, as he lowered his gaze, he saw the distinct outlines of V'ornn male tender parts.

"Are we ready?" Nith Immmon asked.

"As I said." The creature had a voice both silky and throaty. The sound of it set the insects in the pit of Kurgan's lowest belly to scrambling again, as if an unconscious part of him recognized it.

The creature set down its burden, which, Kurgan saw, was a male child. He looked somewhat like a V'ornn, but there were differences, subtle and otherwise. For one thing, he had hair on the top of his head.

"Show me what he can do," Nith Immmon said.

The creature took the child by the hand and walked him to one of the chambers. Kurgan could see that the creature had very long, dextrous fingers. A wave of the creature's hand and one of the chambers opened. It helped the male child in, and the lid came down, sealing the child within.

"Will an exposure of three minutes be sufficient?" the creature asked.

"At what concentration?"

"The goron wave simulates that encountered at Helle-spennn."

"Hellespennn, when the stars fell." Nith Immmon was racked by a shudder. "Commence."

Sound like a knife caused Kurgan to slam his hands to his ears. His eyes began to tear.

When the sound ceased, the door to the chamber opened, and the creature helped the child climb out. Unlike Courion, he appeared unharmed by the terrible radiation.

Nith Immmon held out his hand, and the child walked toward him. He was almost there when his pupils and irises vanished, and he collapsed.

"Another failure," Nith Immmon said sorrowfully.

"This is the longest one has survived," the creature said. "I see progress, not failure."

"That is because we have different priorities," Nith Immmon said. "I seek to prepare us for what is to come and you . . ."

"I create," the creature said.

"Of course. You are Breeder." Nith Immmon put on his helm. "Still, it is a mystery to me, Gul Aluf, that you are comfortable being outside the Temple of Mnemonics without your ion exomatrix."

She smiled. "No. The real mystery is why you lie to me, Nith Immmon, about these experiments."

"Do you doubt my loyalty to the Comradeship, to this very Swarm?"

"Not at all." Her wings flashed up and down once. "But I also know that once these experiments work you will wield almost unlimited power among the Comradeship. Nith Sahor. Nith Batoxxx. Our stewards are gone. There is disunity among the Comradeship—and worse, the beginnings of internecine warfare."

"Worse still, we suddenly are directionless. And why is that? Nith Sahor was betrayed and murdered by Nith Batoxxx and his cabal. Nith Batoxxx was possessed by a Kundalan archdaemon of great power—a power we neither foresaw nor can understand no matter how much we try. Here on Kundala are forces we neither control nor comprehend. Do you not consider the possibility that Nith Sahor was right about how special Kundala is?"

"No. We are V'ornn. The Kundalan are nothing more than animals."

"You see?" Nith Immmon said. "This is why the Comradeship is at an impasse. And for us—at this juncture in our history—any impasse is dangerous."

Riane, Eleana, and Thigpen arrived in Axis Tyr in the evening of what had been a bright brittle early-spring day. The chill was returning to the air, a reflection of winter's grip, but the sysal trees were so bursting with incipient buds that the gimnopedes felt safe flitting through the knobby branches.

The trio had slipped secretly into the city via the network of tunnels the Resistance had spent years digging. Riane could see right away why they needed Eleana. For security reasons the Resistance periodically filled in tunnel entrances, dug others in different locations. It was difficult work, time-consuming, backbreaking, but it saved countless lives. They emerged more or less in the heart of

the spice market, which at this time of day was thronged
with buyers, sellers, idle onlookers, and others bent on illicit deals.

They had flown on the back of the *fulkaan*, the enormous avian with which Riane had been connected in her
former life. The fulkaan had let them down in a dense
copse of ammonwood within five kilometers of the city
walls. From there, Eleana had led them on foot to the hidden entrance to one of the Resistance tunnels that honeycombed the surrounding area.

They passed the glowing windows of Spice Jaxx's,
where Looorm and Deirus congregated in their off-hours
or, in the Looorms' case, off-moments between acrobatic
sexual liaisons with wealthy Bashkir clients. It was also
where members of Resistance cadres sometimes met to
exchange information and to eat heartily before the dangerous trip home to the hillsides north of the city. The
Deirus presence guaranteed that Khagggun and inquisitive
members of other castes would give it a wide berth. It was
comfortable, a hushed and low-lit establishment, the better
to accommodate the clandestine nature of its clientele.

Thigpen curled across Riane's shoulders, hidden beneath her voluminous travel cloak as they wended their
way through the milling crowd, immersed in the babble of
voices, the singsong trills of the spice merchants hawking
their wares. Laughter was passed around small groups of
V'ornn as if it were ludd-wine, and a heady mix of spice
dust sparkled in the dusk. Long shadows sprang up as
lanterns were lighted. A Kundalan male haggled with a
dealer on behalf of his V'ornn master, a Tuskugggun put a
fingertip to her mouth, deciding between two grades of
cinnamon. A patrol hoverpod, weapons bristling, droned
by overhead, making contact with a pair of Khagggun,
who had all at once materialized like spectres from a fog-
bank. The travelers continued in their dogged way to the
edge of the market, whose demarcation was a scraggly
line of Kundalan with lost or maimed limbs, scarred faces,
and hopeless eyes.

Riane stopped to speak to each one, crouching down, touching their outstretched hands, murmuring Venca prayers that would initiate auras of healing around them. As she signaled Eleana to fetch some water, she felt Thigpen's tail curling around her neck.

"This is not perhaps the wisest course of action." Thigpen's whiskers twitched beneath Riane's cloak. "Consider the heightened Khagggun presence."

"These are my folk," Riane whispered back. "It is prophesied that I will bring them out of their enslavement. I will not ignore their torment until that time comes."

With tearful eyes and murmurings of gratitude, they accepted the water that Eleana brought. However, one there was with red-rimmed eyes who rose and slipped into the crowd, shadowing them as they passed on.

Cinnabar Street was part of a rather quiet district lined with expensive artists' villas, the beautifully ornate Kundalan architecture and designs perfectly preserved. High stone walls, expertly carved and patterned, inset with graven bas-relief medallions, preserved the privacy of the owners.

"Look at how they live here amid beauty and tranquillity." Thigpen bristled with anger. "Look, look! Not only V'ornn live here. Kundalan who collaborate with them. For them, the war scarcely exists."

At length, they crossed Constance Street and turned into Divination Street, a wider thoroughfare more appropriate for the beginning of a commercial district, containing armories and large ateliers, bristling unashamedly with wealth and power. There, two sides of V'ornn culture existed elbow to elbow despite being polar opposites. They saw on display the latest suits of armor, loaded with new biocircuits the distribution of which had been sanctioned by the Gyrgon comradeship, new shock-swords, lighter-looking, more lethal even than those Rekkk and Eleana possessed, mean-looking ion maces. And then, in the next shop, photonic sculptures, brilliant, ethereal, lighter than the air itself, which seemed to breathe on their own. In the next, a true oddity, reading matter caught not in the facets of decagons but on supple wrygrass paper, lovingly hand-made, bound with cor-tail thread, surrounded by covers fashioned from the speckled hides of razor-raptors, dyed hindemuth, pebbled searay, even, astonishingly, perwillon.

A brief hush heralded dusk, a lull drifting across the streets. Shops closing, the Tuskugggun armorers and artists needing to return to their hingatta to see to their children. Divination Street saw its crowds melt away.

Eleana went up the wide steps of a large shanstone building that had once been a temple. The V'ornn had turned it into the Bashkir Forum of Adjudication. It was there that Sornnn SaTrryn weighed disputes between Bashkir families.

As luck would have it, the forum was between sessions, and the guards were nowhere about. Their boot soles rang on the green polished shanstone flooring as they wended their way between fluted columns. The harsh bluish light thrown off by the V'ornn fusion lamps seemed to wash out the natural colors of the stones. In the rear, Eleana opened a narrow door so plain it was scarcely visible, and they found themselves in a utility area—a small succession of cubicles with rough-hewn rock walls and ceilings, piled with the rags, brushes, buckets, brooms, and cleansers of the Kundalan work crew. Thigpen, who had leapt down the moment they had come inside, wrinkled her nose at the harsh chemical smells.

"Civilization," she said huffily. "Who needs it?"

"Shhh!" Eleana warned them both.

They stood very still, listening to the soft echo of foot-falls outside. Following Eleana's lead, they crept from cu-bicle to cubicle until they were in the last one. It was smaller than the others, with makeshift shelving. A mag-nificent red-jasper Ramahan altar incised with images of Miina's sacred butterfly had been shoved against the back wall as if it were a piece of junk.

They could hear a deep voice, uttering the harsh, clipped vernacular of Khagggun-speak. "In here, come on."

"Why?" came the higher-pitched voice of a Tuskugg-gun. "This place gives me the chills."

"The only thing giving you chills tonight is me." The Khagggun laughed. "I told you. There's an old Kundalan altar in there."

The voices were rapidly drawing closer, and Riane and Eleana looked at each other. Eleana made to draw her shock-sword, but Riane grasped her hand to stay her.

"Their priestesses sacrificed animals on this thing." Shadows skittered. The Khagggun and his Looorm were in the next chamber. "Climbing on, naked, joining our tender parts where so much blood had been spilled. Trust me, there's nothing like it."

"The last time I trusted a Khagggun," the Looorm said, "I broke my collarbone."

The Khagggun was laughing, in high spirits when he found Eleana in the chamber where the V'ornn had con-signed the altar. She stood with her hands behind her back, her breasts provocatively thrust out.

"What can this be?" He was a big, hulking specimen of the warrior caste. The purple color of his body armor marked him as a foot soldier in the regent's Haaar-kyut guard.

"Listen, skcettta," the Looorm said with a sneer, "work your own territory and get out of mine."

"No, no, this is too good to pass up!" the Khagggun boomed. "Two females for the price of one!" He ap-proached Eleana, who was leaning back slightly, her legs spread. "The altar will receive a good workout tonight, eh?"

He reached for Eleana, but before his meat hook hand could wrap itself around her arm, Thigpen leapt from her hiding place behind the altar. Extruding her long, needle-sharp claws, she bared her teeth at him. Rappa were carni-vores, and had the rending teeth of creatures many times their size.

The Looorm screamed, lurched into the Khagggun. Off-balance, he took a swipe at Thigpen, for his effort feeling her teeth sink into the back of his hand. He whipped her into the wall, then swung his shock-sword free. Riane dropped from the ceiling, where with her body's mountain-climbing expertise, she had found adequate handholds in the pockmarked rock. As she hit the floor, a dagger in her fist, the Khagggun turned to face her, and Eleana drew her shock-sword from behind her back. He heard the telltale sound of the ion flow as Eleana thumbed her weapon to life. With a battle cry, he swung a blind blow behind him that, had she not nimbly danced away, would have severed her abdominal muscles.

He was slowed by his shock that she was a female, and a Kundalan, to boot. She wasted no time, engaging his sword tips with her own, sliding her twin blades down the length of his to the hilt. The ion arc flowing back and forth between her blades caused a powerful feedback loop that sent a nerve-numbing shock all the way up into his shoulder. He yelped, dropping his weapon as much in surprise as in pain.

Riane jammed her dagger into the interstice between the plates of his alloy armor, and he swatted at her, as if she were some form of biting insect. She staggered a little, but held on to the hilt, twisting the blade inside him, bringing a grimace to his face but no sound to his lips. Khagggun were stoics, trained to take physical punishment as well as to give it.

Ignoring the growing pain in his side, he unhooked his ion mace and, in one fluid motion, swung it in a short vicious arc. Eleana leapt back, but a cluster of spikes dragged across the front of her left shoulder, sending an agonizing shock through her. The regent's guardsman took a stride toward her and, grabbing the front of her tunic, lifted her off her feet.

He wrapped the ion mace's chain around her neck and pulled. Riane withdrew the dagger, stabbed again in another spot. The Haaar-kyut ignored her as he continued to squeeze the life out of Eleana. And he ignored Thigpen when she landed on his back. Deftly, she flicked off his helm, sank her teeth into his ear, and scraped both sets of foreclaws down his skull. He screamed as his blood flew, Eleana collapsed onto the altar, her eyes rolling up in her head. Riane scrambled across the floor, grasped the Haaar-kyut's shock-sword and, without a second's thought, drove it point first just above the spot where the hilt of her dagger protruded.

The Haaar-kyut staggered a pace before falling to his knees. His hands were spasming; he had no control over them. His lips were moving. He was trying to contact his Pack-Commander, though his photonic link had been severed when Thigpen had wrenched off his helm.

The Rappa left him to Riane, skittered across the floor on extended claws, jumping onto the altar where Eleana lay. The Haaar-kyut, relentless to the end, grabbed Riane's cloak, pulling her toward him. His teeth gnashed and his jaws came down on her. She twisted, jammed her elbow hard into his throat, and his grip on her loosened.

She ran to where Thigpen was crouched over Eleana.

"How is she?" Riane panted, staring down at Eleana's pale face. "How badly is she hurt?"

Thigpen shook her head. She had unwound the ion mace's chain, which had left deep red welts around Eleana's neck.

Riane conjured Earth Granary, surrounding Eleana with its potent healing and was about to gather her into her arms, when Thigpen tapped her on the shoulder. She turned to see the Looorm incongruously wielding the Haaar-kyut's shock-sword.

"Careful," Riane said softly. "That thing can kill you as easily as it can me."

"Who are you?" The Looorm's eyes were wide and staring. She was clearly panicked.

"I am Riane, this is Thigpen, and Eleana."

"Do you know what you have done? You've murdered a member of the regent's elite guard."

"Not murdered," Riane said reasonably. "It was self-defense."

"Do you think that matters?" The Looorm was wildly

swinging the shock-sword in their direction. She was small and slender, no more than a child, really, and her face seemed all eyes and pouty lips. She looked born to the profession of sex. She was without the traditional Tuskugggun sifeyn, of course, and her skull, perfumed and oiled, gleamed provocatively in the light. "You are Kundalan. You will die for this affront."

"What is your name?" Riane asked, all the while spreading Earth Granary like a balm over Eleana's body.

"What?"

"You know our names. What is yours."

"No one asks a Looorm's name."

"You do have one."

"Why, yes, I . . ." The Looorm's shock had turned to something akin to confusion. "My name is Jura."

"Listen to me, Jura. You have many choices."

"You lie, criminal. My path is laid out for me." Jura tossed her head. "I will run you through myself and collect the vengeance reward the regent is bound to give me."

Riane did not turn to face her, nor in any way move to defend herself. "You are Tuskugggun. Worse, you are Looorm. The only thing the regent is likely to do is throw you on the garbage heap."

"Impudent Kundalan, how do you know—" Jura's jaw jutted in defiance. "How can you say that?"

"We are females. Just like you." She gathered Eleana in her arms, rocking her slightly. "Now do what you will. I have my friend's life to save."

The banestone, black as pitch, heavy as a hindemuth's head, seemed to wink at Kurgan from its hiding place in his residence. As he stared at it, he wondered what it was. Even Minnum was unable to say what, precisely, it could do. The two key pieces of information he had managed to glean were that it was known as a banestone (whatever that was!) and that it was very, very valuable. That was why he had stolen it just before he had made his way out of Za Hara-at. He had thought about ordering Sornnn

SaTrryn to come with him, but had changed his mind. The
SaTrryn had the Korrush in their blood, and none more
than Sornnn, that was clear enough. If he wanted to spend
his time mucking around in the dead city, let him. All the
better to advise Kurgan when the Mesagggun rebuilt it.

Hearing a knock on his door, he put away the banestone,
but, oddly, he still felt its presence, like a heart that had
been pulled from a living victim.

"Come," he said, turning, and saw First-Captain Kwenn
standing in his doorway. A rather smallish Khagggun, possessed of a mild manner uncharacteristic of the species.
But Kurgan had discovered that he harbored under his
placid surface a fierce and determined nature. He could
lull you to sleep with his dull manner, but he had a mind
like a tritanium trap. He never forgot anything.

"Deck-Admiral Iin Mennus has arrived," the head of
the regent's Haaar-kyut said. "Shall I have him escorted to
the great hall?"

"No pomp. This is a social call," Kurgan dissembled.
"Have him brought directly here."

"It shall be done, regent," he said, turning on his heel
and marching out.

First-Captain Kwenn knew how to take orders; he did
not overthink situations. Best of all, he heard things, kept
his snout to the ground. He could find the bones, no matter
how deeply buried.

Kurgan glanced down at his crystal reader. Though he
had already committed them to memory, he skimmed
again the information that had been compiled for him on
the glowing green data-decagon in the reader's slot. Then
he switched it off and looked up at the wall studded with
weapons from all the star-flung races the V'ornn had conquered. Well-oiled blades gleamed darkly, curved, twisted,
straight, hanging side by side with weapons that trans-
muted and discharged all manner of energy. Not a goron
particle among the lot, however. The V'ornn had not conquered the Centophennni. Their battles, when they occurred, were so fierce that all was obliterated in the frenzy.

Not one goron-particle weapon had ever been salvaged, and so the origin of their terrifying power remained an enigma. What he would not give to possess a goron-based weapon!

A discreet cough announced Deck-Admiral Iin Mennus being shown through the doorway. After the Haaar-kyut guard closed the door, the Deck-Admiral proceeded across the room as warily as if he were crossing enemy territory.

"Good evening." To which Kurgan received only the most perfunctory of nods. The Deck-Admiral was not known for his courteous manner or his respect for authority, especially what he considered civilian authority. He was a short, squat Khagggun with a misshapen skull and a hideous scar that pulled down the left corner of his mouth. Any competent Genomatekk could have fixed it. That he had chosen otherwise said something about his fierceness and his pride. "*I am who I am!*" Kurgan could hear him booming.

In fact, though, his voice was as silken as a shock-sword being withdrawn from its scabbard and seemed quite out of place emanating from that brutish physiognomy.

"Quite a collection you have here." The Deck-Admiral stood, spread-legged, in front of the weapons display. He then turned to stare at Kurgan with his small, close-set eyes. "But rather crude, I'd say, as a means of intimidation."

"I thought you would appreciate these trophies."

"Why? Because I am Khagggun? But you know nothing about me, regent."

Kurgan's smile was without a blood drop of warmth. "You are the primary male in a litter of eight children. Your mother is an armorer in hingatta liiina do butha, where she reared her female offspring. Your father distinguished himself in service before dying on the line at Hellespennn. Your first younger brother, Hannn Mennus, is a Pack-Commander with a commendable record of kills and cruelty." Kurgan cocked his head. "How am I doing so far?"

"I had heard rumors concerning your elaborate network

of spies," Deck-Admiral Mennus said sourly. "As well as your vault of dossiers."

" 'Information and vigilance breeds victory.' "

Deck-Admiral Mennus took a Nieobian push-dagger off the wall. "Excellent balance." He ran the tip of his thick, scarred forefinger down the composite S-curve blade. "You speak like a Khaggun, yet I do not think you mock me."

"I have only the highest regard for you, Deck-Admiral."

Iin Mennus returned the push-dagger to its place on the wall. "Regent, I have many duties. My time is limited."

"Are you so eager, then, to spill more Resistance blood?"

The Deck-Admiral shrugged chronosteel-cable shoulders. "What other pleasures do I have?"

Kurgan laughed. "You are too long away from Axis Tyr."

"I do well keeping my distance from a place whose many fleshpots would blunt my most faithful companion, the sword edge of death."

Kurgan held up a hexagonal crystal decanter. "Firegrade numaaadis? A laaga stick to share." Mennus glowered, "No, I suppose not." He gestured. "Won't you at least sit and make yourself comfortable?"

"Comfort is for Bashkir."

Kurgan, looking at the wall of weapons, caressed a fantasy to life, imagining them one by one struck to the hilts in Mennus' flesh.

"Despite my admiration for you, Deck-Admiral, I assure you there will come a moment when you will have crossed a line from which you cannot retreat."

"Shall I treat with respect one who seeks to weaken me by implanting an okummmon in my flesh?"

"Is that why you think I have brought you here?"

"I am the only Khaggun of my rank without one. What else am I to think?"

"And yet nothing could be further from the truth."

"The news is most welcome." Mennus' scar had gone

dead white. "I meant no offense, regent. Khagggun are not diplomats. We are blunt, sometimes to a fault, perhaps. In the shedding of blood, this bluntness serves us well. We have a job to do, we do it, end of story."

Kurgan cocked his head again. "Is there no other way for you?"

Mennus shook his head. "You know there is not."

Having received confirmation of what the data had suggested, namely that this particular Khagggun had no interest in palace intrigue, Kurgan crossed the room, pulled aside a set of thick dark blue drapes, and opened the window-doors onto the terrace. As he stepped out, he heard the Deck-Admiral moving behind him. There was a small low table on which rose a coruscating spiral. At its peak was a shallow veradium bowl filled with five small pentagons carved out of bone. Kurgan and Mennus stood at the sculpted stone balustrade. Beyond had once been Eleusis Ashera's star-rose garden. When Kurgan's father had briefly been regent, he had turned it over to his sorceress-mistress. Kurgan had lately planted rows of orangesweet because Nith Batoxxx had despised the scent. Breathing in the perfume served to bring him a kind of contentment, if only briefly.

At length, Iin Mennus gestured at the coruscating spiral. "I take it you play warrnixx, regent."

"I have a fondness for the game, yes."

"It takes a certain kind of mind to master warrnixx. I would judge your level of expertise."

"And I yours." When Kurgan turned to Mennus he was smiling a little. "I wish to make you my new Star-Admiral."

Mennus' eyes opened wide. "Regent?"

"There has of late been much unrest among the high command. The last two Star-Admirals turned treasonous, plotting against their regent." Kurgan took a step toward his guest. "I mean to stop it right here, right now."

"I am a warrior, regent. I would be useless as an administrator."

Kurgan came even closer. "Between you and me, Deck-

Admiral, I no longer trust the members of the high command. They have, as you so accurately put it, spent too much time in fleshpots, in idleness that breeds envy and rancor. The recent theft by the Resistance of an entire convoy of the Khagggun's newest weaponry is just the latest example of their laxity. They have become rotten. They must be swept into oblivion. Order, stability, and obedience will be restored to the Khagggun. Otherwise, we become vulnerable—to the Resistance and to others."

"The regent must know that I am the last Khagggun to bend his knee to civilian authority."

"Which is why, once you destroy those who have diseased the corps, the others will fall in line without a whimper of protest."

Mennus gripped the stone balustrade with his large, square hands and looked down at the rows of tortured vines newly bursting into flower. "If I were ever to have a garden, which is unlikely, I would sow it with the bleached skulls of our enemies. What do you think I would reap, in time?"

"I do not know."

"Nothing, regent. Absolutely nothing." He turned to Kurgan. "I want nothing more than the continued strength of our Swarm. If I were to accept . . . the entire Khagggun structure would have to be strategically rethought and overhauled."

Kurgan said nothing.

"And there is another thing."

From beyond the palace's thick walls came the ten thousand songs sung by Axis Tyr as darkness crept close, the hush of evening ended, another raucous night stepping out of the wings, eager to begin its dance. Kurgan said nothing. He was content to wait for what he knew would be the Deck-Admiral's final request.

"It is this nonsense about giving Khagggun Great Caste status that is at the root of our rot. The high command is far too busy scrambling to make coin on deals best left to the Bashkir than in honing the edge of death. I know you must agree. During your short reign, you have done everything in your power to wipe away every last vestige of your father's legacy."

"You surprise me, Deck-Admiral. Being cast away in the west countries has done you no harm."

" 'Intelligence and vigilance,' regent," Iin Mennus said.

Kurgan nodded. This interview had gone better than he had imagined. "Give me your arm." They gripped each other's forearms in the seigggon, the solemn blood oath. "It is done. From this day forward, the order for Great Caste status for Khagggun is rescinded. You will make certain that high command report to Receiving Spirit to have their okummmon removed."

"And if they obfuscate or refuse?"

"I commend the members of the high command into your care, Star-Admiral Iin Mennus. Do with them as you see fit."

Jura struck the dead Haaar-kyut in the chest with his own shock-sword. "I have dreamed of doing that." She drove it down again, grunting with the effort, and this time split the alloy armor. "He paid well, but I lost count of the times he hurt me." She looked at Riane. "To be honest, they all hurt me, the males, in one way or another. Oh, they excel in that."

Riane was sitting next to Eleana, her arm around her. Eleana had regained consciousness moments after Jura stopped waving the weapon around. Her breath was a little raspy, and her voice sounded semistrangled. Otherwise, the spell had done its work. Thigpen was crouched beside them, silent, her brushlike tail switching back and forth, content for the moment to play the part of the dumb domestic pet.

"If you transform yourself," Riane said, "it will alter what happens to you."

Jura laughed thinly. "You must be joking." She had a flat, guileful face with a decidedly feral cast, an animal's natural magnetism. Beneath her cloak she wore a tunic through which her enviable charms could now and again be glimpsed in tantalizing fashion. "It was my misfortune to be born into the caste of the lowest form of Tuskugg-gun. I have lived all my life on Isinglass Street. There is no hope of altering anything."

"And yet," Riane said, "in here you have been trans-formed. Do you not see it?"

"All I see is that I am out my rich fee," Jura said tartly. She dropped the shock-sword to rifle through the Haaar-kyut's armor. In a moment, she rose with a stack of coins in her hand. "It is more than I could have imagined." She took a step toward the doorway. "You will not stop me, or turn me in?"

"Go in safety," Riane said.

"Use the coins wisely," Eleana added.

For a moment, Jura stood dumbfounded, then a sly grin broke out across her face. *"Transformation,* isn't that the word you used?" She hefted the bag of coins. "I will re-member what happened here. I will not forget you." Then she vanished with only a whisper of sound.

It had been Sornnn SaTrryn's intention to make all haste back to Axis Tyr, there to return to his duties both as Prime Factor and as a de facto member of the Kundalan Resistance. In this way, he hoped to retain the ear of the regent and to gain knowledge of Marethyn's whereabouts and her well-being.

But the Korrush, as is often its wont, had different ideas. He was not a hundred meters from Za Hara-at when he was met by two Rasan Sul. Like him, they wore thick-striped robes. Like his, their heads were covered with the traditional sinschal. Though one was old and one was young, they both had long, curling beards. Their rugged, wind-roughened features, shadowed and deeply seamed, peered out at him with a gravity, a sense of purpose that could only have been forged in the hostile environment of the Great Northern Plains. The sky was clear save for a single streamer of cloud, long and low and immobile with the weight of memory.

"Greetings, *wa tarabibi*," the old one said. He had sunken cheeks, skin the color of Korrush dust, a soft but forceful way of speaking. His name was Nasaqa. He had known Sornnn since Sornnn was a child. The other one, Baqesh, was his bodyguard. He was large, tongueless at the hands of the Jeni Cerii, very good at what he did.

"Greetings, wise one," Sornnn said. "What brings you to Za Hara-at?"

Nasaqa smiled, showing white but irregular teeth. "I am come to say a prayer for your father here at the Holy of Holies." He stroked his long, tangled grey beard. "He brought you to the Korrush, *wa tarabibi*, but it was already in you to love us."

"You honor me with both action and words." Sornnn knew very well, and Nasaqa knew he knew, that this journey to Za Hara-at was not simply about meditation and prayer.

Nasaqa raised a hand. "Walk with me."

They proceeded around the perimeter of the Za Hara-at dig, at first seeming to make little progress, for the ruined city was huge. Presently they arrived at a low plateau completely removed from the shimmering energy field protecting the V'ornn encampment. In the immediate distance, the squat shanties of the poor village of Im-Thera could be seen, the Beyy Das villagers moving about their chores.

All at once, Nasaqa turned to Sornnn. His eyes were piercing in their intense scrutiny. "Recently, we were visited by the Ghor and learned from them that the Gyrgon have been using their insidious influence with the kapudaan of the Five Tribes. They would have us kill each other off in the frenzy of a religious war."

"Now that you know the truth can't you call a council of leaders to defuse the situation?"

"Some, doubtless, will be dissuaded, but most will not.

The ancient embers of smoldering hatreds and distrusts have been fanned into flames. The majority are convinced that this is the beginning of the *She'ajj*, the holy war promised us by Jiharre. What we will have instead is self-immolation for all the Korrush."

A bird called from the blue roof of heaven, its cry echoing through the barren stillness. They walked on, seeming far away from everyone and everything.

"We cannot allow this, Nasaqa. You and I must find a way to stop this insane talk of war."

"But, you see, the Jeni Cerii are already arming, and the Ghor tell us that the Gazzi Qhan gird themselves for war. Skirmishes have broken out on either side of the two tribes' borders."

"Have the Rasan Sul been affected?"

"Not yet. But it is only a matter of time." Nasaqa raised his hand. "I know what is in your mind. We are already storehousing spices."

Sornnn spread his hands. "My concern is for more than our spice trade, Nasaqa. There is a long-standing friendship between the SaTrryn and the Rasan Sul. Whatever service I may perform, if it is in my power to do so, I will."

"We need your knowledge and your expertise to help us combat the insidious seeds of destruction the Gyrgon have sown. Will you stand by my side when the war commences?"

Sornnn was stunned. "Nasaqa, I am sick with worry for you, for the Korrush, for the business, but I am Prime Factor of all the Bashkir caste. I cannot simply abandon my position. The regent would not allow it. Not to mention the Gyrgon."

Nasaqa nodded. "Your reply was preordained. Indeed, considering the outcome, some of my council cautioned me not to have this meeting."

"Then why did you?"

"Because I believe with all my heart that you will help us," Nasaqa said.

"I regret there is nothing I can do."

"Regret nothing, *wa tarabibi,* and yours will be a happy life," the old one said. "*A falah katra.*" Until we meet again.

While it seemed on first glance that the altar had been shoved against the rear wall of the cubicle, that was not the case. There was, in fact, a little more than a meter of space into which Eleana now crawled. Reaching the center point, she tapped on the rock face in a peculiar rhythm, and a section swung silently inward. She slithered through feetfirst. Thigpen scampered after her, then, Riane, with a last look at the doorway through which Jura had disappeared.

The cleverly concealed entrance swung shut behind them, and Riane looked around. They were in a shaft made of huge square shanstone blocks into which were set, at regular intervals, small niches where oil lamps burned, giving off warms pools of light. They stood on a small landing from which depended an elegantly carved but vertiginously steep shanstone spiral stairway, down which they descended, Eleana leading the way.

Riane did not care for this roundabout route to gain entrance to the regent's palace, but, as Giyan pointed out, they had no choice. Kurgan had had the run of the palace for months. He had been prowling the caverns when she had placed the Ring of Five Dragons in the Storehouse Door. He knew she had found her way in somehow. The underground entrance into the palace cavern via Blank Lane was untrustworthy. Someone must have seen Giyan and Annon exit the palace on the night of the coup because the Khaggggun arrived so quickly after them in Stone Border.

Brushing aside these dark thoughts, she touched Eleana on the shoulder.

"Do not worry," Eleana whispered. "Your spell has done wonders." She took Riane's hand, briefly squeezed it, and for that moment their gazes locked.

Thigpen, running on all sixes and sniffing the astringent air, missed this brief exchange. Her keen ears had already picked up what the other two soon heard: a deep, rhythmic booming as of an animal breathing or a complex machine running. It was neither, however. By the time they reached the bottom of the stairs, they recognized the percussive backbeat of music.

They moved down a narrow passageway whose ceiling was lost in gloom. Its walls were darkly gleaming and seamless.

"Over there is the entrance to a club called Cthonne," Eleana said, pointing to bronze doors, studded with shan-stone cabochons. "It is unknown to either the regent or the Khagggun. Children come here in secret to dance the night away."

"Kundalan children."

"Kundalan *and* V'ornn," she told him. "What would strike them as more subversive?"

"How do you know about it?" Riane asked.

"It is a meeting place, for Resistance and those V'ornn who believe in its cause."

"There are V'ornn who believe in the Kundalan Resistance?" Thigpen asked.

"Besides Sornnn and Sahor?" Riane said to her.

Eleana nodded. "The Deirus, for one. They know what it is like to be beaten down, persecuted, indiscriminately killed."

They were nearing Cthonne's bronze doors, which were half-open. Just outside was a thin, grey-skinned Deirus. He was talking to two Kundalan youths, possibly Resistance. He glanced at them, and Thigpen immediately leapt into deep shadow. It was unclear whether he noticed her or not.

"I wonder what they are plotting." Riane was clearly fascinated.

"Come on, you two," the Rappa hissed with a furtive glance at the inquisitive Deirus. "There's no time to waste."

They hurried past the knot of conspirators and around a corner.

* * *

"You will do what I tell you," Nith Nassam said to Kurgan, "and only what I tell you."

They stood alone in the intimacy of Kurgan's private suite in the regent's palace. Kurgan would have much preferred meeting with the Gyrgon in the Temple of Mnemonics, but it appeared that Nith Nassam had a penchant for intrusion. On the walls were arrayed the regent's collection of weapons, of comfort to him perhaps, though it was ignored by the Gyrgon.

"As you wish."

"Precisely so." Nith Nassam's biocircuit horns sparked gold and green like a starfield in flux. "Tell me, regent, what you know about the Orieniad."

"The Orieniad is the Sarakkon ruling council."

"Tell me something I *don't* know."

Kurgan was silent.

"I see." The ghost of a smile played around Nith Nassam's mouth. "Courion was a member of the Orieniad. Did you know that?"

Kurgan effectively hid his surprise. "No. I didn't."

"Since you are a self-professed expert on the Sarakkon I want to know what such a high-ranking Sarakkon was doing in Axis Tyr. Why was he hiding his identity? What was his business with Nith Batoxxx? It is clear that Nith Batoxxx had layers of identities he hid from the Comradeship. Do this for me, and I will allow you access to Nith Batoxxx's laboratory."

"Consider it done," Kurgan said.

Nith Nassam's smile grew broader. "We shall see," he said as he turned and left.

Kurgan stared after him, his mind whirling. Then he let out a long-held breath. He had just pulled off his tunic when First-Captain Kwenn rapped on the door.

"Come," he said curtly.

First-Captain Kwenn crossed the residence chamber in his crisp gait to stand at the regent's side. His alloy armor shot from its highly polished surfaces a legion of reflections into every corner of the chamber, which was as pleasingly spare as his own small quarters. This regent, so different from the last, had stripped the residence of virtually all of the excesses his father had piled into it.

"Regent, there is a line of functionaries with memoranda, proposed law changes, petitions, Bashkir, Mesagggun, and Kundalan, waiting for you in the great hall. Many have been there since before dawn."

"You know, First-Captain, you have taken on the duties of a court functionary, and this displeases me greatly," Kurgan said tartly. He selected, then rejected one tunic top after another. "I am giving you an assignment. I wish you to find out where my sister Marethyn is. She seems to have vanished. Use all your formidable array of sources."

"Regent—"

"Licit and otherwise, First-Captain. This is an order."

"Yes, regent." First-Captain Kwenn pointed to a tunic, of a deep brown matte fabric, and Kurgan put it on. "There is a possibility . . ."

Kurgan turned. "Yes?"

"There is the whisper of a rumor—and let me emphasize that it is just that, a rumor—of a Tuskugggun in the north country."

"Idiotic! And certainly not Marethyn."

"Nevertheless, I feel I ought to probe further."

"As you like." There was a thoroughness about this Khagggun that Kurgan particularly liked—he was a professional through and through. And he congratulated himself on the sagacity of his choice.

There was a discreet knock on the door, and Kwenn went to see who it was. He returned a moment later. "Blood-Worm is asking to see you directly," he said.

Kurgan turned from his contemplation of himself in the mirror. "Ah, the one-armed one." He laughed to see First-Captain Kwenn wince.

"We have given all our spies code names for a good reason, regent," Kwenn said.

"Yes, but must the names be so foolish-sounding?" Kurgan donned dark leggings, snapped his fingers several times in succession. "Make a note. From now on, we will give them the names of libidinous Looorm."

First-Captain Kwenn winced again. "Regent, the crystalwork involved . . ."

"All right, all right," Kurgan said crossly. "Bring him in. But I warn you, First-Captain, I have but a moment to spare."

First-Captain Kwenn returned a moment later with a filthy Kundalan with red-rimmed eyes. His back was bowed, and he was cupping the stump of his arm in the palm of his hand. Despite his bout with the Khaggun interrogators, there was nothing wrong with his memory. He described in detail the two Kundalan females he had seen.

"Shall I marshal a pack of Haaar-kyut?" Kwenn asked after he had paid the beggar and seen him out.

"Yes." Kurgan held up a hand. "On second thought, First-Captain, I think it would be best if you and I went ourselves."

"Without a proper detachment of guards?"

"Where we are going," Kurgan said in a tone that brooked no further contradiction, "they would only get in the way." He hurriedly finished dressing, donning a traveling cloak. From one of three hidden drawers he chose several small weapons. There was a strange and, to First-Captain Kwenn's way of thinking, unsettling grin on the regent's face. "We would not want to alert our prey to our presence, now would we, First-Captain?"

Giyan was discussing with Konara Inggres the copying and dissemination of the long-lost *Utmost Source,* one of the Sacred Texts of Miina, when the calm core of her exploded. *The opal has shattered,* she thought. Quickly excusing herself, she immediately Thripped into the Kells, there to find Perrnodt crumpled on the floor. By her side was the shattered opal.

"Perrnodt!" she cried, kneeling beside the stricken Druuge. "Oh, my dear, what has happened?"

Perrnodt's pale lips moved ever so slightly, but no sound emerged. Casting Earth Granary, Giyan gathered the Druuge into her arms. But the spell wasn't working. It was encountering resistance of a most peculiar sort. It was as if its healing properties were beings sucked through ten thousand tiny holes in Perrnodt's aura.

Hold on. Giyan communicated mind to mind with the Druuge. *Just hold on.*

Giyan conjured Penetrating Inside, but the simple Osoru spell to divine the nature of things also failed completely. Now she cast Transverse Guest, a far more complex spell in the same category. She could see the energy trails eating their way through Perrnodt's aura like a fistful of squirming serpents. All creatures possessed auras; they were the physical manifestation of the spirit in just the same way sorceresses possessed Avatars, creatures to house their spirits when they traveled through Otherwhere. Those with the Gift, the Druuge very much among them, possessed a heightened aura that, like a castle moat, was part of their protection, in this case, from evil spells and creatures.

Whatever Perrnodt had encountered was so powerful that when she had peered through the light lens of the opal it had seriously compromised her aura. To work so profoundly upon a Druuge, far more powerful than any Ramahan, it must be exceedingly strong. How was it possible? She shivered.

Perrnodt was trembling in her arms. The fistful of serpents continued to eat into her aura, tearing great rents in it. Giyan conjured spell after spell, but nothing in her formidable arsenal had any effect, and she knew that if she was to have any chance of saving the Druuge, she had to find out what happened.

Perrnodt . . . Perrnodt, what did you see when you looked through the opal? Did you find the lost Ramahan?

Perrnodt stirred, and Giyan almost recoiled at the echo of the agony rending her.

I saw them, she said very faintly. *But they are not lost.*

Where are they, then?

Hidden. They have been hidden.

What has happened to them?

They set one upon the other. Those who would not obey were tortured, and when they had given up their secrets they were given to be killed to those who would obey in order to bind them, as proof of their loyalty.

But this is monstrous, Giyan said. *Who would do such a thing? Who are they obeying?*

The . . . Perrnodt writhed in her agony. *The sauromicians.*

Impossible. The sauromicians lack the power.

No longer.

What do you mean?

Tears of blood were leaking out of Perrnodt's eyes, and her head lolled. Clearly, she had fallen into a kind of delirium. Giyan felt despair begin to overwhelm her. Perrnodt was dying. She could not allow that to happen, and yet she was powerless. No Osoru spell was powerful enough to combat this pernicious enchantment.

And then Giyan began to weep, for she knew that she was not, in fact, helpless. There was one weapon in her arsenal that had a chance to save Perrnodt. But it was a weapon she had turned her back on, a weapon she had vowed never to use. Her ability as a seer. She knew the path she would embark upon if she willingly chose to invoke it, because once she opened the psychic door there was no going back; she would not be able to close it again. And, as history had proved, like as not what lay at the end of the path was complete and utter madness.

She was shaking as if with an ague, but as she looked down into the agonized face of Perrnodt, she knew she had no choice. If there was a chance to save the Druuge, she had to take it.

And so she opened the psychic locks she had spent

years constructing as her oracular abilities clamored ever more forcefully to be heard. Time dissolved into a rain puddle from which ripples spread outward from so many points at once that at first she was dizzied and grew afraid. It was as if, sightless from birth, she could suddenly see. At first, there was a sense of a terrifying randomness. And then, all at once, the new world made sense and was thus forever transformed.

She searched amid all the skeins running this way and that, finding Perrnodt's and following its many convoluted branchings—for a life, any life, had a great many possible futures—to the particular end she sought. There she found Perrnodt's shriveled spirit unable to support life in her physical body. As she suspected, knowing how the Druuge might meet her end gave her a clue as to how to combat the spell. She had very little time, she saw, before the process became irreversible.

Perrnodt had not been killed by the sorcerous serpents eating away at her aura, but by a certain xi-wraith. The serpents were but the advance guard, there to open the way so that the xi-wraith could penetrate the aura and enter Perrnodt's spirit through Crooked Spring Gate.

Giyan had had experience with xi-wraiths because her training had made her intimately familiar with the fifteen Spirit Gates that kept the body and mind healthy and free of evil intent. Each Spirit Gate was susceptible to a different xi-wraith, which were created as psychic safeguards against any Ramahan gaining too much power and upsetting the delicate balance between male and female members of the order. Over the centuries, there were those who found ways not only to circumvent the xi-wraiths but to corrupt them to use for their own purposes.

Giyan closed her eyes, went into Ayame, Osoru's deep trance-state. She felt jihe, the moment of disconnection with her corporeal body, and then, as her Avatar, the great bird Ras Shamra, she was passing across the grey, white, and black landscape of Otherwhere.

In the distance, she saw, half-hidden behind the black

line of jagged mountains, the dreaded shape of the Eye of Ajbal, Avatar of a powerful Kyofu sorcerer. From the corner of the Eye, she could see dripping like a tear the xi-wraith as it waited for its chance to infiltrate Perrnodt's aura. The presence of the Eye of Ajbal was further proof—if any was needed—of the extent of the power that had formed behind the Dark League.

She knew she had to work fast to defeat the xi-wraith before the Eye noticed her and turned its black light in her direction. She flew directly at the xi-wraith and began to conjure Great Bell. This particular xi-wraith ate truths, transforming them into lies. The clear, pure tone of Great Bell was the only way to defeat it. The trouble was, she needed to get within a hundred meters of it in order for Great Bell to work. The risk was that the Eye of Ajbal would spot her before she could complete the spell.

She dipped down, skimming just above the shadowless topography of Otherwhere. She found thermals there which she rode, keeping her avian form utterly still. She was perhaps three hundred meters from the xi-wraith, which was now depending from the corner of the Eye like an icicle. As she neared it, it began to take form: a globular body, hairy as a skorpion-spider, from which a multitude of tentacles protruded in a sudden fury of impatient questing. The xi-wraith scented the clearing path to Perrnodt's Crooked Spring Gate.

Two hundred meters, and Giyan did not think she would make it in time. She had to risk flapping her wings, gaining the added speed. She arched them up and down, and again. One hundred fifty meters, and now the Eye of Ajbal seemed to blink and, in blinking, began to turn in her direction.

Giyan felt a flood of terror, and she pushed her Avatar to its very limits, flashing across the landscape. The pupil of the Eye of Ajbal opened, turning a fiery hue as it set its sights on her. Giyan sensed the onrushing peril and banked to the right as a flash of lambent energy sped by her. She banked again, this time to the left, feeling the scorch of the energy blast all across her belly. The Eye was trying to get her to rise so that it could get a clear shot at her. She had to resist that at all costs.

Twenty meters to go and the third energy blast tumbled her over onto her back. She righted herself, flew right into another before she could regain her momentum. Rubble blew at her, striking pinions and breast. She flew through it, heading directly at the xi-wraith. She was close. Almost there. The Eye was readying itself for its most powerful blast, and she uttered the last words, completing the spell.

Great Bell's clear, plangent tone extended outward in waves. When the leading edge encountered the xi-wraith, the tone changed, rising in pitch, echoing through Otherwhere. The xi-wraith gave a little yip of surprise and pain and shattered like a crystal goblet thrown against a shanstone wall.

The Eye of Ajbal had turned directly into Giyan's path, tracking her, waiting to see which way she would bank so it could burn her out of the ether. Instead, she flew directly at it, her heart pounding painfully in her breath. It grew to monstrous size and, this close to it, she could see tiny evil things like weevils or wyr-maggots crawling like veins across its convex surface.

She felt the gathering of its Kyofu power, the imminence of its attack, and still she flew on in a collision course with the dilated pupil. The energy beam commenced to erupt from it, and Giyan entered Ayame, in an instant letting go of her psychic self, removing herself from Otherwhere.

Shaken, she opened her eyes. She was in the Kells in the Abbey of Floating White; she was still holding Perrnodt. Of the sorcerous serpents or the xi-wraith there were no signs. She leaned over, kissed the Druuge's clammy forehead. Pulse and breathing were returning to normal. Perrnodt was safe.

Now she conjured Earth Granary, enveloping them both in its healing warmth. Her head throbbed and her skin felt scorched where parts of her psychic being had been ex-

posed to the near misses of the Eye of Ajbal's pernicious
energy emissions.

It terrified her that the sauromicians had returned,
backed by such power. Who or what could be behind their
rise? What horrific deal had they made in exchange for
this newfound dominion? She shuddered to think. She
looked down into Perrnodt's pale and haggard face and her
fists clenched. Why hadn't Miina killed the sauromicians
when She had had a chance? And then she thought of Minnum and was grateful that the Great Goddess had been
merciful.

She returned her attention to Perrnodt, stroked her
cheek, and murmured to her until the Druuge rose into
consciousness.

"Perrnodt, Perrnodt," she whispered, as the Druuge's
eyes opened. "You are safe now. I have destroyed the xi-
wraith. It is all right."

But then she saw Perrnodt's eyes, eerily pale, opaque as
chalkstone, and she knew it wasn't all right.

Perrnodt, what has happened?

I am blind, Giyan. Her psychic voice was frail and halting. *The Dark League has blinded me.*

Dear Miina! Giyan cried. *How is this possible?*

They have . . . punished me.

Giyan bent over her. Through Earth Granary, she could
sense that Perrnodt was still in shock. She knew that she
ought to wait to continue questioning her, but she could
not stop herself. *Why did they punish you, Perrnodt? What
was it they were so desperate to keep secret?*

The source of their power. . . .

What is the source?

The Others. . . .

The Others? Giyan leaned closer. *Who are the Others?*

Abbey.

Giyan frowned. *Abbey? Yes, you are back in Floating
White.*

No, no, no. . . .

Perrnodt's mind was fading, slipping back into unconsciousness in order to better try to heal the psychic and physical trauma to which it had been subjected.

Perrnodt. Perrnodt! What do you mean? Where are our strayed Ramahan?

No, no no no. . . . Perrnodt's voice grew fainter, then ceased altogether.

5

Down in the Farm

Y ou should not have exposed him to me," Gul Aluf said.

Nith Nassam was startled. "You mean you knew?"

She turned from one of her biovats from which ten thousand thermionic filaments, circuits of elemental particles suspended in water, emanated like hair from a giant's scalp. In the center of the vat hung an adolescent V'ornn to which the filaments were attached. "What did you think you were up to? Kurgan Stogggul caught a glimpse of me, of everything."

"But he saw nothing, he understood nothing."

All around them the deep hum of Gyrgon ion engines. They were in her fiery lab-orb in the Temple of Mnemonics, the official one, the one known to every member of the Comradeship. The Crown of Creation, where the chosen V'ornn were genetically manipulated, bioengineered into Gyrgon.

Nith Nassam laughed. "It was a joke."

"A joke you say." Gul Aluf's expression told him that she was not amused.

"Of course it was a joke, and if you had a sense of humor, you would see it." He crossed his arms over his chest.

"Kurgan Stogggul could have been one of us. He very well might have been, along with Annon Ashera, save for Nith Batoxxx." He cocked his head. "If memory serves, you would have been the assigned Breeder."

"I am not *assigned* to individuals," Gul Aluf said hotly. "I choose my children."

"Is that what you Breeders call us?"

She turned her back on him, continuing with her work. "You should not even be here."

"And yet I am." He waited a beat. "I want your help."

"A foolish desire."

He spread his hands. "Why? You helped Nith Sahor."

"Do not mention his name to me."

"That's right. I remember now. It did not end well."

She adjusted a cluster of biowires, dipped twenty more into a steaming vat of enhanced engineered electrolytes. "It never does."

"I need help extracting and deciphering data from Nith Batoxxx's lab-orb."

She added the twenty to the others, inserting them one by one at key points. It was work that required a great deal of concentration.

"He was your child." Nith Nassam took a step toward her. "You knew him better than any of us—his quirks, his secrets, his methodology."

"Do you really think he confided in me?" She turned around, put her hands on her hips. "From the first he was an anomaly. His brain kept transmuting. I almost terminated his birth."

"Why didn't you?"

She looked at him for a moment, then turned away without answering. "Eventually, he found out. He never forgave me for it."

"Still, he was your child. Help save him. Only you can do it. If you help me, you can rehabilitate his reputation."

She stopped what she was doing. "Why are you so interested in what he was working on?"

He came around in front of her, the steaming biovat between them. "Doesn't it concern you even a little that a Kundalan archdaemon could take possession of him? Next time it might be you or me. In a way, they collaborated—they must have—before Pyphoros took him over completely. If we can extract his files, if we can unravel the thread of his experiments, perhaps we will find a way to protect ourselves."

Though he had a valid point, Gul Aluf was not fooled. He had another agenda, hidden and, therefore, far more important. But what was it? She knew there was only one way to find out, but for the moment at least she was reluctant to act on it.

"I will take it under advisement," she said coolly.

"Thank you."

"And next time, Nith Nassam, kindly ask permission before you enter my Breeding Field."

See those squinty little eyes glowing in the dark?" Thigpen had halted them as they had turned a corner. The darkened corridor, dank, littered with sour smells and refuse, stretched away from them without a soul to be seen. The sounds from Cthonne had faded away sometime ago. "There is a creature dead ahead."

"What is it?" Riane peered into the gloom.

"I don't know." Thigpen's teeth were bared, and her ears were flat against her head. "All I can tell you is that it has a very nasty disposition."

Eleana gave a low whistle of five or six notes and a guttural growl ricocheted off the heavily stained and chipped walls.

"You see?" Thigpen rose up on her four hind legs, her claws unsheathed.

"Calm yourself." Eleana rubbed the place between the Rappa's ears.

"Not now," Thigpen snapped.

Eleana laughed, and called out, "Come here, Muzli, my little darling."

They heard the skittering of claws and, again, that low,

guttural growl, closer this time. Thigpen bared her teeth, snapping her jaws closed with an audible clash.

Eleana crouched down, her arm around Thigpen. "It's all right. I know him. There is no danger."

Out of the gloom, they saw a sestapod appear. Its short, stubby legs ended in large curved claws and its long, flat head with a matching elongated muzzle was distinctly reptilian. Its back, ridged with a triple row of wicked-looking spikes, snaked back and forth. Its waddling kind of walk seemed almost comical until, all at once, it shot toward them with astonishing speed.

It rushed right into Eleana's chest, ducking its snout under her left arm while she rubbed its skull with her knuckles.

"It's a claiwen!" Thigpen cried in alarm.

"Ah, Muzli, ah," she said, laughing. "It's been such a long time I wondered whether you would remember me."

The claiwen rolled its reddish eyes in apparent ecstasy and wiggled its powerful-looking tail so that the spikes on it trembled in a blur. Then it gave a hoarse bark and, slithering around, commenced to lead them down the noisome corridor. They soon discovered an entire encampment, a warren of one-chamber hovels, filthy, crammed with hollow-faced, sunken-eyed Kundalan, who stared at them dully from their positions crouched in their open doorways.

"What is this place?" Riane said.

"It is known as the Black Farm." Eleana methodically followed the claiwen's tail. "It is home to those beaten and broken by V'ornn torture. They can no longer work or be productive in any way, so they are of no use to the V'ornn. Decades ago, they were swept out of the streets of Axis Tyr. The V'ornn have lost track of them, but we have not."

"I never knew of the Black Farm's existence."

"Few do, outside the Resistance and a handful of family members. Every week, a different cadre of Resistance members delivers food and supplies to these folk."

Riane was struck by this. It reminded her of one of her chores when she had been an acolyte at the Abbey of

Floating White. Each month, food and supplies were delivered to the Ice Caves, almost directly above the Rappa's deep cavern homestead. They helped feed and clothe the castoffs, undesirables, and petty criminals excised from Kundalan society, who lived high in the icebound reaches of the Djenn Marre under crushing physical conditions. Among the Ramahan, it was considered an onerous task—almost a punishment—but if she had not been assigned to it she never would have met Thigpen, and so many aspects of her life would have been different.

It wasn't long before Muzli directed them into a side corridor that reeked of stale cooking, stale bodies, fear, and exhaustion. The beast took up a position outside the doorway to a chamber close to the far end.

"This way," Eleana said, leading them through the doorway.

The chamber was neat and clean, though as spare as a prison cell. A pale square of streetlight lit the place through a small window high up in a heavily stained wall. A warm glow and a complex scent of fragrant oils emanated from a Kundalan lamp of rubbed bronze. Beneath their feet was a carpet, stained and threadbare, of Korrush design. On the carpet stood a stoop-shouldered figure, thin as a nail.

"Sagiira!" Eleana cried, and immediately threw herself into his opened arms.

"My child, my child!" His leathery face cracked open, and a wide smile tumbled out. "I had lost track of you, as had all your friends." He kissed her on both cheeks. "They feared the worst, but I had faith."

"Faith, my eye." Eleana laughed as she held him at arm's length. "I would be very surprised if you haven't been following my progress every step of the way."

"My dear, you know me too well." He shook his head. "In my line of work that can be dangerous, you know."

"Just what is your line of work?" Thigpen asked.

"By Miina's robes," Sagiira exclaimed, "what is your name, Rappa?"

Eleana introduced Riane and Thigpen.

Sagiira nodded. "As to my line of work . . ." He held up his right hand. The sixth finger was black as soil.

"A sauromician!" Riane exclaimed.

Thigpen jumped back, her teeth bared. "We are in a sauromician's lair. Eleana, why have you done this?"

Sagiira spread his hands wide. "Listen to me, Thigpen. If the regent became aware of my existence, he would surely seek to incarcerate me. There, you hold my fate in your hands. He and his minions, however, are the lesser of my concerns. If ever the Dark League should discover my whereabouts, it would be the end for me."

Thigpen, ears still flat to her head, was hardly mollified. "Once a sauromician . . ."

Riane leaned down, ruffled her luxuriant coat, whispered, "Have you so soon forgotten Minnum?"

"The Rappa can be forgiven their little paranoias," Sagiira said. "They have been the victims of terrible persecution."

Thigpen eyed him darkly. "Trying to suck up, are you?"

Sagiira smiled indulgently. When they were all seated on the carpet, he poured them a fruit-based concoction from an earthenware jug. "Lately, the Dark League's focus has turned to one purpose." Handing chipped goblets around. "Banestones."

"Why?" Riane asked.

Sagiira watched them over the lip of his goblet. His head, narrow as a ruler, was dominated by almond-shaped eyes, suspended in liquid.

"Whatever his answer," Thigpen growled, "it cannot be good."

"The Rappa is correct. Somehow the Dark League has found the lost banestones—eight of them. The ninth they are still searching for—desperately."

"Miina save us all." Thigpen's whiskers were twitching violently. "I told Giyan. I warned her. But when it comes to you, little dumpling, she is as overprotective as a mother. Where's the sense of sparing you the horrors of the world, I say. Better by far to be prepared."

Sagiira broke into a dry, brittle laugh. "My word, you are such a pessimistic species."

"Pessimism saves lives," Thigpen muttered. "My father used to say that, and he was right on the mark."

"What do they mean to do with the nine banestones?" Riane was concentrating harder.

"Clearly, they mean to harness the energy of the ninth in order to increase their power. Difficult to speculate just how."

"But if we can stop them from acquiring the ninth banestone?"

"The harnessing cannot take place. Separately each banestone is dangerous, but their energy makes their effect unstable, impossible to predict. Putting the nine together focuses their energy, stabilizes it."

"Like the weapon at Za Hara-at."

Sagiira watching them over the lip of his goblet. "I never said it was a weapon."

"You didn't have to."

"Do you know where the ninth banestone is?" Eleana asked.

Sagiira looked shriveled, worn, like the nub of an ancient writing implement. "I know where it *was*. Buried in Za Hara-at and good riddance to it, caused all manner of troubles. But now it's vanished. The Dark League knows this much, as do I. I do not know who took it from Za Hara-at or where it is now. Neither do they." Looked from one of his visitors to the other. "To business, then. One does not need a sauromician's skills to know that you have come for help. What is it that you require?"

"A way into the cavern beneath the regent's palace," Riane began. But before she could continue, Muzli's deep-throated growl brought her to silence.

Sagiira cocked his head, listening to the very air that eddied around them. "Unwanted visitors."

"Khagggun?" Eleana asked.

"Yes and no." Sagiira's eyes closed for a moment, and they could see very rapid movement beneath thin, blue lids. "The regent Stogggul and his Haaar-kyut satrap. They are coming this way." He stood. "Quickly now, come. I will tell you what you need to know."

This is not the safest place for you to be," the regent's Haaar-kyut satrap said.

"I have spent the better part of the last year trying to hunt these fugitives down," Kurgan Stogggul growled. "They have outwitted my best Khagggun. Nothing you say will give me pause. I am going to take care of them myself, First-Captain Kwenn."

"Still." Kwenn held at the end of a straining chain a large, wire-haired wyr-hound. He let it poke its ugly black snout into one miserable hovel after another, snuffling at scents. He had his portable ion cannon at the ready. "One can never be too careful."

Kurgan appreciated Kwenn's strict attention to detail, though he could not admire it. To his way of thinking, tiny imaginations bred tiny thoughts.

"I had no idea there were so many Kundalan living like rat-moles in the bowels of the city."

"As far as I can see," Kurgan said as they pressed forward, "they are welcome to the bowels of this backward city." The wyr-hound left a thin trail of saliva wherever it went. "Who trains these things, anyway?"

"A retired Khagggun named Tong, regent. He only breeds the best. They are exceptionally loyal, you know."

"As long as they do their job."

"Oh, Unu will find our quarry."

"You *name* these things?" Kurgan wrinkled his nose. "That is a bit much, Kwenn."

"Don't you like animals, regent?"

"Not in the least," Kurgan said. "I never can fathom what they are going to do next."

"It is simple, really." Kwenn went into a stinking cubicle on their right, while the wyr-hound terrified the inhabitants. "They are not so different from us Khagggun," he continued upon reemerging. "They respond negatively to fear and aggression, positively to being rewarded, and they require strong leadership." He cocked his head as they made their way down the dank underground corridor. "On the subject of strong leadership, regent, your choice of Star-Admiral will anger many."

"Those Khagggun, whoever they may be, are of no consequence, First-Captain Kwenn, for they shall soon succumb to Iin Mennus' iron fist." Kurgan kept a wary eye on the wyr-hound, whose snufflings he found disgusting. "This change is long overdue. The Khagggun have become soft; they bicker among themselves. Their Bashkir desire for coins will gain them only fat bellies."

"You are right, regent. Great Caste status for us was nothing more than a noble experiment."

"It was not even that. It was an ill-considered deal brokered by my father to gain political control over all Khagggun."

"Then you are wise to rescind the status."

All at once, they stopped. The fur on the wyr-hound's collar stood up. Its ears had flattened, and its long greenish teeth gnashed together. Kwenn pointed his ion cannon down the corridor.

"Listen to me." There was a fierce and determined look in Kurgan's eyes. "Under no circumstances do I want the fugitives killed. Do you understand me, First-Captain Kwenn?"

"Absolutely, regent." First-Captain Kwenn depressed the limiter icon on the ion cannon. "I will hit them with stun bursts."

At that moment, Kwenn was almost taken off his feet by the leap of the wyr-hound. "Here we go!" he said as he dropped the chain. At once, the wyr-hound bounded down the corridor on his powerful legs, the two V'ornn right behind him. Kurgan drew a weapon, a small but lethal-looking push-dagger with a dartlike blade that had been dipped in a Nieobian paralysis gel. The corridor had sometime ago emptied of its shambling residents, who were doubtless cowering at the backs of their mean little chambers.

Up ahead, Kurgan could see a creature, something long and sinuous, moving low to the ground. The wyr-hound leapt upon the creature, its jaws clashing, seeking to snap the creature's neck. The creature—he was astonished to see that it was a claiwen—whipped its spiked tail around. The wyr-hound screamed as the spikes buried themselves in its muzzle and the side of its skull. It dug its claws fiercely into the claiwen's side, but the tail whipped up and back again, and the wyr-hound was thrown against the wall. Even as it bounced off, the claiwen opened its huge jaws and tore out the wyr-hound's throat.

"Unu!" Kwenn cried, and, as the claiwen turned its bloody face toward them, fired off a blast from the ion cannon that dropped the thing in its tracks.

"Look!" Kurgan hissed.

Down the corridor raced three figures—two Kundalan and another kind of beast that Kurgan had caught a glimpse of at Za Hara-at. They tore around a corner and disappeared as Kwenn, leaping over his fallen wyr-hound, fired off another blast that made the air sizzle.

"Concentrate on the female with the yellow hair," Kurgan said as he ran easily at Kwenn's side. "Leave the dark-haired one to me."

We should make all haste for the under level Sagiira told us about while we still have a lead on them," Eleana said as she ran side by side with Riane.

"That is just what we won't do," Riane said. "You heard that sound. The First-Captain is armed with an ion cannon. He doesn't need to get close to bring us down." They whipped around another corner, almost tripping over a half-supine Kundalan just starting out of a doze.

"Then what do you suggest?"

They had reached a section of the underground warren

that Sagiira had described to them. Here the corridor opened up into a kind of plaza with a succession of nooks and crannies created by massive structural columns supporting the buildings above. The plaza was entirely deserted. All was silence, save for the occasional creak of the massive stone underflooring above their heads.

"We stay right here," Riane said.

"What?" Eleana looked around. "And wait for them to come upon us?"

"Yes," Riane said. "Exactly so."

She directed Eleana and Thigpen into niches a bit farther back in the plaza. Then she chose one herself, closer to where their pursuers would arrive.

"Say nothing," she whispered. "No matter what happens, keep absolutely quiet."

Eleana, setting her back against the cold stone column, watched Riane close her eyes. Her lips moved slightly, and a moment later Eleana felt overcome by a slight dizziness. She blinked. It seemed to her as if they were underwater. She thought she could detect ripples emanating from Riane, as of a stone thrown into a lake, spiraling out to encompass the entire plaza. She had been witness to Flowering Wand once before. It was a powerful spell, rendering those within it invisible. Its drawback was that it had a short duration.

Now her thoughts turned elsewhere as her ear detected the pounding of V'ornn boot soles, and into the plaza burst the regent and his Haaar-kyut First-Captain. She possessed a healthy fear of Khagggun. She knew better than most their ferocity and relentless cruelty. But it was the sight of Kurgan Stogggul that make her heart turn over in terror. It was he who had raped her, he who had buried his seed deep in her womb, he who was the father of Sahor, the child she had borne, a child who would have died without the intervention of the Gyrgon Nith Sahor. Now Nith Sahor dwelt within her child, using Gyrgon technomagic to age him from infant to sixteen-year-old in a matter of days.

Her mind was filled with Sahor as she watched Kurgan's clever pirate eyes scan the plaza. She wished that Sahor had not gone to the Museum of False Memory to become its new curator while Minnum stayed on to explore Za Hara-at. She wished that the war was over. She wished to be with her child and with Riane, whom she loved more than life itself. But here she was, deep underground, with nowhere to run, confronting the one V'ornn she never wished to see again.

As Kurgan walked slowly and carefully through the plaza, she felt a loathing that was close to revulsion. The sight of him brought up that beautiful sun-dappled day when she had stupidly stopped at her favorite creek to bathe after completing her act of sabotage against the Khagggun in Axis Tyr. That was when he had spied her and, coming upon her by surprise, had taken her by force. Abruptly, her nostrils were filled with his rutting scent. She felt his rough hands digging into her flesh, his crushing weight on top of her. In her ears his breath panted out his lust.

Tears filled her eyes, and his image swam before her.

"Unu is dead. I will kill them all now."

Kurgan whirled to confront his Haaar-kyut. "You will do as I have told you, Kwenn, and help me capture them."

Their voices came to her as a drifted cloud, slightly muffled, partially distorted by the spell.

"Unu was my favorite." First-Captain Kwenn swung the muzzle of his ion cannon this way and that. "How many nights I slept with him as I trained him."

"If you harm them in any way—"

"They are Kundalan. They deserve to die."

"That is not for you to say, First-Captain." Kurgan took a step toward him. "If you harm Riane or Eleana, I will kill you myself. Is that clear enough?"

"Yes, regent." Kwenn nodded. "Of course. My apologies."

"When we return to the palace I will procure for you another wyr-hound. Right now, though, we have fugitives to find." Kurgan pointed. "You take the right side, I will take the left."

He knew her name! Eleana, shaken, saw the Haaar-kyut move off toward where Riane stood. She held her breath as Kurgan Stogggul advanced in her direction. He worked methodically and thoroughly, peering into each nook and cranny, looking for a door or escape hatch. All too soon, he was less than an arm's length from where she stood. Though she knew he could not see her, still she had pressed herself against the stone as if she could sink into it, vanish for real.

How did he know her name?

He was so close she could smell him now, and she gave a tiny involuntary gasp. At once, his head came around, and he stared right at her. His black eyes searched the shadows within which she was secreted. His nostrils flared, and his eyes flicked back and forth. His hand came up, his fingertips touching the stone beside her cheek.

He could only know her name one way—he had been spying on them in Za Hara-at! What else had he learned? She feared for Riane.

Locked in proximity with him, Eleana felt as if she were suffocating. She could sense the malevolence emanating from him. Felt his overweening ambition, his lust for conquest. And something else that threatened to turn her bones to water—the extraordinary force of his desire. She commenced to tremble, for she knew with every cell of her being that this desire was aimed at her.

Riane had heard Eleana's gasp and how it had instantly drawn Kurgan's attention. Looking at the intense expression on his face, she wondered whether he somehow suspected that Eleana was there. She had been stunned to discover that he knew Eleana's name, and she, too, had come to the inevitable conclusion that he had not disappeared from Za Hara-at as quickly as it had at first seemed. Then she realized what must actually be happening—Flowering Wand was beginning to dissipate.

They had only moments before the spell was gone, leaving them visible and vulnerable to the V'ornn. She had to use her advantage before it vanished altogether.

Kwenn had just passed her when she stepped out of her niche and slammed her forearm into the back of his neck. He pitched forward, his forehead striking the stone wall. Riane jammed her boot into the back of his right knee and, as he buckled, snatched the ion cannon out of his grasp.

The small sounds of the scuffle had caused Kurgan to cease his scrutiny of the place where Eleana was hiding. He turned, the point of his push-dagger coming up, when Riane fired an ion burst into his chest. He flew backward, crashing to the floor, insensate.

"Come on!" Riane cried as she led the way out of the far side of the plaza.

Sornnn SaTrryn returned to Axis Tyr to find it dull as dishwater. He knew he should have been pumped up by the prestige and power that went with being Prime Factor, but all he could muster was indifference. Within twenty-four hours of listening to Bashkir business disputes, he felt as if he had been incarcerated in the Forum of Adjudication for twenty-four years. He found the invidious accusations of his fellow Bashkir almost as risible as their prevarications. Owing to his absence, the backlog of adjudications was formidable, the Forum's session interminable, the recesses, though brief, his only solace.

His mind was filled with the kaleidoscopic Korrush, with brooding Za Hara-at, with the portent of war, and with his disquieting conversation with Nasaqa. And he could not help but wonder how Minnum was getting along without him. He missed the little sauromician, but not as much as he missed Marethyn. He longed for her as one longs for food, for breath. She had, in short, become an essential part of his life, and he could not now live it happily without her.

He was briefly pulled out of his misery by Raan Tallus.

He was the solicitor-general, a clever and powerful Bashkir, who was now administering the Ashera family business. Cool-eyed, dark-skinned, clearheaded. Loved a good verbal sparring match. In short, since he was at the center of a dispute involving not only an emperor's ransom of coinage but also of intellectual property he insisted belonged solely to the Ashera, he brought a single spark of interest to Sornnn's life. Sornnn watched in concealed amusement the ease with which he demolished the opposing Bashkir's arguments while at the same time scoring his own points. It was impossible not to be impressed. On the other hand, the matter was far from the open-and-shut case he would have Sornnn believe, and eventually Sornnn fell back into the prison that his life had become.

Mercifully, the session could not go on forever, and when at last time won him his temporary respite, he roamed the packed streets, restlessly moving from place to place. He walked the entire length of Divination Street just so he could pass Marethyn's atelier. Shuttered now, it had a sad air of abandonment that sent him straight to Gamut, the cafe where they used to meet in secret, but inside the sense of her was so palpable he was forced to leave before he could finish his drink. Divination Street brought him in close proximity with the subterranean club, Cthonne. He went there after midnight, but amid the gyrating throng he could find none of his Resistance contacts.

He went next to the umbilical of the vast all-night spice market, to Spice Jaxx's, where he most often met Majja and Basse, the Resistance members to whom he had introduced Marethyn. They were not there, and the Resistance he did find were from different cells, and so knew nothing of them, or of her. That was frustrating but perfectly normal, the way the Resistance was required to work. Still, he could not help feeling that fate was mocking him. How could Marethyn simply fall off the map?

The next day, during an hour's break—a welcome respite from Raan Tallus' endless oration filled with galax-

ies of witnesses, affidavit-crystals, case-law precedents—
he went to see Tong.

Tong was his father's oldest friend, an ancient and war-
torn Khagggun, who had chosen retirement rather than
having his many-times-broken bones rehabilitated once
more by the Genomatekks. Now he raised wyr-hounds and
led a quiet, unremarkable life.

Tong had his kennels in the Northern Quarter, a rough
area for Khagggun, seeing how it was populated mostly by
the perpetually angry Mesagggun. But there were Looorm,
too, which, Sornnn supposed, was why Tong was there in
the first place. He had never mated; as far as Sornnn knew,
he had no children.

It was Tong who had helped Sornnn's father set up the
traffic routes to and from the Korrush. Routes unknown or
little guarded by the Khagggun so Hadinnn SaTrryn could
move more than spice when he needed to.

Tong was Sornnn's last resort in finding out news of
Marethyn, but he was soon to rue his decision to come
there.

"My friend, I'm afraid I have some bad news."

Sornnn felt a buzzing in his head, and he sat down in a
chair Tong provided for him. Wyr-hound pups nipped at
his legs, begging for attention.

Tong picked one up and set him down in Sornnn's lap,
where Sornnn immediately began to stroke his still-soft
fur. The pup licked his fingers.

"What's happened?" Sornnn said in a faint voice. "Tell
me straight out."

Tong sighed. He had been a massive Khagggun once,
but age and the disabilities he chose to live with had whittled him down. His skin, grey-tinged as the day, lay over
atrophied muscles in thick folds. All the deep copper color
seemed to have been lost on the many battlefields he had
left behind. He still had a keen eye, though, and a taste for
the Looorm he'd bedded in brief bouts between battles.

"Ah, Sornnn, there is no good way to say this." He
poured Sornnn a shot of fire-grade numaaadis. "The cell

Marethyn joined was ambushed while they lay in wait for a convoy of Khaggun war materiel."

The cup slipped from Sornnn's nerveless fingers. He felt his stomach clench, his gorge rising. A great black wall seemed to be rising, obliterating everything in its path. Dimly, he was aware of Tong pouring him another drink, urging him to swallow it. But when he did he choked, spewed the numaaadis onto the ground, where the dogs greedily lapped it up. Dimly, he heard someone saying, "Your source must be mistaken. I don't believe it." Eventually, he recognized his own voice. His vision blurred with tears. Marethyn gone. It could not be. He thought of their love, their time together, so precious, so short. He heard her laugh, the rustle of her clothes, the luster of her bare flesh. The scent of her! How deeply he breathed in her presence. His best friend, his lover, his life. How would he survive without her? He uttered a low moan.

Tong was patient. When he judged Sornnn ready, he went on. "From what I have learned the cell was set up." He took the empty tumbler from Sornnn, but when he went to refill it Sornnn shook his head sharply. "They walked right into the trap."

Sornnn felt his hearts constrict, and he cried out her name. "Surely some of them had to survive," he said in a strangled voice.

"None have been reported anywhere. And that convoy disappeared as well. If it's any consolation, it was a disaster for both sides." Tong's eyes were very sad. "My friend, is there anything I can do?"

Sornnn shook his head. The sweet balm of shock had for the moment removed him from everyone and everything. In his mind he danced with Marethyn, and she spoke to him of all the intimate things he longed to hear. Never her touch, never her voice. Never again. The thought was too final to make sense. In a flood, the bitter tears came, overwhelming him.

Tong took the pup as Sornnn stood up.

"I should go now." He felt dizzy and strangely light-headed, certain that at any moment he would awake to find this all just a terrible nightmare. "My work is waiting."

"*Klagh*." It was the worst of the Kraelian curses, a harsh and guttural sound befitting its ugly sentiment. "Stay here until you feel yourself again."

Sornnn did not think that he would ever feel himself again. Besides, his nerves felt rubbed raw. To look at even one sympathetic face that knew what he knew, that felt his pain, seemed intolerable.

He threw himself into his role as Prime Factor, but all the while it seemed false, two-dimensional, as if he were watching a crystal-vid of someone else's life. Nothing was real, nothing mattered without her. A veil had descended over the world, isolating him; he moved through his life like an automaton, functioning without feeling. He looked into the mirror and no longer recognized the face. By night he wandered the streets, slipped through crowds, pinched his face to make certain he was still there. He was not reassured. By day he was assaulted by slick-talking representatives of Bashkir families jabbering on about the growing Kundalan labor shortage, the need for slave labor would explode as soon as ground was broken in Za Hara-at and work in the lortan mines quickly brought on a pernicious lung disease; how to get in on the coming building bonanza at Za Hara-at; the usual simmering resentment toward Ashera entitlement, their monopoly of the salamuuun trade, their major investment—along with the Stogggul—in Za Hara-at. An overall theme apparent to even sunken Sornnn: a groundswell of curiosity and interest in the rebuilding of the ancient city. Every family, it seemed, wanted to participate. They could smell the coinage accruing. Sornnn could not recall this degree of anticipation among the Bashkir. Their fluttery excitement, like Tuskugggun on their way to a party, only served to depress him further. The thought of a concerted Bashkir commercial push into the Korrush made him want to scream. That was all on the inside. On the outside, he smiled politely, listening to their arguments, rebutting when need be. He got caught up in a whirlpool of linguistics, semantics, staid and static logic, precedents, the emotional pushing and shoving for favorable rulings. Cross-talk voices, raised in anger, lowered in seduction. He interfaced with so many they became a blur, the blur became a pain in his head, closing one eye, a vein throbbing excessively in his skull. Bludgeoning him to a Genomatekk. *Perhaps I am dying,* he thought as he sat, waiting. *That would be fitting.*

Marethyn was dead, and it was his fault. He had brought her into his secret world, had wanted to share everything with her. Lacked the strength to keep her at arm's length, to be friends. It was too heavy a price to pay to keep that wall between them as he did with everyone else. With her, he had wanted it all, had believed that he was in control of everything, and now she had paid the ultimate price.

Not a thing wrong, the Genomatekk assured him after the half hour of inscrutable diagnostics. Nothing organic, that is. He knew what was wrong, as he drove himself back into the desolation of his life. The pain was loss. The loss was Marethyn.

And at the end of another long and grueling adjudicating session, to which he could see no point, he was too despairing to go home. Everywhere else reminded him of her. So he hauled himself across the street to the nearest cafe, a hole called, of all things, Alloy Fist. Its depressing chronosteel interior matched his mood perfectly. The livid blue lighting made everyone look half-dead. That too was apt. He saw that it most of its habitues were grim-faced Khaggun from the nearby barracks. Perfect.

At the bar, he pulled up a stool and ordered a drink. After the first one, he felt even worse, if that were possible. But after the fourth, he couldn't see much reason to leave.

Rekkk, I think she is dying," Giyan said. She held Perrnodt in her arms. The Druuge was as pale as the snowbanks outside. "I saved her from the xi-wraith, but now . . . now she is fading again. I cannot determine what has damaged her so severely, and I cannot find a spell to bring her back."

They, along with Konara Inggres, were in the abbey's infirmary. Enfeebled grey light lay gasping against the windows, a reflection of the fogbound twilight that had enrobed the ridge on which the abbey sat. It was so thick it completely absorbed the lights of the nearby village of Stone Border. Even the upper reaches of the abbey's nine slender minarets were lost to view.

"Perhaps I can help," the Nawatir said. He unclipped his long cloak and wrapped Perrnodt in it. As they watched, it molded itself to her body. At the same time, its edges began to flutter as if in a wind. Perrnodt sighed.

"Rekkk, what is happening?"

"I am still learning about the cloak," he admitted. "What I do know is that it is composed of a material not found on Kundala. It was spun by the Dragons and, therefore, has in its warp and weft a part of their will, their power. It is both a weapon and a defense, though I have yet to discover the extent of its uses." He gently took Perrnodt out of Giyan's embrace and put her on the bed. "Nevertheless, I believe the cloak will heal her." He looked at Konara Inggres. "If you will be so good as to have one of your Ramahan watch over her, I think we should leave her. Unless I miss my guess, her recovery will take some time."

6

Scent of Bitterroot

What is this?" Marethyn Stogggul, holding the glistening dark brown cube in front of her nose.

"Braised bitterroot." Majja was laughing. "I am willing

to wager you never thought you would be eating such basic Kundalan food." The Resistance fighter used a worn wooden ladle to fill her blackened wood bowl from the small cauldron that hung above the crackling fire. Hunkered down beside Marethyn, she began to eat her midday meal. "It smells worse than it tastes, believe me."

Marethyn, long of body, regal of face, an amalgam of cool intelligence and burning sensuality, took a bite, and was surprised. As Majja had said, the acrid, almost rank odor did not translate into the taste, which was mild and not unpleasant. Furthermore, the braising had imparted to the tuber a rich, creamy texture that was almost luxurious.

"Not bad," she said, and the two females laughed together.

Ever since Marethyn had decided to join the Resistance by helping to hijack a convoy of new Khagggun weapons, she had been embraced by them despite the fact that she was a V'ornn Tuskugggun. That was doubtless because she had shown both initiative and courage when the group had been ambushed, losing all but three of their number, including their leader, Kasstna. He was the only one Marethyn did not mourn. He had distrusted her from the beginning, and had made her life with the Resistance miserable, shouting down any suggestions she had, ordering her to perform the most menial and humiliating tasks, including clearing out the camp's offal.

It had been Marethyn who had taken Majja and the male Basse with her as she had boarded the hoverpod, guiding it away from the battle. They had directed her northwest, flying higher into the Djenn Marre, then due west, over the extreme northwestern triangle of the dense Borobodur forest to a great whitish slab of rock known as Receive Tears Ridge. It offered breathtaking views that translated, in Resistance terms, into a great tactical advantage. From it, one could see south into the forest, west to the Three Fish River, and northwest to the waterfall of Little Rushing. At their backs, to the north and northeast, rose the high ragged tors of the Djenn Marre, brooding amidst constantly fulminating clouds. The winds were high, chill, and, at times, pierced through even the thickest fur. Still, they were safe there.

The ridge was misty both at dawn and toward sunset, but at noon the sky overhead was sun-burnished. For a Tuskugggun from the Axis Tyr lowlands, the clarity of the light was extraordinary, especially if that Tuskugggun was an artist.

"We are safe here, if Kundalan can ever be said to be safe from Khagggun packs," Gerwa, the Resistance cell leader said, just after they had arrived. He had greeted Majja and Basse and the contents of the convoy with exultation. As to Marethyn, his reception had been, if not hostile, than decidedly muted.

"After all," he had said, "you are the enemy. Everything you do or say here will be scrutinized, a matter of suspicion."

"You do not owe me an explanation," she had said as they had shared a flagon of steaming ludd-wine, mulled with unfamiliar spices.

"I do owe you that much for the cache of V'ornn weapons you have brought us." Dark eyes and thin, pale lips in a rather narrow face lent him a sinister cast. "But, quite frankly, until I am comfortable with your motivation for joining us you cannot expect to be fully trusted."

"I understand completely. It will be a learning experience," she said, "for both of us."

That particular conversation was already several weeks past, and Marethyn's place in the cell was becoming more readily defined. For one thing, she had gained some respect for Gerwa who, unlike the brutish and hotheaded Kasstna, commanded through cleverness, not intimidation.

He had refrained from ordering her to do the menial tasks that had been her lot before, but occasionally she volunteered for such chores. As a reward, she supposed, Gerwa had assigned her to several recon forays, looking for the myriad Khagggun pairs embedded within the surrounding terrain, put there by Deck-Admiral Iin Mennus in order to ambush unwary Resistance members. Though they did not stray more than five kilometers from the ridge, and though she was fairly certain that Gerwa had assigned a different Resistance fighter each time to keep an eye on her, she was grateful for the missions, during which her mind was engaged and her muscles were taxed.

The fire cracked and sparked, protesting a wicked gust of wind, and the cauldron in its midst rocked a little, creaking like an ancient Kundalan. Majja, hard and lean, black of eye and hair, in peaceful times, might have had nothing more on her mind than which boy to favor. Now rage and a surfeit of hormones fueled her, but war and misery had combined to make her a killer. Unlikely as it might seem, she and Marethyn had become friends; that, too, a product of war.

"You eat bitterroot like a true Kundalan," Majja said. "Too bad Kasstna cannot see you now."

"Kasstna hated me for who I am," Marethyn pointed out. "What I did or said was irrelevant."

"Good riddance to him," Majja said. "Basse and I spoke often of his inability to lead us successfully. His hatred dictated every decision he made; it often clouded his judgment."

She lighted a laaga stick, and for a time they smoked in companionable silence, passing it back and forth between them. Marethyn was thinking of Sornnn. She missed him terribly. At night, she dreamed she lay in his arms, felt the caress of his hands on her body, the flutter of his lips on hers, and she would awake with her cheeks wet with tears. During the day, she did not cry for him; she had more pressing matters on her mind. Often, though, in the languorous moments before sleep swept her away, she had tried to figure a way to send him a message. Too dangerous, not only for herself but for her compatriots. She had their welfare to consider, as well.

The bronze sun beat down, but to the north clouds built against the towering citadel of the Djenn Marre, and thunder commenced to rumble in the far distance, echoing through the ice-gripped interstices between the mountains. The air was turning bitter, a certain harbinger, she had learned, of snow.

They broke off smoking the laaga stick as Gerwa approached them. With a pinched face, unkempt hair and a clenched disposition, product of worry and a sour stomach, he wore thick grey-black furs over his leggings and cor-hide jerkin that stank of smoke and sweat.

Marethyn eyed him warily. "It seems to me that the cache we brought him has become something of a two-edged sword."

Majja nodded. "This cell has now become the envy of every other, and it is Gerwa's responsibility to see that the weapons we stole are given into the strongest and most capable hands. That has made him enemies as well as allies."

Gerwa squatted down. "Do not stop on my account." He took the laaga stick between his lips, inhaling deeply. When no one replied, he shrugged. "The two of you are on patrol. Southwest quadrant. Medda has all the details." He stood and ground the remainder of the laaga stick beneath his heel as he released in a hiss the last of the smoke. "Make sure your weapons are fully charged. You leave at once."

They found Medda and three others at the supply tent.

"We are headed down the southwest slope of the ridge." Medda was charging his ion cannon. "It is the steepest of the descents and the weather is not likely to cooperate. Have a care, all of you." Then he turned to Majja, and said under his breath, "We are taking Kin, Gerwa's younger brother. He is very young and green around the gills. Keep an eye on him."

Marethyn was standing right beside her friend but Medda did not address her at all.

He turned and led them out of the camp and down off Receive Tears Ridge. The top, white as bleached bone, was entirely different from the sides. It was as if a great skull had been partially heaved up from the fiery core of Kundala, its upper cranium exposed and scoured by the ages.

As Medda had told them, the southwest descent was exceptionally steep. They were obliged at times to hold on to the whiplike trunks of immature Marre pines huddled in patches on the stony slope.

Snow did not come but, worse, sleet, which made the footing even more treacherous than it normally would be. Often, they had no choice but to slide on their backsides as a precaution against pitching headlong into the gathering gloom.

Marethyn was entirely calm. In fact, she loved being lost within the Marre pines. Their slender trunks once again conjured up the elfin forms she had imagined when as a child her grandmother Tettsie had taken her into the forests to paint. The rich, resinous scent they exuded recalled long, golden afternoons during which she and Tettsie had had the most fascinating discussions on whether form followed function or function followed form. As a budding artist, those kinds of ontological questions helped her grope toward her own theories of shape and color that brought life to her canvases.

For the moment at least, the sleet let up, leaving evening to frost the sky. For most of their descent they had cleaved to the edge of the precipitous slope, but now Medda took them almost due west, across the slope's face in a gently descending arc. Possibly he had received intelligence from another group just back from their patrol. In any event, he gave the clear impression that he knew where he was going.

There, out of the biting northeast wind, the stands of Marre pines were higher and sturdier; thicker, as well, because they were joined by the more delicate kuello-firs, whose long, lacy needles dipped and rose to the dance of their supple branches.

Their pace slowed, and by then Marethyn was certain that Medda had a destination in mind. The sleet had matted down the needles, icing them in patches. In this pitched terrain, knobby with root knees, it would be easy to break a leg. Unobtrusively, she worked her way until she was directly behind Kin. Just as well, because she had to snatch him up by the scruff of his neck when he skidded on a patch of icy-crusted leaves.

The wind shifted and, for a moment, it was in their faces. Marethyn scented something through the thick pine resin—the telltale scent of hyperexcited ions. Quickly, she reached Medda's side and whispered in his ear.

At once, he hunkered down with her as he waved the others to do likewise.

"Khagggun straight ahead? Are you sure?" he whispered.

"Absolutely."

"My information is that if we move directly through here and turn south, we will have their backs."

She could tell that he did not quite believe her. What if she were deliberately leading them into a trap?

"Either your intelligence is wrong," she said, "or the Khagggun allowed themselves to be seen, then moved so as to catch us."

He looked off into the dripping forest, then back to her. "Unfortunately, there is no way to be sure until it is too late."

"There is one way," she said.

He waited for a moment, judging her, judging the moment.

"Send me to flush out the Khagggun."

"What?"

"I am Tuskugggun. They will neither expect me nor immediately fire on me. But they will show themselves, then you will have them."

Shook his head. "Too risky. You know the location of our encampment."

"Shadow me through the woods. Stay close enough so that you can be certain I do not betray you. Kill me if I do."

He put his back against the bole of a kuello-fir as if to think it through. She knew he would agree. Her plan had no downside. Even as she was thinking this, he nodded. He put his ion cannon at the ready, and the rest of the party followed suit. Marethyn handed him her weapon, rose, and began to walk forward with as little stealth as possible. She wanted the Khagggun to hear her coming. In fact, it was essential she not surprise them altogether, for then, she suspected, with their hair-trigger fingers, they would shoot and ask questions later.

She made her way through the trees, trying to avoid the slickest patches of iced Marre pine needles. She could not hear Medda behind her, but she knew he was there, his ion cannon aimed at the middle of her back. With her artist's sensibilities, the maze of the forest resolved itself into light and shadow, texture and color, forming a pattern through which she could see herself moving. It still quite astonished her that her ability to see, collate, and transform what she saw into art was of such vital use to her in her new life as a warrior.

The waft of hyperexcited ions grew vaguer as the wind dissipated the discharge. Nevertheless, she followed her nose, here and there cracking a dead twig or rotted branch underfoot. Up ahead, in the last of the silverish light, she saw a small clearing, a natural place for a band of weary Resistance fighters to rest. Without breaking stride, she broke out of the tree line and began to cross it. The place between her shoulder blades began to itch as she imagined ion cannons being aimed at her. She paused, turning in this direction and that, as if she had lost her way. What she was, in fact, doing was giving the Khagggun a good look at her face.

She heard a sound then, and froze, a look of fear stitched to her face.

A metallic voice broke through the trees, "What is a Tuskugggun doing out here?"

"Who is there?" she cried. "If it is Resistance, know that I am Marethyn Stogggul, the regent's sister. If you harm me, he will destroy you and your families."

A harsh laugh echoed, and she squinted. She could make out a shape moving silently through the trees, then another.

"Listen to the Tuskugggun!" The first of the Khagggun

entered the small clearing, aiming an ion cannon at her chest. He, like his companion, was wearing specially designed alloy armor that blended in with the forest. She had seen such armor displayed in the shop windows of Axis Tyr but this was her first look at it in the field. "The regent's sister, she says!"

The second Khagggun appeared, a towering specimen with shoulders like a water buttren. "By Enlil's tender parts, what a beauty she is!" He wasted no time, striding to where she stood and peering into her face. "You know, I think she *is* the regent's sister."

"N'Luuura take it!" the first one cried. "Why is she here?"

"I was captured by Resistance," Marethyn said in her best breathless voice. "I waited until they slept, then I overpowered my guard and sneaked out of their camp. I have been walking all day."

"You hear that? She got the best of her guard." The big one's hands roamed over her shoulders and biceps. "Yes, I can believe that." Then he cupped her large breasts. "You will be grateful that we are here to protect you."

"And escort you back to our base," the first one said, "where a hoverpod will take you back to Axis Tyr."

"The regent will reward us." His huge hands were wandering far afield. "As will you, Marethyn Stogggul, for we are your deliverance from the torture that otherwise would have been your fate."

The first one grinned. "You will show us the location of their camp."

"But later." The towering Khagggun backed her against a tree. "In the dead of night." He moved his hips suggestively against her. "When all are asleep and unsuspecting." He held her head in his hands, his lips close to hers. "But now, here, it will be just us, a moment of—"

His head slammed against hers with a sudden crack that made her start, and all at once she was covered in blood. The Khagggun staggered, and she kneed him in his swollen tender parts. He groaned, sank to his knees, and she stepped out of his grasp. The smaller Khagggun was spraying the woods with ion fire. An instant later, he was struck from two sides at once and, headless, collapsed where he stood.

Marethyn's companions broke out of their hiding places, and were making their cautious way toward her. Marethyn went to meet them, but was abruptly jerked off her feet. The huge Khagggun had gripped her ankle. Before she had a chance to recover, he began to crawl over her. He had sustained a hideous head wound and was blind in one eye, but his good eye, red and swollen, glowered at her with such rage and hatred it nearly froze her blood.

She twisted and saw Kin running toward her. But from her vantage point, she saw the green glint of an ion cannon low to the ground like her. All the Resistance members were in the clearing. The huge Khagggun grasped her, bellowing in pain and anger. She spotted his ion cannon, but it was too far out of reach. Twisting back, she dug her thumb into his ruined eye. As he spasmed, he drew his ion pistol from its hip holster.

She groaned at the sudden flare of pain in her side. The huge Khagggun punched her again. Tears came to her eyes. Then Kin appeared, slammed the butt end of his ion cannon into the Khagggun's face. The Khagggun, grinding his teeth in pain and fury, drew Marethyn closer toward him. His burly forearm slithered across her throat, cutting off her windpipe.

"Back off, child," he growled. "Back off, or she dies."

Kin aimed. As if hearing a sound, his eyes cut quickly to the left. Focused again on Marethyn and the Khagggun, he lowered his weapon and took a step back.

The Khagggun grinned through bloody teeth. "That's the good boy."

Medda, crouched to their left, fired his ion cannon and blew a hole the size of a qwawd egg in the Khagggun's head.

* * *

What you mustn't do, Sagiira had told them, *is attempt to enter the cavern by any of the known escape routes.*

Riane, Eleana, and Thigpen crouched in the stifling darkness of the tunnel. They smelled the richness of the earth and the bitter tang of metal. Small scurryings suggested ghostly voices whispering into hidden corners.

It is unclear whether Kurgan Stogggul has knowledge of these routes, but what is certain is that he has embarked on a campaign to find and booby-trap all of them.

Riane caused the Veil of a Thousand Tears to emit a glow, and by its light they crawled forward in the cramped space. Riane and Eleana were on elbows and knees. Thigpen had retracted her claws so as not to make any noise. Now and again, Riane could feel the tickle of the Rappa's long whiskers or the soft brush of her luxuriant fur.

Therefore, the safest way for you to gain access is through the regent's palace itself.

In the smells that now and again wafted their way, Riane could sense glimpses of Annon's old life. By the faded scent of star-roses, which infused the soil around the plant roots even after they had been ripped out, she knew they were traversing a span that ran beneath Eleusis Ashera's beloved garden. Not long after, they came to a fork, and, as Sagiira had advised them, headed left.

They had been reluctant to leave Muzli without knowing whether he was alive or dead, especially Eleana, to whom he had long ago endeared himself. But they had had no choice, and, as Thigpen pointed out, if, in fact, the beast had been killed in trying to buy them time, the very worst thing they could do would be to make his sacrifice meaningless.

The sweet-sour stink of illness and bodily decay followed them down the corridor. Eleana had been weeping, but soon dried her eyes as she forced her practical warrior side to the fore. They were moving so fast, they had overshot the small dimly lit branch corridor to their right.

Backtracking hastily, they went down the very steep flight of stairs as quickly as they were able considering the garbage that lay in bursting bags on almost every tread.

When, breathless, they at last reached a landing, it was only a brief respite, a narrow catwalk, its massive stone blocks pitted and cracked, beyond which was nothing on either side save fetid updrafts, punctuated by occasional muffled shouts of discord and alarm.

They ran along this walkway for what Riane judged to be the better part of a half kilometer. Then, abruptly, she stumbled over another flight of stairs, this one going up, and knew that they were inside the perimeter of the regent's palace.

Ascending farther than they had descended out of Sagiira's corridor, they at length found themselves in a small circular chamber with a ceiling so low they could barely sit up. As Sagiira had said, eight tunnels debouched into this odd place, making it a kind of nexus point.

I cannot guide you farther, for I myself have never been there, nor am I able, the old sauromician had told her. *But, mark me well, it is easy to become lost, which is the point of this chamber, to discourage interlopers who are not Ramahan konara.*

"Now what?" Thigpen had said when they had had a look around at their options. "We have eight ways to go. Which is the right one?"

Riane had been thinking about this. She was struck by Sagiira telling them that he was unable to go here. Why would that be? Then something occurred to her. One of things she had learned in Za Hara-at was that the power bourns that crisscrossed all Kundala deep below the surface were inimical to sauromicians. Furthermore, all Ramahan abbeys were built above major bourn nexus points.

With this in mind, she opened her Third Eye and, as Perrnodt had taught her, searched for the bourns. She could feel them almost immediately. Powerful and networked, they pulsed in her mind like the grid of a glowing spiderweb. With the skein spread out before her like the plan of a metropolis, she turned until she was facing one of the eight tunnel mouths.

"This one," she said.

Such was her conviction that neither Thigpen nor Eleana questioned her decision.

Where the scent of star-rose was strongest, they came upon a bronze-banded hatch of black mortewood. Riane, however, did not use it. They continued on. Gradually, the scent faded, and for some time, there was nothing but the musty smell of the foundation stones. Then, Riane picked up the prickly odors of datura inoxia, then, more pungently, shanin, Pandanus, and latua.

Eleana wrinkled up her nose. "What is that smell?"

"Ramahan herbs, roots, and mushrooms," Riane said. "We are near the garden that Giyan planted. Giyan had me memorize a plan of the palace's interior."

Eleana did not believe her, believing that she had an intimate knowledge of the palace because she was, in fact, Annon. They had reached another mortewood hatch, the next egress point. Riane was pushing it open, was already going through, Thigpen slipping after her. It was now or never. In or out. Despite Giyan's warning about the danger awaiting her in Middle Palace Eleana was not about to leave Riane. Taking a deep breath, Eleana let it out and followed them into musty darkness.

When Kurgan arose to consciousness and discovered a photon cable inserted into the inside of his left wrist he let out a bellow that could be heard in the adjacent wards of Receiving Spirit. A flush-faced Genomatekk rushed to his side from the holoscreen within the observation chamber from which he had been monitoring his distinguished patient's vital signs.

"What is this?" Kurgan demanded.

"Calm yourself, regent," the Genomatekk said. "I am treating you." He was agitated, hearing by second- and thirdhand means the extent of Kurgan Stogggul's ire. "You were hit point-blank with an ion cannon burst. Luckily, it was a low level, otherwise—"

Kurgan sat up and ripped out the photon cable. He saw a pair of Khagggun stationed just outside the doorway. At the sound of his rage, they had lifted their ion cannons to port arms. He ignored them.

"Who brought me here?"

"Why, I believe it was one of your own Haaar-kyut, regent." The Genomatekk glanced up at one of the holoscreens depending from the ceiling. "Yes, here it is. A First-Captain by the name of Gynnn Kwenn. He is being treated just down the corridor for—"

"Cease your jabbering!" Kurgan swung his fist into the nearest holoscreen, shattering it. He detested this place in the best of circumstances. He began to dress. "Make yourself useful. Go fetch First-Captain Kwenn for me."

His leggings had been hung next to the second holoscreen. As he pulled them down, he called to the Genomatekk. "Whose file is this?" he said, pointing to the holoscreen.

"Why, it is yours, regent. It is a complete medical history."

Kurgan felt a little chill run through him. The thought that Nith Batoxxx might have manipulated his genome as he had Terrettt's was always in the back of his mind, though he comforted himself with the fact that he exhibited none of his brother's symptoms.

Still, he could not help but ask; "Do you see any anomalies? Anything at all amiss?"

"No, regent," the terrified Genomatekk stammered.

"Are you certain? Have you examined the file thoroughly?"

"I have, regent. There are no anomalies whatsoever. You are in peak condition. You always have been."

Kurgan nodded. "Forget about First-Captain Kwenn," he said. "I wish to speak with Kirlll Qandda."

The Genomatekk was rooted to the spot. "I beg your pardon?"

"Are you deaf as well as slow?" Kurgan thundered.

"No, but I . . . Regent, Kirlll Qandda is a Deirus."

"That's right and I want to speak with him this instant."

After the Genomatekk rushed off, Kurgan turned his attention to the whorls and spirals of his medical history. What if something was amiss? he wondered. What if this idiot of a Genomatekk misread the data? He shivered and almost recalled him. Perhaps it was better not to know, to continue living his life as he always had. But no, if Nith Batoxxx had done something to him, he needed to know.

Kirlll Qandda entered the cubicle and smiled uncertainly. "Yes, regent. How may I be of service?"

Kurgan pointed. "Interpret this medical history for me."

Kirlll Qandda gave him a brief glance before turning to the holoscreen. He brought up other panels Kurgan had not known were there. He scrutinized everything.

"You are in perfect health, regent," he said when he was finished.

"Absolutely?"

"Yes, of course."

Kurgan felt a slight wave of relief pass through him, followed almost immediately by a spasm of annoyance at allowing himself to sink into a state of spurious speculation. He dismissed Kirlll Qandda with a curt wave of his hand.

Riane felt along the wall, opened another door. A thin wedge of light revealed the inside of a closet. They were on the ground floor of the palace. Just above them, on the second floor, was the regent's residential wing. It was there that Giyan had once had her quarters. That was where Riane was headed, for as Annon, she had stumbled upon a secret passageway to the caverns from the balcony that fronted the chambers of Giyan's suite.

Annon knew perfectly well how to get from the ground floor upstairs without any V'ornn seeing him. He had sneaked in and around the palace innumerable times in the days before his father had been slaughtered by the Stogggul.

Riane heard the tread and clank of Haaar-kyut guards, and quickly ducked back into the closet. The harsh gutturals of the Khagggun rose, then drifted off, fading into echoes. She peered out again and, gesturing, led them down a short corridor made of sea-green shanstone, and into the shadows of a porphyry spiral staircase. Each tread was incised with an image of Miina's sacred butterfly. The trio went up as lightly as a spray of mist and quickly reached the second floor.

Seeing more Haaar-kyut, Riane cautioned her companions back into deepest shadow, where they waited in stillness for the way to clear. Riane then took them through the fourth door on the right.

It was difficult for her, returning to the royal residence where once Annon's father had ruled all Kundala, where, in a different reality, Annon would have succeeded Eleusis Ashera as regent. Instead, both Eleusis and Annon were gone, and the usurper Stogggul ruled in their place.

Seeing the familiar surroundings, which had remained essentially unchanged since the days when Giyan had slept there, brought up powerful emotions. At the same time, she was aware of Riane's awe at being in the holy Kundalan temple. She felt the now eerily familiar dichotomy of Riane's serene and thoughtful personality and Annon's fierce and rageful warrior spirit. The past's sadness, loss, and desire for revenge vied with the present's need for calm, focus, and perseverance. It was difficult being at odds with oneself, odder still to fathom the complexities of two personalities in one mind. Mostly, now, they were in accord, seeking integration and resolutions. But there were still moments, as now, when one or the other sought dominance, tearing a rift in the uneasy harmony. The original Riane's concentration was astonishing. For eons, Middle Palace had been a holy place. Now the V'ornn had desecrated it in their cruel and deliberate fashion. Where was her desire for revenge?

It will come. Have patience. Our revenge begins now.

The voice, wise and true, emanating from her very core,

calmed her, and she felt her focus returning as the V'ornn bloodlust burned away like fire in a crucible.

"Riane?"

She started at Eleana's whisper.

"Are you all right?"

"Yes, I . . ." Riane blinked and nodded. "I'm fine." She gave Eleana a little smile as she led them through the chambers. The air was close and still, stale as a grave, as if no one had breathed it since the night of bloodletting almost two years before. Heavy curtains had been drawn across the windows, and Riane pulled them aside, found the door out to the terrace, and opened it.

At the far end she picked out in deepest shadow the sliver of metal she knew to be there. By the time Eleana and Thigpen had reached it, Riane had pried the hidden door open, just as Annon had done on the night his father had been murdered.

It was not without trepidation that she stepped into the fetid darkness of the vertical shaft and started down the metal spiral staircase. Almost at once, the stink of bitter-root caught in the back of her throat, bringing back Annon's memories of what? Something dark, sinister, rippling, waiting for him on this very staircase, just below where it branched. It exuded the scent of bitterroot, and now, with the rotting smell in her nostrils, she entertained the irrational notion that it still lay in wait for her, that it knew that Annon still existed inside her.

The farther she descended, the faster her pulse raced. Her eyes tried to pierce farther and farther into the gloom. She was searching for the small triangular landing from which the staircase split into three. Annon had chosen the right branch and, before long, had been overcome by the sensation of extreme danger and the certain knowledge that the thing waited for him in the darkness below.

Reaching the landing at last, Riane turned back to her companions, and whispered, "We have come to three branches in the staircase. It is imperative that we take the center one. Is that clear?" She could hear their murmurs of assent. "All right. The landing I am standing on is very small, so we will have to move slowly and carefully because the way is treacherous. Keep in mind that the staircase will give out before you know it and turn into a chute. Just let yourself go, and you'll be fine."

"I will go first. Then Thigpen, then Eleana." She reached up and Thigpen leapt into her arms.

"I do not like this, little dumpling," the Rappa growled. "I do not like this at all."

"Come on." Riane turned around. Just then, she preferred not to think of the bitterroot beast that might be lurking in the right branch, but she did not think it wise to remain there for long. What if it came lunging up from its lair?

"There is the center staircase." She turned to look over her shoulder at the Rappa. "Do you see it?"

"Of course I see it!" Thigpen snapped. "I am wary, not blind."

"I only asked because the branching is complicated here. I will go last so that I can make certain that you and Eleana get safely down the center staircase. Then I will follow. Ready?"

"No. But I very much doubt you will give me a choice."

"You're right about that," Riane said, as she gave the Rappa a nudge. Thigpen leapt, vanishing at once down the center stairwell.

Riane turned back. "All right," she whispered, "your turn now, Eleana."

She reached up and Eleana came into her arms. For a breathless moment, they stood face-to-face. Heat and musk rose between them, and Riane recalled the electric moment not long ago when the two of them had been alone in Za Hara-at.

When we are apart I dream about you, Eleana had said. *When I see you I cannot cool my body down.*

And Riane had seen it in her eyes. *She must know,* Riane had thought with a ferocious lift to her heart. *She must know that her beloved Annon still lives inside me.*

As she swung Eleana toward her, she felt Eleana's eye-

lashes flutter against her cheek. And then Eleana turned
her head slightly, and their lips brushed. Off-balance, Riane shifted her feet. One of them slipped off the landing,
Eleana slewed around, and her boot caught on the back of
a stair tread.

In the blink of an eye, she was wrenched out of Riane's
embrace and, tumbling head over heels, she shot down the
right-hand staircase.

7

Heroes and Villains

Marethyn returned to the Resistance camp a hero.
With an abrupt shift in the wind, the sleet had
started up again but, almost immediately, had
changed to rain. It bounced off the mottled alloy of the
Khagggun armor in which her compatriots had dressed
her. Predictably, she caused quite a sensation when they
returned in triumph, flanked by Majja and Kin, who were
laden with the weaponry of the vanquished.

Medda poured them all drinks, and they toasted one another. Kin did not leave Marethyn's side. He kept looking
at her, touching the Khagggun armor. He stammered
when she spoke to him, astonished to be so attached to a
V'ornn. The smell of the wet Marre pines was like silver
and almonds.

Basse, laughing his sardonic laugh, whispered to her, "It
seems that you have a new admirer."

Marethyn smiled in return, but the truth was she had a
nagging worry. As they were leaving the site of the melee
she was sure she had detected a third pair of Khagggun
boots, though her search had turned up no other evidence.
When she pointed them out to Medda he had had the entire

bunch of them fan out to no avail. In any event, they had returned to camp without incident, and having taken all precautions, they were quite certain at least that they had not been followed.

"You did well, young Kin," Medda said. Over the beaming boy's head, he gave Marethyn a brief nod.

"We are so much better off now that Kasstna is dead," Majja said, speaking of the leader of their former Resistance cell.

"Kasstna was a brave and influential leader," Basse said.

"He was also distrustful and rigid," Marethyn said. "Those traits are not the mark of a good leader."

Majja nodded. "If he had trusted Marethyn enough to listen to her, we would not have suffered such losses in the Khagggun ambush."

"Enough gloomy talk about the past," Medda said, refilling their goblets. "It's time to celebrate!"

Not all joined in the celebration, however. Gerwa's lieutenant, a round-faced Resistance fighter, approached Medda. "Gerwa wishes to see you and the Tuskugggun," he said, adding in Medda's ear. "Judging by his mood and who is with him, I'd get her out of that V'ornn armor, if I were you."

"Who's with him?" Marethyn asked.

The lieutenant looked at her. "Best not to tarry, Tuskuggun. Waiting will only worsen his majesty's foul mood."

Majja helped Marethyn off with the armor while Medda and Basse watched.

"Like what you see?" Marethyn asked archly.

Medda cleared his throat. "You are hairless. I find that curious. But not as curious as why you are helping us."

"You mean you are suspicious of my motives."

Medda said, "We need to meet with Gerwa. His patience often wears thin."

"Then he is not fit to lead." Marethyn quickly regretted her words.

Basse said, "Is that your wish, Marethyn Stogggul? To lead us?"

Marethyn, dressed now in her dark brown leggings and tunic, came up to him. "I have no such thought, nor have I earned the right to have it," she said softly. "But I am perhaps more objective than any of you, and what I see is disorganization, suspicion, petty jealousies, and perpetual infighting among the cell leaders. It is hardly a wonder that you are losing the war for independence."

Medda's brows knitted together. "Say that to Gerwa and see how fast he has you executed."

"That is why I have told you, and not him."

"She speaks the truth," Majja said.

"No one asked you," Medda snapped.

"You know she is right," Majja persevered. "I have seen her bravery more than once. Without her, Medda, we never would have gotten the cache of weapons."

"Bah!" Medda threw up his hands in disgust. "Trust females to stick together!"

"This prejudice was not the way of it in the old days," Majja said heatedly. "Our society was founded on females and males sharing responsibility and power."

"Times have changed," Medda said. "We must look to the future, not the past."

"Stop blindly repeating what Kara preaches." Majja's eyes sparked with anger. "Think for yourself and discover the truth."

"You are not a Follower. You still believe in the Goddess, in the old ways, the ways that made us weak enough to fall to the V'ornn. Kara gives us the strength to break with the old and embrace the new."

"You are wrong, Medda," Marethyn said. "Kara is a religion created by Gyrgon. It is a ruse to keep you Kundalan disaffected, factionalized, cut off from your past."

"Enough, Tuskugggun!" Medda's eyes narrowed. "Again I would warn you to keep your mouth shut." He jerked his head. "Now let us be off to see what Gerwa has in mind for us."

As it happened, what Gerwa had in mind for them was far from pleasant. Standing by his side when they entered his tent was Kasstna, the head of the Resistance cell into which Marethyn had been recruited by Majja and Basse. Gerwa was sitting behind his folding camp table, a crude, hand-drawn map of the immediate vicinity spread before him. Kasstna stood just to the left of him, his legs slightly spread, his arms folded across his massive chest. His brutish, closed face with its rage-fueled, diamond-shaped eyes, was further disfigured by a pair of wounds, lividly fresh, slashed diagonally across the flat planes of his cheeks.

"You are dismissed, Medda," Gerwa said, without looking up from his study of the map.

"I would prefer to stay," Medda said, unexpectedly.

Gerwa looked up. "That was not a request."

"Let him stay if that is his wish," Kasstna said curtly. "He will soon come to regret his folly."

Marethyn could see by Gerwa's quick glance that he was peeved at Kasstna's usurpation of his authority.

Gerwa said, "Marethyn Stogggul, your cell leader wishes you to answer questions he feels compelled to put to you."

Kasstna's irked expression told Marethyn several things, not the least of which was that Gerwa's verbal retaliation had had its desired effect. *There is no love lost between those two*, she thought.

"Question number one," Kasstna said, as he returned his attention to her. "How did the Khagggun know when and where we were lying in wait to ambush the weapons convoy?"

"I do not know," Marethyn said.

"Don't you?" Kasstna unwound his arms and began to stalk around her. "Almost all my cell were killed when we were blindsided."

"We all would have been if I hadn't—"

"Keep still!" he shouted so loudly the cords of his neck stood out. "You will speak only when you are spoken to. Is that clear?"

Marethyn stared straight ahead.

"Question two." Kasstna stood behind her. "Am I to believe that you, a V'ornn, the sister of the regent, did not deliberately set out to infiltrate our cell and set us up for the slaughter?"

"Believe what you will. I did not."

He came around and faced her. "You are V'ornn. Why should I believe anything you say?"

"My actions speak more clearly than any words. Majja, Basse, and I escaped with the weapons cache and delivered them here."

"To further ingratiate yourself with us. To worm your way in." He stuck his face in hers. "To gain our trust so you can undermine us from the inside out."

"It seems to me that you are doing an acceptable job of it on your own."

Kasstna struck her so hard she staggered. Before she could regain her balance, the point of his dagger pricked her side. "I should kill you on the spot, but Gerwa thinks you are too valuable to be thrown in the offal heap with the other V'ornn."

"I hope you are not foolish enough to try to use me as a hostage." She ignored the line of blood that had begun to ooze from the laceration just beneath her right ear. "Like as not, my brother would dance a jig at news of my death."

"Liar!" Kasstna struck her again.

"In fact, it's the truth," Medda said. "According to Majja and Basse, the Stogggul family has more or less washed its hands of her. They are intensely embarrassed by her ongoing efforts to gain Great Caste status for the Tuskugggun. None more so than the regent. Their latest row occurred at the barbaric Rescendance ceremony for their father."

Kasstna shook his head. "Majja and Basse have somehow fallen under the Tuskugggun's spell."

"You accuse your own cell members?" Medda said. "They have spent more time among the V'ornn in Axis Tyr than the three of us combined."

"My point exactly," Kasstna shouted. "They have been corrupted."

"They are part of my subcell," Medda said. "They are brave and fearless warriors."

Kasstna's dagger came up threateningly. "Is this how you maintain discipline, Gerwa?"

"Actually, Medda has a point." Gerwa stood up. "I have kept a close eye on your warriors since their arrival. They hold nothing but hate in their hearts for the enemy. To suggest otherwise is—"

But Kasstna was already holding the edge of his dagger to Marethyn's throat. "You see these wounds?" His voice was throttled with emotion. "Coward! Traitor! You left me for dead!"

"As far as I knew you *were* dead. When we left, we were under heavy fire, and you were surrounded by Khaggun. If we had hesitated, we all would have been killed."

He shook her as he pointed to his cheeks. "I got these at the hands of your kind."

"*My* kind treat me just as you do," Marethyn said. "There is no difference between you and my brother."

Gerwa caught Medda's eye just as Kasstna uttered a guttural cry. It took both of them to drag him off Marethyn. With a deft motion, Medda disarmed Kasstna while Gerwa pushed him back against the wall of the tent.

"That is enough now," Gerwa said in an even tone. "In trying to disgrace me, you have dishonored yourself."

"Get off me!" Kasstna cried. "Do you even know what you are doing?"

"Show some restraint, Kasstna."

"Restraint? Don't make me laugh." Kasstna shook himself free. "You will hand her over. I will take her to the tribunal, where she will be appropriately punished for her crimes."

"I will no longer entertain your accusations," Gerwa said. "And you do not seem in any condition to take anyone anywhere. I would suggest—"

"Are you questioning my order?"

"This is my cell, my territory."

"But she is still under my command, as are Majja and Basse. If you go against me in this, you yourself will be brought up before the tribunal."

In the ensuing silence, Kasstna's evil grin seemed to fill the tent. "You have gained nothing this day, Gerwa. But you have made a powerful enemy." He held out his hand without looking at Medda. "My weapon."

Medda glanced at Gerwa, who gave him a curt nod, and Medda handed over the dagger, hilt first.

"I will take possession of my prisoner now," Kasstna said. "As for Majja and Basse, you can keep them. The three of you deserve one another."

I remember how you once were." Gul Aluf, standing in Terrettt's room in Receiving Spirit, put a hand out and stroked his cheek. "I remember the promise you held." Her hand was damp with his sweat. He always perspired mightily when he slept now. "What happened?"

The late-afternoon sun cast a burnished hand upon the wall as it sank into the west. It was the hour when activity on the Promenade slowed from a roar to a whisper, when the fishing boats lay empty, rocking at their berths while their crews took an early supper, when the great, ornately prowed Sarakkon ships were finished off- or on-loading, when the Sarakkon themselves came out on deck, smoking laaga or drinking their foul brew from tiny, unbreakable cups, when the frenzy of the day slipped away with an inaudible sigh, before the furor of the night began.

"How did Nith Batoxxx go wrong?" Gul Aluf stared down at Terrettt's sleeping face, spasmed in some nightmare. "I checked his calculations myself. Nothing was amiss. He was right. You were a choice candidate. We both agreed on that, and your birth caul confirmed our assessment. What happened? How did you turn out like this?"

She shook her head while she inserted probes from her own palms into his, took measurements, gathered readings, saved them to her personal databank, and withdrew the probes. Her eyes flickered as she compared the new data with the previous set.

"No change." She sighed. "Locked in limbo, in a twilight world of knowing and not knowing, the pendulum swinging first toward genius, then toward lunacy." She sighed again, more deeply this time. "No wonder you are mad. Any V'ornn would be, given the circumstance."

She looked around the room, at his latest paintings—stars and swirls and globules. Her gaze passed over the topographical map of the northern continent Terrettt's sister had put up. On it, he had drawn seven circles, very much like those in his paintings. Senseless, useless. A total waste of a life. But that was the risk you ran when you experimented. It was for the greater good that Terrettt had been sacrificed, she had no doubt about that. But in this case, because Terrettt was a Stogggul, the outcome was awkward. She had argued with Nith Batoxxx, but he was adamant that the Stogggul usurp the Ashera power. The father had been a fool; not so the son, the present regent. Nith Batoxxx knew that, and now she wondered whether he had seen it all, that he had known that Stogggul Kurgan would turn on his weak father and engineer his death. It was no secret to her that Nith Batoxxx had a special—one might say obsessive—interest in Stogggul Kurgan. On one point Nith Batoxxx and Nith Sahor had agreed: the Ashera and the Stogggul had crucial roles to play in the future of the V'ornn on Kundala.

"Poor thing." She said it out of reflex, thinking of the experiment gone awry, mourning the loss. "Poor, poor thing."

Riane hurtled down the stairwell. The instant Eleana vanished, Riane leapt into it after her. A hundred meters of painful, teeth-jarring small-scale collisions, then, like the center stairway, the treads abruptly ended, and she was pitched, feetfirst, down a spiral chute.

This one, however, was far different from the one that

had taken Annon to the cavern just outside the Storehouse Door. This chute was roughly hacked from the bedrock. Sharp outcroppings and jagged edges scraped and struck her like a rageful enemy, bouncing her from side to side.

"Eleana!" she managed. "Eleana, where are you?"

Light rose along with a draft of warmish air, an exhalation from a corpse, and she saw what appeared to be a giant mouth, glowing pasty white, open and waiting for her to plunge into it. Her heart almost froze in her breast. Had Eleana fallen into it?

A jagged outcropping struck her a glancing blow, and she reached up, grabbed hold of it. She cried out; the sudden halt to her fall had almost wrenched her arm out of its socket. Riane swung dizzily, sickeningly, suspended from her precarious handhold, but not for long. She was slipping. She flung out her other hand, but encountered nothing to hold on to. There was a narrow ledge below her. *Can I reach it?* she asked herself. *Is it strong enough to hold me?*

She had no time to contemplate such questions. Extending her left leg, she dropped her handhold, and landed. The ledge held. She threw out her right leg, wedging her boot against the other side of the chute. Now she was spread-eagled just above the place where the chute opened out into the monstrous maw. The illumination, which appeared to rise from the very depths of the pit, was pearlescent. It was impossible to make out its source.

Cut, scraped, and bleeding, trying to catch her breath, she stared down into the pit, and there she saw Eleana, lying on what appeared to be a black-basalt plinth that rose up in the center of the maw.

"Eleana!" Riane called. "Eleana!"

There was no response. Eleana lay on her side like a crumpled doll. *Is she dead?* Riane wondered in despair. *Or simply unconscious?*

In the shadowless light, she could now make out details of the shaft's jaggedly rippled contours. Eight or nine meters above her a narrow fissure presented itself, doubtless cracked open by one of the seismic quakes that periodically ground the bedrock plates of the northern continent. Looking elsewhere, she quickly determined that she could make use of the shaft's erose contours. By employing them as foot- and handholds, she began to make her laborious way downward. The effort was extreme, even for someone used to rock climbing. Drops of her sweat mingled with her blood, vanishing into the depths as she crept ever closer to Eleana.

Finally, she arrived at the very edge of the rock maw. Then she was close enough to make out that Eleana was, indeed, breathing, and she thanked Miina for that. Only a space of several meters separated them, though it might as well have been kilometers wide. *How am I going to reach her without falling myself?* she asked herself.

Blood and sweat dripped dolefully off her into the heart of the maw.

"Eleana!" she called. "Eleana!"

Still, Eleana did not stir. Desperate, Riane swept off a few small bits of rubble from the upper side of a nearby ridge and tossed them onto Eleana. They struck her body without effect. She tried again, aiming this time. The one that hit Eleana's forehead caused her eyelids to flutter open.

Riane called her name, and Eleana turned slowly, looking up at where Riane painfully clung to the rocks above her, calling again, keeping her pitch and tone even, an aural lifeline.

Eleana blinked heavily, her breast rose and fell slowly, as if she were pinned to a dream. Her pupils were unnaturally dilated and unfocused.

Drip-drip of blood mingled with sweat.

Eleana stirred, her eyes moving in the direction of Riane's echoey voice.

"Riane . . ."

"Yes, yes! I am right above you!"

At that moment, the pearlescent glow flickered, and Riane almost gagged, for on a particularly strong updraft of air came the sickening stench of bitterroot. It was mingled with the cloying odors of moist earth and rotting flesh.

The air stirred from below, the flickering increased, a shadow formed. Riane felt her heart racing, and she was suffused with the same overpowering sense of danger Annon had once felt on the stairway above. The difference was that then Annon had had a way out. She did not. She reached for the ion pistol, but it was gone. She must have lost it when she pitched down the stairs after Eleana.

"Riane?" Eleana's eyes were open wide and staring. "I feel a shuddering, a vibration. What . . . what . . . ?"

"Eleana, listen to me." The shadow was coalescing, growing in size and dimension as it rose from the depths of the abyss. "Just stay where you are, all right?" The shadow was obliterating the light as it came. "Don't move!"

Eleana nodded.

The shadow resolved itself further. Some kind of creature, humped, misshapen, huge beyond imagining, was climbing the pillar on the top of which Eleana lay. Riane concentrated all the more. *Drip-drip,* her blood and sweat plunged into the pit. A long, slender tentacle whipped up, sucking the drops right out of the air. Riane's blood ran cold. To her horror, she realized that it was her own blood that had roused the thing, bringing it up from its subterranean lair.

8

Rain

W hat is it?" Rekkk asked. "Is it that you still do not trust me?"

Giyan stirred in the darkness beside him.

Their scents mingled with a hint of dampness, the bitter of old stone. "How can you say that?"

"I will tell you how, my love. You are the most secretive person I have ever met."

"More secretive than Nith Sahor?"

"More secretive than he."

Giyan moved her hands over his bare flesh. "I love to feel the contours of your new body."

"You see what I mean?"

"What? I am being romantic."

"You are avoiding the subject. Again."

Giyan watched the tiny pinpoints of the lamplight as they squeezed in through the intricately carved latticework screens that afforded them absolute privacy. Now and again, as the evening breeze willed it, the pungent scents of herbs wafted in from the neatly rowed garden just beyond the screens. Something else as well, intangible. Among the remaining Ramahan there was nothing but gloom and despair over the loss of their sisters.

"Giyan?"

She pulled her knees up to her breast, wrapped her arms around them.

"You were thinking dark thoughts."

"Have you become a seer now, as well as the Nawatir?"

"They seep out of you like tears."

Giyan remained silent.

"Why won't you let me help you?" His frustration burst out of him at last. "The secrets you carry are too much of a burden for one person."

"This is my fate," she said quietly. "I cannot change it."

"Giyan—"

"Please, Rekkk." She gave a beseeching look. "Ask anything of me—anything else and I will grant it."

"But *this* is what I want." He rose up on one elbow. The pinpoints of light illuminated his face. Bold features, rugged contours. "Don't you see that the secrets you hold so close are a barrier between us?"

"Oh, Rekkk, that is not so!"

"But it is. If you cannot confide in me, then what is there between us?"

"Can you doubt my love for you?"

He sat up, but when she reached for him, he eluded her, moving to the latticework screens.

"Rekkk, in Miina's name, do not do this."

"Like you, I have no choice." His voice seemed to come from a great distance.

"Rekkk!"

He heard the sorrow in her voice, could sense the tears sliding down her cheeks, and his hearts constricted. "For me, love is all-consuming, it is everything. Giyan, I gave up *who I was* for you. Because of my love, I was transformed. Can you not have as much faith in me?"

"It is not the same."

"Of course it is. The trouble is, you won't acknowledge it."

"I—" Gasping. "Perrnodt!" Giyan was holding her aching head in her hands.

"What has happened?"

Giyan shook her head mutely.

Rekkk gathered up their clothes and, grimly, silently, they dressed together, burst out of their fragrant bower, and hurried through the abbey to the infirmary. Perrnodt lay wrapped in the Nawatir's cloak just as they had left her.

Rekkk was alarmed by the ashen color of her face.

"She is dead." Giyan's voice was leaden.

"But how? My cloak was healing her."

Giyan put a hand on his arm as he took a step toward Perrnodt.

"Do not touch her." She pointed. "Look there. Can you see the crust between her eyelids?"

He looked from the dead Druuge to Giyan. "I had best fetch Konara Inggres."

"No."

"Another of your secrets."

She was stung by the sharpness of his tone. "Ah, Rekkk,

this abbey has had more than its share of evil news of late. Right now, there is nothing to be gained by adding to it."

He watched her, mutely, as she took down a basalt mortar from the apothecary cabinets that ran the length of the infirmary. She knelt at Perrnodt's side. The abbey was very still. Bells tolled, echoing through the corridors and courtyards, calling the Ramahan to prayer.

"You see," she whispered, "Konara Inggres is needed elsewhere."

Rekkk stood in uncertain light just behind her. The crust between Perrnodt's lids looked like diamond dust.

"Rekkk, may I borrow your smallest weapon?"

Without a word, he handed over a narrow-bladed dagger. He watched while she manipulated the tip, scooping up some of the crust onto the blade, depositing it into the mortar.

Rekkk leaning closer. "Is this what killed her?"

"Possibly it is the residue."

"Do you know what it is?"

"No." Giyan looked up at him. "But perhaps our resident sauromician will."

K asstna poked Marethyn in the small of the back. "Have I bound your wrists too tightly?"

Marethyn, walking in front of him, said nothing.

"I hope so," Kasstna said. "I hope you lose all the feeling in your hands." He laughed. "Once you were an artist, isn't it? Yes, that is what you told Majja and Basse. You used your hands to splash pigment across canvas." He laughed again. "Now life is different. At the tribunal, if I have my way, I will beat your hands to a pulp." He poked her again, harder this time, so that she stumbled over a kuello-fir root and fell to her knees. "If you ever make it to the tribunal, that is." He kicked her. "Get up." He watched her use the bole of the kuello-fir as she struggled to her feet.

They were perhaps a kilometer east of the cell encampment, hiking across a heavily forested ridge. Marethyn had no idea where this tribunal he was speaking of was located. Not that it would make a difference to her if she did. She had no illusions. She had been in trouble from the moment Gerwa refused to stand up to Kasstna. Had she been too idealistic to have expected him to do so? She had done nothing but help the Resistance ever since she had met Majja and Basse. But then she had to remind herself that she had thrust herself upon them. Even Sornnn had been against her joining. But, then, Sornnn loved her. Wanted to keep her safe.

"You could very easily be killed, couldn't you, as you attempted to escape." Kasstna broke in on her thoughts. He drove her onward as if she were a cor or a water buttren. "That very well might happen. It all depends on your attitude."

"What attitude?"

"Ah, at last. The Tuskuggggun speaks!"

Marethyn stopped and turned to face him. "What attitude?"

Thickening clouds brought about a claustrophobic dusk. The air was gravid with moisture, but the wind was out of the south so at least there was no threat of more snow or sleet. A rumbling had returned across the hills to the south, where the sky was darkest. The willowy tops of the kuello-firs bent and whipped, the friction of their needles mimicking the sound of rushing insects.

Kasstna studied her for a long time. "The attitude you've had all your life, Tuskugggun." He came in close to her, and she could smell his sour breath. "You know what I mean. That superiority of yours. The sureness you have that you are smarter, more clever than anyone else." He cuffed her a little. "You'll have to lose that attitude, Tuskugggun, in order to make it back to the tribunal."

She kept her expression neutral as she slammed her knee into his groin. She watched him, silent, as he doubled over, gasping. She tried to kick him, but he grabbed her foot in midair and spun her off her feet. She landed hard on her right shoulder.

Kneeling over her, his breath sawing through his open mouth, he pushed her down onto her back. Struck her on the side of her head, which made her moan. Clambering over her, he put his cheek against hers and whispered in her ear, "I mean to break you, see? I mean to have you eating out of my hand, I mean to have you on your knees tending to my every whim." He grabbed her head in a vise-like grip. "Otherwise, I will kill you here in the forest, where no one can see, where no one can contradict my story of your attempted escape." His tongue came out, and he licked the shell of her ear. "Is there some V'ornn who loves you, Tuskugggun? Some V'ornn whom you love in return? Think of him now. Because if you continue in this way, you will be dead, and he will not even have your body to mourn."

A staircase, of sorts, hacked into the bedrock of the cavern. This is what Riane had seen from her spider's-eye position. The treads were old and worn, cracked, in some places missing. Nevertheless, it was her only way down, so she clambered to the mouth of the chute. It was by no means easy, but her fingers told her that she had been on more difficult descents. There she hung by tenuous handholds, seeing there was no way to get to the top of the steps. Possibly there had once been a bridge of sorts but, if so, it had sheared off long ago.

She glanced over to the basalt plinth, where Eleana was watching her. Tentacles wrapped ever higher on the column, and below was a bulk so gigantic it was slowly eclipsing the light.

Riane pulled her attention away, began to rock herself back and forth, gaining momentum. At the apex of the seventh forward arc, she launched herself through space. The stairs came up very fast, and she splayed herself, striking the carved rock face. Grabbing for a handhold, finding it, losing it, dropping to find another, better, less eroded, secure. She swung one leg, then the other, levered her lower body onto a tread, felt the rock crack and give, friable, unsafe, then rolled down two stairs as the first one gave way. Rain of blue-grey shards falling into the shadows. The depth could have been eighty meters or eight hundred, a great yawning fissure for some reason built into the foundation of the palace.

Scrambling down the stairs, quickly, carefully, she kept secure handholds wherever she was able. The steps followed the natural curvature of the cavern wall, sometimes carved into the wall itself, sometimes hewn from shallow ledges that protruded out. They were scarifyingly inconstant. They provided Riane with no sense of security at all. She passed the horizontal crevasse, larger than it had looked from a distance, slash of a mouth large enough for several adults to slither into on their bellies. Who knew how far back it went?

She kept descending, concentrating on one step at a time, light step, testing, then allowing her weight to fall forward gradually, listening for the telltale crack that would presage another break. She was almost at Eleana's level, and she risked a glance at the base of the plinth.

The monster was massive, hideous beyond description, and she was seeing only a small fraction of it.

Eleana, seeing the direction of Riane's gaze, said, "What? What is it?"

"Never mind." Gritting her teeth. "Concentrate on me."

As the stairs turned she came upon a bridge of stone spanning the nine or so meters to the plinth, so narrow and of such a hue it had been invisible until that moment.

"Eleana, look here, can you see the bridge?"

"No." Eleana moved closer to the plinth's edge. Looking out, she shook her head. "The span is incomplete." She knelt. "It is broken away where it was supposed to connect."

Moving farther down, Riane could see that, indeed, the bridge had partially crumbled.

"Stay where you are," she said. "I will come to get you."

"No, it's too dangerous. I do not like the way the stones look."

Riane ignored her, stepped out on to the first block of the span. It took her weight, seemed stable enough, and she stepped out fully. Narrow, though, not any wider than the span of her hand. In her memory loomed an escarpment, sharp as a dagger, crusty with ice and last winter's snow, friable as this rock. Dangerous as they come, sinuous as a dune, falloffs of a thousand meters, more, on either side. She had picked her way across. How?

Arms up at shoulder height for optimum balance, fingers loose and cupped to warn of wind gusts, knees slightly bent, hips rolling. Keep the center of gravity low—lower meant safer, more secure. That was how Riane made her way toward Eleana on the crumbling stone bridge. Until the last step which, as she put her foot down, testing, gave way. She picked her foot up just as the stone plunged down.

Lifted foot still in midair, she took an assessment. She was as far as she could go. Still two meters between them, and the creature rising like the moon into sunset, like an eclipse into harvest night.

Into view it came. The head misshapen, looked positively hydrocephalic. Could it be that the tentacles were growing out of either side of a grizzled snout that extended out into a trunk? They seemed able to extend and contract, thin out and thicken at the creature's will.

Dear Miina, it is the Hagoshrin! She recognized it from Giyan's description. She could not tell whether it had more hair or scales, but she could see that in addition to the tentacles it had eight legs, four on each side, which worked in unison. It seemed to need all of them to haul its bulk up the column.

"Hagoshrin, hear me!" she called. "I am the Dar Salaat! Cease this attack at once!"

"Lying infidel!" the Hagoshrin screamed. "I know what you have come to steal! I know!"

"Riane, what are you doing? You will only inflame it."

The muscles in Riane's upper body had been so tightly bunched for so long that they had begun to cramp, and she had lost feeling in her right hand. As she shifted a little to try to loosen up, her left foot slipped, and she almost pitched headlong into the pit.

"Riane!" Eleana swung back and forth like a pendulum.

"It's all right." With difficulty, Riane regained her foothold and her balance, wedging herself more firmly in place. But searing pains were whipping up her arms, and she could feel fatigue slowing her like a gale in her face. "I'm all right."

She could see that she was running out of time. The Hagoshrin had hauled its upper torso above the level of the black-basalt altar, which meant that it was not that far below Eleana.

"Hurry!" Eleana urged. "Hurry!"

"Infidels," the beast howled. "I will suck the bones out of you. I will leave your pathetic, flaccid bodies as a warning for others against further trespass into the Holy of Holies."

Riane unwound the Veil from her waist. Leaving only enough to anchor, she threw the rest in a ball that Eleana caught. There was only enough to tie it around her right wrist; she tied it tight with a proper knot and nodded. Riane moved her left leg back on the stones, bracing herself as Eleana flung herself off the plinth. What if the bridge would not hold? Then they would both fall to their deaths. Too late to worry about that.

Down she went in a shallow arc to the end of the Veil's length, coming up then, twisting, lifting her legs as a child will on a swing, giving her natural momentum a boost. Closer she rose, closer. She reached out for the stone bridge, grasped it with her left hand, arm extended, arcing farther, then, suddenly, shockingly, she was pulled back down.

Riane heard the little cry, saw the end of a tentacle whipped around Eleana's ankle. Then it flattened itself, widening into a kind of strap, and Riane could feel it pulling back. Riane jerked harder, only to have Eleana cry out in pain.

Eleana's face twisted in agony. "Miina, it's going to break my leg!"

Riane eased off, but this only allowed the tentacle to gain purchase farther up Eleana's leg. Riane looked around. *What am I to do?* she thought. *I can't pull her up, and I can't let her go.*

Drip-drip. Her sweat and blood plinked down like rain.

Marethyn went limp. There was no use in fighting Kasstna, not like this, anyway. He had every advantage, and she had none.

"I know when I am beaten," she said.

"You will pardon me if I choose not to believe you."

Like a serpent, Kasstna's head came down, and he pressed his mouth against hers. It was all she could do not to gag. He gave her a short, hard jab to her solar plexus. All the breath went out of her. He sat back on his haunches and allowed her to turn on her side in a fetal position.

"You see what I mean, Tuskugggun?" He untied her wrists. Then, abruptly, his face empurpled, he threw her onto her back. "Do you see what I mean, Tuskugggun!" His spittle spattered her face. He trembled with rage and something even more primitive.

Crossing her hands, he rebound her wrists, pushed her arms over her head, ran a cord to the trunk of the nearest kuello-fir, where he tied it off. His fingers fumbled with the ties of her tunic, and he began to pant as he uncovered her breasts. He used his powerful legs to spread hers as he ripped off her tunic.

"I've never had a hairless female," he said thickly, as his hands pinched her bare flesh. "Though I have heard stories of what it is like to lie with a Tuskugggun."

In order to numb herself, Marethyn turned her mind to the beauty of the world around her. She absorbed the endless fulminations of the dark sky, felt the soft wind rustling over her skin, heard the restless swooshing of the kuello-firs. She let the tactile rumble of the approaching thunder run through her. And then the rain came, hissing down through the forest, turning the nearby glade into a blue-grey blur.

Kasstna pulled down her leggings, raised her thighs, and put an ion cannon to her temple.

"Give me even one small reason to use this," he whispered.

With his bulk about to lower upon her, Marethyn felt the hotness of tears mingle with the raindrops on her face.

Eleana, her dagger out, slashed at the living elastic binding without making even the smallest cut. The Hagoshrin's free tentacle whipped up and, as it had before, snatched the droplets of blood as they fell. Riane could see the end of the tentacle expand into a cuplike shape that had absorbed her blood in a wink.

Riane let go of the Veil with one hand, scooped up a rock shard, and ground it into her lacerated shoulder.

"Riane, this thing has skin like V'ornn alloy. I can't get through."

"Just hold on!" Her teeth were gritted in pain, her shoulder was on fire from the self-inflicted wound. "Get ready to climb!"

"It won't let go. It's got too tight a hold on me—Riane!"

Eleana saw the blood flowing freely from the open wound. The creature's free tentacle whipped up to catch the stream, but it could not expend the tip enough to catch all of it. In a heartbeat, the second tentacle unwound from Eleana to join its mate in feeding.

"Now!" Riane shouted, and Eleana, banged against stone. swung herself up. Riane bent, helping her, the tentacles slithering after them both, the Hagoshrin humped across the entire plinth, in places oozing off it. Eleana whirled, brandishing the dagger's tip, warrior to the last. Riane backed them away, one step, two. The tentacles pursued, narrowing the gap. It was impossible to move fast or to maneuver at all on the damnable bridge. A tentacle reared back and slapped down against the ancient stone. A groaning, a great crack, and Riane lifted Eleana off her feet where the stones were giving way. Another crack, another as they retraced Riane's steps, the bridge falling apart under their combined weight.

Almost at the steps and Riane knew the bridge was failing—all of it. She hoisted Eleana and threw her across the remaining space. Knees, one shoulder, then the palms took the brunt of the impact. But then Eleana was scrambling up the steps.

"Come on, Riane! Come on!"

But Riane had turned. Surely there was some way to reason with the Hagoshrin, some way to convince him of Riane's identity.

"Hagoshrin," she cried, "do you not recognize the Dar Sala-at when you see her?"

"The Dar Sala-at opens the Storehouse Door with the Ring!" the Hagoshrin bellowed.

"I have the Veil." Held up a fistful. "The Veil of a Thousand Tears."

"The Veil is Dragon seed." Eyes blazing, the Hagoshrin shook his head. "I damn all Dragons to the Abyss."

The tentacles, curling, he reached for Riane. The bridge gave one final crack that reverberated through the cavern, and down Riane plunged.

9

Three Little Admirals

Star-Admiral Iin Mennus stood peering into the interrogation cells that lined this section of the cavern beneath the regent's palace. Usually, they were filled with Kundalan, who went under the implements lovingly designed to make even a lump of silicon talk. Not this evening, however. This evening the three cells in front

of Mennus were occupied by three admirals. All of them
had in one way or another proved resistant to the philosophy of their new superior.

By Mennus' side stood two of his most trusted confeder-
ates from his West Country base, Pack-Commander Teww
Dacce and the newly named Line-Commander Hannn
Mennus, the Star-Admiral's younger brother. He had hated
taking them away from what they loved best—
slaughtering the Kundalan Resistance—but the exigencies
of his new post demanded he have those who were absolutely loyal to him close beside him during this dangerous transition phase.

"What is the regent's condition?" Mennus asked Pack-
Commander Dacce.

"Moments ago First-Captain Kwenn informed me that
he is in remarkable shape," Pack-Commander Dacce said.
"For a Bashkir."

Mennus inclined his head, and his brother went to check
on their guests.

"I warrant Kurgan Stogggul is like no other Bashkir,"
Mennus said. "He is a warrior born, and a supremely
clever one, to boot. Treat him as anything less at your own
peril."

"Yes, sir."

Mennus found that he had begun to harbor a certain
fondness for Kurgan Stogggul. This surprised him, since
he had little respect for Bashkir, had had even less for the
boy's father, the former regent. But he had to admit that
Kurgan was special. Possibly that arose from his being
trained by Gyrgon. That would change any V'ornn, even a
Bashkir! But the instinct that had made Mennus a formidable warrior and a great leader also told him that this
Stogggul was different for other reasons. Unlike his predecessors, he was unwilling to dismiss the lad.

"In the matter at hand, Pack-Commander, I want you to
strike up a friendship with First-Captain Kwenn."

"Sir?"

"He has the regent's ear."

"I don't think any Khagggun has the regent's ear."

"You aren't paid to think," Iin Mennus barked. "Just do as you are told."

Hannn Mennus reappeared. He was a small V'ornn, even smaller by Khagggun standards. His bronze skull was as scarred as his meat hook hands. Each scar told its story, the raised, whitish fingers like the pickets of a fence onto which the skeletons of those he had killed had been nailed. His eyes, too, were freakish, pale and glaucous as mistfern, ghostly as moons on water. And, though for the most part calm and calculating, he was given to great gouts of ill temper, during which even those closest to him—if that term could be used—kept their mouths shut and gave him a wide berth.

"Deck-Admiral Whon has gone to N'Luuura," he said. "Deck-Admiral Lupaas is on his way. Fleet-Admiral Hiche is still unconscious."

The V'ornn named were three of the four members of the high command. Years ago, they had banded together to ostracize and banish Iin Mennus to the West Country. *Now look at them!* Mennus cracked knuckles knotty with scars. He had waited long years for this moment. Now, at long last, he would have his revenge.

While Pack-Commander Dacce went off on his mission, the Mennus brothers entered the cell where Deck-Admiral Lupaas lay dying. He was not a pretty sight, which cheered the Star-Admiral immensely. For years, he had been dreaming of a day when he would be allowed full rein, but in truth he had never really entertained the notion that it would ever come.

The powerful body that lay on the blood-dark stone slab had a face that was barely recognizable. With an expert eye, Iin Mennus gazed down at the quiltwork wounds. "You have done a fine piece of work, Hannn."

"Thank you. I appreciate you allowing me the honor. In this line of work, experience is everything."

"Quite right." Mennus nodded. "No matter how good the texts are, they never manage to convey the visceral quality of the real thing. Field training. I insist on it for all my troops. That is why you are the best in your caste." He caught Lupaas' eye, and winked.

The Deck-Admiral's bloodshot eyes tracked him.

Iin Mennus made a clicking sound with his tongue. "Lupaas, can you hear me?"

"I have heard everything," Lupaas said in a gratingly thin voice that spoke of severely damaged vocal cords. "Speaking about me as if I were an example in a course."

"But that is precisely what you are," Iin Mennus said. "An example in Disloyalty 101."

"I have never been disloyal."

"Do you deny being part of a conspiracy to assassinate Kurgan Stogggul?" the Star-Admiral demanded.

"I know what this is about. It is about you!"

"Me? I assure you I could care less about what you or others think of me, Lupaas. My only concern here is in rooting out the conspirators."

"There is no conspiracy."

"We are beyond that," Iin Mennus said. "You have already been implicated."

"By whom?" Lupaas asked. "Let me confront my accuser."

"Deck-Admiral Whon is dead," Iin Mennus told him.

"I do not believe . . . He would never accuse me."

The Star-Admiral shrugged. "It's a razor-raptor eat razor-raptor world. You deny being part of the conspiracy?"

"To my dying breath."

"It will come to that, Lupaas." Iin Mennus bent over him. "I make you this promise."

Deck-Admiral Lupaas turned his head and spat onto the stone wall.

"This is the respect you show your regent?"

"Foolish stripling!" Lupaas turned back. "It was a dark day when he named you Star-Admiral." Eyes filled with loathing. "Who are you loyal to, save Iin Mennus? You never follow orders, you will not toe the line. If your peers despise and distrust you, you have only yourself to blame."

The Star-Admiral nodded imperceptibly, and Hannn Mennus applied himself to his work. Deck-Admiral Lupaas' eyes opened wide, but he uttered no sound of pain. Hannn Mennus ceased his ministration just as Lupaas was about to pass out.

"Really, this is a pathetic sight," the Star-Admiral said. "One of the high command squirming under interrogation. Surely you know your death will be dishonorable."

"What happens to me matters not," Lupaas gasped. "My sons died honorably on the line. My daughter I do not even know, nor care to." Blood leaked out of his mouth. "You are the illustration that proves our system. You are a loose ion cannon, Mennus. You are secretive, selfish, unpredictable, dangerous. In short, you are everything a commander should not be. If we were fighting the Centophennni this very minute, I would use my first round to blow your brains out. I would—"

That was the last word Deck-Admiral Lupaas ever uttered for, with a bloodthirsty cry, Hannn Mennus plunged the implement through Lupaas' hearts.

For a long moment, Hannn Mennus stood panting, while bloody foam bubbled out of Lupaas' half-open mouth.

Iin Mennus said not a word of rebuke. He had always had a soft spot for Hannn and indulged his hotheaded transgressions, this dwarfish Khaggun who had battled all manner of adversity to arrive at this fierce and bloodthirsty state. When his brother had regained control of himself, he said, "Never let your emotions enter an interrogation. That, Hannn, is your lesson for today, one I wish you to take back with you to the West Country now that you are in charge of operations there."

Eleana, braced, had realized the bridge was near collapse. Even so, she was almost pulled off her feet. She staggered, one foot precariously over the edge, heel grinding in rubble, slipping a little. She gained footing then, and hauled Riane onto the steps. The Hagoshrin could not reach them. In its towering rage it began to hurl rocks as large as their heads at them. Dodging and weaving, they ran up, up, until they came to the great mouth in the wall. There was a dry, chalky smell to the sundered rock.

"There is no way back to the shaft." Riane pointed to the protection of the fissure. She gave Eleana a rough-and-tumble boost into the rock mouth, was preparing herself to leap up when a rock struck her on the side of the head.

"Riane!"

Eleana caught her as she was falling back, blood running, that stunned look on her face, reminiscent of her sister playing behind a bush, face stunned just the same as the Khagggun skewered her on the end of his shock-sword, letting her dangle there, screaming and crying, then shot Eleana's mother in the belly with his ion pistol when she ran to her daughter's aid. Funny what you thought of at a time like this.

With a groan like a cry of anguish, Eleana hoisted Riane onto the fissure's lip.

"You have not escaped me," the Hagoshrin screamed. "No one here gets out alive."

Eleana turned Riane over on her back. Riane was fast losing consciousness, eyes beginning to roll up, the way they were when Eleana had found her sister and her mother lying together like dolls. Her mother with one arm flung out around her daughter, seizing her shoulders, as if to protect her during their long journey down. All that blood.

"Riane, please, oh, please stay awake!"

All that blood.

Through the soft patter of the rain Marethyn heard the other sound. Kasstna, peeling off his leggings, grunted like an animal.

"Shut up!" she hissed, straining her ears to determine the direction of the sound.

Kasstna at first did not hear her.

"Shut up!" Louder this time.

He lifted his head. "Wha—?"

"Listen!"

He ground the muzzle of the ion pistol into her temple.

"Fool! Listen! Through the rain!"

His head turned as he cocked an ear. "Voices."

"Khaggun voices," she said. "They are close, and coming closer."

Immediately, he took the ion cannon from her head and rolled off her. He sat on his haunches, willing himself to full alertness as he pulled up his leggings.

"What are they saying?"

"Untie me," she said.

"So you can run to them?" He glared at her, shook his head.

"Untie me. You need my help with them."

Thumping his chest, he said, "I have killed my share of Khaggun."

She cocked her head. "There are three of them. At least. Untie me, Kasstna. I swear I will help you kill them."

His eyes narrowed. "How do I know—?"

"I have not cried out to alert them. I want to kill them as badly as you do."

Still, he hesitated. But then, as if they had crested a rise, the Khaggun voices suddenly became clearer. Kasstna crabbed his way over to the kuello-fir and cut the cord. He pulled her into a sitting position, his eyes bored into hers as he slipped the dagger between her wrists and slit her bonds.

"I need a weapon." Marethyn drew on her leggings, lacing up her tunic.

He shook his head. Then they both moved behind a thicket of underbrush beneath the canopy of kuello-fir. An instant later, three Khaggun came into view. They were mud- and blood-spattered. One, a First-Captain, was holding the head of a male Resistance fighter. They must have just killed him because blood was still leaking from the stump of the neck.

They were laughing as they headed for the nearby

glade. Once there, the First-Captain lofted the head into the rain. It came down on the toe of his boot, and he kicked it to one of the other Khagggun, who caught it on the toe of his boot and lofted it again, this time to the third Khagggun. They played at this grisly game until the head was too battered to kick in a true arc.

"As I told you," one of the Khagggun said, "Kundalan heads are too soft for Pelinq."

"Maybe we should use yours, instead, Third-Major," the First-Captain said, and they all roared with laughter.

The First-Captain crunched the head beneath the sole of his boot. "All right, back to work, you bile-worms. We have had photon telemetry of consistent Resistance activity in this area. That means an encampment. We are going to find said encampment before daybreak, or I will know the reason why."

He led them out of the glade in a westerly direction.

"We have to stop them," Marethyn whispered, "or at least lead them in another direction."

"As you said, there are three of them. And who knows how many more they are in contact with? We can't risk an engagement for which we are inadequately prepared."

"They will surely find Gerwa's camp."

"All the better for me," Kasstna hissed. "I can return to the tribunal with you and claim this territory as my reward."

"You can't be serious. I have friends there. But even if I didn't, I couldn't allow—"

He shook her until her teeth rattled. "You will do as I say!"

She put her head down. "All right."

Snatching the ion cannon out of his hand, she darted through the woods on a parallel course with the Khagggun. Kasstna, cursing under his breath, sprinted after her.

As she ran, Marethyn allowed her artist's eye to merge with the sharpshooter's instincts her grandmother had nurtured in her as she was growing up. The forest became a pattern of dark grey and pale grey, a gridwork through which she glimpsed the Khagggun. A hurried glance ahead revealed a small gap in the natural tree grid coming up. Ignoring Kasstna gaining on her from behind, she drew a bead on the First-Captain. He went in and out of her sight as she passed clusters of evergreens. She counted to herself, slowed her pulse, felt her finger curled around the trigger, so that when the gap opened up she was ready.

She squeezed off a shot. There was a brief bolt of lurid green that took the First-Captain off his feet. He lay in the bed of wet kuello-fir needles, his helmet a blackened, twisted mass.

By this time, his two pack companions had slewed around in her direction, and were raking the woods with ion fire. Marethyn had not slowed her pace. They were firing behind her. Kasstna leapt and skidded into her, knocking her off her feet.

"You fool," he hissed. "Now they are coming after us."

"Better us than the entire Resistance camp," she said. "Besides, I killed their First-Captain. Without a leader—"

"Look out!" He shoved her down as a pair of ion bolts cracked the trees just over their heads, showering them with sizzling bark and needles.

"Come on," she whispered. "We can't stay here."

Marethyn circled around them, heading northeast because it was away from Gerwa's encampment. Kasstna looked livid, but he had regained some of his previous composure. He had drawn a new-model ion pistol he had managed to steal from the cache she had brought to Gerwa. He shook it at her silently, and mouthed, *I will kill you for this*.

Marethyn had no time to think about his latest threat because the terrain had begun to rise more steeply. The rain had not let up. That was a blessing, for it muffled what little noise they made in their haste to flee.

"This is useless, you know," Kasstna said. "Now that you have cast the cor among the perwillon, it is only a matter of time before they find us and, if we are lucky, kill us."

He was right. The Khagggun were using the echo-guidance system hardwired into their helmets to track the two fugitives.

"Then we will just have to kill them first," she said, scrambling up a rise.

"And how do you propose to do that? We cannot take them by surprise the way you did the First-Captain."

"No." She stopped so abruptly he ran right into her. "But just possibly there is another way to surprise them."

Minnum was elbows deep in the rich claylike gums into which the roots of Za Hara-at had been sunk when he felt the telltale tingling at the base of his neck.

"Someone this way Thripps." He ceased his digging and wiped his hands and forearms on the leather apron he had fashioned for himself. He had been at his work all day and saw little of value to show for it, save a headache behind his eyes and some not very expert surveillance on the part of a couple of presumably bored Khagggun. He wished Sornnn was still there. After years as curator of the Museum of False Memory, living the solitary life, he was astonished at how much he missed Sornnn SaTrryn. This was just one measure of how much his life had changed since the Dar Sala-at first poked her half-drowned head above the rim of his cistern that dank and rain-filled afternoon. He had never before had any experience with friendship and responsibility.

Sapphire evening spread its wings over the great steppe. The air vibrated with the *Mokakaddir*, the ecstatic prayer cycle of the Ghor. Ever since the Dar Sala-at had made herself known to this religious sect, a group of them had made camp outside Im-Thera, there to observe the ongoing project of restoring Za Hara-at to its former glory and to pray for the Dar Sala-at's swift return. Sornnn had gone to speak with them daily, returning with dire snippets of news concerning the imminent war among the Five Tribes.

A small whirlwind of red dust gathered itself before him, then released. Within its widening gyre, Giyan appeared. Her face was pale and drawn. Minnum took one look at her and knew he would not like the contents of the basalt mortar she held in the crook of one arm.

"Good fortune to you, Lady Giyan," he said. "What news from the Abbey of Floating White?"

"All evil," Giyan said as she put down the mortar on the remains of a stone plinth. The city of the dead rose all around them in dizzying swaths of temples, plazas, and boulevards, all meticulously marked with mysterious runes meant to invoke at a whispered breath the vast engine of the power bourns that crisscrossed beneath the foundations. "Perrnodt is dead, murdered, unless I miss my guess, by sauromicians." She was looking at him when she said this and saw him wince.

Minnum set about brewing gowit tea. The pungent cinnamon aroma soon suffused the air about them. While the tea was steeping, Giyan said nothing, but sat brooding with her arms crossed over her knees. Minnum poured the deep rose-colored tea into tiny handleless cups.

"To the end of evil days." They clinked their cups together.

He shook his shaggy head ruefully. "Ever since the Dar Sala-at and I encountered the sauromician archon Talaasa here in Za Hara-at, I was afraid of this. When we killed him to stop him from gaining possession of the Veil of a Thousand Tears, we began a war the sauromicians have for some time been longing to wage. Believe me when I tell you, Lady Giyan, that Perrnodt's death is but the opening salvo in their retaliation."

"I had hoped I was wrong, but . . ." Giyan nodded. "What we need to discover is the source of their newfound power," she said. "Perrnodt said something about the Others. Does that word mean anything to you?"

He shook his head.

Giyan put aside her tumbler and took up the basalt mortar to show him its contents. "I found this grit stuck between her eyelids."

Minnum looked at the crystals as if Giyan had produced a deadly adder. From his knapsack he produced what looked like a thin concave implement, but of what material it might be made was unclear. Taking a sample of the grit onto it, he eyed it speculatively. Rubbing thumb and forefinger together, he produced a greenish yellow flame that gave off no heat. This flame he introduced to the crust of crystals.

There was a brief flare, along with a bitter odor that stuck in the back of Giyan's throat. All at once, her eyeballs began to ache, and she was sick to her stomach. She felt a quick plunge, as if she was falling off a cliff. For a split instant, she was assailed by an army of coruscating colors. Then everything snapped back to normal.

"As I suspected," Minnum was saying. "This is the crystal residue of Madila."

"I have never heard of it."

"Unsurprising. Madila is not in any Ramahan plant lexicon. It is an indole distillation."

"An hallucinogen! So that is what I felt just now!"

"Then you can imagine." Minnum nodded. "It is used by sauromicians for a number of purposes including, I am very much afraid, obtaining information from those otherwise unwilling to divulge it." He dropped the crystals back into the mortar. "However, in this concentrated form, Madila becomes a most powerful and toxic compound." His eyes looked bleak. "My Lady, our friend Perrnodt was subjected to a particularly horrible death. The compound quite literally drove her mad before it paralyzed her autonomic nervous system."

Rocking, rocking. Eleana held Riane in her arms. And all the while she eyed the beast, the Hagoshrin, whatever it was. Had there ever been such a malevolent creature? Her head ached, but not as much as her heart. Riane's breathing was quick and shallow. Her shoulder was angry-looking, her swollen, pale face a sure sign of how much blood she had lost. The violent shivering was what terrified Eleana most. Riane was cold as ice. Eleana wrapped her as fully as she could in the Veil, spreading it out, hoping that it could heal her.

Eleana closed her eyes for a moment, recalling how Riane had saved her from drowning when they had escaped from the Khaggun pack and the Tzelos in Axis Tyr. How she had wrapped her and healed her with her Osoru spells. How she wished she could do the same now. Instead, she held her tightly, rocking her a little, and tried to transmit her own warmth through the Veil to her lost love.

She bent over, her hair a bower, drawing them closer. All the loss she had suffered, and now this. A family of two brothers and a sister, mother, father, uncles and aunts, nieces and nephews, who else spinning away from her memory, gone now, all of them ground to pulp under bloody Khaggun heels. And then to fall in love with a V'ornn! Irony sharp enough to carve you, make you weep. But what could you say? A heart will flow where it will, it cannot do otherwise. But how strange life is! Stranger than dreams, more surprising, even, than imagination. The biggest mystery was how a heart so full of hatred and revenge could love at all. And yet the stone had cracked, broken open, revealing inside an organ hot and wet and still beating. Ready.

"O, love, I know who you really are. I thought I had lost you forever. How you came to be inside this body I cannot imagine. I only know that by some blessed miracle you are not dead. You have come back to me. I see how you glance at me, and I know that look. It melted me the first time you looked at me with your V'ornn eyes. I did not care that you were the enemy. I listened to the language of my heart. I knew that I loved you, that I would love you for all time. That I would assault the very gates of N'Luuura if that is where I would find you."

She held Riane more tightly, as if with her own strength she could stop the other's violent shaking. "Annon, Annon, Annon! I never thought I would ever again utter your name without the chill of death running through me. But now you are here inside this body. I feel you. I know you are there. Don't you dare leave me now!"

In her mind's clear eye, Eleana saw her father, hands in soil dark and damp, dirt streaks painting his face, never so happy as when he was teaching her to plant medicinal herbs. He tilled small plots of soil, reclaimed from bedrock and tenacious scrub, for the high hills of the Djenn Marre were generally inhospitable to farming. That hardship did not stop him. When a patch withered and died he pulled out the dry roots and replanted. Celebrated what grew, nurtured what grew poorly. He did not know how to give up. That was her father.

In these memories, in a kaleidoscope of others, her father lived again. But Annon, in the body of an alien, what memories did he have? Overhearing a low conversation with Giyan, she had learned that Riane had no memories, had lost them in a fall. No mother, no father. Brothers, sisters could be alive or dead. A blank slate, or almost so. A life without memories. She could not conceive of such a sad thing.

Rocking Riane. Rocking her and loving her.

Riane, wrapped in the Veil, in Eleana's arms, shook and shivered like a boat tossed on high seas. A storm of gale-force magnitude blowing through her, rattling her insides, trying to shake her apart.

Eleana's father shaking, his eyes red and rheumy, whittled into premature old age by the deaths of his beloveds. Holding Eleana's little hand at graveside, shaking like a leaf all the same, knees turned to jelly, his healing knowledge washed away on a tide of grief. He took up arms the next morning early, before Eleana had awakened, so as not to say good-bye. Not knowing how, or not wanting to, she guessed he was dead by nightfall, fallen hard, died happy, having taken his revenge, slitting the throats of two Khagggun while they slept, dreaming of blood and victory.

Eleana was left alone to train, to learn how to survive, how to kill. Which was, more or less, how Annon Ashera had found her. He turned all her preconceptions about V'ornn on their head. Lost love Annon, returned to her. Rocking her, rocking. She made up her mind. She would not let Riane die. Remembering, then, something long forgotten, the song her father would sing to her, half under his breath as together they turned over soil, planted the mugwort deep, pruned the low branches off sweet clemett. A little nonsense rhyme with a melody so simple and lovely it brought tears to her eyes. Remembering him fiercely. Loving him all over again. Flooding her mind with light and life . . .

Hours later, Riane started, bringing Eleana back to consciousness. The Hagoshrin had made so little progress in its attempts to get to them, it had apparently retreated, for there was no sound of it, and its distinctive scent had faded. Riane opened her mouth and sighed. That was all she did, sigh. Twitched a little. Gave one last shiver and was done with it.

Because Eleana had dreamed of her father and mother alive amid a herd of cthauros, because she had awakened with a heaviness in her heart, she leaned down, and whispered, "Listen to me, Annon. I lied to you when we first met. I told you my parents raised cthauros because we needed them to ride and I knew you would not trust me if I told you the truth, told you I was stealing them. Who would trust a thief? I wish my parents raised cthauros. I wish they were alive." The truth had used up all the energy she had woken with. She lapsed into a state of semiconsciousness, alternately drowsing, starting awake with a fresh jolt of anxiety.

Not long after, however, Riane's breathing slowed and deepened as she sank into the sleep of the exhausted warrior.

I in Mennus stood in the semidarkness of the interrogation cell and picked up a wicked-looking implement from a narrow shelf. In its place, he set up a small crystal recorder and activated it. Then he prodded Fleet-Admiral Hiche as he if were an underdone side of cor meat. Hiche moaned. *So. Not dead*, Mennus thought. *Not yet.*

Stretched out on the stone bench where for centuries Ramahan priests and priestesses had gone to cleanse themselves spiritually by fasting and praying to Miina,

Fleet-Admiral Hiche lay, defeated. He was tall and broad-shouldered and handsome. In short, he was everything Mennus was not. Or, at least, he had been. Twenty hours under the merciless ministrations of Hannn Mennus had tenderized his flesh. His face looked like a pulped orangesweet.

"Little Admiral, can you hear me?"

The lump of flesh lying on the bloodstained bench stirred.

"Look at you, Little Admiral. So diminished." He clucked his tongue against the roof of his mouth. "Such an ignoble end for you. For us, to die is nothing, am I right? But to die in disgrace, a conspirator, a traitor, well, that is *everything*."

Fleet-Admiral Hiche uttered a curse, which turned into a moan as Mennus twisted the implement. "There is a way, though. A way out for you. If you are smart enough to take it."

Hiche muttered something through cracked lips.

"Eh?" Mennus leaned on the implement as he corkscrewed it into the rotting flesh. "Speak up."

"Wh-what . . ."

"What," Mennus repeated. "Yes, precisely. What can you do to save yourself from a dishonorable death?" He bent closer, trying to ignore the stench that wafted up from the Fleet-Admiral. In a conversational tone, he said, "Well, you can clear up something for me. You see, another of the Little Admirals, Lupaas, is dead. With his dying breath he implicated you. Yes, you, Hiche. He told me that you were the instigator of the recent assassination attempt on the regent."

"Fleet-Admiral Lokck Werrrent . . ."

"Yes, we all thought it began and ended with Werrrent and the former Star-Admiral." Mennus barked a laugh. "But of course you know this. Better than I do, I warrant." Mennus' face closed down, and now it was truly ugly. "There was a conspiracy. That is what the Little Admiral Lupaas told me just before his spirit departed for N'Luuura. He named you, Hiche. No surprise there, since you were a great admirer of the former Star-Admiral. So. Who else was involved? If you tell me, I will absolve you. I will grant you an honorable death. You will be at peace, and your family will not be stripped of their rights and your coins."

Eyes muddy with pain stared up at him. "I . . . I was not involved," Hiche rasped. "I know of no con . . . conspiracy."

"In other words Lupaas was lying. Is this what you wish me to believe?"

There was fear in Hiche's eyes, as well as pain. "Not lying," he gasped out. "Possibly mis . . . mistaken."

"About you or about the conspiracy against the regent?"

"Me . . . I . . ." Fleet-Admiral Hiche spent a few moments gasping. The gases he thus expelled were noxious in the extreme. "I . . . had heard of unrest . . . in certain quarters . . . but there is always—"

Mennus twisted the implement buried in the Fleet-Admiral's flesh. "Have you knowledge of a conspiracy, Little Admiral, yes or no?"

"Yes," Hiche gasped. "All right. Yes, there was a conspiracy. Be . . . between Star-Admiral Rydddlin and Fleet-Admiral Werrrent."

"I care nothing for them." Mennus grimly continued his work with the implement. "Giving me their names will not save you."

"What . . . ?"

"Who else was involved?"

Hiche's eyes were squeezed shut, tears ran down his cheeks.

"Who else?" Mennus said, bearing down.

Hiche's chest was heaving, and beneath his closed lids his eyes were rolling. Mennus knew he was cutting it close.

"Rydddlin was too young, too inexperienced to come up with such an audacious plan. Fleet-Admiral Pnin. He was the real instigator, wasn't he?"

"Ardus Pnin?" Hiche cried stupidly.

"Yes." Mennus slowly, agonizingly stirred Hiche's innards as if brewing a stew. "Pnin."

Hiche shook his head from side to side. "No. You are insane."

Mennus bore down, grinding slowly, inexorably with his implement of pain. Hiche's mouth opened in a rictus of agony, his chest ballooned outward. It was the end. Mennus had gone too far. His last breath escaped his trembling lips. This air had form and substance.

"Ardus Pnin distrusted Rydddlin," Hiche sighed with his final breath, "as much as he distrusts you."

With a roar, Mennus swept the crystal recorder off its perch and stomped it to fragments beneath the heel of his bloodstained boot.

A thread, shining, dark, impossible to ignore, had stretched itself from the regent's palace all the way across Axis Tyr to Receiving Spirit. There it intercepted Kurgan.

The banestone called to him.

He returned at once to his quarters at the regent's palace without precisely knowing why. As he crossed the chamber in which he had hidden the banestone, his thoughts were drawn toward Eleana in much the same way that an animal's attention is directed toward the direction of an oncoming storm. He saw her again as he had down in Black Farm, and he felt a painful swelling of his tender parts. He had, by this time, reached the set of scrollwork drawers within which he had secreted his purloined prize, and now he pulled open a drawer and unfurled a piece of bloody robe he had ripped from a particularly resistant Ramahan at the end of a long and grueling interrogation. It seemed appropriate that he wrap the banestone in this grisly artifact.

Naked, dark as a pit, the banestone wove its spell. It had reached into his mind, found the person he desired most, and attuned itself to her. Now it spoke in Eleana's voice. Her laughter echoed in the chamber, causing a shiver of anticipation to slither up his spine and explode at the base of his brain. All at once, he was overcome by a fever for her that was so intense his knees felt momentarily weak. When his eyes refocused, he noticed that he was gripping the banestone with white-knuckled tension and that the veins in his hands coursed as dark as the artifact itself.

It struck him that Eleana was close. He was absolutely certain that this feeling was neither wishful thinking nor a premonition.

Eleana was here, in the palace.

Where are you?

His hands had begun to shake.

I want you. I will have you.

He mouthed these words as he stared into the convex surface of the banestone. No reflection returned his gaze. Rather, it was Eleana herself. The banestone had opened up a window through time and space to show him that the object of his desire was somewhere in the caverns below the palace.

"They are close," the Khagggun said to his companion, as they made their silent way through the kuello-fir forest. "In fact"—he looked up quickly—"they have ceased to flee."

"Good." The other went down in a semicrouch. "We will take them out along with this section of the forest."

The first Khagggun held up his mailed hand. "Hold. For what they have done a quick death is too merciful. Besides, one of them is down on the ground." He glanced at his companion. "And the other is female."

The second Khagggun grinned. "Sex and death. Double our fun."

"Still," the first one said, "let us proceed with caution."

So saying, they separated, converging on the position of the fugitives from different vectors. The rain continued in rather desultory fashion, plinking down through the webwork of branches and needles, creating a melancholy sound much like the dreamy breathing of a restless sleeper. They ignored the tiny animal sounds, the rustling and scurrying across the beds of fallen needles, or the occasional twitterings of warning emitted by huddled birds awakened by scent or sound to the advancing intruders.

The southeast wind brought a clinging mist that rolled dankly through the forest, erasing the farthest visible trees and partially obscuring the rest. The Khagggun made their way through the mottled, lichen-colored landscape until they saw the fugitives. Much to their surprise, they saw a Tuskugggun holding an ion pistol on a male Resistance fighter, who lay on the misty bed of kuello-fir needles.

She turned suddenly as she became aware of them.

"Who are you, Tuskugggun," the first Khagggun growled, "and what are you doing so far from civilization?"

That was when Kasstna, aiming between Marethyn's legs, shot the first Khagggun dead. The second Khagggun leapt back toward the bole of a tree, returning Kasstna's fire.

Kasstna dived into a thick swath of underbrush as Marethyn ran in a zigzag diagonal path in order to get a clear line of sight. He tracked her with his eyes. When she nodded, he knew she was in position, and he commenced a scattershot firing at the remaining Khagggun. The Khagggun returned his fire, and he just missed losing an arm, as a third of the thicket whooshed up in violent green flame. He scuttled through the mist to the bole of a kuello-fir, firing as he went. Kasstna saw Marethyn roll on one shoulder, get up on one knee, and fire. The second Khagggun flew backward.

Marethyn rose and went over to the downed Khagggun to check that he was dead. Then she turned her attention to Kasstna. For a long moment, they watched each other with a kind of wary distrust.

"I have to admit that I may have misjudged you," he said as he walked easily toward her.

Marethyn tensed, and as she raised her weapon, he fired at her in reflex without aiming. She turned and fled, through the forest, keeping the trees between her and Kasstna.

Kasstna made no attempt immediately to follow her. He would find her, he had no doubt of that. He felt the urge to relieve himself, which always came over him after a kill, and did so all over the Khagggun corpse. It was a shame in a way to have to kill these Khagggun. If not for the Tuskugggun's stupid actions, the Khagggun would have discovered the camp, contacted their pack, wiped out Gerwa and his cell. He could have stolen back, liberated the hidden cache of weapons.

He sighed in satisfaction as he finished emptying his bladder. The key to gaining and maintaining power in the Resistance was having access to Khagggun weapons. The more you had of them, the more success you would have against the V'ornn. And that, in turn, would translate into more power. What remained now was to devise another plan to discredit Gerwa and take control of the weapons cache.

One step at a time, he thought. He needed to take the Tuskugggun back to the tribunal. Delivering her would gain him some power in the eyes of the other leaders, and he knew just the way to do it. Twisting off the Khagggun's helmet, he placed it on his own head. Of course, owing to the V'ornn's oddly conical heads, it did not really fit, but with some fiddling he was able to settle it sufficiently in place. He activated the echo-tracer circuitry. A holoimage appeared, nothing more than a blip, really, heading away from him, almost due north.

The Tuskugggun.

Methodically and coldly, he began to slip through the dripping forest after her.

Like a sea creature rising from fathoms deep, the ringing blackness inside Riane's head was gradually replaced by the grey, amorphous light not of a watery sun but of words forming like air bubbles rising to sunlight. These words took on a life of their own, the world melted and metamorphosed, and Riane heard Eleana whispering to her . . .

"I listened to the language of my heart. I knew that I loved you, that I would love you for all time. That I would assault the very gates of N'Luuura if that is where I would find you."

This manifestation of Eleana's heartfelt emotion had long been swallowed up in the hollowed-out intestinal tract of Kundala. And yet it continued to circulate, like a widening gyre of bright-rippled eddies, in the bubbling preconscious of the heroine who lay, healing, in her arms.

Riane, who was yet to wake, had entered that vast whirlpool suspended between time and space. She was Annon again, with his life before him, unsullied by danger, deprivation, or death. There was only the promise of possibilities that, for a scion of the Ashera, were virtually limitless. Into this shadowless Cosmos, Eleana's words stole like sunlight through a glade, causing Riane to conjure in her preconscious a scene she cherished. She had just saved Eleana from drowning in the cistern in the courtyard of the Museum of False Memory, and now in her mind resounded her own words: *I won't let you give up, Eleana. I love you too much to let you die. I will follow you all the way to the gates of N'Luuura.*

That I would assault the very gates of N'Luuura if that is where I would find you.

In this state of semiwakefulness, of timelessness, Riane said nothing, for words circled in the pool of her mind like bright silver fish. Instead, she envisioned Eleana, all the living details of her, the iconic minutiae that crowded, unseen, at the corners of one's vision because there was never time enough to take them in: the sensual angle of her upper leg, the power and promise of her thighs, the languorous arch of her hip, the perfect arc of sun-burnished shoulder that merged so sweetly into the gently muscled arm, the moist hollow on the inside of her elbow, the silken threads of veins on the pale inside of her wrist, the fine down of her, erotic in the flickering light.

I will follow you . . . I would assault . . . A prayer from which she arose, as from a dream of her own fashioning which, in a sense it was, into the reality of the conscious moment when place was fixed and time began again to tick forward.

"Eleana." Her voice was a dry cracked reedy whisper.

"Ah, thank Miina!" Eleana kissed Riane's forehead.

"The Hagoshrin?"

She shuddered. "Look for yourself."

Riane saw the Hagoshrin squatting atop the altar. Held by its tentacles was a body. It was stripping it of flesh. As each bone was exposed, it almost daintily drew the bone out, popped it between its massive jaws, and chewed. When it got to the skull, it wrenched it off what was left of the spine and, holding it for a moment between its teeth as if savoring what was to come, crunched down slowly and methodically, the sound of bone splintering reverberating through the cavern.

"Is that what it plans for us?" Riane looked around. "We cannot go forward, and we cannot go back. We are trapped here."

"Hush now." Eleana rocking her. "All is well. I am here, love."

Riane's heart thudded in her breast. "What?" She was overcome by a sudden display of nerves. "What did you say?"

A slow smile spread over Eleana's face, a shy smile, but one also of great pleasure.

Time seemed to have slowed again to a honey drip. Riane felt the ghost of Annon rising within her, not dead, no, far, far from that—felt his V'ornness, his *maleness* as one feels the pressure drop at the advent of a storm, a soft stirring in the inner ear.

Eleana touched her, a hand on her arm, a warmth, a current like an eddy in the water made by something surfacing. She kissed Riane tenderly on both cheeks. "Annon."

How long had Riane been waiting to hear those words.

It might only have been a year, but it seemed like all her life. All the anxiety that had held her rigid drained out of her, the nerves that had delivered unconvincing denials to her lips had vanished.

"Giyan said you knew."

"She was right."

Riane, Annon, both at once, reached up, brought Eleana's head closer. Inhaled deeply her tangy scent. Her lips opened, and she tasted the tip of Eleana's tongue. Riane gave a little moan of longing, and for a delicious moment the kiss consumed them both in a perfumed cloud of citrus and musk.

Time stopped for them, as it does for all lovers. The one existed for the other in a kind of luminous suspension large as the Cosmos itself. They breathed each other in, felt the other's long-pent-up longing, felt it as their own. Tasted each other, the sweeter because each for their own reasons had assumed it would never be.

For Eleana, Annon had returned from the dead, although it seemed to her that the flame of her hope, her desire, had resurrected him from darkness invisible, had brought him back to her as unerringly as a compass needle finds true north. It seemed magical, impossible, inevitable and right. It did not seem strange to her to touch Riane and feel Annon. He lay just beneath the surface, like a great sinuous fish in a pond revealed by sudden shadow erasing the sunglare. She felt Riane as well, the mysterious one, not only to her but to Annon as well, felt a power and a purpose beyond her understanding. Or maybe it was her own unleashed passion that made breathing a labor. Losing herself, she did not care.

And what did Riane feel? Riane and Annon had so often been at war, at odds, the unfamiliar grappling with the unfamiliar like conjoined twins forced by circumstance to learn too much about each other. As one, now, they rose together to the flame of passion, each bringing different emotions. Annon, who had loved Eleana from the moment he had first seen her through dancing trees, through sunlight and shadow, taking her hair down, slow as the fall of moonslight. Riane, who had come to love her, in part through the force of Annon's feelings, in part discovering the love on her own, a shock, a thrill, a whole new world undreamed of. Two became one, an integration as much dreaded as longed for. Here it was, all at once, in a circumstance neither could have anticipated. They gave themselves up to it, heart and soul.

10

Hagoshrin

Pack-Commander Dacce found First-Captain Kwenn eating a desultory meal in a café known as Alloy Fist. It was, not surprisingly, merely a stone's throw from the main Khagggun barracks and even nearer the Forum of Adjudication, where Bashkir butted heads over who was making more coins. All Dacce knew was that it wasn't him making coins. The V'ornn owners had gutted the interior, incinerating all the heartwood Kundalan fixtures, replacing them with utilitarian chronosteel tables and chairs. Fusion lamps lent the place the cool bluish cast of an off-world grotto.

Dacce did not immediately approach Kwenn, but rather collected a drink from the bar, at which only a solitary Bashkir sat. Dacce thought he ought to know him, but he could not quite place the face. As he passed Kwenn's table, he made sure the First-Captain saw him.

"How goes the interrogation?" Kwenn asked in his typically neutral voice.

"All things considered, I'd rather be in the middle of a war."

"Wouldn't we all."

Kwenn kicked out a chair, and Dacce hesitated just long enough to give Kwenn the idea that he wasn't really interested.

"I see you're wearing the new star."

Kwenn looked down at his uniform. "By the regent's order, all Haaar-kyut must wear it."

"I understand each is coded to your personal DNA."

Kwenn nodded. "It will turn black if someone else— you, for instance, were to try to use it."

Dacce stared at the star. "They say the regent is paranoid."

"Just careful," Kwenn said. "And after the recent betrayals by former Star-Admirals, I'd say he is prudent, as well."

Dacce sipped his drink, not really tasting it, while they chatted about those things of interest to born-and-bred warriors: weapons, training, death. When he had judged that enough time had gone by, Dacce changed the subject. "Tell me something, Pack-Commander, how did you feel about our so-called elevation to Great Caste status?"

"I could have predicted the trouble we would get into," Kwenn said bluntly. "It was inevitable, really. We are bred to defend and to kill. Personally"—he glanced over at the lone Bashkir nursing a drink at the bar—"I have nothing but contempt for Bashkir."

"Save for their wealth. So tell me, how did you wind up working for one?"

"Trust me. Kurgan Stogggul is as far from your typical Bashkir as you could get."

Dacce was reminded of his superior's respect for Kurgan Stogggul, though he still saw no reason to share it.

"Besides," Kwenn added with a lopsided grin, "Bashkir know how to pay. I get a thousand times the coins I received in Khagggun ranks."

Dacce felt a serious flush of anger, not only at the First-Captain but at himself for not being shrewd enough to invest with Bashkir what little savings he had during the time when it was possible. Now he saw himself doomed to near-poverty level. He mentally shook himself. He did not want to look too closely at why a Khaggun longed for luxury instead of the acetic cortasyne rush of battle.

"Do you play warrnixx?" First-Captain Kwenn was asking him now.

"When I have the time."

Kwenn produced a small multialloy cube.

"Play for coins?" he asked.

"Played for more than that on battlefields."

"Shall we say one hundred?"

That lopsided grin appeared again as Kwenn twisted open the cube. A spiral appeared from which a shaft of pure indigo light rose. Out of this fountained twenty-four small decagons, twelve each of red and black, suspended in the beam of the light, while the two contestants put their left hands into the edge of the holographic spiral. Black sparks ensued spiraling around each of the hands before tingling against Dacce. He had the twelve black decagons and would have the first move.

They played quickly and efficiently, as befitted Khaggun. In the end, Dacce won with a daring and unexpected maneuver with his last remaining decagon.

"Well done, Pack-Commander." Kwenn pushed over a pile of coins.

"And you, First-Captain." Dacce deftly swept the coins into his pocket. "I find your defensive strategy most unorthodox."

"Do you have five thousand to go with those hundred?" Kwenn said. "Because being at the regent's side, I am privy to numerous lucrative deals that make Bashkir fortunes."

"Five thousand! I hardly have five hundred!" Dacce exclaimed bitterly. "It is my ill fate to be poor."

"Pity. Twenty-five hundred and we could have been partners, a small dip in a big deal that could have tripled our coinage."

"Triple! But it is now illegal for us to involve ourselves in Bashkir deals."

"It all depends on whom you know and who looks the

other way." Kwenn was staring at the spiral, possibly reliving the game moves. "Are those flecks of blood on your uniform?"

"Admiral's blood," Dacce said. Then, as Kwenn set the spiral for another game, he laughed. "*Little Admirals.*"

Kwenn glanced up.

"That is what Iin Mennus calls them, the members of the high command. Little Admirals." The lights glittered on the warrnixx playing field. "How he hates them. It is palpable, his hatred."

"That is only natural after how they treated him."

"No, no. This is different." Dacce shook his head. "Iin Mennus and his brother have a love affair with torture. It is not enough for them to kill their enemies; no, for them death is the least interesting part of it."

At the bar, Sornnn SaTrryn, whom Dacce should have remembered but did not, pushed away his half-finished drink. He'd finally had enough.

Marethyn knew she was running out of options. The rain had finally stopped. It was growing cold and clear, the worst kind of weather in which to try to hide from Kasstna. Not to mention the fact that she was hungry, tired, and frightened. As she ran through the forest, she could feel her nerves overfiring. There was a bitter taste in her mouth, almost like silicon. Her body had been pumping out so much cortasyne as a means of self-preservation that all her senses felt as if they were on permanent hyperalert, but her thinking was muddled.

As a consequence, she barely reacted as the way ahead pitched upward at a steeper angle. Grasping handfuls of branches, she hauled herself upward, until she became aware that she was leaving a carpet of stripped buds in her wake. She veered to the west, grasping the boles of trees, but these were often either too big around or too slippery to be of much use. Twice, she lost her grip and fell backward, squandering precious time and energy.

Her lungs began to labor as the trajectory she was on

became even more difficult. The last one hundred meters was almost a sheer vertical, but at last she made it up to the crest of the intermediate ridgeline. Above her, the Djenn Marre continued their torturous ascent, thrusting, so it seemed, into the very heart of the heavens. She took the time to do a quick reconnoiter, and discovered the ridge petered out perhaps three hundred meters to the east. With no strength left to climb farther, she headed west.

On the semidenuded ridge, the wind was like a knife against her. She knew she had to find some cover soon, for if Kasstna didn't kill her, exposure to the deepening night surely would. She loped on, feeling her hearts beating wildly in her breast. Presently she entered a line of Marre pines. Their unfortunate location had stunted them, however; the tops barely reached eye level.

At least the ridge was fairly flat, and she could rest her aching thigh muscles. A half kilometer farther on she saw the mountainside to the north falling back. At first it was so gradual that she barely noticed. Then, abruptly, it drew back sharply, as if afraid of the precipice its own towering height had built. Just beyond, she discovered a hollow. It was filled with brush, dense and dusty as a broom. There was a peculiar odor in this area, bittersweet as burnt spun sugar.

With a little grunt of thanks, she made for this best of all possible hiding places. But she had only gone several meters into it when her footing gave out and, with a brief rumble of loose stones, she skidded down into utter blackness and utter silence.

The Hagoshrin was staring up at them with an expression that defied decoding. Riane felt as if she and Eleana were a pair of prehistoric insects trapped in amber. As she had said to Eleana, they could not go forward or back. She looked around her, desperate to see if she could find anything useful that she had overlooked. As she did so, she found once again her elation at finally being with Eleana without the wall of secrecy. She knew Giyan had only her best interests at heart when she had warned Riane of telling anyone—even Eleana, *especially* Eleana—her secret. But Riane's heart knew what was right, what she needed to do, and she had done it. Now there was no going back.

"Riane, look!"

Eleana's urgent whisper broke into her thoughts. She was pointing at the Hagoshrin, which had managed to move forward. Its tentacles reached out, quested along the ruined span, slithering across the gaps in the arch, moving inexorably toward them.

Riane, however, was on her back. Staring up at the ceiling of the crevasse.

"Love, what are you doing? The Hagoshrin is still coming toward us. It's almost at the stairs. What are we going to do?"

"Move deeper into the crevasse."

Eleana followed the direction of Riane's gaze. "And then? We'll just be trapping ourselves."

"Perhaps not. I have noticed that the crevasse is far deeper than I had thought or expected." She slid deeper inside, Eleana following. Riane unwound the Veil, its glow illuminating the rock walls. "Look. Do you see?"

"The rock is smooth."

"That is what caught my attention." They kept moving farther in, which was just as well, for they could clearly hear the dry rasping sound of the Hagoshrin's body against the rock stairs. "My guess is this crevasse is not natural at all."

"It was made by the Kundalan? But why?"

"I am hopeful that if we explore far enough, we will find out."

A scraping sound caused them to turn their heads. By the Veil's glow, they could see that the Hagoshrin's serpent form had reached the entrance to the crevasse.

"Show yourselves, infidels!" it screamed. "You are trespassing on holy ground!"

"Keep going," Riane whispered. As they crawled backward, she kept an eye on the Hagoshrin. Its coils were filling the mouth of the crevasse. It was still coming after them.

The way was becoming more and more narrow. They were forced now onto their bellies, squirming like reptiles, the rock face just above their heads, brushing their shoulders and buttocks.

"It's getting smaller still," Eleana said.

Riane, raising the Veil, saw the space whittled down to a thin opening.

"Your flight is hopeless." The Hagoshrin's cry echoed through the crevasse. "You are trapped."

"I think it's right," Eleana said. "I don't know whether we can squeeze through."

Behind them, rocks skittered. A slithering drew near.

"We have to," Riane said. She smiled, turned Eleana's hand over, kissed the palm. "You first."

"I don't want to lose you," Eleana whispered. "Not now."

"Not ever," Riane said, kissing her tenderly.

Eleana went feet first, wriggling and struggling in a shower of pebbles and loose rock. For a moment, she seemed stuck. Then, in the blink of an eye, she was through.

"Come on." Her voice floated back to Riane. "Hurry!"

Riane slid through on her stomach. Wriggling and squirming as Eleana had. She saw the first coils appearing at the far edge of the glow the Veil threw off. The coils roiled and rose to fill the whole space. Using her elbows, she levered herself backward through the narrow aperture, could feel the rock digging into her back.

She was halfway through when the coil abruptly, explosively expanded. Like a beaten drum the crevasse reverberated with the shock waves. There came a loud crack, and Riane felt the top of the aperture fracture, a terrible weight pressing down on her. Felt Eleana pulling at her legs to no avail. She was trapped.

For Kurgan, carrying the banestone in the crook of his arm like a newborn, it was decidedly odd to hear the sound of laughter in the caverns. He stopped in his tracks, looking around for the source. He had explored far enough to be aware of the peculiarities of the acoustics. You never knew where sounds were coming from. He had often speculated that this was deliberate on the part of the Ramahan who had excavated the space, for he had seen myriad signs that the original cavern had been expanded and redesigned to fit unknown purposes.

The banestone had brought him to an area with which he was unfamiliar. He was far away from where Star-Admiral Iin Mennus had, until recently, toiled diligently and bloodily over his three Little Admirals. He had, of course, violated the protocol of his office by venturing into the caverns without his Haaar-kyut guards. However, he had no intention of allowing anyone, First-Captain Kwenn included, access to the banestone. It was too precious and potentially powerful an artifact. No one must know of its existence; otherwise, doubtless, word would reach the Gyrgon, and they would order him to relinquish it. Eventually, he might decide to do that, but not unless it was under his conditions and not until he had exacted a terrific price.

The ghostly laughter had ceased, and he began to wonder whether he had heard it at all. The banestone was urging him on, pulsing cold and hot. The thought of finding Eleana, of having her for his own, goaded him onward. He felt hot and clammy. He had an abrupt urge to spit.

He shone his lumane ahead of him. He had long ago left the area lit by V'ornn fusion lamps. The rather organic-looking cavern curled around to his left. Upon reaching the elbow, he smelled something dank and foul, the acrid accretion of rot and decay. He played the powerful lumane beam over the velvet blackness, half-expecting to have come upon some secret Ramahan burial site. Not that it would have mattered to him; his mind was filled with Eleana. The banestone was like some strange, sorcerous compass that had locked on to the object of his desire, and was bringing him unerringly closer to it.

The banestone's throbbing became more rapid, and Kurgan kept moving forward, the certainty growing in his mind that he was nearing her position. The lumane's beam revealed to him stone walls unbroken by crypts or any sign that he had entered a Ramahan tomb.

Somewhat farther on, he came upon an enormous sigil deeply incised into the cavern wall. There was something about it that struck him. It seemed that the center of it took the form of a great eye, surrounded by a circle of what could only be tiny pupils.

As he watched, astonished, the pupils began to pulse. But surely that was impossible. They were a part of a stone carving. And yet, now, it was unmistakable. Not only were they pulsing, but they were doing so in sync with the banestone. Abruptly, the banestone chilled in his hand, and the section of the wall into which the pictogram was incised split silently down the middle, opening inward.

The banestone was pulsing more rapidly than ever. Kurgan gripped the tritanium hilt of his push-dagger as he stepped through. His lumane threw out a reassuring beacon of cool blue-white light, revealing what appeared to be a tunnel through the rock, round and hollow as an intestine.

As he began to move through it, the thick stone doors swung closed behind him.

Riane let go of all the breath she had been holding in when the aperture collapsed. Behind her, she could feel Eleana frantically digging at the loose rubble. A space opened just as the coils were about to reach her, and she levered herself backward with all her strength. A shower of rock, a minicascade, tumbling. As she popped through, the aperture, no longer held up by her shoulders, collapsed completely, cutting them off from the Hagoshrin.

They held each other in the semidarkness, breathing hard and shaking with relief.

Eleana stirred, and whispered, "Since we may die in here—"

"We are not going to die here."

She took Riane's face in her hands and whispered fiercely, "Our love is what we have now, in this black and desolate place. It may be all that we have. You must tell me everything."

Riane knew that she was right. She told Eleana how the spirit of the dying Annon had by sorcerous means migrated into the shell of this Kundalan girl. "Riane was dying, too, of duur fever, until I brought my V'ornn strength to her. She had suffered a fall from a great height. Her memory was wiped clean. It is only now beginning to surface in small flashes. I still do not know my own origin."

"But her personality—"

"Is still intact. The process of integration is ongoing. It has been slow and difficult." Riane stirred, abruptly afraid. "And you are not . . . repulsed?"

Eleana laughed. "That is the male V'ornn in you talking. I fell in love with *you*, not who you were or what you looked like. You have come back to me from the land of the dead." Eleana brushed away her tears. "I feel as if I have been given the most wonderful gift."

The inescapable magnetism of love long held in abeyance overcame them again, and, for a time, exquisitely, almost painfully, attuned to each other's touch and breath, they were insensate to everything else around them.

"Listen to me," Riane said, when at last she forced herself to pull away. "No one must ever know what I have told you."

"Who knows besides Giyan?"

"Possibly Sahor. No one else, not even Thigpen. As far as the world is concerned Annon is dead. He must remain dead, for the Stogggul would come after him with all the power at their disposal if they had even a hint he was still alive."

"Not to worry, love." She touched Riane's cheek. "No V'ornn would believe such an outlandish tale."

"This is no joking matter," Riane warned. "And you must never, ever call me by that name."

Eleana's pink tongue came out, its tip questing at the corner of Riane's lips. "Not even when we are alone?"

"Never. Otherwise, sometime when you least mean to, it will surely slip out."

Eleana kissed her. "I understand."

"I mean it. Giyan did not want me to tell even you."

Eleana took Riane's head in her hands. Her gaze locked with Riane's. "I swear, Dar Sala-at, on my life and the life of my son, that I will tell no one. Your secret is like our love; it binds us closer together." She kissed Riane once, twice, three times. "No one will ever come between us now."

They continued to kiss, long and passionately.

After a time, Riane held up the Veil. They were in a chamber hewn out of the living rock. It was square, a vast cube. At its center was a column, square as well, gleaming as if lit from within. Metal. Approaching it, they saw that it ran down through a hole bored into the rock.

"What is this place?" Eleana whispered.

Riane shook her head. She did not know. She inspected the column, saw a pair of narrow vertical channels set into opposing sides. Feeling something surfacing from the depths of Riane's shattered memory, she began to search around on the front of the column and found a lever set flush. Depressing it set in motion an ingenious system of counterweights. Up along the channels rose a pair of leather-bound stirrups and a carved porphyry handgrip.

Eleana staring, openmouthed. "What on Kundala—?"

"It's the way down," Riane said.

"How do you know?"

"I just do." She settled her feet in the stirrups, took a deep breath, and let it out slowly. "Ready to give this a try?"

"Do I have a choice?" Eleana put her arms around Riane, clung to her back.

"Hold on." Riane raised the lever.

The system of counterweights once again began to whir, down went the stirrups and the handgrip, Riane and Eleana with them. Fetid wind rushed up their backs, fluttered their hair. Astonishingly, there was virtually no vibration, which made the ride unexpectedly easy.

"I do not understand this," Eleana said. "Here is a machine, admittedly with a single, simple purpose, that is of a level of sophistication beyond anything I thought us capable of. Could it be V'ornn?"

"The V'ornn never explored this part of the palace, I can assure you."

They were almost at the bottom of the column. The pearlescent glow had returned, giving an almost surreal aspect to this part of their journey. Certainly, they felt the pull of gravity, but their other senses steadfastly refused to confirm their descent.

Arriving with a soft metallic clank at the bottom of the column, they found themselves at the edge of a stinking moat of a viscous, opaque liquid in which could be seen floating huge water lilies, pale and erose to the point of shapelessness. There was a narrow bridge of white granite that spanned a cesspit reeking of rot and bitterroot. In the center was the basalt column that was crowned with the altar.

"The Hagoshrin's lair," Riane whispered.

Walking around the cesspit, Eleana peered down at the water lilies, and a shiver raced up her spine.

"Dear Miina, look!"

Riane studied the flowers more closely, and discovered stirring not some form of sun-averse plant life but the rotting remains of what once must have been corpses. The water lilies were actually patches of skin and connective tissue that had come free of the decomposed flesh. What was particularly disturbing about the grisly sight was that there were no bones or skulls at all to be seen.

"What do you think happened to the skeletons?" Eleana asked, echoing Riane's thoughts. "Dissolved in the moat?"

"By all the evidence, it appears as if the legends about the Hagoshrin are correct," Riane said. "The creature eats the bones of its victims and leaves the rest to rot."

"Ugh!" Eleana shook herself like a wet cor as she made dry land. "I wouldn't want to fall into that moat." She looked around. "How are we ever going to find Thigpen in this maze?"

"Good question." Riane took the lead.

Reaching a wall, they discovered that the chamber at the bottom of the shaft was circular. Embedded within the carved rock were veins of minute creatures, viruses or colonies of bacteria, perhaps, which emitted the shadowless glow. At precise intervals, the wall was incised with a single repeating glyph that looked like a stylized eye with a circlet of pupils. The glyph was not Venca, not any language Riane or, for that matter, Annon recognized. As she possessed a linguist's mind, this fascinated her. Was this glyph part of a language even more ancient than Venca, a protolanguage even, pictograms thought up by Riane's ancient ancestors? Or was it more sophisticated than that, another language altogether, long since fallen from memory like so many things of ancient Kundala buried in this tomb along with the Hagoshrin?

She became aware of Eleana softly calling her name. It appeared as if she had found one section of the wall without a glyph on it.

"Dar Sala-at," Eleana said, "what do you see?"

"A blank wall."

"Come here, then."

Eleana was standing directly in front of the center of the blank area. When Riane came and stood beside her, she saw what Eleana saw: a shadowed archway and, beyond, a lamplit corridor.

Riane moved to her right, and the archway vanished. "More technology we cannot account for," she said.

Eleana nodded. "It seems as if this area of the caverns is better at raising questions than providing answers."

With a palpable sense of relief, they left behind the lair of the Hagoshrin. The corridor was smaller than any other Riane had been in down there and, oddly, was as round as the inside of a barrel. It bore few, if any, traits recognizable as being Kundalan in origin. But if the place was not built by Kundalan, who, then, had created it?

They had walked only several hundred meters when they saw before them a kind of hump rising out of the concave floor. Riane knew what it was even before they neared it.

It was a crystal oculus.

She was elated. Annon had seen the one embedded in the ceiling just outside the Storehouse, the one Giyan told her had been created by a series of sorcerous spells.

Kneeling, she peered down through it and gasped.

"Eleana! Look here!" She could scarcely contain her excitement as Eleana knelt beside her atop the oculus. "We are just above the Storehouse Door!"

At that moment, the oculus occluded. Stress fractures zigzagged through it, and it collapsed, sending them tumbling down into the cavern below.

Riane groaned, put her arm around Eleana's waist as the other shook her head groggily. And there was the Storehouse Door, a mammoth, circular affair, studded with deeply carved runes. In its center was a carved dragon, and in the dragon's mouth was embedded the Ring of Five Dragons Riane herself had placed there.

She rose and stood before the Door. She put her finger in the Ring and heard a deep rumbling. At last, the Door began to open. She would have access into the Storehouse, there to begin her search for the long-lost Pearl.

As she stared, awestruck, the Door rolled open, revealed a dark and odoriferous interior. She called to Eleana, but in that instant two powerful tentacles shot out. Riane tried to back away, but the pain in her head exploded and, before she knew what was happening, the tentacles twined about her waist. Eleana grabbed her, but Riane was jerked away, snatched into the Storehouse, where the Hagoshrin crouched, hungrily waiting.

Eleana leapt after her, but the Door rolled closed, separating the two of them.

* * *

The stench of Marethyn's temporary abode threatened to make her pass out. Even in the darkness, it had not taken her long, stooping, feeling around, to ascertain that she had stumbled into a mass grave. Like one newly blind, she discovered the wealth of information her fingertips could provide. For one thing, she found that all the bodies she touched were female. For another, they wore Ramahan robes. But what would Ramahan be doing there in the wilderness of the West Country so far from a working abbey? Perhaps they had become lost. There could be no doubt that this poor band of priestesses had run afoul of a Khaggun patrol. But if so, why were there no burn holes in their robes, why was there no aftersmell of dissipated ion-fusion weapons?

Marethyn lay back against the steeply sloping side of the mass grave and contemplated a multitude of questions without answers. Could the Ramahan have gotten trapped on this densely forested ridge during the winter? Had they died of starvation and exposure? Running her fingertips over several of the corpses at random, she determined that the bodies were freshly dead. Further, none of them felt emaciated. So, then, what had killed them? That was when she found the first of the daggers. Soon enough, she found others, some still clutched in the fists of the dead. What were Ramahan doing with weapons? Surely, they must have used them to defend themselves because the other explanation was too bizarre. Of course they could not have fallen upon each other.

"Miina? Great Goddess, is that you?"

The faint sibilance made her start. Then she heard a stirring, followed by a small moan of pain. Climbing over the mounds of corpses, she came to a body that moved slightly beneath her touch.

"I am Marethyn," she whispered.

"You have a V'ornnish name and a V'ornnish accent."

The Ramahan was covered in dried blood and nearly dead. There was nothing Marethyn could do for her.

"What happened here?"

"You don't know, do you, V'ornn?" A dry cackle quickly turned into a cough thick with blood and phlegm. "Shhhh." The return of the cackle-cough made Marethyn's gorge rise.

"Won't you tell me something? Perhaps I can help."

"How can you help?" the Ramahan whispered. "I am already dead."

Then she did something strange. She grabbed Marethyn's hand in a dry, trembling grip. "You want to help, V'ornn? Here." She pinched the tip of each of Marethyn's fingers in turn while she counted off, "One, two, three, four, five. What do you see?"

"My fingers."

"Stupid V'ornn. Five pivots. Do you understand now?"

"No, I—" Marethyn stopped in midsentence. The Ramahan was already dead. She sighed, reached out to close her eyes and, with a little cry, snatched her hand away from the empty sockets.

She heard something then, a twig snap or a branch swooshing in the wind. Or was it a furtive footfall? She turned from her macabre encounter and gazed toward the opening down which she had slid.

She listened.

The soughing of the wind. The rustle of rodents. Hearts beating fast.

The skitter of stones.

And then, so abruptly it paralyzed her, she was hit with a brilliant blue-white light.

"You weren't so hard to find, Tuskugggun."

Kasstna's harsh voice seemed to emanate from the center of the light. She shaded her squinting eyes, and he laughed.

"A rat-mole in its hole."

She turned this way and that, but there was nowhere to run or hide.

"How does it feel, Tuskugggun, to be the hunted? To know you are going to die?"

The achingly bright light threw into sharp relief the slashed corpses. Two were locked in a death struggle. *So they* had *fallen upon one another*, she thought distractedly. The Ramahan dead grinned as if urging her to join them. She was trapped, and nothing could save her. She turned back to see Kasstna aiming his ion pistol at her.

"You are far more trouble than you are worth," he said, "so I will kill you and bring your severed head back as a trophy for the tribunal leaders."

Marethyn did not beg for her life. On the contrary, she found that she was resigned to her fate. From the moment she had embarked on this dangerous path, she had always known that her life could end this way. She did have regrets, however. She wished she could see Sornnn one more time. She thought of her grandmother. *Tettsie, I hope for a brief moment, at least, you were proud of me.*

The ion blast resounded shockingly loud in her ears, and she stumbled backward. But, on her knees, she realized that she had lost her balance because of the noise. She remained unhurt.

The light source was canted at an angle that cast her in a penumbra. Quickly, she dragged over a couple of the corpses. Standing on tiptoe on the grisly mound, she gained a handhold and levered herself up.

"Marethyn?" A blessedly familiar voice.

She gained her feet, her hearts beating fast. "Majja?" The bright light filled her field of vision. "Is that you?"

"Here," Majja said. "Help me with Basse. He has been hurt."

Marethyn made her way to where Majja crouched, Basse's head in her lap.

"What happened?"

"He wounded Kasstna and went after him. Kasstna shot him. I think I killed Kasstna, but I can't be sure."

Marethyn found the light source—a battle-grade lumane used by Khagggun—and turned it down to low. By its illumination, she saw that Majja had pressed her hand over a spot on Basse's abdomen. His clothes were soaked in blood, and he was unconscious.

When Majja took her hand away, Marethyn could see a pink iridescence that made her stomachs want to rebel. She stripped off the sleeves of her blouse and, tearing them into strips, wrapped them tightly around the wound.

"How did you find me?" she asked, as much to keep the look of fear off Majja's face as to calm herself.

"Did you think we would just let Kasstna take you away like that?"

"You followed us?"

"I finally persuaded Gerwa." Majja licked her lips. "We must get him back to camp."

Marethyn looked down at the pale, drawn face, and said a silent prayer.

"We cannot move him," she said quietly. "You know that."

Majja's eyes searched hers. "We cannot let him die. We cannot!"

Riane!"

    Eleana, dizzy with fear, pounded on the Door.

"Riane!"

Eleana's shock-sword was out, striking the Door over and over again with heavy two-handed blows. After not too long at this the twin blades exploded into smithereens.

"I am glad I saw that for myself." Kurgan stood grinning at her. "Because if you had told me that Kundalan stone could destroy V'ornn alloy, I would have called you liar."

Blood freezing in her veins, she let go a foul oath, lunged at him, the ragged stump of the shock-sword raised. But rage and terror blunted her reflexes, allowing him to dance lithely away from her rather clumsy attack. His push-dagger was already out, and deftly, gently, almost lovingly, he pricked her side with its needlelike tip.

It did not take long for the Nieobian paralysis gel to

work. Her curses turned to unintelligible slurring. She stumbled over her own boots.

"Come here, sweetling." Kurgan sighed deeply.

Eyes rolling up, Eleana fell into his arms.

Krystren's Journey

Krystren, at the western edge of the island onto which she had been washed up, rolled a cube of worn red jade between her fingers, sea wrack sloshing at her feet. She heard the call of the Sea of Blood. She inhaled the sharp, clean tang of the ocean. In the bright, tender days of her childhood, before the *Onnda* had come to claim her, she and Courion had swum with giant spotted rays and dancing deep-water snapper. The intelligent cephalopods, which he had loved best, she left for him, preferring the cities of coralbright, colonies of shellfish, armies of circling glittery eels. It was for him to peer into the deep, and see there the shadows of immense creatures no Sarakkon had ever encountered.

They had been born in the Great Southern Arryx, an enormous swath of undulating valleys that ran through a chain of slouch-sloped volcanos. Centuries ago, in the Time before the Imagining, it was said that a pair of Dragons cavorted across the Arryx, their sexual couplings creating the first Sarakkon. Perhaps this was true, for all around the Arryx was an arid place. No tree rose from the nutrient-poor soil, no flowering plant pushed up through the sharp-edged igneous rock.

She sat in the lee of a blue-black fang of rock with her

knees drawn up, staring out at the Sea of Blood, and thought of the time she had returned home from the absolute isolation of *Onnda* training to find Orujo moping on the veranda. His family name was Aersthone, but for many reasons they always called him by his given name. He was simply Orujo. He had come looking for Courion, who was away at sea. For two days they sat drinking a highly potent distillation of *oqeyya,* the rare fungus that grew in the caldera of Oppamonifex, regent of the volcano chain, while they spoke of Courion, whom they both loved. When they ran out of the distillation, he suggested they hike into the caldera to gather more of the fungus.

At the summit of Oppamonifex, the air was so thin that those raised in the coastal cities could scarcely catch their breath. Clouds passed ghostlike below them. Wind and sun scoured their faces raw, dried their lips as if they were in the desert. They felt their hearts laboring, the blood rushing through their veins. Peering over the lip into the crownlike caldera they saw an area blasted by natural cataclysm into a landscape both surreal and wondrous, for it looked like nothing else on Kundala.

Krystren had tried to take everything in, to do more than remember it—to somehow absorb it, keep it forever whole and throbbing and alive just as it was at that moment. It was, more than anything else, the spontaneity of their decision, like a color pure, rich, fresh, that filled their hearts with such elation. If only each decision in life could be this quick and clean, a knife slash across the throat.

And she had succeeded, because these were the dominant images that occurred to her now, vivid and breathtaking still after all this time. The wind quartering in off the Sea of Blood smelled of torment, the torment of memory.

"It is so spectacular," Orujo had said, alight in his turquoise jacket at Oppamonifex's summit. "Thank you. I never would have gotten Courion up here."

He spread his arms wide, Orujo the adventurer, who

preferred hanging three thousand meters in the air to sailing on the deep. Which was where the nettles of his relationship with Courion resided.

"Let's see if we can find some *oqeyya*," Orujo had said with his unquenchable enthusiasm, "before we lose the light."

"Are you sure?"

Orujo flashed the smile that Krystren loved and which made Courion weak. "Even you and I will likely never pass this way again."

And so they had begun the precipitous descent, entering the miraculous Oppamonifex caldera, home of living Dragons, seedbed of *oqeyya*, of, so the Sarakkon believe, Kundala itself.

The blasted world opened wide to meet them, the harsh blue sky slipping away just as if they had dived into deep water. The darkness of the caldera rose up, loose rubble and powdery ash slithering away like wild rivulets in a tempest. Glassy fingers of obsidian, wicked as daggers, proliferated on the steep incline. Once or twice, Orujo almost lost his balance as the friable rock underfoot gave way. He laughed as Krystren reached for him. He did not need her arm around his narrow waist but, being Orujo, he enjoyed the attention.

Their descent was methodical and cautious. There was no cause for concern or alarm. High above, in the dwindling oval of the sky, enormous golden-winged vistures circled silently, scanning for prey with telescope eyes.

Orujo's thick, braided hair was pulled back from his face, tied with a band of silver runes, in his thick beard was a cube of red jade, ancient and worn, given to him by Courion on their first anniversary. His slender, open face was alight with the impromptu adventure. Or was it impromptu? Krystren found herself wondering whether Orujo had this in mind all along, a trophy greater than any other to take back to his lover, Krystren's brother, Courion.

By the time they were a third of the way down, the

caldera was pitched at a dizzyingly steep angle. They slowed even more, picking their way carefully down the precarious slope. Above them, the sky was deepening, color impastoed onto the undersides of clouds as the sun swung lower in the sky.

Krystren prudently called a halt, and they drank deeply from their water flasks. Orujo pointed. Below them was a rufous patch of *oqeyya*. He grinned at her, for it was far larger than they could have envisioned, and they said what was in their minds, that spontaneity caused life to be at its most surprising. So much *oqeyya* would make them rich.

If she replayed the next few moments in her mind ten thousand times, Krystren would never quite fathom how he lost his grip on her flask. Perhaps his hand was stiff and sore from being used as a brake to halt his descent. Perhaps the flask itself was overbeaded with moisture. In any event, he lost control of it, and it began to bounce away. She watched Orujo reach for it, his outstretched fingers almost grasping it on its first rebound off the rubble, and then that stretch— the stretch of his beautiful sculptured, hard-muscled body, a body whose every square centimeter Courion knew and cherished—as he leaned out over the sheer slope. In that one gesture was embodied the very essence of his eternally open and optimistic personality, the absolute belief that anything he tried he would excel at. It was a moment, fixed in time as firmly, as irrevocably as the point of a compass, at once exquisite and horrifying.

And so he had stretched past the limit of any Sarakkon's ability, and grabbed the water flask on its way down. The weight, tiny as it was, had unbalanced him.

In a flutter of brilliant turquoise, he fell.

Down into the crisped center of the caldera he had plunged so shockingly, so quickly that Krystren was frozen in place. Rivulets of ash followed him down, disappearing with him, completely, irrevocably, with no trace at all that he had ever stood beside her.

Orujo!

She slipped into the Sea of Blood. Bright plumefish
skirted reefs of coralbright and the ballet dance of the
sea rays as they moved in and out of the slanting shafts
of sunlight. They swam with Krystren, and wept for
Orujo, understanding why a week after dazedly hauling
herself out of the Oppamonifex caldera she was waiting
at the port of Celiocco when Courion's ship had nosed
in. Coming down the gangplank, he had seen the truth in
her eyes before she could say a word, and that night, over
her bitter protests, he had shipped out, never to return
home.

Did he blame her for Orujo's death? He never said.
And yet, his absence had spoken louder than any anger
he might have raised against her, for he never wrote to
her, and despite her best efforts she had failed for years
to locate him. Until she had been summoned by the
Orieniad. Cerro himself had told her that her brother had
been sent on a secret mission on the northern continent,
then charged her with the mission of finding him and delivering into his hands a small, wrapped parcel, sealed
with wax. It did not seem possible that after all this time
she would be reunited with her brother. How would he
greet her? What would she say to him? What was there
left to say?

Only everything.

Everything that had been left unsaid, that had festered
like an unburied corpse in the house of their youth. The
spectre of Orujo's death lay between them like a mysterious fen, fogbound and treacherous, causing them to lose
each other forever. Except now, this mission had given
them one last chance to remember who they once had
been.

A shadow moving in the unknowable deep brought her
up short. She backpedaled away from the searays, from
the coralbright so full of life.

Though Courion had loved them and had professed to

understand them, she had an unreasoning fear of orquidia.
With a spasm of terror, she turned her back on the shadow
and in fifteen long, strong strokes made it back to the
safety of the tidal pool.

The sun had begun to melt into the Sea of Blood, turning the shallow water in which she lazed into a bowl of
liquid silver. She had been on the island for several weeks
now, sleeping during the day, never in the same grotto
twice, making her reconnaissance at night, sticking to the
moonslight.

It had been her initial intention to find a way off the island as quickly as possible. But when she had seen who
was advising the sauromicians, she felt it her duty to
learn as much as she could about the clandestine activities
on the island before she continued her journey to find
Courion in the dense crush of Axis Tyr. When Cerro had
made her privy to the information she required to carry
out her mission he had also revealed to her why Courion
had been sent to the northern continent. He had left it up
to her to connect the dots. So she had stayed in order to
discover how much the *Sintire* knew of the *Onnda*'s
plans.

In the course of her eavesdropping, she had discovered, among others things, that the west side of the island
was the most treacherous for a sailor. It also contained a
hidden grotto choked even at low tide with deadly surf
fueled by fiercely swirling crosscurrents. The discovery
had almost cost her her life. But she had made it inside,
finding an entrance up into the core of the granite towers,
thick now with sauromicians, their new pupils, and their
advisors.

The sun had bloodied the western horizon. The last
crescent thumbnail of it emblazoned the sky with fiery
color. Three of the five moons had risen. It was almost
time for her to make her way into the Chaos Grotto, as she
had named it, taking the winding staircase up into the
heart of the sauromician citadel, there to begin her nightly

session of spying. However, this evening she sat unmoving in the pale green moonlight.

She had heard the whisper behind her, an onshore breeze rustling the hems of long robes. Without turning around, she knew that two males had emerged onto a cave mouth almost directly above her. They stood gazing at the same violet swath of twilit sea that stretched before her. The three moons were in a pregnant phase; their reflected illumination was bright as dawn.

"I would hardly believe it," said a very deep voice she recognized as belonging to Haamadi. "We have successfully killed a Druuge. And without possessing the Veil of a Thousand Tears." Haamadi was the youngest, and newest, of the sauromician archons. From what Krystren had gleaned, he had been elevated following Talaasa's death in Za Hara-at.

"Talaasa's failure was inevitable, as we told you." This voice was higher. "It was a fortunate occurrence not only for you, personally, but for sauromician and *Sintire* alike." The voice possessed the soft whispery insidious intonations of the *Sintire Ardinal* named Lujon. "Through us, you see that you need not rely on the Veil. Through you, we have a long-sought-after toehold of power on the northern continent."

"Leverage over the Druuge, you mean."

"You said that," Lujon said. "We did not."

"No, of course not. You wouldn't." The sauromician snorted. "The perfect symbiosis."

"Is it skepticism, Haamadi, that we hear in your voice?"

"We were born sucking at the great teat of Miina," the sauromician said. "Now we are sucking at yours."

"Caligo and Varda do not see it that way," Lujon said. "They have been archons for many years."

"That is the problem," Haamadi said. "Their frustration makes them impatient. Their impatience makes them incautious."

"You would do well not to discount their experience."

"Their experience is in being thwarted by the Druuge."

"This is why they have asked us for help in locating the ninth banestone."

"And in return you have asked us to use our sorcery to find a certain Sarakkon. Tell me, Lujon, what is so special about this female?"

There followed a short pause. "She is an agent of our sworn enemy."

"And that is all?"

"That is more than enough, believe us."

Haamadi grunted. "And what of the ninth banestone?"

"What of this agent named Krystren?"

Their laughter spilled over the edge of the cliff, echoing harshly across the tidal pool where Krystren sat still, breathless, and, because of her power, invisible to them both.

"We discovered that the ninth banestone was hidden at Za Hara-at," Lujon said. "Unfortunately, it was taken from there before we could get to it. Rest assured that we will discover by whom."

"I am counting on it."

"But having it is not enough, is it? You also have to complete the Cage that has imprisoned—"

"Do not invoke the Dragon's name," Haamadi cautioned. "Not here. Not anywhere."

"And why not?"

"Its power is vaster than your mind can comprehend, Lujon."

Another pause, after which Lujon said, "Raiding a Ramahan abbey has been quite informative. Our knowledge has increased a thousandfold along with yours."

"An unfortunate consequence of our new relationship." Haamadi's innate paranoia could turn any statement into an implied threat. "I foresee a time when your so-called toehold of power on the northern continent will increase to a point when an alliance with us will become disadvantageous to you."

"You feel we are using you."

Haamadi smiled with small, pointed teeth.

"But you are using us as well," Lujon pointed out. "This is the nature of symbiosis."

"No," Haamadi snapped. "The nature of symbiosis is two entities in a *mutually beneficial* relationship."

"Your outlook is entirely too pessimistic."

"I am a realist." Haamadi pointed. "See that tidal pool below us? In it live a myriad of creatures coexisting peacefully. Until, that is, one or another of them gets hungry enough to devour its neighbor."

"What is your point?" Lujon said shortly.

"It matters not whether we rely on the Veil or the *Sintire* for our power," Haamadi replied. "Inside, we sauromicians are as hollow as this rock fortress we are forced to inhabit. We remain stripped of our power."

"The power you were judged to have misused. In that regard, Miina did Her job well."

"Is it any wonder we are impatient to regain it?" he cried.

Lujon, crossing his arms over his chest, said nothing.

Haamadi regarded him for a moment. "You do not like us."

Lujon laughed. "On the contrary. Despite everything, Haamadi, you we like."

"Insofar as *Sintire* can feel anything."

"That is an old lie," Lujon said with some asperity. "We are not machines."

"I have heard otherwise." There was a short pause during which Krystren could imagine Haamadi shrugging. "But perhaps I am misinformed."

"Youth is often tempted to draw conclusions from the flimsiest of evidence."

"That *is* dangerous," Haamadi admitted. "It is also dangerous to believe that age and wisdom are synonymous."

"Both of us speak a rebellious tongue," Lujon said in a contemplative tone of voice, "and yet we represent ancient federations."

"As for myself, I am no proponent of monolithic thinking."

"Come, Haamadi," Lujon said. "Let us drink together.

Sooner or later, we think, we will reach a consensus as to how best to accommodate one another."

"Drunk or sober," the sauromician said, "I will never fully trust you."

"It seems to us that is because you recognize in us something precious to you: the pearl of ambition."

"And if so?"

Lujon forced air between his teeth in a tuneless stream. "We now have a firm basis on which to move forward."

For some time after they had retreated into the rock fortress, Krystren remained in the tidal pool, trying to digest all that she had heard. The implications rippled out in all directions, multiplying dizzyingly. *Sintire* on the *Oomaloo; Sintire* in league with sauromicians. *Sintire* so desperate to find her they had made a deal with sauromicians. She shuddered. On the other hand, she was gaining an understanding of both the ramifications and the urgency of her mission. She could spend all spring eavesdropping on the sauromicians and their new allies, but this conversation had served to make it even more urgent that she find Courion and deliver to him the information she carried.

And so she cast her mind toward how to get off the accursed rock. It was too far and too treacherous to swim to the mainland, and she had not discovered where the *Sintire* had stowed their ship. Besides, she had no wish to alert them to her presence; stealing one of their small boats would only inflame their curiosity, not to mention their determination to get it back.

Something interrupted her pondering. Fifteen meters out, where a short time ago she had been swimming, where the seabed plunged into the deep, she saw a dark stain upon the water. As the tide was coming in, it was slowly making its way toward her. When it was close enough to recognize, she rose and stood shivering on the salt-rich evening air.

It was an orquidia.

Unreasoning panic sent a chill through her, but she found that she could not move. The creature had arisen from the deep, and was now making its way toward her with each successive wave. It must be over six meters long. She knew she should climb out of the tidal pool, gain as much height as she could in order to protect herself. Obdurately, she stayed where she was, even as, one after the other, the creature's tentacles slopped over the rocks into the tidal pool.

She watched the suckers, big as her ears, brown as the algae that turned the bottom of the tidal pool furry, expand and contract as they drew ever nearer. Shame mixed with her paralytic terror. She was deeply, inconsolably ashamed that she, *crifica Onnda*, should feel such fear. Where did it come from, this horror that drained her of rational thought and action? From deep inside her, she realized, in the mysterious underworld where dreams are born, the kind of dreams from which she started awake, her hair plastered damply to her cheeks, the kind of dreams that stayed with her, dulling the day to pastel translucence.

A particularly powerful wave washed the orquidia's head partway into the tidal pool, causing a scream to bubble in her clotted throat. The rubicund beak was curved as a talon, sharp as any raptor's. One terrifying saucerlike eye stared evilly at her, and she felt like vomiting. It was quite some time before she realized that the eye was filmed over. The orquidia was dead, murdered by some enemy in the deep. It moved at the whim of the tide; it was harmless.

Whispering a short prayer to Yahé, she cupped her hand into the tidal pool, splashed water onto her face. She felt like laughing, but she could not rid herself of the shame. That it was involuntary was all the worse, for her *Onnda* training was meant to supplant such vulnerabilities with the iron fists of concentration, determination, and perseverance.

Only Courion knew of her phobia. He had tried to free

her of it, to no avail. Now he would not talk to her. Her own brother.

The orquidia lay spread out before her. Waves lapped its filmed eyes. Six of its twelve powerful tentacles lay limp in the tidal pool. Small fish were sucking tiny morsels off the suction cups. If they were unafraid, why wasn't she?

She rose, at last. Wading through the warm water, she took a deep breath and ripped off the orquidia's beak. Using it in lieu of a knife blade, she began to cut off the tentacles. Then she bound the body with half of them, making it narrower and deeper so that it took on the shape of a canoe. She cut the hollow trunks of dead softwood trees that storms had felled along the shoreline into appropriate lengths, bound them with the remaining tentacles on either side as ballast. She split a branch lengthwise and clambered aboard her makeshift watercraft.

Dipping the branch into the water, she paddled furiously past the surf to get beyond the island's westernmost headland. This was the difficult part, because she was headed perpendicular to the tide. She leaned in, putting her entire body into it, and presently she found herself far enough out so that she quit paddling. Her orquidia craft quickly turned north into the tide, and now the going was a great deal easier. Still, she could feel the current obdurately pushing her in a westerly direction. She concentrated on paddling against it, maintaining a course due north, for the farther west she went, the farther she would be from Axis Tyr and Courion.

It took her the better part of five hours to gain the mainland. When, at last, she clambered off the orquidia, she could barely stand, and her stomach cried out for food and water. Still, sleep was her overriding priority. She crawled through the muck of the tide line, finding shelter between a pair of massive rocks, and set her back into the groove. For a time, she gazed out through soft moonlight and bristling starlight at the rising black hulk of the island known as Suspended Skull. She could not imagine what evil Haamadi and Lujon were plotting.

She fell asleep fingering the worn cube of red jade. In her dreams she rode upon the back of a live orquidia and, strangely, experienced the joy Courion must have felt riding one. Then his ship, cleaving the waves at full sail, struck the orquidia head-on. It split in two, and she burst asunder.

Book Two:
GATE OF
BLINDED PATH

For a sorceress, Third Sight is all important. If Gate of Blinded Path is closed or otherwise impaired, errors in judgment are inevitable. Now the future is filled with brambles and thorns. And many a sorceress has come to a bloody end, trying to claw her way out.

—Utmost Source,
The Five Sacred Books of Miina

11

Einon

With a sigh that caused the sky-blue velvet curtains of his quarters to tremble, Nith Immmon unwound himself from his ion exomatrix. Removing the alloy suit that both protected and hid Gyrgon when they were outside the Temple of Mnemonics was a delicate and difficult task. For one thing, it was laced with skeins of quasi-organic veins and arteries of biocircuits. These biocircuits were chains of computer chips. The chips processed photons through a mnemonic liquid, which both held them in specified patterns and magnified their power. For another, each and every vein and artery was connected to specific pores in Nith Immmon's skin, linking into the Gyrgon's autonomic, endocrine, and nervous systems.

Nith Immmon's hermaphroditic body looked as if it was bleeding from every pore. But instead of drooling down his naked form, the blood followed a spiral course that eventually linked every square centimeter of the Gyrgon's form. A kind of garment was thus knitted, section by section, forming a three-part, body-fitting tunic, leggings, cape with a neck cowl that rose to the level of the Gyrgon's ears, all of a greenish blue hue. It was composed of an exhaustively complex network of quasi-organic biocircuits whose skin, metallic and burnished, coruscated in the light.

The Teyj, sitting on the branch of a small, potted sysal tree whose gnarled roots Nith Immmon periodically pruned, observed this all-too-familiar transformation with a cocked head and a brilliant eye.

"I suppose you must miss this," Nith Immmon said.

The Teyj ruffled its four multicolored wings and gave a little trill.

Nith Immmon laughed. "You always did have a wicked sense of humor, Nith Einon."

I am not Nith now, the Teyj said in Nith Immmon's mind. *My time has come and gone.*

"Tell me, did disassembly pain you as much as it pains me?"

It took me a long time to discover that the pain was part of the privilege of being Nith.

Nith Immmon finished storing the exomatrix and approached the bird. "Your time has not come and gone, Nith Einon. On the contrary, it is my belief that it is just beginning." He held out his left arm, but the Teyj declined to flutter onto it.

"As you wish."

He turned and, making a sweeping pass with his right arm, plunged his quarters into darkness.

A throbbing commenced. Light bloomed in the breathing darkness, at first just a pinpoint, then a pinwheel expanding. Stars burst into galaxies and nebulae, gas clouds, and the unimaginably vast emptiness of space. At Nith Immmon's behest, the starfield shifted and changed, until they were looking at a single shoal of stars.

"Behold," Nith Immmon said. "Hellespennn."

Is this the past or a simulation?

"This is where the stars fell." Objects could be seen moving amidst the shoal. "This is where we engaged the Centophennni." Not vectoring, drifting. V'ornn gravships torn to twisted pieces, reamed inside out, some all but unrecognizable lumps. "This is our end, Nith Einon. Unless we can learn the secrets of the Centophennni, we are looking at our end." A graveyard of almost an entire V'ornn fleet, tumbling end over end in eternal torment. "For the Centophennni are searching for us."

This was a widespread theory even in my time.

Abruptly, the starfield shifted to another quadrant entirely, to another shoal of stars within the galaxy, to more V'ornn gravships torn apart and tumbling like deadweight.

"It is theory no longer." Nith Immmon's sigh rustled the curtains. "Twenty-seven sidereal days ago Fleet 1011 was engaged by the Centophennni. Nineteen gravships. Thirty thousand of us." The image was closer now, the horrifying details piling up into a magnitude that staggered the mind. "All gone."

I see no sign of Centophennni casualties.

"There are none."

Just as at Hellespennn.

There was a kind of numb silence.

How far?

Nith Immmon knew Nith Einon meant how far away was this. "Not far enough," he said. "The Centophennni have gotten the scent of us. Sooner or later they will be coming."

Have you informed Gul Aluf?

Nith Immmon noted that Nith Einon did not mention the convocation or even the Gyrgon Comradeship as a whole. But then why should he be surprised that Nith Einon would know where the true power lay?

"I have not," he said.

Surely that was a mistake.

"I wanted to get your opinion first."

My opinion! Nith Einon tried to snort his derision, but as a Teyj could not snort. What he produced was a sound halfway between a whistle and a caw. *I am permanently disassembled. Why would you care about my opinion?*

"Because you are who you are. And because you are Nith Sahor's father."

Nith Einon fluttered the Teyj's four wings, settling back on the potted sysal tree. *Turn up the lights. I find this starfield depressing.*

Nith Immmon shut down the photon exciter, and raised the lights. "I know what you had been researching just before your death."

I was retired, Nith Einon said shortly. *I had returned to my sculpture.*

"Yes, yes. I am familiar with the stories you and your son disseminated." Nith Immmon waved a hand. "All lies."

Nith Einon pecked at imaginary nits in his glorious jewel-hued feathers.

Drawing up a chair beside the potted sysal tree, Nith Immmon sat down, crossed his legs. "Look here, I know you blame me in some measure for your son's demise."

How quaint a phrase is demise, Nith Einon said acidly. *How neat and . . . antiseptic.*

Nith Immmon opened his hands, palms up.

Oh, murder *will do nicely,* Nith Einon said. *And, yes, I do in part hold you to blame.*

"Unlike Niths Settt and Nassam I did not join Nith Batoxxx in his fatal attack on Nith Sahor."

You feel that you deserve praise even though you did not lift a finger in my son's defense?

"If I had, I would have been murdered as well."

Good riddance!

"But I am still here, and Nith Batoxxx is dead."

No thanks to you. And now you have Nith Nassam to fear.

Nith Immmon sighed. "Nith Einon, I want only to help you."

My son is dead! He and I are both beyond your—or any other Gyrgon's—help.

Nith Immmon sat sadly gazing at the Teyj. At length, he said, "All I ask is a chance to prove you wrong."

Bring back Nith Sahor.

"I cannot do the impossible."

This is the promise we promulgate among the other castes.

"But we are here in the Temple of Mnemonics. It is only you and I. You know better than any our limitations."

If you cannot do what I ask, then we have nothing further to discuss.

Nith Immmon rose and quietly brought the chair back to its original place. He took meticulous care to ensure that the foot of each leg was settled in its exact spot.

Everything in his quarters had the same air of being precisely placed and never moved, or at least, like the chair, not for long. There was a sense of the magic of this placement, as if the physicality of the quarters was part of an unspoken incantation.

"When the Centophennni find us," Nith Immmon said softly, as if to himself, "it will be the end for us."

After all the bloody wars we have waged, the endless destruction we have caused, if that is the consequence of our actions, then we should be strong enough to accept it.

"Since when are you a fatalist?"

It ill becomes you, Nith Immmon, to pretend to know me. Nith Einon lifted one leg, then the other, the only outward sign of his inner agitation. *We Gyrgon—and by extension the V'ornn as a whole—have been going down the wrong road for as long as I can recall. Mine was a lone voice in the wilderness. I was ignored, then, when I would not remain quiet, I was reviled. That animus devolved on my son when he took up the cause, refining the theories I had only time enough to outline.*

"You were not alone, Nith Einon. And neither was he."

Coward! It is too late! Your holoimages of the new front prove it. Now you will reap what your inaction has sown. The Centophennni will do to us what we have done to the Kundalan. If you have even a grain of sense, you can see how perfectly the consequence fits our crime.

"I, for one, refuse to believe that."

Then do what you should have done days ago, Nith Einon advised. *Show Gul Aluf what you have just shown me.*

"Is this another of your peculiarities, consorting with Gul Aluf?"

The Teyj tried to laugh. *Possibly, Nith Immmon, it is the only thing we have in common.*

Minnum's tent within the vast archeological dig at Za Hara-at was abrim with warm lamplight and the smells of roasting slingbok and brewing ba'du. The dwarfish sauromician was at the fire, fist on hip, stirring a flame-blackened pan in which he was stir-frying blood-rose petals in a bit of limoniq oil.

"I did not know you were such a cook," Giyan said, standing just behind him and observing everything he did.

"You may find that I have many hidden talents." He tossed in a pinch of cinnamon. "Living on your own, Lady, makes good cooking a necessity. Especially when you have my refined taste buds!" He glanced over at her. "Pardon my bluntness, but you really should get off your feet. You look exhausted."

"An occupational hazard, I am afraid." Giyan offered him a smile as she poured herself a cup of strong thick ba'du. "But I thank you for your concern."

"Are you hungry? You must eat, at least."

"Everything looks delicious." She bent her head as he offered her a taste of the stir-fried blood-rose. "And it is!"

She sat, then, and sipped her ba'du. Minnum had pitched his tent inside a ruined temple that fronted Reconnaissance Boulevard. Minarets rose in slender but truncated columns, fluted sentinels in the windswept night. She could hear the stirring of Za Hara-at all around her. It was these emanations, she was certain, that made the Khaggun guard uneasy. They ventured inside the ruined city only briefly during the day when they accompanied the architects. At night, they kept their distance behind the energy field the Mesagggun had erected around the V'ornn encampment.

"What have you discovered here?" she asked.

Minnum paused in his stirring for only an instant. He hooked a thumb over his shoulder. "Our prizes are arranged in the corner there."

Giyan rose and went to take a look. Crouched down, she ran a hand over each item, absorbing its internal vibration.

Minnum looked nervously over his shoulder. He had come to have a healthy respect for Giyan's power. He knew she was, among other things, one of the Ramahan Chosen, a seer, and he was terrified that she would somehow intuit that he and Sornnn had found a banestone. She had in her hand the broken idol, half-male, half-female, he had found.

"Curious, isn't it?" he said.

"Extremely." Giyan ran her fingertip over the surface. "It is clearly a deity, but it is not Kundalan. Do you know its origin?"

"I do not, Lady. I confess I have never seen its like before."

"Look at this face. What do you see?"

He shook his head mutely.

"Acceptance and death," she said, "in equal measure."

She put it aside and, after picking through a half dozen other artifacts, came across the ceremonial dagger that had been beside the banestone. Minnum's heart flipped over in his chest, and he cursed himself for not hiding it.

Giyan rose and, with the dagger in the palm of her hand, turned to him. "Where did you find this?"

With a sick feeling, he told her.

"Take me there."

"But, Lady, our supper is almost ready."

"Now."

Minnum knew an order when he heard one. He put down the wooden spoon and set the pan aside. Grabbing a lumane Sornnn had left behind, he took her into the rune-laden streets of Za Hara-at.

As they hurried along, he said, "The temple is on the boulevard Gather the Unknowing,"

"Of course it is."

She was staring at the dagger, which was carved out a single slab of lavender jade. Its hilt and handle had been fashioned into Venca runes. From her scrutiny, Minnum intuited that she attached some importance to it. There had been an urgency in her voice that gave him pause. He thought of the banestone found and as quickly lost. If he had fouled up again, he did not know what he would do.

At length, they turned onto Gather the Unknowing, a wide and, therefore, important thoroughfare. Just past the

Plaza of the Unfinished Rune, the beam of his lumane found the enclosing wall of the temple. Following it around to what was left of the entrance, he took her inside. His skin began to prickle, as if he had been infested with a thousand insects. His shoulders twitched, and he tried to even out his breathing.

The temple had a complicated structure. Even with the roof off and many of the columns destroyed it was possible to get lost within the labyrinthine form, especially at night. A cold wind skittered red dust along the stone flooring. Over the eons the dust had filled in some of the heavily incised runes, giving them an eerily reddish cast.

"It is just here, Lady," he said as he led her down an aisle between two rows of corkscrew green-porphyry columns.

At the aisle's end, he came upon the site. "Sornnn and I determined that there had once been a ceremonial altar here. But it was either destroyed or carried away by looters."

She knelt in front of the dig. As her posture could be interpreted as reverential, he felt compelled to kneel beside her. He wanted to ask her a hundred questions, but he was terrified to speak. He was on probation, after all, and he had every reason to believe that the Druuge were monitoring his behavior. Giyan had the authority to return him to the terrible limbo life he had been living before the advent of the Dar Sala-at at the Museum of False Memory. Having tasted freedom, he did not think that he could go back to the living death to which he had been consigned.

He watched, trembling as if ill with the ague, as she applied the tip of the jade dagger to the bed of the dig he and Sornnn had worked so assiduously. He peered into her face, trying to divine her thoughts, but it remained unreadable. At length, she sat back on her haunches.

"Minnum," she said slowly and deliberately, "what else did you and Sornnn SaTrryn find here?"

"Lady?"

"Do not dissemble," she snapped. Her eyes bored into

his very depths. "You have come such a long way. Do not revert now."

"My Lady, I—"

"Minnum, listen to me. We are in the Temple of the Avenging Spirit. It is a holy place. Well, of course all of Za Hara-at is holy. But this temple is the Holy of Holies. It is place where the entire engine that is this city was controlled. Do you understand me? In the language of Za Hara-at, 'holy' may be translated as 'power.'" She looked around them. "Once, there was power here. The secret is that it abides. The power has never left Za Hara-at. It only lies sleeping, waiting for all the pieces of the puzzle to be fitted into place, waiting for the day of its resurrection."

Her gaze gathered him in, surrounded him, enfolded him. For him, there was nothing else but her.

"Minnum, I will ask you for the second and last time. What else did you find here?"

"There was something else, Lady." Tears began to leak out of Minnum's eyes. "It lay just beneath the dagger you hold."

"I know," she said. "I knew it the moment I held it."

He felt as miserable, as alone as he had in the bowels of the terrifying Museum of False Memory.

"Now you must tell me."

And receive my punishment, he thought. *I am trapped by my own stupidity. How on Kundala could I have lost the thing?* He sighed deeply. "It was a banestone, Lady. Sornnn and I found a banestone here."

Giyan closed her eyes for a moment, and it seemed to him that in that moment she aged ten years. She said, "And where is it now?"

Minnum was weeping again. "Well, that's just it. I do not know."

Giyan sat watching him, silent, patient, waiting as Za Hara-at to avenge itself on those who had been foolish enough to believe that they had destroyed it.

"It . . . Lady, it just disappeared. As of its own accord."

"A banestone can do many things," Giyan said, "but walk off on its own is not one of them. What, then, is your conclusion?"

"Lady, I do not—"

"But you do, Minnum. You did not lose the banestone. It was stolen."

Oh, avenging Miina, now what? he thought. This is what Sornnn had warned him of, what he had refused to believe because the possibility made him deathly afraid.

"Minnum," she said softly, "who could have stolen it?"

"Not Sornnn."

"Don't be absurd. It would never enter his mind."

"One of the Beyy Das, then. The archeological assistants are known for their venality."

"They trade in petty trinkets. Small objects they know they can smuggle out undetected. Of course you know the penalty exacted if they are caught."

Minnum shuddered. "It must have been a Khagggun."

"A Khagggun would never come this deep into Za Hara-at because they escort only the V'ornn architects. Even they who know no fear are afraid of this place."

"Then who?" he cried. "Who could have stolen it?" But he knew. He knew as surely as he knew his own sins.

Giyan rose, and now she led him back down the aisle. Minnum was in an agony of despair. He had known from the moment he had discovered the banestone missing that he had made the gravest error by not hiding it more thoroughly.

When they had returned to the Plaza of the Unfinished Rune, she said to him in her gentlest voice, "I know you think you are about to be punished."

"I do, Lady."

"Well, stop it. We must both turn our thoughts from what has happened to what is about to be." She stopped them near the stone cenote at the center of the plaza. "We must assume the worst has happened."

He almost choked. "The sauromicians."

"Yes. It seems likely that they have stolen the banestone. That would explain how they were able to block Perrnodt's opal exploration, and the means by which they were able to introduce the Madila into her system."

"Lady, what can I do to repair the damage?"

"Not feeling sorry for yourself would be a good place to start. Ensuring that you do not repeat your error would be another." She put a hand on his shoulder. "As for the rest, have patience and faith." She looked around them and took a deep breath of the stirring city. "It is good to be in Za hara-at, Minnum, for I feel as if I have come home."

"I, too, feel an affinity for this place. But this makes my foolishness all the more egregious."

"I don't know about you," Giyan said, rubbing her hands together, "but I am suddenly famished."

They returned to Minnum's tent in time to save the haunch of slingbok from being charred through and through, but the blood-rose stir-fry was beyond redemption. They ate their fill of the meat, along with hunks of spicy flatbread the Beyy Das made from the flour of pedda-pads. Afterward, they drank ba'du until it was gone. Then Minnum broke out a bottle of naeffita, a jade-green liquor, whose smokey richness held hints of cloves, cinnamon, and burnt orange.

They lounged on Han Jad carpets, and, as the night wore on, wrapped themselves in patterned Beyy Das blankets to keep the chill at bay. They spoke of many things important and trivial, happy and sad, and each was pleased to get to better know the other.

"Tell me something," Giyan said at last. "This sauromician herb Madila, is it commonly grown and harvested among sauromicians?"

"Oh, no, Lady," Minnum said. "In fact, because the soil in the Korrush was inhospitable the archons had no access to it for all the time I was there."

"Then we can deduce that the archons have left their exile in the Korrush. More evidence that they have gained a powerful ally."

"I would say that is an inescapable conclusion."

"Since they now have access to Madila, they must be inhabiting an area where the mushroom naturally grows, for they would not have had enough time to sow spores and bring them to harvest."

"Again, a clever deduction, Lady." Minnum nodded. "In my experience, there is only one place on the northern continent where this herb is naturally occurring. I myself used to go there, from time to time, in order to pick it. But that was many long years ago."

"And where would that be?" Giyan asked patiently.

Minnum took a long draught of naeffita. "Ah, in the West Country. High in the Djenn Marre foothills in the far northwest quadrant of the Borobodur forest. On Receive Tears Ridge."

"Prepare yourself, Minnum, for that is where we are bound."

The little sauromician shuddered. "Oh, my Lady, would that you would ask anything else of me."

Giyan's gaze caught his in its web and would not let go. "But this is what I am asking of you, Minnum. We will go together."

"Alone?"

"Why?"

A cold wind had sprung up, moaning through the bones of the ruined city like mourners at a funeral. Minnum grabbed a cloak, wrapped it around him.

"The West Country is dangerous," he said, "and the territory around Receive Tears Ridge most of all."

"I know." Giyan nodded. "The Khaggun patrols."

"The V'ornn and their weapons will be the least of our worries, my Lady." He shivered. "If the mushroom fields are still there, then chances are so are the sauromicians."

Sahor could not sleep. However much he tried to calm himself, he failed. He rose and, lighting lamps that guttered in insidious drafts, padded out of his sleeping quarters and into the warren of galleries of the Museum of False Memory. This curious structure, guarded by gar-

goyled and crenellated stone walls, crouched like a hunch-
back at the end of Fifth Division Street in the far western
district of Axis Tyr. From its ramparts, if one dared to
walk them, could be seen the Great Phosphorus Marsh,
where nocturnal hunters had, for centuries, stalked the
large and dangerous amphibious claiwen. The gargoyles
crowning its forbidding parapets were, in fact, artful de-
pictions of daëmons, those frightening creatures whom the
Great Goddess Miina had imprisoned in the sorcerous
Abyss eons ago, and whose sole purpose, so the legends
said, was to free themselves and overrun all of Kundala.

Sahor was immensely excited to be there. When he had
been the Gyrgon Nith Sahor he and Eleusis Ashera had
spent much time there, learning all they could about the
mysterious treasures housed in the museum. But that excitement, intense though it was, did not account for his in-
somnia. Ever since he had left Za Hara-at, he had thought
of nothing but his father.

Now, as he prowled the dim, packed galleries, he knew
what he must do. In fact, he had known ever since he had
arrived weeks earlier. What had stayed his hand was the
sheer danger of it. He did not know how many enemies
Nith Sahor still had among the Gyrgon Comradeship, but
under Nith Batoxxx that cabal had been both numerous
and powerful. Now they believed him dead. The risk that
they should think otherwise was, at that moment in time,
unacceptable. He was still getting used to his new body,
still struggling with not being Gyrgon, not being Nith. He
did not yet know the extent of his powers; for, despite being reborn through technomancy into Eleana's son, he still
retained much of his Gyrgon DNA. It had been irre-
versibly fused to the child's hybrid DNA.

He paused before a mirror, staring at his face. It was
long, angular, predatory. He could not get used to the cruelty etched by the acid of heredity into its physiognomy.
There was no avoiding the truth. It was the face of
Stogggul Kurgan, the baby's father—*his* father, now that
he was inside this body. He shuddered at the thought. His

father was Nith Einon. To think otherwise was to court
madness. Sahor he might now be, but he could not let go
of his Gyrgon roots.

Swiftly, he returned to his quarters and dressed in patterned black robes of Kundalan design and manufacture.
This was one aspect of his new life that he enjoyed immensely, for as Nith Sahor he had had to keep secret his
love of all things Kundalan.

Clouds made phosphorescent by moonslight sailed in
the black night sky. A small dusting of the brightest stars
could be seen through the harsh V'ornn-made light haze
that emanated from the softly thrumming city.

By back alleys and narrow deserted streets, he made his
circuitous way into the northern district, home to the hard-
working Mesagggun and the alluring Looorm. Several
times he halted, shrinking back into shadowed doorways
or runed arches to avoid being seen by Khagggun pa-
trolling on foot and in hoverpods. Not that anyone would
recognize him, but he had no desire to be stopped and
questioned.

Presently, he arrived at the section of the city that was
his destination, all crooked streets and dead-end lanes. On
Black Chronos Street, he stood watching the dumb,
unlovely facade of the warehouse Nith Sahor had known
so well. Under various false identities, he had over the decades acquired space in several quarters of Axis Tyr, there
re-creating parts of his lab-orb in the Temple of Mnemonics. His devious strategy served two purposes. First, its
forced redundancy ensured that his research would survive
even the most catastrophic cataclysm. Second, it protected
both him and his work from the legion of enemies that
over the years had grown up around him.

That was hardly surprising, given the sundering of the
Kundalan Comradeship. Its shift from the pursuit of science to the amassing of political power had broken the
whole into fractious blocs. It had been the late unlamented
Nith Batoxxx who had engineered this tragic alteration in

the Gyrgon way of life. But it was Nith Einon's central theory that haunted his son's every waking thought. *From the moment we first engaged the Centophennni, nothing inside the Comradeship has been the same*, Sahor's father had posited. *That one act tainted us with what the doctrine of Enlil spoke of as the Original Sin.* How could he be wrong? Sahor asked himself. There seemed little doubt that this fear, as deep-seated as it was unspoken, was what had moved the Comradeship officially to repudiate the religion, to ban its worship, to systematically destroy its priesthood and persecute those who stubbornly refused to surrender their faith in the V'ornn god Enlil. It was not coincidence, Sahor knew, that his swarm of V'ornn had come upon Kundala at just this time. Ever since he had set foot on this planet, Sahor had felt a deep and abiding conviction that the V'ornn had reached a nexus point in their existence. And he had posited his own theory, an adjunct to Nith Einon's: *Here we will make our stand. Here, the great scythe of evolution will reach us. Here, we will, as a species, either survive or be plowed under.*

There were shadows in the street, shifting, and he tensed. But it was only a wyr-hound, thin of legs, belly grotesquely distended, sniffing its way through strewn garbage and regurgitated sewage. All at once, it stopped, lifted its head. Its glittering eyes searched for the source of the scent it had picked up. It watched the shadows, the rhythmic rise and fall of its rib cage its only movement. It growled, baring its yellow teeth as it lowered its hindquarters.

With a swift, practiced stride, a Khagggun emerged from the doorway where he had been hidden and, drawing his shock-sword, dealt the animal a fatal blow.

"Why did you bother?" a voice said from the deep shadows of the same doorway.

"Disease-ridden pests." His companion wiped off the twin blades on the wyr-hound's patchy fur.

"I know you too well." The other Khagggun emerged into the street. "You're just bored."

"Who wouldn't be?" The first Khagggun sheathed his weapon. "Standing out here, night after night, guarding this abandoned building. What for? What have we done to deserve the short stick?"

The second Khagggun shrugged. "Part of the job."

"No. We are being punished, I tell you."

"Well, anyway, it's almost dawn."

"You can play at being the obedient little Khagggun for all the good it will do you. For my part, I've had more than enough boredom for one night. What say we go find some Mesagggun and mete out our own brand of punishment?"

The second Khagggun took one last look at the entrance to the warehouse. "To N'Luuura with it, let's go."

Sahor watched them stalk off in search of bloody mayhem. He might have pitied the Mesagggun those two would ferociously attack, had not his mind been working at fever pitch. He crossed to where the wyr-hound lay in a pool of its own blood and touched it in a kind of benediction. Without it, he would have run afoul of the Khagggun. He knew why they had been sent there to guard this "abandoned warehouse." But who had sent them?

Some clever Gyrgon, one who had been with Nith Batoxxx when he had launched his near-fatal attack, was doubtless behind the Khagggun guard. The fact that the auxiliary laboratory was still being watched so long after his "death" gave him pause. The unknown Gyrgon was ensuring that no other Gyrgon loyal to Nith Sahor would gain entrance without his identity being noted. All this made him approach with extreme caution. He could, of course, have gone to either of the other two locations in Axis Tyr, but there had always been an uncharacteristic sentimental streak in him. His transformation into a hybrid corpus had only enhanced that atypical V'ornn trait. Eleusis Ashera had possessed it; so had his son Annon.

This warehouse was where he and his father had last been together. By means of complex technomancy, he had resurrected Nith Einon. In secret, he had labored many months to manufacture a fiendishly complex bio cortical

net in the form of a Teyj to house Nith Einon's electro-
magnetic force. His father had been with him at the time
of the attack. Sahor had managed to collapse the bio cortical net into a stream of iconic positrons just before the final conflagration that would make the body of Nith Sahor
unable to support life.

Thus he had returned to the place of his father's temporary interment in order once again to bring him back to
life. He could not accomplish that from another location.
He needed to resurrect him from the place where he had
been deconstructed.

It was well that his guard was up. Upon reaching the
musty entrance, he discovered a null-wave net, much like
those deployed in and around the Temple of Mnemonics.
Upon close inspection, however, he discovered that it was
a very special one. Entering it would not only immobilize
any intruder, even a Gyrgon, but it would send a photon
pulse of a wholly unfamiliar sequence that only the Gyrgon who had constructed the net would pick up.

The truly astonishing thing was that he still saw as a Gyrgon *without in any way being connected to the Comradeship neural net*. How this was possible he was yet to
understand.

He went swiftly around to the side of the warehouse. A
dust-blown sysal tree spread a kris-spider web of shadows
onto the blank facade. Scaling the tree, he reached a place
perhaps midway to the sloping roof. There, he stretched
himself full length on a sturdy branch.

Taking out a slender dagger, he tapped its hilt against
sections of the facade until he heard the hollow sound he
had been seeking. He used the dagger point to dig into the
whitewash. Chunks of it pattered to the ground at the base
of the tree. He continued in this fashion until he had outlined a square more or less three-quarters of a meter
across. Then he pushed with the heels of his hands, and the
square fell into the interior. Sahor followed it in.

The single chamber was completely bare, devoid of any
sign of habitation. The first thing he did as he crouched in

the dark was to search for another null-wave net. Finding none, he retrieved the whitewashed wooden panel he had constructed and set it back in place. Needing no light, he crossed to the baseboard in the far corner, pressed the center of it three times, then twice, then five times. A section slid back, and he manipulated a small panel he had hidden within.

In an instant, pale blue fire flared and flickered, causing the entire chamber to shimmer. Into view popped all of Nith Sahor's equipment neatly arranged and cataloged just as he had left it. Quickly, he activated the center touch panels, entering the formulae that would return his father to life.

Nothing happened.

Assuming that in his haste he had made a mistake, he reentered the figures, more slowly this time. An empty void loomed where the bio cortical net should have been. Sahor stepped back. There could be no mistake.

In a frenzy, he entered another formula, one far simpler than the first one. Death was so much simpler to fabricate than life.

In a trice, he was out the escape window he had made, shinnying down the sysal tree. Happily, heavier clouds had rolled in, obscuring all three moons. Only a dismal smudge indicated their location low in the western sky. Dawn was almost upon him.

Like a wraith, he stole silently from shadow to shadow, certain that his movements remained undetected. On Green Canthus Lane, he entered a small, gritty, unmarked tavern. A cadaverously thin, stoop-shouldered Mesagggun stood behind the flyblown counter picking on a plate of grey scraps. Sahor ordered and sat at a corner table, watching two bleary-eyed locals play warrnixx. The stoop-shouldered Mesagggun brought a goblet of crudely made ludd-wine. Sahor drank it anyway.

What worried him was this: some Gyrgon knew the formulae to bring the bio cortical net out of stasis. Whoever that Gyrgon was must have been in on Nith Batoxxx's attack to know of the laboratory's location. Doubtless, he was the one who had set the traps around the warehouse. How he had known about the bio cortical net's existence was a complete mystery, one that Sahor knew he had to solve as quickly as possible. He would not rest until he had his father back.

He was munching on a plate of freshly fried leeesta when the explosion rocked the tavern. Somewhere, crystal windows blew out with the tinkling of tiny bells that filled the awful silence following the percussion. The two warnixx adversaries leapt up and raced out the door to see what had happened. The stoop-shouldered Mesagggun did not look up. He wiped the counter with an unspeakably filthy rag and kept his own counsel.

12

The Forest Primeval

Working together, Marethyn and Majja managed to half slide, half drag Basse back to the edge of the mass grave. Marethyn did not like how much blood he left in the detritus of the forest floor where he had lain.

"Why have we brought him here?" Majja asked, her nose wrinkling with the stink. "There was the pleasant scent of burnt spun sugar back where we were."

"It is already growing cold, and we need a protected spot to keep Basse as warm as possible through the night." Marethyn was using the lumane to probe the darkness below. "We need to get him down there."

"What, into that stinking pit? You have to be joking!"

"Basse will die of exposure if we do not keep him warm. Do you have a better idea?"

"In fact, I do," Majja said. "We cover him with this." She scooped up handfuls of the dried needles that carpeted the forest floor. "We use this all the time as roof thatching for temporary shelters. It's good camouflage, better insulation."

Marethyn nodded. "Let's stay near the pit, though, just in case we need to hide from Khaggun patrols."

"All right." Majja began to cover Basse. "But don't expect me to go down there with you. The place makes my skin crawl." Majja shuddered as the beam of Marethyn's concentrated photonic beam exposed corpse after corpse.

"It can't be that you are afraid of the dead."

"So many Ramahan slaughtered—I'd only heard stories from my parents, whole abbeys of them wiped out. But seeing this with my own eyes . . ." She piled the needles in compact bunches around Basse. "Tradition says that we cannot touch, cannot even approach a dead Ramahan. The Ramahan prepare their own dead. Sacred prayers must be said to guide their spirits." She shook her head. "Though I have to tell you that there are some Resistance who would rejoice at the sight of this slaughter."

Marethyn glanced at her.

"Many in the Resistance are converts to Kara. They have turned their backs on the Goddess Miina because She turned Her back on them. They had begun to resent the power of the Ramahan even before your kind came."

Majja wiped her face with her forearm. "He is as well insulated as he can be. But without medical attention I don't know how long he will last." Majja stood up and went to stand beside Marethyn. "They are also healers, you know. Many carry small leather pouches of herbal mixtures used for treating all manner of ailments and wounds. They are very powerful, so I have heard."

Marethyn played the lumane over the grave pit. There were weapons and blood and ripped robes. "You stay here with Basse. I have the advantage of having already been down there. I'll see if I can find one of those pouches."

Majja wiped sweat off her forehead. "We're going to

need food and water. I'll go forage. With luck I'll be back soon with a brace of gimnopedes or a fine, fat qwawd."

Marethyn nodded and squeezed her friend's shoulder. It was odd, she thought as she slid down into the grisly pit, how you could feel closer to a member of a different species than to a majority of your own.

Together, they notched out a fallen tree trunk then, lifting it, slid it end first down into the pit.

She watched Majja expertly thread her way through the forest without disturbing a branch or bending a needle, quickly disappearing into the undergrowth. She turned and, wrapping her legs around the tree trunk, climbed down into the fetid pit. The stench was almost overwhelming, and she gagged a little. Breathing through her mouth, she bent her back, steeled her stomachs, and methodically turned over the corpses one after another. Once, she slipped and fell to her knees. When her lumane illuminated what she had stumbled over, she gave a little cry.

Despite her resolve, she soon grew dizzy at the grisly work. Nothing in her life could have prepared her for death on this scale. The evidence of suffering and agony, the unmitigated horror of it staggered her, and, without realizing it, she was weeping. Biting her lip in concentration, she redoubled her efforts, for she did not think she could remain there much longer. The first pouch she found had burst open, its contents scattered and useless. The second pouch was saturated with blood. But the third, which had been thrown from the Ramahan wearing it when she had been attacked, was lying in a corner, intact and dry. Stuffing it between her breasts, Marethyn gratefully returned to the crude ladder and scrambled up.

The light was wan in the indigo forest, grey as the faces of the dead Ramahan.

For some time, she knelt, her back bowed, weeping and breathing in the air that carried the faint aroma of burnt spun sugar. She concentrated on that as if it were a lifeline that drew her slowly away from the hellpit below. She felt the soft crush of Marre pine needles against her forehead.

She grabbed handfuls as her fists beat softly against the packed earth. She uttered one sob and stopped, abruptly. The silence of the forest was almost stifling, like the atmosphere grown heavy and charged just before a rainstorm. She lifted her head. No birds twittered, no mammals foraged. Save for the almost imperceptible buzz of insects, the swale was utterly still.

Majja. Where was Majja?

She rose and went to check on Basse. Despite his thick coat of needles, he was shivering. His forehead was hot and clammy when she touched it. He was burning up with fever, doubtless because his wound was becoming infected. If she did not do something immediately, sepsis would kill him.

Brushing aside the needles on his chest, she saw that he had bled right through the impromptu bandage she had fashioned. First, she tore off the lower half of her tunic, then she unwound the filthy, bloodstained cloth. The wound was purple and swollen around the edges. She felt the Ramahan herbal pouch between her breasts and took it out. Opening the drawstring, she smelled the heady, musky odor of herbs and ground mushrooms. She wished Majja were there so that she could ask her advice, but the probability was that she would have no better idea of what was in the pouch or what it was meant for than Marethyn did. But Ramahan were healers, Majja had said so. That was all Marethyn had to go on.

Shaking out a small handful of the powdered herbal mixture, she applied it directly to the wound. Then she rebandaged it with the cloth from her tunic and piled the Marre pine needles over him.

She sat back on her haunches and waited. She was thirsty and hungry and very tired. Putting her back against the bole of a Marre pine, she closed her eyes. Just for a moment, she thought. Just for a moment. . . .

She started awake at a sound, and her ion cannon was out and aimed as Majja appeared. Grinning, she held up a freshly killed qwawd by its feet, shook it in a victory sign.

Hearing a soft moan, Marethyn looked down at Basse. He was pale as moonslight and shaking all over.

She gave a little moan as Basse began to spasm. She heard Majja running up, felt her kneel beside them.

"What happened?" Majja asked breathlessly.

Marethyn briefly recounted what she had happened. "Oh, Majja, what have I done? Whatever was in those herbs has made him worse, not better."

At precisely the midnight hour of a very long and tiring day, Fleet-Admiral Ardus Pnin returned to his villa from delivering his reluctant grandson Miirlin back to his hingatta. To clear his mind of the questions the child asked of him that he could not answer, he took a stroll around the Kundalan garden he had refused to have torn out when he had taken possession of the villa. It was at the center of the property, at the nexus, one might say, of the villa, for there were walls all around it, but none within the garden itself. It was a formal garden, with four rows of smooth-trunked heartwood trees, planted at right angles to one another. They were bisected by paths of green porphyry up and down which he trod. He walked with his square head down, his huge hands clasped behind his back.

He was a big Khagggun, an aged Khagggun, a many-scarred Khagggun who had reached a surfeit of war and death, but could not bear to admit it to himself. In the dead of night, he would descend into a recurring dream in which he was lying on a high bed, a veritable mountain composed of the skulls of his enemies. Scrupulously picked clean, the skulls were, yellow-white like candle tallow, smooth as drowned stones. Just before he woke up, he discovered their mouths moving, sharp, curved teeth nipping at him, tearing into his flesh, rending it from sinew and bone.

He awoke so immersed in this dream he had difficulty remembering he was in his well-guarded villa. His routine from then on was always the same. He would rise and, naked, stare into the night, his mind crowded with the times that he had crunched across battlefield morasses, blood streaming from a multitude of wounds, slaughtering as he went. He had been trained to be an efficient killing machine, and that is what he had become. Save that a machine running at peak efficiency does not dream of being rent alive by its victims. It does not have thoughts that question and, therefore, undermine its sole purpose.

Of late, he failed to find solace even in the libidinous arms of his favorite Looorm. When one was drowning in blood it was difficult to get one's tender parts to swell. Only his daughter, Leyytey, could make him feel calm. She was an armorer, a magnificent artisan. Most of his colleagues knew nothing of their female offspring's whereabouts, let alone their trade. But he had kept an eye on her progress and, unbeknownst to her or her mother, had helped finance her training with the finest armorers on Kundala. Now she had her own atelier and all the top-echelon Khagggun were armed with her creations. It seemed a long time ago that he would visit her in her hingatta.

Truth is, I am getting old, Fleet-Admiral Pnin told himself as he passed between the narrow rows of heartwood trees. A breath of air from the south rustled the immature leaves. *Truth is, I should step aside and let Iin Mennus have his day in the sun.* But he could not; defeat simply was not in him. Besides, he harbored a deep distrust of Mennus. The Khagggun corps was built on rules and regulations, and for a very good reason. Khagggun were created to follow orders, to be part of a unit, a cog in a colossal wheel that kept rolling forward no matter what terrain or enemies or adversity it encountered. In his experience, Khagggun were uncomfortable when the strict limits within which they had been born and raised were altered or lifted. The limits made them feel safe and secure, they ensured that Khagggun would direct their entire concentration on each mission as it was presented to them. To put it another way, they were bred for the trenches. That was their world. Narrow and restrictive though it might seem to members of other castes, Khagg-gun themselves found it was where they operated best.

There had been altogether too much turnover at the top. First Star-Admiral Kinnnus Morcha made a highly political, and, therefore, highly suspect deal to give Khagggun Great Caste status. Now, Iin Mennus, the latest Star-Admiral, had begun to clean out the high command of those against whom he held a personal grudge. As far as Pnin could see, the Khagggun caste was already rotten with questionable politics and personal vendettas. He laid this sorry state of affairs squarely at the feet of the Stogggul family. The moment they had succeeded in murdering Eleusis Ashera and his immediate family, the warrnixx die was cast. Why the Gyrgon would sanction such an action was completely beyond him, but then who could fathom the motives of Gyrgon? Now he saw himself as the last bastion of the old guard, the last sane Admiral in a caste rotted by its taste of ambition and intrigue.

"Such heavy steps," a familiar voice said softly from the shadows. "Surely you will wear away these magnificent porphyry tiles."

Fleet-Admiral Pnin paused in his pacing, his clear-eyed gaze fixed at a spot between two of the largest heartwood trees, where he knew a white marble bench to be.

"Come, Ardus. Sit beside me," the figure said. "For the night is dark, and I am in need of company."

Pnin entered the deeper shadows of the trees, where the villa's fusion lamplight did not penetrate, and settled himself beside the tall, powerfully built figure.

"You all right, Sornnn? Anything I can bring you?"

"Considering our relationship, that is a very odd thing to say."

"I hear the pain in your voice."

"The female I love is dead."

Pnin bowed his head. "I am truly sorry. Is there something I can do? There is nothing I can say."

"Thank you, no."

Pnin laced his fingers together. "How swiftly time passes, Sornnn. The death of someone close does that, you know, makes you see your life differently. It occurs to me that we have been meeting like this for almost a year."

"A Khaggun and a Bashkir, skulking around like clandestine lovers."

"Castes be damned!" Pnin laughed. "I like to think that when he introduced us Line-General Werrrent knew we would become good friends."

"Werrrent is best forgotten since he was implicated in the aborted plot to assassinate the regent."

"Thought highly of you, Sornnn. His hearts were pure."

"He was a traitor."

Pnin sighed. "He was my friend." He shook his head. "The great pity of it is he didn't succeed."

The comment interested Sornnn. As a secret member of the Kundalan Resistance he was always on the lookout for potential sympathizers. He simply never considered that it might come from so high a quarter. Though he did not need to remind himself that this particular quarter might not make it to High Summer. It was Pnin's current troubles that had brought him out of himself, had cleared away the morass of self-pity in which he had wallowing, had returned to him at least a semblance of his old life.

Sornnn watched Pnin out of the corner of his eye with the concern a Genomatekk might have for a patient in critical condition. "I have been hearing rumors . . . Your situation has become untenable, hasn't it, Ardus?"

Pnin nodded. "Fleet-Admiral Hiche, Deck-Admiral Lupaas, Deck-Admiral Whon, my allies in the high command, have been taken into custody by the new Star-Admiral."

"So it is true. The regent has given Iin Mennus the power to do whatever he wishes."

Pnin's voice was very low. "I must assume the worst. My colleagues are all dead, or they will be shortly."

All at once, he gripped his head in his hands. He bent

over, rocking a little. He emitted a string of awkward sounds as drool spilled out of his half-open mouth.

Sornnn dug into a pocket and slipped a handmade pellet, black as mud cake, into the Fleet-Admiral's mouth. He pressed his jaws together, tipped back his head until Pnin swallowed convulsively.

"You have been remiss," Sornnn said. "When was the last time you took the *da'ala?* A week at least, I warrant." He watched the blood come slowly back into Pnin's face. "Why must you test yourself so?"

"I am Khagggun," Pnin said thickly. "I should need no nostrum, Kundalan or otherwise."

Sornnn sighed. "Ah, my friend, what a stubborn caste you belong to. You have a tumor deep inside your brain. You should have long ago gone to a Genomatekk."

"Bah, Genomatekks know nothing." Fleet-Admiral Pnin coughed up part of dinner and spat it out. "Besides, I would be immediately relieved of active duty if it ever came out."

"Then keep to your twice-a-day regimen. The Korrush spice at least keeps the tumor from growing as well as keeping these seizures under control."

Pnin stared bleakly at the shadows that cloaked the garden, and nodded. "One day soon our meetings will come to an end. It is only a matter of time before Iin Mennus comes after me."

"What will you do?"

Pnin sucked in his cheeks. "That, my friend, is the question." He exhaled. "I must now decide whether I have it in me to fight one more time."

Sornnn was genuinely shocked. "How could it be otherwise?"

Pnin could not help but think of his recurring dream. "I have killed too many times, Sornnn. Standing in an ocean of blood. Perhaps I should get out before I drown."

"You are Khagggun. You cannot escape."

Pnin rubbed his temples. "Possibly Iin Mennus would grant me an honorable death."

"You are fooling yourself. He will revel in denying you just that." And Sornnn told Pnin of the conversation he had overheard between Pack-Commander Dacce and First-Captain Kwenn at Alloy Fist, wherein Dacce had talked of the Mennus brothers' fixation with torture.

"If you surrender to them," he concluded, "they will take even longer in killing you. And the very last thing they will grant you is an honorable death."

"If you are right."

"You know that I am," Sornnn said. "Besides, there is your family to think of."

"What do you know of my daughter?" Pnin said a trifle sharply.

"Only what you have told me, only what I have observed the few times we have met."

"Then you cannot tell me why she still loves the father of her son."

"On the contrary. The explanation is simple."

Pnin hesitated only an instant, then he nodded his assent.

"She loves him," Sornnn said, "because he reminds her of you."

The Fleet-Admiral started as if he had been pricked by a sword blade. "If you were anyone else," he growled, "believe me you would be dead by now."

Sornnn sat very still. "I tell you this as a friend, sir, as a friend."

Pnin said nothing for the longest time. He was shaking a little. He tried concentrating on his recurring dream and what it was trying to tell him. He did not want to think of his daughter or of what Sornnn had said about her.

"Please understand that I will help you, Ardus," Sornnn said, "in any way I can."

Pnin's chest felt constricted. He needed to lash out at something, someone, and had to restrain himself. He willed his body to relax, his breathing to slow. He knew that if Sornnn had not made him take the *da'ala* he would have had another seizure. "I will need friends like you," he said, "in the days and weeks ahead."

"Not only me."

Pnin's head swung around. "What?"

Ever since Sornnn had overheard Dacce and Kwenn his mind had been calmly and methodically working out how to use his knowledge to its best advantage.

"Dacce is coin-obsessed," he said. "My sense is that he is deeply unhappy in his current position. That can be exploited."

"But to do so . . ."

"That's right," Sornnn said. "You will need your daughter."

Those Khagggun who had stared death in the face saw in the eyes of Line-Commander Hannn Mennus the same blank stare that hinted of nullity and infinity all at once. It was a curiosity to find it in the newly dead, a terror to observe it in one still living. He had been captured, so the story went, on Lethe, an ash-grey wilderness world once used by the Centophennni as a spyglass to observe, godlike, that quadrant of the galaxy. Possibly they were looking for the V'ornn; in any case, that was the suspicion.

What was known and undisputed was that Hannn Mennus led a scouting pack ordered by the high command to confirm advance intelligence of Centophennni activity. Among the rank and file, speculation was rife that the high command never expected the pack to return. Hannn Mennus was not informed of this, of course. Instead, he led his pack into the inscrutable jaws of death. Every one of them had been obliterated, ashes scattered to the winds. Save him. He had no memory of what transpired on Lethe, and, of course, his Khagggun could no longer give up their secrets. Had the Centophennni ambushed them? But there was no evidence of goron particles. Had Hannn Mennus gone mad and killed them himself, pyred them to N'Luuura? No one could say. And so it remained a mystery.

Perhaps the Gyrgon discovered something during their three-day debriefing of him, prying into the recesses of his brain like fervid speleologists, but, if so, the findings never made their way into data crystals, a fact the speculators found particularly ominous. At length, the Gyrgon released him into the flow of everyday life. There remained about him, however, the stain of an unsolvable mystery, a whiff of suspicion; and if there was anything Khaggun disliked it was those things. He commanded well, employed excessive force and cruelty with abandon. They respected him for that. He was also a canny leader. He had killed many Kundalan, ripping the tongues from their mouths, displaying like so many bird feathers the dried, shriveled remains on the shaft of his fluttering standard.

It was Kasstna's ill fortune to be discovered by a pair of Hannn Mennus' Khaggun. He heard them coming, but wounded as he was he was scarcely in any position to outrun them. Foolishly, he tried to kill them, but his hands were so palsied from his ion cannon wounds that he missed them completely. They came after him. Then he compounded his error by trying to hide from them. He was bleeding too badly and left a trail impossible to miss. Perhaps the loss of blood had addled his brain, for he neglected to remove his Khaggun helm and throw away his ion cannon before they dragged him from his inadequate hidey-hole. Seeing him wearing the contraband ignited their rage, but they were Hannn Mennus' own and he had trained them well. They beat him quietly, calmly, methodically and for a very long time which had the advantage of prolonging their pleasure as well as preventing them from making the fatal mistake of killing him.

Instead, one of them threw him over his shoulder like a side of freshly butchered meat, which by that time Kasstna resembled. In due course, they delivered him to their Line-Commander in the tense and ritualistic manner of warriors who place an important sacrifice before their shaman-king.

Kasstna was at that point in no condition to resist torture—especially the forms in which Hannn Mennus excelled. Besides, Kasstna had no specific sense of loyalty to Gerwa, for whom both the Mennus brothers had been unsuccessfully searching for years. In fact, he had every reason to see Gerwa destroyed. It did not take long for him to spill his guts, both figuratively and literally. He gave the Khagggun chapter and verse on where to find Gerwa's encampment, the size of his complement, and the level of training of his Resistance fighters. But in one matter he perversely held his tongue—the cache of stolen Khagggun war materiel, for even then he harbored the insane hope that he would be left alive to one day soon enter Gerwa's burnt-out encampment and find the weapons that would ensure his entry into the council. He had perhaps five minutes to warm himself in the fire of that improbable dream before Line-Commander Mennus, having determined that he had bled this specimen dry of intelligence, slit open his abdomen.

An hour later, Mennus, at the head of a Wing that comprised fully five packs of heavily armed Khagggun, moved out through the dripping foliage on his way to annihilate the infestation on Receiving Tears Ridge.

13

The Garden of Law and Chaos

Riane had been dreaming of Eleana. It was so peaceful, so perfect she did not want to leave the world she had created, she did not want the dream to end. Then all was grey ash dispersed on the wind, and her eyes snapped open and a chill whipped through her just as if she had been plunged into ice water. Her heart beat so fast it was almost painful.

Eleana!

Where was she? Left alone in the caverns patrolled by Haaar-kyut.

She sat up and found herself entirely alone in the center of a garden. It was, however, unlike any garden she had ever seen or heard spoken of. For one thing, it had the aspect of an oasis in the desert. That is to say, instead of an infinity of sand, all around it loomed the massive granite chambers of the Storehouse—dark, cyclopean, forbidding—grinding and moaning like ice floes to the subtle shifts of the tectonic plates out of which it had been hewn. For another thing, the entire scene was quite impossible. Honeyed sunlight filtered through smooth, curving tri-palm trees, the undersides of their deep green fronds gravid with nut-brown fruit. Flower-lined lawns stretched in every direction, crisscrossed by a formal grid of white-marble paths. At each intersection of the grid, water tinkled in snowflake obsidian fountains, each one breathtakingly carved into the shape of a colossal Venca rune. Gimnopedes swooped and flitted through the fronds, chasing each other in carefree fashion, following soft breaths of air sweet beyond comprehension.

Riane shook her head. First, the sudden loss of Eleana and now this impossible place all set her mind reeling. And then she remembered where she was. The Storehouse was the place she had been trying to get into ever since she had become the Dar Sala-at. The sacred repository where the Great Goddess Miina had ordained The Pearl must be kept. It was written in Prophecy that she would find The Pearl and lead all of Kundala to freedom and their ulti-mate destiny. Now, at long last, she was at the starting point, the place where Miina had cast down The Pearl af-ter the cabal of sauromicians had wrested control of it from Mother and, profaning the Holy of Holies, had gazed into its depths. She had a chance now to right those wrongs, to bring The Pearl back into Miina's White Light.

A sudden shadow, as of a hulking cloud passing before the white sun glare, caused her to turn. She saw the Hagoshrin. Its hideous head with its thick trunk and quest-ing tentacles was turned toward her. Its saucerlike eyes, with their eerie circle of pupils, were fixed on her. The vee slash of its mouth, half-obscured by the ciliated trunk with an obscene hole at the end, opened and closed in terrible silence.

Riane took an involuntary step back, and the Hagoshrin followed her, a movement made all the more menacing by its colossal bulk. She said, "Do you know who I am?"

"I know you." The Hagoshrin possessed a voice like a rasp abrading metal. It sent shivers down Riane's spine, it invaded her brain like a parasite, worming its way past all the psychic barriers she put up. "Do you know who *I* am?"

"You are the Hagoshrin that guards The Pearl. You almost killed me and my companion Eleana."

"That is what I am meant to do."

"You would not listen when I told you who I was."

"Over the centuries, all who have tried to enter this holy place have lied. All who have tried have failed. That was before the Storehouse Door opened for you. You told the truth. You are the Dar Sala-at." Its head shot forward with alarming speed, and its nostrils dilated quickly. "Yes. You are not on the surface whom you appear to be." The eyes squinted. "I discern in you V'ornnish traits. I see fire in your blood. I smell the scent of vengeance on your sweat."

Riane was startled. "You do not seem to be the monster legend paints."

"Legends are dangerous," the Hagoshrin said. "Like history they can be easily manipulated. After all, who is to gainsay those who remain to rewrite them to their own benefit. To the survivors the spoils."

Riane looked hard into the hideous face. It was a struggle not to let that terrible visage color her expectations of temperament and intellect. "This is not how I imagined you would be."

"It is best to have no expectation when facing the unknown." The Hagoshrin bared its enormous teeth, whether in laughter or in remorse, it was impossible to tell. "You are in the Garden of Law and Chaos. Here everything is in perfect balance—Darkness and Light, Good and Evil, Love and Hate, Order and Chaos. Those things that rely on imbalance are rendered inert. The Veil of a Thousand Tears, for instance."

Riane unwound the Veil from her waist. The Hagoshrin was right. No matter how much she tried she could not hear the voices of the Dragons whose tears were enmeshed in the sorcerous fabric of the Veil.

"A good lesson to be learned, Dar Sala-at. Do not overly rely on any single implement, sorcerous or otherwise. Rely rather on your wits."

Riane shook her head. Imagine getting advice from a Hagoshrin! Nevertheless, she knew that it would be well to take its advice to heart. Giyan had told her that the Hagoshrin spoke only the truth. But she was in a daemonically difficult situation. Eleana was alone in the caverns, and who knew where Thigpen had gotten to? Yet she had a responsibility here to fulfill her destiny and locate The Pearl.

As Riane rewound the Veil, the Hagoshrin said, "In the Time that was No-Time, before the Imagining when the Kundalan were born, Miina constructed this place by weaving the bourn lines together. The Garden of Law and Chaos is pure energy."

"A perfect place to store The Pearl," Riane said. "I am come now. Deliver to me The Pearl or lead me to where Miina hid it."

"As you wish, Dar Sala-at!"

The Hagoshrin bellowed so loudly that Riane clapped hands to her ears in a vain attempt to protect herself, for it spoke a Venca word, and there was no protection. It caused the entire garden to tremble. The sun winked out. What was left was a grey light, dim and occluded, filthy as sewage. A fearsome black sphere had formed that seemed all maw. The tri-palm fronds were bent low, their root balls sucked from the ground as they, along with the frolicking gimnopedes vanished into it. The lovely fountains frothed, disassembling. Their plashing water spewed in a thunderous cloudburst. The last vestiges of the magnificent garden was sucked whole cloth into the sphere of the Hagoshrin's powerful spellcasting.

The silence was oppressive, the darkness absolute. The stench of bitterroot took on a third dimension, a sharp-toothed rodent crawling through shadow. Livid bluish light bloomed in four corners, as if there existed within the sphere a cube of lambent energy.

Riane peered into the eerie semidarkness. "Where is it?"

"It will take a bit of time," the Hagoshrin said. "I am not as I once was. Your coming has freed me from this ac-cursed prison but not in the way I imagined. I am coming apart from the inside out. After eons beyond number the sorcery is unraveling."

"This has been your prison?"

The Hagoshrin snorted. "Do you think I would *willingly choose* to be locked away in this Goddess-forsaken fortress? No, no. I was promised all that I wished for—and then I was *tricked*, ensorceled, *burdened* with this agoniz-ing existence. For the love of Kundala, look what has be-come of me!"

"I would think guarding The Pearl would be an honor beyond measure."

"Ah, Dar Sala-at, how much you have yet to learn."

The Hagoshrin rolled the middle part of its ungainly torso over to reveal a huge navel. "Yes, there, you see, it is coming." From its depths, it plucked a sphere that glowed every color imaginable.

"The Pearl!" Riane whispered.

"Yes! The Holy of Holies. The granter of all wishes, the bringer of dreams, the one instrument of all power." The Hagoshrim offered it. "Here, then, is The Pearl."

It felt insubstantial, lighter than air. Riane's hands be-gan to tremble. Here she was on the brink of understand-ing, on the brink of fulfilling her destiny as the Dar Sala-at. With the Pearl she would lead a rebellion such as the V'ornn have never witnessed—the Resistance would rise up and, joined by the entire Kundalan population, throw off the V'ornn yoke and drive the aliens completely off Kundala.

"The Prophecies are true," she whispered. She could not control her trembling. There with her in spirit were Mother and Giyan and all the devout Ramahan who had died at the hands of the V'ornn and the sauromician traitors. All the pain and suffering she had endured, all that had been taken away from her, all the sacrifices she had made—everything made sense now as she saw her purpose taking form in front of her eyes. She was filled with elation and the prick of fear. Here was the moment of Transformation spoken of in both of Miina's sacred texts, *Utmost Source* and *The Book of Recantation*.

"What do the Prophecies say?" the Hagoshrin asked.

"That the Dar Sala-at will look into the depths of The Pearl and see the future of the Kundalan, that she will see the way to their salvation, the return to their former glory."

"Your moment is at hand," the Hagoshrin said. "Fulfill the Prophecy."

Riane stared into the sorcerous depths of The Pearl. At first she saw nothing, a swirl of colors, like pigments stirred in an artist's pot. Then, like a curtain of mist parting, she saw a scene. It was of an armada of ships— V'ornn ships—darkening the sky over the northern continent. As the ships descended through the atmosphere, a group of male Ramahan were seen emerging from Middle Palace, walking through the thronged streets of Axis Tyr to the North Gate. A contingent of V'ornn were already waiting to greet them as they passed through the gate. The V'ornn were unarmed. There were no hostilities, merely an exchange of greetings, then an exchange of cultural gifts.

Riane, stunned, looked up at the Hagoshrin, who was grinning from ear to ear.

"This isn't the future," she said in despair. "It isn't even the past. This isn't what happened."

"Indeed not. What you are seeing is precisely what the

cabal saw, what caused them to open the gates of Axis Tyr—of all Kundala, in fact—to the V'ornn."

Riane was shaking her head. "This cannot be. It is some ruse—"

"You are seeing what caused the Kundalan to be massacred and enslaved without even a modicum of a fight. They believed—because the cabal believed—that the V'ornn were benign. Is it any wonder that the remains of this cabal—the sauromicians—have turned away from Miina, will now fight to the death to destroy Her teachings and Her followers?"

"I do not believe you."

"I pity you, then, for you will remain deluded for the rest of your days. I am incapable of lying."

"Maybe you cannot lie," Riane said, "but surely you are capable of hiding the true Pearl you are sworn to protect."

"I am sworn to protect it, yes. But I am also sworn to deliver it into the hands of the Dar Sala-at. This I have done."

Riane felt as if she were plummeting down an endless shaft. Rage, confusion and despair all swirled inside her like the colors oozing across the surface of The Pearl.

"It cannot be true!"

"I assure you it is."

She thought of all she had been subjected to, coming near to death, Annon's essence ripped out of his body, rudely thrust into a Kundalan shell, healed by some sorcery she could not even now fathom. She thought of all she had been taught, all she had endured within the corrupt confines of the Abbey of Floating White. She was overcome by nausea and a mounting sense of dread.

"But Mother used The Pearl. She told me so."

"Mother saw what Miina wished her to see, no more and no less. Like everyone else, she was convinced that The Pearl was real. The deception had to be absolute in order to fool the sauromicians."

Riane felt Annon's rage—the male V'ornn that was part of her, wanting revenge, needing to slash and burn everything in sight. She clenched her fists, threw her head back, and screamed until her throat was raw and aching.

"I feel your pain," the Hagoshrin said.

"Like N'Luuura you do!" Riane stalked off.

In utter darkness, she stared into an infinity of nothingness. She felt as if she had been asleep for a long time, only to awake into a nightmare. She had trusted in Giyan, in Mother, the teachings of the Ramahan. In the Great Goddess Miina. Was nothing on this world what it appeared to be? She recognized hers as a V'ornn thought and was grateful, for she would need Annon's indomitable strength now more than ever. How grateful she was to be part of this new fused entity, now that the world was spinning around her at a speed and in an orbit entirely new to her. The question was how to proceed. Part of her—the part that was in despair, that was paralyzed with dread—wanted to do nothing more than curl up there in the darkness, go to sleep, and never wake up. Even so, she recognized that as a fantasy, flight from what seemed an unknowable and unknown future bereft of all the supports she had counted on.

She felt alone—and yet she was not alone. Behind her the Hagoshrin was waiting, and right now the creature was her only hope of going on. Because she knew that no matter how deep her despair and desperation went, she would go on. She could do nought else.

Seeing her reappear, the Hagoshrin said, "Yes, Dar Sala-at. It is much to absorb."

"That is an understatement." She was fighting to catch her breath, but she appreciated the Hagoshrin's empathy. "Why would Miina do this?"

"I am not a god. And, in any event, I never had the Goddess's ear."

"But I am written in Prophecy—"

"The Prophecies are the invention of the Five Sacred Dragons. They are spun from imagination, conjecture, wish fulfillment—the hubris of thinking one can control the skein of the future. The truth is that any sense of control is an illusion. One cannot *control* anything. The Cosmos is in entropy. It was born, it lives, and, like all of us who exist within its web, it will die. What any of us does or fails to do will not change it."

"This is insane. It is against everything I know or was taught."

"Think the process through, Dar Sala-at," the Hagoshrin said with infinite patience. "The Pearl was purported to be the source of the greatest power and, therefore, it became the lodestone for the greatest corruption. It was a means to cull from the ranks of the Ramahan all those who were corrupt. It was meant to draw them into a boil that in one stroke could be lanced, freeing the body of the faithful from the poison debilitating it. And Her ploy worked. The Pearl lured the sauromicians into the open."

"But beyond that it failed," Riane said. "Corruption still infiltrates the Ramahan."

"Even after the boil is lanced, there remains a smaller seepage of toxin—from the deepest levels, therefore the most virulent and dangerous—that requires extirpation."

She wanted to spit in the Hagoshrin's face, she wanted to believe that it was demented, but she could not. Everything it said explained so many otherwise unfathomable questions. She had never truly believed that Miina would have created The Pearl only to let it so easily fall into the hands of those who would become sauromicians. Slowly, she let go of the breath she had been holding.

"If you speak the truth, then who am I? Why was I created?"

"Ah, do not ask me for the meaning of life." There was an infinite sadness etched into the Hagoshrin's face. "I cannot even answer for my own poor soul."

"What you are saying is that everything I learned is a lie. I am not the savior of the Kundalan race, I will not be able to deliver them, and we are doomed to the living death to which the V'ornn have condemned us."

"Is that what I have said?"

"So much pain, so much suffering, deaths beyond count, misery beyond measure. Surely this cannot be the fate Miina would want for Her chosen."

"Her chosen betrayed Her and Her teaching."

"But to take such a drastic step . . ."

"Possibly drastic measures were called for. But if you wish an answer, perhaps that, too, will become part of your journey."

She was aware of a numbness setting in, akin to that which binds your flesh in cotton wool when first you are pierced by a weapon, a self-defense mechanism that allows you to fight on despite even a grievous wound. She sat for a long time saying nothing. Her mind seemed to have gone blank, and why not? Everything she believed in was called into question, everything she was so certain she would become was gone. She stared at The Pearl. A bauble, the Hagoshrin called it. It was nothing more than a holoscreen showing the same lies over and over. She opened her hands, and The Pearl dropped, bounced once, twice, then rolled along the ground until it vanished into the blackness of the sphere.

Riane looked up bleakly. "I don't know where to go, I don't know what to do."

"You are the one. Hold tight to your belief, Dar Sala-at, for that which remains after the boil has been lanced, the most virulent of the toxin, requires an agent—fearless, pure of heart—to destroy it utterly and for all time."

"But without The Pearl's power I am nothing."

"No. The Pearl is only an object. We do not better ourselves through objects. Without your belief in yourself you are nothing. This and this alone is what you must take away with you." A tentacle curled around her, almost tenderly. "And now you must marshal yourself, for there is a task at hand both vital and perilous. It involves the banestones."

She told it what Giyan and Sagiira had told her about banestones.

"The banestones, mined by daemons, were originally used in Za Hara-at. They powered the great engine that staved off the destruction of Kundala. After the crisis was averted, Za Hara-at was deemed too powerful to remain intact. By sledgehammer and sorcery it was dismantled, the banestones scattered, buried, so none could reharness their power.

"But someone has. The sauromicians."

"The information you were given is correct. They have eight. They are searching for the ninth."

"Why? What do they mean to do?"

"They are building the Cage of Nine Banestones, for once the nine are linked their power becomes steady, accurate, immense. They will be able to open the Portals to the Abyss and free the daemons. They have already made a pact with the archdaemon Pyphoros. With the daemons and the nine banestones they will be able to resurrect the great weapon of Za Hara-at. They will annihilate those who have sought to destroy them—the Ramahan. Then they will enslave all those who remain on Kundala."

"If I had The Pearl, if it actually existed, I would be able to stop them."

"You must forget that line of thinking, Dar Sala-at. It will only lead to despair."

"What other path have I now?"

"I do not know. But whatever it is you must discover it inside yourself."

"Will you help me?"

"I will try. I have located one of your companions. At least, she says she is your companion."

Riane's heart leapt. "Eleana?"

And out of the darkness popped Thigpen.

"Thank you for that overwhelming greeting," she sniffed as she shook out her fur.

"Thigpen!" Riane knelt down, embraced the Rappa. Briefly, she outlined what had befallen her and Eleana after the mishap on the stairs. Then she turned to the

Hagoshrin. "But what about Eleana, the female who was with me earlier. She was left outside the Storehouse Door when—"

"She is of interest to you, Dar Sala-at?"

"She is my beloved."

The Hagoshrin's hideous head moved from side to side. "I am afraid she is not where you left her."

"Where is she, then? Do you know?"

"She is in the hands of the regent."

"Kurgan!" Riane cried. "How could you let her be—"

"Even if I had known she was your beloved, I would have not been able to save her. The regent has the ninth banestone."

"You knew where the ninth banestone was all along?"

"Of course."

She ran her hands through her hair. "Why didn't you tell me this before?"

The creature shuddered. "Banestones can kill Hagoshrin."

"You have got to get us to Kurgan. Who knows what he means to do with her?"

"Ah, Kurgan Stogggul," the Hagoshrin said, nodding. "He loves her, you know."

Riane's heart skipped a beat, and she felt a sickness in her belly. "What do you say?"

"Foolishly, recklessly, absolutely."

Riane felt as if all the breath had been knocked out of her. "Kurgan loves Eleana?" Riane's thoughts raced back to the golden afternoon when Annon and Kurgan had come upon her bathing in a sylvan creek. "But he only met her once."

"Who can explain love?"

"This is a nightmare. Kurgan raped Eleana. She hates and fears him. You must help me rescue her and get the banestone."

"As you wish." The Hagoshrin uttered three words in Venca and Riane shivered as a current went through her.

The lights winked out, the black sphere was gone. They were in the garden again. Gimnopedes twittered as they darted here and there.

"A word of warning," the Hagoshrin said. "Should we succeed, Kurgan Stogggul will stop at nothing to get her back. You must understand fully the implications of what I say, Dar Sala-at, and act accordingly."

"Fine, fine," Riane said, as she stooped to wake Thigpen.

A tentacle rose and wrapped itself gently around Riane's wrist, making her turn.

"You cannot allow Kurgan Stogggul to see you, Dar Sala-at," the Hagoshrin said gravely. "For if he does, he will hunt you down and kill you."

Riane took a deep breath, her heart beating fast. "I understand. Let's get on with it before—"

"Before I die?" The Hagoshrin laughed dryly. "Yes, yes, best we hurry then."

Amid the humid, ghostly whispered warren of chambers, halls, loggia, oculi, and other ornate unfathomable abandoned spaces that stretched beyond the regent's quarters was a bedchamber. It had ceased to be lived in the moment the V'ornn had arrived and dragged the Ramahan from their lair. In the years since then, it had remained forgotten, unlooted, and unexplored.

It was a round chamber, turretlike, with walls of pale-veined marble into which, at intervals, were sunk a series of voluptuous black-onyx columns. Still and all, it had about it an air not only of desolation but of desiccation and death, which made the high, domed ceiling even more astonishing. On it had been painted a large and elaborate nightlily. It was an exquisitely wrought single-stemmed flower with eight swordlike petals. In its center was a clutch of five slender stamens, ruddy as the Kundalan sun, the anthers at their tips the purest cadmium yellow. How something so *alive* could exist in this musty wilderness was a mystery that would not let him go. There was some-

thing intensely erotic about the nightlily, which as de-
picted was both phallic and softly, dewily open. Though
Kurgan would hardly admit it, even to himself, there was
something intensely attractive as well as repulsive about
the duality.

It was there that he took Eleana, laying her on a vast bed
whose purpose could only be guessed at. He climbed upon
the bed to the fluttering of a century of dust, the senescent
wings of extinct birds. For an eternity he did nothing but
sit on his haunches and watch her face. He was in an agony
of longing. He had dreamed of this moment for more than
a year, could hardly believe it had arrived.

Simply by her existence there the entire bedchamber
had come alive, the marble and onyx gleaming where before they had been dull with dust. The room pulsed with
the triple beat of his hearts, with the rhythmic drumbeat
of blood through his arteries, its ebb and flow through his
veins. Each piece of furniture—tiered tables, deep chairs,
sensual lounges, all in threes—were florid, filigreed, fres-
coed, feverish even for the Kundalan. Light filtered down
from cleverly hidden niches to provide a softly diffuse illumination that overlaid the bedchamber like a diaphanous gown. Now with her there it seemed clear that
the space had been designed for amorous trysts, not religious asceticism. Doubtless, that was why he had first
been drawn to it, why he continued to come back. And
yet, he had felt enjoined from revealing it to anyone else,
including the parade of Looorm, who almost nightly
shared his bed. At last he knew why.

He wanted Eleana, and only Eleana, there.

His hands dug into his thigh muscles so hard the pain finally penetrated his half stupor. He felt drugged, slow-
witted, and dull. All the things he needed to do were swept
away by the indelible fact of her presence. He was
stunned. He wept at his inability to think clearly, and was
shaken by a sudden murderous rage.

With an inchoate cry, he closed his hands around her

neck. His fingers seemed seared by the first contact with her flesh, and his face turned lupine, feral, his nostrils flaring as they filled with her ravishing rosaceous ruinous odor. He was possessed by a throbbing, as of thunder overflowing distant dells. He felt as if he must explode. Instead, his fingers tightened on her windpipe.

Her chest heaved, and she began to choke. He forced himself to pretend that the rippled cartilage beneath the gently veined silken skin of her throat was the stock of an ion cannon.

Her face had turned very white, and she was thrashing. He bent over and pressed his feverish lips to hers, hard enough that he could feel her bared teeth, the life soughing out of her with each beat of her heart. He wanted to possess her and to kill her. He desired her, and he despised her, both beyond measure. His brain was clotted with bloodlust and desire. He wept and called her name. Had he been another kind of V'ornn he might have prayed for deliverance.

In any event, deliverance arrived. His okummmon activated, the telltale tingling running up his right arm, increasing in intensity until, centimeter by centimeter, it led him back from the precipice on which he had been precariously balanced.

He was being Summoned.

Out loud, he cursed the interruption, but as he withdrew his hands, as he crawled off the huge bed and before exiting the bedchamber, he remembered to place the small milky alabaster box on a heavily filigreed table next to where she lay.

He made his way back through the labyrinth into a smallish atrium whose faraway ceiling was pierced by an oculus. He stood for a moment in a shaft of dun-colored sunlight. The thick, dusty illumination that could have belonged to any time of day seemed with its unnatural weight to penetrate clear through him.

He stepped nimbly out of the light and turned the

searchlight of his brain onto other matters. He thought of the banestone hidden like a seed in the alabaster box he had placed beside the bed. The banestone had proved its worth. The Nieobean paralysis gel would not wear off for another eighteen hours. By then surely he would have decided whether to take her or kill her. Either way, she was his.

By the time he had returned to his suite, he was in full command of all his faculties. Just as well, since Nith Nassam was already there. His taloned arms were crossed over his chest. His biocircuit horns were fulminating orange and red as he stood, spread-legged, turning the wall of weapons impotent.

"What have you learned about Courion?" he growled without preamble.

"Nothing as yet. These things are delicate. They take time."

"I am not interested in excuses."

Kurgan had but an instant to decide which tack to take. "Since you have not climbed into the Kalllistotos ring with the Sarakkon as I have, let me explain something to you. They are a deeply suspicious race. It took me a long time just to get them to acknowledge me, let alone allow me into their company. I cannot simply ask them the questions you seek answers to. I gain their trust ever so gently. One false move will sever my connection with them forever. I know you cannot want that."

"You have no idea what I want." Nith Nassam slowly, ominously, unwound his arms. Ion arcs sparked from the tips of his clawed, alloyed gloves. "Know that I have no tolerance for slackers or dissemblers. Nevertheless, in this matter and this matter alone I am willing to give you the benefit of the doubt." He pointed. "Do try my patience, however. Answers must be forthcoming soon."

Kurgan, who now had his own reasons for ensuring the process met with quick success, said, "I understand completely, Nith Nassam. Rest assured that I will have information for you before the week is out."

14

Deceptions

Leyytey, Fleet-Admiral Ardus Pnin's daughter, looked nothing like him. She was small and dark-eyed, but as determined as he ever was. As a little girl, she worshiped him, absorbed every word he uttered to her. Tried her best to please him. He made her laugh, he terrified her, it felt to her that when he walked all Kundala trembled. And then one day when she was sixteen she discovered the truth about him. On the day he lost both his sons at Hellespennn, he mercilessly cursed the twist of fate that had left him with only a daughter. Leyytey's face went white, and she could scarcely breathe. Panicked, she looked to her mother, whose eyes, cast down, refused to meet hers. Her father, made temporarily mad by the death of his sons, continued to rail against her because he could not bring himself to utter one bad word about his dead sons.

She revealed nothing of that in her public life, of course. With the fatalistic conviction of a Khagggun, she could not help believing that his periodic visits to the workshops where she learned her art and later to her own atelier, was for him a kind of perverse self-punishment. And yet, for all that, she could not turn her back on him, could not cut him out of her life. Each time she saw him, however, she was racked with anguish.

And so, toward evening, at the end of her long day, when she saw him stride into her atelier, she was buffeted by these familiar vicious crosscurrents. If she had been born a male like her brothers, she would be standing by his

side, proud and armor-clad, seeking his sage advice before
going to war. She almost never thought of her brothers, but
they sometimes appeared in her dreams as floating faces
with disembodied voices. Often, she was trying to say
something to them, but they could not hear her and, when
she awoke she retained no memory of what she might have
been trying to say to them. They were dead. What was
there to say, anyway? What had she ever said to them—or
they to her—before they had flown off to be ground up in
the jaws of the Centophennni?

She fixed her father in the corner of her eye, watching
him the way a Khagggun would look at a timed fusion
bomb. The irony was that because of her avocation she
knew more ways to take life violently than most Khagggun. The knowledge was a necessity in order for her to design and forge the finest weapons and armor.

As was his wont, Fleet-Admiral Ardus Pnin stood unobtrusively against a wall, hands clasped behind his back.
His curious golden eyes, almost all pupil, watched everything at once. The sight of his merciless scrutiny reduced
her to nothing.

His gaze pierced the gloom of the atelier, alighting only
for an instant on Pack-Commander Teww Dacce, standing
spread-legged in one of the trial booths, testing the new
ion mace Leyytey had made for him. Pnin took a deep
breath and, for the time being, put Dacce out of his mind.

He was fascinated by the cleverly articulated suits of armor. Lit by pools of bronze light, they revolved slowly as
if dancing to an unheard beat. He deeply appreciated the
feel of Leyytey's blades in his hand, the balance perfect to
use sword tip for thrusting or razor edge for slashing, the
heft ideal for cleaving skulls. He liked to watch her agile
fingers, lit by the bright purple sparks from her ion anvil,
stained copper by the metallurgical seeds of her art.

All this remained locked inside his head, theoretical as a
Gyrgon experiment. Child of his she might be, but she was
Tuskugggun. What Leyytey could not know was that deep
down in the shadows of his soul, he possessed no tools for

understanding her. Ever since she had produced her first schematic for a shock-sword at a preternaturally early age, he had not known what to make of her. If she had the mind of a Khagggun, then why in Enlil's accursed name could she not have been born one?

The air cracked and sparked, brittle as mica. It was acrid with ozone and other trace chemicals. Lit by the crimson flames of her ion forge, they began in short sentences, awkward and stilted, that proved them strangers to themselves as well as to one another.

"Daughter, business is good, I see." He hefted a magnificent shock-sword, newly forged, not yet shipped to the Temple of Mnemonics, where it would be ion-charged by Gyrgon. With an expert eye, he assessed the perfect alignment of the twin blades.

"Getting better all the time, Fleet-Admiral." His ion-bound law dictated that she address him formally.

Pnin nodded.

"Miirlin misses you. He does not understand why you turned him out of your villa."

"It will take time for my grandson to learn everything he needs to know."

"Less time than either of us think. He is extremely precocious, surprising his mentors at every turn." Leyytey had mated and bred because she had heard her father say many times that the good warrior lays down his bloody sword long enough to ensure the future of his line. She had cared little for her mate, but his genomic profile was excellent and, in any event, he was her father's choice for her. Involuntarily, her gaze passed over Pack-Commander Dacce, remembering the fleeting furnace of their frenzied mating. After that, nothing. The fire that had flared so brightly had been banked by a surfeit of indifference, though not from her.

"That is good. When Miirlin is of age I will make him into a great Khaggqun leader." The weapon resounded with a proper pure, clean note as he tested it. "Have an heir to continue my line, my work."

Leyytey reacted to this backhand rebuke with a furious blush that was thankfully lost in the rubicund glow. All she had ever wanted was his approval. She felt defeated by circumstance, by the inescapable prison of her gender, the reflection that leered back at her each morning when she stood naked and helpless before the mirror in her bedroom. She wanted to turn away, to look at anything but his intimidating face, so she willed herself to gaze into his cold golden eyes.

"I want Miirlin to be safe."

"I will keep him safe."

"And who will keep you safe, Fleet-Admiral?" To his surprised look, she said; "Isn't that why you placed him back in the hingatta?"

"Willfulness ill becomes a Tuskugggun!" His raised voice was enough to turn the heads of her assistants, who crept, silent and cowed, into the shadows.

Still she would not look away. "I have heard disturbing rumors of late."

He stared stonily at her.

"Rumors that the new Star-Admiral is disbanding the high command."

Pnin's gaze did not flicker. "Pack-Commander Dacce's tongue has been wagging."

"Well? Is it true?"

"He is simply trying to frighten you."

"In that case, he's done a fairly good job of it."

Grasping the shock-sword in a two-handed grip, Fleet-Admiral Pnin held it up so that the blades threw darts of reflected light into the air between them. "I want this weapon."

"No." She took it from him. "It was made for a smaller Khaggggun, one less powerful than you. The balance is all wrong, for one thing."

"Change it," Pnin said. "Change whatever you have to. Make it mine."

Leyytey set the shock-sword down. "As you wish, Fleet-Admiral."

She was about to take her hand away when he put his over it. She looked up into his face, and he leaned in, lowering his voice.

"Not all I wish."

"Another weapon?"

He shook his head. "You must do something for me. Something extremely important." He drew her away, into a corner where the livid light from the ion forge could not reach them. "There is trouble brewing of a most serious nature."

She could not keep the flash of fear out of her eyes. "Fleet-Admiral—"

Pnin put his forefinger across her half-parted lips. "In due course the threat will be dealt with. This I swear. But you must do as I tell you."

Leyytey's body vibrated as if it were a Kundalan bow from which an arrow had just been loosed. "Whatever you ask of me I will do it. You know that." Her father had never asked anything of her.

His eyes raked her face. "It will require all of your discretion, as well as a great deal of guile."

Her eyes watched his carefully.

He drew her farther into the shadows. "It involves Pack-Commander Dacce."

There was an almost painful constriction in her chest. "Please continue."

"Are you certain?"

She nodded, for the moment not trusting herself to speak.

"Tell him you are going to work for the Prime Factor—"

She felt a stab of terror, as if a nightmare she had had as a child had finally come true, as if a stalker from her past had emerged from the shadows to grab her by the throat. "Why?" she said, rather wildly. "Why the Prime Factor? Why, of all Bashkir, the SaTrryn?"

"Tell him in a manner he will not deem suspicious. Tell him that Sornnn SaTrryn has offered you a great deal of coins—more than he could ever imagine."

"A Bashkir hiring me? I doubt he would believe me."

"This story has about it the advantage of being absolutely true," Pnin said. "He knows the SaTrryn livelihood is wrapped up in the spice trade. The Five Tribes of the Korrush are on war footing. Dacce may or may not already know that, it does not matter, because he will find it easy to confirm. Dacce will understand that Sornnn SaTrryn needs to protect the Rasan Sul. The Khagggun will not step in, of course, so what is his other recourse? Arm them himself."

"Fleet-Admiral, how is this—?"

"Listen." Pnin's grip on his daughter tightened and his voice lowered to a harsh whisper. "Less you know the better."

"Doubtless you would tell Miirlin your plan, though he is only nine."

"N'Luuura take it, daughter, will you do it?"

She longed to tell him that she would do anything to help protect him, but she knew he would despise her for saying it, would despise her even more if he should ever learn . . . Her mind shied away from the dire consequences. No, he never would, she would see to that. Ever the good daughter, she said, "I hate Iin Mennus and all he stands for."

The ghost of a smile briefly played across Fleet-Admiral Pnin's lips. "Your filial devotion is noted."

Cocooned within the jellified body of the Hagoshrin, Riane and Thigpen were transported through the labyrinthine substructure of the regent's palace with almost frightening ease. Though the beast was immense, it had a facility for reshaping itself and squeezing insectlike around corners, through echoing air shafts and into musty utility ducts unknown even to most of the Ramahan who had previously inhabited Middle Palace.

"I like this not," Thigpen said testily.

What she didn't like, Riane thought, was that she had

been unconscious during crucial moments and therefore useless.

As if to confirm this suspicion, she added, "I fear this Hagoshrin is as crazy as a sunstroked claiwen. How do we know that it will not crush us on a whim."

"It could just as easily have killed you as rendered you unconscious," Riane pointed out, as the Hagoshrin whipped and slithered into the palace's living quarters. "And, for the record, it is not mad."

"How else would you describe something that insists The Pearl does not exist!"

"I showed you The Pearl."

Thigpen bared her very sharp teeth. "That wasn't The Pearl. I don't know what it was. The Pearl has been lost. Miina cast it out of the Storehouse."

When Riane did not answer, Thigpen said, "What is the matter with you? You will now take the word of a beast who has been incarcerated for millennia? That would drive even a Rappa mad!"

"Giyan said that the Hagoshrin doesn't lie," Riane said sternly. "It is not mad, either."

Thigpen fidgeted for a bit "What's the point, then? Without the promise of The Pearl to save us we are doomed."

Riane who had been in despair ever since she had looked into The Pearl, felt overburdened. She could not take on the Rappa's despair also. She tried to keep in her mind the Hagoshrin's warning to hold fast to her belief that she was the one. But what was the point? Without The Pearl, all Kundalan were doomed. She would not, however, give vent to her pessimism.

"The point is life," she said, trying to convince herself as well as Thigpen. "The point is to go on, no matter what."

"But without The Pearl how will we ever defeat the V'ornn?"

I have no idea, Riane thought. *And that is the problem.*

"I can sense her," the Hagoshrin said, interrupting them. It had slowed to a crawl. "I can scent Eleana as I can scent you, Dar Sala-at, but even could I not, I would have been able to find her. There are three places in Middle Palace that Kurgan Stogggul uses for his private meetings. He confers with the Gyrgon in his weapons chamber, he takes his Looorm to what were the old wash chambers, and he goes by himself to the nightlily bedchamber. That is where he has taken Eleana."

"Is she all right?" Riane asked anxiously. "Can you tell if he has harmed her in any way?"

"I doubt that he has," the Hagoshrin said. It sniffed disdainfully. "He is not much of a regent, you know. Despises the daily tasks, leaves them to his underlings. He will come to ruin over that oversight, mark me."

"If you can foretell the future," Thigpen said rather nastily, "tell us what we will do without The Pearl."

They were tossed around by the Hagoshrin's chuckle. "Tell her, Dar Sala-at."

Riane related how, according to the Hagoshrin, no one could foretell the future.

"No?" Thigpen said with a fierce grin. "Then how do you explain the Ramahan seers?"

"They are like small boats tossed in high seas," the Hagoshrin said. "Once in a while, at the crest of a wave, they may get a glimpse of an onrushing storm. But which storm? There are many realities, many futures. Which one will come to pass? That is the question they cannot answer. Seeing all those futures, the chaos of possibilities, is what eventually drives them mad."

Thigpen clamped her jaws shut and growled deep in her throat. "All you Hagoshrin, you never liked the Dragons, were jealous of their rank and status, coveted their power. But then what else could you expect," she sneered, "from a creature that eats the bones of Kundalan?"

The Hagoshrin winced. "Why is that always thrown up in my face? Is it my fault? Who made me this way? Miina, the Great Goddess. If I am a horror, it is She who must answer for it. I can no more change how I get my nourishment than you can."

"There is more than this one Hagoshrin?" Riane asked as much for her own curiosity as to put an end to their contentious colloquy.

"What made you think there was only one?" Thigpen said. "Have you ever heard of a race consisting of a single being?"

"Then where are the others?"

Both the Hagoshrin and the Rappa shook their heads mutely, and, in silence, they continued their snaking travels through the bowels of the palace.

The keening sounded like death. The ion mace made the eerie sound as Pack-Commander Teww Dacce swung it. The sound was peculiar to the ion-maces forged by Leyytey, owing to the composite construction of the ball. Other armorers had tried to copy her design; all had failed.

"I trust it is to your satisfaction," Leyytey said, coming up beside Dacce.

He did not look at her; he swung harder, the keening rising in pitch. Then he lashed out with his arm, and the ball struck the wall, splintering lathe, plaster, and brickwork.

"It will do," he said.

"I will have to charge Iin Mennus for the damage."

"I will pay for it," he said quickly. Mennus would not pay for it. He would dock Dacce the coinage, dress him down in public, and never let him forget it.

Leyytey peered at the extent of the damage. "You cannot afford it."

"I will pay it off over time," he said shortly.

She shrugged. "It does not matter, really. I am closing my business to the trade."

"What?"

For the first time he looked at her, and she felt a little shiver run down between her breasts. He had always made her feel like that, from the moment they had first met.

When he had abandoned her and Miirlin she had been ill
for a month. The first night, she had wanted to ram one of
her own shock-swords through her gut. She might have,
but for her son. It got better after that, but not much. Not a
day went by that she did not miss him. When they were together she felt complete, competent, serene. She had slept
deeply and dreamlessly in the crook of his arm. Her empty
bed howled at night.

"I have been offered an exclusive contract." She told
him the story her father had given her.

"Work for the SaTrryn? For a *Bashkir* house? That is
incredible."

"Only inevitable," she said.

"Inevitable? Why?"

Then she told him how much the SaTrryn was paying
her and all the breath went out of him. It was interesting to
see the change in him, and she exulted in the effect of her
words. Maybe now he would pay more attention to her.
Maybe now she could win him back.

Maybe she was right because he asked her to dinner.

It was a mixed blessing because he took her to Off-
world, a restaurant on the third floor overlooking the
Promenade and the Sea of Blood. It was one of the few
places that had not been taken over from a Kundalan establishment. The building had once been a warehouse, but
a Bashkir family had turned it into a club downstairs and a
two-tiered restaurant upstairs. It was difficult to get into,
but not for a ranking member of the new Star-Admiral's
staff. It was also the restaurant where they had dined the
night before he had walked out on her, so as with everything surrounding Teww Dacce it tasted bittersweet. There
were fresh wildflowers on the table and not a chronosteel
chair or table in sight.

Lights along the Promenade glittered on the water, on
the sleek hulls of Sarakkon ships. The Sarakkon themselves, tall, slender, their gleaming skin russet as a sunset
in winter seemed like living art with their bejeweled
beards and tattooed skulls. The calls of the fishers, the rau-

cous sounds of the tavern patrons, the roars of the crowd out for blood at the nearby Kalllistotos ring wafted in waves like mist, mingling with the fragrant smoke from the restaurant's open-air grill.

Dacce wanted to know what she had been doing, and he was so attentive that for a time she could deceive herself into believing that things could change between them. But after a time, when it was clear that he was not going to ask her about Miirlin, she looked down at their fingers laced together and tried to accept the truth. It was the coinage she had come into to which he was drawn. She excused herself, stumbled through the low-lit restaurant to the washrooms, where she locked herself in a stall and wept so bitterly she thought her hearts would shatter. The worst part was that she still loved him, fiercely, deeply, sadly. It was as if the more he removed himself from her, the more she loved him. She banged her head against the stall door. How could she possibly be so perverse? But was it perverse to believe that love could conquer everything, that it could turn a seemingly shallow, self-interested Khaggun into a decent V'ornn? For the hope had not yet died that beneath his emotional armor beat the hearts of a male as capable as she was of kindness, love, and devotion. And she was sure that she and only she possessed the key to unlock that armor, to reveal the true Teww Dacce behind that alloy-hard reserve.

She returned to find that he had ordered them drinks, forgetting completely that she did not touch anything fermented. When she reminded him, he told her not to worry. He drank both, one after the other, so quickly it took her breath away. He had begun to drink like this in the weeks before he left her.

And that was how the evening went. She ate, and he drank. He seemed not to be interested in food at all, and he did not appreciate her trying to feed him. He complained bitterly about his position, about how Iin Mennus did not appreciate his skills. He bemoaned his lack of coinage, and she patiently listened, hoping against hope that the conversation would move on. But it did not; and, with a sadness she could not express, she saw it happening all over again, the old dynamic between them returning, unchanged, like a rubber band that snaps back no matter how wide it is pulled. And at last she realized how it was going to be, that it did not matter whether or not he loved her—or even if he was capable of loving her—because eventually he would leave her again, as surely as night followed day.

How then he ended up in her bed, how she ended up crawling all over him, pouring out her need, her pain, her love she never quite understood. She only knew that after a feverish night of nonstop lovemaking that held her for hours quivering and ecstatic in its thrall, she awoke in the ash-grey light of predawn to find him gone.

She had risen from sleep to put her arms around him, found instead bedcovers stained with their mingled secretions. Grabbing handfuls, she had pressed them against her nose, inhaling the scent of him, the last of him, and could not bear to part with it. Tears welled up, unbidden, staining her cheeks even as she wondered how he could be so cruel, how he could have left, stealing away in the night, after what they had shared. What, after all, could it have meant to him?

And she exhaled a heartsrending sob. She gathered herself to hate him, but only wound up wanting him more.

"There is a problem," the Hagoshrin said.

They were jammed in an air duct clogged with soot, ash, and the smell of burnt flesh that seemed baked into the walls. How many Ramahan had died in the initial onrush of the Khaggun attack on Middle Palace? It seemed as if even the screams of the dying had been trapped there, distorting the echoes of their voices.

"You are Hagoshrin," Thigpen said shortly. "Fix it."

"Eleana is being guarded."

"How many Haaar-kyut?" Riane asked.

"The regent's guards would pose little problem, if there were any, which there aren't." The Hagoshrin's voice had taken on a dark, morose tone. "She is being guarded by a sigil of evil."

"And what would that be?" Thigpen said skeptically. Riane could tell she still thought the beast half-mad.

"Dar Sala-at, I do not know how better to say this, but it is a banestone."

"A banestone!" Thigpen cried so loudly that Riane admonished her to keep her voice down.

"How in Miina's name did a V'ornn come into possession of a banestone!" Thigpen was so agitated that her whiskers were twitching madly.

"*How* is meaningless," the Hagoshrin said. "What matters is that it has become attuned to Eleana."

"What does that mean?" Riane asked quietly and firmly. She had a specific mission to accomplish. She was starting to feel in control again.

"That we are already at risk," Thigpen said nervously.

"The Rappa is correct, Dar Sala-at." The Hagoshrin craned its neck, somehow managing to shove its head through the aperture. "Time is of the essence." Its voice came back to them as if from a distant dimension. "Rescuing Eleana has become secondary."

"What?" Riane could not believe what she was hearing.

"It is the ninth banestone, Dar Sala-at," the beast said. "The one that will complete the Cage, the one that will kill Seelin. We must gain control of it, destroy it if we have to."

Thigpen snorted. "There is no way to destroy a banestone."

The Hagoshrin lifted a curved yellow claw. "Ah, but there is. It must be taken into Otherwhere and there cast into the mouth of the white dragon."

"Whose Avatar is that?" Riane asked.

"It is a shared thing and so both more and less than other Avatars," the Hagoshrin said. "It belongs to the archdaemon Pyphoros and his three children."

"We defeated them," Riane said. "I sent Pyphoros back to the Abyss at Za Hara-at."

"And yet the white dragon still sails through Otherwhere. I know. I have seen him."

"You have the ability to Thrip?" Thigpen said. "I did not know—"

"There are many things you Rappa do not know about us." The Hagoshrin sniffed.

"Enough of this." Riane began to squirm her way toward the elongated neck of the creature. "You will retrieve the banestone while I fetch Eleana."

She was brought up short as a tentacle wrapped itself around her waist. "You do not understand." The Hagoshrin's stinking muzzle had turned back to the aperture of the air shaft. "I cannot touch the banestone. It is the one thing—"

"Then you get Eleana, and I will go after the banestone."

The Hagoshrin heaved a sigh, slithering its bulk through the aperture. Riane followed it, levering herself out into the palace corridor—a dark and airless place she guessed must be one of the myriad service hallways that honeycombed the palace's living quarters.

Over the undulating body of the Hagoshrin Riane caught a glimpse of Eleana in the nightlily bedchamber onto which this end of the corridor debouched, and her heart felt squeezed within her breast. She could barely breathe, and there was a roaring in her ears.

She was on her way toward the bed when she heard an explosion so close by it knocked them against the corridor wall, and the Hagoshrin began to scream.

Kurgan, on the run, grabbed the ion cannon out of his bodyguard's grip and waved him and another tense Haaar-kyut off. Had they not became inured to this regent's peculiar whims, they would have flanked him anyway; but neither wanted the public dressing-down and humiliating loss of rank that would be a sure consequence.

As he flew down the corridors, moving deeper and deeper into his residence wing, he was glad to be alone.

No one had seen him bring Eleana up from the nether regions of the palace, and he wanted no such observers now.

The banestone was tolling—an ominous sound in the center of his mind. It was, however, as clear as any Khaggun clarion call to battle.

He saw a noxious Kundalan creature crouched over Eleana as he entered the bedchamber, and he flipped up the photon rangefinder, took a preliminary reading, and shot from the hip. The thing was so big he could hardly have missed even if he were stone drunk.

The blast disintegrated a large patch of cilia that covered much of the beast's seemingly shapeless body. It threw its head back and roared. Kurgan came on, shooting without aiming properly, still believing, despite the mounting evidence, that the ion cannon could put a hole in the thing.

It had Eleana wrapped in one of its tentacles, and Kurgan kept his fire away from her. But another tentacle shot out and slammed him back against the far wall of the bedchamber. Half-dazed, he raised the ion cannon to deliver a blast directly into the beast's face, but the accursed tentacle lashed out, spoiling his aim. Then the tip of it wrapped itself around the barrel of the weapon.

Kurgan was dragged forward, smashed into a chair, overturning it. One leg splintered, flew across to the table on which sat the alabaster box. The table canted over, the box slid off, and Kurgan let go of the ion cannon, leaping and twisting to cradle the box against his chest. His momentum rolled him over into the side of the bed. The lid of the alabaster box popped open, and, as if having a mind of its own, the banestone rolled into his hand.

It felt at once hot and cold. A kind of liquid flowed through him, and he rose, holding the banestone before him, scrambling over the rumpled bed on his knees.

The beast had retreated, taking Eleana with it. How it had found her, he had no idea. But of one thing he was absolutely certain, he was not going to allow it to take her

from him. He was abruptly overcome with a rage that
commanded him to hurl the banestone at the beast. He
cocked his arm back.

"Stop!" the beast cried in alarm.

Kurgan did not know whether he was more surprised
that it could talk or that it was afraid of the banestone, but
its fear was what he homed in on. He threw the banestone
directly at it.

The Hagoshrin was dying. It had felt the life force
draining out of it even before it came to the place
where Kurgan Stogggul had secreted Eleana. Its dying had
progressed. The deliquescing, the warmth that had run
through it, was gone, overridden by a certain sluggishness
of foot, a shortness of breath. That was followed by a terrible systemic weakness. It was so debilitating, in fact, that
by the time Kurgan fired at it, the sting of the ion blast reverberated through its corpus. The stench of its own hair
burning made it nearly faint. Stupid to have attempted this
rescue with death so near, with the terrible danger the
banestone represented. It had tried to tell the Dar Sala-at
the truth about the banestone, although not very forcefully.
The truth was it could not bear to disappoint the Dar Sala-
at, not after the awful shock it had given her. The
Hagoshrin had been astonished by its fondness for the Dar
Sala-at. Odd. Never during the centuries of incarceration
had it ever imagined such a thing. And then there was that
damnable Rappa! It did not want to appear weak in front
of her, not with her already lowly opinion of Hagoshrin.
The Rappa were a clever race, but their weakness was their
hubris, their annoying sense of superiority.

These ruminations, typical of the time just preceding
death, were what made it hesitate, and the hesitation was
fatal. Before it could react—indeed, if it could have effectively reacted at all in its debilitated state—the banestone
struck it square on the forehead. The Hagoshrin went
down as if poleaxed, and lay upon the dusty floor, staring
up at the great mural of the nightlily in its overgrown,

feverish garden. Eleana lay insensate within the cradle of
one tentacle and, becoming once again aware of this, the
Hagoshrin attempted to haul its disgusting bulk up and
make for the air shaft in the corridor. It wasn't so far away,
that dim aperture. And yet, it seemed to be on the other
side of Kundala. Oh, the agony the banestone had inflicted
on him, and now it lay close. The Hagoshrin could feel it
pulsing, feeding, growing in power.

Kurgan Stogggul was scrambling across the floor in
search of the ion cannon still weakly clutched in the
Hagoshrin's other tentacle. The Hagoshrin tried to move it
out of the way, but it saw Kurgan withdraw a thin,
triangular-bladed dagger and, reversing it in his fist, stab
down so that it slit the tentacle down the middle.

Pain lanced through the Hagoshrin, and more of its life
force leached away. Still, it held stubbornly to the ion cannon, while Kurgan tried to jerk the weapon free. If only the
Dar Sala-at understood what the Hagoshrin was doing. If
only the Dar Sala-at would use the Veil of a Thousand
Tears to protect her from the effects of the banestone, for
if she touched it with her bare hands as Kurgan Stogggul
had . . .

The Hagoshrin shuddered as Riane shot across its flank
on her way toward the banestone. It tried to voice a warning, but all that came out of its V-shaped mouth was an unintelligible croak. *To die like this*, it thought, *a hideous
beast, where is the justice in that?*

Riane broke into a sprint at the Hagoshrin's cry of pain.
She had been witness to everything that had transpired, and now she raced down the corridor and into the
bedchamber. Without waiting to assess fully the situation,
she struggled across the Hagoshrin's supine bulk and there
she came face-to-face with Kurgan Stogggul. The regent
looked at her, and recognition flooded his face.

"You," he grated through clenched teeth.

The banestone lay to the right of Riane, dark and evil-
looking. A vibration rippled through the Veil of a Thou-

sand Tears, a kind of reflexive shudder. Riane could hear the voices of the Dragons wailing in her mind, warning her. She still harbored the hope that she could get the bane-stone and save Eleana. She took one step toward the bane-stone, but at that moment the Hagoshrin's strength gave out, and Kurgan wrenched the ion cannon out of its grip.

There was no time for thought, for logic. Riane, reacting on pure emotional instinct, changed directions and scooped Eleana into her arms. Kurgan squeezed off a shot, but the Hagoshrin's head rose upward, taking the violent energy discharge squarely between the eyes. At the same time, its body rippled, pushing Riane across the mountain of its bulk.

Riane, Eleana in her arms, slid to the floor and ran. By that time, Kurgan had managed to change his vantage point. Sensing the beast was no longer a threat to him, he concentrated on Riane.

The Hagoshrin gave one last scream, and Riane threw herself to the floor, her body covering Eleana's as a glowing blue bolt of hyperexcited ions passed over her head and blew out a chunk of the marble wall.

The Veil of a Thousand Tears was singing, and she unwound it from her waist, letting it unfurl as she rose. The Veil was transformative, she knew, and she reasoned that it would not allow the ion blast to reach her in its native form. She turned to see Kurgan's grim face.

"If you fire again, you will harm her as well as me," she said.

She saw Kurgan pull the trigger, just as if she had given him a dare. She lifted her arm, the Veil floating in front of her. When the blast struck the Veil the hyperexcited ions metamorphosed into inert pebbles that dropped to the floor in an impotent clatter.

"You will have to do better than that, Kurgan, to come after me."

Riane and Kurgan stood staring at one another across the gulf of time, race, culture, memory. There was, she was astonished to discover, some elemental force that drew them together as strongly as it repulsed them. There was a circle—the Venca word for it was *yannam*, which signified a mode of knowledge, a way of seeing the world, a particular state of being—within which the two of them existed. Riane could see that it mattered not that Annon had been thrust into the form of a Kundalan female. Just as his love for Eleana survived the transformation so did the peculiar friendship-enmity between Annon and Kurgan.

Kurgan, for his part, was unaware of this, and yet so absolutely was their fate, their *yannam*, tied together, that he sensed something, as one scents a fire long before it becomes visible, before it can be determined whether in the dead of winter it is a blessing or a danger. Riane saw in his face a flicker—not of recognition, that would be impossible—but of that precognitive sensation that crawls down the spine and is called intuition.

"Kurgan, you must give me the banestone," Riane said.

Kurgan laughed, a caustic, unpleasant sound. "I will die before I give you anything you want."

"You do not understand. There are creatures searching for the banestone. They will stop at nothing to get it."

"Really?" Kurgan sneered. "And who are these creatures?"

Of course Riane did not know. *"One banestone they all are searching for,"* the Hagoshrin had told her. Only it had neglected to tell her who *they* were. But even if she knew, she doubted that Kurgan would believe her.

She was caught on the barbs of an insoluble dilemma: try to get the banestone from Kurgan or save Eleana.

As she began to back away into the corridor, Kurgan said, in a matter-of-fact tone, "Leave her here. What could she mean to you? Just another soldier in your doomed fight."

Riane watched his face as she continued to retreat. Either way, she would lose, and something precious would be irretrievably lost.

Then his voice changed again. "Listen. Listen to me." Softened now with his expression. "Why bother?" Cajoling. "She will die anyway." Beguiling even. "If not today, then tomorrow or next week. Like you."

Shadows crept over Riane, stealing Eleana's face. She sensed the corridor behind her, could smell its familiar and comforting fustiness. Almost there.

As if Kurgan realized what she was thinking, his face abruptly twisted, and he shouted; "If you take her, I will track you down, punish her by killing you slowly, piece by piece in front of her. This I swear on my own life."

Riane slipped completely into the shadows and, turning, ran for the air shaft aperture.

With a low growl, Kurgan scrabbled over the inert bulk of the creature. He ran after them.

The banestone, pulsing its eerie power, sank Riane's barb more deeply into his psyche. *You will have to do better than that, Kurgan, to come after me.* Imagine, he thought, furious, a Kundalan taunting him! Again and again, he fired wildly into the corridor, the hyperexcited ions ricocheting off the walls, floor, and ceiling.

The utility corridor was heating up like a porcelain oven. Riane reached the aperture, and Thigpen scrambled away from the edge, where she had been waiting, tense and agitated.

"Thank Miina you're safe," she said. "Did you get the banestone?"

Riane shook her head. She was busy unwrapping the Veil of a Thousand Tears from around her waist.

"Little dumpling, what are you doing?"

Riane had no time to answer her. Wrapping the Veil around Eleana's inert form, she said, "If I'm not back in five minutes, sink your teeth into the Veil and pull Eleana to safety."

"And leave you behind? I most certainly will not."

Riane glared at her. "I am the Dar Sala-at! You will do as I tell you."

"It is because you are the Dar Sala-at that I cannot comply. I am bound to protect you."

"Eleana is my beloved. You are bound to protect her as well."

"She is not the savior of all Kundala."

"Apparently, neither am I." Riane reached out and ruffled Thigpen's fur between her ears. "Listen to me. If I fail to recover the banestone, you and Eleana must survive in order to warn Giyan. You understand *that*, don't you?"

The Rappa sat back on her haunches, her forearms crossed angrily over her breast.

"Thigpen—"

"Yes. All right, by Miina, I understand!"

Riane nodded, then, with a last look at Eleana, she turned and poked her head out of the aperture.

"Come out, come out, or I will smoke you out." Kurgan's voice echoed down the corridor. He had apparently regained his senses, for he had stopped firing.

Dropping silently to the utility corridor's floor, Riane crept out toward the nightlily bedchamber. The razor's whisper of an ion blast caused her to drop to the floor and cover her head.

"I can see you," Kurgan whispered. "Shadow moving against shadow."

Another blast, ricocheting back and forth, searing Riane's shoulders, the backs of her hands.

"I can see it's just you," Kurgan called. "What have you done with her?"

Riane said nothing as she cast Flowering Wand, the simple cloaking spell. Then she began to crawl toward Kurgan. She could see him hiding behind the bulky folds of the dead Hagoshrin.

"What are you doing? You have disappeared," Kurgan cried. "Ah, I see. You've cast a spell."

How could he know that? Riane asked herself and, almost immediately, received an answer.

"The banestone is throwing off shocks. It may not know you yet, but it has attuned itself to your spellcasting." He commenced to move, crabwise, across the mountain of flesh. "Even if you are invisible, it will lead me to you."

Can this be true? Riane wondered. She cast Penetrating Inside to try to learn the nature of the banestone's attuning ability.

"There you are!" Kurgan leveled his ion cannon and squeezed off a shot.

Only Riane's quick reflexes saved her, but the beam of hyperexcited ions struck close enough to sear her lungs, left her gasping and dizzy.

"Keep up your spellcasting," Kurgan crowed in delight as he scrambled closer. "It will lead me right to you!"

How could the banestone counteract Osoru spells? Riane wondered. She had no other means of combating the ion cannon. Kurgan was close enough so that retreat was no longer an option. Surely, with the banestone's help, he would shoot her in the back as she ran. But how was she to fight him?

She switched to the far more powerful Eye Window sorcery that was a combination of Osoru and Kyofu, taught to her by Perrnodt in the wastes of the Korrush. Speaking the Venca runes, she conjured up Reweaving the Veins. But immediately she saw the offensive spell turned back on herself by some mysterious property of the banestone, and she murmured the counterspell just in time.

Kurgan was laughing, holding the banestone high, delirious with its power.

Despairing, Riane cast her mind into its darkest recesses for a way to counteract the banestone. And then she thought of something. Reaching back into the fortress of her memory, passing the twin fountains of MEMORY and OBLIVION into the entryway, down the silent corridor into the proper room. There, *The Book of Recantation* was waiting for her, and she mentally leafed through the pages. Her expertise in Kyofu spells was at best incomplete, but she did not think she had another alternative.

She found the right page and incanted the sigils, invoking Fly's-Eye, a spell that had once been used against her to confuse her.

Almost at once, Kurgan stopped his advance. He looked around this way and that. He put one hand to his head and squeezed his eyes shut. The Kyofu spell was working; he was clearly disoriented.

At a full sprint, Riane broke out of the shadows of the corridor, leapt at Kurgan, bowling him over backward. Riane reached out, but the banestone just evaded her fingertips, rolling down a groove in the Hagoshrin's body. Riane, scrambling over Kurgan's body, stretched for it, and Kurgan brought the butt of the ion cannon down into her stomach.

All the breath went out of her, and she doubled up, gagging. Her grip on Fly's-Eye wavered, and Kurgan reversed the ion cannon, his forefinger tightening on the trigger as the muzzle came level with Riane's head.

Riane slammed her left elbow against the middle of weapon and an ion burst cracked the ceiling, raining plaster down on them. Fighting to regain her breath, Riane kicked the ion cannon away. For that, she absorbed three devastating punches in a row. She thought she heard a rib crack, but it might have been in her mind.

As the two grappled together Riane could feel waves of V'ornn energy pulsing up from her core. That was good, for it increased both her strength and her determination. But at the same time, she felt Annon's conflicted emotions. As much as he hated the Stogggul, when it came to Kurgan, he could not quite give up his childhood friend, could not quite believe that the evil that flowed through his father and grandfather before him had irrevocably infected Kurgan. There was a part of him that still loved him in that intimately interconnected way only children with shared experiences can, part of him that was certain that he could save his friend from his family's curse. And so he held on to him, fairly embraced him, even while they pummeled each other, the love and the hatred commingling until they became indistinguishable.

In this subtle way, Riane was losing the battle, and inside her the Riane personality, that had ceded control to her V'ornn counterpart, reemerged into the light to take control. Blocking down hard on Annon's personality, she used her legs as she had been taught in another forgotten life. She clung to Kurgan as if he were a sheer mountainside, as if faced with a drop of a thousand kilometers, because as on a treacherous ice-encrusted tor she knew that her very life depended on her tenacity and agility. She slammed Kurgan onto his back, saw his eyes flutter, knew that he was losing consciousness, and she rolled over him, down the Hagoshrin's fleshy embankment, following the path of least resistance the banestone had taken.

She saw it gleaming darkly, rolled and tumbled toward it, had it within her grasp when a tremendous blow landed on the back of her head. Everything went sheet-white, snowstorm, silent as the bottom of a well. She could barely hear herself groan as she turned over.

Kurgan reared up over her, the butt end of the ion cannon he had retrieved at head height, ready to drive down onto her neck, cracking her windpipe.

Even through her pain and disorientation Riane tried to get her hands up to protect herself, but her arms felt like stone, and she could hardly move them, let alone maneuver them into a defensive position. She tried to get her brain to work, to conjure up another Kyofu spell, but her mind seemed as leaden as her body. Her last glimpse of Kurgan revealed him, torso arched, muscles rippling.

Kurgan, about to deliver the lethal blow, felt rather than saw a blur of red-and-black fur slam into his leg. When it reached a nerve bundle, he collapsed heavily, tumbling head over heels over the last hillock of the gargantuan corpse to the floor.

As Thigpen darted for the banestone, Kurgan fired awkwardly from his prone position, cursing the creature as it retreated. Keeping one eye on the banestone, he gritted his teeth and began to clamber back up the mountain of stinking flesh until he reached the ravine where Riane lay. But she was gone, and so was the little beast.

Cursing all the more loudly, he tried to go after them, but his leg gave out, and he banged his head on the way down. He fired into the utility corridor, and kept on firing until the weapon's power pak was drained.

15

Along Came a Gul

It was that time of the day when the light was a pellucid blue, the treetops burnished a deep gold, and the shadows grown long. Across a lapidary sky was thrown a paragraph of high, thin clouds in the curlicue shapes of a numinous language. The dense forest of West Country Marre pine cut the wind into innocuous puffs that soughed through the needle-laden branches, causing them to dip and sway like the wavelets of a becalmed sea. Birds sang happily and insects buzzed industriously and every now and again there came the sound of a small mammal foraging through the underbrush.

It was a thoroughly pastoral setting in which one would find the sight of spilled blood particularly shocking.

So it was with Giyan and Minnum as they hiked down a shadowed northern embankment of Receive Tears Ridge on their way to the deep forest where the sauromicians had long ago harvested the mushroom known as Peganis harmelea from which Madila was derived. They had arrived via the network of ancient cenotes built throughout the northern continent. Giyan had learned to use them when she had returned to the Abbey of Floating White the previous year. With the sauromicians abroad and very active, she rightly felt this a safer means of travel than Thripping, which—she suspected—the Dark League now had the means to monitor.

They broke through a gap in the tree line and began to traverse an upsloping highland meadow, lush with waving wrygrass, diaphanous milk-nettle and tall stands of whistleflower, their clear blue buds just beginning to open.

Giyan dropped to one knee, her fingers tapping, tracing patterns on the ground here and there.

"What do you sense, Lady?" Minnum asked.

"This ridge is far from deserted."

"Khagggun?" Minnum spun around.

"Khagggun and Resistance both." She rose. "We are crossing a nexus point of some kind. A battleground, past, future, present."

They continued on with a heightened sense of awareness and were relieved to leave the openness of the meadow behind. Once again, the forest closed about them, but now the Marre pines were interspersed with hardneedled, bluish green kuello-fir, and the rocks held more moss and lichen. The needle bed across which they walked was thick and springy and pleasantly fragrant.

They rose to a narrow ridge. The far side descended more steeply, and they bent their knees as they went to take the strain off their lower backs.

"Look familiar?" Giyan asked.

"It has been many years, Lady." Minnum looked around. "Put me down anywhere in the Korrush, and I can tell you within half a kilometer where I am. But I was never so at home in forests that I could distinguish one part from another."

No more than a quarter of the way down, Giyan stopped. Her nostrils flared, and she swept up a handful of dead needles. They were dark, matted together.

"Kundalan blood," Minnum said, and she nodded.

A little farther on, they came to a pock whose pale lichen was similarly stained. She reached out. "Still sticky," she said.

They continued their descent. She had them pause often, cocking her head as if listening to periodic reports brought to her by the wind. Minnum was very glad to be in her company, but observing her command of sorcery he could not help but feel a twinge of sorrow for all that had been taken from him. It was harder to be sightless if at one time you had had your vision, because it was impossible to forget what was no longer yours, what had once been.

The slope was accelerating its descent. At the same time, the forest became more dense, darker. The tree trunks were thicker, taller. What light filtered down was turned a mottled blue-green as if they were traveling underwater.

"There are fewer animals here," Giyan whispered. "And no birds at all."

This sounded ominous, but at that moment Minnum paused, sniffing the cool, crisp air. "Smell that?"

"The odor of burnt spun sugar?"

He nodded. "The mushrooms give off that distinct odor. We're close now to the harvest field."

They proceeded at a quickened pace. He led the way, winding through damp underbrush and large, moss-encrusted rocks that grew denser the farther they advanced into the forest. All at once, Giyan reached out, pulling him clean off his feet.

His head swiveled. "What—?"

But she hushed him and he felt the ripple in the air around them, a slight darkening against his second sight that signaled a spell being cast.

Hidden within Flowering Wand, an Osoru cloaking spell, the two of them peered back up the ridge. From behind them, Minnum heard what Lady Giyan must have sensed a moment ago: the telltale *click-clack* of Khagggun armor. And then the first column appeared, moving steadily, inexorably along the snaking ridgeline, more than a pack, and then a second column, a third, fourth, and fifth.

"It looks like an entire Wing is on the move," Minnum whispered. "That cannot be good news for the Resistance."

All at once, the column halted. A short, helmed Khagggun at its head swiveled this way and that. His alloy armor bore the insignia of a Wing-Commander.

Minnum felt a shiver run down his spine. "Surely they cannot see us, Lady?"

The Wing-Commander gestured, and a phalanx of Khagggun broke out of the column. They fanned out along the ridge and headed slowly down it toward the thick forested area where Giyan and Minnum crouched.

Giyan cursed her memory lapse. It had been so long since she had had to deal with Khagggun that she had forgotten that their helms were equipped with photonic sensors that could detect body heat. Flowering Wand was of no use against that technology.

As the Khagggun advanced, they swung their ion cannons off their shoulders and toggled the arming mechanisms.

"What are they seeing inside those helms?" Minnum whispered.

Giyan, feeling his shiver, put her arm around him and squeezed him tight.

No talking, she said in his mind. *In a moment, they will be close enough to pick up our molecular vibrations.*

What are we going to do, First Mother?

The Khagggun had moved into a wedge formation with the center Khagggun in the lead. They were in constant communication, a hive mind, as the hardware inside their helms performed multiple scans across increasingly wider arcs of the forest.

Giyan knew that their body heat would soon betray them. She could not let that happen. She looked around. They were crouched between two boulders. She could smell the musty aroma of the moss that lay in thick swaths across the north rock faces. Putting out her hand, she touched the soft wet spongy surface. Cool as stone, cool as metal. She ripped off a piece.

Quickly now, she said. *Tear off as much of the moss as you can find and cover yourself with it.*

But, Lady, why—
Do as I tell you! Now!

They tore great handfuls of the moss, ripping it wholesale off the rock face, and when they had denuded those rocks, they scrabbled behind them for others. Crouched in a fetal position, huddled together, they covered themselves in the cool must of the moss. Small insects wriggling through the moss bottom crawled across their cheeks and arms, bands of tiny cilia rippling, antennae questing. All else was still.

Giyan heard their hearts beating, the blood rushing through their veins. She stilled her breathing to almost nothing, slipping into a meditative state. It took Minnum a moment longer to get his racing heartbeat, his fright, under control. Giyan extended her pool of calm to encompass him, and at length he, too, drifted into the sorcerous twilight.

Above them, the lead Khaggun stopped, and the others stopped with him. He looked to the left, and they all looked with him. They all looked to the right together.

"What do you see?" Hannn Mennus spoke in their ears. "Did you find the anomalies I picked up?"

"There is nothing, Wing-Commander," the lead Khaggun said.

"Two bodies," Hannn Mennus said. "It seemed like two bodies."

"We have registered a brood of six qwawd, two adults, three juveniles, and a pair of snow-lynx."

"No Kundalan."

"No, Wing-Commander."

"The snow-lynx?" Hannn Mennus said. "Coming toward us or away from us?"

"They must have sensed us," the lead Khaggun said. "They have changed direction and are moving away to the north."

"Catch them now, kill them cleanly," Hannn Mennus said. "I want to wear their hides."

* * *

When Sahor, reading dense and difficult texts in one of the myriad lamplit galleries of the Museum of False Memory, heard the sound, he looked up. What he had heard had been small—tiny even—the whispered click of a rodent's claws on the stone flooring, or perhaps the soft metallic clash given off by a nocturnal insect. Transparent wings beating against the windowpane.

It was this last possibility that caused him to approach the crystal window. Beyond the eternal V'ornn-made night glow of the city, the sky was clear and full of stars. He could sense them, rather than see them, burning brightly, enigmatically, semaphoring their Cosmic messages. And where were the Centophennni? Were they seeing the same constellations that were strewn across the Kundalan sky? His new Kundalan body gave a brief, involuntary shudder, his gaze trended downward, and he saw the face.

It was on the other side of the windowpane, pale as ice, translucent as an old holophoto. What did he feel inside? How was he to say? He had been quite certain that he would never see it again, and now that he had been transformed he had in fact put it out of his mind altogether. Now up it popped, there of all places.

The face smiled at him, and he went to the door, unlatched it, and pulled it open. She was wrapped in an ankle-length greatcoat, dark and dusty and travel-worn, though from what he knew of her she never traveled at all. Her face was not dissimilar to other Tuskugggun faces, long and copper-colored, with high cheekbones and a bow of a mouth and dark eyes. Except she was more beautiful—far more beautiful, even in this guise of her own creation. Possibly, though, he was already seeing beneath the photon shell.

"May I help you?" he said. "We are closed."

"You are always closed," she replied. "These days."

They stood facing one another, he in the doorway, she wrapped in her cloak and the early spring night. Insects, roused from their winter dormancy by the change in light and temperature, whizzed and shrieked, softly, shrilly, their linen wings beating against the darkness. There was a sudden heaviness to the air that spoke of a coming change.

"Aren't you going to ask me in?"

"Do I know you?"

Her laughter, deep and clear, a perfect note, was a reminder of the old days, of the pain she had caused him, but also of the incandescence, bittersweet, that had engulfed them both.

He stepped aside and, without a moment's hesitation, she entered. As he relatched the door, she swept off the greatcoat and, with it, the photon shell. And there she was facing him again in all her terrible glory, wings beating, biocircuits spiraling up her gleaming glabrous skull, white pupils dilated in the dimness, lips formed in the familiar enigmatic half smile.

Gul Aluf.

"How did you find me?" he said.

"Offer me a drink," Gul Aluf said. "Please offer me a drink."

He went to a well-stocked sideboard. Minnum had liked his brews. His hand went automatically to the oldest fire-grade numaaadis, which was her favorite,

"Not that," she said. "Something . . . Kundalan." And when he turned to look at her questioningly, she added, "In honor of the new you, something quintessentially Kundalan."

"This is an exceptional ludd-wine."

She nodded her assent.

His hand moved to another crystal decanter. "A favorite of the Ramahan konara."

"So I am told."

The ludd-wine was the color of dried cor blood and almost as thick. He handed her a crystal goblet, and they both took a sip. She wore a sleeveless black ion-mesh tunic that alternately hid and revealed her body as she moved. He had forgotten the lustrous sheen of her skin.

"An acquired taste," he said, noting the look on her face.

"As is everything Kundalan." She put the goblet to her lips, swallowed more this time. "I had another null-wave net in the laboratory," she said softly. "That is how I found you."

"Impossible. I checked."

"As I knew you would."

She gazed at him over the rim of the goblet. Was she laughing at him? It would be so like her to do that.

"That would assume you knew that I was alive."

"I suspected." Her gaze never wavered. "I *hoped*."

He spent some time digesting that last sentence. He discovered, much to his dismay, that he fervently wanted to explore the implications. Part of him, of course, wanted nothing more than to shy away. He had vowed a long time ago that he would never allow himself to become entangled with her again.

She took more ludd-wine, drank it all down. "I know what you are thinking."

"I doubt it."

Her wings beat arhythmically, a habit he had found at first endearing, then as their relationship deepened, frankly erotic.

"As you wish." But her smile—that maddening, ripe, altogether luscious smile—informed him otherwise.

"Who else suspects," he said abruptly. "Who else hopes?"

"None. But Nith Immmon suspects."

"Yes." Sahor nodded. Nith Immmon had been one of his father's admirers. Clever at political maneuvering, quite a bit less so as a scientist. "Of course." And then, sadly, because he could not help himself: "Are you connected with him?"

Gul Aluf moved in her gliding manner. Her feet barely touched the cool stone squares. As she passed the sideboard, she placed her goblet on it. She stopped not a pace from where Sahor stood. She placed a hand on his shoulder. In anyone else it would have been a neutral gesture, but with her nothing was neutral, everything was, like an ion, charged.

"I like your new form," she said. "Yes, I do." Her hand slowly skimmed across his skin. "It is unusual. But so young. So taut. So vital. It was wise of you to manufacture this Kundalan-like photon shell, the better to hide from your enemies. One day you must show me the neural-net schemata." She cocked her head. "But how did you manage to go off-line from the Comradeship's matrix?"

"Nith Batoxxx managed it," he said. "So did I."

"Only the two of you. You can trust me, Sahor."

Of course he could not tell her how he had gone off-line. She still believed him to be Nith. If she got even a hint that he was a V'ornn-Kundalan hybrid . . .

But at the moment he had other worries.

"I won't let it happen again," he said in a voice clotted with emotion.

She leaned her cheek against his chest. "Won't let what happen?"

Her scent was invading him; the only way to avoid it was to stop breathing, and, he suspected, it would still creep through his pores. "Don't say you missed me."

"Even if it is the truth?"

"It couldn't possibly be the truth," he said tartly, somewhat defensively, because he *felt* her voice, as well as heard it. Felt it deep down in his bones as if it belonged there, twined with his marrow.

"Why?"

"Because you left me." His voice was tinged with an anguish that seemed freshly bitter.

"Everything with you is black or white."

"If you think that, then you know nothing about me."

"Quite right. That was unfair. On the other hand . . . Isn't it true that you had begun to despise me?"

He looked around the gallery, vainly searching for a way out. Or was he?

"Why have you come?" He wanted to push her away, to maintain a safe distance, but he found much to his dismay that he lacked the strength to do so. "What do you want?"

"You already know. To confirm that Nith Batoxxx had not killed you."

"And now that you have?"

"You were always far more clever, far more resourceful than he was—smarter, too. It was just that you—"

"Just that I what?"

"Somehow you became a dreamer, when I knew that you were meant to be a leader."

"*You knew.*"

She looked up at him. "I wonder whether you know how much contempt you packed into those two words."

The trouble was he did know.

"You disconnected yourself from the Comradeship at just the time you should have seized power."

"That was *your* wish for me, *your* desire."

"You could have made a difference." She looked him in the eye. "My desire was for you, Sahor."

He felt a spear in his side. "It no longer matters."

"Then why did you ask me if I had connected with Nith Immmon?"

"Knowing you, it seemed the logical question to ask."

"Knowing Nith Immmon, it is most illogical." She returned herself to his body, pressing herself against the length of him.

"Somehow, alliances for you always have a sexual component."

"We both know why you asked."

"Let it go." He closed his eyes. "Everything has changed now."

Small sounds from the deep eaves and the windowpanes, a swift, startled spatter, and then the steadier beat of rain. It had been raining the night she had turned away from him, hadn't it?

"Yes. You. Me. The Comradeship. Everything has changed."

"The Comradeship has devolved into political infighters intent on personal gain."

"It has splintered, yes. Without you—without your vision and your strength—the center could not hold."

"My path is my path."

"How can you be so damnably sure?"

"Because I have already made a difference."

"How? You have been in hiding."

"In ways you could never fathom."

She shook her head, angry at him, impatient with herself for failing to move him. "No matter, because now, something else has . . . We need you more than ever."

So that is why she had set her null-wave trap, why she had patiently lain in wait for him to surface, why she had come tonight. He had been wrong: not everything had changed. Her immoderate ambition, for one thing, remained intact. She needed to make her power play. She was no better than the rest of the Comradeship. Something that had been about to be reborn inside him punctured and sank into darkness.

She stirred, abruptly restless. "You are silent when you shouldn't be."

"I have nothing to say."

"You have not heard me out."

"I have heard enough."

"You *will* hear what I have to say!"

"Your power over me ended a long time ago."

"If you hate me, that is one thing. But don't let personal—"

"Are you serious? *Everything* with you is personal."

"Selfish, contemptuous creature!" At last the outburst, like the first spate of rain. "How can you abandon the Comradeship in crisis? Your species needs you!"

"You are not the least bit convincing."

She sighed, and her wings folded in upon themselves. "I see how it is going to be." That half smile again, hinting at secrets he could only guess at. "We have the Teyj you created." Her arms were crossed over her chest, folded like her wings. "We have your father, Nith Einon."

16

Unforgiven

The SaTrryn were headquartered in a large, rambling villa complex in the far reaches of the eastern district. It was imposing, not to say intimidating, but perhaps the effect was deliberate. The buildings had been magnificently restored to their former luster by a host of Kundalan craftsfolk, much to the invidious talk of the other Bashkir families. It was entirely possible, though, that envy rather than patriotism had given rise to the whisperers. The simple fact was that the SaTrryn had made a fortune in their spice trade with the Rasan Sul, vaulting them to the top tier of Bashkir families. Sornnn SaTrryn's appointment to the post of Prime Factor was merely validation of their status for, in point of fact, they owed their fantastic success to the care and energy Hadinnn SaTrryn had put into cultivating his relationship with the Korrush spice merchants. Sornnn's father hadn't been much of a husband, but he had trained his eldest son well in the intricacies of Korrush lore and etiquette; and it was well that he did, for he died so quickly and prematurely that surely the family business would have foundered had not Sornnn been there to step into his father's position.

However, Hadinnn's presence could still be felt anywhere one cared to look inside the compound. A gargantuan holoportrait of him hanging in the vast echoing front court stared down at Leyytey as she was shown through the imposing polished heartwood double doors. As was the Kundalan tradition, the front court was partially open to the elements and so on this late morning in spring it was filled with sunlight, the sound of twittering gimnopedes, and the scent of neatly planted star-roses. She was shown out into the adjacent garden, to a stone settee beneath a pair of twined sysal trees, and offered a selection of cold drinks by a uniformed attendant. Because it was Kundalan, the settee was more comfortable than it had any right to be. Nevertheless, Leyytey, drink in one hand, did not settle back, but rather perched on the edge. One knee rode up and down, a sign of her nerves. Bad enough she had to see Sornnn SaTrryn, but in the very place where . . .

She caught herself, immediately turned her thoughts elsewhere. The garden had been set square in the middle of the compound. It was planted in the Kundalan manner—that is to say both lushly and formally, with an eye toward the repeating triangles, emblematic of the Goddess Miina, and Leyytey could see how in this setting the repetitions in pathways, flower beds, trees, and other close-sheared foliage created a kind of language that merged with the villas, whose stained-crystal windows echoed the shapes. But though she tried to enjoy the undeniable beauty and harmony of her surroundings, she could not. For one thing, she was being watched by a bronze-and-alloy bust of Hadinnn SaTrryn. She took a gulp of her drink, placed the frosted crystal against her forehead, let the coolness of it sink in.

A few moments later, Sornnn SaTrryn emerged from a shadowed doorway and strode down a green-limestone path toward her. She rose to greet him and all at once became conscious of how much time she had spent dressing for this interview. She had chosen leggings of a mimetic fabric that clung to her like a second skin, a belted chain-alloy jerkin she had designed herself over a milk-white blouse of feather-silk, a favorite Kundalan material. High boots clad her small feet in matte black alloy, her delicate ankles, her muscled calves in cream-colored cor hide. Her sifeyn was also of her own design—ion-forged of a chain mail so fine as to be all but invisible.

Her interest in impressing him so shocked her that when Sornnn greeted her she stumbled over her response. To his

credit, he made no comment. Instead, he sat beside her on
the stone settee.

"Are you enjoying the drink?"

"Yes. Very much." She could not remember whether she
was, but she could not think of what else to say.

"It's iced *gibta*, a concentrated form of ba'du. From the
Korrush. Refreshing, isn't it?"

Leyytey took a sip and agreed that it was. She peered at
Sornnn over the rim. She had not seen him for some time,
so maybe she was mistaken, but he looked thinner, more
haggard than she remembered. He sat very still. She could
see his large eyes watching her, steady as two beacons in
the night.

"Thank you for agreeing to this arrangement," he said.

"You are paying me a mountain of coinage."

"You know what I mean. It cannot be easy dealing with
Pack-Commander Dacce."

Immediately her eyes sparked and her voice got flinty.
"I am not afraid of him, if that is what you mean."

"You misunderstand me, Leyytey. I meant . . . He is a
difficult Khaggun to understand."

"You don't seem to have any problem understanding
him," she said tartly. But it wasn't Sornnn she was angry
with, and she knew it.

"That is because I am not in love with him."

She looked away and felt ashamed of being so transparent. "He came back, of course, after that first night. He
bought me presents. I took him to see Miirlin. In his mind,
he is being kind and loving. To me, it is all brittle and
false. It's perfectly clear what he wants."

Responding to her distress, he said, "It's all right, we all
do foolish things."

"I hate this," she said more vehemently than she had
intended.

"You do not have to go through with it."

She shook her head. "That is not what I mean. I feel as
if I know nothing about love."

He laughed, and the sad note it struck made her turn back to him.

"Oh, when it comes to love I confess I know less than nothing!" he exclaimed. "Love is as mysterious to me as the Gyrgon."

Hearing his words, she looked at him as if for the first time, and she saw through her fear and her memories and realized that he was as lost as she was. He, the scion of the SaTrryn! And she knew with a certainty that floored her that some profound trauma had befallen him, for he bore the scar as bloody, as livid as if it had happened an hour ago.

"I apologize, anyway," he said. "Please forgive me."

Her tongue cleaved to the roof of her mouth. She did not know how to respond.

"We have much to discuss and formal documents to sign," he said as he rose. "The midday meal is prepared. Will you join me?"

What could she say? That she wanted nothing more from the day than to be freed from this grim place, that she could no longer bear Hadinnn SaTrryn's accusatory eyes on her, that she was so afraid of letting her father down that she dare not leave, dare not even give Sornnn SaTrryn a reason to suspect that she knew—

Why hadn't she said something before? Because doubtless her life would have been in jeopardy the moment she opened her mouth. Her father would not have been able to save her; no one could have. And so she had chosen to say nothing, she had chosen to push it away, convince herself that it had happened to someone else. But she had not forgotten, and now that she was here in the SaTrryn compound, now that she was in the company of the oh-so-charming, the oh-so-sad son, she seemed to be awakening from a dream. It had not happened to some other Tuskugggun, it had happened to her. All the self-deception was erupting to the surface to drag her down.

"Leyytey, are you all right?"

Sornnn had a look of concern on his face.

"You're flushed and sweating. Are you ill?"

"No, I—" She put a trembling hand to her brow. N'Lu-uura take it, he was right. Her skin felt hot and clammy.

"Here, sit down," he said, indicating the stone settee.

"I do not require rest," she said sharply. "I am neither a weakling nor a child."

He nodded. "Of course not. I meant no offense."

He was so polite he set her teeth on edge, mainly because she had no reason to trust his sincerity. Leyytey was something of an anomaly among Tuskugggun. She was revered by Khagggun (and even some Bashkir) for what she did even while she was secretly demeaned for what she was. How many of her warrior clients spoke of wanting to bed her in the crudest possible terms, just as if she were a common Looorm. Perversely, her very expertise spurred their libidos like the most potent aphrodisiac. She was weary of being mentally undressed by every male with whom she came in contact. Just as she was weary of being used and tossed aside by the one Khagggun she loved.

Not that she necessarily thought that of Sornnn. In fact, by the time they began the midday meal she realized that she could not quite figure out what he was about, apart from obviously wanting to impress her. If he'd had his way, they would have dined in the enormous porphyry-clad second-floor hall of the villa that lay directly in front of the bust of Hadinnn SaTrryn. Rather than impressing her, its gargantuan size had the effect of making her feel anxious, and she asked if they could move to the lone table on the sun-dappled balcony. It was small, the thick disk of its top a lovely intarsia of perhaps a half dozen woods. It was only after she was already seated on a spiral-heartwood chair that she realized that she had a perfect view of that accursed bust. Hadinnn SaTrryn's accusatory stare had locked onto her like a photon-powered weapon. She lost her appetite but she kept on eating anyway, slowly, methodically, grimly so that Sornnn would not ask

her again if she was all right. Because the truth was she
was not all right. Not by a long shot. Sitting there across
from Hadinnn's son, she was consumed with guilt and did
not know what to do about it.

On the other hand, Sornnn made certain that she did not
have much time to think about it, since he regaled her with
stories about his beloved Korrush, all of which she found
fascinating. It made her realize that she had never been
outside the gates of Axis Tyr, had never really considered
why she would want to. Sornnn's tales made her think
otherwise.

"You understand that I will need to see these Rasan Sul
myself," she said, "before I can make weapons for them. I
will need to assess their size and strength as well as the
manner in which they do battle."

He nodded. "That can be easily arranged. I will take you
myself."

His intense eyes rested on her and, once again, she wondered what he really wanted.

When the plates were cleared away, he said, "I need you
to tell me the truth about something."

"Of course. If I can."

He gave her a thin smile. "Spoken like a Khaggggun."

She felt herself flush at the compliment. No one had
ever said that to her before and meant it. She felt that in
this he was sincere. He had been hurt too badly; he was
not interested in bedding her.

"What is it you want to know?" she urged him, because
suddenly she was eager to find out what was on his mind.

"How do you feel about using him?"

She knew he meant Teww Dacce. "I don't know." And
then, after a short pause: "You said you wanted me to be
honest."

He sat back and pursed his lips. "This must be very difficult for you."

Her innate anger flared once more. "Would you say that
if I really was a Khaggggun?"

"Absolutely."

She sat forward, put her elbows on the table. "Now I need you to tell the truth."

He looked away for a moment, and it seemed to her as if he was studying the bust of his father, as if somehow trying to communicate with him. Then his gaze slid back to her.

"All right. I doubt that I would ask this of you if you were a Khagggun."

Her eyes opened wide. This was the last response she had expected. "I don't understand."

"It's simple, really. When it comes to love and sex, it seems to me that Khagggun—most male V'ornn, actually—have an on-off switch. They tend not to see subtleties or nuances. All the grey areas are lost on them because in such things they are not complex. Frankly, if you were a male, I doubt you could do what we are asking you to do."

Leyytey was stunned. He might have been talking about Teww Dacce, which was how she knew that he was right. She could not believe he had that insight, and, despite her wariness, she felt a connection forming. But then the sun emerged from behind an attenuated fair-weather cloud and Hadinnn SaTrryn glittered in her eyes, and her skin grew clammy again.

"But you are different, is that it?" Too late, she realized how enraged she sounded.

"Leyytey, for your father's sake as well as for mine I want this to proceed as smoothly as possible. Have I done something to offend you?"

"No, I—" Now it was her turn to look away. *Tell him,* a voice in her head whispered recklessly. *For the love of N'Luuura, tell him!* But she only shook her head and looked rueful. "Sorry, I have no excuse. You have done nothing but be extraordinarily kind to the Fleet-Admiral and to me."

" 'The Fleet-Admiral'?" He had a wry look on his face. "Is that how you refer to your father?"

"It is his wish," she said simply, though there was certainly nothing simple about the statement. It was loaded with so much emotional freight she could not bear to examine it.

As if sensing that, Sornnn said, "Relationships with parents are tricky. I was estranged from my mother for many years."

"But you're not anymore?"

"No. There was a misunderstanding. It arose because she and I failed to talk to one another."

"Why do you think that was?"

"We didn't know how to communicate."

"And now you do?" She seemed skeptical.

"I think we were afraid to say what had to be said, afraid that the other would—I don't know, that we would say something unforgivable."

Leyytey rose then and stood looking out into the garden. Her hands gripped the wrought-iron balustrade so hard they turned white as her blouse. *That we would say something unforgivable.* That was just what she felt when her father was around—that she would say or do something unforgivable, that he would go away, withdraw even the unwitting verbal abuse to which he subjected her. Because she knew that that abuse was better than nothing, that she was still his little girl, that skill or competence or success had nothing to do with it, that she would always feel thus.

After a long time, she said; "When it comes to the Fleet-Admiral I have done something unforgivable."

She heard him get up and come to stand beside her. She could smell his clean, masculine scent. "What could you have done, Leyytey?"

"I was born a Tuskugggun."

He sighed. "I felt like that once."

"What happened?"

"I met a Tuskugggun. A very special Tuskugggun. But now she's dead, and for me everything died with her."

Soon thereafter, she went back to her atelier, and that night, when Teww Dacce came like a death moth to a flame, when she twined with him, when she whispered in his ear the things she was supposed to say, she saw Sornnn in her mind's eye and heard his words as clearly as if they were the tolling of a bell.

Blood was everywhere. Minnum and Giyan found patches of it on the forest floor, great, frightening gouts spurted onto tree boles, lichen-matted rock shoulders. The Khagggun Wing had passed by after running down the two snow-lynx. They were magnificent animals, and Giyan wanted to save them, but to do so she would have exposed herself and Minnum. Hearing their death screams, she said a prayer for their spirits.

With the Khagggun's departure, the birds and small mammals had returned, though in their fluttering, their nervous foraging she could detect the patterns of fear.

"Over here!"

Minnum's excited whisper brought Giyan down to a narrow plateau on the slope. He was kneeling amid a tidal pool of mushrooms.

"*Peganis harmela.*" Minnum brushed his hands across the bowed mushroom tops. "This is the harvest glade where I used to come."

But Giyan was walking right by him, through the sea of mushrooms to the far edge of the plateau. Minnum looked up. To him, she had the appearance of a sleepwalker, and when he called her name, when she did not answer, he rose and hurried after her, afraid in his heart of what she saw, of what might be lurking in the dense forest. And he came up short with a gasp as she walked right into the muzzle of an ion cannon.

The Abbey of Floating White was deathly quiet after Lady Giyan left. Konara Inggres had not realized how much life and hope Giyan had brought to the abbey until she was no longer there.

Now the daylight hours were filled to the brim with classes and curriculum and correcting the evil errors in gospel that had been fulminating through the sorcerous syllabus for decades. After a meager dinner—these days she was never very hungry—hours were spent counseling the leyna and younger shima in the wake of the trauma that had beset them. Late at night, almost insensate, she fell onto her cot and slept soundly, dreamlessly for two hours, possibly three. Then, without any transition, she started awake, her heart palpitating painfully in her breast. She lay in a sheen of sweat, listening to her blood rush.

Her mind was besieged by death—Perrnodt's death: abrupt, shocking, horrifying. She was haunted by the sight of those eyes, glued shut and rimed. She sat up and, reaching out in the darkness, emptied the small vitreous tray into her cupped palm. The shattered shards of Perrnodt's opal lay inert and ominous. Their fire had been extinguished. She wondered whether that was an omen of what was to come.

Konara Inggres had risen to power not out of desire, but rather necessity. She had had greatness forced upon her, but still she had been more than up to the task. Her process was simple: she thought, she considered, she acted. She knew no other way to be.

Lady Giyan had departed abruptly, and no word from her all these long days. Where had she gone? What had she found? As she stirred, the Ja-Gaar that slept with her rose and padded to her. Its lambent green eyes watched her, waiting for a direction to which her anxiety would point it.

There came a discreet knock on her door, and she rose soundlessly, drew on her robe, and lighted an oil lamp. She crossed to the door and stood aside for the Nawatir to enter. The Ja-Gaar made no move; like its brethren it loved the Nawatir and obeyed his every command.

He seemed to fill the room, seemed like a planet eclipsing the sun of the flame. His shadow ran along the stone floor, up the stone wall where it mimicked his stillness. She studied his face: the double curve of his full lips, the twin juts of his cheeks, his thick blond hair and beard. His startlingly pale eyes looked back at her enigmatically. Oh, what she would give to know what he was thinking!

"I have heard from Lady Giyan," he said, and the silence stretched on for so long that Konara Inggres ceased to breathe.

"The sauromicians are on the rise," he told her ominously. "We must immediately turn our efforts to protecting the abbey."

"Are we in imminent danger of attack?"

"That I do not know," he conceded. "But what is clear is that the sauromicians must not gain control of Floating White."

She nodded, terrified all over again. With the return of First Mother to the abbey where she had been trained, Konara Inggres had become more optimistic for the future. But now, just as they had defeated the daemonic threat, the sauromicians were rising to take their place. All at once, she was acutely conscious of the Nawatir's strong arm and keen mind. Of course she had the sorcerous Ja-Gaar to help her guard the abbey, but they were only beasts, ferocious and powerful enough to battle daemons as they were. They could give her no guidance, no reassurance. She realized that, for the first time in many years, she felt safe with the Nawatir roaming the abbey grounds, standing spread-legged in the gardens, practicing with his miraculous sword. More than once, she had had to shoo away the younger leyna who, passing on their way to class or prayer, were transfixed at the sight of him. She always lingered, however, watching him in sunlight and shadow, mist and rain and moonlight.

He put his hand on her shoulder. His cool fire crept through her, and she felt a stirring and was instantly ashamed. She pushed herself away and kept her distance. But she could not keep her heart from racing or her pulse from pounding. She recited prayers while he spoke to her, his voice filling the chamber, clasping her as surely has had his hand.

"Konara Inggres," he said sharply, "are you listening to me?"

"Yes, Nawatir." Her cheeks were flaming. "I was thinking of my charges. They have been though so much already."

"Listen to me." He took a step toward her. "The red Dragon, the one who transformed me into the Nawatir, told me of this war. *Be forewarned,* he told me. *Everything—everything you know or have ever believed true—will change.*"

"Mother of Miina." Konara Inggres shivered. "What does it mean?"

"Prepare yourself is what I am saying, for I fear that ere long we will all be called upon to do whatever it takes to safeguard the Dar Sala-at and Kundala."

Then he was gone, and she felt his absence like a wound that would not heal. She put her fist to her mouth and bit down, pain as punishment for what her body felt, what she knew she must not feel. Blood stained her teeth, ran along her lower lip, and she sucked at it, as if she could suck into herself her own feelings.

What he had told her—the implications—it was too much to absorb all at once.

Everything you know or have ever believed true will change.

Change—how will it change?

With a little moan, she turned her thoughts to Perrnodt, aware that the exercise was a salve as well as a necessity. She had considered the implications of Perrnodt's death, the interference with the opal casting, the fact Perrnodt was a Druuge and, therefore, very powerful. Still, an evil of great power had destroyed her. Something stronger, more clever, smarter. She had been working out how to protect the abbey from such a foe and had come to the conclusion that with the limited means at her disposal she could not. She had only just begun the process of determining which, if any, of the remaining Ramahan possessed the Gift that had been so long outlawed in the

abbey. And even if every one of her charges proved
Gifted, it would still take time to train them properly so
that they could protect themselves from a concerted sorcerous attack. That left only her, the Nawatir, and the three
Ja-Gaar. Now was the time to act. She could not put it off.

Dumping the shards on the floor, she rose and went to
her cabinet. She required no light to find what she was
looking for. She held the casting opal between the tips of
her fingers, saw it as clearly as if she were standing in sunlight. She could feel its fire.

The danger inherent in what she was about to attempt
was extreme. She had already considered that fact, had considered the implications for the abbey if she were to die. But
the threat to all Ramahan—all Kundalan, in fact—was extreme. The sauromicians' push to return to power would
mean the annihilation of what abbeys were left, and the
abbey was the last vestige of life on Kundala as it had been
centuries ago, of life as, Miina willing, it would be once
again. First Mother and the Nawatir were right. The abbey
had to be defended at all costs.

Her plan was simple. Communication between the
abbeys, once free-flowing, had broken down at the first
V'ornn assault. Early on, when attempts to contact the
neighboring abbeys had failed, the communication process had been abandoned. Then, when it became known
that the inhabitants of other abbeys such as Listening
Bone in Axis Tyr, Warm Current outside Middle Seat and
Glistening Drum outside Joining the Valleys had been either killed outright or dragged back to the capital to be interrogated and tortured, a strict regime of silence and
isolation had been instituted by Konara Mossa and then
Konara Bartta. There had never been a concerted effort to
communicate with other, more far-flung abbeys, and
within decades even the names and locations of those
abbeys passed from current Ramahan consciousness.

But in the course of her clandestine studies she had
come across a list. It was decades old and yellowed and

frayed at the edges. Insects had eaten into it, making the reading of it more like deciphering a text a thousand years old. Using an inspired combination of cross-referencing and intuition, she was able to piece together the list. The one thing she could not be certain of was whether or not it was complete.

Now, standing in the center of her cell, she said a prayer to Miina and began the casting. Unlike Perrnodt, she was self-taught, because opal casting, like so many other traditions, had been abandoned, then banned outright by the previous administrations. She had learned her lessons in the dead of night, alone and unaided, from books secreted in the Library. Her clever and inventive mind had been her only guide as she mentored herself, and so inured to secrecy was she that no one, not even Lady Giyan, was aware of the full extent of her knowledge and abilities.

And yet . . .

And yet, they had never been fully tested. She did not even know whether to trust fully the texts she had ferreted out in the unvisited depths of the Library, dusty, damp, wormholed, water-damaged tomes with page edges of whole sections blackened, crisped, and crumbling as if they had survived some unimaginable war. Which, in a sense, they had. In her heart, where Miina dwelled, she trusted absolutely. It was her mind, prey to doubts and fears and her own sense of inadequacy (how could she, a self-taught Ramahan, pretend to the power of Lady Giyan or, even, a Druuge!), that threatened to undermine her resolve.

Her palms were clammy. The darkness had taken on a viscous quality. She felt submerged, suffocated, as if she were swaddled in a shroud, and yet she felt certain that turning on a lamp would be a mistake. She had no idea where the notion came from, but years of living by her wits had trained her to listen to her intuition. It had saved her life more than once.

Let no evil see me. This was her watch phrase tonight.

* * *

Giyan stood very still. She was between the limbs of two kuello-firs. Not a breath of air stirred. Minnum tried to swallow but could not.

The owner of the ion cannon was a young female Kundalan, Resistance obviously. So far as Giyan could tell, she was unharmed, not the wounded one who had left blood all over the forest above. But her haggard, desperate expression, her torn and filthy tunic made it equally obvious that she had been in a serious battle.

"Who are you?" the Resistance female, deep suspicion turning her voice into a throaty growl. "What are you doing here?"

Without moving a muscle or giving her the slightest cause for alarm, Giyan said, "Your compatriot. Is he dead or seriously wounded?"

The female's eyes narrowed to slits. "How do you know I have a compatriot?"

"There is blood all over the forest floor," Minnum said. "It is a wonder the Khagggun we saw did not find it."

"They were too busy looking for us," Giyan said. She smiled. "I am Giyan, and this is Minnum. We both have healing skills. Please, if your friend is still alive, take us to him."

The female saw that they were unarmed. Still, had her situation not been so desperate, Minnum judged, she might have chosen to disbelieve them. He could see it in her eyes, in the way they darted back and forth between him and Giyan.

All at once she nodded. "My name is Majja," she said. But she did not lower the muzzle of her weapon, and she watched them carefully as she walked beside them, guiding them down the slope. "I am afraid that Basse is near death. He was hit by ion-cannon fire."

"Where?" Giyan said immediately.

"Abdomen," Majja replied.

Minnum had to admire Giyan. She appeared unperturbed by the V'ornn weapon trained on them. He himself did not feel quite so sanguine. A small beetle was crawling on his arm. He looked at it for a minute before flicking it into the underbrush. The V'ornn made him feel as if he was not more than an insect crawling across their sleeve.

They moved through the forest, silent as wraiths. All at once, Giyan broke into a run. Majja swung her ion cannon around.

"Basse is dying," Minnum said, for he felt it, too, the cold creep of death, slithering through the trees like a damp mist. And he took off after Giyan, for once unmindful of the weapon's threat.

Basse lay on the ground, his life hanging by a thread. As Minnum came up, Giyan was already on her knees beside him. Opposite her, eyes opened wide, was a Tuskugggun dressed—or half-dressed, to be accurate—in standard Resistance issue.

"Now this is really interesting," Minnum said, staring at her.

"What is this?" Giyan's fingers were hovering over a suppurating poultice. She put her head down, then jerked it back up. "Hyoscyamus." She stared at the Tuskugggun. "Where did you get this?" she said sharply.

Marethyn held up the stained pouch she had found in the death pit.

Giyan snatched it from her. "Where did you—?"

"Ramahan are said to be healers," Marethyn began. "I took a handful, I just thought—"

"A handful! Merciful Miina!" Using a coating of matted needles, Giyan scooped the noisome poultice off Basse. Then she put her ear to his chest.

"They weren't healing herbs?" Majja said.

"Black hyoscyamus is used for many things, including healing," Giyan said. With a *rhump-thump!* she pounded on Basse's sternum. "It's all a matter of how much you use." *Rhump-thump!* "A little can heal the most grievous wound." *Rhump-thump!* "A middling amount will induce a trancelike state."

"What are you doing?" Majja said, alarmed.

Rhump-thump! "A large amount will induce seizures and, eventually, cause the heart to stop." *Rhump-thump! Rhump-thump!* "The hyoscyamus was applied externally, not taken internally, so the symptoms take longer to go into effect." *Rhump-thump!* Giyan looked up. "I am not in time. There is nothing I can do. His heart has stopped."

"No!" Majja screamed. Throwing her weapon aside, she dropped to her knees, cradling Basse's head. "No!" But she could feel that he was not breathing.

Marethyn came and slid her arms around Majja's shoulders.

"Wait!" Minnum said, and, turning, scrambled up the slope to the sea of mushrooms. He looked this way and that, frantically searching for the largest mushroom. Considering Basse's state, he needed a fully mature specimen.

"Where are you?" he whispered. "Where are you, slippery fish?"

He found it at the northern edge of the patch, half-hidden by the exposed roots of a kuello-fir. Quick as a blink, he snatched off the cap without disturbing the stem. Cradling it in the palm of his hand, he hurried back down the slope, half-sliding on the balls of his behind because he could not afford to stumble and fall and risk damaging the mushroom cap.

Giyan made way for him as he knelt beside Basse. He opened his fingers, turned the pale cap open so that dark gills were accessible. Using the nails of his thumb and forefinger, he plucked every other gill. He did so deftly and carefully, for to be effective the gills had to remain intact. Tear even one, and he would have to start over with another cap, and he knew he had no time for that.

When he had gone all the way around the underside of the cap, he bade Giyan gather the gills and place them in a radiating pattern on the wound. While she did this, he plucked all the remaining gills but one. He buried the cap beside Basse, then pried open his rigid jaws. Roughly, he pushed back Basse's head so that his mouth was pointing straight up, then he used one finger to depress his tongue. One by one, he dropped the gills into his mouth so that they went directly down his throat.

Seeing that Giyan was finished, he said, "All right, everyone stand away." He glanced around. "Back away, I say!" he shouted, and was gratified to see both Majja and the Tuskugggun comply. Clamping Basse's jaws shut, he rose over him, his knees firmly against Basse's shoulder bones.

A moment later, Basse gasped, and his body arched upward, almost knocking Minnum off. But the little sauromician was prepared, and he held on, pressing downward more firmly as Basse continued to spasm, shaking like a mad wyr-hound.

"What's happening?" Majja cried.

"Look!" Marethyn clutched Majja. "He's breathing!"

Majja was trembling slightly. "What are you doing to him?"

"Bringing him back," Minnum said, "from the twilight world into which he had slipped."

Whispering the spell as if she were praying to Miina, Konara Inggres opened her Third Eye. Immediately she felt the emanations of the opal, and she touched them with her psyche, sensing the conduit, opening her mind to it, following it back to the coolly glowing skin of the opal. She felt each color inside as a pinprick, as if she were being inoculated, shot through with a potent decoction of mushrooms and herbs. Her mind expanded until it seemed to fill the chamber.

And then the colors irised open and, one by one, she conjured up the names of the abbeys on the master list she had painstakingly assembled: Returning Current, Floating Reserve, Correspondence Hall, on and on, journeying through the sorcerous lens of the opal casting to the abbeys, each time on a wave of hope, only to crash into the trough of lifelessness that greeted her. On and on, each wave lower, each trough deeper. The pain of each abandonment was like a grave being dug inside her, growing larger, deeper, darker, and she despaired. Could it be true? Could Floating White be the last remaining inhabited abbey on Kundala?

She was on her way to the Abbey of Orbit Bone when she felt it. It was only the slightest prickling at the nape of her neck, stirring the loose strands of hair there as from the slightest zephyr, but it sent a shiver down her spine. Turning her gaze, she saw the vertical slit, fiery red, lambent orange: the dreaded Eye of Ajbal. It was one of the three most potent Kyofu spells, one that even Bartta had not mastered. But it was rumored that the sauromicians knew of the Ajbal Incantations and had, against Miina's express wishes, used it extensively.

She felt fear swallow her for she was certain that this spell was what had ensnared Perrnodt, what had pursued her through netherspace, what had caught her in its grip. Konara Inggres knew she did not have the expertise to defend herself against the Eye of Ajbal—didn't know if even the First Mother did.

In any event, it did not seem as if the Eye had as yet found her. But it was Seeking. She could feel the emanation of its filaments, sticky as kris-spider silk. From her reading she knew that she was relatively safe as long as one of the filaments did not lock on to her. She could still maneuver in the psychic world of netherspace sandwiched between realms of existence as long as she made sure that none of the filaments sensed her. The problem was, of course, that they winked in and out of her sight according to her own speed. The faster she went—and she was by then of a mind to go as fast as she possibly could because doing so would make it more difficult for the Eye to spot her—the harder it would be for her to keep track of the filaments.

She did not see that she had a choice. Pushing her casting to the limits, she fairly flew through the opal-casting lens until she had come to the Abbey of Orbit Bone. The milk-white granite walls had been built at the base of Little Rushing, the waterfall that fed Three Fish River. Cloaked in eternal mist, dewy with moisture, its blank walls rose ahead of her as if in greeting. But when she pierced the exterior she found the abbey filled with the plucked-clean skeletons of the faithful. They sat or lay in positions of ordinary life, as if death had overtaken them in the blink of an eye, which, she supposed, it had. The dust of what had once been skeletons tended the over-grown garden, lay beside the abbey bell, knelt in postures of prayer. Others, small—leyna surely—were crumpled in rows, along with shards of blackened wood, in classrooms where they had been studying when the end came.

All at once, she looked up and saw the Eye of Ajbal rising over the parapets like a livid sun, and she raced away into the mist, into the mountains, anywhere to rid herself of the danger. But the images from Orbit Bone followed her, mocking in their utter despair. It was one thing to learn about the dissolution of a world, a way of life, but it was something else again to confront it face-to-face. She felt desolate, and once again she beseeched the Great Goddess, begging her for another sign, some fur-ther reassurance that one day soon the tide would turn, that the old ways, the sacred days would return. But this time she heard nothing but the awful, stifling silence that infested Orbit Bone.

In her utter despair, she almost forgot about the last abbey on her list. It was the one she was least certain about, the one at the bottom, where the page was most damaged, the lettering most eaten away.

The Abbey of Summit Window. That was her last hope. And she turned the lens to the west, toward the high, spiked tors of the Djenn Marre, toward the Great Rift and beyond, just to the north, Kunlung Mountain. As always, the mountain was almost entirely obscured by the perpet-ual ice storms that raged in the Unknown Territories. At first, when she had pieced together the master list, she had been certain that she had made some mistake, for what would a Ramahan abbey be doing in such a remote and inhospitable climate? But then, as she checked and rechecked her translations, she had had to accept the fact that there could be no mistake. Summit Window was perched high on the north face of Kunlung, overlooking the Unknown Territories, though what could be seen or even surmised through the blinding storms she was at a loss to say.

Reaching the Great Rift, she lost the last of the filaments behind her and entered fully into the ice storm that filled the rift with an eerie and desolate howling. Not a bird could be seen, not an animal trudged across the trackless wastes. It was clear that no living thing could survive there.

Despite her research, she approached the mountain with a good deal of skepticism. Kunlung was an anomaly, for where the bare jagged rock could be seen through the layers of snow, permafrost, and ice, it was a uniform jetblack. Not a speck of silicate, not a vein of iron or limestone or calcite marred the perfect ebon hue. And there was something else, stranger perhaps even than the stultifying mass of its color. The rock was smooth as glass. How on Kundala could anything be built on such a surface?

And then, as she came around the western shoulder of Kunlung, she saw it. At first, she thought she was looking at another sheer wall of ice and rock, but then she spotted a fortresslike crenellation, then another and another. Moving the lens in closer, she spied behind the crenellations a walkway wide enough for perhaps two Ramahan to stand back to back. It was entirely free of crystallized snow and, with a surge of elation, she felt the spell that kept it clear.

Nearer Summit Window, she could see that the crenellations were not the only aspect that made the abbey seem more like a fortress. For one thing, its walls were massive, thicker on the bottom than on the top, a certain sign that its battlements were heavily reinforced. For another, it featured narrow, almost slitlike windows. They could, of course, be a response to the violently inclement weather;

but combined with the other features, such as an inner wall and a central keep, it was clear that the abbey had been constructed to repel even the most persistent siege. In what era had it been built, Konara Inggres wondered, and for what purpose? It looked ancient, far older even than Floating White, which had long been acknowledged as the oldest of the abbeys.

Her entire mind itching with curiosity, she moved the lens even closer, but when she came abreast of the jutting crenellations, she was brought up short. The lens of the opal irised inward and the colors that swirled through the spectrum of its body were held in stasis.

Konara Inggres heard a voice in the center of her mind. *You fool! What have you done? You have led them to us!*

The prickling at the nape of her neck caused Konara Inggres to turn and, looking up, she saw through a rent in the clouds of ice and snow the fiery red slit of the Eye, turning this way and that. The fresh spurt of filaments it was sending out filled the sky, melting ice crystals and snowflakes alike into rain that froze as it slanted down, turning into an assault of hail that rattled against ice walls and disfigured virgin ice fields.

No! she cried. *It's me they want. It's me they are searching for.*

She backed furiously away from the sorcerous screen. Freeing the opal-casting lens, she plunged through it, withdrawing from Kunlung Mountain, from the Great Rift, from the breathless heights of the Djenn Marre.

But to her terror, she saw that the Eye of Ajbal came with her. Had it seen the Abbey of Summit Window? She prayed to Miina that it had not. And she prayed to Miina for deliverance, for just then the first of the filaments touched her shoulder. She squirmed away, right into the path of another. She gasped inwardly as another half dozen filaments wrapped around her. Immediately, she felt the dreadful tug in her mind and knew that whoever controlled the Eye had cast Sphere of Binding. She felt like a fish caught on a hook who was now being slowly reeled in to be gaffed and gutted. The first connections of the potent spell were plugging into her memory synapses, the better to read her mind, discover her strengths, weaknesses, her purpose. Even as she conjured up Arms Crossed, a defensive spell, she could feel the cold, slithery thoughts of the entity behind the Eye.

Her gorge rose and caught in her throat as the Sphere of Binding shattered her own spell. She cast Wall of Hope, an Osoru spell that she had learned on her own. But either she conjured it improperly or it, too, was rendered impotent by the Eye of Ajbal, which had now drawn closer, its fiery iris opened wide, its orange pupil fully dilated.

A hateful cacophony of thoughts filled Konara Inggres to overflowing. She wanted to scream, wanted to rend her flesh from her bones, anything to escape the madness that was centimeter by centimeter swallowing her whole.

17

Word to the Wise

They sat eating the qwawd Majja had caught and skinned. It was a large bird, and there was plenty to eat. Nevertheless, it was an altogether unpalatable meal. Because of the assumed proximity of the Khagggun, they were unwilling to light a fire. Raw qwawd meat was no bargain even for famished adventurers such as these four.

There was, however, much to celebrate, as Basse was recovering at a miraculous rate. His fever was down, and his breathing was deep and even. Majja, who had thanked Minnum and Giyan profusely, had bathed his head and shoulders with water Minnum had brought from a nearby stream. Once having oriented himself around the mushroom sea, he had mapped out the immediate area in impressive detail. They managed to get the raw slippery meat down with copious mouthfuls of the cold, clear water.

When they were done, Giyan held up the cor-hide pouch.

"I found it down there." Marethyn went over to the death pit whose slotlike opening looked in the gloom like the maw of a gigantic beast. She turned on her lumane, played the beam around the interior. "I counted just over thirty Ramahan."

"I want to go down there," Giyan said.

Minnum shook his head. "Lady—?"

"It's all right. I need to see it for myself. I need to feel the evil that killed them." She turned to Marethyn. "Will you be my searchlight?"

By that time, of course, Marethyn had introduced herself, but not by her full name. No matter. Giyan knew who she was from the time Kurgan had been her son Annon's best friend. At first, she had assumed she was Majja's prisoner, but it did not take her long to intuit the truth. And if it astonished her to discover that the regent's sister was an active member of the Resistance, she did not show it. All the same, it gave her a degree of pleasure.

"Of course I will," Marethyn said.

"Keep a sharp lookout," Giyan said to Minnum, before turning and descending down the makeshift ladder.

The pit was a charnel house. She walked slowly and carefully, moving through the evidence of mass murder with all her senses at full alert. She noticed, as Marethyn did, how many of the Ramahan had turned on one another, but there were two questions she asked that Marethyn lacked the knowledge to ask. The first was what had caused them to fall upon each other. The second was who had given them the weapons to commit these atrocities.

It was difficult to ignore the horror all around her, but she knew that for the moment she needed to hold her feelings in abeyance while she allowed her rational mind to make sense of the slaughter.

Directing Marethyn, she crouched down and looked

into their eyes and ears, she pried open jaws and studied the roofs of their mouths, the insides of their cheeks, their tongues. She repeated this meticulous process until she had examined all thirty-four corpses. Fully a third were so badly mutilated or so encrusted with blood that whatever evidence might once have been there had been obliterated. Still, she did not skip a single one, and it was well that she was so methodical for as she rolled over one of the blood-iest corpses she discovered something beneath it. It was no more than twenty centimeters in length and though entirely covered in blood and gore, she could tell it was carved, could see its outline begin to appear as she cleaned it off. Her heart skipped a beat.

Nearly breathless, she returned to the ladder and climbed out of the pit. She washed the thing she had found and even before all the details appeared she knew what it was: an idol. An idol of the same curious male-female deity, in fact, that Minnum had discovered at Za Hara-at. When she showed it to him, he confirmed that it was, indeed, the same deity.

"What does this mean?" Minnum asked. "That the same mysterious folk who were at Za Hara-at centuries ago are responsible for this slaughter?"

"The Ramahan were infected somehow," she said, her blood running cold. "Possibly in a stew that was fed to them or a tea brewed for them."

"The Dark League," Minnum said.

"One would think so." Giyan was staring at the androg-ynous face of the idol. "An odd thing, though—all their eyes were the same."

Minnum cocked his head. "All of them?"

"Every one. Their irises were so black they merged with the pupil." She looked at him. "Sound familiar, my sauromician? You tell me."

Minnum frowned. "On the face of it—"

"Here." She unwrapped a small cloth. "I took scrapings from their tongues and ears. We have to be certain the sauromicians were responsible. How long will you need?"

"Perhaps an hour. I am going to have to cover every possibility, and some of the tests are quite complicated."

"Anything you need that you do not have?"

"You must be joking." He laughed and opened his jerkin, the underside of which was a warren of tiny pockets and gusseted pouches. His hairy paws swept the air. "Besides, this is the forest. In the unlikely event I am lacking a reagent, I will find what I require right here."

He took the cloth in his cupped palm and went off by himself to do his sorcerous testing.

Majja was sitting cross-legged, with Basse's head in her lap, wiping the last of the sweat off him. The purple swelling around his wound was gone, and he was sleeping deeply and peacefully. Within moments, her head went down on her chest, and she began to nod off.

Giyan and Marethyn crouched over the remains of the qwawd. The night had a velvety quality, a deepness and a certain luster, as if the lichen and the mushrooms possessed a slight phosphorescence. The effect was pleasing, and it was possible to forget the nearby presence of prowling Khagggun packs, if only for a few moments.

Marethyn stretched. "So you are Giyan." She settled herself with her back against the rough trunk of a Marre pine, wrists on knees she had drawn up. "*The* Giyan, mistress of the Ashera?"

"I have seen you several times." Glimmerings of moonslight tracing across Giyan's cheeks like silver snowflakes. "Kurgan spoke of you occasionally."

"Not flatteringly, I imagine."

"Kurgan was always very angry inside."

Marethyn said, "Don't you hate him?"

Giyan knew that was not quite the question Marethyn was asking. *Don't you hate the Stogggul?* was more like it. "Of what use would hatred be?" she said.

Marethyn appeared to consider this assessment for some time. "Do you know the name Raan Tallus?"

"Of course. He was the Ashera family solicitor-Bashkir. When Eleusis became regent much of his time was taken up with the affairs of all Kundala, and he began to give more power over the family's affairs to Raan Tallus."

"I am curious." Marethyn cocked her head. "What did you think of him?"

"Why do you ask?"

"Now Raan Tallus is running the Ashera business as if he were the Ashera heir himself."

"That is most unfortunate," Giyan said. "I told Eleusis that Raan Tallus had ambitions far beyond his caste, that it could make him dangerous, under certain circumstances a potential enemy. All Eleusis responded to was his expertise."

"Which made Eleusis' life as regent that much easier."

"Yes. Exactly. Raan Tallus knew how to make himself indispensable to Eleusis. In any event, by that time, Eleusis was already captivated by Kundalan myth and lore. That was my doing, so I have to take much of the responsibility for Raan's rise to power."

Marethyn laughed a little.

"Have I missed something?" Giyan asked.

"No, it's just that I was thinking, if we were male we would be enemies, we would be choosing weapons and mapping out plans to kill each other."

They heard movement in the darkness, and the focus of their attention shifted. Minnum was making his way toward them through the underbrush.

"I have completed my tests," he said as he hunkered down beside them.

"And?" Giyan arched an eyebrow.

"It is not what I expected." He sighed. "It is most curious. The substance you scraped off the dead Ramahan was used to drive them mad. They killed each other in a frenzy of paranoia."

"Sounds very sauromician," Giyan said.

"And yet it's not." Minnum looked at her. "I swear I checked and double-checked, and I can assure you that this is a by-product of no psychotropic the Dark League uses or is even aware of."

"What is it, then?"

"I cannot be certain, but I think I can make an educated guess," he said. "When I spent time in the Korrush I happened to overhear two Jeni Cerii talking about a compound they had traded for. We were in a tavern, and it was very noisy, but I distinctly heard them say that it was incredibly potent, dangerous even. They had it spread out between them, and when they were gone, I slipped over and managed to scrape up several grains that remained.

"I ran tests on it and found that the information they had been given was correct. This substance was different from any psychotropic you or we used. It had an entirely different chemical makeup. It was very volatile and frighteningly potent."

"What was it?" Marethyn asked.

"It took some doing, but I did find out," Minnum said. "It is called *oqeyya,* and it is a well-guarded secret of the Sarakkon."

"The Sarakkon!" Giyan exclaimed. "What would sailors be doing in the great steppe of the Korrush?"

Minnum scratched at his beard. "Better to ask, Lady, what they are doing here."

Leyytey was fuming. "What do you mean he doesn't trust me?"

"Isn't what I said." Fleet-Admiral Pnin laced his fingers together.

"That stupid, arrogant—! How dare he!"

"For the love of N'Luuura, daughter, why won't you listen."

"It was what he implied. You said Sornnn felt I still loved Teww Dacce."

"In this he is correct. Your hearts have never let go of Dacce."

Leyytey looked into the fulminating core of her ion forge. Her cheeks were flushed but not from its heat. "I have agreed to help you. I *will* help you. Whatever I feel about Teww Dacce is irrelevant."

"Is it?" Pnin performed a deep scan of the shadows in her atelier. It was late, and they were alone, he had made certain of that; but instincts never died. "You need to think this through all the way to the end. If you change your mind midstream, if you weaken—"

"I am not weak."

"If you tell Dacce what we have asked you to do—"

"Never." Leyytey was shocked. "Never!"

"Gratified to hear it. Nevertheless, you must realize that powerful emotions are in play."

What would you know about it, she thought. "It was you who put us together!"

"He is genetically flawless. You were meant to consummate a specific act with him. A breeding, that is all."

"Yes, yes. To perpetuate your precious line! To make you immortal! I did it for you. Only for you!" she shouted. "And look where it's gotten me!"

"Weak-kneed. Typical Tuskugggun argument."

"Then why did you insist that I mate with him?"

Pnin sighed. "I have already explained."

"You *knew* this could happen. You knew it, and yet you went ahead—"

"I discounted the possibility—"

"No, no. You wanted a grandson—"

"—because—"

"—a genetically perfect grandson, and nothing was going to get in the way of that."

"Because," he bellowed, "like any Tuskugggun I expected you to do as you are told."

A shocked silence enveloped them both.

"N'Luuura take it all!" She did not know what to do with her rage. She felt as if she might at any minute explode, turn herself into a living weapon that would impale him with ten thousand splintered bones. Striking out with her hand, she swept her tools off the chronosteel table that stood beside the ion forge. They rang like bells against the stone flooring.

"Daughter." Pnin took Leyytey by the wrists and pulled

her close to him. "What you must do, think of Dacce as a *thing* to be used, manipulated," he whispered fiercely. "The way *he* thinks of *you*."

She stared up into her father's golden eyes. "The way you think of me."

Pnin grimaced. "What grievous sins have I committed to have such an insolent child?"

Leyytey laughed. She could not help herself. She laughed until tears came to her eyes, and he let go of her wrists. Afterward, when she was alone again, alone as always, the laughter stopped. But the tears kept on rolling, building like waves until she could no longer stand. Crouched by her ion forge, she put her head in her hands and sobbed as if she would never stop.

These Ramahan were seduced out of Floating White by sauromician archons," Minnum said. "I mean to say how would the Dark League come into possession of such a thing?"

"Unless," Giyan said thoughtfully, "the sauromicians had somehow forged an alliance with Sarakkon."

"But why?" Minnum asked. "What would the sauromicians achieve from such an alliance?"

"That is what we must find out."

"If I may say something," Marethyn interjected, "I have been down in the death pit." And she told them about how she had stumbled across the dying Ramahan and what she had said. " 'One, two, three, four, five,' she counted out my fingers and then asked me what I saw. When I answered that I saw my fingers, she laughed at me and called me stupid." Marethyn held up her hand, her fingers splayed wide. " 'Five pivots,' she said. Does that mean anything to you?"

Giyan and Minnum exchanged a glance.

"There is an abbey by that name southwest of here near the village of Silk Bamboo Spring," Giyan said.

"But what could she have meant?" Minnum wondered. "That Five Pivots was where they had been or where they were being taken?"

"It does not matter." Giyan rose. "Either way, that abbey must be our immediate destination." She gestured, and the little sauromician got to his feet, the bones of his legs cracking a little as he stretched.

"You are leaving now, before first light?" Majja had come over to them.

"I am afraid there is no time to waste," Giyan said.

Marethyn rose, too. "How can we thank you?"

Majja nodded. "You saved Basse's life."

"You are doing important work here," Giyan said. Her blue eyes settled on Marethyn. "I doubt this will be the last time we see one another, Marethyn Stogggul." She held out her hand, and Marethyn grasped her wrist in traditional male V'ornn style.

"I will not forget you," Marethyn said. "Either of you."

The two had gone to the edge of the small encampment, when Giyan suddenly turned and said, "You are aware of the Wing, aren't you?"

"What?" Marethyn and Majja said at once.

Minnum told them of the long line of Khaggun he and Giyan had encountered crossing the crest of the ridge above them. When he described the leader, Majja gasped.

"Hannn Mennus himself is leading them? Are you certain it was an entire Wing?"

"Absolutely," Giyan said.

Majja shivered. "That means he has been promoted from Line-Commander."

"What direction were they headed in?" Marethyn asked.

"West by southwest."

"Ah, Miina," Majja cried. "Gerwa's camp!"

18

Twilight

R iane, carrying Eleana over her shoulder, emerged from the darkling, claustrophobic twilight beneath Middle Palace into the pallid, noisome twilight of Axis Tyr. She was exhausted both physically and emotionally. True, she had managed to save Eleana from Kurgan Stogggul, but in the process she had missed an opportunity to get the ninth banestone, and she felt defeated. All the despair and desolation she had felt when she had discovered that The Pearl was a fake came rushing back in a bitter black tide. Tears glittered in her eyes, and she felt so betrayed and abandoned that she thought she would dissolve into a cascade of sobs. Then she became aware of the Annon part of her asserting itself, urging her to keep going, and breaking through the depths of her despair came the Hagoshrin's exhortation, *The Pearl is only an object. We do not better ourselves through objects. Without your belief in yourself you are nothing.*

A pair of Kundalan servants cajoled their toddling V'ornn charges down the street. One of the brats bared his. teeth at her. A Bashkir toting up receipts went swiftly by. He was soon elbowed aside by three careless Haaar-kyut, and he cursed them as he lurched; but they were in too much of a hurry to apologize or even to reply.

Thigpen herded Riane into an alley deserted save for a phalanx of half-filled trash bins and a wary wyr-hound that backed away from them on spindle legs.

With a barely audible groan, Riane put Eleana on her feet, bracing her against the stained wall.

"Eleana, Eleana." Her voice was a coarse whisper. "Ah, Miina, what has he done to her?"

"Hold on, little dumpling."

"Thigpen, Kurgan has done something to her, something my sorcery cannot combat." Riane's eyes were abruptly filled with tears. "What if only he can rouse her?"

Behind the Dar Sala-at's eyes Thigpen could see the traumas piling up. She knew they needed a place to hole up so the two could heal and recuperate. The trouble was she had not been in Axis Tyr for more than a century. The changes the V'ornn had wrought stupefied her. Turning her furry back to them, she wept silent tears for a golden age that had been trampled underfoot.

Quickly, she pulled herself together. But a more thorough assessment of her two charges alarmed her. With Eleana still unconscious and Riane almost out on her feet, it seemed clear to her that more than rest was required. A judicious application of appropriate medications was definitely in order. Another problem: no known Ramahan herbalist within kilometers of the city and nowhere to get herbs that she herself could prepare.

"Little dumpling, I am going to Thrip us out of here, to a place where I can get herbs to treat your exhaustion."

"And what of Eleana? I have tried several healing spells on her without avail. It follows that herbs will not work on her, either." She shook her head. "No, we must stay within the confines of Axis Tyr."

"You are ill with fright and fatigue; you are not thinking clearly," the Rappa said gently. "Axis Tyr is dangerous for us on any account, but now that you are so debilitated—"

"No!" Riane said more sharply than she had intended. She scooped Thigpen up into the crook of her arm. "Listen to me," she said in a more normal tone of voice. "I made a choice to save Eleana. It may have been the worst decision I ever made, I don't know. But what I do know is that I cannot leave Axis Tyr. I must remain close to Kurgan now.

I have to shadow him until I can find the moment to get the banestone away from him."

"But by now he will have every Khagggun within a hundred kilometers looking for us."

"Not necessarily. No, if I know anything about the regent, he will think of another way—a less public way—to hunt us down."

"How can you know that?"

"The Hagoshrin was right. He loves Eleana. Because his father had a taste for Kundalan females, Kurgan will do whatever it takes to keep his interest in her secret."

Thigpen sighed. Of course the Dar Sala-at was right. But how were they to get aid and succor in this most hostile of environments? Then she thought of the Looorm Jura, whom they had helped in the shanstone temple. *I have lived all my life on Isinglass Street*, she had told them.

Thigpen felt the tremors going through the Dar Sala-at, and she jumped down. Riane was leaning heavily against a pale wall, supporting the insensate Eleana. Star-roses trailed down from a wrought-iron window box almost to the crown of her head.

"Sorry," she said weakly. "Sorry."

Thigpen could see that she could not go on, that the three of them could not walk another block, let alone trek up to the northern district, where Isinglass Street wound its crooked way up a sharp and unexpected slope. It was narrow, that street, and shadows would be collecting there like gimnopedes nesting in the sysal trees. It would already be full twilight there, but not quiet, no, not quiet in that unlovely district where Looorm and greasy Mesagggun rubbed shoulders and, at times, groins.

When the Ramahan had inhabited the regent's palace they had erected sorcerous fields to prevent Thripping within its environs, but they were now far enough away from it to be able to Thripp. She knew it was likely quite dangerous to Thripp them because the sauromicians' power had advanced far enough that they might be monitoring the activation of the power bourns. Nevertheless, she knew she had to take the chance. Wedging herself between them, she darkened the air with her sacred litany. She found the power bourn flowing deep beneath the bedrock of the city, and almost at once the vertiginous sensation arose like a behemoth from the deep and engulfed them all as, with an enormous effort, she Thripped them to Isinglass Street.

Astonishingly, it was just as she remembered it: the slick roughly laid cobbles, the acute turnings as the narrow thoroughfare wound its crooked-backed way up the steepening slope. The facades of the narrow buildings seemed to tip outward into the street, cutting off the midafternoon sunlight even in summer.

Still trying to act as Riane's dumb pet, she led them to a nearby tavern, where they were able to take a table seemingly carved out of the shadows in the rear.

Riane, who was by then carrying Eleana in her arms, set her down on a deeply cushioned chair. The owner came over. He was a Mesagggun aqueous of eye, vitreous of skull, with the powerful shoulders and bent back of the professional laborer. When he inquired about Eleana's health, Riane told him that she had been ill for days and was now sleeping off her exhaustion. He brought for her a powderleaf tea, touting its healing properties, and for Riane a cup of strong ba'du. For Thigpen there was nothing. He cautioned Riane to keep her pet from bothering the other patrons. Reaching down, he swept the Rappa onto the floor.

Thigpen jumped back onto the chair as soon as he was gone. "You sit here and sip your ba'du, little dumpling," she whispered. "I will return as quickly as possible with Jura."

And so she set off. It happened that she knew the area well, for in the ancient days the northern district was home to the Rappa who served Mother and the Ramahan konara. Though there had been plenty of room for them at Middle Palace, they were more comfortable in less grandiose quarters, where they could maintain the convenient illusion that they were their own masters.

That was the problem, really, she thought, as she started up the crooked spine of Isinglass Street And possibly that was where it all began to go wrong. There once might have been a time when Miina strode across Kundala, when Ramahan and Rappa shared equally in the numinous mysteries of the religion. But then, so subtly that not even the most astute Rappa could have judged the date, the relationship began to change. Just when did the Ramahan— Mother included, oh yes!—begin to view the Rappa as servants, lesser creatures there to do Miina's bidding— and, therefore, *theirs*? Doubtless, the Ramahan would deny this bias, but they would only be deluding themselves. It would not have been so easy, so *expedient* to blame Mother's death on the Rappa had not the priests and priestesses already considered the Rappa as lesser, as *other*.

And so a caste system had developed within the powerful world of the abbeys, one, though unacknowledged, fully as specific, as exacting, as heinous as that of the V'ornn. Because the very nature of a caste system engenders a polarization. It encourages everyone within it to think either *I am better than* or *I am lesser than, I want more or I have nothing, I have power or I am powerless*.

And so the rot had begun from within the very bowels of the system. It is a well-known fact that one of the things daemons do better than any other creature in the Cosmos is smell rot. They are drawn to it like insects to excrement. And so they sniffed out this rot at the very beginning and, insinuating themselves in invisible ways, accelerated the decay.

Thigpen, her thoughts plunged deep in gloom, trotted up the impoverished street. *It just goes to show*, she thought, *that the downtrodden are the downtrodden, no matter what race they belong to*.

It was fortunate that it was the time of the evening when, like finbats, the Looorm emerged from their backwater lairs, swarming throughout the city on their way to assignations or their nightly patrols to drum up business.

Jura was emerging from a shadowed doorway near the top of the street. She looked both sad and irresolute, which lent her the appearance of being lost. When Thigpen trotted up to her, she stopped dead in her tracks. For a moment, she looked blankly at the Rappa then, as if a switch had been thrown, recognition dawned in her vulpine face, and she knelt.

"Well, well, what are you doing here?" she said to herself.

"Jura, we need your help."

The Looorm's eyes went wide and she emitted a tiny grunt of astonishment. "What is this?"

"We need your help, I say."

"You can speak!"

"Yes, yes, of course I can speak," Thigpen said shortly. "There has been an accident."

Jura frowned. "What kind of an accident?"

"Eleana has been hurt. Riane as well."

Jura sat on her haunches staring at the Rappa.

"Will you help us, Jura?"

"I was just on my way to work." Her hands were pale and thin and very soft.

"Riane needs you. We all need you."

"I have been thinking about everything Riane said to me, and it seems that this is work I no longer want to perform." She looked down at her body. "But what am I to do now? I don't know anything else except how to lure males."

"Jura."

At last, she recognized the urgency in Thigpen's voice. "Where are they?" She rose. "Where is Riane?"

"At the tavern near the foot of the street."

"Take me to her," she said.

From a great distance Konara Inggres heard the tolling of the bells. It was the call to prayer, reverberating through the white-stone passageways and cleanly clipped gardens of the Abbey of Floating White. The sound was so sweet it brought tears to her eyes.

Her eyes! They were not glued shut as Perrnodt's had been. She opened them, gazed, startled, up into the beautiful, manly face of the Nawatir. She opened her mouth, but her tongue felt thick. It seemed to have forgotten how it worked.

"Don't try to speak," the Nawatir said. "You're in Floating White. You're quite safe."

All at once, as if returning from a dreamworld, Konara Inggres realized that she was wrapped in his cloak, that she was encircled by his strong arms. She could smell him, a combination of spice and musk, and she did nothing for some time but breathe him in. Her head was in the crook of his arm, and she turned so that her cheek rested against his left bicep. She rested there, luxuriating in the warmth that crept through her extremities. Her lips were half-open. His cloak, his warmth was like a balm, healing the psychic wounds the awful filaments had made in her mind. She thought of Perrnodt blinded, her eyelids glued shut with crystal, and she shuddered.

"It's all right," the Nawatir whispered, rocking her a little. "You're home now. You're safe."

The prayers of her flock flowed through the abbey, a song of joyous praise, spreading Miina's holy light, beating back the darkness of uncertainty. She allowed herself to close her eyes, to be rocked like a feverish child. Her mind felt empty, her body weak, just as if she had passed through a terrible illness.

"Why did you do it?" he asked softly, gently. "Why did you put yourself at risk? You should have come to me first."

She smiled a little, as one does in a dream. "I am sorry." Her voice, a husky whisper, seemed odd to her ears, as if someone else were speaking. "I am not used to having a male around the abbey."

He chuckled and held her all the closer. "You have had

to do so much on your own." She felt his breath, sweet as new-mown grass, cross her cheek. "You have shouldered so much responsibility. Without you, the abbey would have fallen to Horolaggia. The daemons would have taken over. You have great courage and perseverance."

Konara Inggres felt so grateful to him that she began to weep.

Mistaking her emotion, he bent over her, and whispered, "Ah, don't."

His strong, callused hand stroked her tears away. And with that tender touch Konara Inggres felt something that she had dreamed of but had never actually experienced. The spasms began deep inside her, radiating out from that damp place between her thighs. Her nipples felt as if they had been dipped in fire, her mons was bared, split open like a ripe pomegranate, and she gasped once, involuntarily, shamelessly, then clamped her lips together so that she would not utter another. Deep within his embrace, her eyelids fluttered and she gripped him with fingers bled white by the swift, shocking overflow of her passion.

"Konara Inggres, are you all right?"

"Yes," she whispered. "Oh, yes." But she bit her lip until she tasted blood. She was in utter disbelief. Breathless and throbbing, her ecstasy was turned rotten by her acute sense of betrayal. For she knew now what she had been trying to keep from herself. She loved him. Her heart and soul, her mind and her body belonged to him, and she cursed her weakness, berated herself for what she could not control. And yet, she knew that she had to control it. She had to deny her heart what it wanted most, for she loved First Mother, had witnessed the intimate connection between her and the Nawatir, and she would die rather than disturb their tight orbit.

And so she struggled wildly, desperately, to free herself from his embrace, for she felt that if she stayed within it one more moment, she would lose her resolve and be lost forever. But he mistook her weakened thrashing for a recurrence of the trauma she had just suffered and held her all the more tightly.

Swaddled in the Nawatir's semisentient cloak, horribly and beautifully crushed against him, Konara Inggres sank into a well of self-pity. What had she done to deserve such anguish?

Dearest Miina, she prayed, *haven't I been Your most loyal servant, haven't I toiled countless hours to preserve Your teaching, to protect all that is Yours?*

And then from all around her or perhaps deep inside her the Great Goddess miraculously responded.

Are you to be rewarded for being strong, righteous, holy? Are not those things their own reward? Do you think me so petty a deity to dispense happiness like so many party favors? Look to your work, child, for it is hardly begun.

Konara Inggres' shock, like a wave of ice water, both revived her and rescued her from the thrall under which she had been suffering.

"Nawatir, I am fine," she said in her normal voice. "Please let me up."

"Are you certain?" His expression was dubious.

"Quite certain."

He let her go, unwrapping his cloak from around her.

He brought her a cup of steaming greengage tea. She held it with both hands and gratefully sipped the brew.

"Now, if you have regained sufficient strength," he said, "kindly tell me what you thought you were up to?"

So she told him how she had felt they needed reinforcements for the assault that seemed sure to come. She showed him the master list of abbeys, told him how she had searched all of them, how all were bereft of life—all save the Abbey of Summit Window on Kunlung Mountain. "But the Eye of Ajbal found me before I could tell the Ramahan of our need."

"I thought you had taken up Perrnodt's quest to find your missing Ramahan." The Nawatir sat with his hands cupped in his lap. "But that would have been stupid, and you are not stupid."

She had trouble looking at his hands without feeling a telltale trembling in her inner thighs. "How do you know about the Eye?"

"Lady Giyan has had experience with it," he said. "I could feel it. I knew it was searching, and I assumed it was looking for us here. I came to your chamber to warn you. When you did not answer my knock I entered and saw you with this." He held the casting opal in the palm of his hand. "You did not respond. I felt the Eye moving and knew you were in trouble."

"But how on Kundala did you save me from it?"

"I brought you back with this." His cloak rippled to his touch. "Perrnodt was too far gone for it to save her, but I got you wrapped in it in time."

She shook her head. "I do not understand."

"I am only beginning to," he admitted. "The cloak is pure Dragon energy. It fluxes in and out of this Realm, through netherspace, into others. I wrapped you in a lifeline, and it brought you back to me."

It brought you back to me. She knew what he meant, but still . . . She closed her eyes against the return of her anguish. She thought of Miina.

"There is something I must tell you," she said. "When the Eye briefly took me, the intelligence behind it cast a spell—Sphere of Binding. It wanted to know my thoughts, and it began to crack open my mind like a glass jar."

"Did it find out anything?"

"You saved me before it could. But at the same time I was privy to its thoughts."

"Do you know who or what the entity was?"

"No. There was a blizzard, a jumble of words and images. None of it made sense, and most have receded now like dreams. But there is one thing. The Eye of Ajbal was not looking for me, not until it sensed my opal casting."

"Who was it looking for?"

"Someone named Krystren." Konara Inggres frowned in

concentration. "I do not know who that is, but one thing I am certain of: its search was desperate."

It was a Deirus Jura brought to see them. Riane recognized him, slim and grey-faced, dark of eye and wary of mien. He had looked at her when they had passed the partly open doorway to Cthonne on their way into the caverns beneath Middle Palace.

Jura said his name was Kirlll Qandda.

He came with his satchel, a shapeless, old-fashioned cor-hide bag of Kundalan manufacture with many pockets and gussets and a capacious interior, and drew up a chair beside Eleana.

"She's not going to be ill in here," the Mesagggun owner said, hurrying up. "She's not going to die."

But he shut up and backed away, muttering to himself, when Kirlll Qandda stitched him with a piercing eye surprising in one so meek-looking.

"I won't have it," the owner said once, before turning away and vanishing into the kitchen.

"We can ill afford his contacting the authorities," Thigpen said.

Jura nodded and followed him into the kitchen.

Kirlll Qandda commenced his examination. If he was surprised to encounter a talking sestapod, he gave no outward sign of it.

"No sign of a head injury," the Deirus said. "Did she suffer a fall?"

"I think she was given something," Riane told him. "But I don't know what."

Kirlll Qandda nodded. He had completed the gross physical examination, and his fingers, small, almost feminine in their gentleness, probed more slowly, looking, Riane supposed, for tiny abnormalities.

"Her neck is clear, as is her scalp," the Deirus said. "Also her arms. But hold on, what's this?" His practiced eye had spotted the small hole—one of many—in her tunic. But this one was different; it wasn't a tear but went straight in. He pulled up the stained and filthy fabric to expose her bare midriff, a pale, vulnerable swath compared to her sun-browned arms and legs. There on her left side was an angry-looking reddish blotch with a triangular black puncture wound in its center.

"Neat as a surgeon," he said. And Riane thought: *Kurgan.*

"Well, now we know *how* it was administered. The question of the moment is what is it?" Kirlll Qandda opened Eleana's mouth, and, delicately drawing out her tongue, began a careful examination of it. "Did you know that you can tell virtually everything about an individual from looking at their tongue?" he continued in a bright, conversational tone.

Riane shook her head.

"Well, it's true. Each section of the tongue corresponds either to a system or to an organ." He pointed. "It is as I suspected. Here, you see these red spots in a circle? They are in the place that represents the autonomic nervous system. That tells me that she was given a paralytic agent of some kind. The fact that there are five spots is a response peculiar to Nieobian paralysis gel."

Annon had heard of the substance but, of course, Riane could not admit to it. No Kundalan had even heard of the planet Nieobius, let alone anything that came from there.

"It's fortuitous you found Jura," he said, as he rooted around in his Kundalan satchel. "I very much doubt that Kundalan herbal medicine could cope with this."

Neither could sorcery. Riane vowed to remember that. "Is she going to be all right?"

"As soon as I synthesize the antidote and administer it." Kirlll Qandda looked around. "Let us find a more private place, shall we?"

Immediately, Thigpen trotted into the rear of the place, soon returning to inform them of a storeroom that would be suitable. Riane, gathering her strength, scooped Eleana up, and they followed the Rappa back into the gloom of the cafe's interior and into a small, airless cubicle. A curtain of dust motes hung in the air as if suspended in syrup.

Kirlll Qandda hurriedly arranged some wooden boxes into an approximation of a pallet, and Thigpen laid down a layer of clean tablecloths. Onto this, Riane laid Eleana.

Kirlll Qandda was already fitting together a series of mimetic-alloy rods, cones, and ovoids. He took a swab of Eleana's saliva off her tongue and inserted it into the end of one of the rods.

"Try not to worry." He smiled. "It won't be long now."

"I remember you." Thigpen was sitting up on her two pairs of powerful hind legs. Her black eyes were bright as lamps, and her sharp teeth were slightly bared.

"See those teeth?" Kirlll Qandda turned to Riane. "Did you know this beast has the ability to inject a powerful nerve toxin through a tiny aperture at the base of each tooth?"

"Don't change the subject," Thigpen snapped. "And where do you get off calling me a beast?"

Riane shot Thigpen a sharp look, and said, "No, I didn't."

Kirlll Qandda gave a tiny, rueful smile. "It is safe to say that what you don't know about Rappa could fill an encyclopedia."

"And you do?" Thigpen snorted. "I know you, Deirus. No matter how much you obfuscate, you cannot change the fact."

"How do you know him?" Riane asked.

"Tell her." Thigpen crossed her forearms over her breast. There was a very unpleasant look on her face. "I would like to hear your version."

Kirlll Qandda shrugged. "There is not so much to tell."

"Oho!" Thigpen's teeth clacked together warningly.

"Hush now." Riane put her arms around the Rappa's neck, rubbing her knuckles in the spot where Thigpen liked it best, between her ears. She nodded to the Deirus.

"I was on assignment with a Khaggun Death Pack—"

"They broke into the Abbey of Listening Bone!" Thigpen snapped. "What is now the Gyrgon Temple of Mnemonics." Riane could feel the Rappa shivering. "They killed and tortured—"

"It was the day of the occupation. I was dragooned out of my lab. I had no idea what they wanted me to do until I arrived with the Death Pack."

"Did you take part in the torture of the Ramahan?" Riane asked.

"No, I—"

"But you did!" Thigpen barked. "I saw you kill and keep on killing helpless Ramahan who just lay there!"

The silence was so absolute they could hear Eleana softly breathing.

"Time," Kirlll Qandda said, removing the mnemonic stick. He opened Eleana's mouth and pressed the end into the base of her tongue, then he did something to make the stick turn clear. "There," he said, sitting back. "She will awake within the hour. Six hours after that she should be fine, though somewhat weak. Make sure she eats and drinks plenty of water. One of your vaunted herbal tea decoctions wouldn't hurt either."

He turned his attention to Riane, studying her intently. "It looks as if you have been in quite a battle." He reach out. "Do you mind?"

Riane shook her head, sitting still while he examined her.

"These bruises, scrapes, and punctures look recent." He glanced up at her face. "And yet except at their very center they appear to be almost healed." He returned to his examination. "Quite astonishing, really. No ointment, salves, herbs of any kind have been used. I admit I am somewhat mystified . . . and completely fascinated."

"I am Ramahan," Riane said, as if that explained everything.

"Ah, but not your typical Kundalan priestess, not by any means."

He finished examining her. In all that time Riane had not moved.

"Sorcery, yes?" When she remained silent, he shrugged. "I don't really blame you. Were I in your position, I wouldn't trust me either." He looked at her. "What would it take?"

"Tell me," she said softly, "what happened."

Kirlll Qandda had begun dismantling his equipment, stowing it away in his satchel. He stopped and sighed. "It's true, I killed them. The ones that were dying I put out of their agony."

"And the others?" Thigpen growled. "There were Rappa there, flushed out of the shadows where we were too loyal or too stupid to quit Axis Tyr and take to the deep caves of the Djenn Marre."

Kirlll Qandda pressed his thumbs against his eyelids as if trying to blot out the memory. "The others I killed as well. I slit their throats cleanly, neatly, quickly. You see, by that time I knew what the Gyrgon had ordered. They wanted to instill fear among the Kundalan, but they also wanted information. Those who survived the first slaughter were to be interrogated." He took his thumbs away and looked at them. "You both know what that means. You know the unbounded torment the Ramahan would have otherwise suffered."

"Even so," Thigpen growled, "it was not your place."

"I wonder about that every day," the Deirus said as he rose, "because when I dream it is their cries I hear."

You should not have brought him here," Nith Immmon said. "This is very bad. Very bad indeed."

"I gave her no choice, Nith Immmon," Sahor said. "Besides, who will recognize me in my new form?"

"*She* did," Nith Immmon pointed out.

Gul Aluf, her arms and wings folded, gazed at Sahor with her enigmatic half smile.

They were in her lab-orb at Receiving Spirit, where Kurgan had first spied on Nith Immmon and Gul Aluf. The deep thrumming of her ion engines was a background wash. At intervals, heuristic nets hung from the high ceiling, but they were empty.

"She also suspected that I was alive," Sahor said as he walked around the lab-orb, observing everything in the minutest detail. He peered into each of the biochambers and did not like what he saw. "Does Nith Nassam?"

"No," Nith Immmon said with absolute assurance. He cleared his throat. Gul Aluf seemed secretly amused by his discomfort with Sahor's new appearance, doubtless recognizing another superiority she held over him.

Sahor said, "The experiments are at an impasse."

"I do not—"

"Let's not get off on the wrong note." He stopped moving and turned to face Nith Immmon. "This is what Gul Aluf told me."

In response to Nith Immmon's glare, Gul Aluf said, "There is nothing to be gained in holding anything back. Not at this point."

"These experiments are heinous," Sahor said in a cold, clear voice. "Wrong in every way you care to look at them."

Gul Aluf said, "We are talking about our survival."

Sahor took a step toward her. This was why he had kept from her the reality of his transformation. If she suspected, she would demand to know by what means he had merged himself with a Kundalan, for he had employed the formula for which she had so long been searching. "And if, through these experiments we survive, then what?"

"Then we have won," she said. "We will have done the unimaginable. We will have defeated the Centophennni."

"No," he said, advancing farther on her. "I mean what will we have become? What will we have sacrificed so that we might survive?"

"Surely our survival is paramount. Nothing else matters."

"Yes," he said. He was very close to her by then, and her face dominated his vision, his thoughts. " 'Nothing else matters.' That is the V'ornn way. Our proud motto, if you will."

"Nith Sahor—"

He rounded on Nith Immmon. "I am no longer Nith!" He grinned fiercely. "You see how it is, what we have already become? We are cripples, moral cripples. We do what we please with whatever species we happen to come across and conquer."

"It is survival of the fittest," Nith Immmon said, "pure and simple."

"There is nothing simple about it," Sahor said. "And surely there is nothing pure about killing, torture, and rape—the misery and suffering we leave in our wake like a slimy trail. No wonder the Centophennni can track us!"

Nith Immmon, taken aback by this extraordinary outburst, said, "I told you this was a mistake."

"I need him," she said.

"He requires a rest," Nith Immmon said with a sigh. "A good, long rest."

"No." Sahor swung around. "What I need is to stop these experiments right here, right now." Thrusting his face into Gul Aluf's, he said, "Did you really think that anything—your sexual blandishments, your clumsy attempt at coercion—would get me to assist you in this obscenity?"

"We do have your father," Nith Immmon pointed out.

"You have the DNA program I created for him," Sahor said. "You stole it from me."

"You were dead."

"*She* did not think so."

As if they inhabited a prison cell, a claustrophobic silence wrapped them in its shroudlike embrace. Sahor wished them plunged into the depths of the ocean; either that, or into a raging inferno, where all the collected sins of the V'ornn could be swept away. But sins, particularly of this magnitude, could not so easily be expunged. Possibly they never could, but that would not stop him from trying.

"You see, my dear"—Gul Aluf touched him gently, tentatively—"this is why I broke it off. It was because of you. I could no longer bear the brunt of your contempt. You despised me for engineering this experiment—"

"Operating on the hybrid offspring of V'ornn and Kundalan. The offspring of callous rape." She had pushed him, pushed him farther than he thought he could go. "Yes, I despised you."

"I broke it off," she said, her voice very low, "because you would not."

Nith Immmon cleared his throat again. "About Nith Einon—"

"My father is dead," Sahor said without taking his eyes off Gul Aluf.

"I know him," Gul Aluf said. She unwound her arms, unfurled her wings. "He does not mean that."

"It is a program," Sahor said, slowly and carefully: "Nothing more."

Her half smile had returned, but its smugness fatally marred her beauty. "I can take that program and build him again, molecule by molecule, into Nith." The smile widened. "You can have him back again, all of him, as he was."

Sahor shook his head. "You simply do not understand, do you?"

She shrugged. "What's to understand? This is a business transaction, nothing more, nothing less."

"Listen to yourself." Sahor gestured. "A business transaction involving the maiming—and murder—of innocent victims."

"They are half-breeds, they mean nothing to us," Nith Immmon said, hammering the last nail into his coffin.

"That is my point," Sahor said. "They mean nothing to you, and they should."

"Why?"

"Because they breathe, they think, they *live*."

"This is useless," Nith Immmon said impatiently.

Sahor at last rounded on him. "Don't you understand it yet? Don't you see? We are never leaving Kundala. Here is where we will make our stand against the Centophennni. Here is where we will be judged by time, by history. I want us to be a better species than we now are."

"It will not matter if we are all dead," Nith Immmon pointed out.

"It will matter most then."

"Beware of what you wish for."

Nith Immmon held out his hand, and a tiny sphere flew

from it, blue and green. Sahor knew what it was. Two meters above their head, it popped open and he saw the starfield, the constellations so familiar to him since the V'ornn arrived on Kundala. Then he saw the debris, floating dead hunks, turned inside out by goron-particle weapons.

"They are coming," Nith Immmon said. "It will not be long before the Centophennni are here."

"If my experiments are terminated," Gul Aluf said, "we will surely be destroyed when they arrive. We have no defense against their goron-particle weapons."

"We ourselves cannot master the goron particle, cannot harness it," Nith Immmon admitted. "We have tried so many times and failed. Even Nith Batoxxx, who was experimenting with a goron-wave weapon, failed."

"And so your response is to try to genetically engineer the hybrids—"

"The Kundalan have a quality, a resilience," Nith Immmon said. "You were right about that."

"But it's more. Much more." Gul Aluf's gaze did not waver. She had taken his best blow and, for better or worse, had absorbed it. He had, at least, to admire her for that. "Something happens when the species combine, something special. The joining becomes more than the sum of the two parts. Something greater, something possibly invincible."

"The miscegenation does not work," he said. "The two races are physically incompatible."

"But they're not. My experiments have proved that." Gul Aluf looked at him with her penetrating stare. "Right now the compatibility is ephemeral, like a radioactive substance with a half-life of milliseconds," she admitted. "Right now I can't quantify it, I don't understand it at all. I only know it exists." She came up to him, and whispered, "Nith Batoxxx worked on many experiments. The goron-wave chamber was one. We discovered hard evidence of that in his lab-orb. But there were other experiments, hidden from us while he was off-line from the Comradeship's matrix. What was he doing? These others have no idea, Sahor. But I genetically manipulated him. I gave birth to him. I suspect he was working on a project parallel to mine but with the same purpose: to meld V'ornn and Kundalan."

19

Maggot in the Works

When Kurgan recovered sufficiently to lever himself up, he hobbled over to the bed and sat heavily. He stared morosely at the dead beast without really seeing it. He could not care less about it, though he guessed the Gyrgon would have a field day with it. A brief flicker of pleasure at not telling them wafted through him, and was almost immediately expunged. Eleana was gone, and the trysting chamber was as dead as ever it had been. The dust lay heavy as molten lead. Its onyx columns seemed to pitch inward, the gloom was suffocating. He could smell death, snickering in the cobwebbed shadows.

His leg felt as if it were on fire, and when he touched the flesh it felt swollen and pulpy, as if his muscles had melted like wax. There was little point in going after Riane, even less in calling his Haaar-kyut. He did consider summoning his personal Genomatekk, but then thought of a better idea. Scooping the banestone back into its alabaster box, he limped his way through the darkened Kundalan corridors. He stashed the box in a niche he had sometime ago discovered behind his wall of weapons.

The pain in his leg was bad, but not so bad as to impair his keen mind. The stairs were the worst. He held on to the banister for support, but he never broke his stride. He used one of the secret exits the Ramahan had made in the palace and left his heavily guarded precincts without his Haaar-kyut being the wiser.

Outside, the glimmerings of night had begun. The city was awash in the bluish glow of fusion lamps. Kurgan entered the bustling stream of pedestrian traffic on Momentum Boulevard without causing so much as a raised eyebrow. He walked with only the slightest limp, though it cost him in effort and pain, and he wondered idly whether he was bleeding. He felt weak, his entire body throbbed. Pausing at a stall on Aquasius Street across from the forbidding facade of warehouses, he drank a cup of cheap ludd-wine in one swallow. He almost choked on the rawness of it, but felt somewhat fortified by the fermentation. The standing, however, did him no good at all because an odd stiffness had set in.

He headed south again, but by the time he reached Harborside the pain in his leg had reached his thigh, and every so often he would suffer a pinprick of agony in his hip. The crowds had thickened, and the smell of roasting meats and vegetables perfumed the air. Down along the Promenade, tavern doors were thrown open, and the shouting and songs of the Sarakkon spewed forth like heat from a bonfire. Kurgan felt abruptly parched, and he pulled himself out of the mainstream crawl, looking around for another drink stall. Heading for one, he lost a couple of seconds, everything went dark, and he momentarily lost his bearings. Holding himself erect, he felt as if he were in the middle of a dream where he did not know where he was, where he was going, or why. He blinked and swallowed hard. The pain in his leg was like a drumbeat of agony. Then he remembered, and he reentered the loud swirl of Sarakkon, Kundalan, and V'ornn, making his way down the Promenade to the slip where Courion's boat was docked.

Long before he got there, he could see that the slip was empty. He gave out a little groan, his one concession to the pain that racked him, but he kept going, step by step, meter by meter. He stared bleakly out across the Sea of Blood. Where was the *Omaline*? Why wasn't it there?

Bleary-eyed, hanging on the rail, he stared out to sea, but what he saw was not the darkling water, not the smear of orange at the horizon, not the black silhouettes of sails like bird wings. He was trapped again in the hateful vision from his last salamuuun flight, his father bent over the sweaty back of another Kundalan female, her long hair twined in his white-knuckled fists, pounding away with great animal grunts, talking about *him*, about Kurgan. The anger in his voice, in his thrusts, the anger at not getting what he had wanted in his son (he *never* spoke of Terrettt). Nothing Kurgan ever did pleased him. But why should Kurgan try? His father looked right through him, spoke to a nonexistent place over his left shoulder when occasionally addressing him. Except when he dressed him down, then he looked him in the eye, which drove Kurgan to do whatever it took to anger his father even more, to be noticed rather than ignored by this hateful figure from whom, it seemed now, he would never be severed, even though he was quite dead. But death had many meanings. In the mind memories refused to die, rather grew like weeds in a tangle, a suffocating mass, for in every nucleus of every cell in his body his father lived, bred, colonized, his tendencies trapping him at every turn.

He slammed fist against thigh. Each time he did so, the pain spiked up to dizzying levels. He hung upon the sea rail, panting, sick to his stomachs, willing the pain to excise his memories. But finally it got the best of him and he pitched sideways, rolling beneath the sea rail, down onto the gently rocking slip where once he and Courion had spoken of many things the night he had saved the Sarakkon from the immense jaws of the black Chimaera.

"What it all boils down to," the Teyj said, "is that they are right." It spread its four multicolored wings, its beady eyes on Sahor. It was very happy to see him. "I know you despise her, I know you love her. And as for Nith

Immmon, the only thing to say about him is he has the best interests of the Modality in mind."

The Teyj watched Sahor out of beady black eyes as he walked around the circular turret that crowned one of the minarets of the Temple of Mnemonics. From this eyrie, he could look out over the Great Phosphorus Marsh, to the north of which were the raked-out hills being systematically strip-mined of lortan, the mineral-rich substance the V'ornn refined into veradium. At the moment, however, his mind was elsewhere. He was checking every square centimeter.

"They cannot see or hear," the Teyj said. "I made certain of that."

Sahor turned to his father. "I will not help Gul Aluf with her experiments," he said flatly.

Nith Einon cocked his little Teyj head. "From the look of you, it wouldn't take much."

"What does that mean?"

The Teyj flew onto his shoulder and said, "You know what it means. You have broken the genetic code. You have engineered the merger of V'ornn and Kundalan into one being. Our experiments in hybridization are crude compared to what you have done, so crude they always end in failure. What did you think you were doing?"

"Isn't this what you had been looking toward?"

"With someone—*anyone*—else. Not you. Nith have no business muddying the gene pool."

"You haven't gone over." Sahor took great pains not to show his alarm. "You haven't become one of them, have you, Father?"

"It is no longer a matter of them versus us, Sahor. The Centophennni are almost here. You have seen the evidence with your own eyes. The need of the V'ornn Modality is great. You can no longer afford to stay on the sidelines."

"You want your Gyrgon body back. Gul Aluf told me she could do it."

"Much as I appreciate what you have done for me, my

son, you know as well as I that in this form my abilities are
severely limited."

"I cannot believe this is happening, not to you."

"It is live or die now for all of us. You must understand
this."

Sahor did, better even than Nith Einon. He knew the
stakes as well as any of them, but he was aware of perils
unknown to them, pitfalls he dared not tell them. And then
there was his own research concerning the Centophennni,
the indications of which he could surely tell no one.

"All I am saying is there must be an alternative to what
Gul Aluf is proposing. These children are innocents. They
do not deserve the misery and death to which she has consigned them."

"That is the point," Nith Einon said. "If you take over
the program, if you do to them what you have done to
yourself, then they will be spared."

"Spared? Listen to yourself, Father. They won't be
spared at all. They will become our first line of defense
against the Centophennni. They will be goron-cannon fod-
der, the first to fall when the Centophennni find us."

"Or they will perform as we expect them to perform,"
Nith Einon said. "They will defeat the Centophennni and
become heroes."

"Is that what you think?" Sahor snorted. "Since when
does the V'ornn Modality treat hybrids with anything
other than contempt? Besides, if they do defeat the Centophennni, our own Khaggun will see them as a threat. And
if they fear them, they will destroy them." He shook his
head. "Either way they will be doomed."

"Is this your last word?" Nith Einon said. "Because if it
is, then surely we are all doomed."

"You forget Nith Batoxxx's experiments with the
goron-wave chamber."

Nith Einon ruffled his feathers. "That ended like all
other experiments with the goron particle. It never
worked."

"Are you certain? Nith Batoxxx had a great advantage

over all of us. He was possessed by the Kundalan archdae-mon Pyphoros."

"We are talking gorons, Sahor. Of what possible use is a Kundalan creature?"

"It was the archdaemon that drove Nith Batoxxx to con-tinue with the goron-wave chamber long after the real Nith Batoxxx would have given up in disgust. Why? Because the archdaemon knew something about gorons we do not."

Now it was Nith Einon's turn to snort. "This is pure speculation on your part, and wild it is, too."

"Possibly," Sahor said. "I would need to explore the chamber myself in order to find out."

"Nith Batoxxx's lab-orb had been put under Prime Re-striction. Nith Nassam and Nith Immmon have control of it."

"Then let me talk with Nith Immmon."

The Teyj sighed. "I know what he will say. Go with Gul Aluf. Let her give you a tour of her lab-orb. See her method-ology, show some sign of reconsidering your position."

"Father, I will not—"

"If you want him to grant you permission to explore the goron-wave chamber, then you must. There is no other way."

It was difficult to pinpoint the precise moment when Teww Dacce knew something was amiss. It was true that he was born with good instincts, but Iin Mennus, having had the skill to sniff out this asset, had honed the trait to razor-raptor sharpness. Like a razor-raptor, Dacce had a habit of using the tip of his tongue to taste the air, to find hidden within its insubstantiality the warp and weft of intent.

It was not that he found Leyytey's news unbelievable, though typical of him the first thing he had done was re-search not only the SaTrryn but the winds of incipient war fanning the Five Tribes of the Korrush. Not that he cared a whit for the tribes or for the great northern steppe. He had the typical V'ornnish disdain for arid bits of land—and all of the sea—that had no intrinsic value. To his way of thinking a war between the tribes would not be a bad thing (the more Kundalan dead the better!), but he could clearly see how it would be a disaster for the SaTrryn, who derived almost all their revenue from trading with the Rasan Sul.

In his meticulous fashion he followed the skein of Leyytey's story backward until he arrived at the inescapable conclusion that it was the absolute truth. And yet, the tip of his tongue, tasting the air when he and Leyytey were together, warned him of a fulminating intent. Possibly it was how easily he could now have what he wanted most. While he was not as paranoid as many of his caste, he was innately suspicious of all things that came too easily. Time and again, battlefield victories turned into clever enemy traps. It was astonishing, really, the rate at which these ruses were perpetrated.

The coins accruing immediately to Leyytey were real enough—he had asked to see the first installment from the SaTrryn that sealed her new fealty, that would make her comfortable, as she told him, with the reality of having for the foreseeable future only one client. This, too, made perfect sense. If he were in her place, he would have demanded just such a gesture. And now all he had to do was to return to her and her newfound riches would be his. He could become First-Captain Kwenn's partner in his fabled Bashkir deal. Kwenn said they could triple their coinage!

Perhaps it was too small a step to take for such largesse. Or then again perhaps she was just a touch too eager. Eager to trap him into the kind of life that would destroy him. He had no doubt that she loved him. He also could not help feeling that it was toxic. Despite her proficiency at weapons design and manufacture, she was a particularly sensitive Tuskugggun. Not that he pretended to understand Tuskugggun. Not that he had a desire to. Who would? Still, had he known this about her when they met, he would have made polite talk for an evening and walked away. Possibly, he should have done, but the thought of mating with Fleet-Admiral Pnin's only daughter was simply too alluring. He had had such plans then, his cojoining with Leyytey appearing to be his ticket to higher rank, privileges available only to the elite. Typical of his luck, that, too, had come to nothing. And now here he was stuck on the coattails of an irascible and ungrateful Khagggun who had become the new Star-Admiral through nothing more mysterious than the sheer force of his belligerence and vindictive nature.

Lying beside her at night, Dacce was possessed by feverish shivers that caused her to weave her arms around him like a web until he thought he might go mad from lack of breath. His lust for her coins, for the entree it would provide him into a world of riches, was like an ague he had contracted hunting claiwen in the Great Phosphorus Marsh. But the more he ached, the more he hated her; the more he hated her, the more suspicious of her he became until he saw in every gesture, heard in every word she uttered, a plot against him. Her love for him gave his suspicions added credence, for without understanding its origin he perceived it as the most profound threat to his well-being. The more he was drawn to what she had, the more time he spent with her, the more real the threat became.

Again without understanding its origin—or caring, for the matter of that—he commenced to abuse her. Her strange acquiescence enraged him further, causing him to abuse her more deeply, possibly only to get her to react, to fight back, to engage him, to join him in the bitter struggle against himself he was waging in lonely and debilitating isolation.

And out of spite or self-abasement or whatever complex emotion now drove him, he would not touch a coin of her newfound wealth. Not one.

Kurgan was lifted gently out of sleep, out of dreams, out of despair, and deposited into the flesh and blood of full consciousness. He lay for a moment, staring up at the low, barrel ceiling, seeing nothing but Eleana's face. He had been talking to her and she to him. She had spoken as no other female, V'ornn or Kundalan, had ever spoken to him. It was stirring, it was significant, but he could not remember a single word of what she had said. The dream had brought him so close to understanding himself, and now nothing remained. Even the feeling that had embraced him was fading like the fugitive taste of a delicious fruit.

"Kurgan Stogggul."

The voice was familiar, and he turned his head, his gaze skimming across the collection of miniature oiled shells, the globule of seawater housing several exotic species of mollusk, the lovingly preserved ripshark, its sandpaper hide an iridescent orange-red. Kelyx swam into his field of vision.

"You are aboard the *Omaline*, in our cabin," the ship's surgeon said. "Do you know what happened to you?"

"No," Kurgan lied. Strange to say, the pain in his leg seemed to be clearing his head. "I was bitten."

Kelyx was peering at the bandage with which he had dressed Kurgan's ankle. "Indeed you were."

"By some rabid six-legged mammal."

"A fair-sized one, too, judging by the size of the bite marks." Kelyx had unwound the bandage, and he grunted. "If we didn't know better, we'd say it was a Rappa. But so far as we know Rappa are extinct and have been for nearly a century." He applied a soothing ointment that stank of phosphorus and unprocessed seaweed. "In any event, we have treated you for the toxin we found in your system." He smiled. "Even for a V'ornn, you have an extraordinary capacity for somatic regeneration."

Kurgan sat up, but as he swung his legs over the side of the berth he was overcome by a bout of vertigo.

"You heal quickly, but not that quickly."

Kelyx helped him to lie down again, then he sat down by the side of the berth, took out a laaga stick, and lighted it. He inhaled deeply, exhaled slowly, almost indolently, the familiar sweet smell curling upward with the bluish smoke to wreathe the bronze lamp that hung from the barrel ceiling.

There was something odd about that lamp, Kurgan thought.

"How are you feeling?" Kelyx asked.

Kurgan stared at the lamp, a Sarakkon lamp, to be sure, incised with the same curious runes that ran down their cheeks and arms. What was wrong with it? He concentrated.

"Are you thirsty, hungry?"

Kurgan blinked. "I am not on the *Omaline*," he said thickly. "I am not on any ship."

Kelyx took another deep drag of the laaga stick. "We told you he would work it out sooner rather than later," he said, but not to Kurgan.

A shadow stirred, and another Sarakkon appeared in Kurgan's field of vision. He was tall and very slender. His narrow skull was tattooed with a single circle of runes that began on the prominent points of his cheeks and ended at the nape of his neck. His thick beard was dark and unadorned. His mustache was a knife blade, waxed to fine points.

"This is Lujon." Kelyx rose and without another word left the cabin or whatever it was.

Lujon sat down on the chair and crossed his long legs. He wore a black sharkskin vest and high seaboots of shagreen, dyed crimson. His slender fingers were clad in rings of carved chrysoberyl and coralbright. Hands heavily callused, even for a Sarakkon. Like Kelyx, he produced a laaga stick and lighted it. Instead of putting it between his lips, he handed it to Kurgan.

"You have a taste for it," he said as Kurgan inhaled. "This is high-Arryx-grown, very smooth, very potent."

"Where am I?" Kurgan said. "If you have abducted me—"

"*Calmitou*, regent. You fell into our lap." He lifted a hand, let it fall slowly to his kneecap. His gestures were as fluid as they were economical. "Rest assured we have no untoward designs on you." He stood, opened a door that had not previously been in Kurgan's field of vision. "You may leave now if you wish." He watched Kurgan lying on the berth, laaga smoke leaking from between his half-parted lips. In a moment, he closed the door and sat down again, crossing his legs into the precise position they had been in before.

"Are you the new captain of the *Omaline*?"

The corners of Lujon's lips curled up into his beard. "Courion's ship belongs to his family. The next captain will be of the Oronel line."

"Then who are you?"

Lujon sat somewhat forward, inclining his torso toward the berth in the way a Khaggguin aims an ion cannon. "Courion had business with Nith Batoxxx. You were close with that Gyrgon. These facts are known."

Out of nowhere the scent of bargaining mingled with the smell of laaga, and Kurgan smiled inwardly. Providentially, he had been returned to familiar ground, one where he reigned supreme.

"Nith Batoxxx trained me from an early age," he said.

Lujon raised one eyebrow. "Is that so? Toward what end?"

"He told me that he saw something in me. Something extraordinary. He had great plans."

"Then it is a shame that he is dead."

Kurgan, who had been taking the temperature of the conversation, made a decision. "Not really. Nith Batoxxx murdered Courion. For that, I killed him."

"You killed a Gyrgon? Really?" Lujon sat back. His hands were hanging loosely over the promontory of his knees, very still. "The pupil rose up and destroyed the master, is that how it was?"

Kurgan was about to continue the fabrication, but some inner antenna sounded a warning. This Sarakkon knew more than he was letting on. If this was a test, if he knew Kurgan was lying, that would be the end. Looking into Lujon's eyes, Kurgan knew it with a certainty that was absolute. There was an inner calm, a stillness Nith Batoxxx in his guise as the Old V'ornn had trained him to recognize. And all at once, Kurgan was privy to the danger to which he was now exposed.

"No," he said. "Not really."

"How did Nith Batoxxx die?"

Kurgan knew that the truth and only the truth would keep the interview going. "The Gyrgon was possessed by Pyphoros, the archdaemon of daemons. He was destroyed in the ruins of Za Hara-at."

"You were there." It was not a question.

"Yes."

Lujon sat very straight; he was still without holding himself in. He simply *was*. "Tell us why Courion died."

"That I do not know," Kurgan said truthfully. "Nith Batoxxx lured him to his lab-orb in the Temple of Mnemonics and killed him."

He hated divulging privileged information, especially to a Sarakkon, but he did not see an alternative. Besides, as Nith Batoxxx had taught him, sometimes you had to give up something valuable to get something even more valuable in return.

"There is more to Courion's death," Lujon said flatly.

Kurgan thought he smelled the beginning of a conspiracy, a subversion of the status quo, and it interested him, for subversives, by definition, had secrets to hide. That made them both valuable and vulnerable.

"What was the nature of the Gyrgon's experiments?"

"Nith Batoxxx has a chamber in his lab-orb," he said. "In it, he was attempting to control a goron wave."

Lujon rose and walked about the room. The Sarakkon took up one small shell after another, holding each one at his very fingertips, handling them as if they were as ephemeral as mist.

"You would not believe it to look at them, but some of these come from near the ocean floor," Lujon said. "So deep it is like being on another planet. These creatures do not react to light or oxygen or pressure the way you and we do. It is difficult to know them no matter how long one studies them. Their habitat is too remote, too inhospitable, too alien." He turned, with a striped shell in his hand, looked at Kurgan. "He failed, did he not?"

Kurgan felt strong enough to attempt to sit up again. He hoped it wasn't an illusion created by the laaga. If he was startled that the Sarakkon was aware of the goron particle, he was not about to show it.

"We Sarakkon deal in radioactives. We have great expertise in these substances. This is why your Gyrgon decided to spare us, why you have not occupied the southern continent. Radioactive substances on Kundala are different, they are mysterious, they have a sorcerous component that confounds your pure science. And no particle is more powerful, more imbued with magic, than the goron. So much so that it is a mystery even to us."

Kurgan discovered that his leg felt immensely better. The systemic weakness, obviously caused by the toxin, had, thanks to Kelyx's medications, all but completely dissipated. Gingerly, he put his feet on the floor and stood up. A wave of dizziness quickly passed, leaving him feeling light and clearheaded. A by-product of the laaga?

Lujon said carefully, "Why did Nith Batoxxx agree to an alliance with Courion?"

"Oqeyya," Kurgan said. Oqeyya was a fungus that was grown in certain areas of the southern continent. It was dried for three weeks at high altitude, after which it was cured in a mixture of herbs and carna oil before being dried again, washed in seawater, and burned. The green ash that remained had powerful psychotropic attributes. Because of its highly toxic effects to both V'ornn and Kundalan, it was contraband by Gyrgon decree. "Courion had begun a partnership with Nith Batoxxx. With the Gyrgon's help, they were going to find a way to eliminate oqeyya's toxic side effects, to make it as desirable as salamuuun, to make the salamuuun trade worthless to the Ashera."

"This we had heard, but we have dismissed it absolutely." Lujon put down the striped shell.

Kurgan smiled. He loved having more knowledge than his negotiating adversary. "Courion himself told me that Nith Batoxxx had assured him that he had found a way to do away with the toxic side effects."

"Courion lied to you. He knew, as do we all, that *oqeyya* resists compositional analysis. The Gyrgon have already tried and failed. We know that magic is involved, but of course your Gyrgon would resist such a notion."

"Is this magic you could teach me?"

Lujon smiled. "With the right incentive anything is possible, regent."

Kurgan thought of something. "What if Courion was really interested in Nith Batoxxx's experiments with the goron wave."

"Yes, what if? And what if Courion came too close? That is why he was killed."

We need to know. The urgency of those words were not lost on Kurgan. "Who are you?" he said for the second time.

"Unlike Courion," Lujon said, "we do not trust Gyrgon."

"Does that extend to any V'ornn?"

Lujon showed his teeth, large and white with powerful canines. Rending teeth. Carnivore's teeth. "Tell me why it should not?"

"Like you, I have reason to distrust Gyrgon." Kurgan took a last hit of the laaga stick, which he'd smoked to the tips of his fingers. "I wish their power diminished; I wish to undermine their command and control."

"Nothing would please me more," Lujon said with a small smile that could have meant anything. He opened the door.

Kurgan did not know whether he could make it all the way to the door, let alone past it, but he was not about to let the Sarakkon know that. He crossed the small room. The muscles of his leg felt stiff and sore, but not weak.

Lujon led him down a hallway lined on both sides with artwork, all with an oceanic theme. They came out on a

huge room filled with the light of a thousand crimson candles. It appeared to run the entire width of the villa, which
was built of pale, glittering schist and charcoal-grey basalt.
Each stone threw back reflections in its own way, making it
appear as if they were walking through a dense forest of
candlelight. They were arranged in a six-tiered semicircle at
the center of which was a seated statue of a heavily striated
stone set upon a circular stand of carved reddish wood. Its
upper half was female, its lower half male, each in full
flower of their sexuality. Through the exquisite art of the
sculptor, its face seemed to shine with both benevolence and
malice.

Kurgan paused before the curious idol. "This is not
Yahé," he said. "Nor is it any god or goddess I have seen
carved on the prows of your ships or heard spoken of."

"Nor would it be." Lujon made a brief but formal genu-
flection as he came abreast of the strange creature. "The
average Sarakkon would rather cut off a limb than utter
the name of Abrasea, the destroyer, the ravener, the burner.
As you can see, Abrasea is both male and female; the deity
speaks in both a female and a male voice. Abrasea gives
nourishment at the breast even as Abrasea annihilates with
the rigid sword of the male member."

*O*ver here!"
     An immense male with a flaming red beard, flaked
with snow, rimed with ice, was beckoning to her.

"Over here, Riane!"

His blue eyes were laughing as he held out a hand and
drew her upward.

"We're at the top of the world," he said. And pointed.
"You see?"

An ice storm—looking from this immense height as diaphanous and innocent as mist—was stinging the mountainside. But beyond, she could see another massive block
of basalt, rising pyramidal, black and forbidding in the
middle ground.

"Kunlung Mountain," Redbeard said. His skull was as bare and smooth as the ice field below. "Where all the lightning on Kundala has gathered."

"Why?"

"Like us, it is waiting for the day of Deliverance."

"Will it come?" she asked.

"It will come," Redbeard said with such assurance that she believed to the very marrow of her bones. He had that effect on her; he always had.

"And beyond Kunlung?" Now she pointed due north.

He looked at her, and there was a sadness in his eyes that made her want to weep. "I suppose I should not be surprised. We have been traveling a long time, you and I. You were little more than a baby when we left." He nodded. "We are returning, Riane, just as I promised you we would. Beyond Kunlung is home. What the Kundalan call the Unknown Territories. . . ."

Riane heard these voices in discrete syllables, like the slow accretion of time, millisecond by millisecond, piling up like granules of sand on a vast and uncharted seashore. She lay in a kind of twilight haze, suspended somewhere between consciousness and the abyss of her vision.

An instant later, she started awake.

I t's dawn," Kurgan said. "I must have slept the night away."

He stood in front of a wall of floor-to-ceiling crystal windows.

Lujon slid one of the windows aside. "In fact, a whole day and the better part of two nights have passed since we found you at Harborside. At this very moment, there is a major search under way for you."

"That does not seem to concern you."

"Why should it? You will never be found here."

Kurgan frowned. "Is that a threat?"

"Not at all," Lujon said. "Merely a statement of fact."

He led Kurgan out onto the stone terrace. A breeze ripe

with brine swept into the villa. The curtains shivered, but not one candle flame guttered or even flickered. If the Sarakkon were known sorcerers, Kurgan would have suspected that there was a spell at work. He could smell the Sea of Blood, hear it crashing against many-toothed rocks. The villa itself was built into the cliffside, stoutly walled on both the sea and the land sides, once, doubtless, vigorously defended.

Directly below, riding at anchor on the glittering water, was the *Omaline*.

Kurgan wondered if that was how they had brought him here.

"We are precisely twenty and two-tenths kilometers east of Axis Tyr," Lujon said.

"I know nothing of this place."

"It was built by the Ramahan of Middle Palace." Lujon sat on a hammock, one of two, that had been set up with an eye to the view. Between them was a low oiled-heartwood table laden with an assortment of food and drink. "But that was a long time ago."

No one else was on the terrace. So far as Kurgan could tell no one else was in the villa. The sun heaved its bulk into the eastern sky like a ball cast by a giant's hand. The sea appeared to have a streak of molten metal down its spine. Already the chill of dawn was dissipating.

Lujon filled a tumbler with a pale blue liquid. "A watchtower I suppose you could call it. One of many along the coastline."

With an effort, Kurgan sat on the other hammock, found it surprisingly comfortable, as if it had somehow molded itself to his body. He poured himself a drink of the unfamiliar liquid. It was tart and sweet and very cold. "Who were the Ramahan on the lookout for?" he said as he lay back.

Lujon had his ankles crossed like a vacationer on a beach. He stretched his torso, torquing it to the left, then the right, like one of the big spotted felines that prowled the jungles of the southern continent preparing itself for a dash to the kill. "Why, us, of course."

Kurgan felt a little thrill run through him. "And by 'us' you mean?"

"Ah, well, that brings us to the crux of the matter, doesn't it?" Lujon sipped his drink, watching, it would seem, the clouds down at the horizon curling up like paper crisped in the fire of sunrise. The breeze stirred the hammocks. "Courion, first son of Coirn, of the House of Oronel was *Onnda*."

"*Onnda?*" Nith Nassam had told him Courion was a member of the Orieniad, the Sarakkon ruling council.

Lujon, appearing to ignore him, went on. "I mention Courion's name in its full form for a reason. Oronel was one of the two houses that founded *Onnda*, so far in the past I could not possibly give you a date that would be meaningful." Condensation that had formed on the tumbler had transferred itself to Lujon's mustache. He wiped it with a practiced brush of his slender forefinger. "The other family was Aersthone. I am Lujon, fourth son of Luccoro, of the House of Aersthone."

"Is *Onnda* what the Orieniad evolved into?"

"Not exactly." The wisp of a smile informed Lujon's face. "The Orieniad came into being in order to stem *Onnda*'s burgeoning power. It could not, however. *Onnda* was already too entrenched, too influential within our society, and so a schism occurred because only those trained in *Onnda* were skilled enough to check its rise. So we abandoned *Onnda*, the House of Aersthone and those who had interbred with the Oronel whom we could persuade to our cause. And so *Sintire* was formed, and we became the mortal enemies of the Oronel, of *Onnda*. And so it remains to this day."

"So Courion was *Onnda* and you are *Sintire*."

"We are *Sintire Ardinal*. What would you call it? A high priest."

"And Kelyx is your agent aboard the *Omaline*."

Lujon smiled. "A fortunate happenstance for both of us, don't you agree?"

"Indeed I do."

Kurgan set down his glass. This was going well, very well indeed. And to think he had that nasty little beast Thigpen to thank for this unexpected windfall. His stomachs felt hollow, but he had no appetite for Sarakkon breakfast—rounds of dried, salted sea eel and translucent cephalopod in a truly disgusting looking yellowish gelatin. Besides, he had more important concerns on his mind. *"I want to know what such a high-ranking Sarakkon was doing in Axis Tyr,"* Nith Nassam had charged him. *"Why was he hiding his identity? What was his business with Nith Batoxxx?"* In order to gain entrance to Nith Batoxxx's lab-orb, he needed to bring Nith Nassam something of real value.

"You have been using the terms *Onnda* and *Sintire*," he said now. "What exactly are they?"

Lujon laughed, a cruel sound like a coral crab being crushed beneath a seaboot's heel. "It is simplicity itself, regent. We are assassins, trained from an early age, steeped in technique and nuance. Our Oath, our *religion*, if you will, reshapes our brains. We feel no guilt, no remorse as we bring death to the living."

"Riane. Riane, wake up!"
It was Jura's voice, low and urgent.

Riane stirred; she had fallen back to sleep. Eleana was curled up beside her, breathing evenly and deeply. Thigpen was awake immediately, her whiskers twitching against Riane's cheek.

"You have to go. Now," Jura said. "The owner didn't like us, and liked the Deirus even less. I think he has contacted the local Khagggun."

Riane looked around. "Where is Kirlll Qandda?"

"Waiting for us," Jura said. "He has agreed to hide you."

"Where?" Thigpen asked suspiciously.

"In Receiving Spirit."

"I like this not, little dumpling."

"You have to trust him," Jura said. "He helps the Resistance every chance he gets."

"Guilty conscience," Thigpen muttered.

"He says there is a large unused section," Jura said urgently. "No one goes there. It is perfectly safe."

Riane nodded. She was reluctant to wake Eleana, but she saw that she had no choice. "All right."

"You bought into the Deirus' sob story. His is an abused caste, so you forgive his murders." Thigpen's tone was accusatory.

"He saved Eleana's life, he works with the Resistance," Riane said. "I will give him the benefit of the doubt."

She grunted. "Don't expect me to shed a tear for him."

"What I expect is for you to keep a civil tongue in your head."

Jura had brought them cold food and water, stolen from the cafe's kitchen, and they ate hurriedly, not tasting a thing. Riane woke Eleana, who at first merely turned and, sighing, put her arms around her so that Riane was obliged to shake her awake.

"Dar Sala-at." Her pupils were dilated and her voice was thick from sleep or possibly from whatever antitoxin Kirlll Qandda had given her. All at once, her eyes got big, and she threw her arms around Riane. "Dear Miina, I saw Kurgan, and I thought I was lost."

"It's all right now," Riane whispered, and hugged Eleana to her. She explained briefly what had happened, where they were, and why it was now imperative that they move. She got Eleana to eat and drink some, then she helped her up.

The city at dawn had a just-washed look. It was filled with a contented murmur, as of a baby at its mother's breast. As Kirlll Qandda had predicted, Eleana was weak, but her resources were deep and once on the streets in the early-morning air she quickly regained her strength. Riane, who had stuffed her pockets with the cold food, periodically fed Eleana as they proceeded.

It was soon clear that Jura had plenty of experience moving around Axis Tyr without being spotted by Khagggun patrols or those collaborators in the civilian population—V'ornn and Kundalan alike—employed by the Khagggun as eyes and ears. She took them on a course that led them down deserted streets and perpetually shadowed alleys known to her to be free of surveillance. She was confident in her knowledge and never hesitated at crossroads or turnings. She scrupulously avoided parks or plazas drenched in fusion lamplight.

Another good thing: Jura had excellent hearing. She could, for instance, hear the sound of Khagggun hoverpods long before they came into view, skimming the ziggurat rooftops, swooping low over open areas, taking random photonic sweeps.

At this early hour, Axis Tyr shimmered pink in the first gentle spray of sunlight. Those who hurried by were greengrocers and spice merchants preoccupied with the mental lists of the day's chores churning in their heads or half-asleep Mesagggun leading lines of emaciated new recruits on their way to begin the backbreaking life in the lortan pits. No one paid any attention to the small party.

The nighttime chill crept out of the city in a low, thin mist. The wet-stone smell of just-sluiced streets mingled with the piquant tang of orangesweet, dissipating the feral odors of sweat and fear.

They arrived at Receiving Spirit without incident. But instead of mounting the wide front staircase, Jura took them around to the side that overlooked a narrow, rather dismal street. A small door midway down was ajar and, as they approached, it was pulled open by Kirlll Qandda.

He glanced up and down the street. "No problems?"

"None," Jura said.

As they went inside, the Deirus smiled at Eleana. "I see you have made an excellent recovery."

"Thanks to you," she said.

"My pleasure."

"I'll bet," Thigpen mumbled.

"What was that?" Riane turned on her. "What did you say?"

"Nothing," Thigpen said grumpily.

"Quickly now." Kirlll Qandda led them from the utilitarian entryway down a corridor to the left. It was small and cramped, the white-stone walls sloping inward as they rose toward the narrow ceiling. A glow emanated from the stone blocks themselves, which perhaps explained the lack of fusion lamps. Riane could hear a low thrumming, and her stomach tightened in recognition of the vast V'ornn fusion engines designed by Gyrgon for unknown purposes.

"You will be safe here for as long as you want," the Deirus said. "To my knowledge this area has never been used since Receiving Spirit was taken over at the beginning of the occupation."

Thigpen snorted. "How easily that word trips off your tongue."

"What did I tell you?" Riane snapped.

"It's all right." Kirlll Qandda raised a placating hand. "In her place I would feel the same animosity."

They turned a corner, and the Deirus stopped so quickly that Thigpen ran right into him, tumbling head over heels. She picked herself up, snorting and growling at the soft laughter that came from the others.

Kirlll Qandda's strained voice broke into their brief merriment. "Get back." He was clearly agitated.

Riane shouldered around him, the Rappa zipping between the forest of their legs. Special fusion lamps filled the corridor beyond with a low rubicund glow.

"Safe in here?" Thigpen's whiskers were twitching. "You see, I told you."

"What is going on—?" Riane whispered.

"I don't know," the Deirus said.

"Well, we had better find out," she said.

Kirlll Qandda looked fearfully around. "That may not be such a good idea."

Thigpen nodded. "It pains me to agree with him."

Ignoring them both, Riane asked Jura to stand guard while she took Eleana, Thigpen, and Kirlll Qandda with her down the corridor. As they proceeded, she could hear the thrum of the fusion engines more clearly, could feel the vibrations of the hyperexcited ions through the floor. The atmosphere felt charged, heated as if with a team of ion forges.

In the reddish glow, they could see that the corridor reached an unnatural end, having been refitted by V'ornn. The far wall was curved and looked to be part of a large, spherical chamber.

"Gyrgon," Kirlll Qandda breathed. He was clearly terrified. "This is a Gyrgon lab-orb. They fashion it like segments of a fruit. They are portable and modular."

Riane put the flat of her hand against the convex alloy side. "What is inside?"

"Without going in there is no way to tell," Kirlll Qandda said. "From the outside they all look alike."

Riane peered at the locking mechanism. "Get us in."

The Deirus flushed. "No, no, I couldn't."

"You mean you can't?" Thigpen said. "Or you won't?"

Kirlll Qandda licked his lips. "This isn't fair."

Riane rounded on him. "Listen, Deirus. Have you ever been inside a Gyrgon lab-orb?"

"No. Of course not. No Deirus has."

"Nor Genomatekk, either, I'll warrant. I am not going to overlook this incredible stroke of luck." She pushed Kirlll Qandda against the door. "We may be able to unlock the secret of what the Gyrgon are doing with the hybrid children. We may find some way to stop them from continuing their horrific experiments. Isn't that worth the risk of death?"

Kirlll Qandda wiped a line of sweat off his brow. "It's a photonic lock. I may not be able to open it."

Riane put her hand on the Deirus' thin shoulder. "All we are asking you to do is try."

The Deirus nodded. While he turned his attention to the lock, Riane told Thigpen to join Jura in her guard duty.

"Your eyes are better in this low light and so is your sense of smell." They both knew that Gyrgon carried with them the curious scent of clove oil and burnt musk. "I want you to station yourself farther down the corridor where you won't be seen but can see everything." She ruffled the Rappa's fur as she knelt beside her. "And remember," she whispered, "he is a second-class citizen just as you once were."

"As you wish, Dar Sala-at."

As Thigpen trotted back down past where Jura crouched, waiting and listening, Riane rose and turned back to the door.

"It's not photonic after all." Kirlll Qandda's slender fingers were tap-tap-tapping the lock in a rhythm. "It's sonic. Very unusual for a Gyrgon locking mechanism. Whatever is inside must be special, indeed."

"Then you can't open it," Riane said.

"I have been opening what was meant to be closed ever since I was six years old," Kirlll Qandda said. "There were times when it was the only skill that kept me alive."

As he worked, Riane kept one eye over her shoulder, checking on Jura and their continued security.

"Almost," Kirlll Qandda said. "Almost." Tap-tap-tap. *Click!* "We're in."

A circular aperture set flush with the orb's side rolled noiselessly aside, and they saw in the ruddy illumination the black, seemingly bottomless moat that ringed the sphere, the metallic catwalk across which they walked to the lab itself, the lines of chambers lying like the sarcophagi of an ancient race. Kirlll Qandda pointed out the photon lines snaking from each chamber to a central plate in the floor.

As they moved around to get a better look at the floorplate a shadow fell across them, and looking up, startled, they saw an amorphous shape dropping down on them.

E at." Lujon pushed a plate of the cephalopod in jelly across the table.

Kurgan shook his head. "Thank you, no."

"But you must. The toxin has depleted you. You need to build up your strength."

Lujon was looking at him in such a way that Kurgan knew he was laughing at him. He studied the disgusting foodstuff. Did he just see it move? Another furtive glance at Lujon convinced him that this wasn't even the kind of test Courion had been fond of putting him through. He knew that he would gain virtually nothing by eating the cephalopod, but if he did not, Lujon would know that he had a weakness he could exploit.

Without further thought, Kurgan dipped the first two fingers of his right hand, Sarakkonian style, scooping up rings of the cephalopod and its sticky jelly. He ate not just one mouthful, but all of it, careful under Lujon's critical eye not to swallow too quickly.

When Kurgan had finished, Lujon took the plate. "Regent of Kundala you may be," he said, "but you are still a child, you still have lessons to learn." He dumped the remainder of the jelly into a bronze drain set into the lowest part of the terrace. "This orquidia has been standing out for over a week. It is rotten with maggot eggs."

He held Kurgan's shoulders as Kurgan leaned over, retching, and vomited into the drain. "Not the least of your lessons, regent, is humility." He threw the plate away, rubbed his palms together fastidiously. "I haven't thought of myself as a teacher in many years. To be honest, I have lacked the interest." His wrists lay atop his knees. His hands were again ready for anything. "But you interest me. You are not like other Stoggguls; not like other V'ornn, for the matter of that, and I feel as if you have as much to teach me as I have to teach you."

Lujon held out a tumbler of the blue liquid, but Kurgan grasped the entire pitcher and upended it over his own head. He sat there, letting the drippings rid his mouth of the taste of his own bile. There was a moment when the old murderous rage galvanized him. He was a millimeter from leaping up and gripping Lujon's neck in his fingers.

It was not fear that drew him back from the brink of murder and, quite possibly, his own death. Nor was it caution because it appeared as if that had somehow been genetically hard-wired out of him. It was self-interest, pure and simple. Lujon had power—what kind and how much was yet to be determined. Kurgan fed on power. You did not kill the thing that made you stronger. So he spat out his murderous rage with the last horrific chunk of maggot-infested cephalopod. And yet the Old V'ornn had taught him never to let go of an affront until it had been repaid with hills of knives and seas of fire. From now on, whenever he looked at Lujon he would be limned in the color of revenge.

During this lull in the conversation, Lujon had been studying his nails. Now he said, "By the way, your having been so recently in Za Hara-at made me curious."

Kurgan pricked up his ears and waited.

"Recently, we have come into information that an artifact lost there for some time has been found and removed from Za Hara-at. Stolen, you might say, yes. It is black and egg-shaped, not large but quite heavy. It is called a banestone." The Sarakkon's eyes flicked up at him. "Have you any knowledge of its whereabouts?"

"No." Kurgan shook his head. The last thing he would do would admit to having the banestone. "I do not."

"Pity. The banestone has great religious value, though nothing more."

Kurgan bit his lip to keep from laughing in Lujon's face. "What would a Sarakkon religious icon be doing buried in Za Hara-at?"

Lujon sat very still. "I never said that it was buried."

Kurgan's pulses spiked. "The entire city is buried, Lujon."

"Of course, of course." Lujon smiled his ripshark's smile. "The banestone does not have a religious significance for us. It does, however, for the sauromicians."

"Sauromicians?"

"Yes. A group of dissident male priests. They hate and

fear the Ramahan. You know, it occurs to us now that you could use them to destroy the last vestiges of Miina's minions. They would be only too happy to do so."

Kurgan did not care for the dark ripple that had so unexpectedly disturbed the ebb and flow of their newfound alliance. He cared even less for the fact that Lujon was trying to twist him into his own dark design. Lies, the Old V'ornn had said, were like wyr-beetles: where you found one, many must be hidden. "I can make inquiries concerning the banestone, if you like," he said easily. "We are in the process of mapping the city's layout so that it can be rebuilt."

Lujon's smile appeared frozen in place. His eyes had gone icy. "Do you really think that is wise, regent?"

"I can't see why not." The dark ripple was broadening, deepening, and he thought he caught a glimpse of what it might be like to have this being as an enemy rather than an ally.

"Za Hara-at is sacred. It was a site of vast power."

"That was long ago."

"Who knows what lies buried in its ruins?"

"Do you?"

"As you say, regent, that was long ago. So much of the ancient knowledge has been lost."

Lujon did know, or he had aligned himself with the sauromicians in order to find out. Either way, the lies were proliferating. "Precisely our thought," Kurgan said. "We will plunder the old at the same time we build the new. We grow weary of occupying a Kundalan capital. We wish to establish our own. A monument to the new Kundala under V'ornn rule." Kurgan, struggling to define the tremor of intent that was now threatening to break apart their delicate alliance, felt the need to do some serious ion cannon rattling. "You never answered my question. The Sarakkon are a seafaring race. The northern Korrush is very far from any body of water, let alone an ocean."

"Za Hara-at was once the nexus of all Kundalá." It was an answer without real substance, and they both knew it.

Far below, the Sea of Blood churned itself into fragrant foam on the black-basalt rocks. A sea eagle swung across their field of vision, its long wings spread, riding thermals.

"Of course I will do what I can for you, Lujon. Rest assured that every member of the mapping party will be well questioned on this matter."

"Our thanks, regent. Perhaps one of your architects took it as a totem to inspire his work." Lujon rose. The interview was at an end.

20

The Truth About Lovers

When the blood-warm netting—one of many that hung from the ceiling of the lab-orb—fell on Riane, it was Kirlll Qandda who understood what it was, if not how it worked. He untangled it from her and, laying it on the floor, began a quick examination of it.

"What is it?" Riane whispered, crouched down beside him.

The Deirus pointed. "You see these fishlike shapes, they're semiorganic chips. I believe it is a Gyrgon heuristic net."

"What is it used for?" Eleana asked.

Kirlll Qandda rose, and they followed him to the line of coffinlike chambers. Three of them held the bodies of children. They were not Gyrgon, were not V'ornn at all. They looked like Kundalan.

"You are aware, I am sure, of the Gyrgon requirement that all children of mixed species be rounded up and brought here to Receiving Spirit."

Riane nodded. Eleana's face was grim.

"Well, these are those children." Kirlll Qandda stared in

a mixture of wonder and horror. "The Gyrgon are experimenting on them." He examined the holopanels attached to the chambers. "The subjects begin in these biochambers, and at some point I believe they are transferred to the heuristic nets for final somata-honing."

"Why?" Riane was far more horrified than he was, for she saw herself reflected in the faces of the hybrids. "What is the purpose of these experiments?"

"As you must also know, the vast majority of these mixed-species children do not survive." The Deirus shrugged. "It is possible the Gyrgon are trying to find a way to keep them alive."

Eleana was shaking her head from side to side. "It doesn't make sense. The Gyrgon think of us as an inferior race. You would think they would consider any miscegenation an abomination."

"Eleana's right," Riane said. "They are thinking of a specific use for these poor children."

They heard the warning from Jura then and, leaving their speculation pooled with the heuristic net in the ruddy light of the lab-orb, headed for the door. Too late! They could hear voices approaching, and together they rolled the door closed, heard the lock click into place. Then they hurried back across the alloy gangway and scuttled into the deepest shadows they could find. Huddled behind one of the biochambers, they saw the door roll open and two very tall figures enter the lab-orb.

I have you now." There was an unmistakable note of triumph in Gul Aluf's voice. "I have you just where I want you."

"So this is your hive," Sahor said.

"My home away from home." Her eyes were shining in triumph. "The place you swore you would never set foot in."

Then she spotted the heuristic net that had come loose from its ceiling moorings and went over to pick it up. Sahor could see the bits of dried blood and bone that had not yet been absorbed by the semisentient heuristic computer network.

He turned away, scrutinizing her elaborate setup. He was disgusted at what he saw: the coffinlike biochambers, more heuristic nets hung from the ceiling like ominous webs. And then he felt something and immediately a tiny icy thread went through him. He kept his demeanor, the tone of his voice, the language of his body the same, for he knew with utter certainty that if he altered any of them even an iota, she would spot it and become suspicious.

"The heuristic nets are malfunctioning," she said. "I am not certain, but they may be part of the problem. Lately, I have begun work on a complete redesign." She held it out to him, bloody bone chips and all. "What do you think?"

Sahor picked over the network of semiorganic chips and biocircuits. It was based on the same technological platform as the Gyrgon ion exomatrix, and when he asked her, Gul Aluf confirmed this. He saw the problem right away because it was something he had worked on for months while he was still Nith, while he was trying to figure out a way to preserve his dying father's essence in another form. He had only partially solved the problem when he was forced by his father's illness to put his theories into practice. The result was the Teyj-matrix, objectively astonishing, true enough, but for him an unsatisfying victory inasmuch as Nith Einon's powers were severely curtailed because of the matrix's limitations. He had worked on improvements, intending to return his father to a perfect simulacrum of his original body, but circumstances had required that he use it on himself instead. He had put his essence into the fragile body of Eleana's dying son. The infant was half-V'ornn by way of her rape at the hands of Kurgan Stogggul, but his corpus was already rejecting the V'ornn part as incompatible. Injecting himself—the very strands of his Gyrgon-enhanced DNA—had reversed the rejection, reconciled the incompatibility, and from this unique baby he had been born.

378 Eric Van Lustbader

"The concept is all wrong," he said, giving her back the heuristic net. "It won't sustain Kundalan life the way it will Gyrgon."

She scowled. "Why not? I made certain that all the Kundalan biological needs were properly met."

"It's not a matter of biology, but rather automatism."

"It would be just like you to muddy the equation with philosophy."

"We believe that our bodies are essentially machines whose functions are accompanied but not controlled by consciousness."

"Yes, yes," she said, impatient with him. "We Guls teach that within the first weeks of life."

"The trouble," he said, "is that it's wrong."

"What?"

"At least as far as the Kundalan are concerned."

"You will cease this heretical talk immediately!"

"Their consciousness is expanded. It controls, more or less, their bodies."

"How can you—!"

"It is the only explanation for their sorcery." He took her by the shoulders. "Gul Aluf, don't you see? It's all so obvious. You have only to look at the problem in the proper fashion."

"You mean be corrupted by your twisted thinking."

She broke away from him, spread her wings, and, lofted into the dense, stultifying atmosphere of the lab-orb, returned the defective heuristic net to its circuit clamps high above his head.

He took the opportunity to dart his gaze this way and that. No, he had not been mistaken. He sensed Riane, hidden there, still as a shadow. By her side, Eleana. And someone else, a V'ornn, of all things, a Deirus! There were many unexpected mutations that had arisen as a result of his transformation. This was one of them. He could feel Riane as clearly as if he were seeing her. The intruders were crouched behind the farthest of the biochambers, veiled by deepest shadow, but it was on Riane that he was concentrated. Something had changed in her, some doubt had crept into her, eroding the fabric of her belief in herself. What it was or where it had come from he could not say, but its very presence disturbed him profoundly.

All around her he sensed a rippling of the atmosphere, and with a little tremor of recognition he knew that she had cast a spell around them. He did not, of course, know which spell. He had little specific knowledge of Kundalan sorcery. Nevertheless, his ability to sense them was unaffected by it. The innate scientist within him was galvanized as an entirely new spectrum of possibilities opened up to him. Queries stretched out before him like unfinished theories. Queries at the moment without solutions.

Gul Aluf descended too soon, alighting in front of him, forcing him to put aside the mountain of conundrums. He pressed his point. "Listen to me, you said yourself that you have ensured that all the biological circuits were correct."

She watched him with care and perhaps a touch of wariness. "Possibly I made a mistake."

"You don't make mistakes. But just to be certain, I double-checked. The failure of the heuristic nets is not about biology. It does not—it cannot as currently designed—take into account the expanded Kundalan consciousness."

Gul Aluf looked away and, for a heart-stopping instant Sahor was afraid that she had become aware of the intruders in her domain. "I thought only the priestesses—what do you call them?"

"Ramahan."

Her head swung back toward him, and her magnificent eyes raked over him like salt in a wound. "I thought only the Ramahan were capable of sorcery."

"It is a matter of training—and then there is the Gift. Only those Ramahan with the Gift have the ability to grasp Five Moon sorcery, what the Kundalan call Osoru. But there is another discipline known as Kyofu, the Black Dreaming sorcery, that is within the reach of all Ramahan, even Kundalan who have not had the Ramahan's years of training." He could see that he had her full attention. Had she also put aside her arrogance, her adamantine faith in her own point of view? "None of it would be possible without the Kundalan expanded consciousness."

"If all this is true, Sahor, then how is it that we defeated them so easily, so quickly, so thoroughly?"

"The answer is simple enough. Initially, they did not oppose us." He could see her skepticism, and he took her and turned her so that her back was to the place where the intruders were hiding. "While we defeated them easily enough and quite quickly, I would not assume that their defeat is as thorough as it appears on the surface."

She laughed, but there was no pleasure in the sound. "What are you implying? That in addition to fearing the Centophennni we should fear the Kundalan slaves as well?"

"I am saying that we should take the time thoroughly to consider what we do here."

"We do not have that luxury, even if we were so inclined." She wrapped him in her arms. "I accept that you won't help me here, won't help me directly. But won't you let me take you into Nith Batoxxx's lab-orb? If anyone can find what we cannot, it is you."

It was a stalemate. He had not moved her one iota. "Are you certain you want me to see such privileged information?"

"I know you." She smiled into his face, a smile that was all sharp teeth. "You want to know what Nith Batoxxx was up to as much as I do."

It was true, he did. If she was right, and there was any chance that Nith Batoxxx had been experimenting with the melding of the two species, he had to know. Besides, he felt that the longer he had to work on her, the better chance he would have of changing her seemingly intractable point of view.

"I have missed you, Sahor." She cocked her head. Her eyes seemed to see clear through him. "I never should have let you walk out on me." She felt she had him now, and a little shiver ran through her. She put her head against his shoulder and breathed him in.

He could not help a quick glance over to where Riane crouched. He could sense her watching him through the Osoru spell.

But a glance was all he got, because, with a soft rustle, Gul Aluf's wings spread, section by section, the red light running through their gossamer, biochip-studded membranes like veins of photons. From their very tips, they curled around until they had completely enfolded him into her embrace.

"How dare you?" Leyytey was furious. "How dare you speak to my father behind my back!"

"I have a concern," Sornnn said.

"Then bring it to *me*."

Sornnn closed the door behind them. Echoes of their voices bounced off the shanstone-and-porphyry walls. The Forum for Adjudication was huge, cold, imposing, not at all like other Kundalan temple complexes. It was difficult to understand what had gone on inside the building before the V'ornn had occupied it. For once, they did not find the need to transform the interior of a major Kundalan structure to suit their needs. The towering, portentous spaces were totally in sync with the V'ornn psyche.

"I thought it would be a mistake, and your intrusion here is proof enough."

Even this small chamber off the busy main hall—one of many of unknown purpose—had an impossibly high ceiling. It was coffered, the massive wooden beams clad with incised bronze. The square table and chairs were stolid, masculine, slightly ominous. To Sornnn it looked like a war room.

"I considered this too important to wait on a time of your pleasure."

He said nothing.

"Whether or not you feel this visit is inappropriate—"

"You know I do."

"Be that as it may," she continued gamely, "I am here now."

"The adjudication process does not allow for long breaks."

"All the more reason to cut to the heart of the matter."

He crossed his arms over his chest. "As you will. My concern is that you are in no emotional state to make an objective judgment about your behavior."

"Correct me if I'm wrong," she said archly, "but you came to me."

"Possibly that was a mistake."

She shook her head, as if his words were raindrops. "To make matters worse, you are now of the opinion that I could betray my father and you."

"You said 'my father.' "

"To N'Luuura with your condescension!"

"Stop acting like a child with a temper tantrum, and I will be happy to—"

She hit him then, and it rocked him because despite her petite size she knew how to land a blow, putting all of herself into it from her hips upward.

Sornnn, off-balance, sat down hard on a chair and rubbed his jaw. It was numb, but that would not last. It was already on its way to swelling. "Well," he said.

At that moment, the door opened inward.

"Prime Factor?"

Raan Tallus appeared, his smooth skull dark as a Teyj egg. His quick, clever eyes took in the scene with a surface amusement that did not quite disguise his avidity.

"Pardon me, have I intruded on a private moment?" He made no move to leave, but rather shut the door behind him and stood watching them with the anticipation of a spectator at the Kalllistotos. At length, he turned to Sornnn. "If you are in the middle of an altercation, Prime Factor, perhaps you will allow me to mediate a satisfactory resolution."

Leyytey made a little sound. The way he spoke set her teeth on edge.

Sornnn rose. "Merely a difference of opinion, solicitor-general." He saw immediately that refuting the obvious would only make matters worse. "Nothing that Leyytey and I cannot resolve on our own."

Raan Tallus shrugged. He was tall and as powerfully built as a Khagggun. He was dressed in an alloy-mesh waistcoat over a shirt without a single wrinkle. His mimetic-fabric breeches clung to his legs like a second skin. As Sornnn well knew, it was unwise to judge him solely on his attention to appearance. He was possessed of both an alloy-trap mind and a very long memory.

"If you say so, Prime Factor. Please remember that I am always here to help." His smile when it came was like the quick slash of a knife, shocking and unpleasant. "I would be remiss if I failed to remind you of the old saying: 'Don't negotiate where you sleep.'"

The outburst from Leyytey Sornnn was expecting did not come. Instead, she seemed to have lapsed into a glum silence. In fact, Sornnn noticed that she had trouble looking the solicitor-general in the eye.

"I think you have misunderstood the situation," Sornnn said. "Leyytey and I are not sleeping together."

"Really"—Raan Tallus spread his hands—"who could blame you if you were?"

"But we are not."

Into the deep silence that ensued, Raan Tallus interjected like a well-struck dart, "So you have said."

"I will be along presently." Sornnn gestured at the door. "Until then . . ."

"You have only to wish assistance, Prime Factor."

The solicitor-general gave what amounted to a stiff-backed bow before he turned on his heel and left.

An uncomfortable silence descended like a curtain. Here was the other side of the quicksilver mind, the amusingly barbed tongue, returning Sornnn to a certain incident six months before his father's death. Raan Tallus, seeking to expand the Ashera empire, had wanted to buy into the spice trade. Hadinnn SaTrryn had not been interested, and neither was Sornnn when his father apprised him of the offer. *Keep your attention where it belongs*, Hadinnn had said to Raan Tallus. *You have a grave responsibility running the Ashera empire.*

Leyytey finally broke the heavy silence. "I suppose now you're sorry you got me involved."

"We'll get into this some other time. Right now I have work to do."

"You can't just dismiss me like this!"

"Leyytey, I told you at the outset that this was the wrong time to—"

"I hate you!" she shouted. "You and all the males who want to use me, then dismiss me, who think they know what's best for me!"

He sighed. "What happens to all of us when the love you are still clinging to causes you to make a mistake?"

"You have it backwards." She stalked toward him, her face pale and pinched. "What happened to *you*? What sin did *you* commit in the name of love? How long will you keep running from whatever happened, SaTrryn?"

For a moment he was struck dumb. "I have to get back to the adjudication."

"Keep lying to yourself!" she yelled after him. "Self-delusion is such a comforting state of mind!"

Konara Inggres found the village of Stone Border quiet and serene. The many-tiered town with its tumbledown buildings and narrow, crooked streets of endless flights of stairs spread out just below the Abbey of Floating White. Ever since she had been thrust into the leadership role at the abbey it had been her habit periodically to take a meal at a local tavern and listen to the chatter of gossip. She was acutely aware of how isolating life was behind the thick, cold walls of the abbey, and she felt it important that she stay on top of current events, even if they were partially—or sometimes wholly—speculation. In the old days before the coming of the V'ornn, the Ramahan had been the shepherds of the people, keeping them safe and productive, ensuring that the wheel of life kept turning. The old days were long gone, of course, but she did not want to let one of the Ramahan prime objectives lapse.

The tavern she chose, the Blackcrow, was ancient, its stone walls cracked, blackened with decades of smoke and soot from its brawny fireplace. The massive beams of its ceiling were so dark they could have been mistaken for titanic slabs of charcoal, and the heavy scent of charred meats hung in the air, the smoke dimming the illumination from the hanging tallow lanterns.

She left the moons-spangled night, plunging headlong into the raucous, alcohol-soaked atmosphere. A regular in her own way, she caused barely a ripple in the ongoing roar. The nightly tournament of darts, played seriously for serious coins, engendered great gouts of noise from participants and spectators alike, periodically making all other talk, no matter how drunken or high-spirited, inaudible. Many patrons nodded to her and out of deference murmured her honorific. She smiled at them all and bade them good evening as the tavern keeper showed her to a choice seat near the fire, away from the dartboard, which was being repeatedly and ferociously struck like a misbehaving boy's cheek. He hurriedly wiped the rings of cloudy rakkis off the tabletop, brought her a metal goblet of steamed ludd-wine, and took her dinner order, which, in the throaty furor, she had to repeat twice. He hurried off, not to inform the cook, but to break up a nasty-looking fight between putative first- and second-place finishers. Big-shouldered, foul-mouthed, these dart-throwers were no longer able to hold at bay the dread that haunted them day and night, so they beat a heavy tattoo on the face and back they pretended was V'ornn.

For a time, she listened to the conversations around her, lively and sullen, inhaling the life, bursting at the seams, in the short time allotted her. Not far from her a young couple grappled and fondled each other in a public display of passion. Another male, not quite so young, piped up, "Bet-

ter get yer licks in now, Tern, before yer wife finds out."
The male grappler blushed amid a forest of lewd guffaws,
took the girl's hand, and rushed with her into the shadows
of the tavern's rear. No one noticed that Konara Inggres'
face was burning. Why should they? Only she knew that
the hot, humiliating flush of infidelity was what had driven
her out of the abbey that night.

Ordinarily, she was not much of a drinker, but tonight
she felt as if she deserved a couple. Needed them, was
more like it. She wrapped her hands around the warm goblet and took a long draught. She wanted time alone with
her thoughts, needed to get away from the Nawatir. When
she was with him her skin tingled, her heart raced, and her
knees grew weak.

Ever since he had come into her room, ever since he had
held her, she had known she was lost. Fight against her
feelings all she might, the truth was she loved him, loved a
male who belonged to another. And not just anyone! First
Mother herself!

How could it have happened? How could her emotions
so betray her? She had prayed long and hard to Miina,
begging for an answer, but none had come. She was faced
with only silence. And in that silence she saw him, coming
toward her bed in the semidarkened room, saw the concern in his eyes, felt his strong arms holding her, and she
breathed in his scent as a blind one takes in the attar of
star-roses and orangesweet, recognizes subtleties within
them beyond the abilities of others. She wept now, as she
had wept in her room after he had left her, after his
warmth had vanished, after her chance to hold him as he
had held her had slipped away.

She shook her head angrily. How foolish she was, acting
like a teenager with a crush! How futile her feelings, for
they would never be reciprocated, and even if they were,
she would never betray First Mother by acting on them.

With a convulsive gesture, she drained her goblet, swallowing so quickly she almost choked. But the fiery liquid
failed to detach her from her ardor. On the contrary, it

made it more intense, more immediate, more real. He
could have been sitting beside her in the glow of the tallow
lanterns, his muscled thigh pressed against hers, his
warmth seeping through her slow as melted wax.

She barely noticed that her plate of food had been
served so deeply sunk in her shamefully amorous reverie
was she. But a growing hue and cry from just outside the
tavern brought her around. As others rose and hurried out
into the night she was compelled to do likewise. What her
eyes fell upon in the street turned her blood cold.

She shouldered her way through the gathering throng
and knelt beside the young male carried at great expenditure of energy by two of his mates. Low clouds obscured
much of the sky, and it had grown colder.

"Give her room," someone called softly. "It is Konara
Inggres."

"A lantern, please," she called, and someone stepped
forward, holding one aloft so that she could see more
clearly the damage done.

She was only dimly aware of a rustling as the citizenry
stumbled a pace or two backward, but she was equally sensitive to the fact that the intensity of their stares had
heightened. Quickly, as her hand ran over the young male,
she cast Earth Granary, blanketing him with its healing.
But she did not like what she saw. She was all too familiar
with the devastation an ion cannon could produce. This
young male had been shot by Khagggun. A stab of sadness
and frustration went through her. She could no longer protect her flock. Well, then, she would do what little she
could. She intensified Earth Granary and dug in her pouch
for a selection of herbs. The wound was grievous. She did
not know whether he could be saved.

"Who saw what happened?" she asked.

"We did." His two companions stepped forward.

"A marauding pack?" she asked.

"No, Konara." One of the young males got down on
one knee.

"Will he live?" asked the other, his face a mass of worry.

"Run and fetch me a goblet of boiled water," she told the second companion, "fast as you can."

She turned to the other. He had unruly hair and dark eyes. "If not a pack, what?"

"More than a pack, Konara." His voice was trembling. "Many, many Khagggun on the march."

Fear clutched at her throat. If for some reason the Khagggun had targeted Stone Border, she would be helpless to stop the slaughter of innocents.

The other companion returned with the hot water, and she filtered in the herbs, rubbing them between her fingers to bring out the oils. She fed a few drops of the decoction to the wounded male, forcing it down his throat. Then she poured half the contents on the wound.

"Where are Wing-Adjutant Wiiin and his detachment headed?" she asked the companion with the unruly hair. "Did you hear?"

"Yes, Konara." His head was lowered, and his voice was barely a whisper.

"Tell me then," she said sharply.

He shivered, and lifted his head so that she could see the abject terror in his eyes. "Floating White, Konara. They mean to storm the abbey and kill everyone in it."

In a remote corner of the SaTrryn compound was a garden. It was tucked away where no business associate, no casual visitor—no intimate, even—would ever find it unless guided to it by one who knew of its existence.

It was an ancient plaza, lush, exquisite, predating even the oldest of the villas, so that it was possible to believe that the entire compound had come into being solely for the purpose of protecting it from inquiring eyes.

It had been constructed around a tortuosa tree, the massive trunk and gnarled branches listing as if grasping for sunlight. Its broad-leafed canopy provided delicious shade on long, scorching summer afternoons and shelter from sudden autumnal squalls. Its pale new leaves fluttered in spring breezes and in the winter its fingerlike branches caught the snow and held it in squiggly lines like the uncertain writing of a small child. *

The tortuosa tree imbued the garden with a certain gravitas, a fulcrum, so Kundalan lore had it, toward which family artists looked for inspiration and upon which scholars leaned for balance. Life played out within its web, no less complex and mystifying than that which occurred beyond the compound's stone walls.

Two figures sat beneath the tortuosa, playing out the next act in the skein of their lives.

"I did not think you would come," Sornnn said. "Not after our last meeting."

"And if I hadn't," Leyytey inquired, "what would you have thought of me then?"

They lapsed into a small silence while insects whirred and danced in the brilliant light of four pale green moons.

"It's not going to work," she said.

He stirred. "What isn't?"

"Your plan."

Sornnn leaned over and poured iced quilllon juice from a crystal pitcher. He handed her a translucent tumbler.

"How do you know?"

"I can read him."

"Don't be so certain." He put down his tumbler. "He has to take the coins, Leyytey," Sornnn said with great intensity. "For the plan to work, he must take the coins and invest them as it is now strictly forbidden for members of his caste to do."

"He won't."

"Yes, he will. His greed will win out."

"We sit here, waiting, waiting . . ." She shook her head again. "This is taking too long."

"Leyytey you must be patient."

Slowly, she unbuttoned her mesh vest, peeled back her blouse, revealing the inside of the two perfect hemispheres of her breasts. Between them was a vertical welt, dark, raised, angry.

"You do not want to see the others," she said.

For a long moment Sornnn stared in shock, then he took his chilled tumbler and gently placed it against the welt.

"Leyytey, I . . . I am sorry about all of this."

His gesture, so full of tenderness and benevolence, genuinely moved her. "SaTrryn, about what I said before—I had no excuse to speak to you that way."

He smiled sadly. "But, you see, I *have* been running away."

"It feels better now."

He removed the tumbler, and she rebuttoned her clothes.

"Do you want to talk about it?"

"I don't know. I . . ." Far to the north, thunder rumbled like the growl of a marauding perwillon. "I don't think I was truly alive before I met her. She was an artist—very talented. She saw the world in an astonishing way. And she was strong—as strong as any male." He shook his head, confused. "Amazing, really. She taught me so many things I could never have learned elsewhere."

"You are a lucky V'ornn, SaTrryn."

"Really?" He thought about this for some time, wondering how much she had to teach him. "Tell me about you and Teww Dacce."

"Not much to tell, really. There was actually a time I was in love with him—madly, completely, absolutely." She shrugged. "Why not? He seemed attentive, loving, passionate. And he was a powerful Khaggun on his way up. I can see now that he was everything, in fact, I desired from a male. But none of it was real. I saw what I wanted to see, what I *needed* to see." She looked up at him. "In order to please my father."

He said nothing, but he was watching her, and in his eyes she saw something that stirred her. He leaned toward her and she to him. A heat arose between them, drawing them closer. Leyytey knew this strange attraction was wrong, that whatever happened now would do so because of their mutual sorrow, their loneliness. Another false foundation. But she could not stop, for it was not only physical desire that welled up inside her, but an almost desperate longing to open herself completely to him. In this moment of intimacy she wanted to tell him her secret so badly she could taste the truth on her lips even as he tenderly bruised them with his own. He was different from all the males she had ever encountered. She felt as if he held the caustic flame of her life in his tender hand and did not flinch.

All around them the bower of leaves rustled and shook in waves with the stirring of the fitful wind. The moonslight outside where they sat bleached out the colors so that the tiny garden appeared limitless. The four deep red jasper walkways that led from the cardinal points of the compass to the tortuosa shimmered in the monochrome light, ethereal until they arrived beneath the thick canopy of interlaced leaves. There came to them the scent of orangesweet, the attar of star-roses, their ruffled petals turned startlingly black in the drench of moonslight.

Locked in his embrace, she heard herself begin. *SaTrryn, I have something tell you.* She imagined that she said it so softly that at first Sornnn would not be certain what he heard. *It's about Raan Tallus.*

Even though this was taking place inside her head, her hearts were hammering, and she could scarcely breathe. She registered the responses of her flesh with only half her mind. In the other, the imaginary dialogue was continuing.

It's a confession, really.

A pair of gimnopedes flitted through the gnarled branches, pecking at each other in the beginning of their complex mating ritual.

I should have told you sooner.

And what would he answer? *Go on. It's all right, Leyytey.*

But that would be before he was made privy to the secret she had kept inside her.

When I told you I was familiar with Raan Tallus it was because of Teww Dacce. The truth about lovers, SaTrryn, is that they lie, inevitably they lie. The solicitor-general hired Teww Dacce. Not that Teww Dacce told me. On the contrary. But I found out, anyway. Despite his lies. There was only one reason a Bashkir would hire a Khaggun, and it was never, ever spoken about. The only reason a Bashkir hired a Khaggun was to murder someone.

It was Hadinnn SaTrryn. There were tears in her eyes, but Sornnn did not see them. Neither did he hear her. He remained locked within his own thoughts, oblivious to the knowledge she kept inside her. *On Raan Tallus' orders, Teww Dacce killed your father.*

Fleet-Admiral Ardus Pnin was working on command changes, specifically the vexing question of who should take control of the important Sudden Lake Corridor sector, when he heard the sound he had for some time been dreading.

He rose from his desk and walked with an unhurried pace to a window, where he looked out on seven hoverpods descending on his villa compound. *Seven,* he thought. *Bit of an overkill.*

All the hoverpods were etched with the sigil of the new Star-Admiral. They landed all at once, and with synchronized precision Iin Mennus' Khaggun quietly took possession of the compound. Pnin's own guard did not resist, neither did they retreat. They stood their ground while they were disarmed. Not one of them was hurt or humiliated. Pnin was proud of the discipline he had instilled in them.

Sunset cast a melancholy patina across the villa walls. The garden was already dark with blue shadows, leaf-laden branches clattered softly in a brief gust of wind, a final exhausted exhalation before the wind died altogether as was often the case in that lugubrious slide into dusk. Why was it, Pnin wondered, that battlefield deaths occurred in the sheen of sunlight, but the wasting away by illness or old age took place in the dark?

He saw Iin Mennus now, resplendent in his Star-Admiral's armor. He was without a helm and, it appeared, any form of weapon. That could be taken either way—as a sign of respect or of contempt.

The long shadows made Iin Mennus' skull seem even

more misshapen, the scar down the left side of his head deep as an ice crevasse in the Djenn Marre. Pnin watched him striding toward the villa and he stepped away from the window. The interior was preternaturally still, as if the building were already in mourning. He looked down at his impeccably polished boots. They were indigo, the traditional color of death. That was when he realized that something inside him had known the end was here when he had dressed that morning.

He was back, seated behind his desk, when his adjutant showed the Star-Admiral in. Pnin caught the aggrieved look on his adjutant's face. He had revealed nothing to Iin Mennus. Again, Pnin felt pride swelling his chest. He gave his adjutant an imperceptible nod, the door swung shut, and he was alone with the Star-Admiral.

For a long moment, Iin Mennus stood silent, surveying the room. Then, slowly and deliberately, he stripped off his alloy-mesh gloves.

"It is good to be home," he said. And that summed it up—the excision order of the high command, the years of exile, the humiliation, the brooding, the need for revenge, the eventual triumphal return to Axis Tyr, the nexus of power.

He crossed to a sideboard, stood looking at the crystal decanters.

"Drink?" he said.

Pnin's silence did not deter him. He filled two goblets with Argggedian ice-marc, set one down on the desk in front of Pnin. As he did so, he looked at the data-crystal readouts. A sly smile passed across his lips. Or, with his disfigurement, what passed for a smile.

"The command at Sudden Lakes, eh?" The data crystals vanished into his huge fist. "You'll have no more need of these, Fleet-Admiral."

Pnin's continued silence seemed to needle him. He took a quick pull of the ice-marc, grimacing slightly at its acidic strength. Then he downed the rest, put the goblet aside. Hooking a booted toe around the leg of a camp chair, he drew it over and lowered himself heavily into it. Sitting there in his shining armor plate, he looked like some great squat beetle, ugly and dangerous.

"The question is what to do with you."

"Put me in the caverns with the other Admirals of the high command."

"Nothing would please me more," Iin Mennus said. "Unfortunately, that would not be the wisest course of action. You still have too many adherents. Your incarceration and interrogation would likely cause a rebellion. No, better by far to keep you here in isolation."

"House arrest, you mean."

"Under protection, officially." Iin Mennus' grin was horribly lopsided, a travesty, really. "Haven't you heard, the Resistance has put a price on your head."

"You could murder us all."

"Believe me, I have considered that." Iin Mennus made a show of pocketing the data crystals. "However, I have no wish to martyr you. Or to start a civil war."

"Of course not. Get off on the wrong foot with your master."

Mennus frowned. "We are all servants of the regent."

Pnin had a sardonic response to that, but he was acutely conscious of the Star-Admiral's desire to trap him into saying something treasonous. He was not fooled by Mennus' urbane facade. The Star-Admiral would use any excuse at all because he meant what he said—he desperately wanted to interrogate Pnin. He wanted to see him suffer, he wanted to break him. Then and only then would his thirst for vengeance be sated.

"So." Mennus hunched forward, making him seem even more like an insect, if that were possible. "Now your order of excision has been negated. Now I am in charge of the high command. That must displease you greatly."

"I fear for the Modality, if that is what you mean."

Mennus' eyes glittered. "That is precisely what I mean."

"What is it you want, Star-Admiral? Do you want my humble apologies, do you want me to admit that the order of excision was in error? I would, certainly, if your actions warranted it. However, just the fact that you would consider murdering me and all the Khagggun loyal to me is proof positive that the order of excision was not only justified but absolutely required. You are as dangerous to us as you are to the enemy."

Mennus kept his seat, though muscles had begun to twitch in the side of his skull. His lack of height had taught him to avoid standing in a room with other Khagggun whenever possible. "I was almost killed, you know." He ran a fingertip down the deep indentation in his skull. "Close-hand fighting. Carnage all day and night without surcease, a pyre of the enemy growing around me, stinking to high heaven. I dispatched twenty-seven of their souls that day. And then out of nowhere a Kraelian battle-ax." He looked at his fingertip as if expecting to see blood and gore. "I fell, a piece of my would-be killer's axe still lodged in the bone of my skull, but on my knees I slaughtered him."

But, as Pnin saw it, that was not his meaning. This bragging of his battlefield prowess was really a question: *How could you have drawn up an order of excision on such a hero?* That was what ate at him. Which meant that he had not heard a word Pnin had said. Typical of him.

"It is true that I am dangerous," Iin Mennus continued. "Dangerous to those within our own caste who would seek to undermine the Khagggun mission to seek and destroy."

"We are on Kundala now, and it seems we will be here for some time," Pnin said. "If we continue to seek and destroy, there will be only V'ornn left."

Mennus spread his hands. "You see, this is what I mean. It is this soft thinking that is undermining the discipline of the Khagggun."

"The Khagggun under my command are the most highly disciplined in the caste."

Because he could not refute that, Mennus took a different tack. "As a caste, we are becoming bored, listless. We lack direction and focus. The Kundalan Resistance should have been completely wiped out by now. We long ago should have occupied the southern continent."

"I was there in the Great Arryx when the Gyrgon ordered us home. Would you gainsay their decision?"

"I point this out because it has come to my attention that the Sarakkon have become more active of late. More of them are here in Axis Tyr than ever before. We do not even have a coordinated means of keeping track of them."

"They are traders. Why track them?"

"Do you know a Sarakkon named Lujon?"

Pnin shook his head. But of course he did know Lujon. They had met when Pnin had been in the southern continent. No one could have been sorrier than he that the Gyrgon had ordered them home. At the time, he had considered it a serious mistake, and nothing since that time had disabused him of that conviction. Quite the contrary. Pnin knew that Lujon was not just another Sarakkon. He knew that he was not a trader. Lujon had presented himself as a priest, but he was too slick, too glib, too ready with the answers to all Pnin's questions. Pnin had not believed anything he had said.

After the interview, he had made it his business to follow Lujon, not an easy task for a V'ornn on the southern continent. Fortunately, he had found someone on the Orieniad who had agreed to help him. From this, Pnin had deduced that there was a serious schism in the Sarakkonian ruling council.

The member of the Orieniad—Cerró was his name—had introduced him to a Sarakkon by the name of Courion, and it was Courion who had led Pnin into the Axetl River basin, where Pnin had seen the Temple of Abrasea, where he had learned that some among the Sarakkon secretly practiced their own form of sorcery—an astonishing ability to murder.

Then, abruptly, the Gyrgon had ordered him and his Khagggun back to Axis Tyr. He had dutifully dictated his report, but before he could deliver it to the Star-Admiral, he was visited by a Gyrgon named Nith Batoxxx, who requested of him a verbal report, then promptly relieved him of the data crystal, admonishing him never to speak of it with anyone. That was the last he ever heard of the matter.

"This is what I mean," Iin Mennus said now. "Lujon has been making strategic alliances."

"As all traders must."

Iin Mennus glowered. "You cannot hide your incompetence. We believe there is something more to Lujon. We believe he is a smuggler."

Pnin wanted to laugh. Instead, he pasted a blank expression on his face. When Nith Batoxxx had popped up at Kurgan Stogggul's side, Pnin's interest had been piqued. He had discovered that Courion was in Axis Tyr, and he knew that, subsequently, Nith Batoxxx had murdered him. This had put him on high alert, and, in due course, he had been informed the moment Lujon had set foot in Axis Tyr. He knew that he had set himself up in a long-abandoned Ramahan watchtower east of the city. He was under surveillance because Pnin very much wanted to know if he, too, would be contacted by the Gyrgon. Why had the Gyrgon decided to leave the Sarakkon alone when they could have been so easily plucked off the vine? That had been a question that had haunted him ever since the order had been given. He suspected Lujon knew the answer.

"Smugglers abound, some doing business with the Gyrgon," Pnin said with a shrug. "He is one Sarakkon. What mischief?"

"Gyrgon? Involved in smuggling with the Sarakkon?" Iin Mennus snorted. "Now I know that you have lost your mind."

Your intelligence network will have to be better than that if you want to remain Star-Admiral, Pnin thought, but he remained mute. No good could come from provoking Mennus. He did what he always did to calm himself. He looked at the small array of artifacts on his desk: a VIII Dynasty Nieobian prayer vase, a Kraelian idol, a pair of meshed Argggedian crystal spheres, mementoes of wars, of bloody battlefields, of hard-won victories, and of compatriots lost but not forgotten.

They glimmered, as if speaking to him. For many years, longer than he could remember, it had seemed to him as if his life was populated by the dead. The enemy, yes, in great number, but more importantly compatriots, friends, rivals, all brothers-in-arms. The sadness of this host's presence was visited on him, like a pain in his chest that defied diagnosis, let alone a cure. He breathed in the dust to which they had returned. When he ate it was with their eyes watching him. And when he slept there they were again, walking toward him through the unspeakable mire of their own offal.

In many ways, they were more real to him than the living. The world he awoke to each morning was like smoke, a dream through which he drifted, always aware of the dead, of their dark eyes, of their breath soughing through the trees of his garden. He found a curious kind of comfort in their sorrow, for he knew they were waiting for him to join them.

"You are old and weak," Iin Mennus said, intuiting the silence, Pnin's decision not to respond to the verbal challenge. "You have a chance to step aside, to announce your retirement. I give you this one chance, more than you gave me. Otherwise"—he shrugged. "Isolation. Impotence. You will never go beyond these walls again. Not a fitting end for a Khagggun."

Pnin was suddenly tired of the bullying. He wanted nothing more than to put his feet up and close his eyes, fall into slumber, joining again with the host of the dead. That would be fitting for a Khagggun, bereft of a son, a leader who could with his strong arm and keen mind pierce this cloud of conspiracy and pry him from the not-so-tender mercies of the new Star-Admiral, but what, instead, did he have? A daughter from whom, for all her prowess forging weapons, he could expect nothing. She was utterly impotent, incapable of mustering support among those still loyal to him or lending help of any kind. With hearts made heavy by this burden, he rose. In a flash, Iin Mennus drew an ion dagger from a sheath hidden inside his armor and nailed his left hand to the desk.

"Did I tell you to get up?" Mennus twisted the blade an eighth of a turn. Blood began to seep out, and Pnin felt a fiery pain race up his arm into his shoulder and chest. "From now on, Little Admiral, this is the way it will be." Another eighth, and Pnin was forced back into his chair. "Ah, yes. I see we are clear on this point."

K onara Inggres burst through the high bastion gates of the Abbey of Floating White, and such was her agitation that the Ja-Gaar began to howl. At once, the Nawatir came at a run, his long, powerful legs eating up the space between them. It had begun to rain, big, fat drops that shimmered on the ghostly white-stone paving. His long blond hair and beard were jeweled with it.

She had given the remaining decoction to the second companion, instructing him to deliver three drops hourly onto the wounded male's tongue.

"Will he live?" the companions asked again.

"He will," she had said, because their belief would help buoy their fallen comrade, and every little bit helped. But whether it would be enough she did not know.

As she left them, they were carrying him home.

"What is it?" the Nawatir said now. His mysterious cloak whipped about his ankles like a stormy sea. "What has happened?"

As the Ja-Gaar prowled around her, restless, infected by her agitation, she told him what had happened in Stone Border.

"Why are they coming here now?" she concluded. "And why so many of them?"

"Wing-Adjutant Wiiin."

Konara Inggres shook her head.

"Come."

The Nawatir took her by the elbow, led her inside a smallish out-temple. It was pillared but without walls. The rain hammered down on the thick tiles of its steeply canted roof. He told her how he and Eleana had met Wing-Adjutant Wiiin, how Eleana had pretended to be his Ramahan contact, how he had threatened the peace of the abbey if she did not deliver new and relevant information about Resistance activities.

"So Konara Urdma was spying for the Khagggun?"

The Nawatir nodded. "Konara Bartta, as well. It went all the way back to Konara Mossa. She made the original deal with the Khagggun in order to spare Floating White."

"The last bastion of Ramahan culture and training. I have long wondered why we were spared." Konara Inggres let her voice trail off. She shivered at the thought of the evil pact her predecessors had made.

They sat together on the porphyry altar watching the grey rain flash down, bounce against the stone paths. Somewhere, thunder rumbled through the valleys, rolling upward toward them.

"This is my fault," the Nawatir said bitterly. "I completely forgot about Wing-Adjutant Wiiin. He seemed more of an administrator than a warrior, and I did not take his threat seriously."

"Useless to apply blame," she said softly. "What are we to do?"

"Don't worry, Inggres, we will find a way to defend ourselves."

She sat quite still. Her cheeks were flaming, her heart pounding. *Inggres*. No one had called her that, not since she had come to the abbey at a very early age. *Inggres*. It felt so naked, so intimate to be called by her name without the armor of her Ramahan honorific. Unbidden, a thrill ran down her spine, pooled in her loins.

And then he took her hand in his. "Don't lose your faith now. You have been through so much, overcome so much."

"But there are so few of us and so many of them," she said. They were alone in the darkness and the silvery rain. No one could hear them, no one could see them. They were as cut off from the abbey as they were from the rest of the world.

The Nawatir's head lifted. "I was born in fire, bred for battle. There is Dragon spoor in my veins, there is potent sorcery in my cloak and in my steed." He put his arms around her, and thunder rolled down on them. "Ah, you are trembling. I am not afraid, Inggres, and neither should you be."

And then she did the unimaginable, the unforgivable. She kissed him.

Krystren's Journey

K rystren, rolling her cube of worn red jade between her fingers, found herself in a dense stand of trees. Six days ago she had lost sight of the ocean. This was not a problem, for she had been born inland, and had been a girl of teenage years when she had first caught sight of the sea. Unlike her brother, Courion, she had not lost her heart to it, nor could she quite fathom by what mysterious mechanism he had done so.

Crouching down in deep green shade, she flicked away leaf mold and brittle Marre pine needles so that she could redraw for herself the map of the northern continent she had memorized before setting out on her journey. Her slightly curved forefinger made complex designs on the forest floor. She did not need to do this. She knew where she was and in which direction she needed to go in order to arrive at Axis Tyr. Nevertheless, she liked the discipline of physically drawing the map, seeing with her eyes as well as with her mind the countryside that lay before her.

To the northeast was a small chain of rising hillsides beyond which lay the Great Phosphorus Marsh and, just to the east of that, the capital city. Almost directly north was the southern shore of Blue Bone Lake, into which Three Fish River emptied on its downward snaking path from the waterfall known as Little Rushing high in the Djenn Marre mountains.

A noise came to her, soft and moss-moist, barely more than an undertone, and she lifted her head, her pulse racing. She remained still, the branches moving gently into sunlight and out again, sparking pinpoints like diamonds across the moist ground, the gnarled tree roots, her knotted shoulders.

She listened hard, expecting voices, but she heard no voices, at least none speaking a language she knew. It might have been the wind rustling through the long, swaying boughs, but it wasn't. It might have been a pair of birds, busily nest-building, but it wasn't. It might have been foraging mammals, but it wasn't.

What *was* it, then?

She sent out a mind-feeler first south, then east. Nothing. She swept it around to the north, then the west, found it there.

The trouble was, it found her at the same time. Whatever was there was instantly aware of her mind-feeler and grabbed hold of it. Krystren was so stunned that she was unable to retaliate or even to defend herself. She felt herself being reeled in, and by the time she recovered sufficiently to break off the mind-feeler, she was already in the grip of the thing.

Only it wasn't a thing at all. She was in the grip of a wraith—quite the most beautiful wraith she had ever seen. He had a long, slender face with high cheekbones and a cleft chin, and curious, upturned eyes. His body was similarly slim—broad of shoulder and narrow of hip—with muscles that were lithe and elastic, rather than puffed and tightly bunched. His demeanor was confident without being in the least bit smug. In sum, he had the appearance of someone entirely at one with his surroundings.

"Who are you?" the wraith demanded.

By Yahé's grisly teeth, she could see clear through him!

"More to the point," he said, examining her tattooed forehead and ears. "*What* are you?"

"Sarakkon," she said.

"Ah, yes. I knew that." The wraith gave a crafty little smile. "I wanted to see whether you would tell me the truth." He continued with his examination. "Krystren, is it? Krystren, second daughter of Coirn, of the House of Oronel."

"We are first daughter."

"Ah, yes. That's right. First daughter Koroneth died when she was a babe of three."

She felt all the breath go out of her. "You can read the kaldea!"

"On males, it's a belt of knotted sea grape. Females, however, are forbidden to wear the kaldea, and so their tattoos tell the family tale." He cocked his head, his glittering eyes more curious than ever. He was pale blue, and aqueous, so that what could be seen through him was rippled and somewhat distorted. "A long way from the Great Arryx, aren't you?"

"You have us at a disadvantage, sir," she said. "You know all about us while we know nothing about you."

"I know hardly enough about you, Krystren of the Oronel. No, not nearly. But perhaps you are right." He tapped a watery forefinger against a watery lip. "My name is Bryn. I am Hagoshrin."

"Do you think us ignorant of the legends of Miina that we would believe you for even an instant?" she said at once. "Hagoshrin are huge and hideous, with tentacles and claws as large as our arm." She sniffed heavily. "They stink, as well."

"I am what I am," he said. "It matters not whether or not you believe me."

"And in any event," she said quite breathlessly, "if memory serves, Hagoshrin cannot lie."

"That is absolutely correct," Bryn said, "we cannot lie."

"But you are not Hagoshrin!"

Bryn threw his head back and laughed. It was an eerie kind of sound, like the midnight wind soughing through a graveyard, but curiously not an unpleasant one for all that. "Here we have something of a conundrum," he said. "But why not? Today seems full of such puzzles. For instance, I had no idea that Sarakkon could use their minds as you do."

"They can't," Krystren said. "Not as a rule, anyway. But we are *Onnda*."

"That you may be," Bryn said, "but neither *Onnda* nor *Sintire* have learned to use their minds as you do."

Krystren was about to tell him that no amount of cajoling on his part would get her to reveal the secrets taught to her by the *crifica*, when without warning he swept her off her feet. Grasping a low branch, he swung them up so swiftly she thought she had left her stomach behind. All this with appalling ease. Though he looked lighter than air, his strength was impressive.

As he took to the trees, he wrapped one hand over her mouth. "Silence now."

Higher and higher they climbed, as he leapt from limb to limb, zigzagging his way into the upper reaches of the Marre pines until they reached the summit, as it were, of the forest. On the tallest tree they crouched, as the Marre pine leader swayed this way and that in the wind so that Krystren felt as if she was back on the wrecked *Oomaloo,* taking rough seas at full sail.

Bryn twisted them around so that they were facing south, and with his free arm pointed down through the sunlight, the maze of tree branches, needles, leaves.

"Behold they that cometh," he whispered, taking his hand from her mouth.

And she saw them, a small band of armed Sarakkon and

robed sauromicians. They stood shoulder to shoulder like a living wedge within a craft that scudded low over the rocky rising terrain.

"They have found us," she whispered.

Bryn shook his head. "They are for the moment unaware of you. They are on their own journey to the north."

"What is that craft?" she whispered, for the vehicle was like none she had ever seen before. It flashed and coruscated in the sunlight, seemed wispy, virtually disappearing in the shadows.

"Look closely," Bryn said. "Witness the sauromicians' necromancy."

Krystren squinted slightly, shading her eyes, and concentrated on the fast-moving craft. She gave a little gasp, for she could see now that the vehicle was eye-shaped, and it seemed to ripple and pulse as if it were alive. And indeed is *was* alive, after a fashion, for it was composed of alternating layers of smoke and swarms of crawling, buzzing warrior-beetles, the blue-black armor of their thoraxes, the oversize scissorlike pincers glinting and flashing in the sunlight. In the shadows, they turned a deep matte black, merging with the other shadows of the forest while the smoke drifted about in misty camouflage.

"Where are they going?" she asked.

"I believe they are making another pilgrimage to the Abbey of Five Pivots." Bryn looked at her, his glittering eyes for an instant solidifying to a deep and lustrous umber. "But the only way to know for certain—"

"—is to follow them."

"Yes, Krystren of the Oronel. I will take you if you wish it."

In an instant, her mind was made up. Her brother could wait a day or two. Her curiosity was piqued; she had to know what the *Sintire* were up to. And she wanted to know more about this odd-looking wraith. She nodded.

His fierce smile somehow warmed her heart.

* * *

Bryn fed her as they went north—nuts and dried berries mostly, but also little bits of things she could not immediately identify, though by the way she was immediately restored she knew they were proteinaceous and nutritious. Cold water she received from the deep, finely woven baskets of air plants that existed near the treetops. Their shootlike tendrils and paper-thin petals caressed her cheeks as she sipped the nectar. Bryn himself seemed to require neither food nor drink, but she did not want to dwell on his eating habits, for she remembered that Hagoshrin—if that was truly what he was—were supposed to subsist on the bones of other species.

The strange and unsettling craft kept up a steady pace all through the long afternoon and into the evening, save for once when the *Sintire* disembarked. They produced a small idol of Abrasea and went down on their knees, the soft ululations of their prayers echoing through the cathedral of trees.

It was not until perhaps an hour after dark that the vehicle finally slowed, coming to rest on a flat outcropping of pale schist. There, beneath the watery light of three moons, the smoke swirled itself into the shape of a rounded dwelling while the warrior-beetles fanned out in a protective circle around it.

High above, Krystren and Bryn hung in the treetops for a time before settling somewhat lower in the topmost crotch of an ancient Marre pine. While she watched, back braced against the tree trunk, he wove three branches together to make something that resembled both a bower and a hammock shot through with moonlight. He sat back in it, gestured for her to join him.

"It's perfectly safe," he said, "and it has the added advantage of keeping the sound of our voices from reaching those below."

Cautiously, she crept into it, testing with every step, and found it soft and dense, the layers of needles formed from the complex weaving a comfortable and comforting cradle. Bryn watched her with his intense, curious gaze as she assured herself of the efficacy of his handiwork.

"I hold you blameless for not trusting me," he said, as she settled in beside him. "Nowadays it is wise to be cautious."

"Why are you doing this?" she asked.

"Why shouldn't I help you? I do not like the sauromicians, I do not like that they have entered into an agreement with the *Sintire*."

"You know so much about the Sarakkon."

"You Sarakkon were frequent visitors to Za Hara-at once upon a time."

"But that was eons ago." She frowned. "You were at Za Hara-at?"

"In those days, we all inhabited the northen continent, Sarakkon included. Then came the war with the *Sintire*, who wanted to usurp the Ramahan power, who wanted to end Miina's reign and replace Her with the epicene abomination Abrasea. With our help, and the secret help of the *Onnda*, the Ramahan drove them from the northern continent, repelled them when time and again they tried to regain the continent by ship. It was the *Onnda*'s hope that the Ramahan would not banish all Sarakkon to the southern continent, but Miina's Law had been broken, all Sarakkon had to pay the price." He shrugged. "That was also a long time ago."

Krystren stared at Bryn with astonishment. "If you are telling the truth—"

"I always tell the truth, Krystren of the Oronel."

She took a breath. "If so, then you are telling us a piece of our own history we did not know. It is not taught among the *Onnda*."

"Because Miina in her fury wiped it from your memory." Bryn shifted slightly. "But believe me when I tell you that those *Sintire* who have made a pact with the sauromicians know."

The *Sintire* prayers to Abrasea rose to them, dark and haunting, through the gloom.

"How could they?"

"The sauromicians used their necromancy to restore their memories."

Krystren said nothing. Nevertheless, Bryn knew the question she wanted to ask.

"The sauromicians killed young Ramahan and while their bodies were still warm removed their brains. I see the look of disgust on your face, Krystren of the Oronel, and I share it. But this vile ritual is in accordance with the basic principles of necromancy, which uses the unique energy released by the dying to power its spells. And so this necromancy is doubly diabolical, for the spirits of those killed are thus trapped within the evil spells, enslaved, forced into the service of the sauromicians."

As Bryn's words took on power, his form appeared even more insubstantial. "An interesting point to remember: sauromicians prefer not to kill their victims themselves. If they do, they cannot use them, cannot trap their energy. Their spirits escape. They must convince others to murder or impel their victims to kill themselves."

"What a life to be born into." There was a bitter taste in Krystren's mouth. "But in truth not so very unfamiliar, for in many ways it parallels the regimented mind-set of the *Sintire*, whose life is in the service of the hermaphrodite Abrasea. The reaver-nourisher deity requires of its suppli-cants a highly ritualized existence. The High Cathedral is known to us. It is presided over by the *Ardinals*, the high priests. Normally, they do not stray far from the High Cathedral, which they are pledged to protect with their very lives. The fact that a number of them are here on the northern continent is an exceedingly ominous sign."

"Tell me about the High Cathedral."

What was it about Bryn that made her feel safe and se-cure? High above her head, soft, cushiony wads of clouds came alive in the moonlight. She could smell the scents of the forest, along with the bitter metallic tang emanating like a dangerous undertow from the small party in their necromantic smoke dwelling and their guardian swarm.

But where were the insects, the birds? At last she decided to go on. "As you may know, the *Onnda* are divided into seven Bloodlines. The Bloodlines, in turn, are divided into ciths. We were sent by my cith chieftain to observe the workings of the High Cathedral.

"It is located at the lowest point of the Axetl River basin. It is guarded not only by *Sintire* but by packs of carna, vicious, flesh-eating reptiles that congregate in the thick mud at the mouth of the river basin."

"And yet you eluded them all."

She touched him briefly with a tendril projected by her mind.

"Yes, of course," he said.

"Inside, the High Cathedral is womblike, oven-hot even on the coolest nights of winter," she continued. "It consists of a vast globular oratory dominated by an enormous statue of Abrasea. All around the idol, a forest of crimson candles burns constantly. Acolytes tend them day and night, for each candle is replaced before it can gutter and go out.

"We entered through one of five smoke holes in the roof and lay on one of many rough-hewn rafters that crisscross the space just below the ceiling. Even from that height there is the scent of an incense that is a derivative of *oqeyya*. Behind the idol, there is a low doorway, so unobtrusive as to be all but invisible, that leads to a warren of small cubicles, living quarters for the *Ardinals*, as well as a larger chamber for meetings and discussions.

"The *Ardinals'* rule is absolute, their word is Law, for they speak with Abrasea's voice as oracles. There is a pulpit made of a magnificent polished slab of kingga from which they preach the Word of Abrasea. *There will be no other god but Abrasea. Abrasea will destroy all those who do not give themselves over to Abrasea. Eternal agony awaits all those who do not embrace Abrasea.* They say these things over and over in hypnotic fashion until it becomes grooved into the brains of the faithful."

Bryn's eyes continued to glitter with his absorbed listening. "And what goes on when the pulpit is empty, when the faithful have departed? What transpires in the warren of chambers off the oratory? What is the real work of the Church of Abrasea?"

"That is precisely what our cith chieftain wanted to find out."

Krystren had turned over on her belly, the better to keep the smoke dwelling in view. She saw a figure emerge. It was sauromician archon. He wore a black cloak, deeply cowled. Around his neck was a thick mineral chain. From it hung what appeared to be a small dagger that shone transparent in the moonslight. Bryn identified him as Varda. Varda stood for a moment, his hands clasped loosely behind his back. She did not have to use her skill to fathom his intent. He scanned the moonslit forest in every direction, and when he tilted his head back, when she saw his one pale eye, she held her breath. After what seemed like ages, he turned and stalked back into the smoke dwelling.

"Mark that eye well," Bryn told her, "for it was taken from the newly dead and thus possesses necromantic power."

"What sort of power?"

"It can see in the dark. It can see shadows."

"He did not detect us."

"As you discovered for yourself on the island of Suspended Skull, necromancy is deeply flawed," he said. "In this, your mind ability can counter the power of the necromantic eye."

She rolled over to look at him. She knew he wanted to know more about her mind-skill.

"What did you discover in the bowels of the High Cathedral, Krystren of the Oronel?"

She decided this was a question she could answer. "The Church of Abrasea is an autarchy. It was created to control the population. The concept is as evil as its implementation is simple. Everyone must attend oratorio, everyone is accounted for; everyone is told what to think, what to do, everything is controlled. But we also discovered something else, a deeper, hidden personal agenda. There burns within the *Ardinals* the obsession to move beyond the borders of Axis Tyr."

"Toward what end?"

"They covet the lost secrets of Za Hara-at."

She fell asleep in Bryn's arms while he watched over her. In the hours after midnight the forest was usually shimmering with industrious nocturnal life. That night, save for the occasional flurry of wind that dipped and lifted the branches, all was silent. It was as if a dead zone had arisen ghostlike from the moldering ground, inside which no living thing dared to be.

Necromancy, unlike sorcery of any sort, was a finite resource. That is to say, a necromancer needed a periodic supply of the dying to renew and sustain his power. Without death, he slowly lost strength and withered away. The trouble was he was exceedingly persuasive, enticing others to commit for him the one act he could not perform himself. That was altogether unsurprising, for evil was glamorous. It held out the promise of love, wealth, influence, whatever was your deepest desire. Glamor was difficult to resist. It cajoled and bedazzled. And so the sauromicians were never without dupes, never without victims, one by one tossed into shallow graves, their deaths as unremarked as their lives had been.

All this Bryn turned over in his mind as he held Krystren. He listened to her soft breathing, felt her heartbeat, the pulse of blood through her body, and he was filled with sorrow, for she was being sought by the very party that was encamped on the forest floor. And if they found her, they would surely find a way to extract every secret she carried inside her head. He could not allow that, no matter the cost.

And the cost would be great. Miina would see to that. Jealous Goddess! And vindictive. Just look what she had done to Pyphoros and his kind! And wasn't all Kundala the poorer for it? Could the taste of revenge be in the least bit sweet when so much death and suffering was its result? Truth be told, he was disgusted by the machinations of goddesses and archdaemons alike. He was convinced that Kundala would be better off without either. Unfortunately, the Cosmos did not allow for such radical negations of its fundamental Laws. Still, if he dared, he could do what he was able.

Bryn, watching Krystren, was filled with questions. He did not understand sleep, for Hagoshrin had no need periodically to shut down their physical functions. But there was one aspect of it that he envied: the ability to dream. He had heard Kundalan talk about their dreams, and it had taken him a long while to fathom the meaning of the word. Bryn wanted to dream, and he wondered now whether he could enter into Krystren's.

Krystren was dreaming of Courion, of her last sight of him, his eyes red-rimmed and teary. She was running along the crowded quay, waving her arms as the ship her brother had signed on to left the port of Celiocco.

"Come back!" she cried, and held aloft the cube of red jade. "Come back!" She had meant to give it to him, to return the gift he had given to Orujo, but his shock, the misery in his face, had driven all thought of it from her mind.

She saw him staring at her, a look she had seen him throw at others but never at her. He blamed her for his beloved's death. He would never forgive her. How quickly love could turn to hatred!

In her dream, Krystren cried, and Bryn, who had managed through his own arts to insinuate himself into the deepest reaches of her mind, saw what she saw, felt what she felt, and he, too, wept. How dear the love of one sibling for another. How exquisitely close they were, their spirits existing side by side, the one occasionally overlapping the other in a kind of intimate dance. Hagoshrin were absolutely solitary; he had no good analog for what she was feeling.

Krystren woke up, as she always did, at once fully awake. She stared up into Bryn's umber eyes. The forest was steeped in the dewy mist of dawn that swirled like steam about their treetop eyrie.

"Have you been refreshed by your sleep?" he asked.

"You were in our dream. You were in our head." She sat up sharply. Her body felt stiff and cold; her mind just felt cold.

"I took care not to disturb anything." He blinked. "I did not look at any thought or memory."

"You were in our *head*." She pulled away until her back was against the tree crotch. It was as far as she could go. "You know *everything*."

"Not true. I told you—"

"And why should we believe you?"

"I am Hagoshrin. I cannot lie."

She looked at him with those clear steady intelligent eyes. "Our *dreams* are private, personal. How could you do that? What you did was the worst form of violation."

"Truly I am sorry, Krystren of the Oronel. I did not mean—"

"We want nothing more to do with you. We will continue on alone."

"This forest is not safe."

"We are familiar with the enemy. We are prepared."

He believed her, for she had told him about her escape from the wrecked ship, her adventures on the island of Suspended Skull and how she had managed the voyage to the mainland. But her knowledge of the forest was severely limited. He sensed that the *gabir* was not far away. Even he was afraid of the *gabir*.

Down below, the party of sauromicians and *Sintire* was astir. The smoke tent was unraveling like a serpent shedding its skin. There was no time to debate with her. The party was moving out.

"Come. We must go."

"We said we would do this alone."

"Look down," he said.

The warrior-beetles were forming, their mandibles clicking furiously.

"You will never be able to keep pace with them."

Krystren hesitated but a moment. Then she nodded and came away from the crotch so that he could loop an arm around her. They set off through the mist-shrouded trees.

It took several hours for the sun to reach a height great enough to penetrate the dense Marre pines and burn off the morning's damp chill. By that time, she had eaten lightly and drunk cold water twice. But in all that time she had said not a word, and Bryn could feel the coldness emanating from her even as he felt the mental barrier she had erected with her particular skill. He had erred again. Now he would never learn the secret of her ability. He would be utterly alone again, as Hagoshrin were meant to be. As he could not bear to be.

Much to his astonishment, her stony silence and icy looks cut him like the touch of a *gabir*. By entering her dream he had done far more than trespass, he had found the connection to another being for which he had been longing. To have experienced its exhilaration, to know he never would again, drove him to misery.

It was those very thoughts, fulminating unfamiliar emotions, that caused him to miss the first signs that they were being followed. By the time he did pick up on it, the *gabir* was very close.

The instant he felt the first touch of its chill emanations, he whirled to his left, changing course.

"What do you think you are doing?" Krystren said shortly. "We will lose sight of them in a moment."

"That is the point."

He took them even higher, into the swaying crowns of the Marre pines, so spindly that Krystren could hardly believe they would support them. She tried to squirm in his arms, but he held her all the tighter.

"Let us go," she hissed. "We knew we should have continued on my own."

"Don't be a fool. Keep still."

And he whirled, holding her close, and she felt the gorge rise into her throat. She saw the creature crouched on a tree limb. It was pale as snow. Even its eyes—huge, lidless, bone-ridged around their perimeters—were ashen. The face, as well as the body, was terrifically emaciated, so that it appeared to be made of skin stretched directly over bones, all fat, muscle, sinew and connective tissue wasted away.

"What is this thing?" she whispered.

"It is a *gabir*, it has been following us for some time."

"Why?"

The *gabir* was staring at her with a kind of hunger.

"It wants to kill us."

As she instinctively began to extend her mental barrier, he warned her to stop.

"It will use the barrier as a pathway into you."

And already she could see the *gabir* leaning forward expectantly, its long arms and prehensile fingers outstretched as if it could gather in the very air between them.

"Let's get out of here," she said.

"Once the *gabir* has found us it will not let us go."

"But you—"

"I cannot outrun a *gabir*," he said.

And that was when she registered the fear on his face.

"What is it?" she asked.

"The *gabir*—it is neither alive nor dead. The sauromicians leave them in their wake. As I told you, they need the death energy in order to maintain their power. A piece of the victim's spirit eludes the necromancy. Sometimes, it survives only an hour or so. Other times, it lasts for weeks or months. It is stuck inside the dying body and all it knows is self-preservation. So it keeps the body alive as best it can. But since it is incomplete, since the body itself has been mutilated, it cannot be successful. It can stitch up the wounds temporarily, but that is all. This is the result."

Krystren shuddered. "How horrible. Why does it happen?"

"As in many things anomalous it is the doing of a banestone."

Krystren went very still. Her heart was beating fast, and she quickly and efficiently used her training to clamp down on it, for she was terrified that Bryn would sense her agitation.

"A banestone?" she said disingenuously. "What is that?"

The *gabir* had shuffled forward, its head at an angle, as it studied them more closely, and Bryn moved slightly in reflex. She could sense his fear, a dark river running through the core of him.

"Why are you afraid of him, Bryn?"

"Because he is neither of this realm nor of that of the dead, his cells are in flux. Therefore, his touch is toxic to me."

She wondered what the *gabir*'s touch would do to her. "Tell us about the banestones."

"There are nine banestones," Bryn said. "They were mined by daemons in the northern core of Kundala, all from the same rich vein. The Dragons brought them to Za Hara-at, where they were used in the foundations of the nine great temples. They are the source of the ancient city's enormous power. Separately, their power is inconstant, mercurial, unpredictable." With his fingertip, he drew a peculiar nine-sided form. "But when the nine are brought together in this configuration the banestones extract the essential power of the Cosmos from the very elements. They become an engine of incalculable power. So they were at the height of Za Hara-at's glory, when it was needed the most. But the temptation to misuse that power was so great that Za Hara-at was destroyed, the banestones scattered to the four corners of Kundala."

"But the existence of the *gabir* means that the banestones have been found."

"By the sauromicians. They have handled them and be-

come infected with the banestones' erratic and unpredictable radiation. The *gabir* appeared only after the
sauromicians had come into possession of the banestones.
But until the archons have all nine they will not regain the
power that was once theirs."

All of a sudden, the *gabir* leapt at them. Bryn moved to
swing Krystren out of harm's way, but she slipped his gasp
and placed herself squarely between him and the hurtling
gabir. She used her training to take the momentum of the
small body, swing it around, and use it to whirl the thing
away from Bryn. Unfortunately, the *gabir* dug its talonlike
nails into her in a grip she could not break. Down it hurtled, and her with it, crashing through boughs and
branches until they smacked against a tree trunk, fetching
up there.

The *gabir*'s jaws snapped and ground as it tried to bite
her. She could feel waves of coldness sweeping off it,
making her feel as if she were standing on a ship's deck in
the height of a storm. Its cold, she sensed, had the capacity
to flay the skin off her, to numb her through if she kept in
contact with it for too long.

"Get away from it!"

She heard Bryn's urgent voice, saw out of the corner of
her eye that he had stripped a branch of its bark, leaving a
flexible green lance whose end he had bitten into a point.

"The green wood will pinion it if I pierce it through the
heart," he said. "But you are too close. You must break
away."

"No!" Krystren wondered whether she knew what she
was doing. "Stay where you are, Bryn."

She saw the *gabir* looking fearfully at the weapon Bryn
had fashioned, and inexplicably her heart went out to the
pathetic creature. To be killed and yet not be able to cross
from one realm to another, to be a part of nothing, this was
a fate more dreadful than any she could imagine.

She shook the *gabir*. Already, her fingers had grown
numb, and she was gritting her teeth simply to hold the
creature down.

"What is it?" she said. "What is it you want?"

The *gabir* merely rolled its eyes at her and, craning its neck, tried to sink its teeth into her shoulder. She twisted away. She spoke to it again, but it was no use. The thing either could not or would not respond. The cold was beginning to creep up her wrists into her forearms. She knew she would not be able to hold it down much longer.

Then she remembered how Bryn had cautioned her against using her mind against it. Concentrating mightily, she pushed out a tendril toward it, forming it into a sentence.

What do you want?

The *gabir* gave a little start, and she felt it turn its full concentration on her. Its pale eyes were like great moons floating in a sky full of clouds. She repeated her question, holding it out as one would hold out a scrap of food to a starving child.

The crystal dagger, the *gabir* said in her mind. *The sauromician Varda has it.*

Krystren remembered seeing it, hung from the chain around his neck.

If you fetch it for me, the *gabir* said, *I will tell you where to find your brother, Courion.*

How do you know—?

The *gabir* stared at her. *Your desire to find him is so strong I can hear it like a scream in my mind.*

You know where we can find him?

I do. The creature blinked rapidly. *I have caught a glimpse of him.*

Krystren nodded. *All right.*

It removed its talons from her upper arms and immediately she felt the flush of blood flowing back into her hands. She flexed her fingers awkwardly, getting the feeling back. Still, she could sense the *gabir*'s fear, and she turned to Bryn.

"Put the spear aside."

"But—"

"Do as we say, Bryn. The *gabir* will not attack you. We have reached an agreement."

* * *

V*arda never takes it off*, the *gabir* said, *save when the others pray to their deity.*

Krystren repeated this to Bryn, as she had her previous conversation with the *gabir*. She harbored a suspicion that he possessed the ability to hear the creature as she did, but he would not allow himself to be that vulnerable. "It means the *Sintire*," she went on. "When they make their thrice-daily obeisance to Abrasea there must be no weapons visible or in a threatening position."

"I know that. While they pray, Varda goes off by himself to practice his necromancy," Bryn said. "But even when he takes off the chain the crystal dagger is never out of his sight. This plan is far too dangerous."

"We don't say it's not," Krystren said. "But we have no choice. We have to know where we can find our brother."

"What about the warrior-beetles?"

"The *gabir* promises he will keep them occupied."

Bryn watched her for some time. Eventually he concluded that he could not dissuade her and threw up his hands in exasperation.

They traveled on, the three of them plunged into the gloom of an edgy silence. An hour after dark, just as it had the evening before, the beetle craft slowed and came to a stop on a small, heavily wooded rise. The insects spread out in a circle, and the smoke tent was conjured up.

As soon as they smelled the pungent aroma of the incense wafting up to them, they moved into position. The *gabir* vanished as it descended to the ground. At the same time, Krystren and Bryn maneuvered themselves through the Marre pines, following Varda. Directly above the spot where he chose to sit, they crouched on stout middle branches, waiting.

Below them, Varda took off the chain, laying it and its crystal dagger aside. The *gabir* had told Krystren that the warrior-beetles were carrion-eaters. Since he was half-dead, they would sense his presence as food and be dis-

tracted, hopefully long enough for her to steal the crystal
dagger. The thought of the *gabir* being eaten by the swarm
of insects gave her the chills.

Cautiously, they moved down through the levels of
boughs. When they were perhaps twenty-five meters above
Varda's head, they stopped. Krystren had told Bryn what
he needed to do, and now she settled herself to begin her
part. But as she commenced to extend her mind-feeler,
Bryn grabbed her arm. They could hear a low, droning
chant.

Putting his lips against her ear, he whispered, "Have a
care. The sauromician is conjuring up the Eye of Ajbal. It
is by this means that he hopes to find you."

Krystren nodded. There was no time to lose. Ignoring
the sick feeling in the pit of her stomach, she extended her
mind-feeler, lowering it into the trees just past where
Varda sat. Then she fashioned it into a simulacrum of herself. She had to be very careful now, because if she made a
mistake, Varda would be able to use his necromancy to
follow the thread of the mind-feeler back to her as Bryn
had done.

At once, the sauromician's head came up. She could see
it swiveling this way and that, until the necromantic eye
caught sight of "her" flitting through the forest. The chanting continued as if it had a life of its own, but he was up in
a flash, darting silently toward the ghost-image she had
fashioned.

She leapt down, landing on bent knees in order to cush-
ion the impact. Fortunately, the ground was soft with rain
and springy with patches of moss. She scooped up the
chain, slid the crystal dagger off it. Then she stood and
looked up, sighting on Bryn. She would need him to get
back up into the Marre pines.

But at that moment, she sky seemed to crack open. The
moons paled, the clouds vanished in a silent sizzle. She
saw this with the same ability that allowed her to project
the mind-feeler. To anyone without her power, the night remained as it had been. But she saw—and she knew that

Bryn must see it, too—the crack in the sky widen, turn fiery red, and she got her first terrifying glimpse of the Eye of Ajbal.

In an instant, her ghost image vanished. The Eye of Ajbal turned and Varda with it. He knew he had been duped.

Krystren could feel the necromantic forces swirling, gathering, gibbering with glee. She raised her arms so that, as they had planned, Bryn could pull her up to where he crouched. But Bryn was now occupied in defending them from the great flaming orb whose terrifying power had pushed apart the night sky.

Varda trod carefully through the forest. He looked this way and that, his pale eye fully open and unblinking as it searched for her.

"Krystren."

She shivered as she heard him call her name, and she shrank back, moving away from him, not directly but diagonally.

"Krystren."

It was a voice to raise the hackles on even a perwillon's neck.

"I know you're here. It's only a matter of time before I find you."

Great streamers of sorcerous energy emanated from the Eye of Ajbal. It had not yet found Bryn. She could sense him concentrating all his energies on deflecting the streamers without giving it any indication that he was doing it. He did not move; he scarcely breathed. His body had become like mist, floating and insubstantial.

Krystren gathered all this information with part of her mind as she continued to retreat from Varda's stalking. She was well aware that every step took her farther away from Bryn and the safety he provided, but what choice did she have?

She was wholly focused on Varda's frightening, pale eye, turning her energies to keeping herself shadowed from its necromantic gaze. And then she realized her mis-

take, for in the corner of her eye she registered a small repeating movement. Varda's other eye—the dark one—was
blinking in time to the emanations from the Eye of Ajbal.
Of course! The archon had summoned it. They were
linked, somehow.

Now she stood her ground, tried to free her mind from
the fear of the sauromician moving closer and closer while
she bent her will to find a way to sever that connection. It
was a perilous course of action, for, in so overtly using her
mind, she would expose herself to Varda. No matter. The
link between him and the spell he had conjured up had to
be broken. It was their only hope.

Summoning all her strength, she put it into a single
mind-feeler, shaping it, honing it into a great shining scimitar with a blade of razor-sharpness. As she had feared,
Varda sensed the gathering of power and turned in her direction. He had not yet seen her, but he was aware now of
where she was. In her mind, she could see the dark umbilical that connected the archon with the Eye of Ajbal. He
sprinted toward her.

Krystren felt her heartbeat increase, felt the fear
swirling at the edges of her mind, and by sheer force of
will beat it back. She raised the scimitar toward the umbilical and, without an instant's hesitation, severed the link.

"No!"

Varda's cry echoed through the forest. He reached for
her, but she slammed the heel of her hand into his chin,
and, as he staggered to his knees, momentarily stunned,
she darted away, circling around and back. Already the
streamers were fading, the Eye itself closing.

When she reached the spot that she and Bryn had
agreed upon, he had already extended the green branch he
had fashioned into a spear. The moment she grabbed it,
Bryn lifted her off her feet, drawing her up into the ancient
Marre pine. Below them, Varda had his arms open wide,
his necromantic chanting came to them, but before they
could make out a word, Bryn had caught her up around the
waist and was racing through the swaying treetops.

* * *

"B y now," Bryn said, "Varda will have discovered that the crystal dagger is missing. He will have realized that you took it."

"We will deal with that when we have to," Krystren said. She was not thinking of the archon now, or of the *Sintire*'s desperate attempts to find her. All she could think of was that at last she was going to find her brother.

Bryn stood to one side, while she and the *gabir* faced each other in the deep shadows of the Marre pines. Even as far away as they had gotten from the encampment, the forest was preternaturally quiet. Not a breath of air stirred.

She held out the crystal dagger. "We have made good on our promise to you. Now you must tell us where to find our brother."

The *gabir* stared at the weapon with avid eyes. "You must do one more thing for me."

"No. We have done this much at great peril to ourself and to Bryn. We have done what you asked. We have an agreement."

"Never mind." The *gabir* shrugged and looked at her. "In a moment, you will do what I want, anyway."

"Here." She thrust the dagger at him hilt first. "You coveted it. Now take it." She was growing increasing impatient with the creature. Was he now going to renege on his promise?

The *gabir*'s half-dead eyes held hers. "Your brother, Courion, is dead."

"No!" Her body tensed as her mind went into shock. "You are lying!"

"I saw him. I did. In the flashes I get of the Other World, the land of the dead. That is where he is, you see."

"No!" Krystren screamed again and, reversing the crystal dagger, buried it to the hilt in what would have been the *gabir*'s heart if he had a heart.

"Ah, yes." He sighed, his eyes rolling up. "Thank you."

And he sank to her feet, at last dead.

"What . . ." She blinked several times. "What happened?"

"That is what he wanted all along." Bryn came toward her, deftly taking the crystal dagger from her grip. "This was the one thing that had the power to free the *gabir* from the limbo into which he had been cast." He looked at the crumpled form, all bone and shriveled skin, for the first time with a kind of compassion. "He is dead now. Free."

Krystren was shaking. She put her hands to her face and wept into them.

At dawn, they continued their pursuit of the party, which was now not as serene as it once had been. Varda, clearly disturbed by the recent events, snapped at everyone. He even ground a flurry of warrior-beetles beneath his bootheel for no particular reason that they could discern. The others in his party stayed well away from him while he fulminated, intoning spells and incantations incessantly.

Krystren, who instead of sleeping had watched Courion's face revolve in her mind like a ravaged moon, traveled with the archon's crystal dagger in her belt. She had stopped Bryn from throwing it away, wrenching it from his grasp as soon as she had regained her composure. It seemed to throb coldly on her hip, paining her with tiny jolts, doubtless a consequence of its necromantic origin. Nevertheless, she would not part with it.

It kept her close to the *gabir*—poor creature—and, by extension, her brother. Courion dead! She could scarcely believe it. She had never lived a day in her life without his presence or, at the very least, the thought of him being near or far, at sea or on the land. She thought of all the time they had wasted being apart, not talking to one another. The anger he had felt for her—the blame he had assigned for Orujo's death was so unfair. It was only now, in retrospect, that she could see that it had been easier for him to blame her than fully to accept Orujo's death. But how could he have accepted it? He had run away from it, as far as he could go. All the way here to the northern continent. She knew now—and understood it completely—that he had accepted this dangerous assignment precisely because he could see his own death waiting for him in Axis Tyr. He had seen it coming and had rushed headlong into its arms. To escape the terrible loss he could not live with. To seek the oblivion of death just as the *gabir* had done.

Now his assignment lay unfinished. Now the *Sintire* had got wind of it, had sent their best *Ardinals* to stop her. And now she harbored the suspicion that Cerro had *already known* that Courion was dead when he had sent for her. That her brother's sudden demise was precisely the reason for her urgent mission. She was being sent as Courion's replacement. Why else would Cerro have risked briefing her on Courion's original mission? Now she had to finish what her brother had begun.

She knew that the *Sintire* wanted the information locked away in her head, the information she had been charged with delivering safely to Courion. The sauromicians would want it even more, had they any inkling of what she carried inside her. But she also knew that the sauromicians were gaining power each time they raided the Abbey of Five Pivots. That meant the *Sintire* were gaining in power, as well. Before she could think of how to complete Courion's mission, she had to stop this party from gaining entrance to the abbey.

A deathlike silence shrouded them all as they drew close to the southern shore of Blue Bone Lake. On its northern shore, near the fishing village of Silk Bamboo Spring, lay the Abbey of Five Pivots. It was clear, Bryn had said not an hour ago, that this was indeed the party's destination. What their business was there he could not say, but he knew that the sauromicians, being unable to exist within the abbey's precincts, were using the *Sintire* to plunder it of Ramahan knowledge. This, he said, the *Sintire* must do in small stages, for they, too, had difficulty with the power bourns that crisscrossed the bedrock of Kundala.

"Listen to me, Krystren of the Oronel. I know that you still do not even trust that I am what I say I am. I do not blame you. Your deadly cold war with the *Sintire* has made distrust a survival instinct. But now I feel I must do whatever I can to dissuade you from your innate distrust.

"One of my kind indeed looks like the monstrosity you have described. Eons ago, he was enslaved by powerful sorcery in the Storeroom beneath what is now the regent's palace in Axis Tyr, charged with guarding The Pearl. It was that very enslavement that turned him into a monstrosity."

"Who could do that? Who could enslave a Hagoshrin?"

"Only one," he said. "The Great Goddess Miina."

Krystren shook her head as if trying to clear it of a question that had no answer. "Why would she do such a thing?"

"From time immemorial Hagoshrin have been enjoined from interfering with the affairs of the Kundalan, which are the sole precinct of Miina. That Hagoshrin broke this sacred Law and, as a consequence, was punished. The Dragons convened and conveyed their condemnation to Miina. She abided by their decision."

"If that is so, then by helping us you, too, have broken the Law."

He looked away from her, out across the tops of the forest to the glittering expanse of Blue Bone Lake. "Look there," he said softly. "The edifice across the water. White it is, like the very tops of the Djenn Marre. Behold the Abbey of Five Pivots."

Krystren was awestruck. High, sloping walls, seemingly made of gleaming ice, hunkered on the far shore. They were as smooth as obsidian, save for the faintest of grooves that revealed them to have been constructed of massive blocks of this peculiar stone or mineral. Set into the south-facing wall were a pair of arched doors made of cinnamon chalcedony, an exceedingly hard stone. These were guarded by gates whose petrified heartwood bars were thorned along their lengths, spiked at their tops. From inside this imposing facade rose five impossibly slender towers—one inside each corner of the abbey, the fifth in its exact center—crowned by taffy-pull domes of bright silver, inset with stars composed of a myriad of sapphires.

"It is magnificent," she whispered.

"Yes," he said. "Isn't it."

Somehow, she felt her heart lifted by the sight of the abbey, but the feeling was short-lived because already the hue of the sun seemed to have changed. Looking up, they both saw in their mind's eye a certain darkening, a rent forming, fiery edges peeling back like blistered skin so that the Eye of Ajbal could slip through.

"Run, Krystren of the Oronel," Bryn said. She could feel his fear, seeping into her like grey sleet. "Run now and do not look back!"

She hesitated, and he shoved her off their branch. She plummeted through the boughs, the Marre pine needles flicking at her painfully, until she stretched out her arms, caught one branch tip, then another. She slowed her fall, regained her balance, swung onto a far lower branch. She thought briefly of trying to climb back to where Bryn now stood, working his Hagoshrin sorcery in order to fend off the evil spell Varda had cast. But thinking of Varda told her what she had to do. She had severed his link with the Eye once before. She would do it again.

Except this time, when she extended her mind-feeler outward toward the dark umbilical, the scimitar she had fashioned exploded soundlessly into ten thousand fragments. She gasped and, at once, she was overcome by vertigo. All strength left her, and she slipped off her perch.

She was falling again, the boughs whispering and whipping past her. And below, she felt the cold, cruel presence of the sauromician archon and knew that he had set this trap for her. Stupid of her to think that he would allow her to use the same tactic twice.

Her shoulder slapped against a branch, and she cried out as pain tore through her. She tumbled head over heels and lost her bearings. Everything became a green-and-brown blur until she hit another, thicker, branch. She grunted, wrapped her legs around it, and was flipped over by her momentum. Then she hung upside down not more than twelve meters off the ground.

And there below her was Varda, grinning with yellow teeth, his icy necromantic eye fixed on her, quivering. She tried to make her brain work, tried to summon her mind-feeler. But it was shackled, unsummonable, and she heard Varda laughing as he made his way toward her, as green flame crackled at his fingertips. She saw his sixth finger, that black and twisted reminder of Miina's wrath and punishment. It flapped, dead and useless, as he approached her.

She could feel the horror of him, of what he was planning, of what would happen to her in the next twenty-four hours, or thirty-six, however long it would take to break her will, to rape her of all her secrets. She could feel his evil intent spiraling toward her. She grew suddenly dizzy and, losing her grip, fell to the ground at his feet.

He hit her, both with his fist and with the green flame, and she felt such agony as she had never dreamed of. She tried to spin away, but he kept up his assault. She gasped and moaned, and he grinned down at her, thoroughly enjoying his work.

But she was working through the pain, fixing her gaze on his necromantic eye, and this time she did not become disoriented. Her right hand was at her belt, her fingers grasped the hilt of the crystal dagger and, drawing it free, she used his own momentum against him, slashing at him in the instant he drew her to him in triumph.

He leapt back, his fiery white gaze fixed on the crystal dagger, but he was bleeding. His lips curled back in a feral snarl, and he hurled a cold-fire bolt at her. She used her mind-feeler to deflect it, but paid a price, as pain seared through her mind. She staggered backward, and he came after her, hurling one bolt after another.

She turned and fled through the forest, dodging this way and that to avoid the bolts. It was only when she emerged into a small clearing, and saw, to her horror, that the Eye of Ajbal was not gone, as she had supposed, but rode dark and fiery in the sky, that she realized what he was doing. He was herding her. As she watched, stupefied, she saw it turning toward her. It had seen her. It was moving toward her. Someone else must be controlling it.

From the treetops she saw a shadow leap upward. Bryn! The Hagoshrin spread his arms and sailed directly at the Eye.

"Run, Krystren of the Oronel! Run now!"

"No!" she cried, and launched a mind-feeler, but it was too late or her power was inadequate, enfeebled by the aftermath of Varda's spell. Bryn plowed into the Eye and there was a flash that for an instant blanked her mind, a deep rumble in her mind that made her sick to her stomach. She felt his essence wink out, and she screamed again.

But then she became aware of Varda, and another presence. Guazu, the *Sintire Ardinal* that accompanied him.

Another Eye of Ajbal was forming, slowly now, almost painfully as if it were struggling to overcome what remained of Bryn's power. Through a gap in the trees, Krystren could see sunlight winking off the massed carapaces of the warrior-beetle swarm. Those within the sorcerous vehicle were all concentrated on her.

She turned and ran.

Book Three

GATE OF
DROWNED POINT

It is inevitable that we come to the Gate of Drowned Point, for it is the path of sorrow and loss. It is the bleak tunnel, the nadir, and therefore serves as the entrance for Transcendence. Gate of Drowned Point is important because it is clear evidence of the Wheel of Life. It is the end of the beginning, the beginning of the end.

—Utmost Source,
The Five Sacred Books of Miina

21

The Mysterious Vine

The sky was on fire when Giyan and Minnum came in sight of the Abbey of Five Pivots. But for perhaps a mile Giyan, on the alert, had been preparing herself. She had felt the sorcerous rent between the Realms, had felt as if she were herself being cut. She had glimpsed the bleeding folds as the rent widened, and she had trembled a little at the advent of the Eye of Ajbal. Though she immediately knew that it was not seeking her, the very fact of its coming filled her with foreboding.

"They are here, no doubt about it," Minnum said, peering out over the lake to the northern edge of the Marre pine forest, with one hand to shade his eyes. "An archon is needed to summon the Eye." Minnum glanced at the abbey. "Is this where you think the sauromicians have made their base?"

"All signs point to it, save for one," Giyan said. "As you know, the power bourns are as inimical to sauromicians as they are to daemons. This was part of Miina's punishment. The Abbey of Five Pivots was built after the daemon uprising, and so all its power points were built over bourn lines. As a result, sauromicians cannot exist there."

"I do not understand," Minnum said. "Both sauromicians and an archdaemon infested your own abbey."

"Floating White is the most ancient of the abbeys; it was built centuries before Miina sent the daemons into the Abyss," Giyan said. "As such, it does not have the requisite safeguards built in. Many of the key areas, including the Library and the temple the archdaemon Horolaggia used as a base, are unprotected by power bourns."

"Still, the Dark League could be hidden in nearby Silk Bamboo Spring."

"Or anywhere in that forest yonder."

The cold, sorcerous fire crept across the sky like a claw scraping flesh. Giyan's sense of foreboding deepened. She was living in a dream, a dream manifesting itself, becoming reality before her eyes. A reality with which she had recently become all too familiar.

They set off at a fast trot and soon enough came down through the last gentle slopes and onto the flatter terrain that surrounded the lake. The Marre pines and kuello-firs gave way quickly to sysal and curly-bark river lingot, lighter-limbed deciduous trees that required wetter soil. But between these rustling stands they were obliged to cross open ground where their exposure was a concern. Accordingly, she cast Wall of Hope to give them a degree of protection.

It was Minnum's assignment to locate the archon controlling the Eye of Ajbal, so he was in the lead. But the closer they came to the northernmost finger of the forest, the more uneasy she became. Her mind was awhirl with the future, and she clamped down, knowing that way lay madness.

Concentrating fiercely on the present, she opened her Third Eye, went to the very edge of Ayame, the deep trance-state used in Thripping, and cast her sorcerous gaze here and there. The Eye of Ajbal, which had been focused on another spot south of them, began to turn in their direction. The Eyes were attuned to sorcerous activity. But this one must be set at hair-trigger level, for she had not even entered Otherwhere, where it would have been certain to notice her and attack.

At once, she shut down her search, and the Eye, confused, began to swivel back to its original subject. But Giyan's casting, however brief, had been useful, for she had detected a figure fleeing almost directly in their direction. Gently, she used a spell to correct the figure's course, bringing her—for she had seen that much—toward them.

"I have found what the Eye is after, Minnum."

He was panting and moaning through half-open lips. His small body and short legs were ill equipped for so much strenuous exercise.

"Or, rather, who."

It happened they were in the midst of a stand of river lingot, burnished, nut-colored bark exfoliating in ornate curlicues. Minnum took a moment to halt and, bent over with hands on thighs, gulped in breaths between panting out responses.

"Who are the sauromicians after?"

"A Sarakkon," Giyan said. "A *female* Sarakkon, at that. Curious, wouldn't you say?"

"*Most* curious." He shook his head. "Frankly, I am at a loss."

"As am I," she said. "That is why I have brought her to us."

Minnum's head snapped up. "You what?"

"Look, the Eye is a threat to all of us—as are the sauromicians. If they are after this female, then she is likely to be able to help us. At the very least, she will be able to shed some light on their recent activities, possibly the extent of their strength as well."

Minnum grunted. "But evidence points to the Sarakkon being in league with the archons."

"Then why is the Eye searching for her?"

"Perhaps it is a ruse to lure us on."

"Well, there is only one way to find out."

At that moment, a bolt of sorcerous energy lanced down from the Eye into the northernmost tip of the forest. A moment later, a figure burst free and began to sprint across the placidly rolling lake plateau toward the first stand of sysal trees.

"There she is!" Giyan cried. "Now what do you think?"

Minnum squinted up at the Eye. "She'll never make it."

Giyan grabbed him by the front of his robe. "Come on!"

Together, they ran toward the figure. She was still far enough away to lack details. One could even fool oneself into believing that she was an image in a V'ornn holoentertainment, Minnum thought, so that when the Eye blasted her into smithereens neither of them would feel the loss overly much.

"Listen now," Giyan said as they ran. "I will concentrate on deflecting the Eye, but you must try and neutralize the archon."

"What are you talking about?" he cried, deeply alarmed. "I am no archon. I lack the training."

"Remember you defeated an archon in Za Hara-at."

"The Dar Sala-at did most of the work," he pointed out.

"Just do your best," she said gently.

"Here comes the Sarakkon," he said, pointing.

To his astonishment, she had made it as far as the first stand of sysal. But another bolt was loosed by the Eye and with a sickening *whoosh!* that took his breath away the stand of trees burst into flame. A great oily cloud mushroomed up, billowing into a sky crowded with ominous clouds.

From out of the black cloud, they saw her sprinting toward them.

"Good for you, Sarakkon," Giyan said under her breath.

"Now we will see if it is a trap," Minnum muttered.

"The archon, Minnum," Giyan reminded him. "Concentrate on the archon."

Minnum planted his feet and cast a cold-fire bolt into the forest. If he could not find the archon, then he would let the archon find him. Treetops shuddered, leaves shredded and burst in a small emerald plume. In his mind, Minnum felt the great serpent Avatar of the archons, it was uncoiling, writhing its way toward him. He saw its face and he recognized Caligo. It was Caligo who had buried him in the sand of a faraway seashore

when he was young, for the crime of being short. It was
Caligo who had laughed, bringing his cohorts to watch
as the rising tide washed over Minnum, as his nostrils
filled with seawater, as he gasped and choked. *The world
is full of peril for freaks,* he had shouted. Then he had
crouched down, tousled Minnum's wet hair. *Poor Minnum. It will get better.* Then he had stuffed a live crab
into Minnum's mouth. *But not any time soon!*

Minnum loosed another cold-fire bolt, aimed at the head
of the serpent. The Avatar reared back and broke apart like
smoke. Behind it, Minnum could see in his mind's eye
Caligo's familiar face. But then his blood ran cold, for
somehow Caligo was instantly aware of him; the archon
fixed him in his sorcerous gaze, and he felt a pain roar
through him. He cried out, for it was as if Caligo had
pierced him with a firebrand. Like a fish on a hook, he
squirmed this way and that, but he could not break free of
the pain.

He glanced at Giyan, but her attention was fully concentrated on the Eye of Ajbal. It was as if she had ceased
to notice him. He was entirely on his own. Dimly, he was
aware of the Sarakkon female approaching them at a run.
He thought she saw them, for there was an astonished
look on her face. Then the pain whirled him into blackness. He descended into a spiral of agony, lost in the sorcerous whirlpool. He caught one last glimpse of Caligo. A
glistening strand of intestine was wrapped around his left
wrist, and in despair, Minnum knew that this was where
his power was coming from. The sauromicians had re-
verted from Kyofu sorcery to pure necromancy. He had
suspected this during his nightmarish battle with Talaasa
in Za Hara-at, but he dared not believe it. Now he had the
proof, for all the good it would do him.

The cold-fire bolts he threw were immediately absorbed
by the necromantic forces swirling around him. He continued being pulled down, drowning as he almost had when
Caligo had buried him in the beach. He nearly cried in

frustration, and in response he heard Caligo's mocking laughter.

Hello, freak, and good-bye.

Minnum was gasping, and terror filled his heart, for he saw the serpent returning, and he felt sure that at the last moment Caligo would use it to rip his heart out and eat it. To die was bad enough, he thought, but to be eaten alive, to be used as energy against those he loved most dearly was a horror beyond imagining.

The serpent was snaking its way toward him, all glossy scales and glittering eyes and bared fangs. He was falling deeper and deeper, never to rise again. He put his hands over his heart as if to shield it for one millisecond longer from the inevitable end.

It's too late." Leyytey's eyes, in her agitation, shone like one of her shock-sword blades. "Whatever we do now is meaningless. Iin Mennus has my father."

Sornnn nodded. "His office has put out a story that he is under protection from a Resistance assassination plot."

"Of course that's a lie," she said vehemently.

They had met just after noon at a rooftop cafe of Sornnn's choosing that overlooked the bustling Promenade. Brightly colored sails rose from ships afloat on the glittering Sea of Blood. The cafe was so popular they were obliged to wait for a table. Sornnn had gotten them drinks at the bar, and they had taken them to the edge, far from the crowd, where they sat on the thick parapet in the brilliant sunshine.

"They won't even allow me to talk with him. It would compromise their security, they said. It might allow me to find a way to get him out, I say."

"We don't want to do that," Sornnn said quietly. "It would make him a fugitive."

"Better alive than dead."

Not for the first time they heard what sounded like the boom of thunder, but the cerulean sky was studded only with benign white clouds. In any event, they were too engrossed in the exigencies of the situation to wonder about what seemed a meteorologic anomaly.

"Listen to me, Leyytey. Now is the time for cool heads and careful planning."

"We tried careful planning, and look where it got us!"

"Drink your marsh queen," he said.

He had ordered her Marethyn's favorite drink. On re-flection perhaps that had not been the best idea. He felt a void inside him where she had curled, contented as a child. She was gone now. He had to keep reminding him-self of that. Inside, he wept for her, and for himself. He could feel himself once again sliding into despair. At least that was familiar. When he was despairing he never had to remind himself that Marethyn was gone, and along with her the best part of himself.

"SaTrryn . . ."

His attention snapped back at the sound of her voice, so different from Marethyn's, and yet just as pleasing to him. He drank in Leyytey's face. There was a fire in her that was akin to the fire that had illuminated Marethyn from the inside. If only she had stayed an artist. If only she had never left Axis Tyr and her marvelous atelier. But, of course, she had.

"SaTrryn, where have you gone?" She smiled a rueful smile. "Ah, I know. You were thinking about your lost love."

"No, I—"

"It's all right."

She put her goblet to her lips and sipped her marsh queen, then set it aside.

"You don't like it."

She made a face. "Too sweet for me."

It was the tiniest moment, gone unremarked by anyone around them, but it meant the world to him, for he could separate them now in his mind. Marethyn and Leyytey. He saw how he had begun to want Leyytey to be just like Marethyn. He saw how dangerous a path that was, how it would inevitably lead to disillusionment and, quite possibly, anger on his part. When he was with Leyytey he could not think of Marethyn. Or, if he did, he could not compare them, for he would always find Leyytey wanting. The more he compared them the more she would fall short of his expectations, which were, after all, nothing but fantasy.

"SaTrryn." She cocked her head. "You are looking at me so strangely. What are you thinking?"

"I was thinking how glad I am to have met you."

She looked down, staring at her hands. She felt suddenly ill at ease, his kind words scoring into that part of her that stubbornly held on to her wicked secret. She knew she should tell him about Dacce and Raan Tallus, but she could not. Every time she began the imaginary dialogue with him it always came to the same dreadful end. And so each moment she was with him was marked with pain as well as pleasure, for she could see the shape and form of her betrayal, and it made her ill.

"Please don't say that," she said in a thin, tight voice.

"Why not? It's the truth."

It was remarkable, Sornnn thought, sitting beside her, what one could intuit from an expression. In her sudden shyness, he saw the little girl she had once been, the yearning to be accepted by her father, her fierce and uncompromising determination to succeed. But most of all he saw her loneliness. It could not be easy being Ardus Pnin's daughter.

At that moment, the manager approached to tell them that their table was ready. As Sornnn followed her through the crowd, he thought about her half-open lips, about the words that had gathered in her throat. What was it she had been about to say to him?

Once they had settled themselves at the table the mood changed. *By what strange alchemy did this happen,* he asked himself. The sole topic of conversation was how to save Fleet-Admiral Pnin.

"Tell me, what are we going to do now?" she said in a clipped tone.

"I'm afraid there are no easy answers."

This was not what she wanted to hear, and her famously volatile temper flared up again. "Easy. Hard. I don't care. Let's just get on with it."

"Leyytey—"

"No, no. We are running out of time."

He decided it was best to allow her to vent her under-standable frustration. He took a neutral stance, neither pla-cating her nor giving her encouragement where, frankly, he felt none was warranted. Unfortunately, this had the ef-fect of increasing her ire. She accused him first of giving up the moment the situation turned really difficult, then of taking advantage of her. When he compounded his mis-take by pointing out that these were mutually exclusive suppositions, she became angrier still, if that were possi-ble, and threatened to take matters into her own hands, though she refused to elucidate, and he could not imagine what she could do alone.

"I know what you want," she said hotly, undoing all that he had accomplished with her moments before, "and it has nothing to do with my father."

By the time dessert came, the day was turning grey, and he had begun to feel quite defeated.

Minnum, hands over his heart, felt a tickling on his legs, and glancing down, he saw a vine rising up from the depths. He did not think, he did not question, he grabbed on to it. And it began to lift him up, to take him away from the dreadful undertow of the whirlpool, bring-ing him to a calmer place, black as death, but entirely without eddies, so that he could gather himself, try to con-trol his terror.

The pain had subsided, he was very aware of that. He saw that the vine was twined all around him, feelers en-tering his body at various points, and it occurred to him that they were somehow siphoning off the pain, enough of it at least so that he could clear his mind enough to form a plan of counterattack.

Forget about the cold-fire bolts, he told himself. He

thought about the power bourns that ran beneath the bedrock of Kundala. The Dar Sala-at had used one to destroy Talaasa. The problem was Minnum lacked the Dar Sala-at's ability to divine the bourns.

He could feel the pain flaring and receding, and he knew that the vine—whatever its miraculous source—could not protect him for long. He needed to take action and he needed to do it immediately.

He drew Caligo back into his consciousness. In his mind's eye, he saw the face he remembered and despised—the predatory jaw, the wide, almost lipless mouth, the black eyes that had they not been alive with cruelty would certainly have seemed already dead. He saw the bony hands describing complex patterns in the air, and there on his left hand was the sixth finger, black as pitch.

The finger! Yes, that was it!

For an instant, his courage failed him, and he quailed inside, but just then the vine gripped him tighter, lifted him higher, as high as it could take him, he imagined. The rest was up to him. He could not fail those who were counting on him. He could not fail himself.

Redoubling his resolve, he gathered his courage and waited for the serpent to come to him. Closer and closer it slithered. Its tongue flickered out, its jaws gaped open. He could feel Caligo's elation behind the facade of the Avatar. He kept a tight lid on the innate terror he felt at the proximity of the serpent, and when at last it was within spitting distance, he cast Fly's-Eye to send it and Caligo into a chaos of conflicting thoughts.

He flew past the great snake, and now he conjured two spells at once, Sphere of Binding and, to hide it from Caligo, Night Blindness. It was a great effort to cast two spells at once, to balance them one against the other, but he did not falter. He felt the serpent Avatar beginning to shake off the effects of Fly's-Eye, and he increased his speed. He felt Caligo beginning to probe, encountering Night Blindness, trying to figure out what had happened.

Then, as if bursting upward through the last of the

darkness, he reached the speckled light of the forest where the archons stood hidden and projected the fireball of Sphere of Binding, so that it encircled Caligo's left hand, the one with the black finger. Using the spell, he began to bend the finger back.

Caligo, concentrating hard, detonated Night Blindness, and the spell dissipated like mist. Now the two sauromicians were locked in mortal combat. Minnum felt the coldness of the necromantic spells Caligo was using to try to free his finger. It was the one vulnerable spot on a sauromician. Minnum knew that if he could break it off, he would destroy the archon.

But Caligo was now fighting him with every ounce of his being. Minnum could feel his hold on Sphere of Binding slipping and, with it, the spell beginning to come apart. Already, Caligo had regained some control over the black finger, bringing it back from its unnatural position.

Minnum tried Circle of Imprisonment, but Caligo was prepared, for he countered the spell with one of his own. Meanwhile, Minnum's hold on Sphere of Binding was being further eroded to the point where he did not think he could keep it together for much longer. Clearly, conventional tactics were not going to work. He had to think of something else. But what?

All at once it came to him. He loosed two cold-fire bolts in quick succession. Caligo brushed them aside, laughing, but that was all right. Minnum had not expected them to have any effect. Like blowing a kiss, he had sent a composite Sticky Spell inside the second of the cold-fire bolts. When Caligo blew it apart, the composite Sticky Spell adhered to him without his knowing it. For a moment, it did nothing, lying dormant. Then, like a V'ornn delayed ion mortar, it cast its first layer. Working off Caligo's own necromantic energy it began to drain him of power. The harder he fought against it, the more it drained him. But that layer would only last a matter of moments.

Minnum cast Rings of Concordance, tightening them around the archon's left wrist, his fingers. The Sticky

Spell was waning. Minnum, bending all his will to this one task, tightened three Rings around the black sixth finger and bent it all the way back.

It snapped like a dry twig. He felt Caligo's scream, quick and spine-tingling, before it was abruptly cut off. A film of white ash had begun to form on Caligo's body. It spread quickly, inexorably, eating into his flesh, turning it all to a fine white powder.

Minnum staggered back and opened his eyes. He was still within the small stand of trees, and he was face-to-face with the Sarakkon female.

From behind the last in the line of Gul Aluf's biochambers, Riane rose on cramped legs. Though he had been in Gul Aluf's embrace, Sahor had been looking right at her. She knew that it should have frightened her that he could sense her even through Flowering Wand, but it didn't. What was he doing here in the company of this strange creature? Why had he revealed himself to her? She knew that the moment she spoke of this to Thigpen, the Rappa would jump to the paranoid conclusion that Sahor had betrayed them. She herself had considered the possibility but had almost immediately dismissed it. After all, he had seen her and hadn't said a word to Gul Aluf. She pondered this as she and Kirlll Qandda crept out of the lab-orb and met up with Eleana and Thigpen. She wished she could talk to Sahor about what he was up to, but in the present circumstance that seemed unwise

The Deirus led them to the same inconspicuous side entrance by which they had entered. While Kirlll Qandda told the others what he and Riane had observed, she went into a storeroom piled high with crates and old crystal data. She required some peace and quiet to do what she knew needed to be done.

She had to find the banestone before Kurgan used it or it fell into the hands of the sauromicians. To do that she needed to cast a particular Eye Window spell. The Spell of Forever was very powerful, she had only used it once be-

fore. If she was correct, it would lead her to the banestone.
But there was a danger, for the Spell of Forever could only
be conjured up by a seer, and every time she used it the
spell opened her oracular powers wider, sent her tumbling
faster down the path to eventual madness. Still, it could not
be helped. She did not have enough time to locate Kurgan
through Eleana's network of Resistance members and pry
its location out of him.

She was about to begin, to stir the shadows, the echoes,
when Eleana slipped into the storeroom. Riane shook her
head, but Eleana ignored her, dropping to her knees beside
Riane.

"Eleana, please stay outside. What I am about to do is
too dangerous—"

"Love." She put her hand against Riane's cheek. "It is
because of the danger that I have come." She took the ion
pistol that she had held against her leg and stood it butt
first on her thigh. "I will protect you."

Riane felt her heart melt, but she knew she had to be
stern. "There are forces here beyond your ken, forces that
care nothing about ion charges."

"If they are so strong, why didn't they beat back the
V'ornn?" She smiled. "No. I will stay, love. I will protect
you while you send your mind wandering."

Riane opened her mouth to protest, but something in
Eleana's expression told her it would do no good. Besides,
being truthful with herself, she wanted Eleana there.

Riane put her hand on Eleana's. It was a chaste gesture,
but in its very innocence lay a voluptuousness beyond description, for it spoke most eloquently of safety and security. Eleana's scent, bolder than Eleana herself, swirled
around Riane. It was like an elixir. They leaned forward
at the same moment, and their lips grazed. Nothing more
was needed. They were together in the darkness, together
in the moment, together forever. There was no doubt, no
question, no hesitation. There was only the beating of
their hearts like gimnopedes fluttering among the sysal
trees.

Pulling away at last, Riane sank into the level where all energy flowed, to jihe, where she could reach out for Otherwhere. But she did not enter the Realm. Rather, she used her memory to walk through the pages of first *Utmost Source* and then *The Book of Recantation* until she found the minor spells described in each. Mother had shown her how to combine them, and she spoke the Old Tongue that she now knew was close to Venca. She fixed the banestone firmly in her mind, as if it were an actor taking center stage.

Syllables formed into words, words into phrases, phrases into the sentences, and the spell formed. A veil of sparkling lights illuminated the gloom of the storeroom, glittering and winking as they danced and spun. And presently they merged into a small sphere. At first wholly without color, the sphere's center slowly coalesced, moving through the spectrum until it became the deepest purple.

Into this darkness burst a scene, odd to Riane because it contained neither Kurgan nor the banestone. Nevertheless, it was what the Spell of Forever showed her:

A building loomed at the extreme western end of the Boulevard of Crooked Dreams. At that point in the city, the boulevard was scarcely wide enough to be considered a street, let alone a thoroughfare. Like much of the extreme western district, the building was in desperate need of repair. The street in front of it was cobbled with such a mismatched assortment of stone it was hard even on the hooves of water buttren.

The building was dun-colored, dirty-looking, and therefore indistinguishable from its neighbors save for a small, smeared plaque much in need of repair itself. FIREFLY it said, or at any rate, it once had beneath the stains. Riane recognized it as a kashiggen, but judging by its look and location, it was a disreputable one. As she looked deep into the heart of the sphere, she could see Deirus skulking in and out. Annon had known, of course, that there were kashiggen that catered to Deirus, but he had never seen one before.

The scene, passing as quickly as a dream, was flickering

out. In that instant she glimpsed a shadowy figure, no more than a silhouette, high up inside the building. She was about to get a look at its face when the sphere broke apart, and one of the shards struck her. It was not, of course, a physical blow, but rather a mental one, and at once she was thrust into a vision of the future, a possible future, at any rate, one of many.

She saw Seelin, the Sacred Dragon of Transformation. She was encased within an octahedron formed by eight banestones, streaks of curved lambent orange connecting them, though it was difficult to see, everything smeared and dark, as with smoke and flames. They are going to burn Seelin alive! And then she saw something that turned her bones to ice. She saw herself, the ninth banestone in her hand, placing it so that it completed the Cage. Her mind recoiled. But that was impossible! She would do anything to keep the Cage from being completed, from allowing the death of Seelin, whom she loved, whom she needed to be complete.

And then, like a bubble bursting, the vision winked out, and she found herself staring at a neatly stacked pile of alloy crates. She felt sick and a little weak. Gradually, she became aware that Eleana was holding her.

"It's all right, love. I'm here. It's all right."

For a moment, she rested her damp forehead against Eleana's shoulder. The atmosphere was still charged with the dissipating spell.

"What is it?" Eleana said after a time. "What have you seen?"

"I know where the banestone is or soon will be. We have to go there immediately."

They rose and went out to where the others waited.

Thigpen, tugging at Riane's robe, pulled her aside. Riane reached out, and the Rappa leapt up into her strong arms.

"I know we must retrieve the banestone at all costs," she whispered, as Riane ruffled the fur between her ears. "But why risk Eleana again? Leave her here. She will be safe with the Deirus."

Riane raised an eyebrow. "Is that a change of heart I hear?"

"He has proved that he is not a worm to be ground underfoot," Thigpen said grudgingly.

"Well and good."

Eleana craned her neck. "What are you two whispering about? Not me, I trust." She said it lightly, but her furrowed brow betrayed her concern.

Riane shook her head and smiled. She lowered her voice even more when she spoke to Thigpen. "Of course you are right. However, we dare not leave her behind. The banestone has somehow sensitized itself to her aura. Eventually, it will find her wherever she is in Axis Tyr."

"Then let's get her out of the city."

"No time. Will you take her?"

"And leave you to face Kurgan and the banestone alone? I think not."

That was what Riane wanted to hear. "Then better by far that she remain with us."

Thigpen gave her a doubtful look, but all the same she leapt down onto the floor and led the way to the small door beyond which all of Axis Tyr lay in wait like a treacherous companion.

22

Kiss

It was you," Minnum said in a breathless voice. "It was you who sent me the vine."

"I hope it was of some help," the Sarakkon female said.

"Are you serious?" Minnum stood very still, but he was conscious of quaking like a leaf in a stiff wind. He could not stop staring at her—the whorls and spirals of her tattoos, the luscious braid of her hair. Where had all his suspicion gone to? He seemed to be melting into her eyes. Part of her was already inside him. "Without it I never would have been able to kill the archon."

"You killed Varda?"

"You are confused, Sarakkon. The archon's name is Caligo."

"Mother of Yahé," Krystren said, "there are two of them!"

"Worse and worse," he muttered. "We had better tell First Mother."

"First Mother?"

He loved, too, the way she cocked her head, the slight twist of her long, curved neck. "That is what we call Giyan." He stuck out a hairy paw. "My name is Minnum."

She did not hesitate to take it, as many would have. He saw in her eyes not the slightest judgment against his size.

"We are gratified to meet you, Minnum. Krystren, first daughter of Coirn, of the House of Oronel."

Krystren! He even liked the sound of her name. It seemed to reverberate inside him like the clear bronze tone of a bell. He led her at a run to where Giyan was crouched, her face furrowed in sorcerous concentration. The Eye of Ajbal was moving closer.

She looked up at them. "It cannot see us, at least for the moment. But the pressure of its searching is difficult to counteract."

He introduced Krystren, then went on a bit breathlessly. "She knows a kind of sorcery, she can see the Eye, can you believe it, First Mother? Anyway, she helped me kill the archon, Caligo."

"If the archon is dead, who is controlling the Eye?" Giyan asked.

"That's just it," Krystren said. "The raiding party contains *two* archons. We have been following them for many kilometers, but had not realized that. We only saw Varda."

"Raiding party?" Giyan's frown deepened. "Who is in this raiding party?"

"Besides the two archons, a Sarakkon with whom they have made a pact. They've come here to raid the Abbey of Five Pivots. The Sarakkon are helping them in this."

"Miina save us!" Giyan cried. "We must not let them inside. There are untold secrets—"

"We fear they have already been inside," Krystren said. "More than once, we will warrant."

Giyan and Minnum exchanged glances, but there was no time to contemplate the ramifications of this latest disaster.

"Listen closely. I must gain immediate entrance to the abbey." Giyan rose, glanced up at the questing Eye. "They will try to stop us. We will have to separate. I will go to the abbey. Minnum, you must stay here and do whatever you can."

"After Caligo's death, Varda will be on his guard."

"Harry him, distract him," Giyan said. "I need time inside the abbey to make preparations. There is a mechanism inside that will aid us."

"What about us?" Krystren asked. "We want to help."

Giyan smiled at her. "You are brave, my child, as well as something of a mystery. You are willing to work against your own kind."

"To them we are an outlaw, the enemy," Krystren said.

Minnum, himself an outlaw to his own kind, liked her better and better.

She winced suddenly and put a hand to her head. "I cannot blind the Eye for much longer. It seems there are other sorceries at work here."

"It is the archon," Minnum said. "He is a full necromancer now."

"His victims make up the rest of the party," Krystren told them. "He kills them as he needs them."

Minnum nodded. "Eats their beating hearts and wraps their intestines around his wrist."

Giyan winced again. "All the more reason to make haste

to Five Pivots. Krystren, it will be your job to deal with the Sarakkon. All right?"

The other two nodded.

"Good luck," she said. "If all goes well, we will meet in the central tower of the abbey within the hour."

Without another word, she was off, heading toward the abbey. Above them, the great and fiery Eye of Ajbal began to swivel.

"Look!" Minnum said. "It is turning in her direction!"

"Quickly now!" Krystren was already sprinting toward the next stand of trees. "We must engage the enemy!"

M innum squeezed with all his might in an attempt to dispel the image of Krystren from his mind. He ran ever faster, heading toward the whispering Marre pines, but try as he might he could not let go of her. Much to his astonishment, he did not want to. Truly, he had never seen her like before. Had the Sarakkon ever brought their females to Za Hara-at? He racked his brains, but it was so long ago, and Miina had so made a mockery of his memory that all history had fled him. Often, he wept at the accumulation of knowledge and experience he had lost. He did not think it fair, but what in life was fair, especially for a sauromician? Of course, he was not like Caligo and Varda and the others. He was rehabilitated—the Druuge had seen to that.

Stern taskmasters, the Druuge. A thoroughly terrifying bunch, if truth be known. Who could say what went on inside their heads? Who could know what they wanted? The Dar Sala-at, possibly, but that was another matter entirely. One which she would have to discover all on her own. Still, he dreaded her that. Who in their right mind wouldn't?

Which brought him back to Krystren. What was it about her? That she had saved him with her sorcerous vine? That she had eyes as deep as the sea itself? That he experienced a slight weakness when he looked at the whorls of her tattooed skull? He was disgusted with himself, really and truly. Here he was in a battle for his life—for all their lives—and he had a Sarakkon female stuck in his head. He tried to stamp down on the feeling—what was it, anticipation, consternation, a pleasurable combination of both?— he felt when he had been near her. He tried to encapsulate it, hurl it into the darkest recesses of his mind. Inexplicably, it resisted all his attempts to rid himself of it.

In the green-shadowed woods now, he slowed. It had not been terribly difficult for him to locate Varda. It took an enormous amount of sorcerous energy to manipulate the Eye. The sorcery the Druuge had given back to him had made visible to his sixth sense the column of energy that linked the Eye with the archon. He sped onward into the first of the whispering Marre pines, his heart beating like a trip-hammer.

The closer he came to Varda the higher his anxiety level climbed. That was unsurprising. He had no illusions about himself. Despite whatever it was the Druuge saw in him, he knew himself to be a coward. Not that being a coward was all bad. It was his cowardice, after all, that had kept him from participating in the vilest deeds the sauromicians had committed.

The thing that struck him most deeply now as he prowled through the forest, hunched over like a pack animal, was how familiar this sense of anxiety seemed. It was as if he had lived all his life in this state of dread, that any other was so unfamiliar he would not be able to recognize it when it appeared.

But of course that was untrue, for now he did recognize how different he felt standing next to her, and it seemed as if its very uniqueness was what had turned him on his head. Having caught a glimpse of pleasure, having held it in his hands, so to speak, like a beautiful jewel, he wondered how it was possible that he had never been aware of it before. Life for him was misery. It always had been. All he asked now was to stand beside her again. That wasn't so much, surely.

He was so close to Varda he could hear the column of energy in the core of his being. The sound it made was like an animal being skinned alive. The column was all around him. The particles felt like a swarm of biting insects on his skin.

He was badly frightened. Caligo's power had been nothing as compared to Varda's. Varda possessed a capacity for malice that defied Minnum's understanding. In the old days, before Miina had taken away the bulk of their memory and, therefore, their power, he had seen Varda destroy a sauromician with his mind. He shuddered at the thought. He felt as if he were walking through quicksand. How to engage him? He dared not send out a mind probe for fear it would alert the archon, and a full-frontal assault seemed beyond his capacity. He did not know what to do.

And then everything changed because in his mind he heard Krystren moaning.

The true strength in Krystren's training lay in stillness. She was adept, as she had shown on the island of Suspended Skull, at remaining unobserved in the eye of the storm. In her stillness she became invisible.

Within the first few trees of the northernmost finger of forest, she stopped her body, then her mind. She let the fear, anxiety, tension flow out of her into the springy ground upon which she stood. In its place, silence rose up—a silence as formidable in its way as the high walls that girt the Abbey of Five Pivots.

It was no ordinary silence that greeted the morning or hushed the twilight. It was a living thing that once invoked could be molded and used. Wrapped in her silence, she watched sunlight fall upon a leaf. The leaf trembled with the passage of air, and soon enough the shadow of Varda's ally, the *Sintire Ardinal* was thrown across the leaf. He paused, doubtless looking around for her, but though she stood not four meters away, he did not see her.

She watched him with the same scrutiny with which one

examines one's own reflection, quietly assessing, seeking out flaws. There was an objectivity in this, a calculated coolness she found immensely comforting, as if she were an observer able to step outside of Time. It was true that for the most part she found emotions at best cumbersome, at worst a detriment. Emotions could be crippling. Just look what they had done to poor Courion! When it came to Orujo, he had forgotten his *Onnda* training completely.

The *Ardinal* Guazu moved, advancing on her without being aware of it. She remained where she was.

Guazu's small size was deceptive. He was very strong, both physically and mentally. His smile was also deceptive, light and winning, without a hint of the maliciousness that lay on his soul like an unhealed scar.

Now he stopped, one foot in front of the other, in midstep. His head was turning, his glossy avian eyes moving until he was looking directly at her.

As the advent of sunlight in a room reveals dancing dust motes, so her silence caused her to feel a peculiar agitation in the atoms of the air as they began to cluster. Soon, he had formed a small sphere unseen by anyone but her. Guazu pursed his lips, inhaled until his cheeks belled outward. He exhaled, the resulting puff of air propelled the sphere directly at her.

She did not know what it was, nevertheless she could divine its purpose. It was meant to detect her, to catch her out despite her silence. She knew instinctively that when the sphere encountered the aura of her silence it would change speed or composition, something like that. By whatever means, it would give Guazu the information he needed. He would have found her.

His was not a *Sintire* skill, and she had to reconcile herself with the terrifying reality that not only were the sauromicians learning from the Ramahan archives in the Abbey of Five Pivots but the *Ardinals* were learning from the sauromicians. In the conversation she had overheard between Lujon and Haamadi there had been hints of this—the symbiosis they had spoken of—but she had not faced the implications. Now she saw just how big a mistake that had been.

The sphere had begun to rotate, ever so slowly. It was causing a prismatic effect, the color hues shifting ever so subtly, sliding from cold to cool to warm to hot. She stood transfixed, mesmerized by the rotating sphere. It was quite as lovely as it was dangerous, but somehow the danger seemed to belong to another world far away, and it was not until she felt Guazu's powerful fingers around her throat that she understood the enormity of her miscalculation.

She gasped, the hallucinogenic sphere popped like a soap bubble, and with paralyzing strength, the *Ardinal* slammed her back into the trunk of a tree. She struggled, but he had pinned her, not just with his hand, but with his mind. How much had he drunk from the sauromician's sorcerous cup? She felt weak. A curious lethargy ran through her veins, as if she had not slept in weeks. She wanted only to close her eyes, to drift off into his arms, to tell him whatever it was he wanted to know.

And so she began to offer herself up, her limbs going slack just as if she were acquiescing to her lover. Guazu's head was so close to hers, his features blurred. She could feel his breath on her cheek, and her eyelids fluttered. He touched her between her breasts, between her legs. His lips pressed against hers, and she opened her mouth to him. Dimly, she was aware of him inhaling, drawing out of her not only her breath but the secrets she held most closely and dear. In a moment, he would have everything; in a moment, she would be of no more interest to him than a husk he would trample underfoot. But at that moment, she was still valuable. The thought filled her with gratitude. She loved him, she would do anything he asked of her. She . . .

The smallest sound made him detach himself, and she moaned. While she hung there, waiting for his return, he twisted his head this way and that, searching for the noise that was hardly more than the rustle a pack rat might make in its twilight foraging.

Wake up!

She moaned again. Who was that disturbing her?

Wake up, Krystren!

She made a sound, as if she could blow away the annoying voice in her head.

He has ensorceled you. I know the spell well. Here is the counter.

She cried out, for it felt as if someone had thrown acid on her. She felt a terrible tearing, as if her limbs were being rent from their sockets.

"No!" Guazu screamed. "Who would dare . . . !"

But the spell had been ripped asunder. Krystren had regained her senses, she knew what he had done to her, how he had almost sucked her dry. She bent her neck and bit down hard on the hand that was still around her neck. She caught the tender triangle that ran between thumb and forefinger, and she clashed her teeth together through skin and flesh.

Then it was his turn to try and twist away, but she held him fast with her teeth. She used her mind to worm her way between his defenses. The sorcery was new to him, and powerful as he was, there were still great gaps in his knowledge and, thankfully, his ability.

"*Silensia!*" she hissed.

She wrapped her silence around him so that when he opened his mouth to scream nothing—not even the tiniest squeak—emerged. She had weapons on her, of course, but she had no need of them. Using the wedge of her fingers, she punctured the soft spot just beneath the left side of his rib cage. Hot blood flowed, and his thrashing became so frenzied that he tore his hand free. He went for her eyes first, as she knew he would, and she ducked her head away. At the same time, the wedge of her fingers drove deep into him, rising until she gripped his living heart.

She squeezed with all her might.

Minnum felt the life being literally squeezed out of the Sarakkon. It was like a dim shaft of moonlight over the hills and far away. Here, inside him, he was bathed in the sunlight given off by Krystren. There was something about her fierceness that moved him, that sent part of him spinning away like a skate blade on ice. He had saved her life as she had saved his, and his elation knew no bounds. At the sight of her, pink with her enemy's entrails, he felt that he could do anything now, that defeating even Varda was within his power.

He saw her turn at his approach. He had been silent, but she had become aware of him. He saw the smile begin to form on her face, and his heart leapt. There was a connection between them, the intimate bond of life and death, of time condensed, for when you were in battle an hour encompassed a lifetime.

The last of the sunlight fluttered across her face, then winked out as dark clouds formed overhead, but the moment remained in his memory. The glitter of the sea in her eyes, her full lips turned slightly up at their corners, stray wisps of her dark brown hair floating about her face like a corona. The spark of her tattoos, as if they were responding to his feelings.

He was coming toward her, and his heart felt as if it was bursting. There was a moment that seemed to last a lifetime when he thought that the only thing he asked of life was a kiss from her.

Her arm reached out. Was it his hand she wanted to hold? Oh, if only it were so! But now her smile was gone. She shouted, and a bolt of energy he could feel but could not see shot from her outflung fingers, passing beyond his right shoulder.

He was turning when the pain struck him in the back. His eyes opened wide, he emitted a tiny, weak cry, and his spine seemed to shatter. On his knees, his head twisted around, and he saw Varda, tall and cadaverously thin, black-robed, black-haired. His skin had the greenish patina of old copper. This strange hue made his necromantic eye all the more apparent. And then to his horror, Minnum saw a ripple run through Varda's robe, an hallucinatory shimmering like the horizon in the desert.

The robe shone like liquid metal, and then as Varda moved, he could see that it was made not of cloth but of a host of warrior-beetles.

The ice-white orb blazed, and Minnum felt an unimaginable agony. His spine was shattering—tiny shards of bone impaling themselves in the surrounding muscles and soft tissue, minuscule scalpels severing nerve connections, pinging like the plucked strings of bent longbows. At the same time, he was aware of Krystren's psychic energy attacking Varda, making him back up a pace with its ferocity.

But then Varda, regaining his balance, threw his arms open wide and his robe fell apart as squads of voracious warrior-beetles scuttled toward her at his command.

"No!" Minnum cried, and tried to get up, but too many nerves had already been shattered and all he was able to manage was to fall into their path. He still had use of his fists, and he used them as hammers, crushing the clicking insects. Their bites and stings were as nothing compared to the agony that racked him. Though they tore at his flesh with their pincers and their mouths, he ground scores of them into a viscous mulch even as more crawled over him. He flopped over on his back, crushing hundreds more. They spread their translucent wings, then, and took to the air, flying at Krystren in a dark, buzzing curtain.

She stood her ground, but was obliged to turn from attacking Varda to defending herself against them. As a consequence, the archon resumed his attack on Minnum. But the respite that she had provided, though brief, was telling. Minnum ignored the blood dripping from a thousand wounds, forgot about his degenerating nerves. He used every spell at his command, casting them in bunches at his nemesis.

Though Varda had caused his body to fail, his mind was sharper than it had ever been. He felt a pulse deep inside him, a desire, a need to do whatever he could to keep the warrior-beetles from eating Krystren alive.

He was unaware, if Krystren wasn't, that the Eye of

Ajbal, which had been heading toward the Abbey of Five
Pivots, was now adrift as Varda's attention focused on defending himself against Minnum's flurry of spells.

Minnum could see that no single spell alone was powerful enough to penetrate the archon's defensive perimeter.
But it was conceivable that if he kept up the barrage he
could wear down the perimeter to a point where a spell
could make it through.

Behind him, he was dimly aware of Krystren holding
the swarm of warrior-beetles in stasis. But it was obviously a temporary achievement. Already, here and there, a
warrior-beetle broke free to sting or bite. They were trying
to concentrate on her face and neck, where she was most
vulnerable.

He redoubled his efforts and was gratified to see Varda's
defensive perimeter shrinking. He could sense that the archon was obliged to use more and more energy simply to
defend himself. He seemed taken aback by the breadth of
Minnum's sorcerous ability as well as the depths of the little sauromician's determination. Minnum used this advantage to continue the ferocity of the attack, but now he had
run through the entire gamut of spells, and Varda was becoming familiar with their workings. He started to pick
them apart, one by one.

Minnum, realizing that sorcery alone would not win the
day, began to crawl through the stinking mire of ground-
up warrior-beetle corpses. On hands and knees he dragged
himself toward where the archon stood, spread-legged,
grimacing with the effort.

The archon's defensive perimeter was so compromised
that it would have been a simple matter for Minnum to
stand on his feet and, had he a weapon, to bury it in
Varda's narrow chest. The trouble was he could no longer
stand. Worse, the energy he was expending was rapidly
sapping his reserves. He had very little else to give.

But then he felt a thread running through him, ten, then
a score, making repairs in his torn nerves. It was Krystren
coming to his rescue again. He almost wept with joy. Rid-

ing the confidence she had in him, he slowly and painfully
rose to his feet and, swaying, lunged for Varda's vulnerable black sixth finger. But even as he caught hold of it he
felt another burst of agony as another section of his spine
exploded.

He gasped and fell to his knees. He would not let go of
the abominable finger, and with his last ounce of strength
he began to bend it backward. Varda kicked him over so
that he lay on his back. The finger was still in Minnum's
grip, Varda's arm twisted horribly. He would never let it go,
never, until it was broken off and Varda lay dead at his feet.

Without thought to the pain he must be in, Varda
jammed his slippered boot on Minnum's throat and, gritting his teeth, pressed down hard. Minnum, with his last
defensive spell, stopped the boot from crushing his windpipe. He was almost done. He needed to make one last effort, but breaking off the finger was by then beyond him.
He steeled himself to make one more expenditure of the
little he had left. He could do it. He thought of Krystren,
imagined her there beside him, smiling down at him, her
lips coming down over his, the press of her cool lips . . .

One more effort, and he chose it wisely.

Krystren, finally free of the warrior-beetle swarm, saw
the two sauromicians struggling on the ground. She
saw the black sixth finger in Minnum's grip. She knew
how badly he was hurt—the extent of the damage apparent
to her the moment she inserted her healing threads into
him. She had almost cried out, then, unable to understand
how he was managing to continue the attack. She knew
many Sarakkon who would already be dead by now if they
had sustained his injuries.

While the warrior-beetles burned in the sorcerous fire
she had conjured up, she channeled all her mental energy
in an attempt to give Minnum strength where he needed it
most—his hands. She saw Varda's finger being bent farther back.

Then the archon kicked Minnum savagely in the side of the head. Varda turned to her, and she gasped at the power of his mind. He had a lock on her throat, an invisible hand choking her. But at that moment she heard a sound, like a dry rustle, a death rattle. He looked up and his grip on her weakened. By the time she freed herself completely, he had vanished among the trees. She ran to where Minnum lay in a twisted heap. She looked up briefly, saw what Varda had seen: the Eye of Ajbal was growing dark. Like a flower starved of water, its edges were curling inward toward the center.

Giyan! she thought, even as she knelt beside the little sauromician. She was extending her healing threads into him, as many as she could—more than she had ever done before—and they were making their repairs. But it was not enough. For every nerve they knit, four others turned necrotic. Her heart grew heavy. There wasn't any more she could do, save to safeguard his body from being disemboweled by Varda, used for the archon's necromancy. Despite these mournful thoughts, she managed to smile when his eyes opened.

For a moment, Minnum was lost in a cosmos of pain. Then, as she cradled his head in her lap, his eyes slowly cleared, came into focus. His lips formed into words she could not hear, and she was obliged to bend over, to put her ear so close to his half-open mouth she could smell his death.

"You . . . you are all right." His whispered voice lacked both tone and timbre.

"Yes," she said, very close to him. "Thanks to you."

He smiled. His breathing was shallow, his pulse erratic. Still, she kept her threads working, repairing what she could, for the moment keeping the inevitable at bay.

"The Eye is dying."

"We gave Giyan enough time."

"What a hero you are," she said, and meant it.

"Hero."

For a moment, his eyes went out of focus, and she was afraid that he was gone.

But they cleared when she called his name.

"Is Varda still alive?"

He nodded, though the tiny effort cost him. Odd, he thought, how he was aware of every move he made, every word that passed his lips. They were so precious, these quotidian things to which he had never given any thought at all.

"Let me tell you about Varda," he said so softly, she had to bend closer in order to hear him. "I attached Spirit Bell to him. Tell Giyan when you see her."

"I will, but—"

"Promise me!" he said fiercely.

And she nodded. "Of course. I promise."

A great wave of exhaustion overcame him. "I am no hero. I am nothing more than—"

"Hush!" She put a finger to his lips, and his eyes closed. "Hero by deed, hero by heart."

"Krystren . . ."

"Not now," she said. "Save your strength. We are repairing you."

When he opened his eyes they were wet. "I thank you. For everything. But there is no point in prolonging it. We both know what comes."

"In time," she whispered. "But now listen to the Marre pines whispering, feel the cool breeze on your face, smell the forest all around you."

"I want to remember." He breathed it all in—all that she had told him was there, and more. He felt himself cradled so tenderly in her arms. The pleasure of it was overwhelming. It was more than he had ever wanted. He gazed up at her, filling himself with her face. "Disengage them."

"What? No." She held him tighter. "Absolutely not."

"All of them."

She said nothing, she did not trust herself to speak, but she did as he asked.

He coughed, the sound thick with his own blood. "I want—"

"We know what you want, Minnum."

And she leaned over, pressing her lips to his, a taste so sweet he took it with him all the way down into death.

23

The Harder They Fall

Kurgan was in the middle of his interview with Nith Nassam when the banestone called to him. He had told Nith Nassam just enough of what he had learned from Lujon to make his lies seem plausible. He was gratified to see the lamp of avidity alight in the Gyrgon's crimson-irised eyes, for Nith Nassam now believed he knew the nature of Courion's relationship with Nith Batoxxx.

"Not one, but two secret societies, working behind the framework of the Orieniad," Nith Nassam said. "I wonder what other secrets the Sarakkon have kept from us?"

"You could have asked Courion, but unfortunately Nith Batoxxx killed him." All Kurgan wanted now was the promised access to Nith Batoxxx's lab-orb, and this he asked for, as was his right.

Nith Nassam beamed an utterly benign smile at Kurgan. "You will get your wish, regent, when you have brought me the information I want. What was Courion doing in Axis Tyr?"

"I brought you something better," Kurgan said, trying to keep his outrage in check. "Intelligence no other Gyrgon knows—the existence of the *Onnda* and the *Sintire*."

"You have done well. Very well, indeed. But it is only a

start." Nith Nassam grunted. "Get cracking, regent. The faster you give me what I want, the faster you will have what you want."

Kurgan ground his teeth in fury, but said nothing in return. He spat upon the floor of his own chamber the moment Nith Nassam had disappeared around a corner, for he knew now that the Gyrgon would never allow him into the lab-orb. He would milk Kurgan for as much information as Kurgan could deliver. Which was, from then on, nothing. He would have to find another way into the lab-orb.

For the moment, however, that burning question would have to wait. The banestone was calling him, its emanations so powerful that he had a pain in his head. But before he could gather it into his hands he had to suffer through yet another interruption, this time from the ubiquitous First-Captain Kwenn, who had with him straining on its leash the new wyr-hound, growling and mewling so that Kurgan regretted ever replacing the one that had been torn to pieces down in the Black Farm.

"I have told you repeatedly not to bring that filthy creature into my quarters," Kurgan said shortly.

"Yes, regent, but I was feeding him when I was made aware of the situation."

"What situation?"

"I felt I needed to come straightaway."

"N'Luuura take it, First-Captain!"

"That matter you asked me to look into concerning the whereabouts of your sister," Kwenn said. "There have been several confirmed sightings of a young Tuskugggun in the high country of Receive Tears Ridge."

"Doubtless a Looorm imported for Mennus' troops." Kurgan rubbed his temple. The insistent pain was becoming intolerable. "Why do you come to me with something I already know?"

The wyr-hound pup growled louder, possibly in response to Kurgan's abrupt tone.

"The Tuskugggun is not dressed like a Tuskugggun. She is not dressed like a V'ornn at all. She is dressed as Resistance." Kwenn cleared his throat, obviously ill at ease. "Regent, the Tuskugggun is your sister, Marethyn."

"What is that you say?"

"I have an eyewitness account—"

"Obviously, he is mistaken, and you are an idiot! My sister may be many things but a member of the Kundalan Resistance? What do you take me for!"

By that time, Kurgan was shouting. The wyr-hound, straining at its leash, leapt at him, its teeth bared, and the only thing stopping it from sinking them into Kurgan's throat was a tight tug on its leash.

"A thousand apologies, regent." Kwenn, breaking into a cold sweat, wound the leash around and around his wrist. "Please pay him no mind. He is just a pup."

Kurgan, eyes glaring, the pain in his head inserting a red haze between him and the rest of the Cosmos, drew his dagger and, with one swift stroke, slit the wyr-hound's throat.

First-Captain Kwenn gave a little cry as blood fountained. The wyr-hound's paws all tried to leave the floor at once, causing it to collapse on its side, its extremities spasming. Kwenn went down on his knees, but with an oath Kurgan hauled him back up to his feet.

"This is what happens when you disobey me, First-Captain. Now get that carcass out of here before it permanently stains my carpet."

There was rain when the Nawatir set out from the Abbey of Floating White. Rain and a low-lying fog enveloped the night, making it as dank and desolate as a fireless hearth. His narbuck was a part of the elements, and he pranced on the raindrops, leaping upward from one to another, using them as the Nawatir would use stones to ford a stream. As they crossed over the village of Stone Border the narbuck shook his head. The Nawatir could feel the dread anticipation that was spread through the darkened streets like a kris-spider's web. The night was alive with the soft creaks and ion leakage of the Khagggun encampment, which lay just south of the village.

The Nawatir, having once been a Pack-Commander himself, was well versed in the Khaggun protocol for setting perimeters, sentinel deployment, and photonic-grid security measures in hostile territory. He busied himself with identifying each one of the cleverly hidden systems not only because he had to but to keep his mind off Inggres.

The kiss had come upon him unawares, and he berated himself for not picking up on the signs. Possibly he hadn't wanted to. His last night together with Giyan had shaken him to the core. How could she love him, as she professed to do, if she would not confide in him? Every secret she kept hidden from him was another barrier that pushed them further apart. That she could not see it was unfathomable to him. She wanted him to love her, but only so much and no further. That was unacceptable to him—he, a V'ornn, once a Khagggun who had been responsible for Annon's pursuit and death. He shook his head in consternation. Was this the Kundalan concept of love? But he thought not. He had lived long enough now with Kundalan to know that much. No, it was Giyan's way, this half love, this icy distance that pierced his soul. He had tried to love her on her terms, but it was impossible.

Over the sleeping village he arced. The narbuck was weightless in the air, and he weightless with it. The fitful wind blew through his long hair. His beard was stippled with moisture.

He was still a long way from feeling comfortable with hair on either his face or his body. Sometimes he felt like an animal, and his nose would wrinkle with the unfamiliar sourish odor as bacteria colonized the strands. At other times, as when Giyan ran her fingers through his luxurious pelt, he felt a strange, fierce pride, and he found himself pitying the hairless V'ornn.

Clearing the lowest houses, small and rickety, defying gravity, he urged the narbuck closer to the rocky, steeply sloped ground.

Inggres. He had felt her desire for him like a living

thing. The moment her lips had touched his, he had felt a shock of recognition pass clear through him. How long had she leashed this part of herself, how deeply had she buried it?

He had no time to contemplate those questions. The narbuck had brought him to within a stone's throw of the Khagggun encampment. He bade the mount to stop, and as it settled to the bare, black ground, he dismounted and left it there, hidden from even the most suspicious V'ornn eyes.

His sorcerous cloak wrapped itself protectively around him so that, save for a V-shaped opening through which he could peer, he was completely enfolded. In that way, he passed through the perimeter unnoticed. He made his way through the neat rows of off-world enclosures. Here and there he paused, listening in on the latest Khagggun gossip, bringing himself up to date, feeling something of what Konara Inggres had experienced at the Blackcrow in Stone Border. It was not that he was nostalgic for his old life, far from it. But the hurried, sour whispers brought home to him how out of touch he had become as Nawatir, sequestered behind thick abbey walls.

Presently he found himself at the center of the encampment. He saw that Wing-Adjutant Wiiin had been promoted to Wing-Commander, a field position, the Nawatir felt certain, he was ill equipped to handle. All to the good. Since the promotion was only temporary, Wiiin was insecure, which had made him a bit reckless, ordering this raid on the abbey in order to win a quick and easy victory to prove to those above him that he was fit for permanent field command.

The Nawatir stood in a pool of shadow between glaring portable fusion lamps and digested all the news. Across the stony ground was the entrance to Wiiin's enclosure. It was flanked by two Khagggun guards. He listened to their low, halting, desultory conversation, gleaning from it their disgust with this assignment, which promised no glory, only the taint of derision from their comrades in other Wings. Watching their grim faces, he saw for the first time

what had been bred into them—the lust for battle, for
bloodletting—and all they had lost because of it. Their
world was small and dark, dank with death and the stench
of offal glistening on mired battlefields. But in his heart
there was neither pity nor contempt for them; only anger
at the Gyrgon who bred them like water buttren.

With the aid of his semisentient cloak, he "became" a
Khagggun with the rank of Line-General. The color of his
armor showed that he was a member of the regent's Haaar-
kyut. The illusion was visually perfect, but risky. While in
another form, he had none of the Nawatir's powers; he was
vulnerable. He was now a V'ornn through and through. Although another risk remained, he believed he had overcome it. He had chosen the uniform of the Haaar-kyut not
only for the power inherent in the regent's elite cadre, but
for the anonymity it would afford him. Not even Khagggun
officers were familiar with Haaar-kyut personnel, whose
duties were strictly to do the regent's bidding. He stepped
out of the pool of shadow and, nodding to the guards who
came swiftly to attention, passed between them.

The center of Wiiin's enclosure was taken up by two
perfectly aligned tables. On one was arrayed crystals displaying maps of the area, broken down by topography,
population density, climatic anomalies, and the like. On
the second table, more crystals detailed holoviews of the
abbey, both aerial and from the ground. It was the quarters
of an adjutant, not a military commander.

The would-be Wing-Commander stood between the tables, amid a trio of military advisors, two lean and
hungry-looking First-Captains and an older, veteran
Pack-Commander with a closed face and wily eyes that
could sort friend from enemy even among his own
Khagggun.

"A frontal assault will show the value of our strength,"
said one of the First-Captains.

"A feint to the front, while we use a flanking maneuver,
will befuddle and defeat them," opined the other.

"The abbey's walls are thick and formidable. I strongly

suggest we lay siege," the Pack-Commander said force-fully. "That will have the effect both of winning us uncontested victory and demoralizing those in the village."

Wiiin listened to these various strategies while peering first at a map, then a holoview. In his hand he held a photonic pad on which he scribbled with a light pen one plan of attack after another. As soon as he had written it, he deleted it. Clearly, he could not make up his mind.

His advisors had about them the air of silent contempt, but they also exhibited the agitation of animals currying favor from the new leader.

They all looked up, however, when the Nawatir strode into the enclosure, and it was difficult to ascertain which of them exhibited the most anxiety at his presence.

"I am Line-General Kamme," the Nawatir said with just the right amount of acid in his voice. "The regent has ordered me to find out what it is you think you are doing."

Wiiin had only begun to launch into his rationale for sacking the Abbey of Floating White when the Nawatir cut him off.

"This Ramahan abbey has a long history of remaining intact, Wing-Adjutant." His deliberate use of Wiiin's former rank set off a wave of stifled laughter from the two First-Captains. The Pack-Commander was canny enough not to betray his feelings, his expression unfathomable. "It has been a source of invaluable intelligence regarding the movements and composition of the Resistance. The regent wishes to know why you would destroy that."

"Times have changed." Wiiin glared at each of his advisors in turn before deferentially focusing on the Nawatir in his Haaar-kyut guise. "The Ramahan are no longer cooperative. In fact, my own experience with them indicates they are being duplicitous. They flout the terms of the old arrangement."

"The old arrangement, as you term it, was with the traitor Line-General Werrrent, whom you served as adjutant." Instantly, a deathly silence enveloped the enclosure and all its occupants. No one stirred. No one dared even breathe.

"Accordingly, the contact for the arrangement was changed. Of course the Ramahan you spoke with was recalcitrant. You were not her contact. She had no reason to trust you. Just the opposite, in fact."

"You mean the old arrangement is still in effect?" Wiiin fairly stammered this.

"Our new contact inside the abbey is supplying us with first-rate intelligence," the Nawatir lied smoothly. "Therefore, the regent orders you to stand down from this ill-advised attack. The division of the Haaar-kyut under my command has taken charge of the arrangement. It is no longer the responsibility of this Wing." He turned to go, then swung back, riveting Wiiin's eyes with his hard gaze. "Oh, yes. Within a week the Star-Admiral, with the advice of the regent himself, will rule on your 'promotion.' Until then, do nothing, plan nothing. Return to your base"— now his stern gaze took in all of them—"and await forthcoming instructions."

So saying, the false Line-General turned on his heel and stalked out of the enclosure. It was not long, however, before the Pack-Commander caught up with him.

"Line-General, Kamme, a word with you."

The Nawatir did not break stride. "What is your name?"

"Pack-Commander Lucus Jerre, sir."

"I have little time for idle chatter, Pack-Commander Jerre."

"No, sir. I would not expect you to." Pack-Commander Jerre hurried to keep up with the false Line-General's pace. "However, I would very much think that the Line-General would be interested in what I have to tell him."

"Bucking for a transfer, Pack-Commander Jerre?"

They were passing through the glow of a photon torch, and Jerre paused. "Begging the Line-General's pardon, but I have important information concerning the Abbey of Floating White."

As the false Line-General swung around, he frowned. Jerre was staring at him with hard eyes. They were at the fringe of the encampment, and he wanted nothing more than to make his escape without incident. Unfortunately, he was stuck in a charade that had outlived its usefulness. It had served its purpose, and he was impatient to return to the abbey, to tell Inggres that she and her flock had nothing to fear. And it was his impatience that made him miss what was, after all, a very little thing, nothing more than a hint of gesture, a shadow of an expression, a patch of darkness creeping into the intonation.

"Why haven't you gone to your superior officer with this information?" he barked in his impatience.

"Because I do not trust my superior officers." Pack-Commander Jerre drew an ion pistol.

The Nawatir was taken by surprise and his elision made him bristle. "What do you think you're up to?"

"Who are you, Line-General?" He pointed the pistol at the Nawatir.

"You can see by my armor—"

"It is your armor that gave you away, Line-General—or whoever you are." He smiled. "You cannot be a member of the Haaar-kyut, you see, because your insignia is wrong. Or at least, it is incomplete. This new regent is paranoid, and rightly so, I see. Last month he instituted a new security initiative. All his Haaar-kyut wear a specially coded star beneath their insignia of rank." The ion pistol waggled from side to side. "Where is yours, Line-General?"

The Nawatir said nothing.

"Just as I thought." As Pack-Commander Jerre reached for his communicator, the Nawatir slammed the ion pistol aside with a forearm and, at the same time, grabbed the Khaggun's armor and jerked him into deep shadow.

Jerre recovered swiftly, smashing his mailed fist into the side of the Nawatir's head. Lights flashed behind the Nawatir's eyes, and he staggered. Jerre managed to squeeze off one shot before the Nawatir gripped his throat, braced an arm behind his neck, and twisted violently. Jerre's eyes went wide as his neck began to crack. But he would not surrender himself to death that easily, and he stamped his foot onto the false Line-General's instep, loosening the death grip just enough.

He ducked under the Nawatir's grip, drew his ion dagger, and went straight for his antagonist's throat. The Nawatir grabbed his wrist with both hands, turned the point aside. But Pack-Commander Jerre hooked his foot behind the Nawatir's heel and down he went, Jerre on top of him. Jerre smashed the butt end of the ion dagger against the Nawatir's temple, reversed the weapon, and made a vicious swipe meant to slit the other's throat.

The Nawatir brought his right shoulder up so that it struck the underside of Jerre's attacking arm, then, as Jerre compensated, he rolled to the left, heaved the Pack-Commander off him. He struck Jerre between the eyes, then grabbed each ear and slammed his head onto the rocky ground. Again and again he lifted the head and drove it back down until Jerre's eyes rolled up, his mouth went slack, and it filled with blood.

Panting and dizzy, the Nawatir dragged Jerre deeper into the shadows, leaving him behind a rocky outcropping. But the effort cost him dearly. He had taken the ion-pistol blast almost point-blank, and with each triple pump of his hearts he was losing blood.

First-Captain Kwenn was scarcely out the door with the bloody remains of his pet, when Kurgan accessed the secret drawer behind his wall of weapons and drew out the banestone. He sighed deeply even as it burned his hand, for it spoke to him in its voice that was not a voice. It had found Eleana. The pain subsided.

At once, he wiped down his dagger. Then he left the regent's palace by the secret passageway he had discovered. The banestone had a way of guiding him. It almost seemed to be a part of him, as if it was speaking to the core of his being. He felt its magnetic pull and he was flooded with a sense of omnipotence and invulnerability. No wonder Lujon wanted it, for he did not for a moment believe that Lujon would turn it over to the sauromicians if it ever came into his possession. No one would be that foolish, least of all canny Lujon. No, he was playing along with the sauromicians—just as Kurgan himself would have done if he had been in the Sarakkon's place. Gradually, he had seen that power was Lujon's currency, his fondest desire. He knew how to handle Lujon. His lust for power made him transparent. Better, even, it made him predictable. It was like a game of warrnixx. You won when you saw how the spiral laid out six or eight moves ahead. It was a heady feeling, that foretaste of victory.

The banestone led him down the Boulevard of Crooked Dreams, west into an area with which he was totally unfamiliar. But he had been to districts like it, stinking of garbage and urine and mange, populated for the most part by bloated-bellied wyr-hounds and limbless Kundalan. Addiction was their only escape from the mutilation caused by the constant Khagggun interrogations.

He hurried on, his fist clamped tightly around his triangular-bladed dàgger, while the way became narrower and meaner between crowded swayback buildings, the sky a muddy ripple, narrow as a stream. Without fanfare, the street ended as abruptly as a slammed door. He found himself facing a dun-colored building whose crumbling facade was a disgrace. He rubbed clean a small plaque to the right of the entrance.

FIREFLY, he read. A kashiggen, but one, judging by its exterior, that should long ago have been shut down.

As his banestone—for that was how he had come to think of it—instructed, he ascended the cracked and crumbling stairs, cursing under his breath as he almost lost his footing. The interior smelled like overboiled granth and rotting corpses. In the entranceway no lamps of any sort were lit. What illumination existed, grey, thin as tissue, filtered down from a grime-encrusted oculus inset into the high, domed ceiling. There was about the place a stir of echoes.

A prickling along his scalp caused him to brandish his

dagger, tip tilted upward. He felt the quick hot flow of cortasyne, bringing on the bloodlust. His senses were sharpened, honed to fever pitch.

Directly opposite the front door a massive shanstone staircase rose like a crippled spine up the center of the building. On either side were closed double doors of heartwood, their intricate carvings half-hidden under layers of dust, grease and grime. He listened for the voice of the banestone, but it was silent. It pulsed powerfully in his hand, though. Eleana was close by.

He moved in a semicrouch to the door on the left, placing his ear near it. Murmured voices. Stepping back, he kicked the center with booted foot. The doors, which had not been locked, flew open, and he raced in, ready to kill, to take possession of her.

Instead, two naked Deirus, their pale heads popped comically up on scrawny bodies, scrambled off the long, seductive settee. They screamed when they recognized him, dashed out past him. He let them go, looked briefly out a grime-streaked window. The fens of the Great Phosphorus Swamp let go their stink. Stagnant pools shiny as oil. Clouds of insects rising, falling, droning. It looked more inviting out there than in here. He turned on his heel.

The chamber to the right of the entranceway was properly furnished for trysts, all manner of sexual fantasy, but it was empty. That left the stairs.

Up them he climbed in a wary semicrouch. The banestone had taken on added weight, as if Eleana was crouched, waiting, inside it. It was possible to think of it as a hole in the Cosmos, a window into another level where light did not exist.

A flurry of echoes, creaks, and moans, greeted him on the landing. It was as if the building were trying to speak to him, as if it had something on its mind. But of course that was impossible. The building was like any other, nothing more than a pile of granite, marble, and porphyry. A stirring, no doubt about it, as if around every corner someone lay in wait. And so, proceeding down the winding second-floor hallway, he was prepared to defend himself, to kill his assailant if necessary. But the corners, like the sparsely furnished chambers he passed, held only shadows, mocking him in their emptiness.

He kept going, keyed up, no thought of turning back, along a corridor carpeted with a long narrow runner, its jewel-tone colors faded. The walls were badly in need of a fresh coat of lacquer. None of the fusion lamps were working. Old-fashioned tallow lanterns hung from bare wires, giving off the heavy scent of rendered fat and smoky flames.

The end of the corridor offered one last chamber. It, too, was deserted. But he discovered a plate of half-eaten food, a tankard of warm mead, an unlit candle. Small smells of habitation, slightly rancid. He reached out and almost burned himself on the blackened wick.

His reflection in the mirror affixed to a narrow door stared back at him. When had he become so hollow-eyed? With a grunt of disgust, he pulled open the door, his reflection wheeling away from him. Out of sight, out of mind. Peering up, he could just make out a steep flight of spiral stairs. He considered lighting the candle but decided against it, choosing stealth over visibility.

He kept his back against the outer rail of the staircase. The air grew close and stifling. The stench of the moldering past was overpowering. Presently, he reached the top of the spiral and found himself in an attic with a steeply canted ceiling. Joists and crossbeams were visible, thickly laced with cobwebs. Sweet wood must, the sour stench of mildew. Rodent droppings, untidy pyramids across the dusty unfinished floorboards.

A streak of light, the color of a dead bird, slanted in from a dormer window caked with grime, a little finger of water rippling across the arid attic floor. The dormer had been sealed shut decades ago. It would take a cocked elbow or the butt of a weapon to go through it.

Kurgan stopped in his tracks, for standing in the patch of wan light was the last individual he expected to see.

* * *

The Nawatir never recalled how he made it back to his narbuck. Possibly, the sorcerous steed found him. In any event, the next thing he knew he was riding the narbuck into the dense mist, his torso slumped against the animal's powerful neck. His hand was pressed to his wound, but the blood leaked out just the same. He was moving in and out of consciousness. He felt warm and cold at the same time.

The lurching journey was a sickening blur of fog and stars, of wind rushing, of ceaseless shivering, of pain and yawning blackness. In the Nawatir's feverish state, the rhythmic gait of the narbuck sounded like a choir of chanting voices. He felt as if he were being dragged through a rubble pit.

Over the rooftops of the village of Stone Border galloped the narbuck, up the steep slope of the Djenn Marre to the promontory on which the Abbey of Floating White hunkered, pale and pearled in the thick swirls of mist. With a mighty leap, the narbuck sailed over the walls, his hooves clattering in the courtyard, through the triple arches, and into the garden outside Konara Inggres' office, where she anxiously waited with her Ja-Gaar, sipping hot greenleaf tea as an antidote to her exhaustion.

She put down her cup when she heard the sound of the narbuck's hooves, and ran alongside the Ja-Gaar out into the garden, where her worst fears were realized. The narbuck went down on his knees, the better to allow her to swing the Nawatir off his perch. He was still dressed in his Line-General's armor, and he looked like a V'ornn, for he had lacked the strength to command his cloak to return him to his true form.

Stripping off the bottom of her robe, she took his stiff-fingered hand away. She stifled a cry when she saw bone exposed, the Ja-Gaar growling and pacing restlessly as she stuffed the cloth into the wound and pressed down hard in order to stanch the blood. But the wad of cloth was soon sodden. He had been shot by a Khaggun ion pistol, and such was the damage that she knew that it must have been at very close range. She could not understand that. He was the Nawatir. How could he have been injured so grievously?

The narbuck pawed the ground nervously, and the Ja-Gaar circled as Konara Inggres called to two of her leyna to help her carry the Nawatir into the infirmary. There, she dismissed them and, somewhat self-consciously, set about stripping him of his bloody armor. Unfortunately, because it was not real, but rather a part of the individual the cloak had turned him into, it would not come off. Inggres could see right away that if she could not remove the armor she would not be able to see the true extent of the wound and would not, therefore, be able to treat it effectively. His extreme pallor and weakness told her how much blood he had already lost.

Pulling open cupboards, she brought an armful of ground herbs and mushrooms, along with a mortar and pestle and two or three vials of decoctions. The first thing she did was take off the bloody wad and replace it with a pinch of finely ground shanin. The blood flow was so prodigious it took her several times—and several healing spells—to get the proper consistency of herb and blood, but at length the shanin had made a latticework across the wound. At least he would not bleed to death.

Next, she ground Pandanus with a small amount of datura inoxia. Periodically, she added several drops of liquid from one of the vials until she had a thick paste. This she spread over the shanin. But she could see blood still seeping out from around parts of the wound covered by armor, and her anxiety redoubled. He was so weak that she did not think he could tolerate much more blood loss.

She knew that he must be terribly dehydrated, and she set about brewing him lyme-ginger tea, which was both healing and restorative. This she fed him slowly and steadily as she thought about how to return him to his Nawatir state. She knew that the key was his cloak, Dragon-made and, therefore, unknowable. It had not absorbed his blood, though it had been wrapped around him. She did not understand it at all, and therefore she did not know how to get it to change him back. Only he could do that, and he was all but insensate.

Pulling the cloak closer around him, she conjured up every spell she knew of in an attempt to trigger the mechanism, to no avail. A small moan escaped her lips. The last several moments had been taken up with the busywork any Ramahan healer could perform, but now, with all that done, with her spells rendered useless, there was nothing but to watch him sink deeper into the coma that would surely kill him. She did not know how this could have come to pass. She had thought him invulnerable. The Khagggun would be there soon enough, blasting their way through the front doors or through the sacred white-stone walls. Without the Nawatir there were only the Ja-Gaar to protect her and her flock. Not enough. And if he were to die . . . She shivered with anguish, suddenly overcome by the terror of never looking into his beautiful eyes again, of never feeling him breathe, of never touching her lips to his again. Weeping, she bent her head to his, pressed her lips against his still mouth. His shallow breath caught in her throat, and she thought she knew what it was to be on the point of death.

She looked up, suddenly aware of a cold presence, a shadow hovering. Rheumy death had entered the infirmary, holding out its hand for him.

"No," she whispered, holding him all the tighter. "No!"

The presence of death, the imminence of the end seemed to galvanize her, to clear her mind. An idea formed and took hold, and with it came hope. The cloak was Dragon-made, the Dragons belonged to Miina. Miina had once heard her prayers and answered them. Would She again?

Holding the Nawatir in her arms, she forced her eyes shut, slowed her breathing, calmed her racing pulse. Layer by layer, she descended into that place between consciousness and unconsciousness, the place of dreams, of emotions, where all the essential particles of the Cosmos were born, died, and were reborn. The place where Time was banished, where past, present, and future existed all at once.

Dearest Miina, hear me, she prayed. *Here lies Your Nawatir, Your protector, Your strong right hand. He has been grievously wounded, by what strange means I cannot pretend to know, and he is dying. Please help me return him to life. Please help me understand how to return him to himself. He is so brave, so fearless. . . . Where is the justice in his dying?*

Only silence greeted her—a deafening silence through which she could hear the phlegmy sawing of his shallow breaths, the wild beating of her heart.

Where are You, Miina, in Your servant's hour of need? Why have You abandoned those who love You most dearly, who cleave to Your covenants, who keep the flame of Your teachings alive in the gathering darkness? Great Goddess, answer Your most humble servant!

But there came no reply. The ether was still as death, and the darkness she spoke of seemed to close in on them, like a curtain being drawn across the stage at play's end.

And yet there was a voice, deep inside her. The voice of her *own* true spirit, rising, speaking to her in the wilderness of her despair.

I love him. I can no longer deny it to myself, for surely if he dies I will crumple up and perish beside him, and be happy, at least, for that.

She bent her head, and the tears flowed freely, and she held the Nawatir all the more tightly, feeling her love for him surging like a river in spring, like the tide pulled by all five moons. Live wave upon wave crashing onto a shingle beach.

But I will not let him die. I will not!

And beneath her, the cloak began to stir, shift, blur. Responding to the passion of her spirit, the force of her true love, the cloak liquefied, melting into him. And as it did so, his armor disappeared, his V'ornnish features reforming into those of the golden-haired Nawatir. And she cried again, but now with delight and relief, and immediately peeled back his tunic and treated the circumference of his wound, which was larger than she had imagined. And presently, he arose from his terrible coma and drifted into a deep and peaceful sleep within which his body would heal.

And Konara Inggres, having done all she could, having done what was necessary, was at last caught by her own exhaustion, and she lay down beside him, her arm draped across his hips.

Even in her sleep she dreamed of healing him.

There is something unique about each Gyrgon lab-orb that preys upon the observer and casts him in the role of outsider. Possibly it was the intimate relationship the Gyrgon had with their kilometers of neural nets, curled and shining. Where the Gyrgon left off and the neural nets began no one, not even another Gyrgon could say, save Guls, and they were forbidden to speak of it, forbidden to reveal how they genetically manipulated the fathered embryo. Sahor thought he had prepared himself for Nith Batoxxx's lab, but he was wrong. Nothing could have forearmed him for the atmosphere of evil he found there. It was so pervasive it had infected the neural nets like a virus. It made him want to turn around and walk out, it made him want to dismantle the lab-orb and everything in it. He felt as if touching even a single interface would infect him as, he suspected, it had infected the others who had been in here: Nith Nassam, Nith Immmon, Gul Aluf, even his father. Looking around, he wondered how he would be able to protect himself.

"What will you tell Nith Nassam?" he said to cover his apprehension. "Who will you tell him I am?"

"Let me worry about Nith Nassam," Nith Immmon told him pointedly.

"We want your input," Gul Aluf said. "So far, we have been stymied. Nith Batoxxx has locked us out of every data server, every storage neural net."

"We can't access any imaging pathway," Nith Immmon said. "And believe me we have tried."

"Everything," Gul Aluf added, if only to emphasize their frustration.

What they said only increased Sahor's desire to see all of this vaporized in a boiling ball of flame. He wondered how hot the conflagration would have to get in order to purify the space.

Far better that than allow Nith Batoxxx's experiments to come out. He could feel this in his hearts in the same way he had known that the destiny of the V'ornn lay somewhere on Kundala.

But he could destroy nothing. They would not even allow him to walk out now that he was here. He began to regret ever leaving the confines of the Museum of False Memory. Had he stayed there he would never have returned to the warehouse he had set up as one of his auxiliary labs, he would never have fallen into Gul Aluf's trap. But what was the point of regrets? He had missed his father. His desire to be reunited with his father had triggered everything.

Sahor first walked over to the dully gleaming egg-shaped goron-wave chamber because it looked so ominous, because it so thoroughly dominated the space.

"We crawled over that inside and out," Gul Aluf said.

Of course you did, Sahor thought. *It was the first place you looked.*

"It was the first place we looked," Nith Immmon said.

Sahor smiled inwardly and turned his attention to the lab-orb as a whole. He took in the arcana—the waves of redesigned neural nets, holoscreens, the banks of fusion generators, the coils of influx water fibers, thick as his wrist, the curious photon webs. He went to the three separate task stations where Nith Batoxxx plugged himself into various terminals. On the one closest to the wall he discovered a cylindrical slot, far too small to insert a data crystal.

He pointed it out to Gul Aluf. "Do you know what this is for?"

She did not even need to take a closer look. "Another mystery."

Behind the task station were the walls of the original temple chambers, with their intricate and colorful murals, covered now by thickly growing orangesweet, vines curling, all the blossoms opened and perfectly symmetrical. He inhaled their scent.

"Have you found something . . . anything." Nith Immmon's voice betrayed his anxiety.

"Not yet." But this was a lie. The fact was, he knew a lot already. Much to his chagrin, he was coming to understand that he and Nith Batoxxx had been very much alike. He had spent much of his time on Kundala devising ingenious ways in which to keep his research out of the Comradeship's matrix. Apparently, so had Nith Batoxxx. In this, they were closer than friends, closer than brothers. Polar opposites, they were in this the same under the skin. He found it odd and more than a little unsettling that he should feel closer to his nemesis in death than ever he had in life, and yet, because he had studied Kundalan for so long, had even lived among them, this very connection was an affirmation of the Ramahan concept of the wheel of life, constantly turning, transforming, connecting the living and the dead.

"All this equipment, known and unknown," Nith Immmon said. "Gul Aluf has been over it with a single-micron flux."

"We know nothing more than when we first opened the lab-orb," she said in disgust.

Now, as Sahor wandered about, his keen eyes saw things that the others would have overlooked, for it was a fact that the deeper the secret, the closer to the surface it should be stored. No one ever looks for secrets in plain sight—their gaze slides over everyday objects. The expected is dismissed by the brain almost before it is fully seen.

What was it here in this particular lab-orb that they all would overlook? He had made a complete circle, he had seen everything, though he had explored not one centimeter of the strange setups that Gul Aluf—and doubtless Nith Nassam—had spent days trying and failing to parse.

He stood completely still, absorbing the particular quality of the light, the relationship of each object with its neighbors, the patterns implicit within the whole. He inhaled the aroma of the orangesweet. He felt a sudden urge to count the blossoms. Why was that? He breathed in, breathed out. Was it a touch too sweet? Was there a hint of the artificial mixed in with the natural scent? And why were *all* the blossoms fully open?

He blinked.

And then he knew. His heart rate increased. The blood pounded in his ears, making such an infernal racket that he felt sure the others could hear it. He walked to the periphery of the lab-orb, stood near tiers of neural nets that had the appearance of a small stream. Just beyond them, the orangesweet twined up the wall.

"Have you found something?" Gul Aluf asked.

"Possibly."

He ran his fingertips over the neural nets. To the others it appeared as if he was examining them in detail, but he wasn't focused on them at all. For him, they had ceased to exist. He was looking, instead, at the orangesweet blossoms. They were quite lovely—beautiful, even. But you had to suspect. You had to know what you were looking for, and even then it would take someone with Sahor's long-honed skills at deceit to spot them.

A small percentage of the blossoms were constructs. They were photon-flux fields where Nith Sahor had secreted his off-line data.

24

The Black Guard

Marethyn led Majja and Basse west through the thickly forested ridge toward Gerwa's camp. The two Kundalan were hard-pressed to keep up with her long strides, especially Basse, who was not yet fully recovered from his wounds. He was strong enough to keep pace with Majja, though, a fact that astonished them all. Marethyn considered it the greatest good fortune that they had encountered Giyan and Minnum. Without the help of the two sorcerers, Basse would surely have died.

High above their head, scudding clouds thickened, grew steadily darker. An ominous rumbling, far away but deep and angry-sounding, made its way through the valleys. The air turned wet and sticky, making their clothes cling uncomfortably to their skin. In the dampness, all the fecund effluence of the forest floor rose up like mist to envelop them: the richness of humus, the mint of blue lichen, the chalk of rock, the bitterness of exposed roots.

On another day, they might even have taken the time to savor these scents, but not now. All their concentration was on warning the encampment of the imminent attack by the Khagggun Wing. Marethyn had no idea what would happen once they delivered their message. Doubtless, Gerwa would choose to stand and fight, but given the size of the complement, she did not like their odds.

She was running through a number of arguments for evacuating the camp as quickly as they could when they went down into a thickly foliated dell she recognized.

They were not more than half a kilometer from the camp, and she urged them into an even quicker pace.

And so it was that they were fairly running when they came upon it. Marethyn stopped dead in her tracks, her chest heaving, the sweat running down inside her tunic. The others came up beside her and their gaze, too, went to the same spot.

On the far side of the dell, just where the forest rose again to ridge height, stood Kin, Gerwa's younger brother. He was stripped to the waist. His leggings appeared half-burned. He was looking straight ahead with deadly concentration. They waved to him, but his eyes did not move. They called to him softly, but he gave them no indication that he had heard them.

Then they ran to him, spoke to him, shook him, but he did not respond. Basse put an arm across his lean muscular shoulders. Majja passed a hand before his eyes. Marethyn knelt in front of him, spoke to him urgently. Nothing. She put an ear to his chest. His heart beat slowly, but it was as if he had been turned to stone.

"What has happened to him?" Majja asked.

Basse made a little sound. He had taken his arm away. It was covered with blood. Slowly, with trembling fingers, Marethyn turned Kin around. They gasped as one. The flesh of his back had been flayed off. As if her hands on him was a signal, he collapsed without a sound.

"Dead," Basse said.

"It was if he were waiting for us," Majja said.

Marethyn, closing Kin's eyes, wept. She remembered him slipping on that icy patch of leaves, remembered reaching out and clutching him, remembered him slamming the butt of his ion cannon into the Khaggun who had grabbed her. She could not believe that he was dead.

They wanted to bury him, but there was no time, so they went on silently and grimly through the deadly forest. They dared not look in one another's eyes for fear of what they might see. Terror had gripped their hearts and would not let go. Their minds were abuzz with terrible possibilities, but such were their natures that hope still thundered like the heartbeats of their comrades amid the darkness of their thoughts.

Their ion cannons were unlocked and fully loaded. They wanted nothing more than to find Khagggun to frame in their crosshairs. They tasted the bittersweet wine of vengeance, and its bouquet made Kin's death bearable for the moment.

They were within shouting distance of the camp. It was just over the next rise, through the dense stand of Marre pine, but as they moved toward it, they saw something in among the trees. The heavily laden branches made it impossible to discern clearly until they were nearly upon it.

An exhalation of breath escaped them, for a stake had been driven into the ground. It was fire-blackened and blood-spattered. At its top sat the severed head of Gerwa.

It took First-Captain Kwenn a long time to bury his wyr-hound, but it took him longer to sort out his feelings. For one thing, he was a Khagggun; he was bred not only to kill, but to take orders, to serve those above him without question. For another, loyalty was a strict matter of honor to him. It was of no moment that the regent was Bashkir or that he had murdered the wyr-hound. He had done it to teach First-Captain Kwenn a lesson. First-Captain Kwenn should therefore have been grateful. He *was* grateful. Why, then, was it taking him so long to bury the wyr-hound? Why, then, was he weeping at the sight of its pathetic, almost headless body. He thought maybe it was because it looked so helpless. It was an animal, after all. It could not defend itself from the likes of the regent. But maybe that was precisely why the regent had chosen to make it an example, to teach him that animals were not allowed inside the regent's quarters.

Ever since the regent had slit the wyr-hound's throat, he had had a bad taste in his mouth, and nothing he took as remedy removed it. Worse still, he could not stop crying.

This sad state of affairs was not only embarrassing, it was humiliating. Who among his comrades would understand his attachment to the animal? None that he could think of. Save the breeder.

The breeder's name was Tong. Many of First-Captain Kwenn's fellow Khagggun laughed at him behind his back. They asked what kind of life could he have. They joked cruelly that he was already dead. But these Khagggun thought they knew all the answers. First-Captain Kwenn knew they were simply ignorant.

First-Captain Kwenn found Tong outside with his wyr-hounds. A bitch had just given birth, and he was crouched amid a heap of squirming newborns.

Tong rose when he saw First-Captain Kwenn approaching. Perhaps he was bracing himself for a complaint about the wyr-hound he had sold the regent. "It was a difficult birthing," he said, wiping his hands. "She needed all my help, but look at what—"

"He's dead," First-Captain Kwenn blurted out. "To teach me a lesson, the regent slit my wyr-hound's throat."

"*Klagh*." Tong put his fists on his hips. "He was a good and true beast, that one."

First-Captain Kwenn turned away just in time. He vomited up his breakfast and last night's meager dinner as well, for it was at this moment that he realized the depths of his sorrow. It was also the moment when he let himself taste the anger that had turned his mouth bitter.

Tong ignored what Kwenn had just disgorged but not the sentiment behind it. "I think a drink is called for, don't you?"

Kwenn allowed Tong to take him to a pub, a grubby place with greasy walls and a filthy tile floor. It was populated by Looorm even Tong would not touch. At least, Kwenn hoped that was the case.

Tong ordered them spring mead that, when it arrived in huge, overflowing tankards, was sweet and rich and surprisingly good.

"Life is full of mysteries, eh?" Tong wiped foam off his

upper lip with a stubby finger. "Five years ago, I was under Fleet-Admiral Pnin's command. Today, I helped my prize bitch give life to her litter. And now I wonder which of those things gave me more pleasure."

"That is a very un-Khagggun comment."

"Well, First-Captain Kwenn, it is my opinion that you are an uncommon Khagggun."

"Really?"

"You love wyr-hounds, for one thing." Tong had a dry, raspy voice that reminded Kwenn of ggley-threshers at work. It was a solid voice, the voice of experience. "For another, you work for a Bashkir."

"He is the regent."

"Nevertheless, and for all his physical prowess in the Kalllistotos, for all his Khagggun-like bluster, he isn't Khagggun. Never will be."

"Still, he is the regent and deserves our loyalty."

Tong took another great swig of mead. "When I was a boy—that was a long, long while ago, mind—we had nothing but war. We flew from world to world, and we did our work, we killed and some of us, at least, were killed in return. In those days, it was us—the Khagggun—who ruled. Without us, even the Gyrgon would not have survived."

"Everything changes," Tong said. "It's not the same now, not for any of us."

First-Captain Kwenn had to agree. Since the death of the wyr-hounds—both of them—nothing made sense to him.

"See, he had no call to do it."

First-Captain Kwenn quick-swallowed his mead. As it was, he almost choked on it. "What?"

"I mean to say, a wyr-hound is a living being. The regent had no reason to take his life."

His words would be considered a treasonous remark by some, certainly by the regent. First-Captain Kwenn knew that he ought to consider it that himself. He didn't, though.

"I mean to say, there were a thousand and one ways to teach you a lesson, eh?"

It was true. Kurgan shouldn't have done it. In fact, now that he thought about it, Kwenn was filled with doubts, about the regent, about himself.

"How well did you know your father, First-Captain?"

"Not well at all. I don't think he cared much for children."

"Pity." Tong raised an arm, and another round was set upon the scarred table. They knew him well here. "I loved my father, loved him in a way I could not imagine loving anyone else. Except my wyr-hounds. They're my family, you see." He cupped his hands around the goblet, and Kwenn could see how scarred and swollen they were. "I was born into a family of five brothers, but they all died fighting the Centophennni. Bloody frontline work. Never even saw the face of the enemy." Tong shrugged. "What can you do? War is *klagh*." He drained one tankard, began on the next. "My father loved music. Can you imagine? Didn't matter what kind, he loved it all. He particularly liked to listen·to the music of the enemy before he went into battle. He always said there was a great deal to learn from music. It's all mathematical, you see. Logical patterns in the service of creativity. That's why he admired it so. He knew the enemy he fought, except the Centophennni, of course. No one knows *klagh* about them." He shook his head. "My wyr-hounds like music. Can you imagine? I have all kinds because I took my father's collection. And each time I play something, he comes to visit me again. I feel him listening along with them."

First-Captain Kwenn felt odd, then, because he envied this part of Tong's life. It was something he never had, never would have. And this lack made him feel trapped, as if, like Tong, he had been born into a family of brothers who had all died. Only he was nothing like these dream brothers.

"First-Captain, why did you come to see me?"

Kwenn looked away and licked his lips.

"It's not that you want another wyr-hound. It's not as simple as that, is it?"

When Kwenn remained silent, Tong decided he needed to go a step further. "He disappointed me once, though, my father." Tong was staring down into the amber-colored mead. "Did something he shouldn't have. Took my old shock-sword and had it deactivated. Gave me another one, said it was better." His voice had deepened, sinking down with him into his memories. "Maybe it was, I don't know. Point was, though, I loved that old shock-sword. It had saved my life more times than I liked to count. It was stout and strong-willed, and it had never let me down. N'Luuura take it, it was an extension of my right arm!" He looked into Kwenn's face. "My father, he didn't understand, so there wasn't even any point in telling him. But I got it back, and even though you're not supposed to reactivate a shock-sword, I took it to the maker and bribed him to do it." Tong pursed his lips. His cheeks were flushed. "What's right is right. And what's wrong is wrong."

For a long time, Kwenn was quiet. Then, all at once, he said, "Is there a time when loyalty is wrong? Because what I am feeling now . . . I am thinking that I feel trapped by my loyalty." Maybe that was why nothing made sense to him anymore.

"I require more information."

Kwenn thought for a moment. "I have an acquaintance who is under the Star-Admiral's command. We play warrnixx. One day not long ago he told me how Iin Mennus and his brother were torturing their enemies, the former Admirals of the high command. It was a strange conversation, and it affected me, not right away, but . . . He said the Mennus brothers live to torture others, that they're obsessed with it. Afterward, I began to feel a kind of dislocation. I thought, They are Khaggun, I am Khaggun. Do I do what they do? Do I feel what they feel? This dislocation grew stronger until after my wyr-hounds were killed I began to feel like a torch in sunlight. Suddenly I no longer understood my purpose."

Tong rubbed his chin thoughtfully. It was clear he took

what Kwenn said most seriously. "When you are com-manded by an exemplary officer such as Fleet-Admiral Pnin, you never, as you say, feel like a torch in sunlight. Everything you do is right and natural. But when your faith in your commander has been damaged . . ." He shook his head slowly. "Well, you never recover from that."

Now Kwenn knew why he had come to see Tong. He was seeking absolution for what, deep down, he knew he had to do in order to keep living with himself.

"Can you help me?"

Tong's eyes rested on Kwenn. "Give me a moment. I will imagine it."

It was a measure of the rapport that had sprung up be-tween these two Khagggun that Tong had no need to ask Kwenn what he meant by his request. Underneath it all, Tong thought, they were like kindred spirits, one a younger reflection of the other. Or was it the other way around?

Kwenn, for his part, felt a little thrill run through his system, the kind of feeling he got on the dagger edge, when the outcome of a battle hung in the balance.

Tong smiled a little smile. He said very softly, "Here is what I am thinking. If Star-Admiral Mennus is discredited with the regent, the regent will be discredited with the Gyrgon. After all, he has already chosen poorly with his first Star-Admiral."

Kwenn's eyes were hard and glittery. "The regent can be that seriously discredited?"

Tong inclined his head.

"If I do this, I will be no one I have ever imagined."

"That is the point, isn't it?"

This remark caused a jolt to rush through Kwenn. All at once, everything made sense to him.

"Continue," he said.

"There is someone you need to see. His name is Sornnn SaTrryn."

Kwenn rose and threw a handful of small coins on the table. "I'd like very much like to listen to your music now."

* * *

Gerwa's eyes were wide-open, his teeth bared like an animal. There was defiance in his expression, but also pain and fear. Horrified, the three of them stood shoulder to shoulder, knowing the worst had come about. Hope guttered and died, and they felt like the dead themselves as they went the last several hundred meters into the camp.

Razed to the ground, it was all but unrecognizable. What remained was a ring of charred blackness, studded with misshapen lumps which, as they high-stepped over the charcoaled ground, they discovered were the crisped bodies of their compatriots. There were hundreds of them. Had any escaped, save Kin? They could not be certain, but it appeared not.

The stench of burnt flesh was sickening. A greasy pall hung over the scene of devastation that made them queasy. Cinders clung to their clothes, their hair, the backs of their hands. It was the precipitate of death.

Mechanically, they went about securing the site. When they had assured themselves that there were no Khaggun about they reconvened in the center of the circle. There they hunkered down, arms on thighs. They searched each other's faces for an answer, or at least assurance, but they did not speak. So many lives lost, snuffed out like candle wicks, easy as that. They were devastated. There were no words for what they were witness to. What lay about them was too complete, too all-encompassing. It was as if they had entered a different Cosmos, one that did not support life, that was, in fact, inimical to it. All they could think of was how to get back home, how to remake the world as it had been before. But there was no way, and they knew it. They would have to learn to live with what had happened there, but for the moment, at least, this new, bleak reality seemed merely a very bad dream.

Presently Marethyn heard a pair of gimnopedes calling to one another. Looking up through the pall to the high branches of the Marre pines and the kuello-firs, she saw the bright flash of the birds, an explosion of vivid color.

She got down on her knees and with the edges of her hands cleared a space free of black ash. Then she began to draw with her fingertip, not thinking about it, allowing her emotions to guide her. She drew the flash of birds, the skulk of mammals, the swift dart of insects, a river rushing, and trees standing shoulder to shoulder.

"What are you doing?"

She looked up to see Basse, dark-faced, staring down at what she had already begun to think of as a memorial. She was about to tell him this, but his expression stopped her cold.

"Come. We have more important things to do."

When she did not get off her knees, he stuck his bootheel in the center of the drawing and dragged it first this way, then that.

Marethyn rose then and looked past his shoulder to where Majja stood, a little away from them. Majja's eyes were neutral. It was as if she did not want to interfere. Did she agree with him? Was it possible that she, too, did not understand?

Marethyn felt heartssick, then chastened. What was she thinking? After all, these were not her species. She saw how she had been fooling herself into thinking that the essential differences between them could be forgotten. V'ornn and Kundalan, conqueror and conquered. With this devastation, how could there ever be a twining? Possibly even a true understanding was beyond their reach. She felt suddenly ashamed, alone amid her newfound friends. She wondered whether they were friends at all, and this thought chilled her. Could she have been so wrong about them? Could she have been so wrong about her calling, about the hope she felt beating like another heart inside her?

Silently, nursing their own thoughts, shock, disappointments, they proceeded down the slope. It felt odd, almost painful, to cross the perimeter of the circle of devastation.

They all stopped and turned, looking back at it, and none of them felt free.

They advanced deeper into the woods where Gerwa had stashed the war materiel they had brought with them when they had hijacked the Khaggun convoy. Their hearts leapt when they saw the undisturbed earth, and they moved aside the seven stones that marked the cache and set about drawing it out into the light. New-model ion cannons, proximity mines, ion-pulse projectors, they were all there, wrapped in their monomolecular shipping skins.

Much later, after they had armed themselves, after they had killed, cooked, and eaten a brace of ice-hares, they sat around a crackling fire. The flames warmed them, but they also fitfully illuminated the humped remains of the Resistance cell. Marethyn told stories of her childhood, of her grandmother Tettsie, who had been involved with the Resistance. In this way she tried to draw her compatriots out of their shells, but even when they spoke in turn of their own childhoods, their faces were clouded in misery and something Marethyn judged far worse: despair. The heavy blanket of night had dispelled the brief elation of finding the weapons cache intact, of knowing that Gerwa had gone to his death protecting that secret.

Marethyn was grappling with her own dreadful vision. In her mind's eye she saw Kin standing at the far side of the dell. Wrapped in the horror of so many deaths, he had ignored the approach of his own. But perhaps Majja had been right. Perhaps he had known it was coming, but had bravely staved it off until they had arrived. Marethyn suspected that one day, when her grievous wound had sufficiently healed, she would derive some solace from the notion. Now she was simply haunted by it.

By her estimation, Basse was changed the most. Possibly this was not so surprising. She had heard that those who recovered from the point of death were reborn in every way. He seemed to her remote, almost removed from the new reality they faced. He refused the laaga stick

Majja offered him. Even Marethyn took a puff or two to calm her nerves. But Basse sat with his new ion cannon across his knees and stared out into the blackness. Every time his finger slipped into the trigger guard she wondered if he was concentrating all his energies on conjuring up the enemy. He wanted to kill, that much was plain enough to see. But there was about him an icy calm that belied any sense of recklessness. She could almost hear the gears in his mind clicking and meshing, working out how his revenge would unwind once he came upon the perpetrators of the atrocity. But she wondered whether she was right. She wondered if she even knew him now.

At last, her eyelids grew heavy, and she slept.

L ujon," Kurgan said, "what are you doing here?"
"Coincidence," Lujon said.

Kurgan laughed at the lie, the sound cut off prematurely by the whiff of foul smell he swallowed.

"Personally, I do not believe in coincidence." His fist tightened on ion-pistol grips. "What is your business here? Somehow you knew this was my destination. How?"

Lujon spread his hands. "When we walk a crooked path, brambles cannot hurt our feet."

"Meaning?" The reek. Decomposition, bacteria forming colonies, eating into dead flesh.

Lujon pointed to the banestone. "Only a child or a fool asks for an explanation to the obvious, regent."

Kurgan stood his ground. "The banestone told you? Impossible. The banestone is mine."

"What is your explanation then?"

"I don't need to give one." The blades swung by overhead. "I am V'ornn." Drawing his ion pistol. "What are you?"

"You don't want to fire that, believe us, regent."

Kurgan was infuriated. "You are nothing, an insignificant bloodfly crawling on the ass of the universe." Why hadn't he seen that all along? Dimly, he realized that his unquenchable thirst for knowledge, for power, was causing him to miss the small signs of betrayal the Old V'ornn had taught him to seek out.

"The moment we asked you about the banestone we suspected you were the one who had found it." Lujon took a step toward Kurgan. "Foolish to think you could hide it from us."

Kurgan shook his head. "Back off. I will kill you."

"The banestone belongs to us. You must understand this, regent."

"What I understand, Lujon, is your place in the Cosmos. At my feet, licking my boots."

"An uncomfortable position, is it not?"

"Too bad. For you."

"In any event, you do not want to keep the banestone. As long as it is in your possession it will continue to behave erratically. It has already begun to affect you in ways you cannot imagine. But it is not too late. Hand it over and—"

"Stay where you are."

"Give us the banestone."

Kurgan aimed the ion pistol at Lujon's chest.

"Careful, regent."

"This one is mine now, Lujon. You are sorely mistaken if you think I will give it to you."

The Sarakkon had a smile reminiscent of teeth sunk deep into flesh. A carnivore's delighted expression at fresh prey. "It would be disingenuous to expect a V'ornn to treat us with respect, let alone give us anything."

"Respect is for equals. From the moment I met you, you have been operating as if you have the run of Kundala, as if you do not understand your situation at all."

"With respect, regent, it is you who does not comprehend your situation." Lujon opening his left hand, a pearly length of intestine, glistening with secretions, was revealed there. He wrapped it around his wrist.

"What are you—?" Kurgan spat, taking a step back.

Lujon kicking a dark mass in the shadows. Rolling over, a Deirus' pale, unlovely face appeared in dusty sunlight.

Streaked with blood. A newly rendered corpse. The stench rose from the open cavity where his guts had been.

"Necromancy, regent." Dark eyes gauging Kurgan's evolving reaction. "A sauromician specialty, but we are a quick study. Interested?"

Kurgan said nothing. On the other hand, his gaze remained on the grisly bracelet.

"It gives us extraordinary power." Lujon's eyes closed for a moment, moving rapidly beneath the lids. When he looked at Kurgan, he said, "Friends of yours are on their way here. Two females and—astonishingly enough . . ." Cocked his head. "Was this the Rappa that bit you?"

Kurgan silent, watching. Eleana. Hearts pounding in his chest, taste of his own blood in his mouth. No time for self-loathing now.

Lujon's silky voice. "Is this of interest to you, regent?"

"How close?" A hoarse rasp ejected from his throat.

"Our present to you, regent. We would not want it said that Sarakkon aren't generous."

In the middle of the night Marethyn awoke, not with a start but with full consciousness. She had been dreaming of the treacherous slope of the southwest escarpment, of Kin, of him slipping, of her reaching out for him, of her being that tiniest bit too late, so that when she grabbed him his momentum took her off their feet. They were both falling when she awoke.

She was cold and wet. She breathed deeply of the forest air, which never seemed so sweet to her. A rain had settled the pall, the last hovering detritus of death, onto the ground, but it had stopped. The black circle glittered all around her.

Majja was curled up, asleep, but Basse was sitting just as he had been when she had dozed off. She stirred to ease an ache, and his gaze fell against her like the weight of a wall.

She smiled at him, but his eyes locked her out. There was something dark and frightening about them.

"What is it?"

He shook his head and turned his head away. Marethyn scrambled up and moved into his line of vision. She nodded uncertainly.

"V'ornn did this," he said.

A small chill swept through her. And now she understood his expression; she had seen that look of hatred before. "But you know me. You know how I feel?"

"How could I—a Kundalan—possibly know what you feel."

"Basse, we have fought side by side. We are comrades in arms."

"I thought that once."

"I don't understand."

"You think I don't see what is happening here, how you are taking control?"

"I am just—"

"Maybe Majja will put up with it, but I won't."

"What will I put up with?"

At the sound of Majja's voice they both turned. So intent on each other had they been that they were unaware their voices had awakened her. She stood over them, fists on hips.

"What will I put up with that you won't, Basse?"

"She is ordering us around, taking over."

Majja squatted in front of him. "Which orders did you object to? Which ones were stupid or wrong?"

He sat there, silent and unmoving.

"Which ones, Basse?"

He turned his head away.

"Answer me!"

"I don't have to answer to you or to her!"

"Will you go it alone?" Majja asked.

"If need be!"

"But it *doesn't* need to be." She took his hand between hers. "We are a unit, Basse. We have been ever since we were ambushed. We've looked out for each other, faced death together, killed together. What is the matter with you?"

He tugged his hand free. "Look all around you," he said fiercely. "Look what they've done to us. For the love of Miina, she's one of *them*!"

"So you'll condemn her, even after all she has done for us."

"This is war, Majja. We can't afford to trust her."

"Basse, we can't afford not to." She put her hands on either side of his face so she could look into his eyes. "If we forget everything she's done for us, if we forget our connection together, then what have we become? Nothing more than the animals the V'ornn believe us to be. Is that what you want? Really? I can't believe—"

She stopped in midsentence, silently watching the tears roll down his cheeks.

"I've tried to make sense of it, but I can't. I almost died, and the others here, they're all dead. Why was I saved, Majja? Why?" His shoulders began to shake as he took great sobs of air.

"Oh, Basse," she whispered, and enfolded him in her arms. She rocked him back and forth, kissing the top of his head. She looked at Marethyn, who squatted nearby, and Marethyn gave her a sad, little smile.

Long after the others fell asleep, Marethyn remained awake. She listened to the tiny symphony of the forest sounds and was somewhat comforted. How many times had she thought of Sornnn? How many times had she strained to conjured up his face? Though part of her continued to long for his arms, that life now seemed very far away. She could scarcely remember what her atelier looked like, and when she thought about Axis Tyr she kept confusing Divination Street and Momentum Boulevard.

She pulled the night sounds of her new home around her as if they were a blanket. She listened harder, waiting for another, deeper stirring. She wondered if Basse heard the voices of the dead calling him in his sleep. She summoned the thought of Hellespennn. So many V'ornn dead, an entire fleet annihilated. She knew at least a semblance of the anguish Basse must be going through. But how deeply had

his near-death experience changed him? Would even Majja be able to say? She sighed softly. If he did not hear the
voices of the dead, surely she did. With that thought in
mind, she slowly drifted off.

The next morning dawned bright and chill, with none
of the threat inherent in yesterday's incipient storm. Sunlight made bright, quick sparks within the black circle
and a deep blue sky stretched itself overhead. After a
light breakfast, Marethyn filled a cauldron she and Majja
had scavenged with water and put it over the fire Basse
had relit. Last night, they had found it difficult to eat
meat that had about it a blackened edge, but this morning
they ate hungrily, for they knew some sense of normalcy
had to be restored to their lives in order for them to go
about living it again.

Basse avoided her gaze, and she thought it best not to
talk to him. She had awakened with another idea. Possibly
the voices of the dead had whispered it in her ear while
she slept.

As the water heated up, she scooped handfuls of charcoal into the cauldron. Her companions looked aghast.

"What are you doing?" Basse said, renewed anger flush-
ing his face. "Is this another stupid piece of art? Why
don't you go back to Axis Tyr with the other V'ornn?"

Even Majja was uncomfortable. "Those are likely our
compatriots," she said.

Marethyn continued scooping. They did not help her.
Basse glowered but he did not stop her. Marethyn thought
that must be a good sign. When the water was as black as
ink, as thick as blood she stopped. Then she stripped off
all her clothes and threw them one by one into the steaming cauldron.

"Will you do the same?" she asked them.

They stared at her for a moment, then Majja disrobed
and threw her clothes into the black water. Basse stood
watching them, arms folded across his chest. Naked, the
two females took turns stirring the cauldron with a long

green-birch switch. Its delicate color soon turned muddy, then deepest black.

After about an hour, Marethyn took out a piece of sopping clothing. It was her tunic, and it was dyed as black as the switch. She held it up like a standard, which in a way it had become.

"From this moment forward we are the Black Guard," she said. "We are the end of all things. Our clothes are black as night. They honor those who died here, but they also serve notice on our enemies that we wear on our backs their own death."

Majja plucked out her own tunic, held it up. "The Black Guard."

Basse looked on stonily. Majja went to him, put her hand on his shoulder, spoke to him softly. In response he turned his back on Marethyn, on the fire. Majja, talking to him still, managed to get his tunic off him. She threw it into the boiling water. He would not remove his breeches, though, and stood, stolid and stoic, arms crossed over his chest, unmoving until his tunic, black as pitch, was ready. Majja spoke to him again, and he lifted his arms like a child so she could slip it over him.

25

Skreeling

The high doors of the Abbey of Five Pivots were closed, locked tight behind gates of petrified heartwood, as Krystren wearily made her way toward them. Periodically, she turned, searching with her mind for any sign of Varda. Though she found none, the atmosphere had taken on a charged quality akin to that before a violent storm. Above, filthy-looking clouds raced by, their edges torn and ragged. Wind whistled through the crenellated cornices of the abbey's pale walls, causing an eerie moaning. But of the Eye of Ajbal there was no trace whatsoever.

When she was no more than a pace or two from them, the spiked bars creaked open just wide enough for her to slip through sideways. They swung shut the moment she was inside, trapping her in a narrow space with the gates behind her and the arched cinnamon-chalcedony doors in front of her.

She went up to the doors, put the flat of her hands on the mineral slabs. Remarkably, she could find no seam with her fingers. That was why she started when her fingertips sank in nails deep. She pulled her hand free and, a moment later, the doors opened soundlessly inward. She hesitated a moment before she went through. Instantly, the doors closed behind her.

She found herself in a courtyard composed of golden gravel—tiny, round, glinting. It was shaped like two triangles, one facing her, the other inverted, superimposed one upon the other. On the far side of the courtyard rose the imposing column of the central tower, impossibly slender, slightly tapering, whiter than the ice caps of the highest peaks of the Djenn Marre. The clusters of sapphires on the taffy-pull dome sparked and danced in blinding shots of clearest blue.

Unfamiliar and exotic scents came to her, doubtless from the herb beds that rimmed the courtyard on all sides. They should have been overgrown, but they were not. On the contrary, they looked newly shorn and shaped. Likewise, whatever damage had been done by the Khagggun invasion decades ago had been repaired in a way that made it appear as if it had never occurred.

At the bottom of the tower was an open archway, and Krystren felt drawn to it in the same manner in which she had been drawn to touch the mineral doors. In a kind of daze, she walked across the gravel, which gave off only the slightest whisper beneath her boot soles.

It was only when she was halfway across that she suddenly remembered that Minnum was not with her. She stopped and turned all the way around, as if he were lagging somewhere and she only need call his name and he would appear. But he would not appear, not ever again. She felt his death in the same way she would a wound that had not yet healed. There was only the occasional stab of pain, but it ached all the time, and there was a drawing sensation as if a small part of her was gone. She wondered at this, for she had known him a very short time, and yet in all the deeply felt ways that mattered it seemed like a lifetime. They had fought together, had saved each other from death, and for that alone she would miss him. Her head came up, and she looked around at nothing. She felt something near her in the vast geometric abbey courtyard. If it were powerful enough, could your courage live on after you were gone? she wondered. Why not?

She turned around and continued her passage to the central tower's archway. Out of the sun it was deliciously cool. Her nose was filled with the dry, flinty scent of stone. The interior looked like the whorl of a mollusk shell, filled with the limpid blue of twilight, liquid and darkly shimmering, cast through a crystal oculus by the sapphires on the dome. In the center of this blue lagoon an alabaster spiral staircase wound upward. To one side was the polished oval of a small heartwood table with the fine, tapered legs of a forest animal. On the table was a bronze lantern, by the look of it very old.

A hush enveloped her. This was very clearly a blessed space, a temple of chants and spells, where ancient prayers had spiraled like incense. She could feel the holiness as surely as she felt the floor beneath her boots. It draped across her shoulders like a finely woven shawl. It was strange to her conscious mind, familiar to her unconscious, powerful to her whole being. It caused the fine hairs at the nape of her neck to stir.

She ran her hand lightly over the lantern's beautiful filigree before mounting the stairs. She had not gone more than a quarter of a circle when a shadow fell upon her and, looking up, she saw Giyan peering down at her from what at this distance looked like a tiny landing.

"Minnum?"

"Dead. Killed by the archon Varda."

Giyan slumped against the balustrade, so delicate it appeared inadequate to hold her. She passed a hand across her eyes, as if by the gesture she could wipe away Krystren's words and all the sadness and loss it brought.

"Can we help in any way?"

Giyan gathered herself. She extended her arm and opened her hand wide. All at once, Krystren felt herself being plucked up as if by an invisible fist, whooshing up the center of the spiral until she had alighted upon the same landing on which Giyan stood. It was, in fact, not tiny at all.

"He died with great courage," Krystren said in a solemn voice. "He saved us from death at the hands of the *Ardinal*." There was more, of course, but she could not bring herself to utter a word of it. The kiss, the words, all that passed between her and Minnum in those last moments were private. They were preserved for her alone.

Giyan sighed. "I saw this two days ago."

"It's true, then, what we have heard about Ramahan."

"Luckily, only a very few are seers," Giyan told her. "It is a gift and a curse I would give almost anything not to have."

Giyan had been leading the way into a circular room that must surely be within the taffy-pull dome of the tower. Save for three smallish windows, the entire circumference was filled from green-porphyry floor to marvelously muraled ceiling with shelves stuffed with books. It was the abbey Library. On either side of the room stood a matched pair of filigreed tables with articulated sections that lifted up to support at an angle convenient for reading the larger and heavier tomes. The center of the room was taken up with what appeared to be a curious polished brass-and-green-jade ladder complete with a seat on its platformlike top step.

"But if you knew, why did you let him stay? You could have saved him, taken him with you."

"Could I? Minnum wanted only one thing from life—to be considered a hero. He was tormented by his sins, was certain he would never be able to atone for them, never be found worthy. What kind of a life was that? Now, by your own reckoning, he *is* a hero. Besides, I cannot decide who lives and who dies. I see a future, but it is only one of many. I had to return to the abbey. It wasn't a happy choice, but it had to be made."

Giyan went over to the ladder, put a hand on it. "The reason this abbey is called Five Pivots is because the five towers were built to harness the power bourns that run deep beneath the foundation. In order to destroy the Eye of Ajbal I needed the help of this—the *kalqin* links the towers, brings them into synergy, so their power is harnessed, like a lens that magnifies sunlight."

"Could you use it to find Varda?"

"I tried just as soon as I was able to disable the Eye of Ajbal. I could sense him, but I couldn't see him."

"He is near then."

Giyan nodded. "We must be on our guard. He will doubtless wish to exact revenge for the death of Caligo."

"How powerful is he? It is our understanding that Miina stripped the sauromicians of most of their sorcerous knowledge."

Giyan lifted her arms. "Do you see the gaps in the books stacks? The Sarakkon the sauromicians enlisted have raided the Library. Varda and those archons with him have been regaining power almost as fast as they can read. In addition, they are using necromancy, a branch of sorcery Ramahan are almost entirely unfamiliar with. It is forbidden knowledge, and with good reason."

Krystren recalled the terrible truths she had learned about necromancy while with Bryn and the *gabir*.

Giyan ran a hand through her hair. "This is where we will miss Minnum the most." Folding herself heavily onto a wide wooden chair, she sat brooding for a time. "I saw the crossroad at Five Pivots," she said at last, "the parting of the ways at the abbey. I prayed that his future, *our* future would be otherwise."

Krystren saw in her mind's eye the terrible burden Giyan was obliged to carry, and said so. "Even for high Ramahan, we see, prayers are not always answered."

Giyan fixed Krystren with her beryl stare, lines of sorrow etched into her beautiful face. "Miina answers all prayers. It is for us to discover how." She smiled wanly. "Sometimes it takes a lifetime."

In the holy stillness of the Library, Krystren thought of the last kiss, the pleasure on Minnum's face, the look in his eyes knowing that she was holding him. Despite her training, something about him had tugged at her heart. Strong emotion, a stranger, had unbeknownst to her crawled into her house, there to lodge with a passionate tenacity.

At length, Giyan rose slowly, almost painfully. "Come now, we must honor Minnum's life."

Together, they ground soft amber in a mortar and pestle, lit the resulting powder. The musky fragrance drifted upward while Giyan intoned a prayer.

"Great Goddess, welcome Minnum, Your child in heart, spirit and mind. Gather him in Your benevolence and protect him. Celebrate with us the hero he has become, the fulfillment of his destiny. Take his hand, walk with him through the shadows and the light, through the Darkness of Eternity and out the other side. May he be reborn with the knowledge You hold in Your heart, with the wisdom that flourishes in the Realms beyond ours, with a loving heart, with a virtuous step."

Gul Aluf wanted Sahor to stay with her, and he agreed. It took some time and coaxing on her part, but in the end he gave in. He did not want her to know how eager he was to remain in the Temple of Mnemonics.

They had had to leave Nith Batoxxx's lab-orb precipitously because Nith Immmon had been made aware that Nith Nassam was on his way there and, as Sahor had suspected, Nith Immmon did not want to have to explain the presence of what would appear to be a Kundalan in the hallowed precincts of the Comradeship.

Guls did not sleep, exactly, and Gul Aluf was no exception. They did, like all living creatures, require rest and rejuvenation. Even as their physical bodies were renewed, their neural pathways were plugged into the neural nets, where they worked on genetic innovations for the Gyrgon children they were creating. Innovation was the Guls' watchword, none more so than Gul Aluf.

When Sahor, who had been asleep, awakened himself at a predetermined time and saw Gul Aluf in a deep dream state, he silently rose. As he dressed he watched her. While it was true that Gyrgon were both male and female, it was also true that the majority of Niths were more male than female. For Guls, the opposite was true. There was, however, no hard-and-fast rule. The fact of the matter was that some Niths—and Nith Immmon was one of them— preferred the company of other Niths when they coupled. That was, of course, why Sahor had betrayed his true feelings when he had asked Gul Aluf if she and Nith Immmon were together. On a larger canvas, it was also why the Comradeship had cast the Deirus out of the mainstream of V'ornn society. Same-sex love, it was decided, should be the sole province of Gyrgon. It worried and somewhat frightened the Comradeship that the Deirus should exhibit this particular trait, and so it denigrated it, made it tacitly illicit.

Seeing Gul Aluf calm, innocent as a child, made him realize that if he truly wanted to transform her way of thinking, he was going about it in the wrong way, for she would never respond to his arguments; in fact, the force of them only reinforced her own point of view. She had an indomitable spirit, and it was, in part what drew him to her. But it also meant that she would be conquered by no Nith, even him. He knew then that he needed to clear his mind absolutely of any intent whatsoever. Only then would he have a chance of changing her mind.

Why was he thinking about it, anyway? Didn't he love her? And if he didn't love her, what then *did* he feel? If not love, what? Lust? Certainly, the two of them were no good for each other. If the last day proved anything, it was that. And when he weighed her on the same scale on which he put those he did love—Riane, Giyan, Eleana, and the rest—he found her sorely wanting. The truth was he loved the Kundalan more than he loved his own species. In fact, if he were to be brutally honest with himself—and in such dire circumstances why not?—he knew that, excepting his father, he had never loved another V'ornn. When he thought of them the emotion that most often came to mind was contempt.

Pushing these disquieting thoughts aside, he proceeded through the labyrinth of the Temple of Mnemonics. He had to be exceedingly careful, he had to have a map in his head of the maze, he had to wrap himself in shadows as if they were his old Nith greatcoat, he had to think about nothing but getting from here to there. For, unlike other Gyrgon facilities, the Temple of Mnemonics was never idle. Neither were its corridors and cubicles deserted. There was a saying among V'ornn of lesser castes, promulgated by Gyrgon, and it was essentially true: The Temple never sleeps. The larger Kundalan-designed chambers on the ground floor, such as the great listening hall where the weekly convocations were held, were for the most part kept intact. The rest of the original Kundalan structure had been more or less hollowed out, replaced by a three-dimensional grid, a hive of industry tailor-made for a comradeship of technomages. Because they were, at hearts, experimenters, Gyrgon liked their privacy, so quarters were separate, as were their lab-orbs. Viewed as a whole, the schemata resembled nothing so much as a gigantic molecule, which, considering their vocation, was altogether appropriate. The layers of living quarters and laborbs were separated by strategically placed fusion generators, photon links and ion-powered substations. And then, of course, there were the Guls' Crowns of Creation, where the Comradeship was perpetuated.

As he moved through that great geometric tangle, Sahor reviewed the list of his enemies, those Gyrgon loyal to Nith Batoxxx and all that he stood for. Now Nith Nassam had taken Nith Batoxxx's place. There was always one to take up the fallen standard. It seemed decades since the Comradeship had spoken with one voice. He had considered the possibility that it was Kundala itself that had sundered the Comradeship, that this was, in fact, a necessary process, a step in some unknown evolution that had begun the moment they had set foot on this world. He knew Gul Aluf would disagree, and so would Nith Nassam and probably Nith Immmon as well. But then they did not see Kundala as he did. He could they? They still believed that Stasis and Harmony were synonymous. He could not imagine in what part of the Cosmos that might be true. He wondered whether it had ever been true. Certainly, it was not the case there on Kundala, a world that thrived on change. It was altogether possible, he knew, that the Comradeship had long ago created their creed in order to perpetuate its power. He wondered whether those who did not understand the essential truth of change—or Transformation, as the Ramahan called it—would one day be swept aside in Anamordor, the great cataclysm the Ramahan believed was coming. Sahor, too, believed it was coming, with all his hearts and soul.

He scrutinized every Gyrgon who passed him. He listened to snatches of their conversations as he melted into corners, stood unmoving in shallow alcoves, attached himself to shadowed walls. He was still finding out things about his new hybrid self. This ability to blend into his environment at will was one of them. There were so many possibilities and pathways. Nothing like him had ever existed before. He was a living experiment in progress, which meant any Gyrgon in the Comradeship would kill to get his hands on him, split him open, find out what made him tick, why he was still alive.

His progress could be charted best on a warrnixx spiral. There was no direct path from Gul Aluf's quarters to Nith Batoxxx's lab-orb. Even if there had been, he wouldn't have taken it. Two steps forward, one step back. Three steps forward, two steps to the right or left. He was up against many impediments, living and quasi-living, for as he well knew the Temple of Mnemonics was laced with all manner of security devices, and if you were no longer Nith, you needed an encyclopedic knowledge of them to avoid tripping them. Some would set off photonic alarms, others, like the null-wave nets, would enmesh the unwary in a force webbing or paralyze the intruder, still others would kill on the spot. Seemingly innocent-looking ramps, gangways, photon lifts held such thorns, invisible and undetectable to the untrained eye.

Despite all the hazards, Sahor made it to Nith Batoxxx's orb-lab without incident. He had watched Nith Immmon open the photon lock and he repeated the procedure, which was, like everything surrounding Nith Batoxxx, unorthodox inasmuch as it employed the antiquated and, therefore, virtually unremembered Nangian scale. Sahor knew of it, though. It had been first taught to him by his father, who used it in some of his sonic sculpture. Lucky for him, for quite by accident he had discovered that Venca, the original language of the Ramahan, was curiously similar to the Nangian scale.

Closing the access hatch behind him, he activated the lab's illumination at its lowest level. The interior glowed with a nacreous iridescence as if it were the inside of a muodd shell. He stood for a moment, inhaling the scent of orangesweet. Then he crossed to the place where he had been standing when Nith Immmon had ordered them out.

He increased the intensity of the glow as he put his face

close to the blossoms. He marveled at the constructs. They were perfect. Almost. He would have done it differently, of course. The problem was that though Nith Batoxxx had programmed in surface blemishes, the structure of the blossoms themselves was *absolutely* perfect. Each petal was exactly the same height and width. Each blossom perfectly symmetrical. Nature did not work that way.

One by one, he touched them, feeling the difference on their insides where the neural nets held the data. He felt around at the base of the blossom where it met the vine and disconnected the construct. He took it to one of the task stations. The stem fit perfectly into the small cylindrical slot which, it was now clear, Nith Batoxxx had manufactured for it.

He keyed in the datastream and on the task station holoscreen up popped a pair of birth cauls. He froze the images to study them better. He just had time to identify them as belonging to Kurgan and Terrettt Stogggul when he became aware of a subtle change in the bio lab's atmosphere.

He took the artificial blossom from the data slot a moment before the lights went up full. His back was to the access hatch. Whoever was there could not see him palm the blossom. He turned and saw Gul Aluf walking toward him. Her wings were folded tight to her torso.

"I thought we had an agreement," she said. "Why are you doing this to me?"

"I don't think you should take this personally."

"I knew you had found something. I suppose I should not be overly surprised that you have chosen to keep it from me." She smiled with her teeth. "You have chosen to keep so much from me, Sahor."

"You should not use my name here, ever."

"You're right, of course. The walls have neural nets." She stopped very close to him. "Nevertheless, I will do what I want."

"As is your right as Breeder," he said.

"Let us not procrastinate further." She pointed to the holoscreen. "Tell me everything. Now."

Sahor debated the best of several poor choices. The best lies were sown in the seedbed of truth.

"Look." He turned the holoscreen so that she had a clear view.

Her eyes widened. "Stogggul Terrettt's and Stogggul Kurgan's birth cauls."

Was it significant that she put Terrettt's name first? Sahor wondered. "What would Nith Batoxxx want with them?"

For some time, she said nothing, bent over his right shoulder, one palm flat on the surface of the task station, eyes eating up the image. At length, she said, "Go on. What else have you found?"

"That's it," he said.

"That cannot be all." She stood up. "There is more, I know it."

She knew why Nith Batoxxx was interested in the Stogggul brothers' birth cauls, Sahor thought. "Not so surprising seeing them here," he said. "After all, it was Nith Batoxxx who wanted the Ashera hold on the regent's post ended. It was he who pushed the Comradeship into accepting the Stogggul as replacement." He was watching Gul Aluf, but she said nothing. "Even you thought he was mad to want Stogggul Wennn as regent. But he didn't, not really. He saw beyond the weak-willed father to the clever and ambitious son. It was his plan to install Stogggul Kurgan as regent all along. The question is why."

"He raised the boy from before the time of his Ascendance." Gul Aluf's gaze had been drawn back to the images of the birth cauls, as if for her they were magnetic. "He could control him absolutely."

"At least he thought he could," Sahor pointed out. "In the end, Stogggul Kurgan proved too clever even for Nith Batoxxx."

"There is something about the Stogggul line," she said, almost to herself, "something about the brothers."

"Terrettt has been incarcerated inside Receiving Spirit

for years," Sahor said. "He is the victim of an untreatable madness."

Gul Aluf was looking from one birth caul to another. "The madness is a by-product."

"A by-product? Of what?"

"That is precisely what I would like to know."

They both turned at once to see Nith Nassam standing in the open hatchway of the goron-wave chamber.

Minnum was resurrected in Krystren's mind, his kindly face, kindlier heart. His last words.

"In all the sorrow and uncertainty we forgot to say. Minnum told us, made us promise we would tell you—"

Giyan was instantly on alert. "What?"

"What was it?" Krystren, brows knit, cast a different look to her tattoos. Snapped her fingers. "Yes. Spirit Bell. He said, 'I have attached Spirit Bell to him,' or something of the sort."

"Are you sure?"

"Indeed, yes." Could hear again his voice, low and damp with blood, his careful articulation a clue to import.

"Minnum, bless him!, cast a Sticky Spell—one spell inside another, like a seed inside a fruit. Undetectable, it attaches itself even if the outer spell goes awry. They can do many things, Sticky Spells. This one—Spirit Bell—will track Varda wherever he goes."

Giyan, eyes closed, conjured Spirit Bell, found its particular note among a blizzard of others, spent a moment or two attuning herself to it, aligning herself, so that she and it vibrated at the same frequency, tracing it back, softly now.

"I see him, but for some reason I cannot tell where he is." Her voice husky, slightly out of time.

Krystren was forced closer. Head bent, ear cocked. Intent on every word, every nuance in every word. "Is he blocking you?" Her voice also hushed, like a Sarakkon fishing, so as to ensure the evening's dinner.

"Something is."

A little shiver ran down Krystren's spine. "What are we to do?"

"Not to worry, my dear." Giyan massaged her temples with delicate fingertips. "The Skreeling Engine will find him."

She rose and climbed the innocuous-looking library ladder. Gaining the top, she sat and was immediately engulfed in a column of amber light. Krystren stepped back, her eyes squeezed to mere slits. The glare from the column seemed greater in one section. Dimly, she could see Giyan moving her hands, and then the glare began to move, swinging around like the lantern in a lighthouse, a brilliant beam of amber light revolving.

A great juddering almost threw her off her feet, and she ran to the walls of shelves beneath one of the three small windows, thrust books away, clouds of dust rising like bloodflies, as she mounted the shelves to get a view. More books flew off the shelves, not of her doing. They slid across the floor, pages waving like fans.

Out the window, the forest was moving—or, more accurately, the tower was. She could see two of the other towers, also moving, leaning in concert as if they were trees bending in a high wind.

Inside the column of amber light Giyan worked feverishly. She had no experience working the great Skreeling Engine of Five Pivots, though she had read the classic text on it written by Konara Leau in a lucid style uncommon for ancient konara. She drew on that knowledge now, allowed it to mingle with her intuition, for she rang in her mind the particular note that Minnum—Miina keep and bless him!—had with Spirit Bell attached to Varda. She aligned the Skreeling Engine with the tone.

Long ago, when Osoru was still in its infancy, konara had devised the Skreeling Engine as a way of listening to the Cosmos, feeling their way along the buried bourns whose purpose was at that time mostly unknown. What the Skreeling Engine did was listen and report back, and from this data the Ramahan of ancient times began to amass information about space, time, and the interstices in between.

What Giyan was attempting to do now was align the Skreeling Engine with the sorcerous link to Varda the Sticky Spell had left. It was essential to divine where he was and what he was doing. For in truth she feared him, feared what he had become, what he would become if his unholy liaison with the ascendant sauromicians was allowed to continue.

Like a wyr-hound on the hunt, the Skreeling Engine sniffed out the Sticky Spell, opened its eye on the subject. What the engine showed her were tracks like footprints in the snow, the eely wake of a fish's progress through ultramarine water, the path of a storm etched in twilight by plumed spindrift. Darkness made visible by Skreeling.

And in the center of the darkness, Varda, splayed out on a rock barely a kilometer south of the abbey. His torso was stretched like the arc of a bow, arms flung to either side, fingers curled into knots of muscle. His head was thrown back, eyes open and staring. Mouth wide-open. And from its cavity emerged a conversation of sorts, one that did not involve Varda at all. Now and again his muscles jumped as if in galvanic response. While his tongue clove to the roof of his mouth, eyes wide and rolling as if in seizure.

Giyan counted eight distinct voices, though they were not voices at all, at least not in the usual sense. They belonged neither to sauromician nor to Sarakkon, belonged in fact to no breathing being.

A sense of dread wormed its way into her soul, for the Skreeling identified the source of the conversation—not where but what. Eight banestones, linked. Banestones found, somehow, how? In the Korrush, the back of beyond where even the Five Tribes rarely ventured. So there had been a reason for the sauromician flight. It had not been, as had been assumed even by Minnum, a headlong flight to the farthest reaches of Kundala. No. The archons had had a plan in mind all along. And they had spent the years of their bitter exile more fruitfully than anyone could have guessed. They had learned necromancy, waiting patient as kris-spiders for the knowledge to build sufficiently to turn to their search for the scattered banestones. They had used their necromantic arts to find them, for the newly dead could feel the banestones' dark emanations and, forced to speak to their new sauromician masters, revealed the burial grounds. The very first one was passed around from archon to archon, and as their bare skin came in contact with it, the banestones altered them forever. And so the sauromicians amassed the stones one by one, hoarding them, caressing them as a male will a female, sinking deeper and deeper into their spell, until eight had come into their possession. And what had the sauromicians done with the eight banestones? She had recalibrated the Skreeling Engine to home in on the cache of banestones. And again the Engine provided the answer—what but not where.

She gasped. Against all odds, the unthinkable had happened: the Cage had been forged. But for what purpose? Without that knowledge it was impossible to know how to prepare to dismantle it, for different purposes changed the shape of the Cage, which in turn changed the nature of the sorcery invoked. The Cage could be used for many things, provided one had the knowledge: it could imprison Dragons, open the Portals to the Abyss, or, Miina forbid, become the great weapon created at Za Hara-at. How much forbidden knowledge had the sauromicians derived from this Library? There was no way to know unless you could coerce an archon into telling you.

A warning sounded from the Engine, and her attention snapped back. She saw that Varda was now sitting up. She saw his head turning in her direction. Could he have become aware of the Skreeling?

With a bang, she shut it all down, the towers' juddering subsided, the slanting floor returned to level. The amber light winked out.

"What did you see?" Krystren's face was tight with worry. "What did it tell you?"

"Varda." Climbing down from the ladder. "In some way I cannot yet understand he had become aware of me."

"Does he know where you are?"

"I am not certain, but I do not think so. I think I shut down the Engine in time."

Krystren thought a moment. "What would happen if you used the Engine to find him again? Would he be able to locate you?"

"There is no way to say for sure, but it seems likely."

"That is what we thought." A small smile crept across Krystren's face, and she fingered the crystal knife she had stolen from him. "We say let him come."

Before they had a chance to react, Nith Nassam sent a serpent of coruscating light from the fingertips of his ion-matrix glove. Gul Aluf's countermove only split the serpent in two, and they passed through her furled wings, pinioning her in place. A kind of photonic cocoon wove it-self about her legs, torso, and arms, binding her faster the more she tried to shake herself free.

"Are you insane?" Gul Aluf said. "It is forbidden to at-tack a Breeder."

"But not unprecedented." Nith Nassam turned his hand over, and the cocoon quickly wound itself around her mouth. "Now." He turned to Sahor. "What have we here?" Another serpent of light circled his hand, both its head and tail questing, ready at a moment's notice to be sped on its way. "Certainly, you look like a Kundalan." He cocked his head inquisitively. "But you neither speak like one nor act like one."

Sahor held himself still. He knew that Nith Nassam had been both lucky and clever. Lucky that he had been able to attack in surprise, clever to have used photonic lances. Had he chosen, instead, any of a thousand ion-based weapons, Gul Aluf would have been able to fight him off.

But Breeders so highly attuned to photons in their work were vulnerable to photon-based weapons.

"How could you be Kundalan?" Nith Nassam began to circle him. "You are in the Temple of Mnemonics, you know your way around a lab-orb, you are familiar with both a Gul and a Nith." He stopped so that he was just out of Sahor's field of vision. "Not so difficult a puzzle to solve." He smiled cruelly. "Even if I had not heard the Breeder call you by name."

He looped the photon lance around Sahor's neck, forming a loose collar. "If I didn't see you, I would not have believed it. Nith Sahor alive." The photon lance did not touch him, but floated ominously, not a centimeter from his skin.

"So the question is not who are, but *what* are you? A photon shell, a construct? Or something *other,* something we have never seen before?"

Sahor was watching Gul Aluf—more specifically, her eyes. She always did have expressive eyes, no matter which guise she was in.

"Why are you looking at Gul Aluf?" Nith Nassam said. "Do you think the Breeder will be able to help you?" He turned his hand over and with an eerie scratching sound the cocoon drew tighter so that Gul Aluf groaned through her gag.

He turned back to Sahor. "I see that you will need further persuasion." He tightened the photon lance around Sahor's neck. "Do you imagine that you are strong enough to resist me? Ah, Sahor, you have an exaggerated sense of your resiliency and strength. I will break you, one way or another." As it contracted, the photon lance crawled against Sahor's skin like an army of carnivorous insects. "In a moment, I shall instruct the photon lance to create a field of tiny blades. Ever so slowly, they will emerge from the inside of the collar, piercing your skin and cartilage. I will drain the blood, of course. I don't want you prematurely drowning."

Sahor, breath already beginning to strangle in his constricted throat, tried to ignore him. He knew that without Gul Aluf's help he would not get out of this predicament.

"Here they come." Nith Nassam studied Sahor with eyes turned obsidian-black. "Do you feel them, Sahor, the ten thousand tiny blades."

Sahor steeled himself as the pain came crashing in on him.

26

Old Friends

R iane stood in tattered FIREFLY wondering what on Kundala Kurgan would be doing there. Dust and the smell of sex, old now, sour as a Mesagg-gun's armpits. She felt battered and bruised. Ever since she had discovered that The Pearl was a fake, that Miina had lied to even Her most devoted disciples, she had been fighting a dreadful despair. How could a goddess be so vengeful, so righteous, that She would sacrifice thousands of innocents to root out and punish the few Ramahan infecting the collective corpus of the abbeys? How could you continue to believe in such a deity? Why would you want to, anyway?

"Love." Eleana's hand on her arm. "I am uncomfortable staying in one place."

Thigpen nodded. There was about the building, a creepy air of sentience, as if they were being watched by the portraits on the walls, the sculpted figures, sinuous, naked, wrapped around lamp bases or stone bowls, lit by their own reflections in stained mirrors. The trio went silently through the pleasure chambers on the ground floor, for the moment passed up the stair to explore the back rooms—

small servants' quarters, explosive with dust, mold along the bottom of the window sash, mildew, an animal stench, sharp and acrid in the tiny bath. They came next, on the other side, to an expansive, low-ceilinged kitchen. Light spilled through windows that flanked a service door. Beneath the windows were square soapstone sinks large enough to bathe twins, a central island on which had taken place the bloodletting of many a fowl and cor haunch, with a narrow door to the larder beyond.

They heard a sound from the ceiling, a creaking from upstairs, and stood transfixed for a moment, listening. It came again, weight on dried-out floorboards. Stealthy footsteps. Riane invoked Dragonfly by speaking the Venca syllables, saw Kurgan, saw where he was precisely, saw the shadows cast by the banestone he held.

She leaned to whisper in Thigpen's ear. "Stay here with Eleana." In so doing, breaking off the spell precipitously, she remained ignorant of other shadows spreading.

"You are my primary concern, little dumpling." The Rappa bared her teeth to show her resolve. "Even if Giyan had not charged me with your protection."

"I am telling you." She took a handful of her fur, shook her lightly. "Don't let her out of your sight."

With that she was gone, Thigpen giving a low growl, Eleana looking from the Rappa to the doorway to the servants' corridor.

"Don't even think about it," Thigpen said, as Eleana tried to get around her. "There is already more than enough danger in this pit without you adding to it."

"You don't like me much, do you?"

"Don't take it personally."

Eleana looked at the Rappa for a time. "It's my relationship with the Dar Sala-at, isn't it? You don't approve."

Thigpen sniffed. "It's not for me to approve or disapprove."

"I am not trying to take your place, I assure you."

"Don't try so hard." Thigpen trotted around, pushing her snout into this corner and that, nose wrinkling, investigating. "We might as well make ourselves useful. Why don't you take a look in the pantry."

"I'm not hungry."

Thigpen bared her teeth again. "Indulge me."

Eleana went around the island and opened the narrow door. Stepped inside to the scents of spices and dried foodstuffs. The moment she was inside, Thigpen slammed the door shut, wedged a shim of wood she had ferreted out from beneath one of the sinks into the gap between the door bottom and the sill.

"Sorry," she muttered as she scampered out. "My responsibility is to the Dar Sala-at. I promised I would protect her, and that's what I'm going to do."

Eleana hammered on the door, shut tight and unmoving.

Nondescript almost to the point of invisibility, First-Captain Kwenn caused barely a ripple in the gallery gathered in the Forum of Adjudication despite the fact that Khagggun rarely looked in on Bashkir adjudications. He took a seat and stared down at the arena-like gallery floor.

The aggrieved parties in the current dispute sat at either side while in the middle stood the Prime Factor, the adjudicator. It took Kwenn only a few moments to recognize Sornnn SaTrryn as the figure at the bar the afternoon he and Pack-Commander Dacce were playing warrnixx. He was tall, handsome, and impressive in his official uniform. Kwenn studied him for a while, allowing the barrage of arguments to flow around him without paying attention to the details. There was something about the SaTrryn's eyes, the way they seemed to take in intent, what was beneath the surface gloss of legalese, that made Kwenn suspect that he was good at his role. He liked particularly Sornnn's economy of movement. He possessed a certain grace Kwenn did not automatically associate with Bashkir. He was a far cry from the sad-looking Bashkir bent over his drink at Alloy Fist.

Seeing the Prime Factor in the flesh brought home to Kwenn with a terrifying finality what he was about to do.

He knew that the moment he accosted the SaTrryn, the moment he uttered the first word, he would be committed. There would be no going back, no saying, sorry, my mistake.

But very soon the tightness in his chest that had been his companion all the way down to the Forum vanished. In its place, he found a sense of freedom he had never felt before. This was his decision. He felt as if it was the first one he had made independent of the intricate web of his caste obligations. There was no Khagggun training that covered such a circumstance. For the first time in his life he was entirely on his own.

It seemed forever before there was a break in the proceedings. During that time Kwenn had ample time to discover that he had no interest in becoming Bashkir. He couldn't imagine any Khagggun who would. Save Dacce. Dacce was an entirely different matter altogether. Somewhere along the line he had acquired a thirst for coin. That made him a mercenary, a dangerous tendency, especially for a Khagggun for whom loyalty was supposed to be a bred-in-the-bone trait.

At the break, Kwenn made his way down to where the SaTrryn was standing. He had to wait as the Prime Factor was in a tense and heated discussion with Raan Tallus. The SaTrryn cut it off abruptly, and Kwenn heard the word "inappropriate."

As Sornnn turned away from Raan Tallus, he came face-to-face with Kwenn.

"Well," he said without missing a beat, "what is a Haaar-kyut doing here?"

"Actually, I came to talk to you, Prime Factor."

"An official visit? I should be offended the regent did not come himself."

Kwenn smiled. "Not at all." Now that the moment had arrived, it was odd how light he felt. There was a certain freedom in following the dictates of your hearts, in having nothing more to lose. "This conversation is strictly between you and me." He looked around the milling Forum. "Is there somewhere more private we could go to?"

"Alloy Fist is nearby."

"A game of warrnixx perhaps?" He saw the closed look on the SaTrryn's face and was immediately sorry he had been flip. "At this point, you're right to be wary. Just give me a chance to prove you wrong."

They wound up walking instead, through a fine spring drizzle that brought the pungent odors from the outdoor food stalls. They stopped at a brazier, bought skewers of grilled meat, which they ate as they strolled. Kwenn, without seeming to, steered them clear of Khagggun patrols.

"I have a problem," Kwenn began, "and I don't know what to do about it." He had been up all night thinking of what to say and how to say it. Tong had told him that the SaTrryn was someone he could trust, but there remained the question of how to gain the SaTrryn's trust.

"I am not of your caste," Sornnn said. "How can I help you?"

"It is precisely because you are not Khagggun that I have sought you out, Prime Factor. It is your role to find answers to vexing problems."

Sornnn, who was thinking about his failure with Fleet-Admiral Pnin, finished his skewer and said nothing.

Kwenn decided to put more than his toe into the water, "Also, our mutual friend Tong suggested I talk to you."

Outwardly, Sornnn did not change, but he had suddenly gone on alert. "I have known Tong all my life. He is of good hearts."

"Great hearts," Kwenn said. "By all accounts that is true also of you."

Sornnn stopped. "What question do you wish to ask me, First-Captain?"

Kwenn looked around at all the passing faces. He was searching particularly for the regent's vast network of spies he himself had set in place. He recognized no one. No one was paying them the slightest attention.

"You must understand, Prime Factor, that what I say next will put me in great jeopardy."

"Are you sure you want to continue?"

"Absolutely." Kwenn licked his lips. "All my life I have been in training. I have killed with more weapons than you could name. I am small, as you can see. Because of that, I trained myself strongly in hand-to-hand combat. In the Kalllistotos, before I became known, I made a lot of money wagering on the long odds the others put on me. I have killed many enemies and have thought little of their passing. I never considered the blood on my hands. Now it seems to me as if I am living two lives. One is the life I have always known, the life of killing and of obeying orders. The other life is unknown to me. In this second life I am like an observer of my other self, and I tell you, Prime Factor, that I do not care for what I see."

Sornnn was intrigued but still wary. "This is all very interesting, First-Captain, but—"

"I want to discredit the regent," Kwenn said. "To do so the Star-Admiral must be discredited."

Sornnn frowned. "You are either confused or mistaken, First-Captain. I have no interest in—"

"Prime Factor, please. This is not a trap."

"I will report this traitorous talk." Sornnn craned his neck. "Where is a Khaggun patrol when you need one?"

"You will not find one," Kwenn said. "I have taken us on a route the patrols do not use. Tong said—"

A sudden fright went through Sornnn. "If you have hurt Tong, if you have harmed him in any way . . ."

"Prime Factor, I swear to you—"

Sornnn held up his hand. He thumbed the Khaggun Tracker Tong had given to him long ago, and when he saw his friend's face a wave of relief swept over him. The two of them spoke for a few moments until Sornnn was satisfied. Then he signed off.

For time, he stood looking thoughtfully at Kwenn. At last he said, "So everything you have told me is the truth."

"Yes, Prime Factor."

Sornnn nodded. "It seems we both want something, First Captain." Something akin to hope was stirring in his hearts, and it did not only concern Fleet-Admiral Pnin. "There is a way now that we can accomplish those ends."

He took Kwenn to Leyytey's atelier, but she was not there. She was not, in fact, anywhere, and by then Sornnn knew all her habits and preferences.

"It looks as though the Fleet-Admiral's daughter has disappeared," Kwenn said.

Kwenn's words made no sense to Sornnn. It was not in Leyytey's nature to retreat from adversity. Then his heart sank, because he knew where she must have gone.

Riane climbed the stairs at FIREFLY, heavy with so many misgivings she preferred not to consider them. With Eleana and Kurgan so close it seemed to her that she was thrust back into Annon's old life, when Annon and Kurgan, best friends, had come upon Eleana bathing. Hot sun drifting through the sysal trees, spangling the water, lending it a dreamlike appearance. Eleana reaching up with bare arms, soft down golden, elbows bent. Letting her hair down in long, luxuriant folds, a bedsheet inviting. Both of them running, wading into the streambed. But it was Kurgan who had taken her by force, Annon trying and failing to stop the rape. Was it then their friendship took a dark turn? Was anything ever the same afterward? It seemed to Riane not. After that, one long unending nightmare, starting with Eleusis Ashera's slaughter and ending there. Then. The principals reunited.

Riane on the second floor, stepping carefully, silently, along the threadbare runner. Stains everywhere. Chambers empty as the eyes of the dead. The odor of desperation seeping like sweat out of every wall.

In this miasma, she returned to Dragonfly, honing the spell to its narrowest possible beam. Her only thought was of Kurgan and the banestone. Approaching the last doorway in the corridor, she vowed that the opportunity to secure it would not be wasted, not again. So preoccupied with Kurgan and the banestone was she, that Riane again missed the shadows coiling like smoke. Afterward, she would have rueful cause to remember the Hagoshrin's admonishment: *Do not rely overly on any implement, sorcerous or otherwise. Rely always on your wits and you will never be disappointed.* Without knowing it, she was relying on emotion, relying on sorcery to protect her. She saw Kurgan, saw the banestone, a dark egg that seemed to pulse before her eyes. Clearly, Kurgan was not yet aware of her. He appeared to be talking to himself, talking, perhaps, to the banestone which, she saw with a thrill of horror, he was holding in his bare hand. *You must not touch the banestone with your bare hands.* The Hagoshrin's words were clearly etched in her memory: *It will change you in ways no one can predict, and not for the better.* What would it do to Kurgan? For despite the blood feud between Ashera and Stogggul, despite the fact that Kurgan's father had been responsible for the deaths of all the Ashera on Kundala save Annon, the spirit that survived inside Riane could not forget that once Annon and Kurgan had been best friends. Hunting together, confiding secrets, confessing sins, sharing everything. Such a bond was not easy to forget, nor to forgo. It remained, like a blood oath. It abided in spite of time and terrible events.

And so Riane stood transfixed by the past and, thusly, the present and the future were formed.

There was another, however, who was not so fixated, one who ran, claws retracted for silence and for speed who, at the last moment, shot past her, through the doorway and into the hands of Lujon.

Thigpen's jaws snapped, her claws came out, drawing blood. Then the *Ardinal* flung her headlong across the chamber at the mirror. The mirror in which, without realizing it, Riane had been staring at Kurgan's reflection.

Thigpen vanished *into* the mirror.

Riane sprang into the room. Lujon emerged fully from the shadows where Thigpen had spied him, a sharp-toothed rock in a befogged bay, waiting for grief to form around him like a shipwreck.

"Eleana!" Kurgan roared. "Where is she?" Launching himself at Riane, he was stopped in midstride by Lujon and lifted off his feet. Whirling, he pressed the slender muzzle of the ion pistol into Lujon's rib cage, pulling the trigger.

Nothing happened.

"Surprised? We told you to be careful." Lujon, reached for the dagger, completely ignoring the inert ion weapon.

Employing Ka Form, Kurgan went hand to hand. He had been well trained by the Old V'ornn, had contested with combatants older and larger than he in the brutal Kalllistotos. For his age, he was an accomplished fighter; but he was saddled with the disadvantage of having both to protect the banestone and to keep an eye on Riane. Lujon, on the other hand, was Sintire trained from birth to be an expert assassin. Now the sauromicians had taught him in the black arts of necromancy which, unlike the white sorcerous arts, was not difficult to master. A firm hand, a few pointers on how to slice into the newly deceased, a strong stomach, and here and there a few words to learn. Any surgeon would do nicely.

As the Old V'ornn had taught him, Kurgan used the edge of his hand like a wedge, breaking the two lower ribs on Lujon's left side. At almost the same moment, Lujon, heel of his hand forward, struck him a tremendous blow on the bridge of the nose. A sharp *crack!* resounded off the walls. Kurgan's head snapped back. Lujon used the massed points of his fingertips on Kurgan's exposed throat, drew back his other hand to gouge out his eyes and use them, no doubt, to augment his power.

Riane conjured Try in Mind, a hammer of energy beating Lujon back. Kurgan dropped to his knees, retching, one hand to his throat, the other fiercely gripping the banestone. Lujon raised the arm with the necromantic talisman, tapping into the energy of the newly dead.

A darkness spilled into the room, running like tar, stinking like the pits of the damned. The air turned gelid; Riane had trouble moving, it was like trying to run in a dream. Lujon drew out a slim rod familiar to Riane. An infinity-blade wand! Milk-white, smooth as silk, just like the one Minnum gave her from the Museum of False Memory. The Sarakkon touched the tip of it to the nearest banestone and it glowed a fiery crimson. It was clear that somehow the wand had absorbed goron energy from the banestone. The goron-particle beam, opalescent, glistering, expanded outward like a great fan, a gigantic scythe sweeping through the space between them, about to slice Riane's head off.

She conjured Mounting Irons, felt the gelid atmosphere thaw, took her opening, and leapt, rolling beneath the great energy blade, fetching up against Kurgan. Out came her own wand and, mimicking the Sarakkon, she tapped it against the banestone. She thumbed the gold disc, causing the opalescent beam to shoot out. She lifted it slightly so that it intersected the great scythe.

Shock registered on Lujon's face as resistance tremored the scythe blade, as energy fought energy, but, recovering quickly, he shut down the beam, swept the wand down, reignited it as a sleek wasp-shaped blade. Riane had limited experience with the goron-particle beam, had only used it against Gyrgon ion-based weaponry. She was clumsy and slow, and did not immediately understand the need to turn it off and on again in order to change its shape. Lujon's energy blade almost disarmed her, slicing inside her defense. She quickly shut down her own beam, rolled, reignited it in the shape of a double-edged ax, and swung it at Lujon's left side with all her might. He grimaced, his broken ribs grinding into fascia and muscle, which was just what she intended, for it caused his arm to lag his eye. Bringing her ax down in a two-handed blow, she engaged his beam with hers. Sparks flew, and there was a scorched stench as of flame against flesh, a juddering down her arms into her chest. Teeth chattering, heart pounding, she felt hooked up to a gigantic engine, which, in a way, she was.

Riane was at last making some headway, Lujon's knees were buckling, as he struggled against the perfect angle she had chosen. And that is where it should have ended, Lujon's position crumbling, Riane's goron-particle ax splitting him in two. But Kurgan had recovered sufficiently, wiping blood out of his eyes. He had not seen Lujon powering the infinity-blade with the banestone, was not even aware of the infinity-blade's existence. Remembering in his befogged state how the banestone had killed the powerful Kundalan monster, he reached out.

"No!" Riane yelled, divining his intent.

He was determined, he would not be stopped, and pressed the banestone against Lujon's bare flesh.

Riane felt the charge against her increasing exponentially. Her energy ax sundered in two, loosed gorons through the chamber. Lujon, eyes blazing, swept his arm in her direction, and she flew backward, arms and legs in a tangle, infinity-blade sputtering and keening. He formed his beam into a poleax, drove it at her, meaning to skewer her against the wall. She twisted away, shook her wand, reformed her infinity-blade into a kind of webbing that hooked the leading edge of the poleax, sweeping it away. With a grunt, Lujon pushed through the webbing, hooked it up and away.

Riane went scrabbling after the wand, almost had her arm severed for her effort. Lujon laughed, toying with her, his power growing still, his energy beam far stronger than hers. Still, she could not give up and pounced on the wand, reactivated it, brought it to bear. He moved her around the chamber with it, and every step she took brought the leading edge of gorons closer to her flesh. She could feel their searing energy, the skin on her forearms burning. Lujon drove her, at length, into the corner by the narrow door to the attic, where the mirror gleamed, reflecting the goron particles in a kind of fireworks splendor. The beam swept toward her again, glennan going down before the scythe, and she knew she could not counter it, could not even deflect it sufficiently.

No time to think or react, a deathlike hollowness rising in her chest as she leapt at the mirror, passed through it.

Into the Other Side.

27

Pnin's End

Because of his status as one of Star-Admiral Iin Mennus' inner circle, Teww Dacce had been assigned a villa. It wasn't a large villa, at least by Bashkir standards. It was certainly more humble than that to which he aspired. Still, it was far more than the barracks in which he had lived in the old days.

Dacce being Dacce, he had filled it with antiques, rare and collectible artifacts, the better to proclaim his true status to acquaintances and compatriots. Slave to his aspirations, he had made a rather desperate attempt to mimic a Bashkir's domicile.

It was late when Iin Mennus had finally dismissed him. During the short walk home his head was so filled with the Star-Admiral's orders that he arrived at his front door not remembering how he got there.

Inside, the villa was dark. He fumbled for the nearest fusion lamp, but it would not come on. Neither would the second one. He was on his way to the third when he stumbled over something that should not have been on the floor. He swung around, startled, but before he could completely regain his balance he felt a shadow movement. His reaction was cut short by dual knife edges at his throat.

"If you move. If you give me any reason at all, I will slice you open like a ripe clemett."

"Leyytey." Teww Dacce had frozen in place. Now a smile spread across his face. "You never had a penchant for rough sex play before."

He yelped as the shock-sword bit into his skin and drew blood.

"You have mistaken what I say for the last time." The slightest twist to her hand caused the blades to bite deeper. A slow drip of blood commenced. "Do I make myself clear?"

He nodded, all at once confused. When it came to Leyytey he was totally at sea.

Leyytey had taken Teww Dacce hostage, though perhaps that was not precisely correct. With a shock-sword at his throat he was surely her prisoner. But, really, Leyytey was not thinking clearly, because she had run out of patience. All she could think of was the dire circumstance Iin Mennus had put her father in. She was tired of listening to males drone on about ways that might or might not work. She was going to free him. She had not considered the consequences, though to be fair to her current state of agitation, had she done so she surely would have dismissed them.

She told herself that she had chosen to take Teww Dacce hostage because it was the only method at her disposal to free her father. Her former lover was in the Star-Admiral's employ. He had access to Fleet-Admiral Pnin. All of this was irrefutable, of course. Nevertheless, she was also motivated by an element of revenge.

Nothing felt so sweet as to hold the keen edges of a shock-sword to his throat, to see the look in his eyes when she lit one of the fusion lamps she had doctored. There was an equal measure of satisfaction and sadness at being witness to his utter confusion. She steeled herself, knowing what his confusion would morph into.

Rage caused Teww Dacce to clench his fists, caused the cords on the sides of his neck to stand out, turned his voice guttural.

"Have you lost your mind?" he said thickly. "What do you think you're doing?"

She tightened her grip on him. "Shut up."

"I am on the Star-Admiral's personal staff. Do you know what they will do to you?"

"I said shut up!"

"They will kill you, Leyytey. And past due, I say."

She punched him in the side as hard as she could with her balled fist. Wind whistled out of him, and he jack-knifed over.

"Here are the rules, Dacce. One: speak only when I address you. Two: obey all orders. Three: make no sudden moves. Think you can remember those?"

Silence.

She poked him, hard. "I am speaking to you."

More silence, obdurate and sullen.

Leyytey grasped his right hand around the wrist and, before he knew what was happening, sliced off his smallest finger.

He screamed and fell to his knees, holding his maimed hand. There was blood everywhere. A string of foul curses fell from his lips. His eyes looked dull and red-rimmed. He was squeezing hard on the stump of his finger.

"It's not too late. Call a Genomatekk. They'll reattach my finger. They do that, and I'll forget all about this."

She hit him then with the heavy butt of the shock-sword. Not in the face, of course. He would need that unmarked for her plan to succeed. Anyway, it hurt him more to do it in the place where she had punched him. He gagged a little at the pain, and she raised his head up with a hand under his chin.

"Do I have your attention now, Dacce? How gratifying. Because I never had it before."

He stilled his panting breaths before he managed to say, "What do you want? To beat me to a pulp?" He began to laugh. "I will kill you for this. I will put your severed head on a pike outside the Star-Admiral's pavilion for all to see."

She saw then that brute force wasn't going to get her what she wanted, and she stepped away and raised the intensity on the fusion lamp. Then she swung her shock-sword, first to the left, then to the right. She slashed into the antiques and the artifacts, stomping on them as they hit the floor. Whirling around the room, shock-sword whistling, her breath coming fast. Dacce watched her in stupefaction.

"What have you done?"

"I thought it was time to redecorate." She kicked at the shards of porcelain and fired clay and crystal, the shreds of textiles and twisted metal alloy. "I have broken everything, Dacce. Everything you love and covet is gone." She knelt down in front of him. "What's the matter? Don't care for the new look? Too late. It's too late for everything, Dacce."

She saw understanding come slowly to his face, and it was not a pretty sight. Longed for, it now only deepened her disgust.

"What do you want?"

"I want you to take me to my father. I want you to free him. I want you to get us both out of there alive and safe."

He realized that she was perfectly serious. The horror of it was that he could do all that. Iin Mennus had given him the power. Not that he would survive it. He seriously doubted if any of them would, but he also knew that would not stop her. Nothing could. She was on a collision course, and unless he was prepared to die right then, nothing would derail her. He closed his eyes for a moment. He had never known her. Why should he have? She was Tuskugg-gun. She was nothing. The essential problem now was that she knew him. She knew that he would not opt for death, would not call her possible bluff if there was even an iota of a chance that she would kill him. Still, there was one last card to play.

"If you kill me, you will never see your father again."

"That may be," she said without hesitation. "But at least I will have had the satisfaction of watching you die."

Dacce's last chance went up in smoke. She had not hesitated to slice off his finger and, he knew one thing about her because he had observed it firsthand in her atelier: she was as good with her weapons as any Khaggun.

"I will do what you ask of me." His head sank to his chest, but he was already calculating the scenarios where, on the way to Fleet-Admiral Pnin's villa or, failing that, inside it, he would take her by surprise, plunge her own shock-sword through her hearts.

E ven if you do not speak, in the end I will win." An entire array of scalpels, pincers, bone forceps, and curettes appeared from the palm of Nith Nassam's ion glove, a bouquet of dreadful blossoms he began to pick through with obvious relish. "Because I will dissect your *mute* body and find all the answers I need."

Gul Aluf's eyes had never left Sahor's face. He became aware of a tiny shiver in the air, a wavering like heat rising. Her fierce concentration was stirring ions to life, but slowly, ever so slowly.

There came for Sahor a moment of disconnection, a moment when neither Gul Aluf nor the lab-orb existed. His universe spiraled down to the size and shape of Nith Nassam. In a way, even he himself ceased to exist inasmuch as he lost any sense of himself inside his body. It was as if he had become incorporeal, an amorphous globule of spinning atoms, mere electrons, neutrons, and protons, invisible even to a Gyrgon's eye.

Sahor saw Gul Aluf's narrowed eyes spark, and she had done all she could, sending a narrow-cast ion beam straight at the photon collar tightening around his neck. When it burst asunder, Sahor commenced his attack.

He was no longer Nith, however, and the first strike of hyperexcited ions from Nith Nassam struck him full in the chest, drove him to his knees. Nith Nassam turned. "And for your part in this . . ." He leveled a photonic stream at Gul Aluf, rendering her unconscious.

He frowned deeply as he stalked after Sahor. "That should have paralyzed you. What is this shell of yours made of?"

He reached down and grabbed Sahor by the bleeding throat. His other hand drew back, ion sparks fizzling off it in all directions. He hooked the first two fingers, and twin beams shot out. Sahor tried to look away, but the photonic beams caught his eyes and held them. Apart from a flare of lambent blue light, he was blind. He felt the beams crawling along his optic nerves, tracing pathways to the deepest centers of his brain there to take possession of his autonomic nervous system. Once that occurred, he knew, Nith Nassam would control his body completely.

He fought back, using his mind, but he lacked sufficient knowledge of his own new self to choose the right pathway. Millimeter by millimeter, the photons were crawling toward their target. All his senses now were flickering, fading out of his control. He had only moments to decide what to do.

But which way to go? He was filled with turmoil: fear, rage, loss made his mind turbid, unable to reach a clear conclusion.

Clear.

Sahor let go of everything. His fear, his rage, his sense of impending loss. Even as the photons crept along his optic nerves, a limpid pool of calm began to spread inside him. He did not think, he did not hope, he did not expect . . . *anything.*

And into the perfectly clear pool of nothingness came an image. In his mind's eye he saw Nith Nassam. How? But of course. He had somehow followed the twin beams of photons back to their source, and they revealed everything he needed.

He tapped into the beams and amplified them beyond their capacity. Like water seeking its own level, the overcrowded photons reversed themselves.

Sahor heard Nith Nassam scream, and then the blinding blue light vanished, leaving him dazzled and panting, but free. His rage returned, redoubled in strength, and he rushed at Nith Nassam. This was a mistake. Nith Nassam, in his pain, lashed out with his ion glove fully activated. It struck Sahor full on the cheek. Agony raced through him, and he doubled over, retching and shivering.

Nith Nassam took hold of him and threw him across the lab-orb, and he struck the goron-wave chamber. Only its convex surface saved him from cracking his ribs. As it was, he fought for breath, hanging on with rubbery knees.

Nith Nassam advanced toward him. He was not about to give Sahor another chance to counter. Blood dripped from one eye, but he ignored that. He was healing himself even as his ion flash caught Sahor in the solar plexus.

Sahor, clinging to the side of the goron-wave chamber, felt his fingers encounter the activation panel. From the moment he had entered this new body, from the moment he had worked his Gyrgon DNA through the spiral of Kundalan DNA, merging them, creating something entirely new, he had seen something there that had fired his interest. He had been planning a scientifically correct series of experiments leading to a trial with himself as the subject. But now, here he was on the point of being dissected, and his only hope lay in taking that idea to its final trial without knowing whether it would kill him. *But better that*, he thought as he activated the goron-wave chamber, *than to let Nith Nassam learn the secret of what I have become.*

"What are you doing?" As the chamber whined into life, Nith Nassam took an involuntary step back. "Are you insane? Close the chamber door before—"

His voice was choked off as Sahor stepped into the goron-wave chamber. Sahor's entire life, everything he believed or ever would believe, was balanced on this one instant. Scientists—even technomages—were not supposed to use intuition. There was a scientific method, exacting, painstakingly worked out, that needed to be followed. Intuition took no known path, intuition relied on faith, and was therefore anathema to Gyrgon. And yet as Sahor's father had pointed out to him more than once, some of the most exciting discoveries had come from Gyrgon who had had the courage to take that leap of faith.

Sahor's father had taken the leap of faith himself. And Sahor, ever since he had set foot on Kundala, had in a very real sense been guided by his own heightened sense of intuition. In fact, it was his theory that Kundala itself had somehow been responsible for bringing his intuition to the surface, making it accessible to him. For that alone he would be eternally grateful to this place they had stumbled upon over a hundred years ago in the midst of their interstellar trek. Even if he were now to take his last breath inside the goron-wave chamber.

The instant Sahor set foot in the interior, Nith Nassam slammed shut the access hatch behind him. Sahor felt as if he had entered a dream. There was no up or down, no north, south, east, or west. He had entered a current, which encompassed Time, Space, the Beginning of All Things, the End of All Things. All existed at once, superimposed, layer upon layer, like a hall of mirrors that kept showing you the same image in different ways. If he was being assaulted by goron particles, he did not feel it. The beam passed through him, doubled back, doubled again, bouncing off the different images of himself even as it revealed them.

And Sahor knew that he had been right, knew why he had been sent to Kundala. For Kundala was the key, it always had been, hanging in its remote section of the Cosmos, slowly spinning, waiting for him to arrive, waiting, in fact, for that very moment. For Sahor at last knew what he had suspected almost from the moment he had landed there. Kundala was alive in a way no other planet they had ever visited or had heard of was alive. Possibly, even, Kundala itself was Miina, the Great Goddess.

He opened his eyes, blinked like a newborn, and looked down at himself. For a moment, he could see through his skin to his organs, through his organs to his bones, through his very bones to the marrow, where, spiraled in a continuing loop, was the hybrid DNA that had made all this possible.

He spun the wheel on the inside of the access hatch and it opened. He stepped out. While Nith Nassam was still goggling at him, he raised his arm, sent a bolt of goron-based energy into him. The Gyrgon fell to his knees. His eyes lost focus, and his mouth worked spastically. Yellow powder dribbled out, all that was left of his teeth. Then, his eyes turned absolutely white, both pupils and irises obliterated by the dreadful radiation, and he fell over, dead.

Gul Aluf was still unconscious; she had seen nothing, and that was how he intended it to remain. Even knowing the danger she represented, it was difficult so close not to be filled up with her. Her haughty expression, her sense of owning him body and soul. How she used her expertise at genetic manipulation to coerce and control, how it gave her a sense of entitlement. Her allegiance to Nith Batoxxx because she had created him, birthed him. He remembered also feverish nights with her, the pulse of lust a taste neither could get enough of. How they broke Comradeship rules, together delinking from the Comradeship for short periods of time, alone together, able to bestride Kundala like colossi, drunk on their own lust, becoming for a time demigods capable of anything.

He could feel the goron charge dissipating like steam from a vent. Soon, it was gone altogether. Would the next charge last longer, remain permanently, would it do so if he stayed longer inside the goron-wave chamber, if he were able somehow to amplify the wave? Those were all questions he was determined to answer. But right then he had others, more pressing, that required his attention.

He had to take advantage of Gul Aluf's condition to extract all he could from Nith Batoxxx's secret experiments. He reinserted the data blossom in its specially made slot, brought up the files. Quickly scanning them, he could see that Nith Batoxxx had been obsessed with Stogggul Terrettt and Stogggul Kurgan. More data spiraled by, and a shock went through him. Could what it indicated be correct? Nith Batoxxx had genetically manipulated Stogggul Terrettt. An experiment not fully thought out and unsupervised. Of course, it had gone wrong. But what had been his aim? What had he wanted to create?

"I see you have managed quite well without me."

Sahor turned, but he already knew, the voice so familiar to him. "Father," he said.

Nith Einon was looking at the fallen Nith Nassam. How long had he been in the lab-orb before speaking? "Killed by goron particles. Fascinating." He appeared exactly as Sahor remembered him: long and lean, the violet eyes set in the sober scholar's deeply lined face. The artfully constructed latticework of tertium and germanium circuits at the crown of his head was perfectly intact.

"Gul Aluf did not tell me that she had resurrected you."

"She wanted to surprise you. I see that you are."

"I am wondering what she demanded of you in return."

Nith Einon frowned. "It's not that I didn't appreciate your keeping me alive. But the truth is, it got cramped inside the Teyj. Couldn't flex my muscles."

"You didn't answer my question."

"You are no longer Nith."

Sahor did not like the tenor of the conversation. Outside the same, nevertheless this Nith Einon seemed a stranger to him. "What did she do to you?"

"She gave me life, nothing more."

"I know her better than that."

Nith Einon used a hand to brush aside his son's words. "Believe what you will. You always have. My only concern is for stopping the Centophennni."

"That is why she resurrected you. To be an ally."

"I am curious as to why it isn't your overriding concern."

"I love the Kundalan."

"At the expense of your own species. You love them too well." He had turned his attention to the holoimages Sahor had brought up. "So Nith Batoxxx was experimenting on Stogggul Terrettt."

"Whatever he was doing to the ativar failed." Sahor pointed. "But look here. There seems to be a difference in Kurgan's ativar also."

"Not the same as Terrettt's. Perhaps with Kurgan he did not fail." Nith Einon clasped his hands behind his back,

craned his neck. "Nith Batoxxx trained Stogggul Kurgan
from an early age. He must have had plans for him. Great
plans."

"But what were they?"

"That is what I mean to find out."

Behind them both, Gul Aluf, having been brought to
consciousness by Nith Einon the moment he entered the
lab-orb, avidly listened to this conversation. Her hearts
leapt when she saw the holoimages of Stogggul Kurgan's
brain. So Nith Batoxxx had succeeded, after all! Why had
he not told her? Of course, the Kundalan archdaemon possessing him had interceded. She knew now what she had
to do. As soon as she was alone she would Summon
Stogggul Kurgan and she would finish the process her son
had started.

F leet-Admiral Pnin was staring at a skull. It was a
Khagggun skull. He held it in the cupped palm of his
hand. It was a lovely thing, really, symmetrical, smooth as
a sea stone, the rich color of clotted cor cream. Its eyeholes were dark and hollow, absolutely devoid of life or
even the echoes of life. No mark of the deathblow or any
sign that it had ever been in battle marred its smooth, gently curved surface, familiar as his own reflection.

A sudden jolt of anxiety caused him to look around.
Was he once again dreaming of the mountain of skulls?
Yes, there it was beneath his buttocks, but as he looked
more closely he saw that all the skulls had been cracked
open like so many nutshells so that whatever anguished
animus they had carried inside them was now gone. They
lay still and quiescent, so much detritus waiting for the
slow accretion of time to grind their empty husks into dust.

All save this one skull, cream-colored, glowing. It lay
comfortably in his hand as if it belonged there, as if it had
always been there. He lifted it until it was at eye level,
peered intently at the eyeholes. Had he seen a flicker of a
shadow there? A quick, darting movement. And then
through the right eyehole slithered a serpent, black and

oily with a head like a baby's fist. The head pulsed like a heart and, as it did so, Pnin clutched his own head. The old pain was back, racing through his brain into his neck. And with a start that jolted his hearts he knew why the skull looked so familiar. It was his own skull. And then he realized that the serpent was the tumor growing inside his brain, pushing against delicate tissue and nerve bundles and . . .

He awoke with a start, jerking forward in the chair in which he had fallen asleep, gasping a little. He was in his villa, which smelled vaguely, unpleasantly, uncharacteristically, of exhaled breath and stale food. But then why not? It had been invaded, locked down tighter than a claiwen's anus.

The fumes of his nightmare still swirled like strong liquor, so real—more real than this forced incarceration, which, in no time at all, had come to seem to him a kind of interment, a sad and bitter end to a Khagggun's life. As he had once been haunted by the battlefield dead, he was haunted now by the loss of the smallest and simplest of freedoms—not to wander the streets and byways of Axis Tyr, not even to walk in his garden, which he could only look out upon and which more than anything else gave him the sense of being a prisoner—all denied him by Iin Mennus. Mennus had been clever to enisle him, for he found it all but unbearable.

There was a scent of ion leakage from the guards' weapons that had seeped into every nook and cranny of the villa, even his narrow Khagggun's bed. It was the first thing he smelled in the morning and the last thing he smelled at night. It was a familiar odor, one that had been a part of his life forever. In this context, he found it offensive. There was a flat, lifeless quality about it that, without the verve of battlefield blood, spoke of tyranny most repellent and egregious, and yet at the same time petty and self-serving.

He pressed thumbs against eyelids at the first telltale throbbing in his head. How long had it been since he had taken his last dose of *da'ala?* He could not recall, which was in itself a bad sign. Putting a hand to his forehead, he felt the cold sweat and was about to wipe it away when he noticed Iin Mennus standing in front of him. Mennus was holding out a cloth, and he took it, humiliated, as he wiped his skull dry. Crumpling up the damp cloth, he held it against his temple, as if he could drive away the throbbing that was building into pain, the black serpent with the baby's fist head awake inside him. He knew all too well what would happen to him if he did not take *da'ala* soon, but he could do nothing as long as Mennus was there. He would die rather than reveal this fatal weakness to his nemesis.

But instead of leaving, Iin Mennus had settled into a chair. He sat facing Pnin and in an uncharacteristically expansive tone told Pnin that he had ordered dinner for both of them brought in from his favorite cafe.

"While we're waiting," he said, producing a photon exciter, "I thought I would show you the new composition of the high council."

Pnin grunted, unconsciously rubbing the biobandage that was healing his wounded hand. "What is this, a new form of torture? I am uninterested."

Iin Mennus shrugged his meaty shoulders. "You will look anyway, Little Admiral. I want you to see the shape of the future." He thumbed the tiny black hexahedron and a series of three-dimensional images popped into the room. One-two-three-four, there were the faces of the new high command. Pnin looked at them, curious despite what he had said. He didn't recognize any of them by name but he knew them just the same: young and ambitious, with death in their eyes and blood on their hands.

"Who are these Khagggun?" he asked. "Not Admirals, surely."

"No, indeed." Iin Mennus rubbed his hands together. "Former Pack-Commanders, all of them."

"What?"

"That's right." Mennus leaned forward, his expression more lupine than ever. It was clear he was enjoying himself immensely. "I have handpicked the best four under my command and promoted them to the rank of Fleet-Admiral."

"But that is absurd. It takes years to work your way up the chain of command. And for good reason. A Fleet-Admiral must have experience at every level of command beneath him in order to control his troops effectively."

"That is the conventional wisdom, yes. But look where the conventional wisdom has gotten us. Stuck in a conservative, unimaginative rut. New blood, new ways of thinking, this is what is called for."

"No, no, no!" Pnin was shouting, which was a mistake, for it set his head to pounding even more deeply. "The conventional wisdom was set in place eons ago to ensure honor. Don't you understand, Mennus? Without honor, what are we?"

"What you must understand, my dear Little Admiral, is that honor—your dearest benchmark—is a hindrance to the acquisition of new experience. And new experience is the seed of knowledge, of moving boldly forward, of taking what by birthright is ours. The conventional wisdom—this *honor* of yours—makes us soft and stupid, and that I will not abide."

"You are insane."

"Really? If that is your assessment—"

"It is a condemnation. You are the personification of evil."

"If that is your *assessment*, Little Admiral, then I was wise to cull you from the Modality." Mennus hunched forward on the edge of his chair. "Your conventional wisdom has been around so long it digs into ground it has long ago depleted. Being old, it is considered *good* even if its value has vanished. History tells us that whoever dares to overthrow existing custom, which may in fact be bad though it is considered otherwise, is at first condemned as *evil*. But later, when the existing custom is not reinstated, when it fades from memory, when the new custom is accepted, then this instigator is hailed, deemed of the deepest, truest *good*." He sat back. "And so it shall be with me."

Mennus' bit of philosophizing was all the more frightening because it had about it the strength of logic. History is long, memory is short.

"You see how it is, Little Admiral," Mennus said smugly. "There are no truths, only interpretations."

Pnin's headache was worse than ever. He pressed the crumpled cloth against his right eye, which felt as if at any moment it would be spat out of its socket.

"And those, like our own misguided priests who continued to preach the gospel of the false god, Enlil, who hold such strong convictions, must be eradicated, for convictions are the pillars on which conventional wisdom is built, and are, therefore, inimical to new thinking."

A sharp knock on the front door, thankfully, spared Pnin any more of this deeply odious tirade.

"Ah, our dinner has arrived." Iin Mennus jumped up. "I don't know about you, Little Admiral, but I am famished."

He proceeded into the entryway to discover that the two guards outside had ushered in not dinner but Pack-Commander Dacce. Much to Mennus' surprise, he had with him Pnin's daughter, Leyytey.

Leyytey took in the scene all at once, with a warrior's eye to the details of stance, expression, visible weapons. But something else just as compelling drew her attention. She stared from Mennus to her father. She was frankly appalled at how he had treated her father. It had never until now occurred to her that her father was old. In his lined face, in the way he carried himself, she saw that age had dug its trembling fingers into him most deeply. He had always been to her a magnificent mountain of strength and canny ability, a powerful engine that had been turned on at birth and had never stopped. Perhaps she was reacting to the strange and frightening watery opaqueness of his eyes, or, more accurately, what lay behind it: the acknowledgment that he had relinquished his hold on life, that he had already sounded the retreat into death's cool embrace.

Whatever it was, she knew that she had come not a moment too soon.

Dacce's face registered his own astonishment. "Star-Admiral, I did not expect you would be here."

Mennus pursed his lips. "What is the meaning of this, Pack-Commander Dacce, and why is my being here relevant?"

"Uh, I brought the Fleet-Admiral's daughter—"

"I'm not blind. Fleet-Admiral Pnin is allowed no visitors, including members of his family."

"Yes, of course," Dacce said. He was trying desperately to show the Star-Admiral the stump of his finger without letting Leyytey see what he was doing.

"Stop fidgeting and get her out of here," Mennus barked.

"Just a moment," Pnin said. He had risen stiffly from his chair and come padding silently into the entryway. "I had ordered a shock-sword remade to my specifications."

Mennus whirled on him. "A warning, Little Admiral. Retreat to your study and await dinner."

"I want to speak with my father," Leyytey said.

"You will speak only when asked a direct question," Iin Mennus snapped.

Leyytey picked up on her father's cue. "I cannot finish his new shock-sword without speaking to him."

"He has no need for any weapon now. You will leave instantly."

"I have a right to see him."

"You have no rights, least of all in my presence. You may think you do because you are a weapons smith, but you do not. You are Tuskugggun. Nothing you do can change that."

"I do not care what you say," Leyytey persisted. "I am here. I will speak with him."

The Star-Admiral, cranky in any case because of his growling stomachs, had had enough of her insolence, and he signed for the guards to take her forcibly.

"Star-Admiral, there is no need for violence," Pnin said urgently.

But no one was listening to him. As Leyytey shifted her attention to the oncoming guards, Dacce whirled and slammed both fists into her chest.

Leyytey cried out, stumbled backward, and Dacce came after her. Pnin was himself on the move, unwilling to allow his daughter to be overwhelmed in an unfair fight. But Mennus signed to his guards, and they restrained Pnin, keeping him back from the fray.

Seeing Leyytey draw a shock-sword, Mennus called to Dacce, threw him his own hilt first. Dacce caught it, a feral look in his eye that warmed the Star-Admiral's hearts. If anyone was going kill the Little Admiral's daughter, let it be Dacce. It would serve as an excellent object lesson for both consort and father. What were Tuskugggun but trouble? He had always believed it, and she was the living proof.

Meanwhile, the combatants were circling each other, their knees bent, their backs slightly hunched. Dacce's hearts raced. This was what he had always wanted but had lacked the courage to perform, a quick, peremptory strike to end it all—the lost resolve, the broken promises, the brilliant future he had envisioned for himself the first time he had bedded her. A stupid fantasy that had eaten at him through the years. Every time Leyytey made him go to the hingatta to see Miirlin—the bitter fruit of their joining—he was reminded all over again how the golden future had died stillborn. It was all he could do, in fact, not to strangle the curious child with the penetrating grey eyes and the preternatural mind. It was as if Miirlin knew every secret thought in his head. He could not admit to himself that he feared the child, so he despised him instead.

Their shock-swords clashed, sending showers of hyperexcited ions sparking toward the ceiling. Leyytey was breathing easy for the first time since she had learned of her father's being put into "protective custody." She had inherited her father's penchant for action. Her hearts burned with the Khagggun's bloodlust for battle. Not, however, against other races, but against the injustices heaped on her and her caste by her own race. The gene sequence that caused xenophobia programmed into all Khagggun by the Gyrgon was nowhere to be found in her DNA. Rather, she, like Marethyn, like most Tuskugggun had their society given them a chance, possessed the ability to see a situation from different sides and, therefore, come to a conclusion, a compromise, somewhere more or less in the middle.

However, there, at that moment, there was no room for compromise or common ground. There was only the thrust and parry of shock-swords, the panting of heated breath, the will to live. She had recognized from the moment Mennus had thrown his weapon to Dacce that the combat was life-or-death. At the end, one of them would be left standing. Only one.

She feinted to the right, went left. Dacce, canny as he was, did not take the bait. His blows rained down on her. Obviously, he had decided to take advantage of his superiority in strength, weight, and height to beat her down. Again and again, he drove his shock-sword at her in short, powerful blows, discovering a rhythm, quick, brutal, relentless, that should bring him victory. All he needed, she knew, was to wait for her to make a mistake, to slip up on her defense. Even a small miscalculation in a parry would allow him inside her perimeter, and once there he could deliver the killing blow in the blink of an eye.

Back across the entryway he drove her until she was literally against the wall. She knew she could not let it go on like this. He was dictating both the pace and the manner of the combat. Her arm was growing weary. Already jolts of stray ions had caused three of her fingers to go numb. If the lack of feeling went any farther, she was done for.

She tried to change tactics, tried to go on the offensive, but he would not let her. His brute force, coming at her like an avalanche, gave her no opportunity to turn the tide. She could hear Mennus urging him on, and the two guards bickering over a wager because neither one wanted to bet on her.

A particularly vicious blow drove her to her knees. Dacce was grinning, an expression so familiar she felt despair flood her. Wasn't this what she had always wanted? A chance to prove herself the equal of any Khaggun in front of her father. And now that she had gotten what she so desperately craved, she was failing. Perhaps she had been wrong all along. Perhaps it was true what the males believed, that Tuskugggun had no place in their arena.

Another blow slammed her hard against the wall, the pain jarring up her spine. There was laughter among the guards, more wager negotiations. The odds must be getting long indeed.

And then, on the verge of defeat, she heard her father say to his guards, "I will take your bets. How much, how much?"

He was willing to wager on her! The knowledge ran through her body, banished her self-pity, galvanized her. In her mind, she saw an array of all her weapons, their careful manufacture, balance, and cutting capabilities. No V'ornn knew them better than she did.

As Dacce's next blow descended, she countered it, but at the last possible instant allowed her wrist to turn. To Dacce it seemed as though, tiring, she was on the brink of being overpowered. His blades scored down hers all the way to the guard, where he brought even more leverage to bear.

He expected Leyytey to resist him, but she did the opposite. Her elbow caved, her defense appearing to crumple, and Dacce leaned in even more, pressing his advantage. At that moment, Leyytey reversed her blade, slamming the heavy butt end into his chin. Dacce's head snapped back, his shock-sword traveled unimpeded to the floor, where such was its momentum that the dual points stuck in the stone flagging.

She slashed at him and, cursing, he backed quickly away without his weapon. She came after him, murder in her eyes. But Mennus interceded again. He held out his hand and one of Pnin's guards filled it with an ion flail, which he threw to the Pack-Commander. Dacce, the predatory grin back on his face, deftly caught it, whirled the studded globe around his head. Leyytey kept coming.

He said, "That's right," and loosed the mace directly at her head.

Leyytey raised her shock-sword so that the blades trapped the whistling chain between them. When it struck the base, a feedback formed, a bolt of hyperexcited ions racing down the chain into the ion mace's handle.

Dacce grimaced with the pain, but somehow he managed to hang on, drawing back on the mace, bringing Leyytey to him. He smashed her in the nose with the flat of his hand, reached for her weapon. But this time she was ready, and she swiveled away from him, allowing the momentum of his lunge to take the upper part of his torso past her.

Afterward, her mind would see it in a strange kind of slow motion: he disengaging the shock-sword blades from the ion-flail chain, she drawing back her arm, her muscles bunched, the thrust coming all the way from her pelvis up through her torso into her shoulder and arm, the twin blades humming, fairly quivering with anticipation as they cleaved the air.

The hot stink of hyperexcited ions was in her nostrils as she sank the shock-sword through muscle, fascia, and organs. She might have lacked a Khaggqun's strength, but with a surgeon's precision she severed Dacce's spinal cord. He was dead even before he hit the floor.

No one moved, not a word was uttered. The atmosphere was stultifying.

"Render unto me my coins!" Fleet-Admiral Pnin bellowed in triumph.

"Take her into custody!" Mennus ordered. "She is formally charged with and summarily convicted of the willful murder of Pack-Commander Teww Dacce."

"You can't—"

"This is my domain, Little Admiral." He whirled on Pnin, aiming his ion pistol at the Fleet-Admiral's hearts. "I can do as I please."

The two guards flanked Leyytey, each grabbing an arm.

"I will now have the exquisite pleasure of executing your daughter while you watch."

A slow smile spread across his face. "Unless, of course . . ." He allowed his voice to drift off, bait in the water.

"Unless what?" Pnin asked. He was fighting the pain in his head, he was fighting to enunciate clearly, fighting to keep his tongue from feeling like cotton batting.

"Father, don't," Leyytey cried. "This is what he wants."

"Star-Admiral," Pnin said slowly but nevertheless firmly, "spare my daughter's life, and I will do what you want."

"No!" Leyytey struggled against her guards, but they had disarmed her, wisely pinioned her arms, and now held her fast. She was acutely aware that she had twice called him "Father" and he had not admonished her. Better to think of that than to admit that her coming there had made matters worse.

"I want your submission, Little Admiral, complete, absolute. I want you to appear before your followers and endorse me, endorse the new high command for that matter. And then you will announce your retirement from active duty. You will say that you will be advising me in all matters of policy. When that is over, we will retire to the privacy of the caverns beneath the regent's palace, where you will divulge all your secrets, every last one."

Mennus signed to his guards, who put their shockswords against Leyytey's throat and her abdomen. "Make your decision now, Little Admiral. Does she live or does she die?"

Because First-Captain Kwenn was in charge of the regent's Haaar-kyut, he encountered no problem with the guards ringing the periphery of Fleet-Admiral Pnin's villa. It was astonishing, really, the power he could wield simply by invoking Kurgan Stogggul's name. He also discovered, through one of the more voluble guards, one of those still loyal to Pnin, that Leyytey was already inside the villa with Pack-Commander Dacce and the Star-Admiral himself.

"I suppose it has occurred to you that we may be too late," he said to Sornnn, as they hurried through the lushly planted grounds.

"Ever since my beloved's death, the possibility occurs to me every day in every way," Sornnn replied.

Kwenn grunted. "I just assumed that you and the Fleet-Admiral's daughter—"

Sornnn laughed grimly. "Had we been idiotic enough to get together, I daresay inside a week we would have murdered each other." Then, realizing that Leyytey might already be dead, he shut his mouth and signed to Kwenn.

They skirted the front door, swinging around through slender sysal trees to the rear of the villa. Kwenn could not know it, of course, but Sornnn was intimately familiar with the layout of Pnin's villa, having for years clandestinely slithered in and out under cover of darkness. He knew, for instance, that Pnin had a habit of keeping one sliding crystal door unlocked, and he prayed now that the Star-Admiral, lulled by his complete and bloodless takeover of the compound, had not bothered to have the guards check such details.

"On the other hand," he whispered, just before his fingers touched the slider, "if the Star-Admiral has harmed either Leyytey or Pnin, I will kill him myself."

Kwenn was used to being with the regent, a Bashkir who spoke his own mind, who possessed both nerve and determination. His original assumption about them—correct inasmuch as it was a cliché, and clichés are given life from a slow accretion of behavioral patterns that creep into the collective caste consciousness—was that they were wily but soft as cor cheese, obsessed as much with their sybaritic lifestyle as they were with coins. Kurgan Stogggul had exploded that assumption, supplanting it with another, even worse: that Bashkir were bombastic, egotistic, needlessly cruel. To have found one who was as brave as a Khagggun, but also loyal and kind was a revelation he was not likely to forget. In that instant, an unshakable bond took shape between them.

The crystal gave way to Sornnn's touch, and the two of them silently entered the villa, crept through Pnin's bedroom with its narrow, precisely made bed, the chronosteel stand with his armor glowing, down a corridor bereft of light or artwork, in time to hear Star-Admiral Iin Mennus say, as only he could; "Make your decision now, Little Admiral. Does she live or does she die?"

An instant later, as they burst into the entryway and saw Dacce lying in a pool of his own blood, everything seemed to happen at once. Seeing them, the guard closest to them drew Leyytey's own shock-sword away from her abdomen and came at them. Mennus turned toward the commotion. Kwenn drew a small shock-dagger from a sheath hidden under his arm and flung it expertly into the guard's cheek.

As Sornnn began to shoot past him, bending low, aiming for the second guard, Iin Mennus swung his ion pistol, tracking him, about to squeeze off a shot. Leyytey screamed a warning to Sornnn even while she lunged for the shock-sword the stricken guard had taken from her. Pnin grabbed at Mennus' arm and uttered a guttural groan. His eyes rolled up in his head, his legs turned to jelly, and he collapsed, thrashing and frothing at the mouth so vigorously that Mennus glanced at him.

While Kwenn efficiently finished off the wounded guard, Sornnn had slammed into the other one with his shoulder. The Khagggun spun away, off-balance, pulling Leyytey with him so that her fingers grasped for and missed the shock-sword. Sornnn pummeled the guard with both fists, striking blow after blow on the Khagggun's face until he had no choice but to let go. Leyytey leapt for the shock-sword just as Mennus recovered from the startlement of seeing Pnin's seizure. He aimed at her, and she saw that she was too far away from him, they all were. In a moment, he would pull the trigger. There was no strategy possible. There was just action or no-action. Shock-swords were for hand-to-hand combat, but Leyytey had never been satisfied with forging so limited a weapon. Her shock-swords were different from any others. She had already drawn back her arm and now, in a powerful sideways motion, she flung he shock-sword directly at Mennus. The dual points, vibrating no more than a few centimeters from each other, struck their mark. Impaled through the throat, Star-Admiral Iin Mennus was flung violently back until he struck the wall, pinioned there as the hyperexcited ions boiled his blood to paste.

In the last moments of his life, he goggled at her. And he died disbelieving what his own eyes told him was the truth. Killed by a Tuskugggun. Impossible. That was no way for a Khagggun to die.

Leyytey, for her part, had no eyes for Iin Mennus. As he was dying in disbelief, she was on her knees, cradling her father's huge square head in her lap.

"Sornnn!" she cried. "Sornnn, what have they done to him?"

Sornnn, leaving First-Captain Kwenn to finish the second guard's unenviable journey to the gates of N'Luuura, ran back down the hall to Pnin's bedroom. There he found the vial of *da'ala*, returning with it on the run, prying open jaws tightly clenched and dispensing it into the Fleet-Admiral's mouth. The effect of the Korrush spice was nothing short of miraculous. Pnin's spasms lessened both in intensity and in duration, and within moments he was sleeping quietly.

Leyytey looked at Sornnn. Her lips moved, but nothing came out.

Seeing the two of them like that, crouched over the Fleet-Admiral and in desperate need of privacy, Kwenn went silently out the front door, there to deliver the news that the order for "protective custody" had been rescinded, and to announce to the Fleet-Admiral's patient Khagggun that the time had come to reassert Pnin's control of his own compound. Fleetingly, he wondered what the regent, who hadn't been heard from in a sidereal day, would make of these events. More tellingly, he had a personal interest in what action the Gyrgon would take.

Meanwhile, inside the villa, with the stink and offal of death all around them, Sornnn and Leyytey carried the Fleet-Admiral's body to his bed. He was very heavy, but neither of them seemed aware of it.

When they were certain that he was comfortable, it seemed as if they both wanted to speak at once. Sornnn led her through the partially open slider out into the back garden. They sat on the same bench Sornnn had occupied with Pnin that night not so long ago when they had schemed a way out of his predicament. It is safe to say that neither could have predicted this outcome.

Above, the trees sprayed the darkling sky with green and gold. Gimnopedes dipped and twittered. But the stench of death clung to their clothes and nostrils.

Sornnn finally found his voice. "Was that the first time you have killed?" It was not what he had meant to say. It was simply what had come out.

She nodded.

"It's not easy, is it?"

Her eyes filled with tears. It was clear she was holding them back with a great force of will. She began to tremble, then she could hold out no longer and put her head in her hands.

"Leyytey," he said softly. "Leyytey."

She told him, then, what had happened. When she came to the part about her father wagering on her, Sornnn broke out into laughter.

It made him happy in a way he had not believed he would ever feel again. "Ah, Leyytey, your father must be so proud of you." He took her hand, prying it away from her tear-streaked face. "At last he understands."

"You think so?"

"Yes, I do. But you will find out for yourself when he wakes up."

"I confess I am terrified of the moment. It seems to me that I have been terrified of him all my life."

"And there he was, lavishing such attention on you."

"I was always afraid that I would in some way further disappoint him or that he would find fault with what I did."

"He loves your work. He told me that from the moment you first began turning out weapons, he took them into battle and would use no others."

"Really? He said that?" Her eyes were made wide and candid by the magnifying lens of her tears. She shook her head. "What happened to him back there? How ill is he? Is he going to be all right?"

"He has a kind of brain anomaly, a tumor."

"It's inoperable?"

"I doubt it. But you know what would happen to him if he disclosed his disability to the Genomatekks."

"He was going to sacrifice his life to his career?"

"In so many ways he had already done that. Why not this one?"

"Because it is insane."

"Not to him it wasn't. It made perfect sense. Being Fleet-Admiral is his life." He sighed. "Listen to me, Leyytey. It is not only *he* who needs to understand you. *You* have to try to understand him. It's the only way for the two of you, now, you see?"

For some time she remained lost in thought. The moonslight that had fallen upon them in their leafy bower faded as high clouds sailed past. Sornnn found the utter darkness, no matter how fleeting, somehow comforting, as if time had stopped and he could pretend that Marethyn wasn't dead at all, but alive with her new Resistance comrades somewhere in the high ridges of the Djenn Marre. She was right there beside him, so real he could almost reach out and touch her beautiful, proud face.

Presently the moonslight returned, and the beatific image retreated to its proper place.

Leyytey stirred and straightened just as a Khagggun would. "I was so unkind to you—"

"Forget it. Old news."

"Thank you for coming, Sornnn. Thank you for your loyalty to my father."

"We have that, at least, in common, don't we?"

At last she laughed with him, and, reaching out, embraced him as she had never been able to do with her brothers, long dead, and afterward—too late—missing them terribly, had ached to do with all her hearts.

28

Necromancy

Among the Ramahan, little is understood of necromancy," Giyan said. "It has never been studied like other forms of sorcery because it was considered too dangerous, too evil."

She and Krystren were in the abbey's Temple of Flowing Out, waiting for Varda. The sun had vanished behind a dirty grey pall. A shadowless light, filtering like a shroud through the doorway, filled the temple with a certain tension. She had shown Varda where she was, and he was coming to destroy them. They had a plan, but would it work? Krystren knew full well how clever and powerful the archon was.

"The Hagoshrin know all about it," she said softly.

"I suppose I should not be surprised. Hagoshrin eat the bones of their living prey."

"Giyan, everything you thought you knew about Hagoshrin is false." Twelve thick columns held aloft the high, vaulted ceiling. Shadows clung like billows of smoke to the curled, hornlike capitals and, above them, the infrastructure of the massive three-tiered architrave. The air was resinous, the residue of centuries of burned incense. "I know because in the forest south of here I came across one."

"A Hagoshrin? Really?"

"His name was Bryn." And so began Krystren's tale of her encounter with the Hagoshrin.

"He looked like *what?*" Giyan turned to her as she described Bryn's physical appearance. "He told you that the other Hagoshrin's punishment was what turned him into a hideous beast?"

"Yes."

"But that is monstrous."

"And in helping us, Bryn, too, willfully broke Miina's edict."

"Why would he do that?"

"Because he was basically good. And because he was unspeakably lonely."

Giyan shook her head. "Miina, Great Goddess, what is Your will?"

"He crawled inside our head while we were asleep. We were so angry with him. You should have seen his face, Giyan. Like a boy slapped by his mother. We thought he was trying to learn the secret of our mind-feelers, but all he wanted was to feel closer to us."

Giyan thought about this for some time. "Poor Bryn," she said at last. "Poor Hagoshrin."

Krystren liked this mysterious female tremendously, felt a curious form of kinship with her that she was at a loss to explain. "Bryn said that the very presence of the *gabir* means that the sauromicians have gained possession of the banestones."

"In fact they have eight," Giyan said bleakly. "There remains only one more for them to find." A sound not unlike a roof tile slipping brought them to silence. They stood very still, listened. Nothing. They returned to their conversation, but their tension level had ratcheted up several notches.

Giyan had released most of the safeguards she had activated when she had gained access to the abbey's Library.

To have deactivated all of them would doubtless have made Varda suspicious.

"How does a Sarakkon know about banestones? Bryn?"

Krystren nodded. "We are *Onnda*." So began her careful explanation of the secret Sarakkonian society and its blood nemesis, *Sintire*.

Giyan was silent throughout, concentrated fully on each word. When Krystren was finished, Giyan said, "Yes, but you have left out the crucial part. Do all *Onnda* possess your sorcerous skills?"

Krystren smiled, liking Giyan all the more for her keen intelligence. "No. Just as few Ramahan are seers, so few *Onnda* know what you call sorcery. We are also *crifica*. But it is not sorcery. We are taught to use our minds in a particular way."

"Show me."

Krystren sent out a mind-feeler. At once, she could "see" into Giyan's mind, like peering through a stained-crystal window. She saw the V'ornn child Annon, Giyan's love for him, her mourning.

She said, "We are so sorry about Annon."

"As I am for your brother's death."

"So the connection is two-way."

"I apologize."

Krystren shook her head. "No need. You have taught us a valuable lesson." She sighed. "If it is fate that we should never see Courion again, then so be it. We each chose our fates when we became *Onnda*."

"These words lack the emotion I saw inside you."

"Now you *should* apologize."

They listened to the soughing of the wind, but there was scant comfort in the sound. Krystren looked into Giyan's eyes. "It is widely believed that during training *Onnda* lose all their emotions, that it is better that way, easier to kill. No remorse, no guilt, nothing to mourn."

Giyan gazed back at her in silence.

"Obviously, you know our secret now. We loved Courion. We felt remorse when his lover died in a fall as we were hiking in the caldera of Oppamonifex. We felt guilt when Courion blamed us for Orujo's death. We are sick with mourning at our brother's death." Even then, she could not bring herself to mention how Minnum's death had affected her. That was too private. And, thank Yahé, Giyan had not seen it.

In fact, Giyan had seen it. Though it told her a lot about Krystren's nature, though she rejoiced for Minnum, she was nevertheless aware that she had trespassed on something profoundly personal. Leaning forward, she put her hand over Krystren's. "There is no shame in this. Quite the opposite."

"Not for *Onnda*. We were sent here on a secret mission to deliver something of value to Courion. In our heart we thought only to postpone our reunion because we were afraid of confronting him, afraid of his anger, afraid that we would no longer be brother and sister. Instead, we find that he is dead, that we will never know how he felt, whether he forgave us or would have forgiven us. On top of that the *Sintire* had foreknowledge of our arrival here and are using all their skills to capture us."

Giyan's eyes had closed, and now a shiver ran through her body. "He is here."

"Here, inside the abbey?" Krystren stood in deepest shadow.

Giyan's eyes opened. "Here, inside the temple."

Eleana, jammed against the pantry door, had stopped her pounding the moment she heard the eerie screaming from upstairs. She instinctively crouched down, hands over her ears. Her blood curdled. What was happening? She kept dead still, put her ear against the door, listening hard.

Silence. And after a time, the tread of footfalls on the stairway. One set. Only one. Pressed her ear all the harder so that when the footfalls reached the ground floor she could tell by the stride that it wasn't Riane. Too long, long legs a prerequisite, a male. Kurgan.

Coming her way.

Shrank back, turning in the semidarkness, scrabbling at the foodstuffs on the shelves. The pantry was deeper than she had realized, the rear wall hewn out of the bedrock. She pushed the foodstuffs out of the way. She could not now hear the footfalls. Were they still coming her way? Sweat broke out at her hairline, on her upper lip, salt dripped into the corner of her mouth.

Crawling onto the lowest shelf, squeezing all the way into the back, she curled up like a fetus. Moving the foodstuffs back in place in front of her, a wall against the possibility—

A screech and she froze. The door opened and light flooded in, did not reach her. Still, she was there, breathing, eyes squeezed shut. If she couldn't see him, he couldn't see her. An instinctual response. Unbidden, the image of Kurgan bloomed in her mind. She could see him, smell him, feel his hands on her, moving, parting her flesh, and a great sob welled up within her. She bit her lip to keep it bottled up. Inside her, terror and rage fought a pitched battle.

It was the silence that induced her to open one eye. Through a crack of light in her wall she could see a sliver of face, a dark beard, mustache like the blade of a dagger. Tall. Taller than Kurgan. Who then? As he turned, she saw the swirl of tattoos across the side of his head. Sarakkon!

In one hand he held a small milkwhite wand like a weapon. In his other hand, the banestone. Held it up as if it were a lantern or a torch, moving it here and there in the pantry, apparently to no effect. Eleana knew he was using it to look for her as Kurgan had, but for some reason it was not working for him. He turned and stalked out.

How had he gotten the banestone from Kurgan? What had happened to Riane and Thigpen? She shuddered with an ague of dreadful but unfounded conclusions.

When she was certain she was alone, she raced upstairs, found no one, nothing save Kurgan's ion pistol, which she appropriated. What could have become of Riane—and for

that matter, Kurgan? The Sarakkon! He might have the answer. Following him was far better than any other possibility she could think of. She turned, raced back down the
corridor, slid down the bannister to the ground floor, and
out the front door.

Since the street was a dead end, there was only one way
for the Sarakkon to go. She saw him turning a corner,
slowed down by something, possibly an injury to his left
side. She tore after him.

In the old days, before the coming of the V'ornn, before
the sauromician uprising, before everything changed,
there had been much blood spilled in the Temple of Flowing Out. Sacrifices of qwawd, gimnopedes, even cor to
propitiate Miina were commonplace, especially during
festivals, which in the Ramahan calendar, were legion.

Giyan, her senses open and attuned to the peculiar reso-
nance of the temple itself, was abruptly aware of the
blood, as if she had entered a slaughterhouse. And then, as
she caught a glimpse of Varda with her Third Eye, she
knew her own mental reference for the stench was mis-
placed. What she was smelling was the whiff of necromancy that surrounded him like a buzzing cloud of
bloodflies.

Her vision showed her first that Varda was wearing an
articulated metal glove over the hand with the vulnerable
black finger. Then it revealed to her the white necromantic
eye that Krystren had warned her about. The eye was moving this way and that, independent of his other eye, piercing the gloom like a searchlight. Alarmed, Giyan moved,
so that it became aware of her.

It rolled in her direction, and she could see what Krystren never had, that the eye, plucked from the head of his
victim at the moment of death, was insubstantial. It had to
be; it was dead tissue, and by the immutable laws of the
Cosmos dead tissue began after a very short time to de-
compose. The necrosis was being held in a kind of stasis
by the necromancy, and while it gave the dead eye great

power, it did so at a cost of tremendous energy. That, too, was an immutable law of the Cosmos. Giyan knew that if she could find a way to increase the load of energy Varda expended to fuel the white eye, she would have a chance to defeat him.

Across the interior of the temple Varda paused. He saw Giyan as if through veils of sand, her image indistinct, inconstant, but undeniably there. He fixed his white eye on her as she slipped behind one pillar, then another, saw her through the porphyry as a shadow, two-dimensional, outlined like an aura. Dimly, he was aware of how much he relied on his necromantic eye. Why shouldn't he? The other archons were covetous of it; it set him apart from them. He had taken an enormous risk in channeling the eye from the newly dead, for in the Korrush where they had begun their study of necromancy in depth, he had heard tales of sorcerers eaten alive by the necrosis of the dead, since an organ torn by necromancy from the dying was infected with the agonized spirit of the victim. For this reason, it had to be handled with the utmost care, and a great deal of energy had to be expended in keeping it functioning. But he had had to do something, for the young archon Haamadi was not like the others. Only the white eye ensured Varda's superiority. Haamadi's unassuming persona might fool the others, but Varda saw it for what it really was, understood his ambition to be one archon over all. He had proved remarkably useful in holding the stolen Ramahan in thrall and it had been his idea to create a false Dar Sala-at—a male whom the Ramahan would readily follow. He possessed an astonishing sense of the psychological makeup of others. Yet another reason for Varda to be wary of him. Now, with Caligo gone, it was up to Varda to keep him in his place, to make certain that whoever replaced Caligo as the third archon was Varda's choice.

He returned his furious attention to Giyan. His white eye had been tracking her even as she tried to elude him. It galled him no end that Giyan could move freely about the abbey, while he was confined to those buildings not built atop bourn lines. The Library, which was of intense interest to him, was guarded so thoroughly by power bourns that he had had to use the Sarakkon *Ardinals* to gather information by proxy.

It was not lost on him that he had found Giyan in the Temple of Flowing Out, one of the few structures in the abbey *not* built atop a power bourn. So she wanted to engage him, was deluded enough to believe that she could defeat him. Well and good. The Ramahan abhorrence of causing pain and suffering ensured that they had no working knowledge of necromancy. She knew neither its origins nor the extent of its power. Such ignorance would spell her doom.

For many reasons, not the least of which was to savor the moment, he took his time stalking her. She was the one who knew enough about the Skreeling Engine to snuff out the Eye of Ajbal. He was already imagining reaching into her brain to extract all her knowledge, an entire Library's worth. And what was the first thing he would do with his new knowledge? Turn around and wipe out the Sarakkon *Ardinals* who, already it seemed to him, had an overinflated opinion of themselves. They had been beaten out of the northern continent once before. It would not be so difficult to do that again.

As he narrowed the distance between them, he used his white eye to probe her defenses, to get a sense of the ultimate extent of her power. Already, he knew that she was no ordinary Ramahan konara; she was something special—which would make raiding her brain that much more delicious.

He waited for his moment, waited until she was behind another pillar. Then he shot twin bolts of cold fire from his fingertips, which first bracketed the pillar, then coiled around her and, pulled her tight against the cool, smooth porphyry. With a sudden movement, he squeezed. The coils sliced through the stone pillar in half a dozen places, causing the heavy carved capital and the uppermost section of the pillar to which it was attached to come crashing down.

Thunder of stone grinding against stone echoed through the temple vaults as Varda sprinted through the choking clouds of dust toward Giyan. As he did so, a shadow dropped from the upper reaches of the architrave where it had secreted itself. Onto his back crashed Krystren.

They fell to the stone floor, gasping and struggling. Varda tried to twist himself onto his back, tried to fix her with his white eye, but he felt the painful clamp of a powerful spell. Giyan, having somehow extricated herself from the falling debris, was trying to overpower him. He was about to laugh at her pathetic attempt to trap him when he caught sight of the crystal dagger in Krystren's fist. With her free hand, she was trying to rip off his metal glove, trying to expose his black finger to the dagger's blade.

Pulling on the glove, he tried to protect his hand, but Giyan kept changing her spells, and he was growing dizzy with trying to counter each one in turn. The glove was more than half-off. In a moment, she would sever his sixth finger, and he would be done for. Where was that *Ardinal*?

Krystren, fighting with every ounce of her strength to sever Varda's black finger before he could turn his necromantic eye on her, could tell him just where the *Ardinal* was, because his strong arm was around her throat, his powerful presence behind her, trying to wrench her off Varda. In defense, she bent over double, in offense, she kicked backward. But, improbably, he seemed prepared for this maneuver, and he tightened his grip on her throat, choking off air.

"Don't make us kill you."

The voice, so chillingly familiar, froze her long enough for Varda to break free of her. He chopped down on her wrist, and the crystal dagger went skittering across the floor into shadow.

"It can't be." Her mind a seething morass of shock and denial.

"Oh, but it is," Orujo Aersthone, her friend, Courion's lover, said. Back from the dead.

Eleana was almost overcome by the miasma of stench as she made her way through the underground labyrinth toward Black Farm. After spending a fruitless half hour searching for him, she gave up. The strange wand the Sarakkon had was much on her mind, so she decided to pay another visit to Sagiira. If anyone she knew could tell her what it was and whether it had been used to spirit Riane and Thigpen away, it was the old sauromician. Perhaps he could also tell her where the Sarakkon had gone.

She had first met Sagiira as a small child, taken by her mother into Axis Tyr as cover for a Resistance mission. All had gone well, Eleana enjoying the new sights, sounds, and smells of the big city, until a melee had unexpectedly erupted, at the height of which she and her mother were separated. She was about to launch herself, bravely but foolishly into the midst of the fighting when she had been caught around the waist from behind and dragged out of harm's way—in this case from a broad but potentially lethal swipe of a Khaggun shock-sword.

Over her protests, Sagiira had whisked her away underground to the Black Farm, where she would be safe. The trouble was she hadn't wanted to be safe, she wanted to be with her mother, helping in the struggle against the feared and hated V'ornn. To that end, she had run away almost as soon as he had brought her to his quarters. He had turned his back to make some tea for them, and she had scooted out, only to run into Muzli's gaping jaws. Her yelp of surprise had brought him, not at a run but a slow walk. He could see that she was petrified, would not take a single step for fear Muzli would chomp down on her leg or some other even more vital part of her.

He had laughed, a clue to Muzli that everything was all right, and the claiwen crept closer the better to nuzzle his snout against her legs. That made her laugh, and so began their friendship.

Years later, she had killed a Khagggun Third-Marshal who had gotten his nose too close to Sagiira's business, dragging him away with the help of her Resistance cell members, dumping him in the Great Phosphorus Swamp, where doubtless Muzli's distant cousins had made of him a tasty meal.

Eleana, her mind full of the past, found Sagiira's quarters easily enough. Nearing them, she felt a pang of sadness, for no Muzli came stampeding toward her to press his long ugly snout between her legs. She thought of his eyes rolling up in ecstasy as she scratched his scaly hide, his loyal fervor, his undying love for his master. These melancholy thoughts brought her to the open doorway to Sagiira's quarters, but he was not there. Back in the reeking corridor, she accosted an old woman limping by, who told her to look for Sagiira in the infirmary. She was gone before Eleana could ask her where the infirmary was, and three others either did not know the way or gave her faulty directions. At length, she found a small boy to take her hand in his filthy one and lead her through corridor after corridor to a large doorway. There he left her, unwilling himself to enter.

The stench had been bad enough in the corridors, within the room was so unbearable that she was obliged to put the crook of her arm over her nose and mouth in order to keep her stomach from rebelling. She proceeded down a narrow central aisle past four tiers of pallets, two on either side. The infirmary was crowded, and it was not easy looking for him among all the volunteer workers. She had just about given up when she heard her name being called.

She turned and, heart in her throat, saw him not administering to the ill and wounded as she had expected, but lying on a pallet, himself a patient in this dreadful place. At once, she ran to the pallet and knelt beside him, pressed like a dead leaf his crepey hand between hers.

"So good to see you again, my brave one." His voice had a thin, reedy quality that seemed to pierce her to the marrow.

"Sagiira." Peering down at his ashen face. "What has happened to you? Are you ill? I will get you whatever medicine you need."

He shook his head, his hair, damp and lank, lying on the thin pillow like a scatter of bones. "I am ill, but not in the sense you mean. No medicine can help me."

His voice had grown faint, and she leaned closer. As she did so, she noticed a kind of calcification, crystals crusting the corner of his mouth.

"Ah, you see it." His eyes searched her face. "I have been caught, in a manner of speaking, by those who have been searching for me. I have been poisoned by my brethren."

"Sauromicians!"

"Yes."

"Dear Sagiira, isn't there anything I can do to help you?"

"Not a thing. Whether I live or die is entirely up to me." He squeezed her hand. "Now tell me why I have the great pleasure of seeing you again."

So she told him about the Sarakkon and the strange silvery wand he carried, what it sounded like and looked like when he turned it on.

"An infinity-blade," he said at once. And began to tremble so badly that Eleana scooped him up in her arms and cradled him. With her sleeve, she wiped the crust off his lips.

"Careful," he said. "Madila in this concentrated form will drive you mad if you ingest it."

She could see more of it on his tongue. In response to her motion, he stuck out his tongue. Ripping off the hem of her sleeve, she took the crystals.

"Wrap that up tightly and don't leave it here," he warned.

"Don't worry." She tied off the twist of fabric and slipped it into her pocket. "Now what can you tell me about this infinity-blade?"

"Describe the Sarakkon in more detail."

She did as he asked, telling him of the Sarakkon's

height, his dark beard, mustache like a dagger's blade, the swirl of tattoos across the side of his head. Sagiira, eyes closed, nodded. His skin so thin, his pulse revealed itself through bulging arteries.

"I have seen him," he said in the dry, papery voice that so frightened her. "He has been in the company of sauromician archons, and will be again." His eyes opened, fixed on Eleana. "I have looked inside his mind. His name is Lujon. His infinity-blade is one of two the Sarakkon possess. They were discovered at the bottom of the Oppamonifex caldera—the great volcano on the southern continent. Since found, they have had a storied history—one stolen again, blood spilled, lives lost." He shuddered again. "Too much to take in."

"Don't try," she said, seeing how much it took out of him. "Concentrate on fighting the Madila." She held him tighter. "Sagiira, can you tell me where Lujon is now?"

Sagiira's eyes were closed. Little shivers like the death throes of a bird ran through his body. Eleana held him, said nothing. She concentrated, straining to direct her energies in helping him stave off the pernicious effects of the Madila. He gasped once and was still, the shivers gone. His breathing was shallow but even.

"Boarding a ship named *Omaline*." Dry lips moving in a whisper against her cocked ear. "They are preparing to set sail. Go there. Quick as you can."

"I don't want to leave you."

He smiled, his eyes pale and watery. "My brave one, you have quite literally lifted me from my deathbed. Now go. They are bound for the island of Suspended Skull. I see that your friend Riane will be there presently." He grasped her wrist with his long, bony fingers. "You must be there to warn her. Though there seem to be power bourns beneath Suspended Skull, that is an illusion. One of many in and around the island. In fact, it is the only place on Kundala where no power bourns exist at all."

Sagiira watched Eleana vanish down the crowded corridor before he raised himself up. He moved easily, without real effort. He went to the door of the infirmary to make certain she had left. No one paid him any attention. Returning to the mean room, he lifted the rug, opened the trapdoor beneath. Levering himself into the blackness, he held out his hand. In it, appeared an orb of light that burned cool and steady. By its light, another figure could be discerned, gagged and cruelly bound with ion whips. As the eerie glow advanced on the filthy, emaciated creature, his features became plain. In every detail, they were identical to the Sagiira who held the cold light in his palm.

"It has not been easy keeping you alive," the impostor said to the real Sagiira. "How many times have you tried to kill yourself during the eighteen months I have kept you incarcerated. I have lost count."

Sagiira cringed away from the cold light, averted his face, covered his nearly hairless head with grimy fingers.

"You do not react well to pain, do you, dear Sagiira?" The impostor put his hand on Sagiira's head in a gesture of absolute possession. "At least, not the sort at my disposal."

Sagiira's eyes got big around, and the bony shoulders began to shake.

The impostor nodded. "As you have intuited, time to extract more knowledge."

Sometime later, the being known to Eleana as Sagiira emerged from the prison he had in secret fashioned for the real Sagiira. He emerged into the corridor, heading in the opposite direction Eleana had taken. He was soon out of the Black Farm and, by a hidden stairway known only to him, ascended out of the reeking bowels of Axis Tyr. By the time he had reached the outer gates of the Temple of Mnemonics he had resumed his real shape.

"Nith Immmon," one of the Gyrgon guards said as he passed into the first antechamber. "It is good to have you back."

The sudden appearance of the *Ardinal*, a Sarakkon that Krystren clearly knew, gave Giyan a choice: continue to engage Varda in their psychic duel or go after the crystal dagger. Having learned from Krystren its power, she whirled and threw herself into the shadows where it had vanished.

Unfortunately, Varda had the same idea. They collided, fetching up against the ornately sculpted plinth of a column. The moment she touched him, she saw the Ramahan being herded into the death pit, being told to drink the potion laced with toxic Madila, the psychotic fury unleashed by the drug. Saw all this through Varda's eyes, filtered by his brain so that she felt what he had, the almost sexual excitement at the nearness of death—so many deaths at once, such a rush of energy released!—positively giddy with it. They had not known which way to turn first when the moment came upon them—*pom, pom, pom*—like shots fired in a string, the deaths coming fast now, too fast to keep track of or to make use of, but, oh, the ecstasy of the long-drawn-out moment, the intense shiver of delight it delivered to him!

Giyan, horrified, recoiled from the contact, and in that instant Varda gathered the dagger to him, kissed it like a long-lost child at the spot where handle and guards crossed, and jabbed it at her stomach. The blade slid through her first, hastily erected defensive spell, in the process bringing her pain. As cold fire swept up her arm, the stench of rotting corpses, decaying flesh, the miasma of the open grave, assaulted her. The point of the dagger pierced her robes, but as she was rolling away, the edge tore through the silk and nothing more.

What was it about the dagger? Giyan asked herself as Varda pursued her. She needed an answer, knew she would not be able to defeat him without it. She raised her forearm, a clumsy gesture, the blade scoring her skin, drawing blood. The pain all but made her faint. It had attacked all her nerve endings at once, producing a pain cascade that in someone not similarly trained would have shorted out the nerve circuits, causing instant unconsciousness. Giyan, prepared for this eventuality, had cast a series of defensive spells one inside the other to keep herself safe. Wise that she had done so, for the pain cascade burst through the first three spells, was slowed by the fourth and was, at last, stopped by the fifth. Quickly, she cast another as reserve.

By the feral grin on his face it was clear that Varda was pleased with her loss of blood. In an odd way, so was Giyan, for at the instant the blade sliced through her skin her Sight had given her a clear picture of the crystal used for the blade. It was white quartz, mined in the northern-most reaches of the Korrush, a stark landscape, where bleak foothills rose toward the rugged, snow-shrouded spires of the Djenn Marre. The dagger was shaped crudely, possibly by Varda himself. But there all resemblance to a traditional weapon ended, for it had been exposed to necromantic forces, wrapped in glistening strands of intestine, pulled still pulsing during the victim's death throes. It had been immersed in warm heart blood while Varda chanted over it, invoking the spirits of the newly dead, coercing them while they were vulnerable to incarcerate themselves inside the crystal, forced to lend it their unwilling energy.

In fact, she now had some of that energy inside her, and she was using First-Gate Correspondence to release it into its constituent parts. The resulting warmth flowed through her, first healing her wound, then arming her against Varda's next assault. He feinted left, drove right. With a shallow sweep of the dagger, he slit open her belly from one side to another. No blood flowed, however. The incision closed itself almost immediately, the two flaps of flesh meshing, remerging into one.

Seeing that happen, Varda slipped the dagger into the belt at his left hip and fixed her with his white necromantic eye. Giyan, caught in the unholy gaze, could not look away; nor could she even blink. She felt the full force of the archon's power concentrated in that gaze, felt the loosed spirits inside her quail and gibber incoherently, felt his exhilaration in reasserting control over them.

And that was when she saw what she had to do. The black finger, the necromantic eye, these were only outward manifestations of a power that had a fixed place in the Cosmos. It was Varda's obsession with controlling as much spirit force as he could that defined him. It was what had made him order the massed deaths of the Ramahan, why he had insisted on the alliance with the Sarakkon who could enter the Abbey of Five Pivots at will without worrying about the power bourns.

The eye that held her was powerful, but not as much as he believed. But Giyan, mindful of who Varda was beneath his archon's persona, fell back, allowed him to believe that she was entirely paralyzed. He struck her, and again, put his hands on either side of her head so that she could not turn away. On top of her, he partook of the contours of her body with rough mouth and even rougher hands. His eye bored into hers until Giyan did feel the dread paralysis begin to seep through all her defenses. It was time, and she knew it. He was close enough, reveling on the brink of victory. She could feel his ardor, feel him swollen, and she spread her thighs just enough to get his attention.

At the same time, she slipped her hand to his left hip, drew the dagger out of his belt. She held it firmly in her hand, for one thrust was all she would get, turned it just so, slamming it at the perfect angle against the fluted column. The tip sheared off and at once she felt the quick beat of the imprisoned spirits and she drove the blade, shattered point first, into Varda's white necromantic eye.

He reared up, bellowed terribly. He twisted this way and that, flailing, scratching, biting. Through all of that she did not let go of the hilt, but rather twisted it until the blade was plunged to its limit, piercing straight through his eye socket, releasing all the pent-up spirit energy into his brain. His body thrashed, green fire crackled, arcing off him. He screamed, and the green fire flared up and burned her, but still she held on while he thrashed and moaned and tried his best to kill her. But the spirit energy was moving the crystal blade through his brain, slicing and rending, and at last the green fire winked out, and his body lay still. Silence from his mind. And then a rushing as of wind in a tunnel passed by Giyan's right ear. Whispered in ghostly chorus, "*Thank you.*"

Orujo, taking full advantage of the shock of surprise, drew Krystren out of the temple. Rain obscured the dull sky, turned the surrounding buildings to vague, bulky shapes hunkered on their calcified haunches. When the smell of the ground and the foliage began to revive her, Orujo struck her again, driving a knuckle into the soft indentation behind the orbital bone, and she collapsed in his arms.

In the middle of the garden the fitful wind showered them with brief gusts of rain. He held her tight, and she did not attempt to break away.

"*You're dead,*" she whispered.

He laughed. "Apparently not."

"But we were there. We saw you fall to your death."

"Ah, the power of assumption." He smiled at her. "You saw us fall—"

"It was a long way down."

"Yes, a very long way down. And so you assumed we fetched up at the bottom of the caldera, every bone in our body broken. But the truth is it was all planned. We needed to get to the Oppamonifex caldera and we needed a witness—a credible witness, we might add—to report to Courion that we had died." He shrugged. "Who better for that messenger's job than you, Krystren?"

"But you were his lover, our friend."

"True enough. And do not think that we did not enjoy our time with the two of you. But, truth be told, a good part of the pleasure was in keeping our secret, in playing a predetermined role. We are *Sintire Ardinal*. But you have already guessed that, haven't you?"

"All the time you were with Courion you spied on him? You pretended to love him?"

"Nothing was pretense. That was how we succeeded." He shook his head. "Do not hate us, Krystren. We do not think we could bear it."

Krystren stared at him silently.

"You must understand. We know everything. We know Cerro charged you with bringing the wand to Courion."

"One of the wands you found at the bottom of Oppamonifex. Why didn't you die?"

"You do hate us."

"You should have died in that fall. Anyone else would have."

"So. We will tell you whatever you wish to know. Do you remember the jacket we were wearing?"

"Vividly. It was turquoise."

"It was made for us by the females of the High Cathedral. It opened up"—he let go of her, threw wide his arms—"into wings that slowed our descent, that broke our fall. And so we landed in the arms of Abrasea."

"So what you want is the wand."

"We have to admit that Courion got under our skin. Poor us. We were unprepared for that. We had to adjust. In retrospect, we should have figured it out sooner. He was unique, your brother. As are you." Slid the back of his hand along her cheek. "This is all so needless, you know. Join us."

"Join you? You and your sauromician allies have been trying their best to track us down and kill us."

"Not us. Never us. We are not like the others, Krystren. We have been trying to find you on our own."

"You are just like them. Duplicitous, power-mad, evil."

He shook his head. "We are the only one who can protect you now. With us you are safe, Krystren. Believe that."

"Why should we?"

"Now that Courion is dead, it will be so easy to leave your old life behind. Just take our hand, and we will slip away together. No one will know what happened to you."

"We will know."

"Do you think we enjoy this? Do you think we want to hurt you? We will make it worth your while. Come with us, and we swear you will not be sorry."

"We trusted you once, and you lied to us."

"Listen to us." Put his lips beside her ear. "You are our only link to Courion. We cherished him."

"Even while you were betraying him?"

"You of all people should understand how that is possible. Can we not love and hate our parents at the same time? Can we not hold two opposing emotions in our hearts? We are made masters of rationalization, are we not? We are trained to compartmentalize everything. In that way, no emotion can overwhelm us. But once in a great while an emotion is so intense it breaks even our bonds. Tell us that is not so. Tell us you have never had it happen."

Krystren, thinking of the love she felt for Courion, for Minnum, said nothing.

"Training—even ours—only goes so far, isn't that your experience? It certainly is ours." He held her now, but not as an enemy. Not even as a friend. "Come with us to the island of Suspended Skull. We want you beside us. We want to take you for our wife, to cherish you, to protect you. Linked this way, we will honor his memory together."

The rain was soft now, tiny pinpoints, gentle as dew. Mist crept through the garden, obscured the five towers. Even the temple looked indistinct, far away.

"How do we know it's us you want and not the wand?"

"Your brother is dead, Krystren, your mission no longer exists. Tell us, what is your purpose now here among the Kundalan?"

She stood very still, watching him.

"Don't give us the wand." He shrugged. "In fact, don't even tell us where you have hidden it. We need time to win your trust, we know. Let us prove that everything we have told you is true. Let your heart guide you, Krystren. That is all we ask."

"Give us one reason why we should trust you."

"We cannot, Krystren. You know we cannot. All we can say is that the past is the past. Everything else lies before us."

At last, she nodded. "All right. We will allow you to

prove yourself. But do not expect anything to change quickly."

"We will expect nothing. Nevertheless, you have made us very happy. Let us make all haste now."

He took her hand, but as they were about to depart, a figure emerged from the mist and called Krystren's name in an urgent tone.

"Giyan," she said, turning back.

"Where are you going?"

"Do not interfere, Kundalan." Orujo took a step toward Giyan. "This is none of your concern."

Giyan ignored him. "What form of fell coercion is this?"

Krystren pushed Orujo back. "We are going with Orujo of our own free will."

Giyan directed her right hand downward, her fingers splayed outward. They heard a deep rumbling, and the ground shook as up from the rock-bed depths arose a column of light force—a sinew of power bourn drawn from its natural course by a powerful spell. It coiled itself around her wrist, flickered from her fingertips, and she held it out, a threat and a promise.

"I do not believe you," she said.

"The truth is we do not belong here. My beloved brother is dead. We belong with our kind."

"But this one—"

"Giyan, please. Do not provoke a needless confrontation." Krystren pushed Orujo back into the mist. "Our mind is made up. We are going now. We beg you to forget we ever met."

With that she turned and, together with Orujo, vanished into a thick swirl of mist.

Giyan called her name again, but the sound was muffled and instantly died away. In any event, there was no reply. Still she went forward a few paces to stand where Krystren had stood, as if there was something in that spot that would reveal the Sarakkon's inexplicable behavior.

In fact, there was. Giyan's gaze was drawn to the ground at her feet, where dark markings mingled with the boot prints of Krystren and Orujo. Dropping to her haunches, she read what Krystren's busy fingers had written in the damp ground.

SUSPENDED SKULL. WHERE THEY ALL ARE.

Immediately, she rushed off, climbing the stairs to the Library, where the Skreeling Engine hulked, waiting.

Eleana, keeping herself well hidden within the crowd along the Promenade, eeled her way toward the Sarakkon ship *Omaline,* which lay to tied up at the seventh slip, but she stopped well short of her goal. Her keen Resistance eye noted several Khagggun out of uniform, posing as Bashkir and Mesagggun. They were keeping the *Omaline* under surveillance. Sagiira had been right. From the activity of the crew it was clear the ship was making ready to set sail. As she pondered what to do next, she wondered whether Riane and Thigpen lay in its hold, tied up or in irons, or worse.

As if galvanized by the thought, a scheme occurred to her. She pinched her cheeks hard to start the tears flowing, then ran as fast as she could. Looking over her shoulder, she slammed right into one of the out-of-uniform Khagggun, who caught her before she hit the ground. As he looked her up and down, it was easy for her to act terrified, for her to blubber that she had glimpsed a Sarakkon—here she gave an accurate description of Lujon—with a Khagggun weapon hidden under his vest.

Her story was enough to send the already on-edge surveillance team into action. Declaring themselves to the startled Sarakkon crew, they swiftly and authoritatively boarded the *Omaline,* looking for Lujon. As their interrogation occupied the crew, it was a simple matter for Eleana to slip through the sea rail, climb down to the dock itself, and from there lower herself unobserved into the water. Swimming under the surface, she soon came to the place on the hull of the *Omaline* where the bow hawser arced down just above the waterline. Grasping it, she hauled herself hand over hand up its thick, slippery length to the foredeck, where she hid behind the mass of a huge iron-and-wood capstan, molding her body to the sculpted bowsprit until, peering through a deadeye, she saw her opportunity. Creeping down into the hold, she shook herself off and began her careful search, hoping to find Riane and Thigpen. In fact, she found nothing, not even a single box or sack. The ship was without cargo, which was extremely odd for a Sarakkon vessel. She was just beginning to ponder this conundrum where she felt the ship begin to move. Apparently, the Khagggun had found nothing and had no reason to keep the *Omaline* in port.

Using all the stealth at her disposal, she crept up the steep companionway and dared to look out past the rolling deck. There she saw the Axis Tyr harbor growing ever smaller. There was a stiff breeze, freshening out of the southeasterly quarter. She could hear Lujon calmly giving orders as the ship headed west to its unknown destiny, carrying her along with it.

29

The Shallow Grave

*T*hink of a pinhole in our Realm," Giyan had said. Riane had gone through the pinhole, into the null-space between Realms. She recalled Thigpen saying, *A shallow grave. Nasty, nasty.*

Where was Thigpen?

She herself was drifting. Awash on a current slowly moving, dragging her out into the deeps of a bottomless sea.

She opened her mouth, felt as if water had rushed in. Null-space filling her up with darkness, like a tube expanding in her throat and stomach. It was as if everything she had known or understood to be true had been reversed. Instead of standing on solid ground she floated in air; instead of breathing air, the atmosphere was solid. No wonder Thigpen had called it nasty. It was inimical to life, hence the name null-space. The interstices between Realms, what kept them from flying apart, was necessarily like glue.

She was aware of nothing save the need to breathe, the sure knowledge that she would not be able to do so. Then her hand floated up in front of her face. It was still clasped tightly around the infinity-blade wand, and her mind flashed. She was somewhere, where?, cold, white. Wind howling. She heard a familiar voice saying to her, *"Worlds . . . worlds within worlds . . . on top of each other like layers of an infinite cake . . . and in between . . ."* What? Remembered snatches from Riane's damaged memory, fading in and out like sunlight through a maze of forest branches. *"In between there is a way to cut . . ."*

To cut? Riane depressed the tiny gold disc. The infinity-blade flamed on, a torch in the night.

". . . there is a way to cut. . . ."

There *was* a way, Riane knew it. She had to go still, completely still, trusting in the knowledge Riane had been given. She emptied her mind so that the damaged memory could surface fully. She saw her arm at work, moving the infinity-blade. Pure instinct, or rather instinct directed by deeply seeded knowledge.

Light. Pearlescent. A glow, a glimmering rift opening, widening. Where did it lead? Annon's question, the need to empty her mind again. Nothing would work if her mind was full of questions. The infinity-blade sliced open null-space, led her on. Floating. Then, all at once, as the rift opened farther, she accelerated through.

Out the Other Side, to where?

Face like a crumpled cup, and feeling the same, Ardus Pnin groaned. He rose on one elbow, looked blearily around his bedroom, and spat heavily into a shallow alloy pan, thoughtfully provided. He looked down into a river of spittle, threaded with his own dark blood, and began to piece together recent events.

Leyytey, standing in the hallway just outside his door, turned to Sornnn when she heard her father call her name.

"Come in with me," she said.

He shook his head.

"He will want to see you."

"Time enough for that." Sornnn kind but firm. "First things first."

Leyytey entered the room with her hearts in her mouth. She felt about five years old. Her father was sitting up, arms stiffly at his side, she saw with a shock, in order to hold himself upright. Sunlight spilled in through the open slider, soft rustling of the leaves, bright chatter of gimno- pedes. Otherwise, all was quiet.

"I need something to eat."

Not a word about her, or what she had done.

A tray with food and drink on a sideboard had been awaiting his pleasure. She brought the tray over, seeing every crease in his face, a victory or defeat, rise up like a monument, like a hand ready to slap her down. As she slid the tray onto his lap, she thought, *How will my life change, ever?*

"What is this?" Staring down at the food.

"Eat it," she said. "You will feel better."

He did not look at her, took up his utensils. Chewing desultorily, as if what she had prepared had no taste, as if he were eating sand and rock. "Where is Sornnn?"

"Just outside. Shall I fetch him?"

"You know what I hate?" Stopped eating altogether. "I hate that sniveling, anxious-to-please tone."

She stood, stunned, her cheeks flaming. All her stomachs hurt at once.

"And stop looking at me as if I am being dragged to the gates of N'Luuura." He commenced eating again, this time with a fair amount of gusto. "This slingbok stew isn't bad." he said, swallowing. "You make it?"

A favorite of his, remembered from childhood. "Yes." Hard to find her voice. Her head was swimming in a sea of fog.

"Good as it is, I wouldn't want to see you make a habit of it." He finished everything on his plate, drank the goblet of water, and did not, surprisingly, ask for fire-grade numaaadis. "You have more important things to do with your time than cook, or blend into a hingatta, for the matter of that." He sat back, still not meeting her eyes. "You never blended into anything in your life. I always liked that about you. Gave me a little kick, you know, inside." He cleared his throat. "Well."

When Leyytey took the tray from him he turned his head aside.

"Are you tired?" Setting the tray down, old plates, cracked and worn around the edges.

"So now you know," he said gruffly. It was an answer, in its way.

"Yes. I've seen the worst. It hasn't changed anything."

"Hasn't, has it?"

"No."

Kept his face averted. "A child shouldn't ever see her father like this. Especially not a Khagggun child."

"I think a Khagggun child can handle it better than others."

He closed his eyes then, and began to laugh. He laughed harder and deeper than he could ever remember. It felt good in a way that was foreign to him. "You just—" His laughter continued. "You just can't help being contrary, can you."

"I'm right, though."

"Yes, you are." He looked at her now, assessing her as he would a potential weapon, a shock-sword to which he could trust his life and the lives under his command. He did not find her wanting. "Get me those guards. I have a mountain of coins to collect from them."

"They're dead," she said.

"And Mennus?"

"Threw my shock-sword at his neck. I didn't miss."

"Well," he said again.

"Your Khagggun are back in charge. Guarding you with their lives."

"Well, well, well." Smoothed the bedcovers over his legs, the better to assuage his nervousness. "You've got a strong arm, Leyytey, to go with your keen mind. And courage enough for two Khagggun."

At his invitation, she sat on the edge of the bed.

"You have to do something about it." She meant the tumor growing in his brain.

"Am doing something. This spice Sornnn's giving me."

"A temporary measure. I am looking at the downside."

His lips pursed out.

"I don't want to lose you."

He made a little noise in his chest.

"I know a Genomatekk is out of the question."

"Glad we don't have to clash over that."

"But there is another option. Sornnn knows this Deirus, Kirlll Qandda."

"You're joking, surely."

"He's as qualified as any Genomatekk, better than most. And he won't say anything. Sornnn trusts him."

Made that sound again in his chest, letting it out slowly. "I will think about it."

"That's all I ask."

Sunlight creeping toward them across the floor, they could feel its warmth, the promise of it. A breeze stepped inside, stirred the room as if it were a goblet of ludd-wine.

"Still miss my sons," Pnin said. "But not nearly as much, it seems, as I used to."

Leyytey, lighter than air, felt her insides melting. Did not know what to say, so she said what was in her hearts. "I'll never get over being frightened of you."

"Is it such a bad thing?" Picking at the covers. "I'm your father, aren't I?"

It was as close as he could come to asking forgiveness. Something unfamiliar welled up in Leyytey's throat.

"Father . . . ?"

"Yes." He did not scold her or contradict.

"There is something I must tell you." She looked down at her hand as he took it in his. He knew this was hard for her. Had he heard something in her voice or did her expression betray her? Either way, the warrnixx die was cast. So she told him about Dacce, how he had been hired by Raan Tallus, how he had murdered Hadinnn SaTrryn, the poison she had kept bottled up inside her.

After she was finished, after the silence was done, he said, "Why have you told me this?"

"I want you—" Looking up into his face. "You can take care of it, see justice is done."

He nodded. "I could, indeed. But I won't."

"Why?"

"Not me you need to tell, and you know it." Squeezing her hand. "It's for the son to see justice done."

A stirring at the doorway made them both look up.

"Sornnn," Pnin said. "A good day, this. A great day."

"Yes, sir, it is."

"What do you think of this daughter of mine?" His face brightening every moment, the creases less deep, less telling, color returning like sunlight out of clouds. "Isn't she something?"

Sornnn smiling. "She is indeed."

"Now we need to turn our attention to the chain of command." He was sitting up straighter. "First thing, I want to find out the fate of the other Admirals—Hiche, Lupaas, and Whon."

Sornnn said, "The Haaar-kyut commandant First-Captain Kwenn, can help us with this."

Pnin nodded. "Second thing—" His eyes were bright, fiery even. "Leyytey, what do you think the second thing should be?"

Leyytey blinked. "I beg your pardon?"

"I'm always telling you what I think. Time the tables were turned. I'm asking for your opinion."

She took a breath. Her hearts hammered in her breast. She did not want to let him down. And then she saw the look in his eye and knew that she couldn't. She also knew that she had a very clear idea of it. "With the Star-Admiral dead that leaves you as senior—and ranking—member of the high council. I think you go in and assess those whom Mennus promoted. You don't like them, you demote them. I think you form your own high council."

"What about the regent?"

"What about him?" she said. "He is Bashkir, and you are Khaggun. It is high time the Khagggguns' fate was returned to their own hands."

"And the Gyrgon?"

"Rumors persist that since Nith Batoxxx's death at Za Hara-at the Comradeship is engrossed in internecine fighting. Besides, since we defend them, a strong Khaggun caste is in their best interest."

Pnin, working his way slowly out of bed, strength and renewed life flowing back into him, a long-pent-up river. The voices of the dead were silent now. "What did I tell you, Sornnn? She really is something."

A black whirlpool was sucking at Hannn Mennus. By all rights he should be back in Axis Tyr finding out the details of his brother's death. Holding interrogations, exacting a terrible revenge. Finding out why the regent hadn't already ordered it done. He spat into damp, blood-soaked ground. What could you expect from Bashkir?

He looked down at two of his Khaggun. Dead. Like the other outrider guards. No warning, no sound, nothing

tripped on the periphery alarms. He bent down, took between two blunt fingers a square of black-dyed cloth out of
each of their mouths. Like the others. He had a whole pile
of black squares, extracted from the mouths of his good
warriors. All dead. Hannn looked around, hands on hips.
His Khagggun were staring at him, thinking what? Who
was killing them? Who would be next? In this atmosphere,
he could not even contemplate leaving for Axis Tyr, no
matter the reason. It could be misinterpreted. He felt the
black whirlpool sucking away his troops' confidence in
themselves, in him.

The sky was grey, neither high nor low, absolutely featureless. He stood in the pouring rain. No wind at all, the
silver needles coming straight down, the trees useless.
Their stares were darkening, his Khagggun were more
hesitant by the hour. When had any of them gotten a decent night's sleep? When had this nightmare started? He
could not recall.

At first, he had made the obvious assumption that they
were under attack by some ragtag remnant of Gerwa's Resistance group, out on a recon when he had staged the raid
that had obliterated the camp. Basking in triumph, he had
paid scant attention to the black squares of cloth. By the
time the second set appeared in his Khaggguns' mouths
he'd had to change his thinking. Hadn't changed his tactics, though. Drove his troops harder than normal, broke
them up into hunting packs, dividing the terrain into radiating sectors, keeping strict photon contact between them,
standard operating procedure. They had found nothing for
their toilsome work. And in the night, three more dead,
mouths stuffed, the black cloths stippled with hoarfrost,
fluttering in the wet morning breeze.

The black whirlpool was sucking at him. If he didn't do
something soon, he would go under. He moved them to
night patrols. What had come of it? Griping, the patrols
slowed, another two dead, found at noon. A spike in his
troops' anxiety, paced by a drop in morale. He knew they
did not trust him, not really. How could they?

They had no idea what had happened on Lethe. Neither did he, only knew he came back without his pack, should have fallen on his shock-sword. He would have, actually, but his brother had stayed his hand. He had always listened to Iin Mennus, following in the trajectory of his older brother's career, lifted by the invisible hand of his success. And what now that he was gone? No one to guide him, temper his hand. No one to tell him to stop dreaming about Lethe.

The air steamed with his breath, the rain pelted down. All of them standing, looking at the newly dead. Awaiting orders. What had gotten to them was the black cloths. Not Hannn, though. His concern was how his Khaggun had died. All ion blasts, very concentrated. Wicked stuff. Very efficient. By which he was forced to conclude that the enemy—whoever they might be—were in possession of ion-based weapons of the latest design. How in the Kraelian hellpit could that be?

He could call and ask for reinforcements, of course, but, considering Lethe—*always* considering Lethe—how could he possibly take that route? He would lose whatever respect his Khaggun still had for him. It would confirm the worst rumors about him: that he was unfit to lead, that he could not get the job done. That he was going to lose his Khaggun all over again.

And yet he stood transfixed, rain drumming against his armor, seeping into the cracks, running down the back of his neck. Black squares in his hand, stiff with blood and mucus. Transfixed by the notion that this was Lethe all over again. A situation out of control. A situation for which he had no solution. They would all die, he knew it, knew this time that he wouldn't survive either. Not that he had any great desire to. When he thought about it—which he did all the time—he had never really survived Lethe. What had returned was a shell, an automaton that walked and talked, ate and eliminated. Good for killing, yes, very good, indeed, for the already dead had nothing to lose. But for anything else, useless. Stayed alive for Iin, because of him. But now there was nothing. Standing there in the rain, between two more of his dead Khagggun, he was suddenly sick of life, enraged at seeing it all around him. How dare anyone laugh, or even smile! What was there to cause happiness? Not him, surely. For death was all he knew, all he ever would know.

He shook himself. What had his brother taught him? Introspection led to maudlin thoughts, and maudlin thoughts were the bane of Khagggun, they made you weak in arm, uncertain in mind. When he drew across his shoulders the cured snow-lynx hides the seeping stopped. Rain beaded up on the luxuriant fur; he was warm and dry. He ordered the Wing Deirus to prepare the bodies, ordered the others out on patrols, a new design, crisscross patterns, back one another up; sent pairs of snipers into the high trees in a fan pattern to lie in wait all day, all night, if need be, spelling each other.

"We'll get them," he said. Moving through the troops, lips cracked in a livid grin. "You'll see. We'll get them." Let the black squares flutter to the ground, where they were trampled underfoot.

A shallow grave," Sornnn said. "That's what they call it in the Korrush."

He and First-Captain Kwenn were down in the interrogation cells. This section of the caverns beneath the regent's palace was rank with the stench of fear and death. Dried blood and fecal matter. Insects, white in their lightless abode, crawling.

"These cells need a good disinfecting," Kwenn said.

They were looking at what remained of the three Admirals, the Mennus brothers' hideous work.

"How do we tell him?" Kwenn meant Ardus Pnin.

Sornnn picked up an alloy implement, crusted with blood, bits of bone, grey matter. Indecipherable save to a torturer. "We must simply tell him. He values the truth, always."

"Even when it is so bitter?"

The implement rang dully when Sornnn put it down. "Especially then." Looked at unseeing eyes, chests pried open, bones protruding, viscera laid bare. A textbook of pain and suffering. "I don't know about you, but I need a breath of fresh air."

They mounted the fusty stairs. Outside the main hall, Kwenn gave orders for the remains to be removed, the cells flushed. Avoiding those on line who wished word of the regent, he slipped them out a side entrance into one of the palace's gardens.

The sky was a filthy grey, a solid sheet, dull and heavy. Looking more like winter than spring. They strolled beneath sheared sysal trees, Sornnn snorting to get the reek out of his nostrils. He stopped to inhale the pleasant tang of orangesweet.

Kwenn watching his Haaar-kyut patrols in the performance of their duties. He was a stickler. "What did you mean, a shallow grave?"

"In the Korrush, when the enemy captures and tortures your warriors, he leaves them where they lie. The pawing of the animals creates a small depression where the bones molder. No spirit can rest easy in such a place."

Kwenn smiled. "I believe I would like the Korrush."

"It is clean, brilliant, vast. Things are what they seem."

"Unlike here." A heavily armed hovercraft passed by overhead, dipped in brief acknowledgment as the pilot recognized him. "This regent is as much a puzzle as his father was."

"Both Stogggul," Sornnn pointed out.

"Precisely so. What could the Gyrgon be thinking, backing the Stogggul?"

"Who can fathom the Gyrgon mind?"

They continued their walk, trying to clear their heads. The sysal, thickening with green, shielded them from the fierce-looking sky. It was very still. Ominous weather.

"For instance, the regent has disappeared." Kwenn continuing his train of thought.

"Is that unusual?"

"Not for him. He's got a pocketful of secrets. Just one of them would make my career, I warrant."

Sornnn paused to stare into a porphyry fountain. "I would think your career already made."

"You don't know the regent as I do. He can turn on anyone at any time. I mean, look at his sister."

"His sister? Oratttony?"

"No, the other one. Marethyn."

Sornnn froze. "What about Marethyn?"

"The regent lost track of her, so he asked me to find her. I did. But he wouldn't do a thing, wouldn't even believe a word—"

In the midst of his stupefaction came wildly beating hearts. "Wait a minute. Stop." A white-hot flame had ignited inside him, a wild flare of hope. "You found her?"

"Sure I did." Leaning in, lowering his voice, though only the plashing water could eavesdrop. "If you can believe it, she's gone and joined the Resistance."

"I heard . . ." His voice caught in his throat. "I heard that she was dead."

"No. Not at all. My source saw her with his own eyes."

Wa tarabibi. My beloved. Knees weak, Sornnn felt suddenly light-headed. His ears were buzzing. "Where?" Voice no more than a croak.

"In the West Country. Near Receive Tears Ridge."

"I don't believe it."

"Neither could my informant. He saw her in a fight. Said what a fierce warrior she is. Imagine! A Tuskugg-gun!" Kwenn looking quizzically at Sornnn, who was laughing so hard tears had come to his eyes.

30

Emergence of Things Past

The view was breathtaking. Seen through a steep col, thrusting into the crystalline cerulean sky, was Kunlung Mountain. Even though it was set in the midst of the Djenn Marre's highest peaks, still it towered over all of them, its head and shoulders whipped, roiled, distorted by permanent ice storms. It was whiter than bleached bone, but here and there were glimmerings, like gems of the same berylline color as the sky, life within the monolith, revealed to Riane, so newly come to this creased and pitiless realm.

The wind howled like a daemon being slaughtered, great plumes of dry snow swirled across razorback ridges and deep defiles, cracking crevasses and sheer ice walls, everything large, too large to take in, let alone understand. Yet all this blasted bleakness, this yowling, tumbled, treacherous sea of ice, all this was prologue, leading to what lay behind her. With a seer's premonition, she turned. She was on a steep ice- and snow-encrusted mountain slope just below the place where colossal walls jutted up. An edifice that looked carved out of the mountainside itself—a castle or fortress, but was in fact neither. She knew that, knew what it was. It was an abbey. She had been there before, though she could not quite remember when. She beat her fists against her forehead, frustrated by memories that flickered tantalizingly before her, only to vanish into the darkness of her unremembered past.

It was very cold. Unprepared for the fierce weather, she shivered, cast Inner Circulation to insulate herself. The rarefied atmosphere sawed in and out of her lungs, made breathing painful. She could only imagine the effect on her skin were she not so well protected.

Still, she could not remain there indefinitely; she needed to gain entry to the abbey. But how? No door, no gateway, not even a practical approach presented itself to her no matter which way she looked. She slogged west along the ice field, then east, looking for a way in and finding none. At the end of the trek, back more or less where she had begun, she was exhausted, for the snow was almost hip deep, layered on top with a friable crust of ice. She was obliged to battle for each step, to crack through the ice and plunge into the densely packed snow beneath.

She stopped, opened her Third Eye, moved into the trance-state of Ayame, preparing to Thripp inside, found she could not. Her eyes snapped open. This was a first. How was it possible? She tried again. Skimming the periphery of the abbey, she discovered innumerable sorcerous safeguards to prohibit Thripping into it.

Returned to the normal world, she stood with hands on hips, wondering what to do next when she spied a figure coming up the slope at a fantastic speed. It was moving not in a straight line, but tacking this way and that, using the gusting wind as would a sailboat on the ocean.

Details emerged through the snow clutter: a male, big-boned and muscular, wrapped so completely in layers of spotted white fur that only his eyes were visible. He was leaning forward, shoulders and hooded head projected ahead of his body, his long, powerful legs pumping rhythmically in concert with his arms.

He had seen her by then, and he changed course slightly, heading directly toward her. By that time, she could see that he wore low boots on the undersides of which were attached long silver blades that allowed him to skate across the ice field. It was a fantastic sight, really, this male skimming over the ice as lightly as if he were a water spider on a pond. Where was he coming from? she wondered. Where *could* he be coming from? He had emerged from the north, but what was there save Kunlung

Mountain and the Unknown Territories, where it was well known no one could survive for more than a few hours, let alone live?

And yet, there he was, skating toward her in long, swooping S-shaped tracks. He was traveling at such a rate of speed she felt sure he could not stop in time, but again her assumptions went by the wayside as, at the last possible moment, he turned his blades to the side and, in a great shower of snow and ice, came to a halt not a half meter from where she stood. He was not even breathing hard. His large eyes were, like hers, a clear, brilliant blue. He grinned and bits of a thick red beard appeared from the edges of his furry hood. His mustache, exposed, was white with clustered snow crystals, but the face was unmistakably that of Redbeard, the same as was set into the entryway of her memory building.

He was grinning. "Stay right there." That booming voice resounded in her head, familiar, comforting.

I know him, she whispered in her own ear. But because she had learned in this world to be, above all, cautious, all she said was, "My name is Riane."

Her simple response appeared to bring him up short. Iced eyebrows condensed across the bridge of his hawk-like nose. "I became aware of you when you entered null-space. I thought I had lost you forever."

"Lost me? I do not understand."

"Do you remember nothing?"

"In truth, your face is familiar to me. But as for your name or where you come from . . ." She shook her head helplessly.

His lips pursed, and for a moment he seemed lost in thought. At last, he said, "I am Asir." He pronounced it *Ay-seer.*

Her fine ear caught his accent. He was from neither the low country around Axis Tyr nor the high plateaus. Not from the West Country. She saw his eyes go to the infinity-blade wand clutched in her right hand, and she put it away at once.

There seemed to have formed between them a lake of questions neither of them was yet prepared to venture into.

"Asir, how do you know me? What is this fortress that seems so familiar to me?"

"In time we must both learn everything there is to know about one other," he said. "But for the moment we must remove ourselves. A storm is quartering in from the northeast. These storms are not pleasant. The Great Rift channels them, magnifying their strength like a lens."

Without another word, he skated away from her. Was he just going to leave her there, alone and unaided, to face the terrible storm? Did he mean for her to follow him? If so, how? She had nothing resembling his miraculous skates. But no. When he had gained sufficient speed, he made a sharp turn, leaning into it at a forty-five-degree angle, looped back to where she stood, transfixed by the sight. Without warning, he scooped her up, taking her right off her feet.

Swooping off, he made three more S-shaped turns, cutting them more sharply than he had lower down because of the increased steepness of the slope. How swiftly and surely they flew up the last levels of the ice field! Wind whistling in their ears, snow bursting in their faces, they passed into the penumbra of the overhanging abbey walls, which, closely observed, had more the feeling of cyclopean cliffs rising to dizzying heights.

The moment they came to rest in a shallow niche in the wall, a kind of crenellation that ran, so far as Riane could see, the entire height of the wall, Asir set her down, detached the long, knife-edged blades from his boots.

Then, startlingly, he put his arms around her, drew her close.

"Riane," he said, "put your arms around me."

"What?"

"Do you not remember?"

"No. I—"

"Now!"

Something in his voice—not exactly a command, but

something like it—made her obey. She was pressed fully against his furs. Their warmth gave rise to a stir of echoes: the smell of cured leather on their underside, the bitter tang of ice particles, tiny as needle points, clinging to the outer layers of the fur, and, beneath, the dark, mysterious musk, all that remained of what the beasts had once, in life, been. She could smell him, as well, a not unfamiliar swirl of spices over a light scent of male sweat. Her eyes began to close, her mind drifting off. More echoes, just out of reach.

"Hold tight."

A curious sensation in her stomach told her even as she disbelieved the evidence of her own eyes that they were rising off the surface of the ice field.

Straight up they ascended, and then regaining her wits, she saw with her keen gaze that no snow or even wind touched them. They were in some form of invisible shaft—a spell shaft, doubtless—up which they were drawn like smoke in a flue. She was keenly aware of Asir studying her with his bright blue eyes. She wished she could read his expression, wished she knew where she knew him from or how.

As they ascended, she noticed that the abbey's outer wall lacked both window and balcony, as befitted such a forbidding fortress. Layer upon layer of massive stone blocks, seamlessly set, impenetrable, impervious to either wind whip or ice lash, this was all she saw, for she faced inward. What Asir saw over her shoulder she could only imagine.

Their aerial journey ended on a platform that emerged from the blank wall. As they stood upon it, it began to re-tract into that same blank wall.

Feeling her tense, Asir smiled and turned her in his arms, so that she faced outward and, he, his bulk, his warmth, protected her. She gasped, for the sky was gone and, with it, Kunlung Mountain. What remained, what came howling, raging through the magnifying lens of the Great Rift, was a fist of opaque whiteness. Like a door slammed in her face, the storm cut off the outside world. Only a cell remained, monochromatic, featureless, malefic, fast closing in.

"Deadly," he said as he turned her back to him. "Even to us."

Us? she wondered. *What did he mean by* us?

He had a gentle smile. It made her want to believe him, want to like him. The white-stone wall was coming closer, and still no opening presented itself. None did, ever. Asir held her tight, and she had no other option but to hold as tightly to him. The storm roared at her back, advancing on them like the first wave of an enemy assault. She thought of being caught in a vise, of the storm flattening them against the stone, white on white, the color of their blood soon whipped into a froth and whirled away into the maelstrom.

There came a moment of utter darkness, of disorientation, her stomach seeming to plummet as it did when she entered *jihe*, just before she reached Otherwhere. This sickening sensation did not, mercifully, last long. Instead she became aware of a warm light pressing gently against her lids, and she opened her eyes.

Asir had pushed back his hood, the flame of his full beard and hair startling, his wide grin as warming as the goblet of hot spiced wine he held out to her. He had taken off his gloves. His hands were square, immense, ridged with veins and callus. They were the hands of someone who worked the land, who knew the ins and outs of things, who could find in his surroundings, no matter how barren and desolate they might be, the means to survive. These hands, wrapped around her goblet, then around her own hands, as she took it from him, reassured her. She was aware of his power, but also of the vein of gentleness that ran through him.

"Drink now," he said. He looked as if he could not take his eyes off her. "I will return within a short while."

The wine was delicious, warmed her immediately, left a complex spice tingle on the back of her tongue. She looked around. The antechamber was not large, not small. It had a high, vaulted ceiling suspended upon the brawny shoulders of carved pillars. Great lanterns of iced bronze hung from chains, exuding an amber glow, but she could smell no oil nor tallow. The center of the anteroom was covered with a carpet of dark, muted tones, a pattern not unlike that of Asir's furs. With a start, she saw that it was a pelt, upon close inspection a single pelt, but from what immense beast she could not imagine. The Annon part of her remembered rumors he had heard while in the regent's palace that fantastic beasts roamed through the ice storms of the Unknown Territories, beasts long lost even to the present-day Kundalan. Riane wondered whether she was looking at proof of those rumors. Both of them—the fused entity that was the Dar Sala-at—felt a nervous anticipation at being here, for they both suspected that they were on the verge of a profound discovery.

The furniture consisted of a matched pair of lounges, upholstered also with pelts of spotted white fur, luxuriantly thick, soft as silk. She sat back in one, abruptly spent. Her nostrils burned, and her head throbbed. At what altitude was she? High, very high.

The sound of bells, light and airy, accompanied the massed voices of a choir raised in what might have been a psalm that was yet again tantalizingly familiar. It was beautiful, and a certain quietude descended upon her. She sipped more wine and listened to the echoes die away. When it was over, she cocked her head, aware at the very edge of hearing of a deep and rhythmic thrumming, huge engines buried deep as the secret of the past.

Soon thereafter, Asir appeared, escorting a female in white robes with deep blue trim. Riane put her goblet aside and rose.

"Riane," he said in his booming voice, "this is Amitra."

The female was standing unnaturally still, her face was very pale, her eyes open wide. So profound was her shock that she could not keep it from registering on her face.

"Can it be?"

Riane had no idea what she meant.

Like the anteroom, Amitra was not large, not small. Slender and upright as a pillar, blond hair framing an oval face, full lips, trembling now, resembling nothing so much as a petite bow. She gathered herself, recalling most if not all of her natural serenity.

"Tell me something, Riane," Amitra said. "Does anything here appear in the least bit familiar to you?" Her voice held the clear timbre of a precisely struck bell.

"Everything, I would say."

Exchanging a quick glance with Asir, she said, "And what about us, Riane? Asir and me." The two of them watching her intently.

"I wish I could remember." She put a hand to the side of her head, massaged her temple. "I have had a . . . bad fall. And then I grew ill. I almost died of duur fever."

"Asir, do you hear?"

"She is not the same as she once was, Amitra. Even you can see that."

"Asir—"

He shook his head sternly. "We must know."

He gestured, and the twin lounges disappeared, along with the pelt. The stone flooring was laid bare, in its center a sigil was incised, what looked like an eye. The circle of pupils in its center began to pulse in a particular rhythm. The stone down the center of the eye split open, the sections opening downward. Up through the opening rose a square column of gleaming metal, dark, depthless. Vertical channels ran down each side. Reaching just above the level of Asir's head, it stopped. He went to it, depressed a lever. Up along the channels rose a pair of leather-bound stirrups and a carved cat's-eye handgrip.

Asir motioned to Riane as he put his feet in the stirrups, but she shied away.

"Asir." Amitra seemed alarmed. "This is not the way."

"Tell me another."

Riane withdrew her wand, thumbed on the infinity-blade.

"Look, now," Amitra said. "Look what you have given rise to."

"Her training has stood her in good stead, Amitra. With it, she escaped null-space."

"You said you found me when I entered null-space," Riane said. "How?"

"Besides." Asir apparently ignoring her. "I am only doing what is necessary."

"If only you would trust her."

"It is not her I am concerned with. It is our enemies. What if she has fallen into their hands, what if she is being used as a weapon against us, have you thought about that?"

"Every day and every night since she was lost to us."

"What is going on here?" Riane said, brandishing her infinity-blade. "Who are you two?"

"Riane, we want to tell you. More than you could possibly know." Amitra took a step toward her, hand held out, palm up. "But we have to make certain."

Riane squeezed her eyes shut for a moment. Had they drugged the wine? Was she still in null-space, hallucinating?

"Your mind is not clear. You yourself described the reasons why."

"My mind is perfectly clear," Riane said. "It's my memory before the fall that has failed me."

"It has been two years." Asir said. "A lot can happen in that time."

"I could have become a weapon for your enemies."

"Yes."

"It depends who your enemies are," Riane said. "Because that is precisely what I have become—a weapon aimed squarely at the V'ornn. The only weapon in the Kundalan arsenal."

Asir and Amitra exchanged another charged look.

He put his hand on the transport lever. "Will you come with us now?"

"I need time."

"Time is running out," Asir said. "Believe me."

Riane shook her head, and Amitra, clearly distraught, made a complex weaving in the air with her hands.

"Don't." Asir removed himself from the stirrups.

In Amitra's hands was a mirror in a lovely painted wood frame. "You brought her inside. You brought her to me. What else did you expect?" She said, "Riane, please be good enough to stand between us."

Riane hesitated only a moment. She desperately needed to know why everything there seemed so familiar. So she did as Amitra bade, taking her place between them. Then Amitra held up the mirror and together they gazed at their reflections.

"You see it, don't you?" Amitra whispered.

How could she not? The resemblance to both of them was uncanny. She had Amitra's face, mouth, hair, Asir's eyes and nose.

"You are my parents," Riane whispered. Her throat was tight with awe. "My parents!"

"Your mother and father," Asir said. "The question now remains, who are you?"

Kurgan hung by his ankles, suspended by an aged and grimy hempen rope from the groaning attic rafter in FIREFLY, trussed like a qwawd for the fire, bleeding dolefully from a hundred wounds. His mind, fled far from the trauma of his violent encounter with Lujon, was elsewhere.

He stood upon the pitching deck of Courion's ship watching the storm approach. The sky was low and dark, the smothered light beneath it livid. Waves rose, coiled, crashed down in an eerie silence. In the troughs it was like the blackness of a well, scuppers running full and frothy, seething like an army with its bloodlust up. At the crests there existed a delicate balance, then the ship half heeled over with a curious lightness, an exhilaration not unlike that of a hoverpod as it hits an air pocket.

Courion, close behind him, hissed in his ear, "This is what it means to be Sarakkon. This is what it means to be alive." Down into another trough they plunged and, timbers groaning, up the other side, climbing the translucent wall of water which curled, on the brink of inundating them. "And what are you, V'ornn? Nothing. You are dead."

Kurgan was silent, without a ready answer to the truth. Save for his time with Annon Ashera he might have thought of himself as born dead. Without his friend—his blood enemy—he was nothing. In a mirror, he had no reflection. Without Annon there was no way to define himself, no way to know what it was he wanted. So much that he had desired, fought for, schemed, plotted, lied, cheated, killed for had been made his. To what end? He was being eaten alive by the rage of being subservient to Gyrgon, by the jealousy of knowing the only female he loved, ever could love, cared not for him but for dead Annon. If only time could be turned backward. If only it was three years ago, he and Annon hunting qwawd and gimnopedes in deep forest glades. That was a happy time! And then Eleana had entered their lives and ruined it all. Over her, their friendship fell apart; because of her, he had begun to hate Annon and, on the night of his father's coup, had betrayed him to the Khagggun who were searching for him, buying his way out from under the oppressive thumb of his father, into their good graces. Best friends, worst enemies. Now all gone, washed away on the tide of bloody history.

Plink-plink.

What was that, the sound of a metronome?

Insensate, he could not know it was the drip of his own blood pooling on the dusty floorboards below him.

His mind swept far away to the high seas, on Courion's yawing ship as a wave struck abeam, the Sarakkon crew working to bring the vessel back on course. And Courion hissing in his ear in a voice that sounded so much like his own, *And what are you, V'ornn? Nothing. You are dead.*

*M*other. Father. My parents. A warmth flooded Riane's entire being. Her eyes were wet and stinging, and for once Annon was completely quiescent, taking a backseat to the roil of her deeply felt emotions. Save for how he felt about Giyan, he had no experience with this sort of emotion. He had admired and loved his father, but no such overt emotion had ever passed between them. It was not the V'ornn way. And as for his mother, he did not even have a clear memory of her.

The enormity of the moment made her heart thunder, turned her knees weak. No longer to be adrift in a tide of unknowing. It was only in retrospect that she could appreciate what a terrible thing it was to be cut off from your own origins, to face the past and see only a mist, amorphous and impenetrable. But within her elation came the all-too-familiar realization of who she really was. She was not the Riane who had gone climbing with her father, who had slipped or got caught in an avalanche and fell away from him, from her mother, from her life. Another Riane now stood there, flanked by parents who could not know unless she chose to tell them how radically she had been altered. How could they possibly understand how she had been invaded by a V'ornn—saved by Annon's V'ornnish strength when the duur fever threatened to snuff out her life? How could they possibly accept their child back now that she was part V'ornn herself? What if they rejected her? She had already seen how suspicious her father was. What would happen if she gave him just cause for his suspicions?

"Darling, what is it?" Amitra held her at arm's length, a concerned look on her face. "What's the matter?"

A quick flash of panic. "Nothing, I—" What if her parents were psychic? What if they could read her mind? Was it so outlandish to think that? They were unlike any Kundalan she had ever met. She had no idea of their powers. She realized grimly that she was every bit as suspicious as her father. Or was that simply Annon's thinking?

"Riane," Amitra said, "you told us that you had become a weapon against the V'ornn. Would you tell us more precisely what you mean?"

Still, she hesitated, doubts swirling. She looked at them. *Mother. Father.* The familial tidal pull was too great to ignore.

"I have become the Dar Sala-at."

"Dear Miina!" Amitra's hand clutched at her throat, and she almost staggered.

"Riane, we knew when you were born that you were destined for great things," Asir said. "And then when you found the fulkaan's eyrie, when it bonded with you—"

"But we dared not hope." Amitra took a step toward her. "Who are we to bear the Dar Sala-at?"

"Amitra, consider the particular logic of it," Asir said. "It was you who learned Venca virtually overnight, you whose memory was better even than mine." He kissed her on both cheeks.

"Now we must show you the rest of your home," Amitra said, her eyes shining.

"With pleasure. But first there is something I must do." Riane recited Venca syllables, and reached through the mirror. Moved closer until both arms had sunk into the Other Side up to her elbows. She held her hands very still, concentrated on the current. Like one sightless she allowed her sense of touch to take over, felt the slight surge and suck of the null-space current and began to pull on it. Solid as it was, it responded. Hand over hand, she pulled it slowly toward her. Presently something soft and furry brushed against her, and she grabbed it.

She pulled Thigpen out of the Other Side by her tail. Not a dignified reentry to be sure, but at least the Rappa was safe and sound.

She cradled Thigpen in her arms, held her close. To the others' credit, they said not a word. Thigpen's eyes opened, and she shuddered.

"Ah, little dumpling, what are you doing here with me in the Other Side? It was foolish to come after me."

"If I hadn't, you would still be lost in null-space." Riane stroked the soft fur. "But we are no longer there. We are inside the Abbey—" She gave Asir an inquiring glance.

"The Abbey of Summit Window."

At the sound of the strange voice, Thigpen sat up, peered at the two older Kundalan over the crook of Riane's elbow.

"Thigpen, meet Asir and Amitra," Riane said. "They are my parents."

Thigpen, taking in their features, cocked her head. "Your parents, at last. Yes, I see. Mysterious folk, hidden away here on the edge of the Forbidden Territories."

Riane reached down, plucked up Asir's long, silver skate blades.

"Careful now," he said, as the light skittered along the knife-sharp edges.

"Even with these," she said, "even with speed, your weight, not to mention our combined weight, should have put you—and us—through the ice crust." She put the skate blades down. "These shouldn't work, and yet they do."

He looked at her with an expression she knew well. It was the look of a teacher, waiting for her pupil's answer, following the test, about to find out whether they had passed or failed.

"They must be ensorceled," she said.

"Well, that is a matter entirely of semantics."

Riane frowned. "I do not understand."

"This and other questions we will answer," Asir said. "But not here. Come." He stepped once again into the stirrups. "As I said, time is running out."

Riane signed to Thigpen, who leapt up onto her shoulders. Wrapping her arms tightly around Asir's waist as he directed, she pressed herself against his broad, muscular back. She inhaled the scents of cinnamon and nutmeg. She saw Amitra disappear. Asir told them that she was climbing into another set of stirrups on the far side of the column. He depressed the lever, and down they went, smoothly, soundlessly.

"I have seen this mechanism before," Riane said.

"Then you must have been exploring the cavern below the regent's palace." Amitra shook her head. "A very dangerous place nowadays."

At the base of the column, they slowed to a halt and she climbed off. The deep thrumming magnified.

They were in a circular chamber filled with cascades of trees, flowering plants, small evergreens. The air was warm, humid, perfumed. Light slanted down from an unknown source. A liquid gurgling could be heard, then a small waterfall came into view.

Asir said, "The Druuge—the first Ramahan—were here once. They built the abbey, and then, later, with the great climatic upheavals, left. It lay abandoned for many years, waiting. And then we took it, made it our home." He regarded Riane. "This is where you were born and raised."

"You remember nothing of it?" Amitra said.

"I can read and write Venca, I am an expert mountain climber, and my lungs are strong, so I know I was brought up high in the Djenn Marre. But as to how I acquired those skills . . ." She shook her head.

"Your memory—"

"I can remember everything, save my life before the fall. Now and again bits and pieces emerge. I remember you, Asir."

"But not as your father."

"I thought you might be my teacher, my mentor."

He smiled. "True enough."

He led them to the center of the trees, into a glade. But it was unlike any in a natural forest, for at its precise center was a gleaming metal hatch with what appeared to be a wheel on top. Asir put both hands on the wheel. His muscles corded as he spun it to his left. With an audible sigh, the hatch opened. The great thrumming became much louder and more distinct.

They descended a vertical metal ladder into a space so vast its bedrock walls were barely visible. Standing upon a grated platform, they stopped and peered down at a gargantuan array of spotless thrumming machinery.

"Engines!" Thigpen exclaimed. She looked from Asir to Amitra and back again. "You are Tchakira."

"What? The undesirables, the insane, the outcasts? Impossible!"

Amitra smiled. "Tchakira are indeed believed to be the insane; we are the undesirables, the outcast. But there are many more of us than is known by the Ramahan."

A wave of consternation passed through Riane. "The Ramahan of the Abbey of Floating White bring food and clothing and medicines to the Tchakira, they leave them in the Ice Caves above Heavenly Rushing, far from here. I myself did so two years ago. That was how I discovered you, Thigpen."

"And I thought it was the other way around!" Thigpen leapt to the floor, began to sniff her way around the couple.

"The perwillon must eat what you bring," Asir said. "We have been gone from that place for many years. We moved into the Forbidden Territories."

"The Forbidden Territories are uninhabitable," Riane exclaimed. "Khagggun expeditions have gone in, none have returned."

"They would have returned," Asir said, "had we wished it. The Forbidden Territories are our home, a secret we protect most fiercely."

Thigpen, who had been patiently quiet, could contain herself no longer. "But Tchakira?"

"Ah, yes, I see." Asir knelt beside the Rappa. "You think of us as the dregs of Kundala because that is the societal belief. Odd, coming from a species that has been used and, to a large extent, abused by the Ramahan."

Thigpen sat back on her double haunches, her long whiskers twitching in anxiety. "The very thing you bring up has made us overly suspicious. You are right. I am too quick to judge, inclined to think ill of everyone I meet," she said.

Asir smiled and rubbed his knuckles in the fur between Thigpen's ears. "The truth is that in the Time before the Becoming, Kundala had technology. Not, at that time, anywhere near that of the V'ornn. But we are great experimenters—we forged alloys, used electricity, powered turbines. Long ago, however, the Ramahan forced us out. Made Kundala revert and forget what had once been."

"What?" Riane shook her head. "Why?"

"They perceived us as a threat to their theocracy, and perhaps they were right, for science and religion are most often at odds with one another."

She was thinking with Annon's memory about the Gyrgon who maintained their power through new technology, the careful distribution of which they controlled. But for a difference of philosophy we could have exerted and maintained a similar stranglehold on Kundalan society. "So they ostracized you," she said.

Asir nodded. "We designed Za Hara-at. It was the daemons who built it. There was good purpose in it, but because of the banestones, because of the enormous power in the city, fear seeped into the Ramahan, and all who had been in any way attached to the construction were deemed tainted, made outcast."

Riane gripped the railing as she leaned over, looking straight down. "Where does your power come from?"

"The same source as your infinity-blade."

Riane took out her wand. "Goron particles?"

Asir nodded. "Null-space—the fabric between layers of the multiverse, what binds them together—is almost pure goron energy. We have learned how to harness it."

Riane was startled. "The V'ornn have a mortal enemy that has pursued them across the Cosmos, a species known as the Centophennni. They use gorons as devastating weapons."

"Our knowledge of gorons is far more limited," Asir said. "We have not yet learned how to make goron-based weapons."

Riane brandished the wand. "What do you call these?"

"We did not make them," Amitra said.

"Then who did?"

"We do not know," Amitra said.

"Tell me"—Asir gestured—"where did you get your infinity-blade?"

"It was given to me by Minnum, the Curator of the Museum of False Memory."

"Could this Curator tell you the origin of his exhibits?"

"He said he did not know where anything in the museum came from," Riane said.

"Pity." Asir nodded. "We have been searching for a clue to their origin ever since we discovered three of them at the bottom of the caldera of Oppamonifex, the largest volcano on the southern continent. Unfortunately, our agents were set upon by Sarakkon. Two of the infinity-blades were lost there."

They ascended the alloy ladder, back to the soughing forest that seemed light-years from the throbbing machinery below.

Amitra put a hand on Riane's shoulder. "A great shadow lies over us all. You have felt it, have you not?"

Riane nodded, a lump in her throat.

Amitra gazed at her lovingly. "You see why we were hesitant, Riane? Our existence must remain an absolute secret until the time is right to strike back."

"Unfortunately," Asir said, "the sauromicians have forced our hand."

"They have achieved a major victory," Amitra said.

"Not yet. Not quite yet." Asir held up a finger. "It is true that they have found eight banestones, but they have yet to find the ninth. Where it is we have no idea."

"But I do," Riane said.

They looked at her with shocked expressions and led her to a bench in a grove on the far side of the forest, where they sat in a group, Thigpen at Riane's right knee. There, she told them of her attempts to get the ninth banestone, first from Kurgan Stogggul, then from the Sarakkon named Lujon. "The Sarakkon have allied themselves with the sauromicians," she concluded. "But why or where Lujon is taking the ninth banestone I have no idea."

"Certain elements of the Sarakkon have long coveted control of the northern continent because they seek the mysteries hidden within Za Hara-at," Amitra said. "Plus, they harbor a grudge." She told them briefly of how in ancient times the Sarakkon had been defeated by the Ramahan and banished to the southern continent.

"What will they do if the Cage is completed?"

"They have caught one of Miina's Sacred Dragons," Amitra said. "They will use her to open all the Portals to the Abyss. The daemons will arise once more."

"Why do the sauromicians want to ally themselves with daemons?"

"Because daemons built Za Hara-at," Asir said, "the sauromicians assume they are privy to its secrets."

Riane, having already battled one archdaemon, shuddered. "I didn't know a Dragon could be caught," she said, "let alone imprisoned."

"It isn't easy, but it can be done." The tip of Amitra's forefinger moved from light into shadow and back again. "The Dragons thrive in brilliant sunlight, in star-spangled velvet night. Otherwise, they keep to the heavy mists that becloud rain-forests and giant waterfalls, for their nemeses are dawn and dusk, those moments before the sun rises and just after it sets. Surprise a Dragon at such a time, and it can be captured, for then it can neither think clearly nor move quickly." Her forefinger hovering in the penumbra between light and shadow.

"Can the Cage be built with only eight banestones?" Riane asked.

"Yes. And it can imprison a Dragon." Asir nodded. "But only for a short time. That is why the sauromicians have been so desperately searching for the ninth and final banestone. With that, the Dragon's fate is sealed."

"But do we know for certain that they have imprisoned a Dragon?"

"It is a fact that one of them is missing."

Riane's heart in her mouth. "Which one?"

"Seelin."

"The Sacred Dragon of Transformation." A terrible fore-boding engulfed her, for Prophecy spoke of Seelin being the Dar Sala-at's personal Dragon. "How can we save her?"

"You must obtain the ninth banestone before the Dark League uses it to complete the Cage."

"I know who is in possession of it—the Sarakkon named Lujon—but not where he is."

"You do not have to know," Amitra said, "for it is in-evitable he will go to where the sauromicians have built the Cage."

"Do we know where that is?" Riane asked.

Amitra opened her hand. In it was a square of raw silk, which she unfurled. Wrapped within it was what looked like the nail from a gargantuan beast—fully twenty cen-timeters long, slightly curved, the most beautiful coral color.

"This is the talon of the Dragon, Seelin." She placed it in Riane's hand, curled her fingers around it. "We found it at the spot where the sauromicians trapped her and took her."

Riane found her mouth dry. "Where was that?"

"At the bottom of Oppamonifex. The same place we found the infinity-wands. These volcanos used to be the Dragons' playground."

Riane discovered that her fingers had begun to tingle where they were in contact with Seelin's talon.

When she told them that, Amitra exclaimed, "You see, Asir, it is well we waited. It is as the Prophecy foretold. Our daughter will find her."

Asir said, "You will take the talon with you into null-space. It will guide you to where Seelin is. You and this particular Dragon have an innate affinity for one another."

"Now listen well to me." Amitra's elation was tempered by concern. "You must not touch the banestone with your bare hands. If you do, it will change you in ways no one can predict, and not for the better I'll warrant."

"I understand. When I get the ninth banestone, what then?"

Asir and Amitra exchanged a charged look. Again, Riane wondered whether they were somehow communicating with one another the way she and Giyan could.

Amitra leaned forward, took Riane's hands in her own. "Seelin has already been in the Cage for some time."

Riane's sense of foreboding increased. Into her mind sprang something the Hagoshrin had said, unremarked upon, but now full of dire meaning. *In fact, it might already be too late.* She said, "What does this mean?"

Amitra squeezed her hands all the tighter. "Remember what I told you about not touching the banestones? One banestone does not affect a Dragon as it would you or me, but if one is caught within the banestone energy field . . ."

"You mean Seelin has been altered?"

Amitra nodded. "I am afraid so."

It might already be too late.

Riane felt a bleakness in her soul. "Is there nothing I can do?"

"One thing and one thing alone," Asir said, his voice echoing ominously. "You must take possession of the ninth banestone and with it kill Seelin."

31

Pools

"Beautiful, isn't it?" Leyytey set the hovercraft down at the edge of a field of wrygrass.

Sornnn held up a cut-crystal bottle of fire-grade numaaadis. "A perfect place to celebrate."

She powered down the engine, and they clambered out. By tacit agreement they left the hovercraft behind, the last vestige of the city's tyranny. The rich scents of growing things, of dew and sweet pollen, loamy soil surrounded them. He followed her lead across a patch of hardscrabble that led down to a meandering brook, sun sparks darting like fish. Crossing that, cresting a small root-knotted knoll, they found themselves in a stand of heartwood trees. They sat for a time in the dappled shade, side by side.

She had been the first person Sornnn had wanted to tell. Marethyn alive. He was elated to share more good news with her. She was like some mysterious blossom, beautiful and thorny, roots sunk deep into the ground. Armored and tenacious. Only in moonslight, in secret, only he could see. She might have been his sister, save for other feelings he held for her, deeper, unsure, pleasurable in the enigma they presented. Out across the wrygrass insects droned in the building heat of the day. Small clouds like puffs of snow. A fitful crosswind cooled their cheeks.

"We're only, what, ten kilometers from Axis Tyr?"

"Less," she said. She was still trying to sort out her feelings. When he had told her she had felt so many things: happiness for him, of course, an odd kind of deflation, a sense of the ground collapsing beneath her feet, buildings tilting. Everyone looked strange. Had she grown to love the SaTrryn? Was that her problem? What would be the point? He loved Marethyn, that was clear enough. He had been sinking without her. Perhaps, if Marethyn had been really and truly dead, saving Pnin would have been enough to save him. And then she might have had a chance. Now she would never know. "But it seems like more, doesn't it?"

"What a relief to be clear of the city!" He wrestled open the sealed stopper, poured them both a generous amount. "Thank you for suggesting this." They clinked crystal and downed the heady liquor. Without asking, he refilled both goblets.

"Whose villa is that?" Sornnn used the bottle to indicate the Kundalan facade visible on the far side of the field. There was a wall, incised with a decorative pattern, beyond which the cerulean tiles of the pitched roof gleamed like the brook. "I imagine it must have a beautiful view of the shoreline."

"You can see kilometers out to sea." She threw the numaaaadis into the back of her throat, swallowed convulsively. "It used to belong to a prominent Kundalan family. Intellectuals. The father was a scholar, the mother a renowned herbalist. Ramahan came from near and far to share her wisdom and buy her wares. They had three girls, and she was training them all."

"What happened to them?"

"All dead. But that was a long time ago."

Sornnn gathered a handful of dirt, tiny pebbles, seed-pods, dried twigs, let it all sift through his fingers like sand in an hourglass. The wrygrass lifting like combers as the wind bustled through. A gimnopede trilled once and was still. To one side of the villa there was a fenced-off area in which three roan cthauros grazed and snorted.

"And now?" Sornnn holding the bottle by its long neck. "Who lives there?"

"Full-time, no one. Most days it's very quiet there. Utterly still. The sea looks perfectly flat from this high up, like you could walk on it all the way to the horizon." She rose, and together they continued their stroll closer to the hissing wrygrass, the somnolent cthauros. "Occasionally, though, Raan Tallus comes out from the city, usually with an entourage, but sometimes alone. He's an expert rider."

"I did not know that." Sornnn studied her sun-glossed profile. "How do you know?"

She took a deep breath, felt as if she were at the southern edge of the villa's property, sun beating down on the back of her neck hard by the cliff, steep and rockbound. A wildness in deep contrast to the softly waving wrygrass, the tranquillity of the cthauros pen. She felt as if she were stepping off the edge. Falling. She drew courage from her father.

"Dacce would tell me about it."

"I don't understand. Teww Dacce and Raan Tallus could not have been friends."

"No, certainly not." The most curious thing had happened when he had told her that Marethyn was still alive. She had felt closer to him than she ever had before. Possibly it was because he had come to her first, had wanted to confide in her. His altered reality had not changed the way he felt about her. Not in the least bit. What did that say about them? Were they friends? If so, what did that entail? She had no experience in the matter of friendship, especially one that seemed so mysterious, so precious. Yes, that was the word. *Precious.* "Dacce and Raan Tallus had a certain business arrangement."

They had come close enough so that the cthauros, scenting them, lifted their heads. Watching with their huge brown eyes, velvet ears turned, alert. One of them stamped a tufted foreleg in warning.

She turned her head, could see him working out the parameters, he had a very keen mind, she knew that already. It was one of the things she found so attractive about him. The other, of course, was that he saw her in a way other males had failed to do.

"Dacce was taking a foolish risk," he said. There were grave consequences for Khaggun caught murdering Bashkir for hire.

"You already know his ambition. It drove him to take foolish risks."

Sornnn nodded. All this was true. "Who did Raan Tallus want killed?"

"I am afraid it was your father."

Reliving the horror of Hadinnn SaTrryn's sudden and premature death all over again, Sornnn experienced it now from some godlike perspective, watching all the participants, including the ones he had not been aware of before. They moved as if in a staged drama, and he a director stripped of his power, reduced to watching the fell event unfold with a fateful inevitability. And yet, deep down, he was astonished to discover not an iota of surprise. It was as if part of him had known it all along—or suspected it—but refused to admit it. Raan Tallus had wanted a piece of the

SaTrryn spice trade. When Hadinnn SaTrryn refused, this was the egregious response. In light of that, he had to ask himself how long Raan Tallus had been plotting to take over the SaTrryn business.

The day seemed completely different now, everything heightened, the smells of the fields, the bars of sunlight, the brachiated shadows, the wind rippling the wrygrass, the piercing cry of a blackcrow. They all spoke to him in the voice of dreams, omens, predetermination. His father rising up beside him, walking with his old familiar lilt. The dense, spicy smell of him, the brush of his shoulder and hip.

"Sornnn?"

Had to clear his throat first. "Yes."

She took his hand, and he squeezed back.

They had kept on walking and were now in sight of the western side of the villa. Someone was there, a solitary figure. Raan Tallus. Sornnn did not break stride but now it all seemed clear to him, laid out like an architect's holo-print, dimensions measured, angles calculated, length, width, height. Nothing left to chance. She had thought of everything.

Only one thread left to unravel. "You told me you know about this place because of Dacce. That's part of the truth but not all of it."

"No." That one word squeezed out of her, more difficult to say than any other in her life. This was why the knowl-edge had lain like a stone in her chest, why she had tried several times and been unable to tell him. Because she knew he was smart enough to work this out. She knew he knew already, only wanted her verbal confirmation. Still, it was difficult. Her throat was hot and full. She felt suffo-cated by the past, the mistake she had made.

"You were here yourself," he said, "without Dacce."

Of course he knew. She felt oddly proud of him. They kept walking, she made certain of that. The figure of Raan Tallus was tense and coiled, a spring about to be released. Staring into a portable data-screen, totally absorbed.

What plots were being hatched on that readout? What evil concocted in the vast silence of this bucolic setting? *I need to be here, I need space to think,* he had once told her, laughing. *Solitude casts a spell over me, and I in turn cast a spell over others.*

"I offered myself to him as a kind of revenge, to get back at Dacce. To make him jealous. At least that's what I told myself." The floodgates, once opened, thrown wide. The fierce joy of confession thundering through her. "But there was something else at work, something more powerful than simple revenge. My affair with Raan Tallus was a way of punishing myself. I could not break with Dacce, so I found another relationship that debased me further."

"Before or after?"

Her hearts contracted. "I was here with him before I found out what Dacce had done, what Raan Tallus had ordered him to do."

He nodded, seemed satisfied by her answer. They stood under the protection of another stand of heartwood. He still held her hand. He found that he did not want to let go, that it served as a kind of conduit. He felt her pain, and he fancied this connection would allow him to take it away. "It is difficult to live with such self-loathing." How he knew, having spent weeks blaming himself for Marethyn's death, hating himself for it. To think she had had years of it. He wanted to take her in his arms and hold her, but he did not think it proper, did not in fact know whether it was what she wanted or needed. He felt her thorns, even then. It was a good feeling because they were a vital part of her. "It's good that you told me. Everything."

"How many times I wanted to, SaTrryn! But I was afraid."

"Of what?"

He saw her look down, followed her gaze to their clasped hands. "I want to thank you."

Her eyes flicked up to gaze into his.

"For this gift. You have prepared it perfectly."

"Thank you, SaTrryn."

She put her hand on the back of his head, kissed his cheek tenderly, and he hugged her to him. They remained like that for a moment, dappled sunlight and shade moving over them with the swaying of the heartwood leaves. Sornnn thought how much she had come to mean to him.

"I want to continue our business arrangement," she said, when at length they drew apart. "I want you to take me to the Korrush."

He grew silent for a moment. Of course, he welcomed Leyytey's offer, but before he could return to the Korrush he needed to find Marethyn, he needed to see her, taste her, feel her. To assure himself that she was, indeed, alive and well. If Leyytey was with him, that might present a problem. She was, after all, a Fleet-Admiral's daughter. "Are you certain?" he said. "It was part of our scheme. I would not hold you to the contract you signed."

"I know, SaTrryn. But this is what I want. To forge my weapons for your tribal folk. To help them survive their war. There is a purpose in this that I think I have been searching for all my life."

A certain tension seemed to drain out of him, as if he had been vibrating all the time she had known him, and now, finally, he had come to rest.

"He likes to ride." He was staring through the glare of sunlight at Raan Tallus. "What else does he like to do?"

Wing-Adjutant Wiiin and the Khagggun Wing had decamped the highland slopes south of Stone Border, glumly wending their way back whence they had come. Wiiin himself was silent as the grave, seeing his career over, his head on a pike in front of the Wing-General's offices. Deep in mountain forests, green-black, dripping with dew, he took his own life, botching that, even, no clean line of death for him, but a slow, agonizing bleed, pecked at by carrion birds, by foraging mammals with sharp teeth and glittering eyes, out of sight of those who had laughed at him, whom he had sought to command. With him died any suspicion as to the cause of death of the officer who had attacked the Nawatir in his guise as Khagggun.

All this Konara Inggres saw with her Third Eye. She should have felt compassion for Wiiin, so clearly a fish out of water, but she could summon none. Because of him the Nawatir had been gravely wounded. Instead of moving with a spell to end Wiiin's suffering, she did nothing, withdrawing her consciousness back to the abbey.

Moonslight slanting in through the barred windows of the infirmary illuminated the Nawatir's face in a pool of celestial light. What emotions now stirred her—emotions she thought long ago atrophied. She had betrayed First Mother, not only in her heart but in every cell of her body. Her lips still burned at the contact with the Nawatir's mouth.

She prayed now, as she had been praying since that one fateful kiss, beseeching Miina for guidance, for resolution. For peace. But it was a fool's endeavor, she knew that well enough. Miina was not concerned with the private lives of Her children, nor should She be. It was for Inggres and Inggres alone to solve a puzzle that could not be solved.

She ceased her prayers, but remained in a position of reflection. There was only one course open to her—the one that had always been there. Continue. What was in her heart must remain there, packed away, sealed. Forever untouched. He must never know what she felt for him. She could tell no one, least of all First Mother.

She put her head down. Felt, despite her resolve, the tidal pull of him. Burning from throat to cheeks, she put her hand on the Nawatir's chest. Her heart thrummed in her throat. Her body felt thick and swollen. The Ja-Gaar watched her incuriously with the cabochon jewels of their eyes, their tails swishing back and forth like the metronomes used at choir practice.

Besieged by anguish, she whispered his name, using a voice, a tone she would never use again. How acutely she felt her breasts, her belly, her thighs—so aware of them that the silk seemed to abrade her flesh. How pleasurable the pain! How deeply inside her she must bury it.

"Inggres."

The sound of his voice, though low, gave her a start. There was a ringing in her ears, over which she could barely make out her stuttering reply. "I am here."

"I am not dead."

"No, Nawatir."

"Take my hand."

She hesitated only a fraction of an instant, and he was too groggy to notice. She slid her hand into his, felt a connection all the way through her bones. His touch felt so right.

"You are here in the abbey," she whispered thickly. "Safe now."

"Thank you." He pulled her down toward him, the smell of him like attar. "Inggres."

His lips brushed hers and she shivered. Their breaths commingled.

"No, Nawatir. No." Resisting him, herself. "This is wrong."

He kept his hold on her, incredibly strong, despite his wound. "Is it? Why?"

"You know why."

"I love you, Inggres."

Her loins were melting. She longed to give in, ached for their physical merging. It seemed as if she had wanted nothing so badly in all her life. But of course it was a lie, and she caught herself at it, hauled herself back from the brink. Still the incredible pull of his sexuality sought to seduce her; but she had her wits about her again, she knew right from wrong. Absolutely.

"I just nursed you back to health. What you are feeling is natural, but it is not real."

"You are wrong. I know what I feel."

"I doubt that you do. Not at this moment, anyway."

His gaze slid away from her. "How can you know that?"

"You and First Mother are bound together."

"She cannot love me. She will not confide in me."

"Nawatir, has it not occurred to you that it is precisely because she *does* love you that she does not confide in you?"

"That makes no sense."

"Oh, but it does. Consider that she is First Mother, consider further that she is a seer. They say that all seers go mad eventually. Do you know why? Because no one—not even Ramahan—are strong enough to hold inside them all the skeins that might evolve into the future. Think, Nawatir! If you see that something will happen in the future, you must always doubt your actions in the present. If you take action, will it prevent that future? Will it cause it? And if you take another action, what then? What if you take no action at all? You see? It is enough to drive even the best minds mad. That is her fate. She cannot change the fact that she is a seer, though for years she tried to deny it. But she can protect you from it."

"I do not want to be protected."

"You cannot know that. I doubt that you even fully believe it. It is your male ego, Nawatir, that has prevented you from seeing it. You felt hurt by her act of kindness and generosity. I think you owe her an apology."

He let go of her, lay back on the bedding. Stared up at the ceiling.

"Is that the way it is, truly?"

Her heart broke for him, and for herself.

There were four possible ways to get rid of Sornnn SaTrryn, none of them easy. Raan Tallus had been months formulating plans, paring the possibilities, calculating odds, and honing those that remained. Moving precipitously against the SaTrryn was not a viable option for a number of reasons, not the least of which was that he was Prime Factor. Another was that he was a favorite of the regent, judging by the amount of time the two had spent together recently. They had even, according to Raan Tallus' information, traveled to the Korrush together several times. It was one thing to engineer the murder of a Bashkir who toiled in virtual anonymity as Hadinnn SaTrryn had, quite another to do the same with someone in the glare of the public eye.

Which was why it was taking him so long to move against the son, why today he was spending his solitude at the villa double- and triple-checking his plan of choice. He was not a Bashkir to leave anything to chance, prided himself on preparing for every eventuality before putting his plans into motion. So it had been with Hadinnn SaTrryn. He rubbed his eyes, put his holopad aside. He had been at it since before dawn and was now in need of a break. Time for a long, bracing ride along the black cliffs.

Advancing on the cthauros pen, he saw Nem, his head held high, stamping his foreleg. He looked around, put his hand up to shield his eyes, searching for the source of Nem's agitation. Seeing no one, he lapsed into deep thought and considered once again how, through the sheer force of his genius, he had turned the past on its ear. He had proved wrong those who believed in determinism. It had been his misfortune not to be born Ashera, further to be born a Tallus. His father had been a minor Bashkir in every sense of the word, content to be a functionary in the regent's court, content to simper in the shadows others cast, doing their bidding. How he had sired a consummate risk-taker, a child of high ambition, was anyone's guess. Many was the time Raan Tallus harbored the suspicion that he was not his father's child at all. Fantasy or no, the notion made him happy, and so he kept it close to him like an heirloom to admire.

What he wanted, then, from a very early age, was to be Ashera. Since he was not, he contrived to inveigle his way into the heart of the Ashera empire. And when Eleusis Ashera became regent he saw his opening. He had already studied Eleusis and so made the new regent aware in as many ways as possible how well he understood him. That was Eleusis' weakness. He saw what Raan Tallus contrived for him to see: that the two of them vibrated to the same exact pitch, and that he responded to blindly, in a rare instance ignoring Giyan's wise counsel. For it was true that Eleusis, like all Ashera, was inherently lonely. The Ashera's success and lofty status was mostly to blame, for while the head of the other Bashkir families outwardly respected the Ashera, their jealousy and envy inwardly seethed.

Eleusis took to Raan Tallus as a trusted friend. Why wouldn't he? Raan Tallus was scrupulous never to let him see his other face. The grasping, covetous, treacherous face that no amount of charm or real talent could hide from Giyan.

And now Raan Tallus had all that he had wished for. If not Ashera in name, then in fact. Until the day Ashera arrived from another swarm, he ran the empire. And each day he drew the cords of power more tightly around him. Nothing, no one would interfere with this accumulation. He had sacrificed everything, dedicated his life to the Ashera. Who deserved this reward better than he?

Fueled by his self-righteous ruminations, he arrived in high spirits at the cthauros pen. Yes, he thought, swinging open the fence, the best decision he ever made was to use Ashera coins to buy this villa. Coming out here like clockwork once a week allowed him to think clearly and formulate tactics, for he had no doubt that running a Bashkir empire was like being in a war. Being first in, last out, taking and holding the high ground, maintaining a high degree of maneuverability, knowing the competition's strengths, weaknesses, tendencies, and how to use them as weapons—the accumulation of such knowledge would serve any Khaggun general well on the field of battle.

He led Nem out of the pen, swung the fence shut. Grasping the cthauros' mane, he leapt astride the great six-legged beast, headed out for his ride. The thundering hooves, the rhythmic gait exhilarated him. He did not return to the villa until twilight. By then he was dusty and tired and ready for something to eat. But first a swim to stretch out cramped muscles, to get the blood flowing freely, to rid himself of small aches and pains piled up by the tension of everyday life. The air was still, breathless, the distant sea a ruffled coat of fleece. A seabird lifted from its cliffside nest. A black sail, two, Sarakkon on the long voyage home.

He spent time brushing Nem's coat, feeding the cthauros, speaking to them as if they were his children. He cared more about them than he did most V'ornn. They were incapable of disappointing or betraying him.

At last, he took his swim. He had deliberately put it off in order to allow the anticipation to build, to better savor the quick, breathtaking transition from the dusty heat of his ride to the cool silkiness of the water. As he walked across the porphyry terrace he watched the last of the sunlight chop itself to tiny scimitars. He picked up his pace, shedding his clothes as he went. Naked, he dived into the stone pool. It was deep and dark, perfectly round. The water, very cold, very bracing, struck him like a blow, snapped his drowsing mind back into full awareness. The water closed over him, chilling him, cleansing him. He dived so deep that at the apex of his arc he could almost touch the bottom with his outstretched hand. Then he turned up, heading for the evening. A good meal, a crackling fire to balance out the spring chill.

Rippling shadows lay upon the surface, making hypnotic patterns. There was a fire in his lungs, growing, a kind of pleasurable ache as he felt another kind of anticipation, of drawing a cool breath of the coming night deep inside him.

Up he shot, but near the surface something slammed into the top of his skull. His upward momentum ceased at once, his limbs pinwheeled as he was turned upside down. Half-stunned, he struck out for what he assumed was the surface, but he had become disoriented. Another blow to his head finished the job. He lay spread-eagled in the pool, blinking, trying to gather his thoughts which seemed to explode in his head like a string of flashes. He tried to reach for one, failed. Opened his mouth, swallowed water, and immediately began to choke.

Dimly, he was aware that he was not alone in the pool. He reached out instinctively for help, received another blow to the head in reply. He blinked, tried to focus. Was that Sornnn SaTrryn? Surely not! He must be hallucinating.

His lungs were on fire. He had to breathe, but he could

not. He had to reach the surface. He kicked, his legs moving powerfully. He should have shot to the surface, but he was not moving at all.

He flailed out stupidly, his fists encountering another body. It was then that he realized what was happening, realized that Sornnn SaTrryn was not only in the pool with him but was responsible for keeping him under.

I have to breathe!

Froth trailed upward from his grimly tightened lips. His fingers sought purchase, to hook the SaTrryn's mouth, gouge his eyes. There were flashes of blackness now, a certain numbness in parts of his body. Turbid water full of treacherous currents, forests of bubbles. He thought of all his meticulously laid plans, the sleepless nights lost to the minutiae of his scheming, thought of Hadinnn SaTrryn waxen, stiff, lifeless. Coming to pay his respects to the family, taking the measure of Sornnn SaTrryn, gauging how difficult it would be to take him down. Flashed on the absurdity of it. What was the point of planning anything when this could happen? A starless night staring at him with a blackcrow's face. How much time had passed? Raan Tallus took one last desperate lunge at his assailant.

Inhaled.

32

Crown of Creation

Gul Aluf, wrapped in her black traveling cloak, stood in the attic of the ramshackle kashiggen known as FIREFLY. In her arms lay Kurgan, more dead than alive. When he had failed to respond to his Summons she had used the signal from his okummmon to trace him.

She had found him hanging upside down from one of the ceiling rafters. Below him, a turquoise pool of blood, indigo at its drying edges. She observed the raw bruises, contusions, lacerations. Three cracked ribs moved beneath her probing fingertips. She had little curiosity about who had done this to him, she only cared whether he lived or died. That, it seemed, would be up to her.

She took him through the grimy window she had kicked in, up onto the roof, then piled him into her hovercraft, climbed in herself, and took off, heading to the Temple of Mnemonics. There, she took Kurgan directly to her lab-orb, the Crown of Creation.

In a way, she thought as she stripped him and hooked him into the alifanon, a surgical net, it was a lucky stroke that she found him near death. That way, she did not have to waste time forcibly subduing him, for she had been clandestinely observing him long enough and knew enough about him to be certain that he would fight her every step of the way. She drove water-based cortical leads into his temples, the base of his neck. Nith Batoxxx had affected him in many ways, not the least of which was the unexpected consequence that made Stogggul Kurgan unafraid of Gyrgon. That was a dangerous trait in any V'ornn, but especially in a regent. Eleusis Ashera, too, had in his own way defied Gyrgon law by studying the Kundalan, taking for his mistress a Ramahan priestess, identifying with them. That was why the Comradeship had sanctioned Nith Batoxxx's petition for his demise. What was it about Kundala, she wondered as she attached more leads to the soft place just beneath his sternum, the base of his spine, on either side of his groin, that caused V'ornn to go native? Her attempts to return to intimacy with Nith Sahor were partially driven by the need to have this vexing enigma unraveled. But part of her knew that he would never trust her, never divulge the answer to even one question for which she sought an answer.

It was with reluctance and a certain sense of agitation that she had informed Nith Immmon of her decision via the Comradeship central neural net. He took it well, gave only a token argument, went off as she instructed him to find Nith Einon.

She returned to the work at hand. When she had Kurgan completely hooked up, she closed her eyes, bringing up on her mental screen the image of his brain. She examined the spot to which Nith Sahor had been pointing. The ativar. The most primitive section of the V'ornn brain, smaller in Gyrgon than in any other caste. Well, almost all Gyrgon. Not her, not Nith Batoxxx. And certainly not Nith Sahor. They all had genetically heightened ativar. What was most curious to her, she thought as she brought up a holoimage of Kurgan's brain on her own screen, was how differently each of them reacted to having an abnormally large ativar.

Of course she had given one to Nith Batoxxx, and she had no doubt that part of her attraction to Nith Sahor had to do with the consequences of his heightened ativar. She did not know how she had gotten hers, suspected that it was a simple matter of a genetic mutation. What a heightened ativar did was to make you stronger, smarter, better than those around you. Size, she had discovered, had nothing to do with it, else why would Gyrgon, the dominant caste, have smaller ativar than other V'ornn. But it was a terribly tricky thing to do deliberately, hence the spectacular failure of Stogggul Terrettt.

She filled the alifanon with amniotic fluid until Kurgan was completely covered. Then she went to work on his skull, her nails extruded, turned to photon scalpels to pare away skin, all the layers beneath to the bare bone, a beautiful thing. While the fluid soaked into him she began to devise the skein of the cortical net she would implant in him. It would, of course, have its root in his ativar, so she worked backward, starting from there. It did not take her long. This was her work, after all. She was a gifted Gul. It was not strictly a scientific process. There was much about it that responded to intuition, which was why only Guls were designated Breeders. Save for Nith Sahor and possibly his father, she knew of no Gyrgon who showed the slightest degree of intuition.

From her point of view, the trouble with Nith Sahor was that she simply did not understand him. What did he want? She could never guess. He did not think like a V'ornn, much less a Gyrgon. Often he acted like a Kundalan. That was particularly disturbing because of his heightened ativar. So far as she knew, his, like hers, was a genetic mutation. There was no doubt that he understood the Kundalan better than any V'ornn. What was his almost mystical link to them? And, in any case, where was the virtue in that? Could he be insane like Stogggul Terrettt? Would she be able to convince anyone else of that? Once, she had been certain she could control him, even up to the moment of their reunion at the museum. Then she saw that he had the power, if not to defeat her, then to resist her. Even Nith Einon did not have that. She had searched long and hard for a way to bind him to her. It took giving him back his life to make him an ally.

She finished the skein of the neural net and was bending over to begin attaching it to Kurgan's nervous system when she saw the odd scar in the hollow of his throat. Taking up one of her instruments, she directed a photon beam at it. A raw patch appeared and immediately new unblemished skin began to knit itself over the wound. But even before it was fully healed, the scar returned. Gul Aluf peered at it, touched it. It was impossible, but true. The scar was permanent, beyond even her capabilities to heal. What could possibly have made it?

She shrugged, returned her attention to fitting the neural net, always a tricky undertaking. Nervous systems did not like being invaded, let alone being tampered with. Her wings unfolded, and she placed the end of one, where the membrane was thinnest, between Kurgan's bared skull and the neural net she had constructed. A Gul's wings were not only for flying. The membrane allowed the neural net to imprint itself on the skull, ensuring that the complex nervous system that ran beneath would become used to the interface without being disturbed.

Her mind kept coming back to Nith Sahor. It was axiomatic that what you could not control you had to kill. She wondered whether it would come to that. She knew it would not be easy for her to kill him, either emotionally or in actuality. She had to admit that she bore an uncommon affinity toward him not only because of his power, his intellect, but because at her core he frightened her. She was like a child who adores being swung upside down because the fear it produces is exhilarating. For she had to admit that these days not much else exhilarated her. Truth be known, she detested being in this backwater, had protested vehemently when her swarm had decided to investigate Kundala. And so it rankled her all the more that Nith Sahor should be so besotted with the place, causing her to consider madness as an explanation. And if he was in fact mad, then he would have to die. Insanity in Gyrgon could not be tolerated; the other castes must never know. Even Nith Einon would have to agree with that.

Time, as Guls said, to build the more perfect beast. She lifted her wing, removing the membrane. Then, slowly, almost reverentially, she placed the neural net onto the skull. It sat there for but a moment. She trained a photon beam on it, and there arose the scents of clove and burnt musk. Slowly the neural net began to embed itself into the bone. Settling there, its tendrils attached themselves to the neural pathways, widening them, causing them to branch out, extend their reach through the brain, into the spinal cord, then into all areas of the body.

She stood upright. Now time to rest for both of them, for reassembling life was a most difficult and exacting task. Tomorrow at this time, or perhaps a few hours thereafter, Kurgan would regain consciousness as Nith. He would be Gyrgon just as Nith Batoxxx had planned.

L ong before the Centophennni set up their galactic spyglass, Lethe had been inhabited by the Vogul. It was unclear why they had left Lethe, possibly the Centophennni had driven them away. In any case, they had left behind inordinately well preserved remnants of their civilization.

Their belief system was simple: they were born from a female and to a female they returned. Death came to them as the female that birthed them, taking them down a long tunnel into the Under-of-Things. A primitive belief, to be sure, but one all the more powerful for that.

When Hannn Mennus went to sleep that night, surrounded by six Khagggun he had designated as his personal bodyguards, he dreamed that he was back on Lethe—dark, still, dead Lethe—taking the journey to Under-of-Things. Not a moment ago he had been standing on a crag, surrounded by what was left of his Khagggun. He was alone, unable to understand what had happened to them or to him. Then he peered more closely, saw that they all had Iin Mennus' face. Everywhere he looked his brother's filmed eyes stared at him.

When Death arrived, a tall female whose face was shrouded in mist and shadow, he felt relieved, wanted to go with her, wanted to leave the silent accusation behind. She took him by the hand and began to lead him to Under-of-Things.

They seemed to be walking down a colossal sewer pipe, for they were slogging through a river of blood. He wrinkled his nose. It should have smelled, but it didn't. He had no faith in the female, but he followed her just the same. Why? He had never followed a female, including his mother, the memory of whom was as dim as the light in this sewer. The story went that he bit his mother's teat when she had tried to feed him. He had almost killed her being born—big for a baby, an empty promise, for he had failed to grow to the expected size. So he had spilled her blood twice, and now here she was, Death leading him down to the Under-of-Things.

He awoke with his hearts hammering and the overpowering need to spit. He rose, fully awake, signaled to his six guards, who though tired dared not even close their eyes for fear of being caught dozing. Leaving Pack-

Commander Twaane in charge, he set out with his small band of guards for Axis Tyr. He no longer cared what his Khagggun would think of him. The dream had left an unpleasant taste in his mouth that no amount of spitting would get rid of.

They traveled swiftly and silently through the forest, over treed ridges, mossed swales, in a virtual straight line. So anxious was he to arrive in Axis Tyr that he ignored the difficulty of the terrain, pushing his cadre as he pushed himself. Not one word of complaint was uttered, but that did not stop their minds from working overtime. They no longer understood their commander; they wondered if they ever had.

Midway between midnight and dawn he called a halt. It was then that he realized that there were only five guards. He turned the heat seeker in his helm to maximum, but, apart from the odd small nocturnal mammal, there was nothing to pick up. He sent three of his Khagggun out in a basic triangle from their position. Only two returned. That left four guards and himself.

He thought seriously of going after the perpetrators, thought even more seriously of setting the forest aflame, making one gigantic pyre to burn them all, but the truth was he no longer cared. Also, it would greatly inconvenience him by forcing him to detour around it. So he urged the cadre onward at an even more urgent pace. His dream had made him desperate to reach Axis Tyr, to see his brother one last time. To avenge his death. He took the lead, slashing the underbrush with his shock-sword, hacking away, hearing the high whine of the hyperexcited ions.

He heard a sound and, turning, saw one of his Khagggun drive the points of his shock-sword through another's armor. Shock froze him as a shadow emerged from the forest. The guard nearest Mennus leapt between him and the shadow. An ion cannon burst blew open his armor, and he fell, writhing. Mennus ducked and rolled along the pine straw. Drawing his own ion cannon, he fired wildly at the shadow, missed, saw tree limbs crashing down, sent it darting back through the gap between the trunks of a pair of Marre pine. At the same time, he saw another shadow, signaled to the one remaining Khagggun, who nodded and went after it. Then he turned and, without aiming, shot from the hip, clipping his own Khagggun, who was already bleeding like a stuck cor. By the time he kicked the corpse out of the way, there was nothing else to see.

There was a strong temptation to go after whoever was impersonating one of his Khagggun, but instinct honed to a knife edge told him that form of pursuit would be futile. Instead, he took to the trees, climbing through the densely needled branches of a Marre pine. He moved carefully from tree to tree more or less in the direction the shadow he had shot at had come from. It was also a temptation to move quickly, but again he restrained himself, crouching on a branch, completely still, even his eyes. Willing the enemy to come to him. Waiting. That was the hardest part for him. He was impatient to continue his journey, just as impatient to discover who it was clever enough to kill off his Khagggun. He was unused to Resistance having the firepower to inflict so much damage. Plus, and almost as worrisome, their tactics had completely changed. He had become conditioned to the ragtag way they approached the field of battle. Never any sense of an overall plan. Even within Resistance cells it always appeared to him that each individual made up his own mind how to act. It made them all the easier to kill once you found them. This was something else altogether.

He saw movement below him and to the left. He put his shock-dagger between his teeth, but held himself back, waiting that extra moment to assure himself what he was seeing was not his own Khagggun. Then he left his perch, leaping onto the back of the semicrouched figure.

He landed on his knees, having knocked the wind out of the figure. It was dressed entirely in black, an interesting innovation, he thought, as he plunged the dagger into the spine, put one hand over the mouth, endured a painful bite, twisted the blade until the lips went slack.

He went tracking through the darkness, searching for more prey.

Nith Immmon unfolded his arms when Sahor approached Gul Aluf's lab-orb. He was standing in front of the access panel, which was sealed shut.

"I want to see her," Sahor said without preamble.

"Impossible. She has left word—"

"Are you her lackey now?"

"Just so you know." Nith Immmon refolded his arms. "There is currently a debate raging within the Comradeship whether or not to charge you with the murder of Nith Nassam."

"Gul Aluf knows I did not murder him."

"Does she?" Nith Immmon showing his teeth.

"Ah," Sahor said. "I see how it is."

With no more than a whisper, the access panel to the lab-orb cycled open. Nith Immmon moved aside as Nith Einon stepped through into the corridor.

"I do not think you do, Sahor," Nith Einon said. "You are no longer welcome here."

Something inside Sahor went cold. "Father, what are you doing speaking in a Gul's voice?"

"I am speaking with the Voice of One, the voice of the Comradeship."

"The Comradeship has been fractured for too long for me to believe that."

"Believe what you will, Sahor. The imminent threat from the Centophennni has united what was once split. There is once more a single Gyrgon voice."

Out of the corner of his eye, Sahor watched the small smile play across Nith Immmon's lips. So they had given Nith Einon everything he wanted. His body, re-formed, renewed, rejuvenated, and returned to him was only part of the price he had exacted from them. His return to power was the other part. The Comradeship spoke with his voice.

"You see, when you unlocked Nith Batoxxx's files you

obviated the need for your reluctant services," Nith Immmon said.

"They grew tired of your reluctance, bored by your arguments," Nith Einon said. "Quite frankly, so did I."

"This is a mistake, Father. A terrible miscalculation on
your part."

"I no longer know who you are, Sahor. I am fearful for
you. To be honest, there are those in the Comradeship who
think you mad. They argued for incarceration in Receiving
Spirit."

"Nith Einon talked them out of it," Nith Immmon said.
"But from this day forward you are banished from the
Temple of Mnemonics, enjoined from having any contact
with Gyrgon."

"Especially Gul Aluf."

"Why especially her?"

The two Niths were silent and unyielding. Sahor was in
a state of shock. He could accept—even halfway expect—
such treachery from any Gyrgon save his father.

"Neither of us knows the other," he said. "How did that
happen?"

"The equation is a simple one, really." Nith Einon had
never looked so imposing or threatening. "You chose the
Kundalan over us, Sahor. Your fate and theirs are one.
And, really, isn't that what you wanted all along?"

Darkness was Basse's friend, despite the fact that he
was not equipped with the benefits of a Khagggun
helm. He had been born into darkness, it seemed, and in
darkness he found comfort. Though his night vision was
excellent, he used the full range of his other senses to
guide him.

His nostrils flared. He scented the Khagggun just as if
he were an animal. He judged him to be not more than a
hundred meters north by northwest of his present position.
He was standing still. His helm turned from side to side as
he decided which way to go next.

Basse waited until he had made his choice, then circled

around, wanting to come at him on the oblique, not quite from the rear and not from the side. Something in between. That way, he judged, he would be able to get in close and slit the Khagggun's throat before he had a chance to react. No good using the ion cannon. Majja had failed to take out Hannn Mennus. He did not want to give his position away.

The Khagggun paused and, with him, Basse. They stood still and tense, almost like mirror images. Basse, one eye on the enemy, listened to what the forest was telling him. It was unnaturally quiet. Those who made the forest their home knew when death was stalking. They were hidden away now, safe in warrens, high branches, beneath piles of fallen needles, slipping into sleep. There was something wrong, Basse could feel it, something was missing that had been there moments before, a void that made him want to retch. Perhaps it was his own death. He wiped his face, thinking of an open grave, and returned to stalking the enemy.

As the Khagggun moved so did Basse, pacing him, turning as he turned, always on the oblique angle he desired. Closer and closer. There were only fifteen meters left between them when the Khagggun stopped beside a tree. Basse's ears pricked up when he heard the sound of water running briefly. Smiling. He had the moment he had been waiting for.

But even as he began his run he knew something was wrong. Too late now to break it off, he was committed. His shock-sword was at the ready, vibrating points held higher than the hilt. He filled his other hand with a dagger, saw the shadow moving at him at the same oblique angle he had on the Khagggun. He recognized Hannn Mennus at the moment Mennus barreled into him.

Thrown off stride, he spun to one knee. Mennus came at him with his own shock-sword. The Khagggun against the tree turned. His armor gaped open, and, with a deft twist of his wrist, Basse threw the dagger, an underhand motion, a flat trajectory, powerful and true, he had practiced since he was six. The dagger buried itself to the hilt. But now it was too late to avoid Mennus' blow, which came whistling down in a trajectory to cleave Basse's skull.

Livid blue-white light exploded, the percussion burst sending Basse tumbling head-over-heels backward. He shook his head, rose on one knee. Hannn Mennus stood, weaving slightly. There was a ragged hole in his chest plate. He was looking at a figure in Khagggun armor advancing on him.

"Who . . . who are you, traitor?" Mennus managed.

The helm came off, revealing Marethyn's face. Mennus cursed mightily. His arm came up, the ion cannon in it, and Marethyn fired at the same place she had hit him the first time. Blood fountained, and Mennus was blown backward, arms thrown wide.

Basse got to his feet, started walking. He saw Marethyn stalking over to Mennus. He was not yet dead, a tough V'ornn even by Khagggun standards.

"I curse you to every level of N'Luuura," Mennus whispered through bloody teeth. He began to gurgle, drowning in his own blood.

"Don't die," Marethyn said. "Not yet." She took out her shock-sword and, with a slow, deliberate stroke, severed his head from his neck. The extremities jerked and spasmed to be subjected to such gross insult. The sphincter let go, and foulness rose into the air.

She plucked the severed head off the ground, tucked it under one arm.

"We must find Majja," Basse growled, "and remove ourselves from this cesspit."

They set out in a tight spiral from the place where they had launched the initial attack. They went together, cautious and tense. Moving across a hummock, she stumbled over a huge root. She looked down. No, not a root. Something else, and she held Basse back. Then her heart seemed to stop beating. An arm, the elbow cocked, rising like a pale fern. She signed to Basse, who knelt with her.

They saw the body, wetness all around, as if she had stopped to drink her fill of rainwater.

No, Marethyn thought. *No!*

Basse turned the body over, made a small noise, put his head down.

Marethyn touched Majja's face, wiped the blood out of her eyes and nose. She put her ear to Majja's chest. No pulse, no beat. This was a mistake. Surely she was only grievously wounded, shock must have caused them to miss the signs. She sat up, slammed her fist into Majja's sternum, began to pump with the heels of her hands, making a steady rhythm.

"Come on, come on," she chanted.

"What are you doing?" Basse looking at her.

She kept up the pump, what else was there to do? If there was even one iota of a chance that she could bring Majja back . . .

"She's dead." Basse lifted her pallid hand. "Feel her. Cool as stone."

Marethyn, ignoring him, gripped by desperation. Pumping away.

"She's lost too much blood."

"Stop it!"

All at once Marethyn's teeth were chattering. She sat back on her haunches, closed her eyes. Majja couldn't be dead, she couldn't. She had grown up with a sister who despised her. It was only now she realized how much she had come to rely on Majja, how much of a buffer between her and Basse—all the Resistance members who feared and distrusted her—she had been. Like an older sister she had looked out for Marethyn. Like an older sister she had accepted the differences in Marethyn and had loved her just the same. What was she going to do without her?

Rain began to patter down. Leaves dipping, dripping. Slippery needles. The fecund smell of fungi.

Basse looking on, expressionless, as she wept.

* * *

After Sahor had gone, after they had been assured of his exit from the Temple grounds, the two Niths made their way to Nith Batoxxx's lab-orb. Nith Einon keyed open the access panel, and they proceeded inside.

Nith Einon identified a false orangesweet blossom, plucked it off the vine. They were trembling, for they both felt the tide of history pulling them onto the shore of great discovery. It had been thus when Nith Glous had discovered the multiverse, when Nith Hunnn had perfected the grav drive that allowed V'ornn ships to "fall" between multiverse layers, travel thousands of light-years in the space of a triple heartsbeat. Now, on the verge of discovering a way to save themselves from annihilation by the Centophennni, they felt the same electric exhilaration those genius Niths, all the others in the Catalogue of Greatness must have felt. Their connection to the accomplishments of the past filled their veins with a tingling, and their chests felt tight with sudden pressure.

They exchanged a meaningful glance as Nith Einon held for a moment the data blossom above the slot. "This is worth everything," he said.

"It is a shame Nith Sahor does not share your dedication to our continued survival."

"My son is not himself, it is true. He has become self-hating. Like Eleusis Ashera, he has allowed the Kundalan to infect him."

"Is he mad, then?" Nith Immmon fidgeted by his side. "Were the others right to want him incarcerated and under constant surveillance?"

"My suspicion is rather more benign, though no less sad. I think he has become deluded. I believe that he thinks of himself as something of a mystic. Mysticism, as I have no need to remind you, has no place in our world. Equation after equation has proved its invalidity."

"Ah, I see. Mysticism is the cornerstone of the Kundalan worldview."

"That is as may be. But as for me, I cannot fathom what

fascination they could possibly hold. Forget the Kundalan. Forget Sahor."

So saying, he placed the stem of Nith Batoxxx's data blossom into its slot. Two sets of Nith eyes were focused on the holoscreen as the longed-for data came up in a series of whorls. They had just started to read it when it was wiped out, leaving a black screen hanging in front of them like a starless sky.

Nith Immmon turned to Nith Einon. "What happened? What did you do?"

"I did not do anything." Nith Einon's fingers were working the controls. "One moment the data was there, the next it was gone."

"Where did it go?"

"It is nowhere in the databank."

"Well, download it again from the blossom."

"I have already tried that." Nith Einon's voice had turned sharp. "The data blossom is dead."

"What do you mean, dead?"

"It is useless. The data inside it is gone."

Nith Immmon plucked another one from the vine. "Here. Try another."

In fact, they tried three more blossoms with no result, including the original one Nith Sahor had inserted in the slot.

"It's a virus," Nith Einon said.

"What?"

Nith Einon was grinding his teeth in fury. "My son inserted a virus into this system."

"Get it out of there."

"Too late." Nith Einon slammed his fist into the control panel. "It has infected the data blossoms. It has eaten every bit of data that was ever in there."

Nith Immmon went searching through the orangesweet vine on the wall. "What about other data blossoms? There must be more here."

In fact, there was only one. He held it up triumphantly.

"What would you do with it?" Nith Einon asked him rhetorically. "It was made to fit this system and no other."

"I know my son too well." Nith Einon took it from him, examined the "petals." "You see here? It is sabotaged. Were we successful in solving the riddle of this system, were we to build another slot for the stem, the data blossom would self-destruct instantaneously."

"Damn him to every level of Argedddian purgatory!"

Nith Einon placed the data blossom in Nith Immmon's hand. "Wear it as a badge. It is of no other practical use."

Marethyn and Basse had been trudging through the forest for close to six hours without a single word having passed between them. If asked, Marethyn would not have been able to say what was on her mind. But no one did ask, and, in any case, she was thinking of Majja.

Burying her had been difficult for both of them. Neither of them had wanted to let her go. What she had meant to Basse was yet another mystery. Had he loved her all the while he was fighting beside her? For all Marethyn knew of them they were blood sister and brother, though she doubted it because the Resistance frowned on more than one family member inside a single cell. From his face, his demeanor, she could tell nothing. Whatever he might be feeling occurred so deep inside him not a trace of it reached the surface.

Consequently, Marethyn traveled with a degree of unease. Possibly, this was his intent. He had made his prejudices known. As far as he was concerned, no matter what she did, she was first, last, and always V'ornn. Not to be trusted. And yet, following the burial he had made no sign of breaking away from her, going his own way. By a kind of unspoken agreement, they had begun to circle back toward the last known position of what was left of the late, unlamented Hannn Mennus' Wing. What they would do when they came upon them was unclear. They were exhausted both physically and emotionally from their long and wrenching ordeal. What they needed most now was several days of hot meals and uninterrupted sleep. Neither, however, harbored any illusions. Time enough for rest when the war was won.

Long, thin clouds raked the sky like claws, scudding south, as if fleeing the Djenn Marre. The head of Hannn Mennus, grim and silent, was darkening, the skin going from bronze to charcoal grey. Also, it had begun to stink. Basse had stuffed the neck with dry Marre pine needles and that had helped. Strangely, they now loved the head, as if inside it the last of Majja still lived and breathed, as if keeping it close would keep her near them.

Chirruping night clutched them to its bosom, and at last they realized that they could go no farther without eating or sleeping. They roasted meat stripped from a qwawd they caught. The juices ran over their fingers as they pulled the meat from the fire. Soon enough their mouths were coated with grease. Still, they had not spoken. Basse barely looked at her, stared instead into the filmed-over eyes of Hannn Mennus, thought his inscrutable thoughts. Slept like the dead, while Hannn Mennus stared infinity in the face.

At first light, on Marethyn's watch, she saw movement in the misty forest. She swung her ion cannon and called softly to Basse. He awoke, as was his wont, completely out of a deep sleep, got to his feet, saw that they were no longer alone.

Figures appeared out of the mist, silent, their weapons at their side, pointing to the ground. Until they were standing in a rough semicircle around them: what appeared to be an entire brigade of Resistance.

One of the males stepped forward. He had a face like a rock, battered by time or circumstance, grizzled with moss. His clothes, like the others', was in tatters. Here and there, you could see muscle or the curve of bone beneath sun-bronzed skin. He addressed Basse in a deep voice. "I am Dunna."

"I am Basse and this is Marethyn." He and Marethyn stood side by side. "Are you leader of this brigade?"

"Hardly a brigade, Basse. We are the remnants of many cells, all that is left from Hannn Mennus' relentless attacks." He licked his lips. "We have heard tales, seen evidence with our own eyes. We have been searching for you. We want to join you."

Marethyn said nothing. She was aware of some of the Resistance fighters looking at her out of the corner of the eyes, but as for Dunna, it seemed as if she did not exist at all. She knew what would happen here if Majja were still with them. But Majja was dead, and there was only Basse. Angry, enigmatic Basse. Her hearts were in her throat, knowing that her fate was in his hands. If he denounced her—though the accusation be false—she could see that they would fall on her, rend her limb from limb. Their sunken eyes were dark-rimmed with too many defeats. They were desperate for leadership, desperate for hope, desperate to participate again in victory.

Dunna moving from one foot to another, impatience intruding on his deference. "So, what do you say?"

"I say nothing." Basse hooked a thumb at Marethyn. "My Commander makes all the decisions."

"Your Commander?" Dunna goggled. "This Tuskugg-gun?"

"My Commander created the Black Guard, conceived of its tactics. You have seen the victorious results with your own eyes. And there is more. Hannn Mennus' Wing is demoralized, in disarray." Basse picked up Hannn Mennus' head, held it high up for them to see. "As for the feared Hannn Mennus himself, here he is. My Commander killed him." He shook the head, a shower of blood-clotted pine straw falling. "I follow her wherever she leads. If you wish to join the Black Guard, you will give her your strong arm, your brave heart, your absolute loyalty, as I do. Nothing less will suffice. The Black Guard accepts only elite warriors. You will have to prove yourself worthy to Commander Marethyn."

At length, Dunna turned to her. "Is this true, Commander? Did you in fact kill Hannn Mennus?"

Marethyn was understandably stunned. She wanted to make eye contact with Basse, possibly to make sure he hadn't lost his mind or, worse still, was joking. The only thing that stopped her was that she knew Basse did not joke. Still, she had the presence of mind to address Dunna directly. Taking her cue from Basse, she said, "You have been told it is by a member of the Black Guard. If you need confirmation, if you doubt what he has told you, then you have no business being with us."

"I meant no offense, Commander. It is just that . . ."

"Yes?" Pulling herself up to her full height. She could feel the black cloth of her blouse fluttering against her ribs.

"Nothing." To his credit, he met her eye. "I speak for all of us, Commander, when I say that we fervently wish to become members of the Black Guard."

"You may walk with us, Dunna. You may fight with us in our next battle. If you follow orders, if you are found worthy by Basse and me, then will your clothes be dyed black like ours."

"That is fair, Commander. We thank you for this kindness."

As he turned to address his ragtag compatriots, Marethyn shot Basse a look. Their eyes locked, she gave him a small nod, and a grin broke out on his face. Not that it lasted long, not that it needed to. It was unmistakable and indelible, and when she grinned back she was flooded with a fierce pride.

33

Island of the Damned

With the precision of a surgeon, Riane emerged from null-space on the blistered shore of the island known as Suspended Skull. Directly in front of her a tidal pool shimmered blue-black in the first glimmerings of dawn. The tide had pulled back sufficiently, leaving in its wake a wide sampling of its infinite bounty: sideways-scuttling crabs, whorled whelks and tiny poniwinkles, three sleek fishlets, trapped now in this enclosed world. All crowned by a twined wreath of sea wrack, dark and podded. She wondered what Thigpen would make of this. The Rappa did not care for the sea or those things that swam in it. Not that it mattered. She had stayed behind because Amitra had told her that those few Rappa who had tried to land on the island with their Ramahan compatriots had died.

Suspended Skull, a roughly oval tower of tumbled rock and tenacious, wind-lashed mortewood, was the last bastion of land jutting south into the Cape of Broken Meridian. A mean and bitter place, drenched by storms, scoured by wind, the seas all around aboil where the crosscurrents from those two vast bodies of water, the Sea of Blood and the Illuminated Sea, were thrown together.

It was true that Suspended Skull was rarely spoken of, and then only in hushed tones. The Kundalan fishers avoided it because of the razor-sharp reefs and treacherous currents surrounding it. The Sarakkon believed its waters infested with black Chimaera, which the bravest of them hunted but most feared. As for the Ramahan, they had their own reasons for shunning this unlovely ridged pile of rock, for they had knowledge of ancient legends that spoke of a sorcerous pit beneath Suspended Skull, conjured in the Time before Time, that led deep into the bowels of Kundala, where roiled and slunk the spirits of those damned creatures that had lived at the Dawn of Time.

All this was not to say that the Ramahan had never inhabited the island. In point of fact they had, in an age long beyond the memory of even the oldest Druuge. What they had been doing there was anyone's guess—possibly they had gone at the behest of Miina, there to fulfill a specific purpose known only to Her. What was incontrovertible was that on its extreme heights they had erected an abbey of sorts. Riane could see it high atop the looming cliff face, wreathed in mist and rent cloud. It was by more modern standards rather crude, owing as much to the island's lack of natural resources as to the supposed temporary nature of the mission. The abbey—or what roofless ruins remained of it—was known as Loathsome Jaws. Speculation was that the odd and somewhat unpleasant name was related to whatever it was the Ramahan had been sent there to do. All this Amitra had told Riane before sending her on her way.

Riane staring at the tidal pool, the morning sun reflected in its surface, an orange-carmine line drawn as if by a fingernail, saw in her mind's eye the flame from Asir's infinity-blade pushing back hard against hers.

"You have already had some experience in using the infinity-blade against traditional V'ornn weaponry," he said. "But against another infinity-blade the strategy is radically altered."

When Asir said this they had been standing upon a bridge of ice that arced into the mist just beyond the forest. The bridge was so narrow that Riane had had to stand with one foot behind the other. If she lost her balance, she had no idea how far she would fall—a meter or a thousand meters—in the swirl of dense mist there was no way to tell.

"The first thing you must learn," Asir had said, "is that gorons do not work like other forms of energy. They do not emit radiation as a continuous stream but in rapid bursts. The trick comes in putting yourself in sync with the bursts, moving to their rhythm. Here, I will show you."

He moved forward, engaged Riane's infinity-blade. But as Riane moved forward into the parry, Asir spun. His infinity-blade slid at an angle with him, and Riane's momentum carried her forward, awkward and slightly off-balance because the resistance was not where she had been expecting it. Instead, Asir's blade came at her from the side. She ducked under it, lunged and, again, he spun, using her own momentum against her. His blade struck her wand, and it went flying away into the mist.

"Do you see what I mean?" He held up his hand and the wand reappeared. He flipped it to Riane. "Now, again, my girl."

But it had been difficult concentrating. He was her father, *her father!* She could not get the thought out of her mind. It was only after he had disarmed her for the third straight time that he stopped the exercise. "What is it?" he had said. "I know how quick a study you are."

"I want to know . . ." She shook her head. "There is so much about you and Amitra, about my childhood and growing up I cannot remember." She was trembling a little. "And I so want to know . . . everything."

In two great strides, Asir gathered her into his arms, holding her tight.

She buried her face in his massive shoulder. "What am I missing?"

"It's difficult, I know, but try not to be impatient." He kissed the top of her head. "Memory is a tricky thing. The more we try to remember, the more elusive the memory becomes. Now." He held her at arm's length, his great grin seeming to burn away her heartache. "Let's get on with it."

Riane, staring down into the tidal pool, remembering her lessons, hand gripping the wand. This time she would be ready for Lujon. A distant movement picked up in the corner of her eye, made her look up, and immediately she crouched behind a huge basalt boulder. A Sarakkon ship was rounding the headland. On its foredeck, she spied the very one she had just been thinking of: Lujon.

When the *Omaline* dropped anchor off the western shore of Suspended Skull, Haamadi was there to meet it. The ship, having safely navigated the treacherous underwater labyrinth of reefs and lethal whirlpools that encircled the rocky island, lay to, its sails reefed, while Lujon and three of the crew took a small boat through fanged rocks to the minuscule beachhead.

Lujon, watching the young archon's face, as the small boat wallowed in the angry, swirling swells, was filled with apprehension. He had no illusions regarding the pact he had made with Haamadi, whom he knew to be as treacherous as the local currents. Those in *Sintire* who saw themselves on an equal footing with the sauromicians were deluding themselves. He, too, held a burning desire to profit from the secrets buried in Za Hara-at; but to prostitute themselves, to become in effect the slaves of the sauromicians, bowing to their every whim, that was too high a price for him to pay. Therefore, he had decided to break with his brethren, to make a pact with Haamadi, the smartest and most ambitious of the sauromician archons, in order to ensure his own survival. He had already proved of use to Haamadi, providing information about *Sintire*

The prow of the small boat grated onto the beachhead, and two of Lujon's crew jumped out. Using ropes, they pulled the vessel farther out of the water. Lujon stepped onto the beachhead, gripped Haamadi's arm.

"Did you get it?" Haamadi asked.

This abruptness, which bordered on rudeness, Lujon had first attributed to youthful exuberance. But further study had made it clear that this was the archon's true nature.

"We taught the V'ornn regent a lesson, Haamadi," Lujon said as they walked up the narrow strand. "We left him hanging from his heels, dying from a thousand cuts."

This news mollified Haamadi only temporarily. "But what of the ninth banestone?" he hissed. His tallow-colored skin was pulled taut over razor-edged bone, his earlobes unnaturally elongated by polished knucklebones that had been thrust through them. The skin of his forehead was pierced by a ruddy rune. "Do you have it?"

They stood in the shadows of overhanging rock, at the mouth of what Krystren called the Chaos Grotto. The sea surged at their feet, spumed and opaque.

"We were unable to obtain it," Lujon lied. He had no intention of giving away his most valuable leverage against the archons. "Kurgan Stogggul took it from Za Hara-at, but since he had no idea what it was, he soon abandoned it."

"Where?"

Haamadi's face had grown dark, but Lujon was prepared for this.

"Somewhere in the Korrush. He did not remember exactly where. 'One kilometer looks just like the next in that • filthy place.' Those were his exact words."

"Bad news comes in packs." Haamadi turned his head and spat into the churning sea. Together they mounted the stairs, which wound in a rising spiral like the shell of a giant sea mollusk. Reflections from the churning waters below cast long fingers that seemed to grasp at them. Lujon watched Haamadi out of the corner of his eye. Broad of shoulder, slim of hip, with a face like an open book and a way of speaking that made you feel as if he were communicating with you alone. His light eyes did not wander, and there was a calmness about him that engendered trust. All of this was a deception, of course, but an impressive one at that. "Both Varda and Caligo are dead, which means our access to the Abbey of Five Pivots is no longer available. Our enemies are arrayed against us."

Though Haamadi made a good show of collegial concern, Lujon was canny enough to detect the light of triumph deep in the archon's eyes. With Caligo and Varda out of the way there was no other sauromician of sufficient strength to challenge him. If he wanted to remain the sole archon to lead them, he would get his wish without opposition. Lujon was still calculating the odds of whether this turn of events would benefit him or not when they were accosted by Fer, the young male they had chosen to impersonate the Dar Sala-at. He was flanked by two grim-faced sauromicians who, it was clear as they bowed, deferred to Haamadi. The matter must have been urgent for them to have allowed him to come partway down the staircase that was, for the most part, off-limits to him. Fer was a tribal orphan, half-lame, whom they had found in the wastes of the Korrush near the ruins of Za Hara-at. Varda had been on the verge of killing him for his life force. Haamadi's intervention had angered Varda, even after the archons as a group had approved Haamadi's plan to use the boy as the false prophet. Varda collected grudges the way others gathered knowledge.

Fer informed Haamadi of a change in the overall demeanor of the Ramahan they had seduced out of the Abbey of Floating White. They were growing restive, querulous, asking questions for which he could provide no answer that satisfied them.

This was cause for alarm, even in Haamadi, because it was his charmed tongue that had persuaded the Ramahan of the authenticity of this false Dar Sala-at in the first place, and through necromancy had performed the sorcerous feats that had maintained the Ramahan faith.

"Is there a leader among the Ramahan?" Haamadi said to Fer.

"Sir?"

"One who is more puling than the rest, one who is asking the most questions."

"Yes," the boy nodded. "Nesta."

"Find her, keep her close for a half hour, then fetch her for me," Haamadi said at once. "We will be in my study."

Fer nodded and with his escort went to do the archon's bidding.

When he was certain they were alone, Haamadi ascended four more steps. He pressed his palm to an almost undetectable depression in the rock wall. A door opened, and they entered a short corridor, whose glassy walls and reddish glow revealed its unnatural origin. The corridor led to another cave. More glassy walls, a deeper reddish glow. Another hidden door opened in the center of the rock wall against which Krystren had weeks ago fallen asleep.

Within was the thick-walled keep. As the sauromicians had discovered, it was the reason the Ramahan had come to Suspended Skull in the first place. For in the very center of this chamber's stone floor was a bronze-and-copper plate—round, thick, incised with runes that resisted translation by even the sauromicians' most potent necromantic spells. Still, they had managed to open the plate, for it was a door of sorts to a chamber carved deep into the bedrock of the island, a place of heat and fumes, where the sauromicians discovered the bones of creatures whose physiognomy defied analysis. They only knew that the bones were ancient beyond reckoning.

Haamadi and Lujon put their feet on the bronze stirrups attached to the square alloy pole, Haamadi pulled the lever, and they descended the vertical shaft at a dizzying rate, slowing just before they came to the bottom.

And there was the Cage, faceted like a mammoth jewel. Within it, Seelin, the Sacred Dragon of Transformation. The creature appeared unmoving, its eyes closed.

"Is it dangerous?" Lujon said.

Haamadi went up to the cage, turned one of the bane-stones so that the beam of energy emanating from it struck Seelin's head.

"Wake up, you filthy beast!" he shouted.

The Dragon opened her huge golden eyes, stared at him with a terrible hatred. "What do you want?"

Haamadi, if for no other reason than innate cruelty, played the beam over the Dragon's body so that she shud-dered in pain.

"Making sure you aren't getting too comfortable," Haa-madi said.

Seelin glared impotently at him, so that he laughed.

"Listen to me, beast. The ninth banestone is on its way. When it arrives, you will do whatever I tell you to do."

"Never," Seelin said.

"Never say never." Haamadi manipulated the banestone further, and the Dragon writhed in a crescendo of agony, culminating in her passing into unconsciousness. Slowly, almost reluctantly, Haamadi returned the banestone to its previous configuration. He did not want to let go of it.

Lujon peered at the beast more closely. The wingspan alone looked to be wider than the vast chamber itself. "It is not dead, is it?"

"The Cage is not yet complete. We have the Dragon, but cannot yet compel it to do our bidding."

"We see."

"I wonder," Haamadi said pointedly. "You should not have returned without it."

Lujon's training made it easy to hide his anger. "We will set sail again on the morning tide if that is your wish."

"My wish is for the ninth banestone," Haamadi said shortly. "But you already knew that."

Haamadi made a curt gesture, and Lujon followed him up out of the ancient crypt, into the rock caves, and thence to the Abbey of Loathsome Jaws. During their time on the island the sauromicians had rebuilt the abbey to their liking. They had restored the roofs, shored up the crumbling walls, and used their necromancy to remove what traces remained of Osoru sorcery. On the island, they had no worries about hidden power-bourns—they were free to move about as they liked. They kept the original footprint of the abbey: large wings on the eastern and western ends connected by a central axis of great rooms and temple spaces, once sanctified to Miina. The largest of them had been converted into a barracks to house the Ramahan, which was guarded day and night by smiling sauromicians in whose company Fer, in his guise as Dar Sala-at, intoned prayers of enlightenment and false hope.

The archon study—now solely Haamadi's—was in the western wing, where half of the sauromicians lived, the other half being housed in the eastern wing, effectively surrounding the Ramahan. It was a low-ceilinged space, like all the chambers in the wings, with a window overlooking the turbulent sea and fulminating sky. Occasionally, the plaintive cries of cliff-dwelling seabirds could be heard echoing among the guano-sprayed rocks.

The study was sparsely but comfortably furnished—a table, chairs, a lone settee no one ever sat on. The sauromicians, so long exiled to the Korrush, had adopted many tribal habits, among them sitting cross-legged on jewel-toned carpets, drinking ba'du or herbal infusions from cups of hammered brass.

Now, however, neither of them took their leisure. Haamadi paced up and down, hands clasped loosely behind his back.

"Tell us something," Lujon said easily. "How vital to you is this ninth banestone?"

Haamadi paused. "It is everything. We have already befriended the daemons. Once we free them, they will owe us a debt. And how will they repay this debt?"

"By disgorging the secrets of Za Hara-at, buried for centuries."

"Precisely."

"Why should you trust them?"

"Who says I do?" Haamadi smiled. "With the Dragon under my control, I have the power to send them back to the Abyss to rot for all eternity if they do not comply with my request."

Request. Lujon thought bitterly. As if Haamadi was used to making a *request* of anyone!

At that moment, Fer arrived, escorting Nesta into the study. The Ramahan was young and fiery. Haamadi remembered her as being one of the first to be won over. Her innate intelligence was undercut by an impatient spirit; she wanted to be konara before her time. Haamadi was familiar with the type—there were too many like her in the ranks of the sauromicians.

"The Dar Sala-at tells me that you are unhappy," Haamadi began in his most beguiling tone. "How may I help you?"

"For one thing, you can tell me what happened to our sisters."

Haamadi spread his hands. "But you were already told. There was an accident on the ridge. It was regrettable, but—"

"We never saw them. We were never allowed to bury them or give them a proper funeral."

"They were already buried," Haamadi pointed out in his reasonable voice, "by the mudslide."

"Then we should have been allowed to dig them out, to

give them dignity in death. Why did you not give us that opportunity?"

"You never mentioned this before." Haamadi was looking deep into Nesta's eyes. "Why now?"

"We have been talking among ourselves."

"Yes, but what started you talking?"

"I do not know." Nesta shrugged. "What does it matter?"

"Indulge me for a moment, I beg you. What started the talk?"

Nesta shrugged again. "For me, it was a dream."

Haamadi came and stood close to her. Fer stood just behind her, rapt, his eyes locked on the archon. "What was this dream?"

"I saw my sisters. They were dead in a cave. They had weapons—knives and such—and there was a curious froth on their lips."

"A dream is just that," Haamadi said with some intensity. "A dream."

"This seemed more real," Nesta said defiantly. "A number of the other Ramahan had the same dream."

"Now that *is* interesting."

"We thought so, too," she said. "We demand an explanation."

Haamadi looked to Fer and nodded. "The Dar Sala-at will provide all the explanation you need."

With that, Fer drew a dagger and, lifting Nesta's chin with one hand, slit her throat with it. Her eyes went wide, a scream stillborn on her lips. Haamadi leapt back at the first fountain of blood. As she collapsed, he dug at her with his taloned fingers, making two incisions. He ripped her heart from her chest and, in seven huge bloody bites, swallowed it. Crouched over her, he dug into the second, lower incision, drew out the glistening strand of her intestine. Wrapping it around his left wrist he began a series of chants, rocking back and forth on the balls of his feet.

Lujon watched this with a combination of fascination and repulsion. It was not the first time he had witnessed this necromantic rite, but the shock of it did not seem to wear off. There were many among the *Sintire*, he chief among them, who believed that it was essential for them to appropriate this powerful sorcery from the sauromicians. His efforts had been slowed, however, by opposition from a faction led by Orujo. Orujo was also an Aersthone, one of the original family that had broken away from the yoke of *Onnda* and he therefore commanded great respect. Lujon knew he had to be careful when dealing with Orujo, but the more he was exposed to the power of necromancy, the more impatient for it he became.

Haamadi's eyes were fluttering. He was infused with the power of the trapped spirit, and unconsciously Lujon moved nearer, as if he might absorb some of the unnatural strength. Strange sounds came from Haamadi's mouth, an echo of tongues unknown, a chittering of unnameable things. Presently, his head tilted back, his eyes opened, their pupils dilated.

"It is that damnable priestess, Giyan," he whispered in a dry and reedy voice unlike his own. "She is using the Skreeling Engine at the Abbey of Five Pivots. Ah, I see her plan! She is feeding the Ramahan the truth about everything."

A slow smile crept across his face. Even for Lujon, it was eerie to see Haamadi's hands moving over the body as if of their own accord, extracting liver and spleen, scoring them with bloody fingernails as long as an animal's.

"We shall see now how it goes." Haamadi's altered voice echoed through the study. The carpet was soaked through with his victim's blood. "Osoru against necromancy. Now she will see the true power of the dead come to life!"

Activity aboard the Sarakkon vessel lapsed into somnolence as soon as Lujon and Haamadi had disappeared into the shell-like cave. Riane did not move, however. She was well aware of how many individuals must be on the island and was taking no chances of being

spotted by a stray sauromician or Sarakkon sailor. She had
crept around so that she had a better look at the sea-cave
mouth, which was aboil with choppy water. As she did so,
she saw a shadow lowering itself down a line of rigging
into the water. Almost immediately, it disappeared underwater only to appear meters away from the ship, a face
only, nose and mouth above the heavy chop of the swells,
taking in a long, deep breath before disappearing again.

By the time the face surfaced again to inhale another
breath, Riane had worked out the place where the stowaway would come ashore. She moved perpendicular to the
underwater swimmer, and when the face surfaced again
her heart leapt in her breast, for the stowaway was close
enough now for her to make an identification. Eleana!

How had she come to be on Lujon's ship? Riane wondered as she waded out into the heavy surf. There was a series of upthrust rocks between them and the ship which,
she was certain, was why Eleana had made for this spot.
But the suck of the surf was very strong, just beyond the
comber line was a dangerous rip current moving very fast
from east to west.

She could see that Eleana, tired from her swim in, was
struggling in the rip current. Stripping off her jacket, she
plunged into the curl of a huge wave and stroked powerfully out. Already, Eleana was west of where Riane had last
seen her, and Riane dived down deeper, swimming along
the very bottom below the worst of the current. Above her,
Eleana took a breath and, head over heels, went under. Riane scissor-kicked, jetting upward, grasped Eleana around
her legs, pulled her down through the current.

At first, Eleana, terrified, fought her, but then, concentrating fully through the turbulence, she recognized Riane
and, jackknifing her body, swam joyously into her arms.
Together, they kicked along the rocky bottom until they
were clear of the rip current, surfacing with gasps, riding
the waves in a spray of foam and ozone-rich air the rest of
the way into shore.

They leaned their backs against a pair of upright rocks,

allowing the fitful sunlight to dry their clothes. Riane had retrieved her jacket, which had been warmed by the sun.

They stared into each other's eyes and, for that moment, nothing else existed for them. They told each other what had transpired from the moment they had been parted on the ground floor of FIREFLY to the moment Riane had grasped Eleana around the legs. Revelation tumbled from their mouths, one after another.

"Your parents! Oh, Riane, that's so wonderful!"

They laughed and cried and embraced again. This time, it lasted a long time. They tasted the salt of the ocean on each other's lips.

Then, all at once, Eleana pushed Riane to arm's length. "Miina," she cried softly, "look at you!"

Riane was dressed in the style of her parents: three-quarter-length leather breeches, indigo raw-silk blouse, wide, triple-tongued amber-colored leather belt. Her waist-length jacket was of undyed woven wool with stand-up collar, wide, three-quarter sleeves and wide cuffs, a Venca rune in black embroidered across its back. On her feet were supple, thin-soled, ankle-length boots.

"This is the style of the Tchakira," she said.

"Is that who you are now?" Eleana frowned. She was still coming to terms with who the Tchakira were. She had many years of socially ingrained prejudice to overcome.

"I am many things, Eleana," she said softly. "As are you. One of them does not preclude the other."

"I know, love. I know."

Riane took a quick peek from behind the rock. "I saw Lujon and Haamadi go into that sea cave. It's obviously the way in, but it is likely to be heavily guarded. The best way to get inside the sauromicians' lair is for us to Thripp."

"We can't." Eleana put her hand on Riane's sleeve. "Sagiira warned me that there are no power bourns beneath the island."

Riane shook her head. "Sagiira must be mistaken. I can sense them deep in the core of the bedrock."

"I know what you are feeling, love. Sagiira told me that the Ramahan had come here long ago to try to conquer death."

"As the Gyrgon are trying to do."

"The reason there are no power bourns here, the reason you feel something, is that somewhere deep below us lies the Underworld, where the spirits of the dead reside before the Great Wheel returns them in one form or another to life."

That jibed in its way with what Amitra told her she must do when she arrived at the Cage. She nodded. "If Thripping here is impossible, then we will have to enter the sea cave."

"Perhaps we should wait until dark."

"We cannot afford to wait. Lujon has the ninth banestone. He has already touched it with his bare hands; who knows what fell changes it has wrought on him. I must intercept him before he gives it to the sauromicians and they complete the Cage." Riane took a deep breath. "We go in *now*."

The pain began behind Giyan's eyes. Not a moment before, she had been sitting in the Skreeling Engine, feeling like a beam of honeyed sunlight the slow seep of acceptance from the Ramahan to whom she had beamed the truth. She was caught up in the Engine's power. The pain spread rapidly to clamp her brain in a kind of vise that squeezed tighter with each beat of her heart, each breath she took.

She had opened her seer's mind to the Skreeling Engine, and it had amplified her ability so that she merged with the Engine. Together, they had manufactured the dream that had set the Ramahan into a quiet uproar. Now her seer's mind grasped what even the Druuge Perrnodt could not. In her mind, she caught a whiff of the open grave, of blood running, terminal scream bubbling, and a stench rising. She saw with a flash the swift draw of blade across throat, white obscured by a gout of brilliant scarlet, and felt the precious life force snatched like an infant from its crib, an act of such violation her instinct was to recoil in horror. Face-to-face with the hideous essence of necromancy, of the dreadful path the sauromicians had chosen, she gathered herself. Like Perrnodt before her, she chose to fight the pain with sorcerous spells and, as with Perrnodt, her strategy proved disastrous, for the more spells she conjured the deeper the pain went until it had inflamed every nerve in her body. Writhing in agony, she fell off the Skreeling Engine. She tried to think, but her mind was aflame. There was a bitter taste in her mouth. She had the good sense to turn her head, spit out the white crystals. More were forming inside her mouth. Madila, the drug they had used to kill Perrnodt. She spat again, but it was more difficult that time, took an inordinate expenditure of energy. Her motor skills were being seriously impaired. She was about to try another spell—the most potent one in her arsenal—when a warning bell sounded deep inside her pain-racked brain. *Think,* she berated herself. *Think!*

Perrnodt must have tried this tack. It hadn't worked. Slowly, Giyan realized why. It was not that the spells were not working, they were actually making the pain worse—they were being used against her! Was that how necromancy worked? She did not know, but she vowed to find out. If she lived through this—an outcome that was becoming more problematic with every moment that elapsed. She had to try something else. What?

K rystren arrived back on the island of Suspended Skull with a keen sense of foreboding. When she looked at Orujo she saw her own death. It was not that she feared death, it was simply that she had never before understood how close she was to it. A hairbreadth, that is all there was separating life and death.

Orujo smiled at her, and she saw a death's-head, she saw the image of her own executioner. He took her hand.

"You are cold, Krystren. We will build you a fire in one of the abbey's hearths."

His solicitousness, the kindness and consideration he had shown her on their swift journey back south, set her teeth on edge. Everything with him was skin-deep. When on their unhappy journey had she realized that he wore a mask even with himself?

All during that journey she could not get Giyan's face out of her mind. Her shocked expression, the helpless corner into which she, Krystren, had pushed her. She prayed to Yahé that Giyan had found the message she had written in the dust.

She had no idea what Orujo planned for her, she only knew it was not what he had so craftily told her. But then neither was her acquiescing to his blandishments, which was motivated by her desire to infiltrate to the heart of the *Sintire* mission there on the northern continent. Her own mission had been made moot by Courion's death, but that did not mean she was simply going to roll over and defect as Orujo wanted her to do. The two of them were playing a deadly game of clandestine motive. The only question was who would discover the other's secret first.

She smiled her most brilliant smile when Lujon met them in the entrance to the Abbey of Loathsome Jaws. She had never met him or even seen him, but had heard many tales of his prowess and his cruelty. The story was told among the *Onnda* that he hated everyone and everything, that his ancestors had been killed when the Sarakkon were driven by the Ramahan from the northern continent, that he lived only for revenge.

"Welcome back, Orujo," he said, his hard gaze on Krystren. "Though you must explain why under the circumstances you should be welcome here."

"Krystren is under our protection," Orujo said.

"Why is that?" Lujon spread his hands. "Did you strike your head? Are your brains addled? Have you lost your memory? Your mission was to find her, take her infinity-blade wand, and kill her. Kindly tell us what has changed?"

"We have a chance to get the infinity-blade wand *and* the knowledge inside her head."

Lujon looked skeptical.

"Think, Lujon, of all the *Onnda* secrets that will be

ours! We will finally have enough to break them once and for all, scatter them to the four winds, oust Cerro, take our rightful place at the Orieniad. At last we will rule!"

Lujon took a step toward Krystren, put himself in her face. "And if she is playing you false? If her motive is to gain *our* secrets?"

"Then we will kill her ourself."

"Indeed." At last, Lujon shifted his gaze to Orujo. "Are you not besotted with her?"

"We are *Sintire*. Our ancestors founded *Sintire*. Nothing will prevent us from doing our duty."

Lujon nodded. "You have sworn this before us and before Abrasea. Let it be so." He lifted a finger. "And if by chance you fail or falter, then know that without a moment's hesitation or regret *we* will kill *you*."

Necromancy depended for fuel upon the life force of the newly dead. Giyan used the last of her energy to concentrate through the pain that had now gripped her heart in a cold and clammy grip.

Nesta. The murdered Ramahan's name was Shima Nesta.

Her seer's mind found the essence of Nesta. It was wrapped around the wrist of a sauromician archon, slaved to his will. It was weeping uncontrollably. With her seer's mind, she spoke to what remained of Nesta, gave it hope.

This act of compassion cost her, for the archon became aware of her extraordinary skill and, after a momentary shock, applied his necromantic power to stop the communication. He did it, quite naturally, through Nesta's essence, compelling it to turn itself full force on Giyan. It was that force the archon had used to introduce the Madila into her.

Giyan began to froth at the mouth, and she fought the urge to swallow, for she knew that if she did the Madila would spread throughout her system, and she would not be able to stop its pernicious effects. She spat again, but her tongue felt thick and useless. She was able to push a very small amount of the crystals out of the corner of her mouth. Her mouth was filling up with bitter-tasting saliva faster than she could get it out. She had to swallow. It was an automatic response. In a moment, it would all be over.

It was her prowess as a seer that saved her, for half-paralyzed, she saw before her a vision of the Ramahan rising up from the torpor of delusion, saw them turning on the sauromicians, experienced their realization that they had been captives, that they had been duped by a false prophet, that they had been played for fools. And it was that vision—that future—to which she turned her mind, to which she directed all her energies. She no longer thought of her own plight. Her life was insignificant when faced with the continued incarceration and abuse of her Rama- · han. Young and foolish they might be, so had she been at their age—foolish and headstrong and unmanageable. She rode the wave of love for them into their minds and hearts. The seeds of their delusion had already been planted through the Skreeling Engine. Now she whispered to them as if she were the Great Goddess Miina Herself of what they needed to do to fight the sauromicians, to win back their freedom. And she felt them as they rose as one. She felt the anger in their hearts, though she did not fuel it. She did not have to, for their rage at what had happened to their sisters while they themselves had stood by, complacent and unaware, was more than enough to energize them. Her mind was filled with their rebellion, as all over the Abbey of Loathsome Jaws they awoke from their somnambulists' trance to mount a simultaneous assault on their captors. The sauromicians were taken completely by surprise. So well trained to repel attacks from the outside, they were unprepared to deal with an internal uprising.

Giyan, having done her part, found the massed rage of the Ramahan feeding back on her, fueling her own psychic battle. She found the strength to rise on all fours. Head hanging down between her shoulders, she vomited up all the Madila, then crawled into an adjacent room, turned the tap, and plunged her head in a basin of freezing water. The extreme temperature revived her. She opened her eyes underwater, felt the frenzy of movement, saw dead faces of sauromicians staring at her with the thousand-kilometer stare. Rinsed out her mouth, the last dregs of the deadly crystals swirling down the drain.

34

The Difference Between Death and Life

At the very last moment, as they were about to enter the sea-cave mouth, Riane held them back. Eleana opened her mouth, but Riane shook her head sharply, and they retreated back to the cover of the large boulders, where they crouched down, huddled with their knees touching.

"I am aware of six sauromicians. We will never get through that way," Riane said.

"Even with your sorcery?"

"I have limited experience with sauromicians and none at all with necromancy," Riane pointed out. "With so many in close quarters the odds are too great against us."

"Then we are lost."

"Not necessarily." Riane was eyeing the rocky scree. "See that cave about halfway up the cliffside? I can climb up to it."

"What good will that do?"

"Watch."

Eleana craned her neck, stared at the cave mouth. In a moment, she saw movement—sauromician or Sarakkon, she could not tell which—and she knew that that cave must also lead up to the abbey above. She also knew what that meant.

"In that case, love, I will only slow you down," she said. "I should not come with you."

Riane took her hand. "Perhaps it is just as well." She gave a quick glance at the ship at anchor. "It is best there is someone here to keep an eye on the Sarakkon."

Eleana nodded. "If the sauromicians call for Sarakkon reinforcements, I will find a way to delay them."

"I know you will." Riane kissed her on both cheeks, then a long ecstatic kiss on the lips.

As she was about to go, Eleana pulled her back down. "There is something I want to give you." She dug in her tunic, produced a twist of cloth. "This is Madila—a very powerful drug the sauromicians used to try to kill Sagiira." She pressed the twist into Riane's hand. "Miina grant that it prove useful to you." With that, she cuffed Riane on the shoulder. "Now go." Her eyes were melting. "And please, love, be careful."

"There is no one I would rather was here with me," Riane whispered. "I trust you with my life."

"As I trust you with mine."

Riane rose and, without a backward glance, made her way to the base of the cliff. It rose spiked and nearly sheer, but she had encountered cliffs like it before in the high Djenn Marre—cliffs more difficult for the cold, the wind, the treacherousness of ice underfoot and hand. She was not daunted.

With unerring instinct Riane chose hand- and footholds that were both secure and advantageous. She was able to seek out the best of her choices, as if the cliffside had been schematized in her mind, mapped and analyzed by the scanning she had done when she had first appeared on the island. The cliff face existed both whole and parceled in her mind. As she climbed steadily upward, her mind moved from section to section, remembering fissures, impassable overhangs, treacherous porches of friable rock, walls of smooth glassy surfaces, inviting indentations and blessed lips on which to lever herself up or to rest—places to avoid and those to which to gravitate.

As she neared the mouth of the cave, she looked for a ledge beneath the lip in which to gather her strength, both mentally and physically. There was no perch of suitable width, but she made do with a slight indentation in the cliff face against which she could press her body. She could hear the waves crashing below, hear the raucous cries of the pelagic birds that swung through the air on their way to and from their eyries. One such nest was, in fact, not far from where she leaned against the cold rock wall. It was nesting season, the little ones ravenous, but not yet ready take wing.

She slowed her breathing, opened her Third Eye, and listened for sounds of movement in the cave mouth just above her. She heard nothing, felt nothing, but she was not emboldened. She did not know the extent of necromancy's powers either to stop her probing or become aware of it. Mindful of this unknown, she extended her consciousness very slowly until she had swept the lip and was certain no one lurked there. But what about farther inside the cave? She was just about to continue her ethereal probing when, with a startled cry, a mother bird, returning to her nest, decided she was too close and flew at her with talons extended.

Riane, forced to defend herself, lost one handhold. She did not want to harm the bird, but the thing had already bloodied her and would not back off, so she conjured a minor Venca spell, catching the bird as it plummeted down, insensate. She was reaching out to carefully place the bird back in her nest when she was wrested out of Riane's grip.

She looked up to see a sauromician wringing the bird's neck. "Filthy screamer." He grinned lasciviously down at Riane. "And what have we here?" Discarding the dead bird, he reached down, and hauled Riane up into the cave.

Something Riane had said stuck in Eleana's mind after she had left. Riane said she had to get to Lujon before he gave the ninth banestone to the sauromicians so they could complete the Cage. Eleana, as she always did in war, had put herself in the mind of the enemy. She did so unconsciously, and though she knew little about Sarakkon, still she knew they were first and foremost traders, and traders were always looking for an edge. What was troubling her was this: if she were Lujon, why in the world would she simply hand over something as valuable as the ninth banestone? Wouldn't he be more likely to keep it hidden somewhere while he negotiated with the sauromicians for its price? Might he not have already done so before he set out to find it? She did not think so because his hand was so much stronger with the banestone in his possession. No, the more she thought about it, the more convinced she was that Lujon had not had the banestone with him when he met Haamadi.

She turned, looking out past the breakers to where the *Omaline* rode at anchor. The ninth banestone was aboard that ship, she had no doubt of it. She had no desire to plunge herself back into that rip current, but she did not see that she had any choice. Besides, Riane had shown her how to dive deep beneath the worst of the current's pull.

Steeling herself, she slipped back into the blue-black ocean. As the freezing water closed over her and she dived beneath the first wave, her thoughts were only of Riane.

Limp in the sauromician's grasp, Riane felt the coldness of his necromancy creep over her like a fist of vipers. He had grabbed hold of her spell, used it like a handle to lever his mind into hers. Stunned by the invasion, she lay spread-eagled, the Riane part of her paralyzed, in the sauromician's control. But Riane's palace of memory, hidden in the deepest recesses of her mind, remained undisturbed by the necromantic spell, and it was there that Riane had retreated.

Within the protection of the palace she thought in overtime. She had been trapped by using a Venca spell. Sagiira had cautioned against trying to access the power bourns, which would have involved Osoru sorcery. Both of these sorceries were practiced by those who, like her, had the Gift—those whom the sauromicians had systematically tried to excise from the body of the Ramahan before being sent into exile. It would make sense that they would gear their necromancy toward those with the Gift. But what about Kyofu, the Black Dreaming sorcery the sauromicians started out using?

Riane, obliged to call upon the small catalog of Kyofu spells she knew, chose Fly's-Eye, because it caused a chaos of thoughts in its victim. She was prepared to cast it when she reconsidered. Even if Fly's-Eye worked, even if, crippled as she was, she was able to defeat this sauromician, then what? She did not know where Lujon was, did not know the layout of the caves or the abbey above. The sauromician did. Why not allow him to carry her into the heart of the enemy, where she needed to be. Surely Lujon would be there or, if not, close by.

The sauromician, whose name was Banne, took his prize through the hidden door in the rear wall of the cave, past two more sauromicians, up a flight of stone steps, past another three sauromicians, more in the corridor down which they trod. Banne shouted out to those who queried him. He turned to the left, the right, then left again, finally mounting another, wider set of stairs, passing between still another set of sauromicians, through a corbeled archway and into the abbey proper.

At length, Banne brought Riane into Haamadi's inner sanctum. The blood-soaked carpet had been rolled up and placed against one wall, but the Ramahan Nesta's violated body was where Haamadi had left it. Though the archon was not in evidence, Lujon was there with Orujo and Krystren. The stench of death hung rankly in the thick atmosphere. Flies buzzed, congregating in the glistening cavities, feeding, laying eggs. No one save Krystren seemed to notice or to be in the least bit disturbed.

Banne asked for Haamadi.

"The archon is otherwise occupied," Lujon said, asserting the authority he believed to be his. "Turn the prisoner so that we may see her face."

"Out of my way. I answer only to Haamadi." Banne was puffed up by his great good fortune. Haamadi would reward him handsomely for his vigilance. Besides, he did not trust this Sarakkon, and to that end he conjured a Kyofu defensive spell which, though basic, was certainly enough to rebuff any possible attack from a Sarakkon.

"Ah, look what we have here!" Lujon had maneuvered so that he could see Riane's face. "We know this one."

"You do?"

Lujon nodded, at once seeing the need to be conciliatory to get what he wanted from this sauromician lout. "Her name is Riane. We encountered her in Axis Tyr when we strung the V'ornn regent up by his ankles and bled him dry."

"What do you know of her?" Banne looked dubious, but he was not yet ready to concede that Lujon was lying to gain some advantage.

Lujon flicked his wrist. "She is something of a sorceress."

"A Ramahan?"

"She is far more dangerous than any Ramahan I have yet met."

"How so?"

There was no possibility that Lujon would tell Banne that Riane had in her possession an infinity-blade. "Her repertory of spells is larger than even a konara thrice her age. Her sorcery may not even be Osoru in origin."

"I would know more of this."

"That could be arranged." Lujon saw that in response to his hand signal Orujo had stepped into Banne's field of view.

"All we would ask is a moment or two to study her," Orujo said.

Banne turned to him, laughing. "You cannot be serious, Sarakkon."

"Oh, but he is," Lujon said softly as he placed a hand on

the side of Banne's neck. Using the necromancy he had
learned from Varda, he broke through the feeble defensive
spell Banne had erected. Temporarily stopping the flow of
blood to the sauromician's carotid artery made him lose
consciousness. Lujon caught him as he collapsed, while
Orujo gathered Riane into his arms.

"What shall we do with her?" Orujo asked.

Lujon did not immediately answer. He had pulled off
Banne's protective glove, grasped his black sixth finger
and, wrenching it with a small grunt, broke the bones and
twisted it off. Within moments, the sauromician shriveled
to a pile of white dust.

"Haamadi will be cross with you," Orujo said with
ironic understatement.

Lujon grunted. "We no longer care about Haamadi." He
briskly slapped his hands together to rid them of the
residue. "We have the ninth banestone."

"And this one?" Orujo hefted Riane. "The young sorceress?"

"Riane? Kill her."

Orujo locked the crook of his elbow against Riane's
throat. Krystren wondered what she should do. She could
not let an innocent girl be cold-bloodedly murdered, but
she did not see how she could stop it without giving herself away.

A reprieve of sorts came from the most unlikely source.
Lujon said, "Wait a moment, we have a better idea." He
gestured. "Put Riane down and step away."

Unhesitatingly, Orujo did as he was ordered.

Lujon, grinning his feral grin, took Krystren's hand in
his. "Now is your chance, my dear, to show us where your
loyalty lies. If you mean what you say, if you wish to be a
part of us, then kill this girl." He kissed the back of her
hand, smiled almost kindly into her eyes. "We promise
you that when you do we will trust you absolutely."

Two of the *Omaline*'s crew, muscular, mustachioed,
tattooed, smelling of spice and brine and dried

searay were leaning against the starboard taffrail, smoking laaga sticks, so it took Eleana longer than she had anticipated to get back aboard. Once on deck, another vexing delay ensued. A Sarakkon sat against the open hatch of the aft companionway polishing his high shagreen boots with wax derived from the distilled oil of onaga, a deep-water snapper.

She waited, willing herself to be patient, until, called by the second mate, he pulled on his boots and went about his late-morning chores. Whipping through the hatchway while no one was looking, she half slid down the companionway stairs, made her way to the captain's cabin where she knew Lujon had been quartered during the voyage from Axis Tyr.

The door was locked. She knelt down and studied the keyhole up close. Several times during the voyage, she had observed Lujon coming and going from the cabin. He was always careful to lock the door after him. She had seen the size and shape of the key, had seen how he turned it in the lock and, therefore, had an essential understanding of what type of lock she was dealing with.

One of her main assignments when she was with the Resistance had been getting in and out of facilities within Axis Tyr. She had been trained in the intricacies of locks and keys by an old veteran whose legs had been severed by a Khagggun shock-sword. She had an aptitude for it, for opening locks required both a steady hand and an intuitive mind. "Locks are alive," her mentor had told her. "Whether they are opened with Kundalan bronze keys or V'ornn photon keys, they respond to your affinity for them."

Eleana put her hand on the lock, tracing its outline with her fingertips. The shouts of the crew, the call of the seabirds, the creaking of seasoned timbers, the wind singing through the rigging drifted down the companionway. The heady spiciness of the narrow corridor's oiled wood paneling in her nostrils. She centered herself.

Inserting a thin strip of alloy into the keyhole, she

closed her eyes, pictured in her mind the key. It had five indentations. Each one of them corresponded to a base pin inside the lock cylinder. The idea to opening all locks of this sort was to gain control of the shear line—the place where all five pins lined up and allowed the cylinder to rotate, the lock to open.

She moved the strip in until she reached the first of the five base pins. By delicately and gently turning the strip she pressured the pin upward, mimicking the action of the key, into its shear-line position. Inserting it deeper, she did the same with the second pin. When all five had been manipulated upward, she turned the strip precisely as she had seen Lujon turn the key.

The cylinder rotated, the door opened, and she slipped inside, only to find the second mate whirling on her, the gleaming blade of his dirk at her throat.

Krystren did not glance at Orujo; to look away from Lujon would have been a mistake, and she knew it. Courion had always told her that being in a position of power was more a matter of perception than anything else. On the one hand, she was effectively Orujo's prisoner. On the other hand, neither he nor Lujon suspected that she was *crifica*. If there was a time to use her hidden power, this was it.

Kneeling beside the girl-sorceress, she drew Riane into her embrace, pressing the left side of her neck into her own biceps, and placing the heel of her hand against Riane's right temple. How simply death could be effected, she thought, not for the first time. Just a swift jab of her hand would crack the lower vertebrae in the neck. Bang! That would be it. Lights out.

Krystren took a deep breath and sent out a mind-feeler. She revealed none of her astonishment that it was met by an ethereal tendril from the girl-sorceress's own mind.

"Go on," Lujon urged, eyes filled with an unnatural luster, a bald avidity. "What are you waiting for?"

Knowledge flooded through Krystren and Riane, moving back and forth with synaptic speed. Within the blink of an eye, they learned many things about each other, found they had common goals in a difficult situation, linked themselves together, formulated a plan of action.

As Krystren moved over Riane, ostensibly to kill her, Riane withdrew her infinity-blade. Out of sight of the two Sarakkon, she thumbed on the wand. As the goron-energy blade manifested itself, Krystren reared back, slamming her elbow into Lujon's midsection. Then, twisting to her feet, she turned to Orujo.

Lujon recovered and switched on his own infinity-blade all in the same instant. "Better this way," he said. "Now we know where everyone stands, eh, Orujo? And you, Riane, we are grateful to Krystren for giving us the opportunity to kill you ourself."

He engaged her blade and, as he had done before, pressed his attack. This time, however, Riane was prepared for him. Instead of directly parrying, she spun, ducked, touched his blade with hers, spun again. As Asir had taught her, she felt for rhythm of the goron-energy pulses, began to move in concert with them.

Lujon, try as he might, could not touch her with his blade, and he became increasingly frustrated, moving after her. Deft as he was, Riane time and again outmaneuvered him. She spun and wove in a tight circle, never covering much distance. That further frustrated Lujon. He tried thrust after thrust, slicing through dead air where she had been standing not a split second before.

Krystren, for her part, did not attempt a physical assault on Orujo. Instead, she sent a mind-feeler directly into the center of his brain. His shock and defensive reflex massed themselves like thunderheads on the horizon, but she kept him from reaching her with his lethal hands and feet.

"What . . . what are you doing?" he whispered hoarsely.

"It was you who killed Courion."

"We were nowhere near him when he was killed."

"However he died, you are to blame," she said bitterly.

"We fell in love with him. You must believe that. We hadn't meant to, but the heart wants what it wants."

"If that is the truth, than your crime against him is all the more horrific."

"Why can you not understand—?"

"You are a fool to seek understanding."

"How can you be so cold?"

You betrayed my brother's love, she said directly into his mind. *That we can never forgive. Never.*

Orujo's eyes opened wide. "You are *crifica?* How? How did we not know?"

That is the trouble with your kind. Increasing the pressure on his brain. *What your arrogance provides you, what you think of as your strength, is really your weakness.* Krystren concentrated fully, channeling all her fury, her pain, her loss into a last lethal stab that caused the cells in the innermost part of his brain to explode.

Orujo's eyes rolled up, and she saw him spinning away from her, plunging down into the caldera of Oppamonifex. This time there was no specially sewn jacket to save him.

Lujon lost patience. Three teeth lay in his palm—Ramahan's teeth, necromantic talismans he rolled back and forth with the pad of his thumb. His eyelids fluttered as the teeth clacked together to the rhythm of his spasming eyelids, and the last of the life force trapped within the teeth at death was released.

A phantasm arose, an animal unlike any of flesh and blood, fierce and unrelenting, as devoid of intelligence as it was of remorse. There was no opportunity to reason with it, no chance to avoid it. The infinity-blade was as useless now as if it were made of paper, for it swept through the necromantic *anima* without effect. Lujon directed the *anima* to attack, and it had no choice but to obey.

Krystren had turned, was planning how best to help Riane, when she heard a rustling from behind her that made the hair at the back of her neck stir. She whirled, to witness the resurrection of the dead, for Orujo, stirring, opened sightless eyes. He rose jerkily, awkwardly.

"Surprised?" Lujon gave a harsh laugh. He had reanimated Orujo's corpse.

What a prize we have found us!" The second mate, grinning evilly, ran the blade across Eleana's throat. He did it gently so as not to pierce the tender skin. "How well will we be rewarded when we bring you to Lujon!"

He was big and burly and volatile, with a mean streak that propelled him into fights with lesser mates. Many feared him. Even the first mate was wary of him.

"How well, indeed," she said, "when Lujon discovers that you were crawling around his locked cabin."

Taking advantage of his momentary surprise, she struck his throat with the point of her knuckles and, as he rocked back on his heels, she struck him a two-handed blow on the bridge of his nose. As it splintered in a welter of cartilage and blood, he roared, charging her, taking her right off her feet, slamming her against the cabin bulkhead. Her head snapped back, hit the bulkhead so hard that she saw stars.

Time enough for him to wrap his salt-hardened hands around her throat. He squeezed as hard as he could, and she heard a roaring in her ears. Her lungs labored. She lifted her legs, wrapping them around his abdomen, but he kept slamming her back against the bulkhead so that she went in and out of consciousness. With a strength fueled by desperation, she kicked with her heels, striking the backs of his knees so that he fell, taking her with him to the floor.

The dirk he had dropped when she had attacked him was partially under her hip. She fumbled for it, grasped its grip, plunged it into the middle of his back. He reared up, letting go of her, his hands scrabbling backward to pull out the blade.

She gasped and groaned, sucking in great lungfuls of air. Bracing her aching back against the bulkhead, she kicked him on the point of the chin. She heard his neck snap, and he fell over on his side.

For a long moment, she crouched like that, bracing against the bulkhead, bent over, hands gripping her trembling thighs, as she brought herself back from the brink of oblivion. Then she stumbled over the corpse, staggered to the opposite side of the cabin, where a built-in rack held bottom-heavy decanters of liquor. She uncapped one at random and, tipping back her head, drank deeply. The resulting fire in her throat and belly soothed the pain in the rest of her body. She felt all over to make certain no bones were broken, but she could not touch her neck, which hurt so badly it brought tears to her eyes.

Decanter in one hand, she sat on the sea berth, concentrated on breathing while she took an inventory of the cabin. It was lined in oiled wood, dark and gleaming with runes. A brass lamp hung by a chain from the canted ceiling. A searay, pebbled skin stretched across its back and wings, hung on one bulkhead. In the other was inset a globular tank in which swam a beautifully colored fish, which now and again nibbled at the smooth edges of the rock-strewn sandy floor of its little world. Dried urchins, shards of coralbright, the lacquered shells of many a distant shoreline filled cases and vitrines cleverly built into the bulkheads. But it was the floor that most interested Eleana. Using the heel of her boot, she struck each and every floorboard. She was listening for a hollow sound, looking for a hidden cache where Lujon would have stashed the banestone.

On her hands and knees, she felt under the berth, her head immediately pounding painfully as the blood rushed into it. She had to pause several times to allow the throbbing to subside. Finding nothing, she checked the berth itself. Then one by one the cabinets, vitrines. She removed the searay, tapped the bulkhead behind it. All to no avail. Where had he hidden the banestone?

Presently she found herself back on the berth. She took another swig from the decanter, stared at the fish. "If only you could talk," she said. "I bet you know where he hid the banestone."

The fish ignored her, swimming languidly from rock to rock, nibbling at what, bits of algae? Eleana rose and put her nose against the crystal of the tank. Maybe the fish had answered her. That one rock it was circling—black, egg-shaped, absorbing all light. Dear Miina! It was the ninth banestone!

Feeling around above the tank, she discovered the access panel and opened it. Leaning in, she found herself looking down into the open top of the tank. The fish swam lazily below her. Dipping her hand in, she reached down toward the half-buried banestone, but as her fingertips neared the fish, it swung around. Its jaws hinged open, baring twin sets of razor-sharp teeth. She pulled her hand out an instant before the jaws snapped shut.

Looking around, she saw a net with a long handle, obviously used to take the fish in and out of the tank during periodic cleanings. She used it to scoop up the banestone. It was heavier than its size would indicate, and the handle bent a little as she drew it out of the tank. The fish followed it upward, swimming near the surface. It seemed to watch her somberly as she reached to cup her bare hand around the banestone and in triumph draw it out of the dripping net. At the very last moment she stopped, looked at the fish and smiled.

"I understand," she whispered. "I remember what Riane told me."

Eleana found a sailor's foul weather scarf in a drawer, dumped the banestone into it, and wrapped it up without ever letting it touch her skin.

Giyan, revived and revitalized, turned her attention to Haamadi. She needed to keep all of his attention directed at her so that the Ramahan would have a chance to free themselves. Toward that end, she entered Ayame—Otherwhere—and gained possession of her sorcerous avatar, the great bird Ras Shamra. Through the lens of Otherwhere she could see Haamadi, could feel the wellsprings of his power. What dreadful power source had he tapped into, how many innocent victims had his minions killed for him, to have amassed such power?

She engaged him through her avatar, bringing to bear all her sorcerous energy, all her considerable intellect with the sole purpose of pinning him down, of defeating him. But she soon discovered another of necromancy's chilling peculiarities. It was dumb. That is to say, it did not respond to intellect the way all the other sorceries—even Kyofu—did. It fed on fear and superstition—the dumb arts, as they were known among the Ramahan, so-called because while they were powerful enough among the ignorant, they became impotent in the light of rationality and knowledge.

She saw him stripped of his necromantic artifice—saw the shriveled thing he had become, grey, lined, drained of life, for necromancy extracted a high price for its power. He had no aura—none at all. He was like one dead. That was the difference between a magician who relied on fetishes and an ecstatic who opened her soul to the Cosmos. Here was a direct manifestation of Miina's special genius. By giving the exiles a black sixth finger she had, in effect, turned them into fetishists, and so had condemned them to this terrible living death.

There was one curious feature of Haamadi that set him apart from other sauromicians: a halo circled his head like the rings of a distant planet, what was left—fragments, really—of the spirit energy of those newly sacrificed. Caught in his low orbit, they screamed with terror, with the desire to be freed, to be allowed to go where the dead must rest before returning to the Great Wheel in whatever form the Cosmos had chosen for them. This was necromancy's most heinous crime—it violated the basic laws of the Cosmos, the ebb and flow of life into death and into life again, the grand cycle of renewal that was, at its core, the reason the Cosmos had come into existence.

Giyan grimly directed her spells to the rings of the dead.

* * *

Under Lujon's necromantic tutelage, Orujo's corpse swiftly gained in coordination. Krystren learned the hard way that it not only possessed extraordinary strength but also the unnatural ability to move from motionlessness to full-out speed without the transition necessary in a living being. The corpse slammed into her with such force that she went tumbling head over heels, all the breath driven from her chest.

Orujo, eyes whitened with a translucent film, grabbed her off the floor, held her with her legs dangling, her boots off the floor, and threw her against the wall. White-hot pain lanced through her shoulder, her left arm hung useless at her side.

The reanimated corpse stood over her, spread-legged. Grabbing her dislocated shoulder between thumb and fingers, it squeezed until the tears overran her eyes, rolling down her cheeks. She sucked in her breath, bit down on her lower lip in order not to cry out. Krystren tried a mindfeeler, but there was nothing to attack, just a grey-matter sponge that sucked up her energy, trapped her feeler inside it. Pulling her in.

Eleana, cradling the banestone, warily entered the Chaos Cave. So far, she had seen no sign of a sauromician either on the narrow rocky beach or in the sea-cave mouth. She had looked up toward the cave into which Riane disappeared, but the ledge was likewise deserted.

The eerie feeling she experienced upon climbing the spiral rock stairs was heightened when she came across the dead sauromician. He was sprawled across several stairs, his eyes open in stark disbelief. There was blood everywhere.

He was not the last dead sauromician she discovered on her way to the abbey. She counted half a dozen. All of them looked as if a pack of rabid wyr-hounds had fallen upon them. This could not be Riane's work. Who was so savagely attacking the sauromicians in their own sanctum?

All such questions were driven from her mind, however, when passing through the carnage in the central part of the abbey, she entered Haamadi's study to discover Riane in pitched battle with Lujon.

The instant the *anima* entered her, Riane quailed at its cold clutch. Her nostrils were clogged with the stench of offal. She wanted to drop the infinity-blade, to tear her clothing off, to rip her skin, rend her flesh from her bones, anything to rid herself of the abomination Lujon had loosed upon her. She knew instantly why the Ramahan had shunned necromancy, made it anathema, unholy. She felt as if every cell in her body was being turned inside out, as if light was dark, as if day had turned to night. Could there be anything more dreadful than experiencing death while still alive? She found herself thinking of null-space, the terrible feeling of reversal, of it being inimical to life, and her mind made the leap, the connection it needed.

Even as the *anima* sought to suffocate her in a pit of death, she slid her hand up the wand and into the pulse of the goron-energy stream. The initial jolt almost finished her, but she quickly adjusted to the pulse of the stream, found that it began to seep into her wrist, travel up her arm, into her shoulder. When it reached her chest, it collided with the *anima*, which emitted a scream that echoed painfully through Riane's body and mind. The *anima* twisted this way and that, trying to get away, to no avail. Riane kept the goron stream trained on it even as it shriveled and blackened into a twist of nothingness before vanishing completely.

Riane's instincts had been correct. Null-space, filled with goron energy, was a place of living death. While the *anima* in its insubstantial form had been unaffected by the gorons, once inside Riane's body it had become vulnerable.

She could feel Lujon's mind gathering itself for its most powerful necromantic assault yet, and she knew she had to stop it before it began. Enfolding a goron pulse in her fist, she flung it at him. It struck him full in the face, burning through his eyes, nose, and mouth. He danced a silent, spastic jig, the skin burned off his face, the flesh flayed from the bone so quickly that the blood was boiled away before even a drop was spilled. What remained was a bare skull on a body in the process of shutting down. Its legs tangled, and it tripped over its own feet, stumbling over Nesta's corpse, before crashing into the desk and crumpling into a heap.

35

The Ninth Banestone

What have you done?"

"I have brought you the ninth banestone." Eleana unwrapped the Sarakkonian scarf, held out the dark, egg-shaped object to Riane. "I thought you would be pleased."

"Of course I am pleased." Riane's eyes were wide and staring. "Where did you get it?"

"On the ship. I figured Lujon would not take his most valuable bargaining chip with him when he confronted Haamadi."

"Miina be praised, that was brilliant!" Riane hugged her. "But how on Kundala did you manage to sneak in here without being noticed? The enormous risk—"

"The sauromicians are dead," Eleana said. "All dead."

"Giyan," Krystren said. "We left a message for her on the ground of the Abbey of Five Pivots. She must have found it. We are willing to bet she used the Skreeling Engine to somehow destroy the sauromicians."

"In that case, we had better find the Cage of Nine Banestones," Eleana said.

Riane nodded. "I have got to save Seelin. There is no time to lose."

The moment Riane had dispatched Lujon, Orujo's reanimated corpse had collapsed into a stinking heap. Of Haamadi they could find no sign, and they were all afraid that he had made his way to the Cage.

"We have seen the Dragon," Krystren said. "We know where it is imprisoned."

She led them out of the abbey and into the rock corridors of the sea caves.

The way was etched in Krystren's memory. They kept descending, the crash of the sea booming through the ear of the cave, giving it the quality of a goddesslike voice speaking to them in a language beyond their understanding. Presently they entered the cave with the unnaturally smooth walls and the peculiar ruddy glow. Krystren placed the flat of her hand on a spot on the rear wall. A door opened, and she led them into the thick-walled keep, windowless and ominous. The sickly red glow enveloped them all. She pointed to the square column in the center. "The Cage is down there. You put your feet on those stirrups—"

"Pull the lever and down you go." Riane nodded. "I know. I have ridden one of these machines twice before."

"*Twice?*" Eleana said.

"That is for later." Riane turned to both of them and said rather formally, "Eleana, Krystren, I cannot thank you enough for the help you have given, for the dangers you have braved. But now I must go on alone."

"What are you talking about?" Eleana cried. "I have come this far. Do you think I would not accompany you all the way?"

Krystren said gravely, "After what we have been through it is our right."

"I do not doubt the truth of your words," Riane said. "However, where I must go now you cannot follow. I am the Dar Sala-at. It is only for me to do. And I need you both to find out what has happened in the abbey. If all the sauromicians are indeed dead, then someone must take control of the Ramahan, prepare them for the long journey home." Her eyes were pleading. "Please. I cannot explain further. Do as I ask."

"All right." Eleana bit her lip to keep herself from adding "love" to the end of her sentence. She was acutely sensitive to the Sarakkon female's presence and how it constrained her from uttering words of love. She could not even give her a proper farewell.

Krystren, after a long moment to show her displeasure, gave a reluctant nod.

"Good," Riane said. "Then do as I have bade you. I will rejoin you shortly."

Giyan was tiring. Even for her, this was a monumental struggle. By concentrating all of her energies, she had managed one painstaking layer at a time to free the spirits trapped within the rings of the dead that circled Haamadi's head like a necromantic aurora. But her success did not come without a severe price. The effort of fighting Haamadi's necromancy every step of the way depleted her. But the sauromician archon without his rings was himself stripped of much of his power. At some point she became aware that he was trying to pull away from her sorcerous grip. Giyan was instantly alert to his change of tactics. Why would he be giving up fighting her? Had he conceded defeat? But immediately her seer's finely honed instincts sensed that this was not his way. He had caught a whiff of something beyond her ken. What could it be?

And then, as he fought to pull away even harder, she had a vision: Haamadi down in the crypt deep beneath the Abbey of Loathsome Jaws, locked in mortal combat with Riane. Between them the ninth banestone. They fought, and Haamadi won. She saw him take the ninth banestone, complete the Cage within which Seelin, Miina's Sacred Dragon of Transformation lay dying. She saw the spark and cold flame, felt the enormous power of the nine banestones flowing into Haamadi, saw him grow to outlandish proportions as he fused with the aura of power bestowed upon him by the banestones. Nothing could stop him now. Nothing.

At the bottom of the shaft, Riane let go of the hand-grips and stepped away from the Tchakira machine. She found it fascinating that at some unspecified time in the past they had been there on Suspended Skull.

The sight of the Cage of Nine Banestones blotted out all other thought. It towered over her, the eight bane-stones pulsing their goron-based energy in crisscrossed lines that imprisoned Seelin, the Sacred Dragon of Transformation.

"Seelin!" Riane ran toward the Dragon, who lay with her eyes closed, great forepaws placed one over the other. The Dragon was identical to the one in Annon's memory. Her body was huge, sinuous sea-green. Her powerful forelegs were attached along their upper surfaces to a thin-veined membrane, triangular as a sail, moving like spin-drift, gleaming prismatically. A long tail whipped back and forth like surf against a rocky shore. She had one set of forelegs and two sets of back legs, all tipped with long coral talons (one of them missing), a long, tapering, reptil-ian skull and enormous golden eyes. Gleaming teeth of pearl protruded out beyond the silhouette of her head. A pair of horns, corkscrewed like waterspouts, grew out of the thick scaly ridge of bone above her eyes.

She crept as close as she could. "I've come to free you! Seelin, wake up! It's me, the Dar Sala-at."

"There you are wrong."

A young boy, no more than Riane's age, had appeared, coming off the Tchakira machine. She could see from his dark skin and sharp features that he was a member of one of the Five Tribes of the Korrush. Oddly, he was dressed in the persimmon-silk robes of a Ramahan konara.

He smiled at her, and said silkily, "As every Ramahan here knows, I am the Dar Sala-at."

Riane now knew the means by which the sauromicians

had persuaded the Ramahan gullible enough to believe them to leave the Abbey of Floating White. They were told that they were following the true savior.

All at once, the youth's eyelids fluttered, and almost instantly he went rigid. His eyes rolled up in their sockets, and he began to shake as if in the grip of a violent seizure.

Riane took a step toward him, away from the Cage. "What is the matter with you?"

The false Dar Sala-at collapsed, his skin dull as if in death. But a moment later he shook himself like a wyrhound throwing rain off his pelt. His eyes opened, and Riane gasped. They had taken on a golden, feral hue. As he rose, he bared his teeth.

"I am the archon Haamadi. This boy, Fer, is mine, body and soul," the youth with the feral eyes said. "You do not believe me? Watch!"

As if released from an invisible leash, Fer leapt at Riane. Riane could feel, like a current from a V'ornn ion engine, the animal energy with which Haamadi had infused the boy. He came at Riane like a rabid wyr-hound.

Riane allowed her spirit to sink into herself, to walk the corridors of her memory palace until she came to the room where she had mentally stored the texts of Miina's sacred books. Fire. She went to the section on the Five Elements, read the Venca text.

Her mind made the extrapolation. She spoke the Venca syllables, creating the spell as she went along. "*Nazha.*" Water. "*Nazhima.*" Ocean. "*Imken.*" Current.

Riane kept chanting, weaving the spell tighter and tighter, could feel the fire retreating, lying low, as if caught in a sudden downpour. He swung down to strike her, and she grabbed the front of his robe, used his own momentum to bring him close. She could smell the animal stench on him. Teeth bared, mouth half-open. Breath like a charnel house. Riane grabbed the twist of cloth Eleana had given her and jammed the Madila crystals into his mouth, striking him in the larynx with the edge of her hand, making him swallow convulsively.

His feral eyes glared at her. He opened his mouth, tried to stick two fingers down his throat. He shrieked then, hands to his head. Sweat flew off him, and he arched back, his head cracking against the stone. Foam was bubbling between his lips as Riane rose, gasping with pain. His heels and fists drummed a tattoo on the floor. His eyes rolled in his head.

Where was Haamadi? She could not think about that now. She was here with Seelin, with the ninth banestone. Difficult as it would be she knew what she had to do. There was no time for second thoughts or hesitation.

Blood was beginning to leak from Fer's ears as Riane staggered to the Cage and unwrapped the ninth banestone. All at once, she recalled her vision of the future. She had seen herself in this cavern, completing the Cage. Seelin's eyes opened. She looked nearly dead. She could no longer move. Amitra had been right. There was only one way to save her.

Riane stepped inside, placed the ninth banestone, completing the Cage. There came a lambent flash as the goron energy completed its circuit. The light went out in Seelin's eyes. Riane went over and touched the Dragon's snout. There could be no doubt about it, and she wept. She could not help herself.

Seelin was dead.

The moment Riane completed the Cage an opening had appeared in its bottom facet. Her grief had momentarily blinded her to it, but now it revealed itself to her. Without a second thought, she levered herself into it. Down she went.

If you are successful, Amitra had said, *you will find yourself in the Underworld our ancestors tried—and failed—to reach. It is a dangerous place for one still alive. We cannot tell you what you will encounter. But it is where Seelin's spirit will go after she has died. There you must find her and bring her back to our world, the world of the living.*

There was no sense of falling, no sensation of gravity,

period. But there was illumination, as if the way was lit by
reed torches. She saw, buried in niches she passed, curled
bodies, some young, others old. They lay in a kind of re-
pose so that it was possible to believe that they were only
sleeping, until you saw their eyes, which were all the
same, grey and filmed, staring at nothing or at everything.

Her nose wrinkled at the profound stench of decay, and
she shivered, certain that she was traveling through the
land of the newly dead. With each level she descended
more and more bodies lay curled. Waiting, but for what?
They were roused, their heads turning in her direction,
their lips pulled back in animal snarls. If they were dead,
how could they be aware of her?

A V'ornn female sat cross-legged. As Riane came
abreast of her niche, she reached out. Had she been waiting?
Though dead, she had the strength to pull Riane to a stop.
She looked at Riane with her grey, filmed eyes, and, with a
start, Riane realized that it was Kalla, Annon's mother.

She blinked several times, as if this would clear her
mind. The part of her that still recalled Annon's V'ornnish ways was certain that she was hallucinating. What
was a V'ornn doing in the Kundalan Underworld? Or was
there only one Underworld for all the races that spanned
the galaxies? *Why not,* she thought. *Isn't death the great
leveler?*

"You look so different from the boy I dandled on my
knee." Kalla gazed at her with her sightless eyes. "Here,
daub this on."

Riane saw that she held out a small black pot. She took it
from her, but the foul odor forced her to turn her head away.

"Rancid oil," Kalla said, laughing. She had a beautiful
smile. "Put it on, and no one will be able to tell you are not
dead like the rest of us."

"Mother, I do not understand."

"Why do you call me mother?"

"You are Kalla. Annon's mother."

"I am Kalla, that much is true. I was Eleusis Ashera's
wife, but Annon was no child of mine."

"What? What is that you say?" Riane felt sick. A dizziness enveloped her. "How can you not be Annon's mother?"

"I bore my husband three females, but alas for us, no boy-child."

"I do not understand. Annon was Eleusis' son and heir."

"That he was. But the female who bore him was a Kundalan sorceress, his mistress Giyan."

Annon was a half-breed? Giyan was his mother? The annealing flash of revelation illuminated even the remotest corners of Riane's mind. So many thoughts flashed by, so many of Annon's memories, so many odd things—his love of Kundalan culture and language, his secret antipathy to V'ornn arrogance and superiority; tiny occurrences, words, glances, between him and Giyan, between Giyan and Eleusis. Unexplained until now. Like a telescope that is suddenly brought into focus, Riane saw the true nature of Annon's origin, but seeing it was not enough. The enormity of it was too much to absorb so quickly. Understanding would take time.

"I have waited a long time to tell you this, Annon. You should know your own mother, shouldn't you? You should know that I, loyal wife of Eleusis, was cast aside because I could not provide him with that which he desired most: a son, an heir." Kalla's lips turned up in a bitter sneer. "He turned to *her* to love, to penetrate, to seed her womb. And she, in her sorcerous ways, contrived to conceive the boy-child that would bind him to her forever. You, Annon. You are that boy-child."

She put her head down, cradling it in her hands. "You hate me now, don't you? The messenger of ill news is always sent to the slaughter, isn't that so? Well, what can I expect? Never loved in life, despised even in death, for even here Tuskugggun are not honored. That is my lot. Foolish creature, then, to complain! I am Tuskugggun. I never should have expected more."

Riane put her hand out.

"No, do not touch me!" Kalla cried. "It is not allowed for the living to touch the dead."

Riane, ignoring her, pulled her close, cradled her as once Giyan had cradled Annon. Kalla was cold as an icicle. "How could I hate you?" she whispered. "You were my father's wife. You were loyal to him. You never gave away his secret, even on the point of death. I am certain he loved you for that, as do I."

Kalla began to weep, or tried to at least. "You see how it is," she said miserably, "the dead cannot shed tears." Shaking Riane off her, she returned to the subject at hand. "Have you anointed yourself?"

Riane began to smear on the rancid oil. She was trying not to think of why Giyan had failed to tell her that she was Annon's mother. Did she not want Riane to know? Was she ashamed of birthing a half-breed? "You know where I am going?"

"I hope you will find what you are looking for." She wagged her crooked forefinger, caught in a power loom. She had not wanted the Genomatekks to replace the fractured bone. "But beware the Daemon."

"Daemon? But, Kalla, all the Kundalan daemons are imprisoned and V'ornn do not believe in daemons."

"Listen to me." The crooked finger wagging. "She guards the dead, she decides their disposition, where they go. She will know where to find the one you seek."

"But Kalla—"

"You will have to throw yourself on her mercy, ask her for the favor. Beware."

Riane staggered back, but Kalla came after her, holding out a gnarled hand. "Take this," she whispered, and dropped what appeared to be a smooth oval stone into Riane's palm. "This will guide you back here, it will help you ascend with your burden back to the land of the living."

And all at once Riane was falling again, this time tumbling in a welter of sparks and flames. She closed her eyes against the vertigo, and presently she arrived. Finding herself on solid ground, she tapped it with her knuckles. At least it seemed solid enough.

Reed torches flickered in the distance, casting long-shadowed light, like a watery winter's sun sliding into the shallows of dusk. She was on a road that wound through dark countryside. She followed it, almost immediately losing track of time. The light never changed, not a breath of air stirred. Though she saw the silhouettes of trees and shrubs, she could smell nothing at all. No birds twittered, no insects buzzed. All was still as the grave.

She passed others, all walking with a somnambulist's tread, their eyes, fixed and staring, registering her as one of their own—because of her smell, she surmised. She did not attempt to talk to them, but hurried on, disquieted to be in their eerily silent company.

Presently she came upon a dark-flowing river, which she passed over using the arch of a narrow bridge. The bridge was most curious, being composed entirely of bones. Four piers that supported it were, in fact, warriors with terrible wounds and cold, staring eyes, who held the arch upon the bulging muscles of their shoulders.

On the other side, she found herself on the extreme edge of a battlefield. For as far as she could see in every direction, dark figures had at each other, swinging weapons, hacking off limbs. But again, there was no sound. Everything appeared to be happening in a vacuum.

"Do you feel it? The desire to join the dead?"

Riane started at the sound of a voice, a beautifully modulated voice, at that. She turned and saw a female. She was tall and slender, with a high-domed forehead. Her skin was white as snow, her hair the same hue, long and flowing, almost prismatic as ice will be when struck by sunlight. Long face, sad eyes. Bloodless lips.

"I feel nothing," Riane said. Was this the white-bone daemon Kalla had warned her of? "It is as if there is a pane of crystal between me and them."

The ice-colored female nodded. "That is good. You will not die soon."

"You know I am alive?"

The ice-colored female laughed. "Your stench will fool the others, but then they are dead. What do they know?

The idea of life is beyond them now." She nodded toward the battlefield. "Here are the warriors, fallen all, continuing their battle unto eternity."

"Is this N'Luuura, then?"

"Call it what you will," the ice-colored female said. "The song remains the same."

"Are you a daemon?"

"My name is Sepseriis. I am an archdaemon."

"Then I am somehow in the Abyss."

Sepseriis shook her head. "Not at all."

"But I thought Miina consigned all daemons to the Abyss."

"I am the only one She spared. I am therefore despised by my kind, even by my father and stepbrothers."

"But why did the Great Goddess spare you?"

Sepseriis smiled. "Someone must shepherd the dead, care for the flock." She gestured. "Now come. We must hurry. If you are to retrieve the soul of your Dragon, you must do so quickly, for after a certain time it will no longer be possible."

They crossed the blood-spattered battlefield, crunching silently through gore and bones that seemed meters deep one moment, then to have vanished the next. But then again, Riane thought, wasn't that the nature of things here? How could you kill something that was already dead?

They walked for a long time. Now they were in rolling pastureland, filled with flowers of every color and description. Trees dotted the landscape, though the sky was dark, low, and ominous as a cavern ceiling.

They came at last to a wall. It was very high and thick and seemed to stretch to the horizon in either direction.

Sepseriis said, "That which you seek is on the other side of this wall."

Riane saw no gate. Nor were there any seams on the stonework, not hand- or toe-holds that would allow her to scale it.

"How do I get past it?" she asked.

"You must hurry," Sepseriis said as if she had not heard

Riane. "Seelin is running out of time. In moments, it will be too late. Her soul will remain here. You will not be able to bring her back to life."

Riane inspected the wall most closely. Even with her skills, she could see no way to scale it. "But how am I to—?"

Sepseriis had made a gesture, and Riane looked down at her feet at a box that had not been there a moment before. She bent down and picked it up. It was made of wood, olive-colored, highly grained. She turned the box in her hand. The workmanship was exquisite.

She could see that the box opened from the top, and she slid the cover off. Inside was what appeared to be a child's toy, carved out of the same olive-colored wood. She took it out, saw that it was a cthauros—but a most curious one, for its color was that of the first tender shoots of spring.

"Qelar will take you to the other side," Sepseriis said.

"This toy?"

"Qelar is no toy."

Riane remembered Kalla's warning about making a pact with the white-bone daemon.

"Only I know Qelar's secret," Sepseriis said. "If you try yourself, you will fail."

Riane saw a Venca rune incised into the side of the tiny saddle. It was the rune for "Larger." Did that mean all she had to do was intone the rune and Qelar would become real size? A glance at Sepseriis told her that was too easy an answer. She turned Qelar around and around, thinking.

"The Dragon's time is almost spent," Sepseriis said. "I will tell you how this works, and in return one day I will come to you and ask a favor. You must grant it, whatever it might be."

That did not seem like a favorable bargain. Riane did not want to take it. But what other choice did she have? Unless . . .

She stared at the rune and realized that if you reversed it you would get the rune for "smaller." Holding the toy tight in her fist, she spoke the Venca word for smaller.

An instant later, she found herself on the ground beside the eight-hoofed steed. She was very small indeed. Sepseriis towered over her as if she were Kunlung Mountain itself. Beside her, Qelar snorted and ducked his head. He was no longer made of wood—or had Riane been mistaken in the first place? Whatever the truth, it no longer mattered.

Putting her hand on the steed's gently curving neck, she mounted him. He snorted again and reared up; she held on by gripping his mane. Then the steed leapt over the wall. On the other side she found herself on the edge of an ocean—grey, pacific, endless. A shale beach was strewn with shells. The tide was coming in, for with each wave— impossibly huge in her diminutive state—a few more shells got drawn back into the water.

Desperately, she roamed the strand, peering at each shell in turn. But all of them were grey, brown or black— spotted, striped, smooth, pebbled—inside their whorls pale and empty, devoid of life. All at once, she saw a shell rolling into the surf. It was blue-green, iridescent, sparkling. She lunged for it, grabbed it just as it was about to be sucked out to sea. It was tear-shaped with a spiked tail that rippled like the ocean's tide. It tingled in her hand just like Seelin's coral talon. She drew a deep, awestruck breath, for she knew that she was holding the Dragon's soul, her essence, her spirit.

Though Seelin's body was huge, her essence was tiny. Now Riane understood the secret Sepseriis believed only she knew. Had Riane been her normal size, she surely would have overlooked this minuscule thing.

Reaching up, she grabbed Qelar's mane, hoisting herself onto his back. Digging her knees into his flanks, she turned him loose to leap back over the wall.

Sepseriis was gone. So was the battlefield, the black river over which the bridge of bones had arced. All that remained was the winding road, down which Qelar began to pound.

From the trees that flew past on either side, she heard

the voice of the white-bone daemon. "I provided you with Qelar. Without him you never would have crossed the barrier, you never would have found that which is so precious to you. Remember this in the time to come. Remember what I have done for you."

Riane gave the steed his head and he began to enlarge and she with him until both were their normal size. He pounded along at such breakneck speed that quite soon he had reached the limits of his domain. The stone Kalla had given her had begun to glow. She held it up as a guide. Ahead lay the ascent back to the cavern and the Cage of Nine Banestones.

Riane dismounted, thanked the steed, and, with a slap to his flank, sent him back to the mysterious place from which he had come. Then, with the iridescent Dragon's tail curled around her neck, she began her ascent out of the Underworld.

36

Resurrection

The Cage was waiting for Riane when she returned. Her first instinct was to resurrect Seelin, but she knew that should the Dragon awake still within the Cage of Nine Banestones, the shock might be enough to destroy her utterly. Inside the Cage, she could feel the banestones' insidious power, like insects crawling beneath her skin.

As Amitra had described, she found the west-facing banestone and turned it forty-five degrees to the south. As she did so she heard an eerie keening, as if someone were dying. Moving always to her left, she turned each of the banestones in the same manner. At last, she came to the ninth banestone. This, she turned forty-five degrees to the east. The banestones ceased their emanations, the Cage disappeared.

Hurrying to Seelin, she crouched over the gigantic curled body. The giant orbs were closed, and when she ran her hand over the scales from rib to rib she could discern no trace of either heartbeat or respiration. Seelin was, indeed, dead.

For the first time, she noticed that the Dragon was so pale its blue-green color was almost blanched out, and she began to tremble. What if Seelin was beyond resurrection? Would she, as Dar Sala-at, be able to go on without the aid of the Dragon?

Putting those black thoughts aside, she bent to her task, kneeling to feel along Seelin's left front foot. Her hand moved along the thick pads, to the long wickedly curved talons. There were seven of them, a deadly forest within which she desperately searched. Amitra had told her there would be an opening somewhere there, and she found it at the base of the seventh talon, an opening that seemed too small to accommodate the Dragon's spirit.

Nevertheless, she pushed the spirit globe into the cavity, and as she did so, she felt it widen. All at once, the spirit was sucked inside the Dragon. At first nothing happened, and she worried that she had found the wrong opening. Then, as she continued to watch, she observed a small bulge as it made its way through Seelin's foot, her leg. It its wake Riane was thrilled to see the color returning to those parts of the Dragon's body through which it had passed. Now Riane could see that it was growing, as if it was getting from the body as much as it gave off. By the time it reached Seelin's abdomen it was as large as a banestone. Through its proximity the lungs began again to work and Seelin took her first shuddering breath. Then it entered the Dragon's heart and Seelin's golden orbs opened and she smiled at Riane.

"I have been waiting an eternity, Dar Sala-at." Her voice, though still diminished, caused the cavern to reverberate.

"Rest easy." Riane put her hand on the Dragon's flank. "You have returned from the land of the dead."

Seelin's long, spiked tail moved, curling slowly, gently around Riane, drawing her against the Dragon's heart, which beat like an enormous bass drum. Seelin sighed, her eyes closed. In her fathomless sleep her tail uncoiled enough for Riane, after one long caress, to step away.

It was just as well the Dragon slept, for Riane and Giyan needed their time alone together. Giyan had arrived from the Abbey of Five Pivots just after Riane had begun her eerie journey into the land of the dead. She had made the journey south to Suspended Skull on the back of the fulkaan, the fabulous creature psychically tied to Riane. The fulkaan had been searching for Riane when Giyan, seeing it through the Skreeling Engine, had summoned it.

Riane and Giyan sat upon Seelin's scaly back. Her wings were folded high like the walls of a cathedral, enfolding them on either side, protecting them, giving them the privacy they required. Her long, spiked tail curled around her flank, swishing slowly back and forth with each breath she took.

Riane told Giyan what the spirit of dead Kalla had revealed about her origins.

"Why did you not tell me you were Annon's mother?"

"Do you hear what you said, Teyjattt? You did not say, 'Why did you not tell me you were *my* mother?' You said, 'Why didn't you tell me you were *Annon's* mother?' " Giyan ducked her head, whispered, "You are no longer Annon. Annon is dead."

"Then why do you call me Teyjattt?"

"My mistake."

They sat watching each other with a wariness that made Giyan want to weep. What terrible fate had contrived to take her only child away from her? She had saved Annon from death, that much was true. But where was he? What had become of him? Looking at Riane now, having heard the news of the existence of her parents, of who they were,

but not yet having absorbed its implications, its ramifications, still she knew enough. Annon was gone. Only her
extreme love for him had kept him alive in her mind.

"I have to let you go, Teyjattt," she said, rising. "That
will be the last time I call you by Annon's nickname."

Riane reached up, took her wrist, held her. Giyan
looked back over her shoulder.

"Dar Sala-at."

"Do not call me that. Please." Riane tugged a little, and
Giyan sat back down opposite her.

"I know you must be angry with me," Giyan whispered.
"Do not deny it; it is only natural. But if you can, temper
your anger with this thought: How difficult would it have
been for Annon to grow up knowing the truth? How easy
would it have been for him to have made a slip to someone
close—can you imagine if it had been Kurgan? I made the
only choice I could make, but never think it was an easy
one. Never think there was a single day afterward that part
of me did not regret what I had done, that longed to tell
you, that ached every time I looked at you."

Everything Giyan said was true, and hearing it did miti-
gate her initial anger. But there was something else Giyan
had not mentioned, possibly because it was too painful.
Riane could not imagine the tempest of emotions that
must be roiling Giyan now that she knew about Amitra.
She had not had her child for so long, and now that he did
know she was his mother, he had found another one.

What an impossible situation this was! And yet, perhaps
because they were both in it together, there was a chance it
would bind them to one another.

Riane leaned in, took Giyan's hands in her own. "Now,"
she said, "I want you to tell me everything. Everything I
suspected, everything a child of yours should know."

"Really?"

"Annon is not dead. He exists as part of Riane, as part
of this fused identity. He is no longer what he once was,
but then neither is Riane, neither are you." There were

tears in her eyes. "I just found you, Mother. I will do anything not to lose you again."

Giyan, weeping, gathered her child into her arms.

Riane asked Eleana to help her pack up the nine banestones. Asir had told her that immersing them in seawater would dampen their radiation for a period of ten to twelve hours. They had built a container, which Krystren had designed along the lines of a Sarakkon ship, to be watertight. In truth, Riane did not need help, and everyone knew that, especially Eleana.

"Giyan has agreed that it will be best for me to take the banestones to the Abbey of Summit Window for study and safekeeping," Riane said. "Seelin will take us there. I cannot wait for you to meet Asir and Amitra. I know you will love them as I do." She paused at the somber expression on Eleana's face.

"Love, there is something I have to tell you."

Riane felt a small clutch in her stomach. "What is it?"

"Let's sit down." Eleana took her hand. "Please." She led her to a rock ledge in the crypt, where they sat side by side. "This is so very difficult to say."

"Why?"

Eleana looked at her. "Because I am afraid?"

"Afraid?" Riane laughed. "Of what?"

"I am afraid of you, love. Of disappointing you, of not doing what you expect me to do."

"I don't expect—"

"Oh, yes, you do." Eleana pressed Riane's hand between hers. "Just think about it for a moment."

After a moment, Riane nodded. "What do you want to tell me?"

"Oh, love, do you see how it is? That coldness creeping into your voice. Like Giyan, you can be cruel at times, though I know neither of you means to be. But you are so driven, you have a vision of the future, and you mean to take everyone in your orbit with you."

Riane swallowed. "What are you saying? That you no

longer believe in the fight for the freedom of Kundala?"

"Of course I believe in it, fervently, completely, absolutely. Never, ever doubt that, love. I would willingly give my life for the cause. But it is because my belief is so strong that I must disappoint you." She took Riane's hand, brought it to her lips, kissed it. "I want to return to the Resistance. I realize how much I miss it, how I long to be a vital part of the struggle."

"You already are a vital part of the struggle. Right here at my side."

"At your side, yes." Eleana stroked Riane's cheek. "Oh, love, don't you see that I will never be who I was meant to be if I remain always at your side. I love you most desperately, but I have to have my old life back—at least for the time being."

"But I need you here." Riane's heart was beating so fast she could hardly think straight.

Eleana smiled. "Did you need me to help you pack the banestones? No, love, you are the Dar Sala-at." Tears tolled down her cheeks. "You are the power and, Miina willing, the glory of Kundala. You worry about me, I know. That can be a dangerous distraction." She stood, and Riane with her.

They embraced for a long time, drinking in the smell and the feel of each other they had come to know so well, to love so deeply.

"When this is over and Kundala is again ours, we will be together again," Eleana whispered fiercely. "By everything I love and hold dear, this I swear to you."

Kurgan was brought to full consciousness with an entirely new set of senses. Before that, he had hung in a twilight world filled with nightmare images of his defeat at the hands of the duplicitous Sarakkon *Ardinal* Lujon. He felt again the terrible agony of being struck by the infinity-blade—not full on, for that would have killed him—but rather a glancing blow, the coruscating edge of the light blade (it appeared to him as light, though it was in fact a fo-

cused beam of goron particles) just glancing the side of his
head, an almost delicate tap-tap-tap that had set the
synapses in his brain to random firing without his volition.
Conscious but utterly helpless, he had watched as Lujon
had thumbed the wand, sheathing the light blade. Watched
as Lujon's balled fist sank deep into his solar plexus.
Watched Lujon's right knee rising up to strike his chin with
a sharp snap. Watched the floor come up and hit his cheek
as he collapsed. He must have blacked out, for his next
memory was of the attic, seen upside down. Blood throbbed
in his head, and there was pain in every square centimeter
of his body. Mucus crept slowly out of his nostrils.

Lujon stood in front of him. Every so often he would
strike Kurgan with the edge of his hand, the blunt blade of
his calloused fingertips, the heel of his hand. These blows
at first seemed random, but each one caused such excruci-
ating pain that Kurgan soon realized that they were well
thought out. Carefully timed as well. The agony of one
had faded just enough to give him the illusion of respite
when the next one was delivered with admirable dexterity.

He wanted nothing more than to defend himself, but his
legs were trussed at the ankle and his arms, hanging down
below his head, felt like lead weights. He could not move
them at all. Even the simple act of clenching his fists was
beyond him.

Pain again, a rat-a-tat of cracks exploding in his chest,
cascading up to his brain. White light and shivers, exacer-
bated when he gasped in a breath. Long ago, in intense physical training, the Old V'ornn had cracked one of his ribs.
This was the pain racking him now, only worse. Far worse.

The sensations bombarded him, bringing him out of his
nightmare memories. A sound from deep inside him, he
was certain, familiar as the soughing breath of his father
kept in an adjacent place in his memory. Kurgan opened
his eyes and saw the wing beating up and down as if fanning him. Translucent, reticulated, it seemed to him both
beautiful and frightening.

"How are you feeling?" Gul Aluf moved into his field of

view, which was still restricted by his prone position in the alifanon. More than half the fluid had been drained away, so that his back and shoulders, the back of his skull were still bathed in it, soaking up the rich nutrients.

"I don't know."

"Of course you don't."

"Are you . . . are you Gyrgon?" His voice was a hoarse croak he did not recognize.

"I am Gul Aluf. What is known as a Breeder. I make Niths what they are."

He tried to make sense of this, thought of the rubicund light emanating from the hatchway of the lab-orb Nith Nassam had taken him past. The same hue that shone here. "Where am I?"

"Better to ask *what* am I?" Smiling down at him in a variant of the guise that Sahor knew best, a ravishing Tuskugggun mask, this one drenched in unmistakable sexuality, the better to manipulate her new "child."

"I do not understand."

"Look at yourself."

Kurgan did as she bade, and almost screamed. "I am male . . . *and* female."

"Isn't this what you have always wanted?"

"I am . . . am I still Kurgan?"

"You are Kurgan, and more."

He could sense differences in whatever he looked at. It was as if he could see the whole thing, rather than just the side facing him. He could understand spatial relationships in a way he had never imagined before and sense the weight and density of objects at a remove from him. Also, but more gradually, he noticed the shift in colors, as if a wider spectrum of light was now available to him. How light reflected off a surface could not only tell him whether the surface was curved or flat but also revealed the composition of the object.

He turned his gaze on Gul Aluf. "What have you done to me?" There was a buzzing in his head, as if he were inside a hive bursting to overflowing with scuttling insects, he put the heels of his hands to his ears as if to blot out the sound, but it was coming from inside his head.

"You are beginning to understand, aren't you?" A mirror appeared between her two hands, and she angled it so that he could see his astonishing reflection.

His skull was a mass of flickering biocircuits that wound in a double spiral that began on the top of the occipital bone, ran up, meeting and blending at the crown of his head, then separating again as they came down behind his ears and into the nape of his neck. He had eyes that looked like cabochon rubies with bits of silver in their centers. "Enlil be damned!" Voices. He was hearing a thousand, ten thousand voices communicating in neat, orderly conversations, tier upon tier upon tier. He knew now who they were, and in the fulfillment of his desire his hearts leapt.

Gul Aluf, reacting to his expression, laughed in delight. "Welcome to the Comradeship, Nith Kurgan."

Silver rain filled the sky with spears. High in the mountains just above Receive Tears Ridge, Sornnn SaTrryn set the hoverpod down in a small glade in the Marre pine and heartwood forest. Puddles with stippled skin lay in the hollows. Downed logs, smeared with lichen, glistered and dripped. Colonies of unlovely mushrooms sprouted beneath slender fingers of ferns.

"How can you be certain she will come?" Leyytey asked, as he shut down the engines.

"I have something she wants." Sornnn sat with his feet dangling over the side pearled with raindrops. They wore water-repellent traveling cloaks over traditional Korrush robes. "In a war, you compel your enemy to come to you by providing something he wants. You prevent him coming by damaging him."

"Marethyn is not your enemy."

"The principle is the same."

She nodded. The glade, turned desolate by the rain, made the surrounding forest seem gloomy and ominous.

Sornnn wished he was as confident as he seemed. In fact, he had no way of knowing whether Marethyn had received the message he had sent to her via his usual contacts at Spice Jaxx. The security surrounding her—put in place, he had no doubt, by Marethyn herself—was both fierce and absolute. He had told Leyytey that on his way to the Korrush he would stop. After having first heard that she was dead, then alive, he had to try. He would be at these coordinates for precisely one hour. Then he would be gone. He dearly wanted to see her, but if for some reason she could not come, he would understand.

It sounded good at the time. The trouble was he knew that if she did not come, though he would accept it, he would *not* understand. He possessed a desperate need to see her face, to talk with her. When one has been told the one he loves is dead, and then, sometime later, that she is in fact alive, there is an imperative deep in the bones to see, smell, feel her. To know absolutely and without hesitation that she is, indeed, alive and well. Taking someone's word for it will not suffice.

Leyytey fidgeted. "Perhaps I should hide."

Sornnn shook his head. "We have been over this. She or one of her Resistance would find you."

"But I am Star-Admiral Pnin's daughter."

"She is the regent's sister. She will understand."

It was still for a time, save for the rustling of the rain through the trees. A golden gyreagle circled twice overhead and vanished behind the treetops. A cluster of saw needles, their six wings an iridescent blur, whirred by.

"Thank you, SaTrryn."

He looked at her. "For what?"

"For trusting me with this."

"It's nothing." But in fact he had thought long and hard about what to do. In the end, he realized that if he could not trust her, if his instincts had failed him, then it was time to retire from the family business.

"It's everything," she said softly, "to me."

He took her hand.

"You still love her, SaTrryn."

How to answer her? The easy answer was Yes, but when it came to Marethyn Stogggul nothing was easy. "I loved who she once was," he said soberly. "I do not know what she has become or whether there is room in her life for me."

Her unasked question hung in the air between them. How to answer her? Yes, he loved her, too, but in what way he had yet to determine. Besides, she was far too smart and clever to ask this of him now or anytime soon. They were together, about to make their contribution to a folk on the cusp of war. For the time being, at least, that was sufficient.

He heard something, and his hand slipped from hers. Leyytey had been prepared for this. Still, she discovered that she was holding her breath. Her hearts pounded furiously in her chest. She found herself afraid, but of what? She wanted Sornnn to be happy, but she wanted the same for herself. As the first of the Black Guard appeared at the periphery of the glade, she was acutely aware of her lack of control of the situation. The two of them could be dead inside of thirty seconds should the Resistance wish it, and there was nothing they could do about it.

"Sornnn SaTrryn," Basse said, "please step away from the hoverpod."

Without a backward glance at Leyytey, Sornnn slid down the convex side. He showed his hands as he walked toward Basse. It had taken Sornnn a moment to recognize him, so profoundly changed he seemed to be.

"Long time, Basse."

"Indeed."

"Majja?"

Basse shook his head, and Sornnn felt a weight in his heart.

"I mourn for her."

"As do we all."

The glade was now entirely encircled by members of the Black Guard. They were well armed, Sornnn saw, with the latest Khagggun weapons, and from the way they held them they looked like they had been well drilled in how to use them.

"Has she come?" Sornnn was able to restrain himself no longer.

Basse stepped aside, and Sornnn at long last saw her. He exhaled long and deep as Marethyn strode toward him through the dripping Marre pine. Like the others, she was dressed all in black. Like Basse, she looked different, though more subtly, her features reshaped by events he could not even guess at. As for her body, she appeared taller, all the fat had been stripped off her, leaving strong muscle and sinew. But the real transformation had occurred from the inside out. It was astonishing to see her in command of a large cadre of heavily armed, battle-hardened Kundalan.

"Sornnn." She had not lost that way of speaking to him that made him melt.

"*Wa tarabibi.*"

They embraced in the center of the clearing as her cadre and Leyytey looked on. They spoke softly so that no one else could hear what they said.

"It was only recently that I felt it was safe enough to send you a message."

He did not want to let her go. He could smell the forest on her. She had become a part of it. He felt her strength, the balance of her, knowing that in this wild and dangerous place she had come into her own.

"It was terribly unfair, I know that. And then when I got your message . . . To think you believed me dead!"

He pushed her away at last. "And now, look at you."

"So far from Axis Tyr."

He knew what she meant. "It's all right," he whispered. "It is what was meant to be."

"I've missed you, Sornnn."

"And I you. But . . ."

"Yes, but . . ." She kissed him fiercely, desperately. "War is a difficult master."

He was at once elated and saddened beyond words.

"And who is this?" Glancing at the hoverpod. "Leyytey Pnin, the armorer."

Of course she would recognize Leyytey. Their ateliers were not so far apart. "War has come to the Korrush. She has agreed to arm the Rasan Sul."

"Also, she wants to be with you."

"Marethyn . . ."

"It's all right," she said. "Who among us wouldn't?"

The answer was strung like a curtain between them.

"I do, Sornnn." She traced the line of his jaw. Her finger a lightning rod for the profound emotions drawing them together, pushing them apart. Her eyes were full and round and glistening, as if at any moment she would be overcome. But she wouldn't, not in front of her cadre. In this, she had become as strong as any male. "You know I do."

He took her hand in his. "Marethyn, what will become of us?"

"Who can say, Sornnn? But, then, who ever could?"

Giyan, First Mother, returned to the Abbey of Floating White with a full heart and at the head of a long line of Ramahan acolytes. Those who had not left the abbey received them with unconditional love and an understanding of their confusion, guilt, and fear of retribution. Konara Inggres had prepared her charges well, Giyan thought.

And yet, there was a subtle difference in the atmosphere. She was aware of it the moment she crossed the outer threshold to the sanctified ground, as a master chef returning to his kitchens will taste a difference in the food prepared by his underchef no matter how subtle the difference. Something of the one who prepared the food finds its way into the final product. Like a sleuth, it is the master chef's duty to determine the alterations. She became even more aware of it at the feast Konara Inggres had ordered for the return of the young Ramahan. She sat between Konara Inggres and the Nawatir at the head table, overseeing the orderly ranks of the priestesses as they raised their voices in humble prayer of thanksgiving and began to pass around the steaming plates of food. Konara Inggres had been properly deferential, even effusive in her joy at their return, but there remained in her a core of withholding that Giyan had not observed before. When Giyan told her about Krystren, about how she helped win back the Rama-han, how she took charge of the Sarakkonian vessel and sailed back to the southern continent, she could tell that Konara Inggres' mind was elsewhere. When she tried to hold her gaze, Konara Inggres' eyes slid away too quickly. She started at the sound of a dropped plate, at a burst of honest laughter.

Giyan wanted to ask her what was the matter, but it was neither the time nor the place. Besides, her mind was filled with the Nawatir. He, too, had embraced her upon her return, and she had reveled in the feel of his powerful arms around her. Until, that is, the contact brought on a vision. She saw a dark room, ancient and musty. In it were the Nawatir and Konara Inggres clasped in a feverish embrace. And where was she? In the corridor outside, her back turned to them. She clamped down mentally, trying to snap the skein of the vision as she had been able to do as a young girl. But, as had been happening lately, she was unsuccessful. The visions had become too strong, her power as a seer unleashed. Instead, she became a trapped witness to a future that might or might not occur. She heard their whispered words of endearment, watched their clothes slowly melt away, smelled the heavy musks of their bodies mingling. Assaulted by their moans of delight, their cries of fulfillment, she rose from her seat and stag-gered into the shadow of a column against whose cool sur-face she rested her head.

Gradually, her mind began to clear, and she could breathe again. Aware of a presence behind her, she turned.

"Are you ill, First Mother?" Grave concern had darkened Konara Inggres' eyes. "Is there anything I may fetch you?"

Yes, Giyan thought. *A different future.* But what she said was, "Return to your charges. I am fine. Just a little fatigue is all. It will pass."

"I beg your pardon, First Mother. The feast was a bad idea. After the battle you and the Dar Sala-at just fought the best place for you is bed."

"No, no, Konara Inggres. The feast is precisely what the abbey needs now."

Konara Inggres held out a hand. "Allow me to escort you to your quarters."

Giyan held her eyes for a moment. "The Nawatir may do that. Your place is with your Ramahan. After their long ordeal, they need the reassurance only you can provide."

Konara Inggres ducked her head. "As you wish, First Mother."

"Konara Inggres . . ."

"Yes, First Mother."

Now was the time to say something, Giyan knew that. But she could not get the words out of her throat. "Nothing," she said hoarsely. "Please tell the Nawatir to come find me."

"At once, First Mother." But Konara Inggres hesitated.

"Yes, what is it?"

"Perhaps it is not my place to say, First Mother." Konara Ingress' head was down, her eyes averted. "But while he was recovering the Nawatir said some things."

"What things?"

"About the disagreement you had before you left."

"You are right," Giyan said coldly. "It is not your place to say. Now go and—"

"But I must say it," Konara Inggres blurted out. "He resents your keeping secrets, is hurt when you push him away. It makes him think that you do not love him anymore." Her eyes flicked up for just an instant.

"Go fetch him," Giyan said in a half-strangled voice.

Watching Konara Inggres as she bent over the Nawatir to whisper in his ear, she wondered how far things between them had progressed. Had they spoken into each other's eyes, had their lips met? Had their bodies twined in carnal lust? That Konara Inggres loved the Nawatir she had no doubt. The question was how did the Nawatir feel. Despite his blowup, she knew what she and the Nawatir had together. How could that be torn asunder in the space of a few weeks? And yet, the vision haunted her, undermining her faith.

"Nawatir," she said as he came up to her, "how are your wounds?"

"Never mind my wounds," he said. "Inggres tells me you are feeling poorly."

Inggres, is it? she thought. "Let us go into the garden. I am in need of some fresh air."

Beneath the cold clear stars they sat on a carved stone bench. The treetops rustled. The black bulk of the Djenn Marre loomed in the background. They were utterly alone.

He has to tell me. I will not ask him. But the moment she thought this she knew she had committed the sin of pride, and was ashamed.

She took his hand in hers, steeled herself. "What happened while I was gone?"

For a long time, it seemed, he said nothing, and Giyan felt herself to be in an agony of suspension and lost longing. What would she do if he loved another?

"It began," he said at last, "when you refused to share your burdens with me."

"Nawatir, please. There are reasons—"

"I know the reasons. Inggres explained them to me."

"She did?"

He nodded.

"And what of Inggres?"

"She is a great leader, a stalwart Ramahan, an exemplar of the faith."

"What else is she?"

"Giyan, she is true to you, to Miina. Sometimes I think she possesses more faith than the two of us combined. She will not allow anything to sway her from her chosen path."

"Even you."

There was a small silence. What Giyan had really wanted to ask was: *Has anything happened?* But of what use would the answer be to her? And then she realized that in his own way he had already provided the answer, and her heart melted.

"Giyan, I beg you to forget this. If she knew what we exchanged here, it would crush her. She lives to serve Miina, and you."

"I will say nothing, do nothing to jeopardize our confidence."

He brought her hands to his lips. "Thank you." Gazing into her eyes. "Giyan, I will ask you one question, and that will be the end of it, all right?"

She nodded, swallowing hard.

"Do you love me?"

At once, her eyes filled with tears, and she threw her arms around him. "Oh, Rekkk; I love you most fiercely." Her eyes closed as she felt his warmth envelop her.

"It's all right then," he whispered, pulled her closer. "Everything is all right."

Krystren, the stout boards of her brother's ship beneath her boot soles, was thinking of Courion. She went around the captain's fan-shaped cabin—Courion's cabin—touching the runes carved into the wooden walls, the metal surfaces, the etched windows. She held in her warm palm small objects Courion had collected—bright shells, a tiny preserved coral crab, a bronze sculpture of a paiha—the mythic gold-and-black bird of prey with healing powers—a pair of lapis warrnixx dice, a tiger-eye sphere incised with runes—feeling their weight and their heft, the smoothness or roughness of their surfaces, wondering what lay beneath. She smelled her brother's spices, the sharp aroma of onaga wax. Staring at the dragonfish in its spherical tank, she poured herself a tumbler of Sarakkonian brandy, drank deeply of it, wondering if Courion had drunk from that very tumbler. Skirting the bunk, over which spread the lacquered wings of a monstrous searay, she passed before a mirror and paused as if suspended in the moment.

She stared at the face reflected there, searching each feature as if the image were of someone she had heard about but never actually seen. Whose sea-green eyes were those, whose thick hair? She downed the rest of her brandy and went up on deck.

The sky was enormous, a pellucid cerulean. Grey-and-white seabirds dipped between the masts, called raucously to each other, keeping a keen eye out for dumped offal. Clouds building on the southern horizon felt to her like harbingers of home. Though, surprisingly, she had made friends—good friends and true—on the northern continent, still she was anxious to see the port of Celiocco.

The *Sintire* plot to gain power had been thwarted, but what worried her was her own assignment. Why had she been sent to deliver an infinity-blade wand to Courion? Was it as benign an assignment as helping him defend himself against the *Sintire* incursion, a way to even the odds? Or was there a more sinister purpose?

The breadth of the sea had provided the space to think about recent events in a clearer light, and what she saw disturbed her deeply. What if the infinity-blade wand was the beginning of *Onnda*'s own push to gain the secrets hidden in Za Hara-at? Would Courion have been a party to such aggression? She hoped not, but she had to admit to herself that she could not be certain. How well had she known her own brother? About as well, she surmised, as he had known her. Which was to say not well at all.

Every aspect of her journey had opened her eyes to the world around her, which was full of wonders beyond the imagining of the Krystren who had set sail from Celiocco in search of her brother. The most astonishing thing of all was that during the journey she had discovered not only friends, but herself. She had become someone whom she doubted even Courion would recognize.

The wind was up, the sails snapping. They were making good headway. She turned her gaze back into their wake, to the smudge on the horizon, low and long, all that remained of the northern continent. Whatever *Onnda*'s plans, she knew she had been changed by this mission, by her contact with Giyan, Riane, and Eleana. It had been unexpectedly difficult to leave them. When Giyan had asked her to stay she had almost said yes. And when she had asked Riane whether, perchance, she had come across Courion in the Underworld, Riane had been so kind. The cube of worn red jade rolled across her fingertips, from Orujo to Courion to her. With the merest flick of her wrist she sent the cube flying over the taffrail into the oncoming waves, where it vanished without a ripple or a wake. Time to acknowledge that Courion would, unlike Orujo, never return.

She tilted her face into the sun, made a sound the wind took away. Already, she missed her newfound friends. What a curious and marvelous sensation! She knew she could never be a part of something that might hurt them. They had awakened emotions in her she thought long dead, feelings she was unwilling to give up even for her discipline. She never thought she would have friends, never thought she was capable of having them. If *Onnda* was, indeed, plotting its own way into Za Hara-at, planning to kill and to steal, she knew she would have to find a way to stop it.

From beneath her leather jerkin she withdrew Varda's crystal dagger. Running her fingertips over it, she thought of Bryn and of Minnum, and for a moment, at least, they were alive again, fiery as the sun in her mind. Was that a tear in her eye? Presently the calls of the crew drew her back to the world.

The comforting roll and pitch of the *Omaline*, the great expanse of aquamarine swells, the rigging singing in the wind all came to her, and she turned her face to the south. It was still a long way off, but if she breathed deeply she thought she could already smell the heady scents of home.

* * *

"I have a place inside my head where I put the things I want to remember," Riane said. "You taught me how to do that, didn't you?"

Asir smiled. "In fact, no. You inherited that gift from me."

Amitra put her arm around Riane's shoulders. "But we gave you the tools to use that gift."

"The palace of memory."

Her parents nodded in concert. "We showed you how to construct it."

On the broad back of Seelin, her beloved Dragon, in the midst of a howling ice storm, she had arrived at the Abbey of Summit Window. With her, she brought the two infinity-blades Asir's agents had found and lost to the Sarakkon. One she had taken from Lujon, the other Krystren had willingly given her. In her mouth, Seelin carried the nine banestones safe and secure in their seawater-filled container.

Asir, Amitra, and Thigpen had greeted her with tears and great hugs. Her parents accepted the bounty she brought with both delight and a grave sense of responsibility. They all spent some time with Seelin, finding her fascinating but reticent, save with Riane.

"This is an enormous victory," Asir had said.

"More even than we could have hoped for," Amitra had said.

"I knew you could do it." Thigpen bounded into her arms, nuzzling her with her black-and-red muzzle while Seelin's breath fulminated. The Dragon was polite but eager to be reunited with her brothers and sisters.

Now they were seated at a table, eating a hearty meal of polar-seal stew and hot spiced mead. They used wedges of a flat, unleavened bread to sop up the gravy and smaller bits of savory meat while Riane held them spellbound as she told her fabulous tale.

Afterwards, because it weighed even more heavily on

her mind now that Seelin was safe and the banestones recovered, she had turned the subject to memory. "Still, after all that has happened, I find myself wondering whether it is all there, whether I will ever have access to my own memories." Riane shook her head. "There are so many rooms inside the palace closed off to me, locked with the word *Oblivion*."

"There is certainly enough empirical evidence that severe trauma can have that effect on minds such as ours," Amitra said.

"Is there no hope, then?"

"Of course there is hope." Asir rose. "Do you feel up to trying?"

She nodded, and they left the table.

She allowed him to lead her into the densely forested area. Past the tinkling waterfall there was nothing save a pearly mist billowing. Immersed in it, she quickly lost touch with direction or any sense of where she was.

Taking her hand, he said gently, "This is your home."

"I know that."

He stopped their progress through the mist. "You know it intellectually, I have no doubt of that. But do you feel it, here?" He touched her heart.

Home. How could one solitary word create such a wellspring of emotion? *Home*. How long had she been searching for this place in her mind? Now she was home. She was compelled to say it.

"Home."

"Yes, Riane," Asir said. "Now face into the mist and *feel* that you are home."

She turned her face into the billows of mist, but there was nothing to see. For a moment, she grew afraid—of the future, of the past, both unknown. And the present, so perilous and uncertain. For that moment, she felt like a ship fogbound, unable to read the sun or the stars. Lost at sea.

Then a wind came up. She felt Asir at her back, felt her mother's love, and the unsettling feeling passed. She heard her father's words and felt herself home. Felt hard, felt with all her might.

And gradually the mist parted or, then again, perhaps something was emerging from its depths. In any case, its symmetrical outline grew clearer with every moment as her unconscious mind conjured up her memory palace.

Amitra could scarcely contain herself. "Oh, darling!" And put her arms around her daughter. Hugged her tightly to her. "You see, Asir, there it is! Perfect! Intact! There is nothing wrong with her."

"This is what saved you." Asir stood by her side, huge, imposing, oh so comforting. "Whatever happened to you, Riane, over the past two years, whatever ill fortune may have befallen you, you are here now, the core of you, because of this, of what we taught you, what you yourself created."

"Here is where you reside," Amitra said, as they began to walk toward the memory palace. "To whatever faraway climes your destiny may lead you, home is always with you."

Riane reached out, opened the gate, brought her parents into her sacred precincts as she must have done many time before, because it was they who had taught her how to build it stone by stone, for it existed not only in her mind but also in one of the billions of interstices that lay between worlds. Her own mind acted as the portal for her, and for those she wished to bring there.

On the edge of this unknown, she felt compelled to ask them the question that had been in her mind ever since they had shown her their great underground engines.

"It was you who had the technology," she said. "It was you who had the power."

"Yes, of course, we could have fought the Ramahan." Asir and Amitra once again exchanged glances. "But that only would have proved their point, that we did not believe, that we were, therefore, anathema to Miina. The bulk of Kundalan society would have turned against us.

No, far better to leave. Despite what the Ramahan think, we believe in Her, in the Prophecy of The Pearl and the Dar Sala-at. We would not interfere with Her design."

"What design?" Riane fairly shouted. "There is no Pearl!"

"How would you know that?" Amitra said.

"Dear Miina," Asir whispered. "She has spoken to the Hagoshrin."

Amitra stared at Riane. "You were inside the Storehouse."

"The Pearl was a bauble confected by Miina." It was astonishing how profoundly she was offended by the thought, how full of rage she was again at being so duped. She hated Miina, if the Goddess actually existed or ever had existed, could not comprehend such cruelty. "The vaunted Prophecy in which millions of Kundalan believe, which was their only hope, is false."

"You are only half-right," Asir said. "It is true that The Pearl the Hagoshrin showed you was nothing more than a bauble, but as for the Prophecy of the Dar Sala-at and The Pearl, that is as true as it ever was."

"How?" Riane shook her head. "The Hagoshrin cannot lie."

"Indeed. But the Hagoshrin can be deceived by Miina. However, I see the doubt in your face." Asir held out his right hand, palm up. "Behold."

A coruscating light formed just above his palm. It spun, throwing off jeweled pinpoints of light. And when it slowed and eventually stopped Riane could see that it was identical to The Pearl that had come from the Hagoshrin's navel. He held it out to her, and she took it, discovered that it was, indeed, the same bauble.

She looked at Asir. "*You* made The Pearl?"

Asir laughed. "Oh, I am not *that* ancient, Riane. My great-great-grandfather.   *Your*   great-great-great-grandfather manufactured it to Miina's specifications."

"Then the Great Goddess exists."

"Oh, yes. Indeed, She does."

"I hate Her," Riane said.

"You do not know Her," Amitra began, but Asir stopped her.

"This was prophesied," he said. " 'The Dar Sala-at will at first see only needless cruelty in the death and suffering that has preceded her.'"

"Oh, my dear!" Amitra gathered Riane to her, enfolded her in her arms.

Riane's face was pressed into the side of her mother's neck. She inhaled the scent of her skin, her hair and felt intoxicated by the familiarity. That peculiar warmth had stolen over her again, and she reached around, hugged her mother as tight as she could. She never wanted to let go.

"It has all happened for a reason." Asir standing, looking at them. "The decision to climb Snake Face instead of trekking the long way through the coll. The friable ice, the sudden thaw. You being taken away from us by the avalanche and now returned. In each and every one of these things I see Miina's hand. It was meant to be. It could not have happened otherwise. It was part of the process of creating the Dar Sala-at."

Riane, her eyes tightly shut against the tears, wanted to believe him, but she couldn't. She opened her eyes, looked at him. "What about The Pearl? It's a fake, a conjuror's trick. It doesn't exist."

"This, yes." Asir snapped his fingers, and The Pearl vanished. "A conjuror's trick, as you say. But let me ask you something. Do you think Miina foolish enough to create something of such power and scope as The Pearl, then let everyone know where it is?"

"But the Storehouse, the Hagoshrin . . ."

"All vulnerable, as the sauromicians proved during their uprising."

"Then She knew it all would happen."

He nodded. "And so she laid the bit of cheese"—he produced the false Pearl again—"in the center of her trap."

"Then The Pearl—the *real* Pearl exists?"

Asir said, "Miina created The Pearl for the Dar Sala-at. Therefore, The Pearl exists."

"Where is it?"

"Until a moment ago I had no idea." He lifted an arm, pointed to her memory palace. "Remember I said that in everything that has happened to you I see the hand of Miina? Even the avalanche, you losing your memory—they were all part of Her plan, for it was during the time when you were unconscious that she seeded The Pearl. Your loss of memory was a by-product of the seeding."

Riane stood rooted to the spot, stunned. "I don't understand." But that was not entirely true. For the first time she could feel the hand of the Great Goddess guiding her, past and present. She remembered how an owl—one of Miina's messengers—had led to Riane's discovery after her fall. She remembered the gyreagle whose talon had been ripped off inside her—the talon that had led her as Annon to the Door of the Storehouse. Most of all she remembered the Khagggun pursuit of Annon and Giyan that had made Giyan take refuge in Stone Border, and how that pursuit had forced Giyan to perform the dangerous rite that had migrated Annon's life force into the dying Riane. For the first time, she began to see the grand design of Miina's plan.

"You see, Riane, The Pearl is not a *thing,* it is not something you can hold and look into. It is not, as you so accurately put it, a conjuror's trick. The Pearl is a storehouse of knowledge. It is *information*, pure and simple. Information with the potential for power so vast, so sweeping, that Miina knew it must be for the Dar Sala-at alone. There must be no possibility whatsoever that it could fall into enemy hands. The consequences of that are too catastrophic to contemplate."

Riane looked with awe and wonder at the edifice she herself had constructed. "You mean it's there?"

"Where safer to store The Pearl than in the eidetic memory of the Dar Sala-at? Especially since she herself would be ignorant of the fact until she was experienced enough and strong enough to know how to use the knowledge. This information is for you alone, Riane. No one else may see it or read it. You will be our guide, our prophet, our oracle. In this way you will deliver us from the bondage of the V'ornn."

Riane turned, staring in wonder at her palace of memory, at the high wall with its basalt gate bound in incised bronze, the pink gravel of the treeless courtyard raked into its perfect wave pattern, the black-basalt path that ran straight down the middle to the front steps of the symmetrical building, and the two carved-stone fountains on either side. As she did so, the word OBLIVION vanished from the basin of the fountain on the left, and she knew that when she went inside it would be gone from the doors behind which lay a treasure trove beyond any imagining.

Riane, on the pebbled path to her memory palace, watched by her parents, took her first momentous steps through the thunderous silence of past-present-future toward her destiny, toward the center of herself. Toward The Pearl.

Major Characters

RIANE—The Dar Sala-at, savior of Kundala; the V'ornn Annon Asgera's essence migrated to a Kundalan body

GIYAN—Kundalan Ramahanm nother of Annon Ashera

ELEANA—former Kundalan Resistance fighter; Riane/Ashera's beloved

THIGPEN—Rappa; Riane's companion

KURGAN STOGGGUL—B'ornn regent of Kundala; sworn enemy of the Ashera

FIRST-CAPTAIN GYNNN KWENN—Kurgan's Haaar-kyut commandant

MINNUM—renegade sauromician

COURION—Sarakkonian captain

KRYSTREN—Sarakkom Onnda; Courion's sister

SOMNN SATRRYN—V'ornn prime factor; spice trader with the Rasab Sul tribe of the Korrush

MARETHYN—former artist' beloved of Sornnn Sa Trryn

SAHOR—the former Gyrgon Nith Sahor, now reborn in a body that is half-Kundalan, half-V'ornn

THE NAWATIR—The Great Goddess Miina's warrior; former V'ornn Pack-Commabder Rekkk Hacilar

NITH IMMMON—Gyrgon ally of Nith Sahor

NITH NASSAM—Gyrgon ally of Nith Batoxxx

GUL ALUF—Gyrgon Breeder

DECK-ADMIRAL IIN MENNUS—the new Star Admiral

PACK-COMMANDER TEWW DACCE—Iin Mennus' trusted aide

LINE-COMMANDER HANNN MCNNUS—Iin Mennus' brother

FLEET-ADMIRAL ARDUS PNIN—Iin Mennus' enemy
LEYYTEY—armorer; Ardus Pnin's daughter
KIRLLL QANDDA—V'ornn Deirus
SAGIIRA—blind sauromician

KONARA INGGRES—Ramahan, acting head of the Abbey of Floating White
PERRNODT—a Druuge, one of the first Ramahan

MAJJA—female Resistance fighter
BASSE—male Resistance fighter; Majja's compatriot
KASSTNA—Resistance cell leader
GERWA—Resistance cell leader
MEDDA—Resistance fighter
TONG—retired Khaggun; wyr-hound breeder
RAAN TALLUS—solicitor-general, administering the business affairs of the Ashera family

HAAMADI—sauromician archon
CALIGO—sauromician archon
VARDA—sauromician archon

LUJON—Sarakkonian Sintire Kardinal
GUAZU—Sarakkonian Sintire Kardinal
BRYN—a Hagoshrin

ASIR—leader of the Abbey of Summit Window
AMITRA—Asir's wife

V'ornn Societal Makeup

The V'ornn are a strict caste society. Their castes are broken down thusly:

GREAT CASTE:
Gyrgon—technomages
Bashkir—merchant-traders
Solicitor—Bashkir
Genomatekk—physicians

LESSER CASTE:
Khagggun—military
Mesagggun—engineers
Tuskugggun—females
Looorm—prostitutes
Deirus—physicians relegated to taking care of the dead
 and the insane

Pronunciation Guide

In the V'ornn language, triple consonants have a distinct sound. With the exceptions noted below, the first two letters are always pronounced as a W, thus:

Kagggun—Kow-gun
Tuskugggun—Tus-kew-gun
Mesägggun—Mes-ow-gun
Rekkk—Rawk
Wennn Stogggul—Woon Stow-gul
Kinnnus—Kew-nus
okummmon—ah-kow-mon
okuuut—ah-kowt
K'yonnno—Ka-yo-no
salamuuun—sala-moown
Olnnn—Owl-lin
Sonnn—Sore-win
Hadinnn—Had-ewn
Bronnn Pallln—Brown Pawln
Teyjattt—Tay-jawt
seigggon—sew-gon
skcettta—shew-tah
Looorm—Loo-orm
bannntor—bown-tor
Kannna—Kaw-na
Keffir Gutttin—Kew-fear Gew-tin
Ourrros—Ow-roos
Jusssar—Jew-sar
Julll—Jew-el
Nefff—Newf

Batoxxx—Bat-owx
Boulllas—Bow-las (as in, to tie a bow)
Hellespennn—Helle-spawn
Argggedus—Ar-weeg-us

When a Y directly precedes the triple consonant, it is pronounced EW, as in shrewd, thus:
Rydddlin—Rewd-lin
Rhynnnon—Rew-non
Tynnn—Tewn
but:
K'yonnno—Ka-yow-no

Because the following word is not of the V'ornn language, the triple consonant does not follow the above rules, thus:
Centophennni—Chento-fenny

Triple vowels are pronounced twice, creating another syllable, thus:
Haaar-kyut—Ha-ar-key-ut
leeesta—lay-aysta
mumaaadis—mu-ma-ah-dis
liiina—lee-eena
N'Luuura—Nu-Loo-oora

Normally, in V'ornn, the Y is pronounced EA, as in tear, thus:
Gyrgon—Gear-gon

Sa is pronounced SAY, thus:
Sa Trryn—Say-Trean

Kha is pronounced KO, while Ka is pronounced KA, thus:
Khagggun—Kow-gun
Kannna—Kaw-na

Ch is always hard, thus:
Morcha—More-ka
Bach—Bahk

Skc is always soft, thus:
skcettta—shew-tah